# The Lazarus Conspiracies

## Richard Rose

Savant Books
Honolulu, HI, USA
2013

Published in the USA by Savant Books and Publications
2630 Kapiolani Blvd #1601
Honolulu, HI 96826
http://www.savantbooksandpublications.com

Printed in the USA

Edited by Wallace Klein
Cover design by Daniel S. Janik
Cover photo by Jorge Medina Photography

13 digit ISBN: 9780988664081
10-digit ISBN: 0988664089

# Dedication

To Kay, my beautiful wife, my true love,
my best friend, soul mate and inspiration.

# Acknowledgments

Grateful acknowledgments to:

Detective John DeBartolo, Chicago Police Department, Special Victims, retired, for helping me with the police procedural details of the novel.

My editor, Wallace Klein, for his dedication, hard work and invaluable assistance.

Irene Michaels for providing her beautiful face for the book cover.

Mary O'Doud for proofing my first draft.

Richard Rose

# Preface

Once an author gets an idea for a mystery novel, thriller or adventure story, the research needed to bring the story to life can become an adventure in itself. Such was my experience with *The Lazarus Conspiracies*.

Two of the main characters in the book, Mack McPherson and Otis Winstrom, are Chicago Police Department Special Victims detectives, so my adventure began when I sought to acquire firsthand knowledge of the police procedures these protagonists would have to know for their story to feel authentic. Thanks to the able assistance of Detective John DeBartolo, now retired, I was able to enter into the world of a real Special Victims detective.

I'd read about John in a *Chicago Sun Times* article, which covered his long distinguished career in Special Victims, during which he'd cracked several "heaters"—cop lingo for headline grabbing cases. Fortunately, when I called John to ask him if he'd help me with the book, he generously agreed. Through him I was able to hang out with detectives at Area 3 Detective Division Headquarters and at a neighborhood bar appropriately named "The Slammer." This gave me the opportunity to learn not only how Special Victims detectives perform their duties, but also how they interact with each other after hours. And I can attest that they are indeed, as Shakespeare dubbed King Henry's loyal men, a "band of brothers."

John also invited me to join him in his unmarked police-issue Crown Victoria on actual cases, even some in high crime areas of Chicago. Although he warned me not to venture into those neighborhoods alone, I must confess that on a couple of occasions I didn't heed his advice. Instead I dressed down and grew a two-day five o'clock shadow, then visited a seedy transient hotel frequented by drug pushers and prostitutes and a neighborhood of refuse-littered sidewalks where steel gates guarded the storefront doors and windows after closing time. This phase of my research came to an abrupt end when I told my wife where I had been.

A less hazardous but no less depressing phase of my research came when I explored the sad plight of the homeless. I needed to do this because another main character in the book, Willie Butler, is a vagrant. I began by visiting some of the shelters and taking a tour of a mission with its pastor/director. Good for openers, but to make the character come alive on the pages of the novel, I needed to get to know someone who lived on the street, to see how he thought, lived and survived.

I chose the only one I knew, a grizzled rangy veteran of the streets whom I will call "M." When he needed some "good time money," as he called it, he would sell a publication called *Street Wise*, as other vagrants do, for a dollar a copy, sixty cents of which he pocketed as his meager profit. M had what he called a "good corner" in the financial district in front of a Starbucks, which is where I first encountered him and then became a loyal client. M eagerly accepted my business proposal. For an agreed sum of cash and a cup of coffee, we would meet at Starbucks and I would give him a copy to review. This required several cups of coffee and cash disbursements, but was more than worth it. M told me what was inauthentic in my writing, especially in dialogue, as street people have their own unique street jargon. As a bonus M volunteered some horror stories of life on the street and in flop houses—stories that nearly curdled the cream in our Starbucks coffees.

In time our Starbucks meetings ended, and I became just a buyer from M of the *Street Wise* paper. But there was an unexpected epilogue to the story of M that began with a phone call from the Law Office of the Public Defender. The attorney who called informed me that M was occupying a detention cell at First District Police Headquarters as a consequence of a physical altercation with his girlfriend. M would be grateful, he said, if I would post his bail. Since this was not part of our business arrangement, I politely declined. However, the persistent public defender called me again the next day with an update. M had been transferred to the Cook County Jail and was getting "antsy." Surrendering to a sense of moral obligation to my erstwhile informant, I agreed to post M's bail provided the amount was reasonable. The public defender quoted me three hundred dollars in cash, ninety percent of which I would get back if M showed up before a judge in two weeks. And how long would it take for me to do this, I asked? He assured me that I would be out in an hour at most.

So that evening I headed for the Cook County Jail in southwest Chicago. Upon seeing the high walls, barbed wire and machine gun towers, I began to get a little "antsy" myself. That feeling continued through two security check points and into a crowded room where friends and relatives of the incarcerated waited to visit or post bail bonds. Finding the only vacant seat on a bench next to one of the visitors, I asked how long he'd been waiting. "Four hours," he said, which somehow didn't surprise me. This prompted a cell phone call to my wife requesting that she have a sandwich and a double martini waiting for me at midnight.

It turned out that I did get a check for two hundred and seventy dollars from Cook County several weeks later, as M had shown up for his court date. However, the next time I purchased a copy of *Street Wise* from M at his corner, I advised him to get a new girlfriend, because I wasn't going to spend another evening bailing him out of the Cook County Jail. Although this episode doesn't appear in *The Lazarus Conspiracies*, I have written it down and stored it on my laptop for future use.

The adventure continues. A sequel is on its way.

The Lazarus Conspiracies

Richard Rose

"We commit his body to the ground;
earth to earth, ashes to ashes, dust to dust."

*The Book of Common Prayer*


"Burn in hell, you sonovabitch!"

*Mack McPherson*

## Thursday, April 25

*7:15 a.m.:* Detective Michael "Mack" McPherson parked on West Diversey Street across from the Crawford Hotel and waited for Jason Fry to come out of the building. The Crawford, a crummy transient flophouse sandwiched between a Korean laundry and a currency exchange, had been Fry's home since he was released from prison two weeks earlier. Air conditioners protruded from some of the dingy windows of the drab, five-story building. Next to the entrance was a faded sign: "VACANCIES. WEEKLY RENTALS AVAILABLE."

Mack knew that Fry would leave the hotel at 7:30 a.m. He knew Fry's routine down to the minute because he'd been tailing Fry since Monday morning, sticking to him like a fly on shit, waiting for him to make a wrong move. He'd blown a week's vacation to keep Fry company—a week that he could have been hiking through the mountains of Colorado with a backpack and a fly rod, a week he could have been away from the shit he had to deal with every day on the streets of Chicago, shit he'd been dealing with for twenty-one years as a CPD Homicide detective. But giving up a week's vacation would be a small price to pay if this time he could nail Fry for good. Hell, getting vermin like Fry off the streets forever was worth a hell of a lot more. Maybe even his badge.

Mack kept the engine of his 1939 Lincoln Zephyr running so he could play the radio without draining the battery while he watched Fry. He'd bought the once-elegant sedan from a high school buddy who made a living restoring old wrecks and selling them to vintage car buffs. Mack couldn't afford to buy the car restored, so his friend let him have it "as is" for ten grand, with the understanding that Mack would fix it up himself. Mack was happy to do this in his spare time, whenever he could afford the cost of parts and materials. Although he was a pretty good mechanic, it took Mack three months of hard work on his days off to finally get the engine purring. Even then, before he could drive it, the Zephyr needed new brake linings and whitewalls to replace the threadbare Goodyears. Although the car was now safe to drive, it was going to take a few more paychecks before Mack could pay a body shop to repair the dents and rust patches that disfigured the faded olive green exterior—work he didn't have the tools or facility to do himself. But at least he could listen to music, thanks to the AM/FM radio he'd installed with his last paycheck.

Mack tapped on the steering wheel with a drumstick in his left hand, keeping the beat to the swinging sound of "Tuxedo Junction." For Mack, drumming was as natural as breathing. Even his feet kept time to the beat, his right toe tapping out four beats to the bar, his left foot coming down on the twos and the fours, typical swing style.

A loud car horn interrupted his concentration, throwing him off the beat. Mack looked out the open side window at a grimy purple van that had pulled up alongside him and stopped. The driver, a bearded young man with a shaggy mane of shoulder-length hair gave him a big grin and held up two drumsticks.

"You're a drummer, huh?"

"Yeah. Mostly jazz and swing."

"Cool. Wish I could play jazz. Rock's my thing, ya know."

No surprise there, Mack thought. Most drummers didn't know the meaning of syncopation.

"Nothing wrong with rock," Mack said, not meaning it. Boring.

The young man started to reply when the horn of a car behind him sounded an impatient blast. The rocker gave the driver the finger. "Gotta go," he said, saluting Mack with his sticks. "Stay cool."

Mack grinned and returned the salute as the van growled away.

"That was 'Tuxedo Junction' as rendered by the Glenn Miller Orchestra in 1939," the DJ said when the song ended. "And you're listening to WZZB, 97.7 on your FM dial, your station for jazz with yours truly, Fred Buckley, your host for the next two hours."

Mack laid the drumstick on the dash and took a sip of the coffee he'd picked up at a 7-Eleven on his way to stake out the hotel. He was not a tall man, but he looked bigger than his 5'11" frame due to his muscular upper torso, the result of regular visits to the gym. His hips were a little snug in the faded Levi's he often wore, but with exercise and a discerning eye on his diet he was able to keep his waistline at 34" and his weight at 167 to 170. All in all he gave the appearance of an aging halfback who could still outrun his age. Most people would put him in his early to mid-thirties. He was forty-four.

"Now let's turn the calendar ahead to 1958 and the cool sounds of Miles Davis playing 'Autumm Leaves'," the DJ continued. "Davis is ably assisted by Cannonball Adderley on alto sax, Hank Jones on piano, and Art Blakey doing his special thing behind the drums."

Mack knew the Davis rendition well, a slow, melancholy improvisation of the lovely tune, straight-on jazz at its best. This time the music washed over him rather than through him. As the band played on, Mack fingered his right ear for a missing lobe, the casualty of a shootout with a gangbanger when he was a beat cop. It was a gesture that Mack performed unconsciously whenever he was thoughtful or worried.

Mack was worried now. If Fry didn't make a move before Monday, Mack would be back on the job, leaving Fry a clear field to seek out his next victim. Mack knew of at least four little girls Fry had raped and then carved up like a butcher in a meat market. But knowing wasn't enough. He hadn't been able to prove it. Not yet. Maybe he could prove it this time, or, better yet, stop it before it happened.

Mack set his coffee cup back into the holder on the dashboard. Fry had come out of the hotel and was walking down the street toward his parked Cherokee, a battered hulk that hadn't seen a drive-through carwash for months. Mack knew what Fry's routine would be for the day. He would stake out one grade school at eight in the morning when the kids were arriving, spend some sack time in a park, then check out another school during lunch recess, grab a bite and a beer, then hang around another school at 3:30 watching the kids who loitered in the playground after school ended.

Fry got the engine rumbling and headed east. Mack did a 180 and followed. At Broadway Fry turned north to a McDonalds, where he got coffee and something to eat at the drive-through window. Fifteen minutes later he ate his breakfast across the street from Pierce Elementary School on West Bryn Mawr. Mack sipped his coffee and gnawed on a bagel he'd bought at the 7-Eleven, watching and waiting. Nothing happened. After the bell rang and the sidewalks and the schoolyard emptied, Fry cranked up the Cherokee and drove off.

Except for a trip to a public restroom, Fry spent the rest of the morning sacked out on a bench in Lincoln Park. Mack watched from the Zephyr, which was parked on North Simonds Drive facing Lake Michigan near Montrose Harbor. It was hot for April, too hot for the sweatshirt he was wearing, and since the Zephyr had no air conditioning, Mack kept both windows down to catch the cool breeze off the lake. It was a weekday, so there wasn't much activity in the park. A few cyclists, joggers and mothers pushing their infants in strollers were using the bike path that stretched for miles along the lakefront. An occasional dog walker ambled by, pausing at a bush or tree. In the distance a few sailboats drifted lazily across the cobalt blue water of the lake.

Fry woke up from his nap around quarter to twelve. He stretched, headed back to the Cherokee, and cranked it up. A few minutes later he was cruising west on Addison. Mack lagged three cars behind the Cherokee. At Sheffield Mack almost lost him. He was distracted by the earlybird fans filtering into Wrigley Field. It was a perfect day for a ball game, and Mack was thinking how nice it would be to sit in the bleachers with a beer and a brat, watching the Cubs take on the Mets. As the light flashed yellow, Mack had to goose the Zephyr across Sheffield before a wall of traffic could block his way.

Fry turned south at Ashland Avenue. Mack followed, his olive green sedan reflected in the storefront windows—a pizzeria, an Ace Hardware, a 7-Eleven—as he passed. Mack had to stop and wait while Fry got a six-pack of beer at a liquor store and then a Big Mac at a McDonalds. When Fry came out of the drive-thru, he turned back north on Ashland and headed up to Barry, where he turned west.

Directly around the corner on the right was Burley Elementary School, an aging three-story brick building with tall, arching windows supported by a ground floor of granite. Fry proceeded to the next street, Paulina, where he turned north to Fletcher. At Fletcher, he headed back east and parked where the street dead-ended at the rear of the school playground. Mack followed, but eased the Zephyr to the curb just around the corner on Fletcher. Removing a pair of binoculars from the glove compartment, he trained them on Fry. With the binoculars he could observe Fry washing down his Big Mac with a Coke while he watched the kids frolicking on the playground. Would this be the place where Fry would select his next victim, Mack wondered? Time would tell, but Mack was running out of time. All he could do was wait and hope that Fry would give him the opportunity to nail his ass before another little girl was raped and slaughtered.

*12:20 p.m.:* Jason was watching a little girl on one of the swings. She reminded him of his little sister, Eve. He'd hated Eve as a kid, still hated her. It was fucking little Eve who'd ratted to his mother about his jacking off. His mother! A religious freak who had dragged Eve and his older brother Morgan and him to church every Sunday to hear "the Word of the Lord." His mother had beat the living shit out of him, so it would be like getting even again to do his sister's look-alike. He decided against it, though. Raping his little sis had more than evened the score. And although it had landed him in a juvenile correction shithouse for two years, it was worth it. Not only was his little sis a mental case for life, he hadn't had to endure any more fucking sermons.

Jason was musing over this when he saw *the one*. Dangling by her spindly legs from the monkey bars, she stood out because she was the only Chink amid the swarm of Caucasian, Black and Hispanic kids scurrying like ants around the playground. Six years old, maybe seven, scrawny but cute, especially the Kewpie Doll mouth on her tinted moon-shaped face. Another turn-on was the way her long pigtail swung back and forth, back and forth, back and forth, like a pendulum ticking away the hours, the minutes, the seconds…to the moment when he would have her. He'd never done a Chink before. It could be just that simple. Whatever it was about her, Jason knew that she was *the one.*

Jason gulped down the last of the Coke and pitched the container on the floor, where it joined a clutter of wrappers, napkins and empty beer cans. His cock was getting hard. In his mind he could see how it would be, how it had been before—her eyes popping out of her face, pleading for mercy. Her eyes would squeeze shut when he entered her, her screams muffled by the duct tape covering her mouth.

When he finished, he would wait for the sobbing to subside, for her eyes to flutter open. Hope would flicker there. Hope that he would let her go now that it was over. As if to reinforce that hope, Jason would smile and stroke her cheek. He would allow her this brief moment to think of home, the comfort of her bed, the protecting arms of her mother.

And then he would show her the knife. The Case hunting knife. The "Kodiak," named after the bear, with its stag bone handle and 440 stainless steel blade, curved at the tip, and razor sharp. The sight of the knife would petrify her with horror. Most of them passed out. If she did, he would revive her with smelling salts. She had to endure the final, agonizing heartbeats of her life. The knife slicing into her abdomen. The gush of blood. Her intestines slithering out of the gaping wound like garden snakes.

Distracted by his thoughts and now throbbing cock, Jason hadn't notice a burly white kid and his black buddy swagger up to the monkey bars.

The little Chinese girl didn't see them either until she felt her pigtail being pulled.

"Stop it! Stop it!" she screamed.

The white kid was tugging at her pigtail while his black sidekick looked on with a sadistic grin.

"Stop it! Stop it!" the white kid mimicked, and tugged harder.

As the Chinese girl clung to the bar with her legs, she flailed helplessly at the white kid with her fists.

"Look out, man," the black kid jeered. "Little monkey bitch gonna take you out."

The white boy laughed like a hyena. "Monkey bitch, monkey bitch! Come on down out of your tree, monkey bitch!"

"Maybe like if you said please," the black kid said.

"Right. So will you please come down, monkey bitch?" He didn't wait for an answer. He hit her. A vicious punch to her stomach that took the wind out of her. Her legs almost lost their grip on the bar, but somehow she managed to hang on.

"Maybe if you asked again," the black kid said. "Like po-lite-ly."

"Right. So will you pleeeeze come down, monkey bitch? No? Well guess I got to insist." He raised his fist to strike again.

"Knock it off, you little bastards!"

The boy's fist froze. He was staring at the young man on the other side of the lock-link fence. So was his black buddy. For a moment they almost laughed. The dude was a lightweight, 5'2", maybe 5'3" at best. Not much taller than they were. And slim. Shit, almost scrawny.

But the laughter died in their throats. Maybe it was the way the dude clutched the fence, fingers curled around the links, knuckles white. But more likely it was his eyes. Pale gray. Mean.

"You touch her again, you little shits, and I'll tear this fence down and kick the livin' shit out of you!" Jason meant it. She's mine, you little fuckers!

The boys only got the first part of the message. The spoken part. It was more than enough. They looked at each other for about one second. They didn't need to discuss this. The guy was one very bad dude.

"Yeah, sure. We was only kiddin' around, you know," the black kid said with a sick smile.

"Help her down!"

"Yeah, sure, okay." The burly white boy lifted the girl off the monkey bar and gently lowered her to the pavement.

"Now apologize!"

"What?"

"Say you're sorry, you little shitheads!"

Both boys stammered the words.

"Now get lost!"

The boys were only too willing to comply.

"Are you okay, honey?"

The little Chinese girl was just getting her breath. Her stomach still ached from the punch the big, nasty boy had given her, and she'd been too distraught to take much notice of her benefactor. When she looked at him she saw a young man with a face like the guys in TV beer commercials. A Chicago Cubs baseball cap covered most of his short-cropped blond hair. A Chicago Bulls sweatshirt draped over his faded jeans rounded out the image Jason Fry wanted to convey. Mr. Chicago Sports Fan. Mr. Nice Guy.

"I said are you okay, sweetie?" Mr. Nice Guy asked again.

"Yes...thank you."

"Hey, I'm just glad I was here to help. What's your name, honey?"

"Mei Wong."

"Mei Wong. That's a very pretty name, honey. Mine's Steve. Glad to meet you, Mei Wong."

The school bell rang, sending kids stampeding toward the rear entrance of the school.

"I've got to go now," Mei Wong said.

"Right. Well, you take care now, honey."

Jason watched little Mei Wong scamper across the playground. When she reached the entrance, she turned. Fry gave her a little wave. She waved back, then entered the building.

As he slid behind the wheel of the Cherokee, Jason couldn't suppress an outburst of laughter. What luck! What fucking unbelievable good luck! The little shitheads had done him a huge favor. They'd set him up as the Chink cunt's benefactor. Mr. Super Nice Guy. A guy you could trust.

Now all he had to do was follow her home. Maybe he'd take her then. More likely not. Momma Chink probably picked the little cunt up. No matter. It would happen. And when she came to from the chloroform some dark night in a secluded spot in one of the forest preserves, she would realize that Momma Chink was right. Never trust anyone you don't know, Mei Wong. Too fucking late, Momma Chink.

A sudden inspiration! He'd left the others where he'd done them. What if this time he brought the Chink cunt back to the playground, tied her upside down to the monkey bar? They would find her dangling there, as he'd first seen her, except this time her guts would be spilling onto the pavement. Yes! It would be risky, but he'd taken risks before. He'd also been careful. He'd used a condom, latex gloves, a bodysuit and bathing cap, even washed his victims out with bleach after he'd raped and gutted them to destroy anything the cops could use to DNA him. Of course, there was the one time, but that hadn't been his fault. Just a bad break.

Jason started the engine, but didn't drive away. Not yet. He sat there, staring at the monkey bars. An idea, a stupendous idea, was taking form in his brain. Why not bring them all back to the playgrounds? The media would have a field day with it. He could see the headlines: "MONKEY BAR MURDERER CLAIMS NEW VICTIM!" "POLICE BAFFLED." "MAYOR DEMANDS ACTION." This would be a national story. Every newspaper in the country would cover it. TV, too. Especially TV. They loved this shit. With this new grand plan came a rush of adrenalin. It felt good.

*2:15 p.m.:* Mack entered Rex's Rendezvous and was nearly overwhelmed by the pungent stench of cigarette smoke. Rex's was a neighborhood bar on West Lawrence near Broadway, a bad neighborhood with a high crime rate that even the presence of the Aragon Ballroom a block east could not redeem. Once a proud showcase for big bands and jitterbug contests, the Aragon rarely opened its doors anymore except for an occasional rock concert or prize fight. Police blue and whites cruised the area regularly, but it was up to the business owners to look after their own security with alarm systems and iron gates pulled across the doors and windows after closing time.

Mack paused for a moment to scan the bar, a long, narrow room, dark, drab and depressing. The place was nearly empty. Only three of the bar stools were occupied, and these by three frail-looking old men, nursing beers and chain smoking, their ashtrays clogged with butts, as they stared like zombies at the TV over the bar. The Cubs/Mets game was on the screen, but the sound was nearly smothered by piped-in country western music.

Moving to the bar, Mack saw Fry hunched over one of the two video games next to the restrooms near the rear exit. Mack felt the weight of a snub-nosed .38 revolver under his sweatshirt, the muzzle tucked into his Levi's. He'd taken the revolver from the body of a gangbanger two days after he'd learned that Fry was out. A drop gun. Nobody knew he had it.

Mack was suddenly thirsty. All he'd had to drink that day was a coffee and a Diet Coke, and his throat felt like he'd just woken up with a killer hangover. A beer would taste good. He moved to the bar, looking in vain for a bartender.

"Does this place have a bartender, or is it self-service?" he asked the nearest old man.

"Takin' a piss," the old man rasped, his eyes still transfixed on the TV.

Mack watched a bloated man in his sixties zip up his fly as he exited the restroom and shuffled up the aisle. It looked like a supreme effort for him to lift the bar gate and move behind the bar.

"What'll it be?" he wheezed.

"Do you have Amstel?"

"Amstel! Get fuckin' serious!"

"Make it a Miller Lite."

The bartender grunted. Pulling a bottle of Miller from an ice bin, he uncapped it and plunked it down on the bar without a glass. Just as well, Mack thought, if this jerk was responsible for washing the glasses.

"That'll be a buck and a half."

Mack extracted a dollar from his wallet and laid it on the bar with two quarters. No tip. The bartender didn't look surprised.

Mack took a long swig of beer before moseying past plastic booths and frayed beer posters toward the rear of the room. Fry was too much into the video game to notice him. It was a combat game. Mack stopped behind him to sip his beer and watch. The little creep was pretty good. When an armored vehicle attacked, Fry blasted it with a rocket, then quickly gunned down a guy in fatigues who appeared in the window of a compound. Another guy peeked through the leaves of a palm tree, rifle poised to blast Fry. Fry got him first.

Mack almost felt like applauding. Instead, he laid his right hand on Fry's shoulder, gripping it hard. "Look out for that tank, Fry!"

Fry's head spun around.

On the video screen a tank fired its cannon—"KABOOM!"—and then a voice, "YOU HAVE JUST BEEN KILLED IN COMBAT. GAME ENDED."

Jason Fry felt like he'd just stepped into an empty elevator shaft.

"McPherson! What the fuck are you doing here?"

"Having a beer, like you. And enjoying the ambiance of this charming establishment."

"Fuck you, McPherson! If this is a bust…"

"No bust, Fry. I'm not even on duty."

"Yeah? Then what in the fuck is it if it's not a bust?"

"I missed you while you were off the street and wanted to renew our acquaintance."

"Bullshit!" Jason studied the face hovering over him—the face of the man who'd busted him two years ago. Rugged, handsome in a way, he supposed, like the fucking Marlboro Man, with a jutting, cleft chin that seemed to be inviting someone to take a punch at it. A little older since he'd last seen him, given the creases around the eyes and mouth and the flecks of gray in his dark brown hair. Like then, the cop's face showed no hostility. He almost wished it did. What it showed was purpose. Dedicated, unyielding, unconditional. Fucking scary!

"No, really. I mean it. You can't know how much I've looked forward to this moment," the cop said, his lips creasing into an unsettling smile.

Jason hated that smile. The cop had been smiling that smile when he'd cuffed him and read him the *Miranda*. What did it mean? Was McPherson enjoying some private joke? And the eyes. Gun-metal gray. It was like looking into the muzzles of a double-barreled shotgun.

"Get off my ass, McPherson. I did my time."

"Yeah, I know. Two years, just two years when you should have done twenty, and in Mantino, a country club for the criminally insane—thanks to that loony judge who bought your delusional bullshit—that you had no recollection of what you'd done when you raped and brutalized that little girl. Well, Donna Moyer remembered, all right. And she remembered enough to ID you."

Tell me about it, asshole, Jason thought, and all because of a fucking dog. A fucking Great Dane who belonged to some asshole campers out at the Cook County Forest Preserve in Blue Island. Some basic animal instinct had made the dog attack him just as he was ready to carve up the little bitch. He'd had to use the knife on the dog, and during the struggle the bitch had taken off into the woods. There'd been no time to go after her. He could still hear the shouts of the campers calling for the dog. "Brutus! Brutus!" A fucking brute, all right. The fucker had done a real job on his arm. Eight stitches and a tetanus shot.

"Yeah, well that's all behind me," Jason said. "I got rehabbed at Mantino, and I'm ready to lead a normal life."

"Rehabbed my ass! You may have conned the shrinks at Mantino into thinking you were cured, but you can't con me. You're a sick, sex-crazed predator, Fry, who killed and will kill again. Donna Moyer lucked out. She lived. But by my count there were at least four other little girls who weren't so lucky."

Five, asshole, Jason thought. Six if hadn't been for that fucking dog. He'd gone to a doctor in Hammond, figuring that if he used an out-of-state doctor, gave a phony name, everything would be cool. Wrong. Somehow the fucking cop had run down the doctor, showed him some mug shots of suspects. His was among them, due to an assault charge two years earlier. He'd beaten that rap because the kid hadn't been able to make a positive ID. Not this time. This time they had his blood, thanks to fucking Brutus. And with his DNA as evidence, there'd been no choice but to plead temporary insanity and take his chances with the court.

"You got no proof I killed anybody," Jason said with as much bravado as he could muster. He picked up his bottle of Bud Light. "You couldn't prove shit then and you can't now." He raised the bottle to his lips.

"True. But I can discourage you from doing it again. I watched you this afternoon, setting up a little Chinese girl as your next score."

Jason choked on the beer. "You watched me..."

"That's right. And I'll keep on watching you. Look over your shoulder, Fry. You won't see me, but I'll be there, just waiting for you to screw up. And the next time it won't be a cushy resort like Mantino. It'll be a long stretch in Joliet and quality time with a roommate who'll romance you like a horny baboon."

"You can't do that! It's illegal, it's stalking, it's..."

"I know. Harassment."

"I got rights, McPherson! I got rights!"

"Not in my book, you don't," the cop said. He took a drink of beer. When he lowered the bottle, he was smiling that fucking smile again. "Tell you what I'll do. You like combat games, right? So let's play a little combat game. Just you and me."

Jason watched McPherson take out his handkerchief, remove something from underneath his sweatshirt and lay it down on the game. It was a .38 caliber revolver.

"So here's the deal. You go for it. If you kill me before I put a bullet in your head, you claim self-defense and maybe you walk. Otherwise, I'll make your life so miserable you'll wish you were back in Mantino."

Jason didn't care for either alternative. But his eyes lingered on the .38.

"What about it, Fry? Do you have the balls?"

Shut up! Shut up! Shut up! Jason's head screamed. God, how he hated this cop. For a moment he was tempted to do it. Grab the gun and blast the bastard. He even watched his hand inch toward the revolver. Then he pulled it back.

"Fuck you, McPherson! You think I'm fuckin' stupid?"

McPherson only shrugged. "Have it your way. But I'll leave the gun anyway, just in case you change your mind." He drained the bottle of beer with one swig, then set it down next to the revolver. "Have a nice day."

He turned and started to move away, then turned back. "Just remember what I told you, Fry. You keep lookin' over your shoulder."

Jason watched the cop saunter down the aisle toward the front door. His back was a tempting target. Very tempting. Jason reached for the gun again. This time he took it.

Mack exited the bar and took a deep breath of fresh air to get the stench of cigarette smoke out of his lungs. He couldn't understand how people ever got used to that smell. From the time he was nine years old and saw a cigarette butt in a urinal, he never gave smoking a second thought.

Well, here we go again, he thought, and wondered how long his luck would hold out. Maybe this time it wouldn't, especially if Fry was as good with a gun as he was behind the controls of the combat game. But what choice did he have with monsters like Fry on the street?

So the game was on, and he'd just have to see how it played out. One thing Mack knew for sure. Fry would use the .38. And soon.

*6:12 p.m.:* Jason flung his empty beer can at a monster cockroach. Godzilla, Jason called him. King of the roaches in his one-bedroom paradise at the beautiful Crawford Hotel. Godzilla had been dining on a fragment of a potato chip on the floor of the kitchenette. The can clanged off the pocked linoleum and skidded, a near miss that sent Godzilla scurrying under a refrigerator that rasped like a dying man on a respirator.

Jason chortled. "Get you next time, fucker."

Sprawled on a sagging sofa, his bare feet plopped on a plastic coffee table, he continued to channel surf the TV with a remote. Not much choice. The Crawford Hotel didn't offer cable for its flow of residents, so Jason settled on the six o'clock news on one of the local network channels. The picture of the spiffily dressed anchorman was blurry due to the damaged master antenna, the casualty of one of those storms that gather momentum over Lake Michigan before punishing the city. This required frequent adjustments of the rabbit ears to improve the quality of the picture.

Jason didn't feel like screwing around with the rabbit ears, but he could use another beer. Holding the remote, he got up, padded over to the fridge, took out one of the four remaining cans of Bud Light and popped the tab. He was about to take a swig, when something on the news caught his attention. A lady reporter was interviewing a tall young black cop about a missing kid. Mary something. He'd done a Mary once. Mary Simpson. He remembered all of their names. In fact, he remembered everything about them, especially the details of their last moments on earth.

Jason turned up the volume with the remote so he could hear better over the drone of the window air conditioner. The cop was telling the reporter bitch how he'd found little Mary with her daddy's ex, but didn't answer the bitch's questions about the kid's momma. Probably a hooker, Jason thought, a junkie as well. Most hookers did drugs. Not Jason. Drugs were one thing he avoided like the plague. They mess with your head, and Jason needed a clear head to do what he had to do without ending back in the joint.

Jason took a swig of the Bud and flopped back onto the couch. The reporter was interviewing the little cunt's parents now. How sickening, Jason thought. The assholes were crying, thanking the cop and God for the return of their fucking kid. He was about to change channels when the camera moved closer on the little bitch. Jason blinked. Damned if she didn't look like the Ramsey kid.

Now there was a major score. Jason was envious of whoever had done *her*. He wished he'd been in that basement with her and let his imagination feast on the thoughts of what he would have done to little JonBenêt.

Jason shrugged off the fantasy with a swig of beer. Mei fucking Wong would have to do. But that wouldn't happen if McPherson was allowed to live. Jason reached over to the end table and picked up the .38 the cop had given him. Big mistake. Jason's old man had taught him how to use a handgun when he was a kid, along with a variety of other weapons. They'd hunted together—ducks, deer, squirrels, rabbits, you name it—Jason had killed more than his share. But killing them was only part of the thrill. What really turned him on was skinning, gutting and dismembering their corpses.

Jason heard something scuttling in the kitchenette. Godzilla was dragging the potato chip toward his lair under the fridge. Smart fucker, Jason thought, pointing the .38 at the cockroach. For a moment he was tempted to blow the fucker away. Instead, he smiled and sighted along the barrel. "Bang, bang, McPherson. You're dead!"

*8:27 p.m.:* Mack was swinging with Count Basie. Perched on a stool behind the Remo drum set, he was playing along with Basie's 1937 recording of "One O'clock Jump." It was tempting to get carried away and rush the beat, forgetting that the drummer's primary function is to hold the groove. Basie's dynamo rhythm section made it almost effortless. At the end Mack did a one-bar flurry on the snare and tom before a climactic stroke on the crash cymbal.

"Not bad," Mack said, as he fingered a remote to turn off the CD player, then the stereo. He reached down for his bottle of Amstel Light on the floor and drained the last of the bottle. He was still on a jazz high, a high that only jazz musicians could fully appreciate. Jazz fans and aficionados could share it to some extent, but you had to be a part of the music to fully experience the feeling. Mack moved from behind the drum set, which occupied an exterior corner of his third-floor loft apartment. He kept it there to maintain friendly relations with his neighbor. The boom of the bass drum could penetrate an interior wall, even with a pillow inside the drum to dampen the sound. Fortunately, the walls were well insulated, thanks to a savvy developer who had rehabbed the one-time warehouse into loft apartments. Mack's 1,300 square feet of hardwood floor and twelve-foot high ceiling provided plenty of breathing room, with only the bathroom and bedroom partitioned off. The large windows of his northeast corner unit allowed in enough sunlight to heat the room in cold weather. It had proven to be an excellent investment. An original buyer a little over three years ago, he'd paid $175,000 for his one-bedroom unit, which would now sell for more than $300,000.

Mack had worked up a thirst behind the drums. Another beer would hit the spot. He moved to the open kitchen that was separated from the large room by a two-seat oak wood bar. The bar wasn't an antique like most of his furnishings, but it had an antique look. The refrigerator, electric stove, microwave, and Dell computer on a vintage roll-top desk seemed out of place in this environment. Mack opened the door to the fridge. Not much inventory: three bottles of Amstel, some Diet Cokes, a box of millet rice cereal, and half a carton of skim milk. He'd have to make a shopping expedition to Whole Foods. Might as well do it tonight, he thought. He could put together a healthy Caesar salad with chicken strips and eat there.

Mack removed a bottle of Amstel, twisted off the cap and flipped it into a trash container on his way to a 1906 barrister bookcase. He lifted up and slid back the glass door of the top unit and pulled out a second edition of *Grant's Memoirs* from his collection of Civil War history books. He read three or four books simultaneously, mostly histories and bios, and wanted to get back to Grant's account of his Vicksburg campaign.

Mack, Grant and the Amstel moved to Mack's favorite chair, an oak rocker with a carved top and Brentwood arms, at least a century old. He settled into the rocker's embrace and took a long pull at the beer with a sigh of contentment. The chair was like a throne, the room his private kingdom. His Shangri-La. It was a Shangri-La he shared with few people. His most frequent visitor was Maria, his maid, a sweet little Mexican lady he'd hired after busting her scumbag hubby for robbery and assault. Maria had a three-year-old son to support, so it seemed like the right thing to do.

Mack looked around the room with a bemused smile. He could always tell when Maria had cleaned. Not only was the apartment spotless and heavy with the orange scent of furniture polish, but some of his things were no longer where they were supposed to be. That was because Maria had her own idea of where his things belonged.

Damn, Mack thought, but not with anger. She'd moved Ulysses again. For some reason Maria thought he belonged in the shelter of a potted ficus.

"Next time she does that, give her hell, Ulysses," he said to the bronze statue of an aging Greek warrior that resided on an old piano stool under the ficus, on the other side of which stood a two-foot tall replica of Michelangelo's *David* that Mack had bought for himself years earlier when he graduated from the police academy.

Mack took another swig of Amstel, set the bottle on an ornate French end table, and opened the book to where the bookmark protruded. He left the book open on his lap. Grant and Vicksburg could wait for a few minutes while he relaxed. Rocking gently, soothed by the soft whirl of a barroom ceiling fan and the metronome tick tick tick of the grandfather clock that occupied one corner, he could feel the tension draining from his body.

The clock was his latest acquisition. To get it, he'd been forced to outbid the antique dealers at the auction of a deceased old lady's cherished possessions. It was worth it. Like the rest of his furniture, he'd restored the cherry wood himself. It was a craft he'd acquired as a boy from his grandparents, along with a discerning eye for genuine bargains. When his granddad retired from Sears Roebuck, Ed and Marsha Henderson had moved from Fort Wayne to North Webster, a small lake town in northeast Indiana, and invested their life savings in an antique store.

His mother ran the store now. After his dad died, she'd gone there to help out, and stayed. Mack knew his mother would live the rest of her life in the cozy, three-bedroom A-frame with its 50 feet of lakefront. Why not? In addition to raising two active and sometimes difficult boys, she'd taught English and history in Chicago's public high schools for thirty years—a job often deserving of combat pay. The little lake community offered a tranquil alternative to the noise and stress of the big city.

Mack felt a twinge of guilt. He hadn't visited his mother since Christmas.

Okay, he thought, with another swallow of beer. Next month he'd make the three-hour drive to North Webster on one of his two-day breaks, maybe over Mother's Day, take her out for supper at The Frog Tavern, get her tipsy on two martinis, buy her some grilled salmon—half of which she would take back for Mazie, her cat—and listen to her reminisce for the umpteenth time about how she'd met and fallen in love with his dad when the Les Brown band played a spring prom gig at Ball State, where his mom was getting her master's degree.

Mack's gaze fell on his parents' wedding picture. It shared the marble top of a massive Victorian sideboard with other family pictures and his dad's trumpet. His mother, a lovely lady with long auburn hair, was wearing a no-frills wedding dress and beaming through her freckles. She looked like a little girl next to his father in his black pants and white tux jacket, the formal attire the band members wore on their ritzy gigs. His dad's swarthy, handsome face had aged prematurely through the years, but to Mack his mom still looked like a little girl. A few more wrinkles, true, and the auburn hair had grayed, but she was still as alert and feisty as ever.

Feisty was putting it mildly, Mack thought. She was one tough little lady. It was his mother who usually meted out the punishment when Mack and his brother Kenny got out of line. Mack winced at the memory of the flyswatter's sting on his bare butt. Their dad preferred the yardstick to the fly swatter, but rarely used it. When he did, Mack was the primary recipient. "You're the oldest, Michael," his dad would lecture him, "and it's up to you to set the example for your brother." True, Mack conceded, but he knew there was more to it than that. Kenny was a musician, like his dad. A natural. He was already pecking out tunes with one finger on the piano when he was three. By seven he was playing the clarinet and saxophone with more than considerable skill. Being a natural, Kenny got away with more shit than Mack did. It would have been easy for Mack to resent this, but he didn't.

"Did I, Kenny?" he said to the picture on the other side of the trumpet.

It showed an eleven-year-old Mack, big for his age and muscular, with one protective arm around the shoulders of his skinny, younger brother. They were posing on the pier of their grandparents' lake home, where they spent most of their summers. They had just finished a three-week program at Camp Crosley, a YMCA camp on neighboring Lake Tippecanoe. Other than having to attend religious services at the camp, Mack and his brother hadn't put in much time at Sunday school or church. Their dad, a Catholic, was too busy on the road with bands to deal with their spiritual needs. Their mother gave it a try, but preferred to leave the job to their grandmother, a devout Methodist. She was a strict old lady, who made Kenny and him do a number of chores, but never insisted that they go to church with their grandfather and her. She used a more subtle method to bring the word of the Lord into their lives. She left a Bible in their bedroom. Mack often read passages from the Book at night, sometimes aloud to Kenny, before succumbing to the day's exhausting activities.

Mack remembered some of the passages from the Bible and found them sometimes contradictory. The Lord's Prayer told you not to trespass against those who have trespassed against you. In other words, if someone slugs you, don't slug him back. And yet another quote in the Bible argued for an eye for an eye and a tooth for a tooth. In short, get even. Mack preferred the second option.

With that thought he reached for a chain around his neck and drew up an attached bronze medal from under his shirt. It was a medal Kenny had won for third place in a swim meet when he and Kenny were at the YMCA camp. The third place acknowledgement was engraved on one side. On the other side were the words, "YMCA—Serving God by Building Healthy Minds, Bodies and Spirits."

Mack gripped the medal, his eyes drawn to the photo again. Just two sunburned kids in swim trunks without a care in the world.. A screwed-up world, Mack thought. An unjust world. How unjust Kenny would never know. But Mack knew.

*9:10 p.m.:* Jason Fry was angle-parked in a red Cutlass between a Land Rover SUV and a Chevy Impala. His position on the east side of May Street north of Carroll gave him a clear view of the entrance to the six-story loft building on the southwest corner, where McPherson lived. Two warehouses and a truck lot occupied the other corners. Jason smiled. Aside from some Italian restaurants on Grand Avenue and the few loft conversions, the neighborhood was dominated by warehouses, industrial buildings, trucking companies and meat, fish and poultry packing houses. After sundown there was little traffic, practically no one on the streets. Perfect for what he had to do.

He'd followed the same game plan he'd used to abduct the girls—rented a car using a phony driver's license, then replaced the plates with stolen ones. Stolen plates were reported, but the cops never bothered to look for them. If someone witnessed the shooting and was astute enough to ID the Cutlass and get the plate number, it would lead the cops exactly nowhere.

Jason hefted the .38 in his hand, pointed it toward the entrance to McPherson's building, and aimed it as though he were going to take the shot. Suddenly aware that someone might see him, he quickly pulled the gun away from the window and set it down on the passenger seat. Don't be stupid, he told himself, no use taking chances. Gotta stay focused, gotta stay loose.

*9:14 p.m.:* Mack sat with his eyes closed, still afloat among the memories of his parents, his grandparents…and Kenny. The beeping sound of the cordless phone jolted him back to the present. He reached over to the end table and grabbed the receiver. Probably some damned telemarketer, he thought. "If you're selling, say goodbye."

"Hi there," a familiar female voice purred into his ear. "Horny?"

Mack laughed. "Not until you called."

"Flattery will get you into my pants every time. Got any plans for tonight?"

"Well, I thought I'd just sit me here rockin', chained to this ol' rockin' chair."

"Sounds like the lyrics to a song. Elton John?"

"Hoagy Carmichael."

"Hoagy who?"

"Carmichael. As in 'Star Dust,' 'Georgia On My Mind' Carmichael."

"Before my time. But I've got something on my mind, and it's not Georgia."

"Such as?"

"Such as you get your horny ass out of that ol' rockin' chair and bring it over here."

"I'm practically there. One problem. I may be horny but I'm also hungry."

"So pick up some Chinese on the way. I wouldn't want you to pass out from malnutrition before I have you for dessert."

Nothing subtle about Inge, Mack thought. "How about the wine?"

"Chardonnay is chilling in the fridge as we speak."

"Okay, I'll stop at Jimmy Wong's for the food. Give me an hour."

"Make it half an hour. I'm horny, too, my dear."

Mack grinned and cradled the phone. Some kind of foxy lady, Inge. He'd met her five years ago after a shootout during a robbery in progress at a convenience store. The two perps died of the slugs Mack and his partner pumped into them, but not before Mack caught a bullet in his left thigh from an AK-47. The bullet had to be surgically removed. No problem there, but it had damaged the hip joint and muscle. This provided him with an all-expenses-paid vacation and one hell of a lot of pain during the initial recovery phase of exercise programs and therapy.

He'd picked a physical therapist at random from the list provided by Blue Cross Blue Shield, which insured the CPD. The West Bank Wellness Center had four therapists on staff, but Mack had gotten the personal attention of the owner. Big surprise. Not only was the owner a lady, but what a lady! Early forties, tall, with a strong but lovely Nordic face, long blonde hair and the legs of a runway model.

A friendship had developed during those rehab rituals. Mack would tell Inge about the latest case he was working, a book he was into, whatever. She opened up to him as well. An early divorce from a shiftless husband had left her with two boys to raise and a pile of debts. The boys were out of college now, and the debts long gone, thanks to a thriving business.

Mack liked that about Inge. Here was a lady who could take care of herself. At least financially. As for her other needs, they weren't discussed. However, one primary need was revealed during his last visit to the clinic. During the usual after-workout massage, she leaned over and whispered in his ear, "How would you like to fuck me?" When he recovered the power of speech, he told her that he would like it just fine.

This had taken their relationship to a new level, one that was still going strong. It was a no bullshit relationship that could only exist between good friends. Love did not enter into the mix. Love could have messed things up. So could marriage. Mack was thankful that, to date, the subject of matrimony had not come up. He'd gone down that road once before and was not looking to go there again.

This was on his mind as he pushed himself out of the rocker. Marriage was not for cops. For bankers, stockbrokers, used car salesmen, plumbers, whoever, but not for cops. "Right, Ulysses?" he said to the statue. No comment from Ulysses, but Mack knew he understood. He took a swig of Amstel and set the half-empty bottle on the piano stool next to the statue.

"You finish it, buddy," he said, patting the warrior on the helmet. "I'm outta here."

Mack moved to the entrance and removed his holster with his service revolver from one of the four brass hooks of a 1903 hall tree. He unbuckled his belt, slid on the holster and its occupant and buckled up without thinking about it. He felt naked without the familiar weight of the revolver on his right hip. Then he remembered that Inge would give him her usual lecture about the number of accidental deaths that occurred each year from handguns—statistics she either gleaned from fellow NRA haters or just made up. She got really pissed when he forgot to remove the revolver before he was invited to share her king-sized playpen, even though he assured her that the only thing that would go off resided between his legs.

Chuckling over this thought, Mack decided to humor her by not packing the .38. He hung it back up, took a windbreaker off another hook and slipped it over his sweatshirt. Then he set the entry alarm next to the door and left the apartment.

*9:25 p.m.:* Jason was getting antsy. The dash clock of the Cutlass showed he had been there for nearly half an hour. Maybe the fucking cop was going to stay home all evening. Probably anchored in front of the tube with a beer and a TV dinner. Okay, so he'd give it another half an hour, then call it quits for the night. But if necessary, there would be another night, and another, and another, until he finally got his chance to use the .38. Jason was hoping he'd get that chance tonight. He wanted this over. He wanted the cop dead. Dead and out of his life, forever. But whatever it took, he would make it happen.

The clanging of warning bells behind him suddenly punctured the quiet. Startled, Jason spun around and saw signal lights flashing red, guard rails descending. Moments later a Northwestern commuter train pulled by two huge diesel engines rumbled over one of the four tracks that stretched through the western burbs as far as Geneva. When he looked back at the loft building, he tensed. Someone was coming out!

Shit. It was only some guy with a dog on a leash. Jason swore again. They were crossing the street and headed his way. Jason ducked. No use taking a chance of being seen. He heard the beast give a couple of angry yelps. Probably had to take a piss, Jason thought. A big fucker, the dog, like that fucking Brutus. Jason could still feel the beast's teeth tearing into his arm. The memory sent a surge of fear slithering down his spine, and his hand sought the comfort of the snub-nosed weapon on the passenger seat.

Jason waited a few more seconds before he sat up and looked back. The guy and the fucking dog were crossing the railroad tracks. Jason relaxed and removed his hand from the gun. Jumpy, he told himself. You're too damned jumpy. Sure, you want to get this over, but you gotta relax. You got all the time in the world. So stay loose, okay? It will happen.

Mack exited the loft building. For a moment he paused under the metal canopy that protected the entrance on May Street. It had started to drizzle. The wind had shifted off the lake, plummeting the temperature thirty degrees in a matter of minutes. Typical Chicago weather, he thought. Zipping up his windbreaker, he debated whether to take the Zephyr or the Bonneville. He kept the Zephyr under a canvas cover in the fenced-in rear lot, where an access card was needed to open the electronic gate. The Bonneville was more accessible. It occupied an assigned spot along the north side of the building. In view of the weather, the Bonneville was a given.

Mack pulled up the collar of the windbreaker and was about to make a dash for the car when he heard a dog barking. It was a familiar bark. Caesar, he thought, his upstairs neighbor's Great Dane. Up the street he could see Larry, watching his roommate hose down the base of a utility pole. Mack smiled. The dog was damned near as big as its master.

The smile quickly faded. He was remembering another Great Dane, the one who'd saved Donna Moyer from Jason Fry. Mack had almost forgotten about Mr. Fry. He would be looking to keep their rendezvous with the .38. Maybe he was out there now, somewhere in the darkness.

Mack took a long look in both directions. A few cars were strung along both sides of May in front of the loft building. In the next block to the north three vehicles—two cars and an SUV—were angle parked on the other side of the street. The SUV looked like a Land Rover. No maroon Cherokee. Not that Mack expected to see one. Fry wouldn't be stupid enough to use the Cherokee. He'd probably be driving a hot car with stolen plates.

Mack hesitated. He was tempted to check out some of the cars, when a blast of cold spray slapped him in the face. To hell with it, he thought. Get to the Bonneville before it really starts to come down. Lowering his head against the wind, he charged into the night.

Jason smiled. McPherson had left the building and was moving fast toward Carroll Street. Going for his car, Jason figured. He'd cased the area earlier. A few cars were T-parked in numbered spaces along the north side of the building; the rest were in a large enclosed lot in the rear. Jason didn't know where McPherson's car was located. It didn't matter. He was ready.

As Jason expected, McPherson headed west on Carroll. The moment he was out of sight, Jason scrambled out of the car with the .38 and darted across the street. The cold drizzle sent a shiver through his body. Shit! Shoulda brought a jacket. To hell with it. He had a job to do. He slid swiftly along the aluminum siding of the warehouse and peered cautiously around the corner. The cop was standing next to a hunter green Pontiac Bonneville SSE with his back toward Jason, digging the key from the pocket of his jeans. Jason was impressed. The SSE was hot shit on wheels. McPherson knew his cars, all right. Jason gave him that.

He'd also give him a slug from the .38. At fifty-some yards it wasn't a sure kill, but the odds were good enough. He gripped his right wrist with his left hand and extended the .38. The cop bent over to get something. Must have dropped his key, Jason figured. Good. It gave him a couple more seconds to take careful aim. He could feel his heartbeat accelerating. The high of the hunter with his prey in his sight. The moment before the kill. The cop straightened. His back offered a bull's eye. Jason took a deep breath, released it. His forefinger pressured the trigger.

Mack thumbed the unlock button on the car key. As he opened the door, he was startled by the sound of Caesar barking again. But this time the barking was frantic. A split second later Mack heard a shot and saw a bullet spider the rear side window at his elbow. Mack didn't hesitate. He dove onto the front seat and, keeping low, reached over, opened the glove compartment, and grabbed another gun, a 1942 Victory Model Smith & Wesson he'd bought as a back-up weapon. Lucky he'd stashed it in the glove compartment, because it was clear now that Fry had taken the bait and was out there in the dark with the .38 gunning for him!

Jason couldn't fucking believe it! He'd missed! He'd missed because of another fucking dog. Like that fucking Brutus that had sent him to a hospital and ultimately to jail, this fucker's barking had shaken him up enough to make him jerk the trigger instead of slowly squeezing it. And there'd been no chance for a second shot, because the cop had taken cover inside the car. All he could do now was get the hell out of there before the cop could come after him.

When there were no more shots, Mack sprinted to the corner in time to see Caesar chasing a rat along the gutter, dragging Larry behind him. There was another rat on the run, as well, and he was scrambling to get inside a Cutlass parked up the block on May Street. Mack dashed back to the Bonneville, folded himself in behind the wheel, cooked the engine, and backed and gunned the SSE.

Mack made a tire-screeching left turn off Carroll onto May heading north. Ahead Mack saw the Cutlass crossing Kinzie and speeding toward Grand Avenue. He also saw the warning lights flashing and the barrier arms descending at the Northwestern tracks ahead of him. He couldn't see the train yet, but he could hear the rumble of the two diesel engines and the warning blare of the horn. For a second he almost hesitated, but he knew he couldn't afford a delay. If he waited for the train to pass, Fry would be long gone. Mack had no choice. He had to get to the other side of the tracks before the train cut him off.

He cranked a hard left and waltzed the Bonneville around the first barrier arm. For a heartbeat he was almost blinded by the intense glare of the diesel's headlights bearing down on him and deafened by the scream of its horn. As fast as he could he cut a hard right and completed an inverted S around the other barrier arm. The twin diesels thundered by behind him. Close!

Jason sped through the tunnel under the North Central Railroad abutment, then braked hard to hang a sharp right onto Hubbard, flooring the accelerator as he came out of the turn. Jason knew he had to get downtown and into heavy traffic. If the cop was chasing him, chances are he wouldn't risk using his gun where people could get hurt. Jason could also ditch his .38 in traffic. Besides, Jason told himself, with his head start, the cop would probably never catch up with him anyway.

Wrong! As he looked up and glanced into the rearview mirror, Jason saw the Bonneville round the corner with the agility of a NASCAR racer. Shit! That car could fly, and McPherson knew how to drive it. Jason tried not to panic. Stay focused, stay cool, he told himself, as he sped past the blur of bizarre murals on the wall of the railroad abutment and blew through the stops at Aberdeen and Carpenter. Another glance in the rearview. The Bonneville was riding his ass, but there were only a few more blocks to Halsted…and heavy traffic…and safety. Just a few more blocks and…

Jason felt his blood jump at the sound of a gunshot and a bullet puncturing the rear windshield. Reflexively he jerked the wheel to the right, causing the Cutlass to jump the curb and head straight for the streetlamp at Morgan. He yanked the wheel hard to the left and managed to steer the Cutlass back off the curb just in time to avoid a head-on collision with the lamppost. He swallowed hard. His throat felt like burnt toast. He had to do something—and fast—before the cop fired again.

Take evasive action. His only chance. Keep the cop busy at the wheel so he couldn't use the gun. He pumped the brakes, cranked a hard right at Peoria. The Cutlass screeched around the corner, its rear end banging against the cement lane divider of the underpass. The impact slowed the Cutlass, jolted Jason. He fought for control, then accelerated through the tunnel.

Mack downshifted and swung the SSE into the underpass around the left side of the divider. The Bonneville sideswiped the wall but drew alongside the Cutlass as they sped out of the underpass. Grabbing the Smith & Wesson from his lap with his right hand, Mack fired three quick shots through the open passenger window. He saw one round spark off the hood of the Cutlass, another shatter the side mirror. A spray of blood on Fry's shoulder told Mack that at least one slug had found its target.

Jason felt the punch of the bullet. It tore into the biceps of his left shoulder and pushed him against the wheel. Oh Jesus, I'm hit!

Jesus! Jason had a flashback of his mother using the Bible to sledgehammer God and Jesus into his head. The Ten Commandments, Sermon on the Mount, the Last Supper, the Crucifixion, all that holy shit clogged and slowed his brain in the split second he had to react.

But there was no time to react. Looming ahead was the big double gate of a fenced-in truck lot that dead-ended Peoria at Kinzie. But Jason couldn't pry his foot off the gas or turn the wheel. His body was like a dead battery. He didn't even feel the impact when the Cutlass rammed through the gates. Then a surge of pain in his left shoulder cleared his brain. The Cutlass was barreling between a row of truck trailers toward the rear of the lot, and directly ahead was a huge diesel tank enclosed by a link fence!

Jason managed to pry his foot off the gas and stomp on the brake pedal. The Cutlass scratched across thirty feet of dirt and gravel. Jason had a fleeting glimpse of a sign on the fence—"NO SMOKING"—before the impact ballooned the airbag and plunged him into a black pit of unconsciousness.

Mack drove into the truck lot and parked. Removing a box of shells from the glove compartment, he fed four rounds into the empty chambers of the revolver. He flipped the cylinder shut and slid out of the bucket. It had stopped raining. He left the Bonneville near the entrance and walked toward the Cutlass. As he got closer, he angled around to the driver's side to check things out.

Fry was slumped over the wheel. His left shoulder was oozing blood. He wasn't moving. If he could move, he wasn't going anywhere. The Cutlass was wedged in a tangle of fence, the hood accordioned against the diesel tank. They'd have to cut the bastard out of the wreck with a welding torch. On second thought, no welding torch. Not with gas spurting from a busted fuel line.

Mack stopped just shy of the spreading pool of gasoline, his Victory Special leveled at the motionless figure behind the wheel. He was taking no chances with Mr. Fry. He heard a moan from the wreck. The creep was stirring. It would be a rude awakening.

Jason inhaled the pungent odor of gasoline. That was his first sensation. The second was the throbbing pain in his left shoulder. The third was the voice echoing in his head, "Fry…Fry…Fry…Fry…" The darkness began to dissolve. He blinked at the steering wheel. "Looks like you'll live…live…live…live," the voice echoed again.

Jason slowly raised his head off the wheel. It felt like it was filled with cement as he swiveled it toward the sound. A blurry image took shape.

"McPher…McPherson."

"Too bad," the cop said, his voice no longer echoing. "I was hoping to save the taxpayers the expense of your room and board for the next twenty years at the Joliet Hilton."

Jason made an effort to move. No good. The steering wheel had him pinned against the seat, and the motor was damn near sitting in his lap. He felt like a sardine in a can someone had stepped on. If that wasn't bad enough, he saw blood seeping from a hole in his sweatshirt.

"Get me outa here! I'm hurt!"

"Really? Yeah, I guess you are. How does it feel?"

Jason tried to talk again but coughed up a spray of blood. The cough triggered a sharp pain in his chest. Shit, I'm busted up inside, too, he thought!

"Goddammit, I'm fucking bleeding to death! You can't just stand there and let me die! You gotta help me!"

"Help you? I was planning to arrest you for the attempted murder of a police officer."

"Yeah, yeah, yeah! So arrest me, but get me outta here, get me to a hospital! You're a cop. It's your duty!"

The cop didn't respond. He just stood there, smiling at him. That fucking smile that bugged the shit out of Jason. His private joke smile.

Mack thought about it. Maybe he should let the bastard die. He could just walk away, get into his car and take off. By the time somebody found Fry, he'd be a corpse.

But Fry was right. It was his duty to help him. Besides, twenty years of hard time would be a kind of slow death in itself. Of course, when Fry got out, Mack would be waiting. Fry would know that. He'd have an eternity to think about it.

"All right, Fry. I'm going to be a good cop, do my duty. First I got to recite the *Miranda*…"

"Fuck the *Miranda*! Just get me some help!"

"Okay. I've got my radio in the car. I'll make some calls. But while I'm gone, I want you to remember some names. Shelly Hart, Heather Wagner, Gretchen Mayer and Mary Simpson. Remember them, Fry? Sure you do. They're the four little girls you did. They bled to death, after you raped and butchered them. Now it's your turn. But at least you've got a chance. So you just sit there and think about them. Maybe the paramedics will pry you out of there in time to give you a transfusion. Maybe not. We'll see." Mack turned and walked away.

Jason felt something snap in his brain. The smile! Now he understood it. It was the smile of an executioner. An executioner who was mocking his victim before the axe fell! Only one thought consumed him. Wipe the smile off the cop's face! Kill him! Kill him, even if he ended up on death row! If he did, it was better than that smile haunting him for the rest of his life!

Jason looked for the .38. Where in the hell was it? There…on the floor of the passenger side. Could he reach it? Rage fueled his adrenaline, gave him the strength to get through the pain as he struggled against the wheel and leaned down. His hand inched for the gun, his fingers numb, fluttering. Just a little further. Almost there. Almost…

Mack winced at the sting of the bullet. It grazed his left arm at the same time that he heard the shot. He hit the ground and rolled toward the rear of a truck trailer. A second bullet kicked dirt into his face. Another roll brought him behind the big, dual wheels of the trailer. He peered around the wheels, the gun extended. A third shot sounded. The bullet ricocheted off the rear of the trailer inches over his head.

Mack lowered the gun. No need to return fire now. The last bullet, the one that had glanced off the trailer, had also sparked off a rock, and the spark had ignited the pool of gasoline. Fry's doom was sealed.

Jason screamed. The ground was suddenly alive with flames. Now he could account for the stench of gasoline. The fuel line must have ruptured, and something had touched off the gasoline. Fear blocked out the pain now and gave Jason the strength to push his shoulder against the door. It didn't budge. The crash had fused the door against the mangled frame. Still, he kept pushing and yelling "Get me out! Get me out!" while he watched the flames lick closer. Closer. Toward the fuel line. Toward the tank.

"Oh, God, help me! Please help me!"

But God wasn't listening.

The explosion filled the Cutlass with a whoosh of white heat. In that instant Jason saw himself standing in front of his mother's open grave, watching the coffin being lowered into the earth and remembering his thoughts at the time. Don't bury me. Don't put me in the fucking ground where the maggots and worms can fuck with me. Burn me. Cremate me. In an incinerator or wherever they do that shit. Just don't bury me!

Jason realized in that same instant that he was getting his wish. He was being cremated. Problem was he wasn't dead. He was alive…and screaming.

Mack ran. Away from the inferno. Away from the agonizing screams that penetrated the crackle of flames. Away from the stench of burning flesh.

When the diesel tank blew, the explosion pounded his eardrums and hurled him to the ground. A wave of scorching heat washed over him. Mack felt a burning sensation on his back and realized his windbreaker was on fire. He rolled in the dirt until the flames were snuffed out, then pulled off the smoldering jacket.

Mack pushed himself to his feet. It seemed to take all his effort. His legs were wobbling. He turned to look at the flaming holocaust. Billowing fireballs illuminated the whole area like a midnight sun. The heat was intense, but Mack could not move away. Or look away. He just stood there, the Smith & Wesson dangling in his hand, and watched. After all, this was his moment. The end of Jason Fry. The end of a monster.

Suddenly he felt nauseated. He coughed up a bitter residue of beer and spit it out. His stomach was churning. So was his brain. This was it. He couldn't do this again. It had to be the last time.

Last time? Mack wondered. He felt the YMCA medal, heated from the fire, burning against his chest, as he watched the conflagration. Fry's funeral pyre. Should he at least recite something from the Book? His grandmother would have done that. She would have said something. Forgive him, oh Lord, for he knows not…knew not…something. Mack grimaced. Ashes to ashes would be more appropriate. As for words from the Book, he had his own epitaph for Mr. Fry:

*"Burn in hell, you sonovabitch!"*

## *Friday, April 26*

*7:32 a.m.:* Mack was pissed. Not that he hadn't expected the call from CPD Headquarters that interrupted his shower. He had. He just hoped it would come after he had time to have a decent breakfast and coffee and call Inge to tell her that nothing but a bullet could have prevented him from keeping their date. But that would have to wait.

Since the Bonneville was in serious need of repair and would have to be left at a body shop for at least a couple of days, Mack took the Zephyr instead. And although there was no time for a leisurely breakfast, as he was already running late, he was still a bit woozy from the previous night's events, so he made a quick stop for coffee at a Starbucks on Wells, hoping that the coffee would at least help clear his head. It did, a little, and he was taking his last sip as he approached the CPD Administration building at 3510 South Michigan.

At the entrance to the large parking lot at the rear of the building, Mack stopped to show his ID and sign a register for a policeman at a guard shack, who took down his license number. Mack parked the Zephyr in the guest area and walked to the rear entrance of the modern five-story structure that had replaced the cramped, vintage building on South State Street a few years earlier. From the outhouse to the penthouse, he thought, and smiled.

Mack entered a cavernous lobby and showed his badge to a young uniformed officer, one of four cops manning the box-shaped front desk. "Detective McPherson. Got an appointment with the Super." By "Super" Mack was referring to Superintendent of Police Franklin Campbell Hollender, whose cluster of offices and large staff shared the fifth floor with Internal Affairs. It was not a floor most cops were anxious to visit. Especially Mack.

"Just a minute, Detective." The officer picked up a phone and poked some numbers. "This is Officer Reed, front desk. I've got Detective McPherson here and…" The party on the other end cut him off. Mack couldn't hear the response, but the officer was looking at him as if he were scheduled for a lethal injection. The officer hung up the phone. "Go on up, Detective. Wait, you'll need a pass."

"Right."

The officer gave him a clip-on pass, which Mack affixed to the breast coat pocket of his wrinkled beige suit that looked like it came off the rack at a Salvation Army outlet store. He thanked the officer and proceeded to a bank of elevators. A tall, heavyset man in his forties rose from a nearby bench to greet him. Unlike Mack, the man was garbed in a neatly pressed dark blue suit with matching tie and spotless white shirt. His polished black shoes glistened.

"Hello, Jack. You look like you're decked out for a wedding."

"More like a funeral, I'd say. You're late."

Mack glanced at his wrist watch. 8:14 a.m. "Exactly fourteen minutes and twenty-three seconds late. I had a kinda rough night."

"No shit!"

Mack observed the splotches of crimson seeping into the rugged face topped by a crop of receding dark brown hair. The fact that his best friend and boss, Commander Jack Casey, did not extend his hand was also no great surprise, given the circumstances. Instead, he pulled an inhaler out of his pocket, sniffed, then snorted.

"Allergies again?"

"Fucking ragweed. Let's get this over with."

An elevator door parted, disgorging three uniformed officers and a plainclothes detective. Mack and Casey entered. Casey stabbed the "5" button with his finger. They had the elevator to themselves all the way to the fifth floor, which gave Casey his chance to begin a variation of his usual lecture.

"You've really done it this time, buddy. You know that, don't you?"

"Right."

"You're one of the best cops on the force, but you're not satisfied to just bend the rules, you gotta fucking break them!"

"Well, you know how I hate red tape."

The joke failed to amuse Casey. "Damn it, Mack..."

The door opened, and Mack stepped out before Casey could finish. After a uniformed officer behind a desk checked their passes and IDs, they proceeded down a hallway amid a crosscurrent of cops and administrative personnel. The lecture resumed.

"How long have I been tellin' you to cool it? How long?"

"What say we take in a Cubs game this Sunday? The Pirates are in town for a three-game series."

"Fuck the Cubs! You screwed up, buddy, big time. The mayor is taking *mucho* heat on this. This time I might not be able to square it with the super."

"Woods is scheduled to pitch. Should be a great game."

"I give up! I fucking give up!"

Mack didn't have to look at Casey's face to know that the crimson splotches would be deepening to burgundy. He'd seen his friend's Irish temper aroused on many occasions going all the way back to their days together at the academy, when a hard-as-nails sergeant instructor chewed him out for not advising a perp of his rights during a training exercise. The budding friendship blossomed during the two years they shared a cruiser as beat cops. After passing the D-2 exam, their professional and personal association continued as Area Two Homicide detectives.

When they reached the door to the superintendent's offices, Casey paused to grip Mack's arm. "Don't make this any tougher than it's gotta be. I do the talking. Period."

Mack gave him a little salute, and got a look of exasperation in return. In fact, Mack was very uncomfortable that he had put Casey on the hot seat, and his awkward attempts at humor were just his way of trying to sidestep the guilt he was feeling. He loved the big guy but he had become one gigantic pain in the ass, to the extent that it was straining their personal relationship. The fact that Casey was his boss didn't help. Unlike Mack, Casey was ambitious. Although Casey had never confided this to him, Mack suspected that he harbored aspirations of someday occupying the office they were approaching.

This thought flashed through his mind again as they entered an outer reception lobby that reminded Mack of a dentist's office, only larger—sofas, cushioned chairs, bland paintings on the walls. Two people were browsing through magazines. An attractive young lady behind a tidy desk looked up from her computer as they approached.

"Go right in, Commander," she said to Casey, her voice conveying the proper respect for his rank. Her furtive glance at Mack did not.

The next room was a large beehive of activity. Mack noted two offices, one marked "General Counsel," the other "Administrative Assistant," as Casey led the way past staff personnel at their work stations toward the superintendent's inner sanctum. The Super's personal secretary, a stocky woman in her fifties, occupied a desk outside the door. Mack wondered if she moonlighted as a lady wrestler. She was wearing a drab-looking business suit and little makeup. The glower on her masculine face was ominous.

"Hello, Pat. Nice to see you again. You're looking great," Casey said, turning on his Irish charm.

It didn't work. "Good morning, Commander," she said perfunctorily. "I'll see if the superintendent can see you." As she punched in the numbers on her phone, Mack watched her eyes fasten on him like leeches. "They're here, Superintendent." Pause. "Yes, sir." Then to them: "He'll see you now."

Mack and Casey entered a large corner office that offered a panoramic view of the lake to the east and skyscrapers to the north through floor-to-ceiling glare-resistant windows. Among the amenities were a conference table, built-in bookshelves, wet bar, computer workstation and bathroom. The bulldog face of Mayor Timothy J. O'Connor glared down from the largest of many framed photos and expensive looking paintings that covered the walls. Not bad, Mack thought. Bill Gates couldn't have had it any better.

The man behind the sprawling desk, however, was not Bill Gates. This was Mack's first face-to-face with the recently-appointed superintendent, who had replaced the popular Arthur Couch, retired after being diagnosed with lung cancer. A hard act to follow, Mack allowed, but so far Hollender was making no effort to win the respect of the rank-and-file dicks. Maybe that would come. Maybe not.

"Good morning, Frank," Casey said.

Hollender did not respond. He was reading the *Chicago Tribune*, and judging by the scowl on his angular face, it wasn't the comics. Now Mack realized why the dicks referred to him as "The Hawk." He had a beak-like nose and alert eyes that seemed to be scouring the terrain for a rabbit to have for his next meal. At the moment Mack felt like he was the rabbit.

"Sit down, gentlemen!" Hollender said, not looking up from the newspaper. Mack realized that this was not intended as an invitation. It was a command.

Mack and Casey settled into two cushioned chairs facing the desk. Hollender continued to read, pausing only to pour himself a tumbler of water from a silver pitcher and take a drink. Mack was familiar with the tactic. Make us sweat. While he sweated, Mack took in The Hawk's stylish pin-striped charcoal suit, starched pale blue shirt and navy tie. The gold tie clip, diamond-studded cuff links and Piaget wrist watch were not there to be overlooked. Mr. Vanity, Mack thought, but human enough to have a wife and kids, judging by a framed picture on a credenza of an attractive lady flanked by a pretty girl and handsome young man.

Hollender finally looked up from the newspaper. "You've read this, I presume?"

Casey shifted in his chair as if he was having a hemorrhoid attack. "Ah, yes."

The Hawk ran a hand over a thick mane of styled white hair. His eyes then panned to Mack. Mack thought they looked like two frost-coated windowpanes.

"And you, Detective McPherson?"

"No, sir." Why start the day with a migraine, he could have added.

"I suggest you invest fifty cents and buy a copy. This time you made the front page," Hollender said, dropping the *Tribune* on the desk in front of them. The headline blared: "MAVERICK COP KILLS AGAIN!" The superintendent picked up a gold-plated pen and pointed it at Mack like a rapier. "You were also featured on the editorial page."

Mack could only imagine what the op-ed had to say. The *Tribune* had trashed him before.

Casey shifted in his chair again. "Look, Frank, let me explain…"

"I've read your report, Commander. And yours, McPherson."

"Then you know I acted in self-defense…" Mack began.

The Hawk came up out of the big, leather swivel chair as if he'd been goosed with a branding iron. "You shut the fuck up! You talk when I tell you to talk! I had my fill of you before I even took this job! You've got a reputation for taking the law into your own hands. Never proven, but I know the score! Every officer on the goddamn force knows the score! Some may approve of your methods, but if they do, they're deluding themselves, because you're only making their job harder…their job and the mayor's. The mayor is busting his ass to keep the media behind him on his tough anti-crime campaign, and so far the media has supported him. But this…" Hollender snapped the end of the pen against the newspaper.

For a moment Hollender didn't speak. Out of breath, Mack wondered, or just a dramatic pause to let his words sink in? He was taller than Mack expected —six four at least, lean and fit-looking. Probably a runner. Now he was leaning across the desk, palms against the surface, close enough for Mack to inhale his lime-scented after-shave.

"I don't know how you did it, McPherson, but I'd bet my last dollar that you goaded Fry into that shootout. That's called entrapment, Detective, and that's exactly what the media is alleging."

Mack wanted to tell Hollender what the media could do, and opened his mouth like he was going to do so, but felt the toe of Casey's shoe hit his shin hard enough to make him wince.

Hollender settled back into the swivel chair, folded his hands and cracked his knuckles before continuing. "You're making a shitload of trouble for the department, Detective, and much as I'd like to have your badge right here and now, I haven't sufficient evidence to take it. But as of this moment you are no longer working Homicide. I'm dumping you to Special Victims!"

"Special Victims?"

"That's right. There's an opening at Area Three, and you're filling it. And get this, McPherson: You get out of line again—just once—and you'll find yourself on suspension and Special Affairs looking up your asshole with a microscope! Do I make myself understood?!"

Mack was afraid that if he spoke, the wrong words would come out, so he just nodded.

Hollender shot up out of his chair again and leaned over Mack, his eyes glaring. "Well do I?!" he nearly shouted.

Mack flushed. "Yes, sir," he replied in a subdued voice.

Hollender relaxed. "Good. This meeting is concluded."

Mack rose, as did Casey, and moved to the door. His brain was churning.

Special Victims! Missing persons, domestic violence, child and elderly abuse, shit like that? Jesus! He'd fucking die of boredom long before his pension kicked in. For a moment he was tempted to do Hollender a favor and turn in his badge. But no. He wouldn't give the asshole that satisfaction. He'd just live with it, gut it out. At least for now. As he left the office the migraine he'd been trying to avoid all morning slammed into his head.

*12:34 p.m.:* Mack sat down at the bar of The Billy Goat Tavern, a cozy, decades-old establishment on East Hubbard, and ordered a double Jack Daniel's on the rocks. The hour-long workout in the weight room of the Lakeshore Athletic Club down the street had helped him calm down somewhat, but he still needed an alcoholic tranquilizer to finish the job. At least the headache was gone, but the anger, although more and more muted with each sip of Mr. Daniel's, was still festering in his brain.

What really pissed him off was the knowledge that he had absolutely done the right thing, and now was being punished for it. He'd taken a monster off the streets, one who was on the edge of kidnapping, raping and butchering another helpless little girl. Mack had watched Jason scoping out the schoolyards. He knew beyond the shadow of a doubt that Jason would kill again. He had no choice but to bait him into attacking him. What else was he to do? Wait until Jason brutally killed another child, and then go after him and try to prove it? Tell himself, "Hey, Mack, don't feel guilty about it? You followed the Rules. It's just the System, that's all. Not your fault." No, he couldn't do that. Results mattered, and in Mack's book, they mattered a whole lot more than process. The System was a lumbering bureaucracy trapped in a forest of rules—impotent, incapable of responding to real danger, in real time. So Mack had to pursue the truth, wherever it led, and act on it timely, whatever the cost. He knew this. He'd done this before. Still it pissed him off that he was being punished for breaking the rules when he should have been getting a medal for saving a young girl's life.

He was still on a vacation day—his last—despite his visit to The Hawk's lair, so he figured he might as well get smashed. He also decided to check in at Area Three Headquarters that afternoon, just to get acclimated to his new environment. He knew some of the dicks in Homicide over there but none of the guys in Special Victims other than their commander, Frank Cronin. Cronin had worked in Area Two Homicide before transferring to Special Victims. A good cop and a nice guy, Mack remembered. At least he'd have a boss he could get along with. He hoped.

The aroma of sizzling hamburgers finally seduced Mack. He finished off two large patties, each smothered with onions and pickles. Thanks to a draft of Miller Lite and another shot of Mr. Daniel's, he was feeling no pain when he left the Billy Goat. He picked up his car at the lot next to the club and drove to Area 3 Detective Division Headquarters to check out his new job.

*2:10 p.m.:* Area 3 Detective Division Headquarters was located in a two-story brick building that shared the northwest corner of Belmont and Western with the Circuit Court. Mack parked in the back lot and entered through the rear double-door entrance. A sergeant at the lobby desk informed Mack that the Special Victims unit was on the second floor. Mack ascended the steps, walked down a hallway and entered a reception room. A uniformed lady desk officer made a quick phone call to the commander that got Mack into the adjoining squad room, where a dozen or so dicks were busy at metal desks. The door to the commander's office was open, so Mack knocked on the frame. Cronin looked up from a pile of reports on his desk and grinned.

"Hey, Mack, come in."

Mack entered a spacious office with three large windows that overlooked Western Avenue. Cronin rose and came around the desk to shake his hand. Cronin's hand was small, but his grip firm.

"Good to see you, Mack. It's been awhile."

"That it has, Frank."

More than awhile. More like eleven years, Mack thought, gazing down at a face that looked like it had been chiseled out of granite. Cronin's crew cut had grayed, and he'd put on a little weight, but it looked like solid muscle. "The Fireplug," they called him. The moniker still fit.

"I assume you got a call from downtown."

"I did. I wasn't expecting you until tomorrow," Cronin said. Then with a sly smile: "I guess you've been celebrating your new job."

"I thought you appreciated good whiskey when you smelled it," Mack said. "I see you're still into the stogies."

"Yeah. Had to cut down, though." Cronin removed the stub of an extinct cigar from his mouth and regarded it with a look of affection. "I remember the days when they let us dicks smoke inside. Now I got to go into the parking lot to finish this."

"Things are tough all over."

"That they are, especially here. I'm sorry about your run-in with the brass, Mack, but I'm glad to have you with us." Cronin gestured to the detectives in the squad room. "We're understaffed and unappreciated."

"So what else is new? Hope I can be of some help." Mack wondered if Cronin was really glad to have him on board, given the baggage he brought with him. If he wasn't, he didn't show it.

"Are you kidding? I only wish I had more guys with your experience."

"Experience, yeah, but not in Special Victims."

"No sweat there. I'm teaming you up with one of our veterans. He'll bring you up to speed in no time. Come on. I'll introduce you."

Mack followed the commander out of the office and through the squad room. As they approached the open door of a small office, Mack grabbed Cronin's arm.

"Hold it a second, Frank."

Cronin looked up at him with a questioning frown.

"Don't tell me *he's* my partner?"

Mack was referring to the lanky black kid hunched over a computer. The clean-cut face looked familiar, but Mack couldn't place him.

"Yeah, that's him. His name's Winstrom. Otis Winstrom. So?"

"You said a veteran. Winstrom looks like he just walked off a high school basketball court."

"Funny you should say that. Otis played basketball for Indiana. Pretty good, I understand. I don't follow college ball."

Mack did, and now he made the connection. "Winstrom. Yeah, I remember him. Point guard, all Big Ten. Might have made the pros. Wonder why he turned down big bucks for a badge."

"Good question. I'm sure he had his reasons. And don't let his boyish looks fool you. Otis is sharp as they come. He should be, with Tony G looking over his shoulder for the last three years."

"Well at least that's something," Mack said.

He'd heard of Tony Giordano, Tony G to his fellow dicks and the media. He'd been a super cop in Special Victims for years. In fact, his retirement had rated him a feature article in the Sunday supplement of the *Sun Times*.

Otis knocked off a big case yesterday," Cronin said. "The little Pletcher girl."

"That so?"

Mack was impressed. The disappearance of the little girl after she left a private school near her home on North State Parkway was a high-profile case, a "heater" in cop lingo, thanks to her father's status. He was a big-time lawyer with *mucho* clout at City Hall. According to the media, Winstrom had found the kid with the lawyer's first wife in a transient hotel room on West Wilson, where the ex was turning tricks to finance her drug addiction. Mack had to admit that Winstrom must have something on the ball to have tracked her down in less than twenty-four hours, and said as much to Cronin.

"Yeah," Cronin said. "Otis doesn't know it yet, but I'm putting him in for an honorable mention."

"That so?" Mack said, trying to remember the last time he'd gotten an honorable mention. "Is that why he rates his own office?"

"It was Tony G's. Otis inherited it when he left."

Mack was willing to bet that this pissed off the veteran dicks who had worn their badges a hell of a lot longer than the boy wonder. Add to that his dapper attire: a coal black suit, peach-colored shirt and coral silk tie. Saks Fifth Avenue or Lord & Taylor at worst.

Mack grimaced. "Okay, Frank. Let's give the kid the bad news."

Busily writing detailed notes in a case file, Otis Winstrom was feeling a surge of exhilaration. The feeling always came when he was close to solving a case. Otherwise, he would have noticed that he had visitors before he heard Commander Cronin's voice.

"Got a minute, Otis?"

Otis looked around. The commander was standing in the doorway with another man, a big guy, at least he looked big next to Cronin. He'd seen the guy somewhere before, but couldn't place him. He had the look of a dick, however, and at the moment not a happy one.

"Hey, lieutenant, dig this," Otis said, gesturing to a pretty face on the monitor. "Sandy Phillips, an Allstate employee, worked with John Elward, the guy reported missing last Saturday. I was working the case with Tony."

"Oh, yeah. You got something?"

"I think so. Elward disappeared about the same time Sandy took a vacation in the Bahamas, and I'm betting that they're together there right now soakin' up sun and strawberry daiquiris."

"How do you figure? It could be a coincidence."

"I don't think so. I got Elward's and Sandy's profiles from Allstate, and guess what? Sandy listed Elward as a reference on her job application. And they both attended New Trier High School, class of '85. So much for coincidence, I'd say."

"I'd say so, too. Good work, Otis," Cronin said, beaming.

The other guy was smiling, too, Otis observed, but the smile was bemused, if not derisive. "So the guy's shacked up with his old high school sweetheart. Sounds like an episode out of a TV soap opera."

What kind of bullshit is this? Otis thought. He stood up, got into the guy's face. "I don't think I know you." Most guys would look away. This guy didn't even blink. If anything, his smile was even more sardonic.

"Otis, I'd like you to meet your new partner," Cronin said. "Detective McPherson."

At first the name didn't register. Otis was too busy dealing with the news that he had a partner.

"I thought I'd be working alone, Lieutenant."

"Mack's been reassigned to Special Victims, Otis, and all the other guys are already teamed up, so…"

"So you drew the wild card," Mack said.

Wild card. Wild for sure, because now Otis realized who McPherson was! "Reassigned, huh? Guess you had a little problem downtown."

"Just a little," Mack said, extending his hand.

Otis hesitated, then took it. "I hope Special Victims isn't too low-profile for a hot dog like you," he said, trying not to wince at McPherson's vise-like grip.

"I think I can handle it."

Yeah, Otis thought. But can I?

*8:34 p.m.:* Otis and his wife, Ava, were celebrating with dinner at Le Petit Gourmet, a small but fancy four-star restaurant tucked away on a side street in downtown Wilmette. Actually, it was a double celebration: Otis for the honorable mention he'd received for finding the Pletcher child, Ava for an outstanding teacher's award from the English Department at National Louis University in Evanston, where she taught Freshman English and French. For Otis, however, the celebration was muted by the news that now he not only had a partner, but one who very well could jeopardize his career.

Otis tried not to think about this as he took another sip of chardonnay at their candlelit table. Despite his concerns about his new partner, Otis was feeling no pain. The mellowing out process had begun earlier in the evening with the bottle of Dom Perignon he'd brought home and continued with the two straight-up Gray Goose martinis he'd consumed with the appetizer of sizzling escargot in the shell. While Otis and Ava nibbled at an outstanding Hollandaise-laced asparagus salad, they discussed their options for a forthcoming weekend trip in their El Monte RV. Ava opted for one of their favorite places, the Dells, a cluster of lakes in Wisconsin. Otis was all for it. He was itching to use his new Martin fly rod, while Ava graded papers and caught up on her reading. They would share long hikes along the many trails that meandered through the lush woodlands, pan fry the trout for supper, wash it down with some chilled Chablis and go to sleep early after making love in the RV's over-the-cab bunk.

As they talked about it, Otis thanked the Almighty again that he had found a bride who loved getting close to nature as much as he did. More, in fact. Ava was into the preserving forests and endangered species movements big time— causes he fully supported until they veered into the realm of the absurd, at least in his mind. They had occasional debates over whether the Spotted Owl or Farmer Jones had the law on his side. Ava maintained that the owl was there first, and that Farmer Jones had no choice but to leave unmolested a tract of land inhabited by the feathered creature. Otis pointed out that Farmer Jones owned the land and had a legal right to earn a living from it. Ava would counter that the Law of Nature prevailed, so screw Farmer Jones. These debates always resulted in Otis waving the white flag. He realized there was no way a man could win an argument with a woman anyway, especially a woman dedicated to a cause.

Otis was grateful that the Spotted Owl debate did not resume during the ensuing mouthwatering bites of grilled Norwegian salmon over a bed of spinach and sips of chilled chardonnay. He was glowing like a roman candle at a Fourth of July picnic and looking forward to the best part of a wonderful evening. Frolicking on the feathers, as Otis liked to quip. That's when Ava dropped the gauntlet on the white linen.

To Otis it didn't look like a gauntlet. Not right away. It looked like an invitation, which is what it was.

"It just came today," Ava was saying. "You haven't forgotten, have you?"

"Forgotten? No way," Otis lied, reaching for the embossed five-by-seven card. He held it next to the candle lamp and tried to keep his mellow smile in place as he made out the text. Another high society deal for a charity, this one the Ravinia Benefit, an annual fundraiser for the Highland Park-based summer music festival. Like the other events Ava insisted they attend, it would force the guys to pull their tuxes out of the plastic dry-cleaning bags and provide their spouses the opportunity to showcase themselves in their latest designer gowns.

"The theme is a Viennese Fantasy," Ava gushed. "My idea, by the way. Or did I tell you?"

"No, but you're forgiven," Otis said. Ava was on the women's committee that planned the event, but had not revealed the details. He observed that the music of Johann and Richard Strauss would be rendered by the Chicago Symphony Orchestra.

Ava took a sip of wine, then continued with enthusiasm. "My concept was to have a huge marquee tent decorated to resemble the Schoenbrunn Palace Conservatory of old Vienna."

"Outasight. What did they do there? Rock concerts?"

"Not exactly, mister funny man. It was a famous nineteenth century music school."

"A little early for the Stones, I guess?"

"Just a little. Oh, and Nina Kotova is the guest cellist. I heard her play at Carnegie Hall when I was in New York last year, remember?"

Otis did. Not the cellist, but the annual shopping expedition to New York that Ava made with her mother.

"She's pretty good, I take it."

"More like awesome, my love, and gorgeous to boot, so be prepared to be blown away."

Otis would take Ava's word for it, as he had regarding the many artists he'd heard performing under the stars at Ravinia Park. He had to admit that he'd enjoyed their musical outings. They would sit on a blanket, sip wine and eat fruit, cheese and other goodies from a deli box, occasionally making their way through the throng of people who covered the sprawling lawn to the pavilion, where they could catch a glimpse of a Pavarotti, Lang Lang or Joshua Bell over the shoulders of other spellbound onlookers.

Otis took another look at the card. The date of the event was May 14, to begin at 6:00 p.m. "I see they're doing the concert right after the cocktail party this time." As he remembered, dinner had always preceded the concert. Not that he cared. The important thing was that they hadn't done away with the cocktails. He would need a couple to fortify himself for the rest of the evening.

"Yes, it's a huge change," Ava said, spearing the last morsel of salmon with her fork. "The board felt that having the concert first would give people a chance to relax throughout the dinner, you know, then mingle, be with friends who love Ravinia."

"Right," Otis said, dreading already the prospect of mingling with Ava's highbrow friends, all of whom would no doubt be on hand. Ava was born and raised in the very affluent black community in Glencoe, the crème de la crème of the North Shore burbs. This was a far cry from the mean streets of East Chicago where he had grown up and survived. Rubbing elbows with North Shore royalty would be as uncomfortable as the starched tux collar he'd be forced to wear. But what the hell. It was a big deal for Ava. Not only was she on the planning committee, her mother, Maureen, was the chairwoman of the Ravinia Women's Board.

"Guess your mom will have to make a speech," Otis said, reaching for his wine glass.

"Yes. She's already having a minor anxiety attack. You know Mother. She dreads making speeches. I just told her to make it brief, you know, just a few words to thank people for their support and...are you all right?"

The answer was no, but Otis didn't say so. He couldn't. He was coughing. The wine had gotten halfway down his throat when he looked again at the date of the event on the card. He had seen it before but it hadn't registered in his brain. It did now.

Ava handed him his glass of Perrier. "Drink some water, dear."

He took a long swallow, and the coughing subsided. The problem did not.

"I told you to chew carefully," Ava scolded, but her face showed concern.

"It wasn't a bone. The wine must have gone down the wrong pipe."

A dubious look from Ava. She always knew when something was bothering him. Otis hoped she wouldn't push it now. Change the subject, he thought.

"How about some dessert? I could deal with the chocolate mousse."

"Not for me. I've had more than my calorie quota for today."

"So do I have your permission to pig out?"

"You do. Besides, you couldn't put on weight if you tried."

Otis flagged their waiter, ordered the dessert, two cups of espresso and the check. Ava waited until the waiter had departed before she began the interrogation.

"What is it, dear?"

So much for diversionary tactics, Otis thought. "What is what, darling?"

"What is the problem?"

"No problem. I just remembered something I forgot to take care of at headquarters."

Otis tried to make his response sound casual, but Ava wasn't buying.

"It's the benefit, isn't it?"

"What? No way."

"I know you don't like these events, but they're important. They raise money for so many worthy causes."

"I know they do, darling. That's not it."

"Then what is it?"

Shit, Otis thought. Might as well tell her. She'd stay on his case until he did. Nonetheless he took a long sip from his wine glass before coming clean.

"Well, darling, it's just that the retirement party for Tony G...you remember?"

"Yes."

"Well, it's the fourteenth. The same night as the benefit."

"Oh, no!"

"Yeah. Some kinda bad timing, right?"

"I'm so sorry, dear. I know how much you were looking forward to it. But I'm sure Tony will understand."

"Understand? Understand what?"

"Not being able to be there."

"Ava, I gotta be there. And I would hope that you would want to be there, too."

An incredulous look from across the table.

"Couldn't you skip the Ravinia deal just this one time? I mean, there's always another benefit, but there's only one retirement party for Tony."

"Skip it? Get serious. After all the work I've done helping to put it together? I think it would look just a little odd if I wasn't there."

"Okay, okay, I understand. You go ahead and go. I know it's important to you. But you gotta understand that Tony's party is important to me, too."

"As important as pleasing me?"

"Come on, Ava. He was my partner, for Christ's sake!"

Ava's lips pursed. "Please keep your voice down."

Otis was vaguely aware that heads at neighboring tables had turned their way. "Okay. Sorry," he said, lowering his voice. "I'm just saying…"

The waiter appeared with the dessert and espressos and the check. After he left with Otis' Visa, Otis continued. "I'm just saying that I spent three years with the guy. He taught me everything I know. Being there for him is the least I can do to show my appreciation."

"We'll discuss it later," Ava said.

Otis didn't want to discuss it later. He wanted to resolve the issue now, before he could lay a guilt trip on himself. "What's wrong with talking about it now?"

"This isn't the place. Now if you don't mind, I'd like to finish my coffee."

Otis started to respond, then swallowed hard. Okay, but this time it won't work, he told himself. No way he'd cave in on this.

Otis nibbled at the dessert without enjoying the rich chocolate that melted in his mouth. Ava made small talk, as if nothing had happened to disrupt the evening. Otis responded with few words. He was too busy trying to keep his anger under control. It was an anger fueled by frustration. Women just didn't understand, maybe couldn't understand, some things that were important to a man. Not letting a buddy down was one of them.

Another one was even more crucial. It concerned his job. Ava had always considered it beneath his talents and made no secret about it. Ever so persistently she was nudging him in another direction. Go back to college, for openers. He'd majored in criminal justice at I.U., and could get a law degree at the University of Chicago in two years. If things got tight financially, her parents would be more than willing to take up the slack, especially since a job would be waiting for Otis at Schwartzberg, Sweeney, Dalton and Morgan, the prestigious law firm where Arthur Nesby, Ava's father, was a senior partner.

This was Ava's campaign. Her mission. Otis thought about it again, as he sipped his espresso, and wondered if he'd be able to hold out. Not that he wasn't ambitious. Someday he expected to make it all the way to the top as Commander of Special Victims. This goal, however, was not shared by Ava. Ava was a lady who knew what she wanted and would wage war to get it. Otis hadn't realized this at the time, but there were some warning signals early in their relationship. Not that that would have made any difference. Otis was hooked the first time he saw her.

Otis smiled wryly now at the irony of that first encounter. It happened at another social shindig for charity, the annual Lincoln Park Zoo Ball. Otis was not there as a guest. He was one of the beat cops assigned to the event for traffic control and to beef up security. He was stationed just outside the main entrance on Cannon Drive when he saw this sexy lady emerging from a Mercedes limo with her escort. She was wearing a sleek, strapless royal blue gown that fit her tall, slim body like another layer of skin. The vision hit Otis in the gut like a blow from a heavyweight with a brass knuckle. When he got around to noticing her face, he took another blow to the stomach. Light skinned, with high cheekbones, a delicate nose, full sensuous lips and mischievous, emerald green eyes that seemed to be saying, "Wouldn't you like to know what I'm thinking?"

He never expected to see her again, let alone get an opportunity to invite her into his life. And if he did, would he even have the nerve to do it? They obviously moved in very different social circles. But he did see her again, a few minutes later, returning for the makeup purse she'd left in the limo. And thanks to a junkie, he got lucky. The junkie was waiting in a clump of bushes near the staging area for the limos. He jumped Ava, ripped off her necklace and took off. Otis easily ran him down—heroin addicts are not exactly Olympic material—and made the arrest.

When Ava thanked him for the return of her necklace, Otis asked for her name, address and phone number. Of course, she'd have to come down to headquarters the next day to make a statement. No problem, Officer, she told him, her mischievous eyes taking him in with approval, Otis thought. Still, it had taken him a week after she made the statement to work up the nerve to call her. She hadn't seemed surprised to hear from him. Otis would learn later that Ava had already checked him out. Maybe that's when her plan for him first entered her mind. The mission.

Otis finished his coffee while they waited for the waiter to return with the bill. Otis was hoping that their argument would not interfere with his plan to indulge in some feather frolicking when they got home. However, Ava's lukewarm response to his attempts to make small talk on their way home was definitely not a good omen.

*10:35 p.m.:* Otis poured the remnants of the Dom Perignon into his champagne glass. Although they'd drunk more than half the bubbly on the rear deck of their modest two bedroom bungalow when they started the evening just a few hours earlier, they'd saved the last of the bottle in the fridge to top off the night when they returned home. Putting the bottle down on the night stand, Otis settled back into the feathery embrace of the mammoth, goose down pillow in his terry cloth robe and waited for Ava to join him in their king-size bed.

Otis took a sip of the champagne, and grimaced. Flat! Symbolic of the evening, which, like the champagne, had lost much of its effervescence. Oh, well, Otis thought, the best was still to come. A little lovin' would dispel the cloud that had rained on their parade and restore the romance and magic with which the evening began.

Otis took another sip of champagne. Ava was taking a long time in her traditional before-sex shower. Too long. To Otis the hiss of the shower began to sound more and more like the hiss of a snake. Your basic Adam and Eve garden variety, he thought with a sloppy grin. Shit, he was getting smashed. No, not getting. Gotten. The flat champagne was barely noticeable, just a drop in an already full bucket. The amazing thing was that the alcohol hadn't subdued his desire for the lady in the shower, as witnessed by the swelling hardness under the terry cloth.

The shower continued hissing. Otis picked up the remote from the night stand and turned on the TV. A few laughs from Leno or Letterman might help to lift his mood, which was beginning to flag. No such luck. The *Deadline Chicago* broadcast that aired during the second half of the ten o'clock evening news on WFFD was in progress, and the host, investigative reporter Mark Jacobs, was devoting the entire fifteen-minute segment to roasting none other than Otis's new partner. To Jacobs, Jason Fry, the reformed sex offender, was another victim of the vigilante cop's warped sense of justice. A film clip of firemen hosing down the flaming diesel tank that had become Fry's funeral pyre, and McPherson brushing off a lady reporter who was trying to interview him on the scene, was all Otis could take. He pushed the power button.

Otis finished off the champagne with one gulp to steel himself for the clincher. The snake in the bathroom had stopped hissing. Would Ava emerge from the Garden of Eden in a sexy negligee, bringing with her the mingled scents of lavender and Joy perfume? Or would she make her appearance in her own matching robe, lavender scented but minus the Joy, which was an indispensable part of their before-sex ritual? Otis could only hope that Ava would put aside their unresolved conflict. At least for tonight.

The sight of this lovely lady entering the room still took his breath away. But Otis watched her with a sinking feeling as she padded in her foam slippers to the vanity, sat down and began to apply a moisturizer cream to her face. Otis now accepted defeat. Ava was wearing her robe over the negligee, there was no scent of Joy, and the moisturizing routine always occurred *after* sex.

Otis looked down at the bulge under his robe. What a waste, he thought, and reached again for the remote.

## *Tuesday, May 14*

*6:15 p.m.:* Megan Herbst looked anxiously at the ornate French wall clock. Her daughter Katie's party guests would be arriving soon, and her dad still wasn't home. He should have walked in the door at least half an hour ago, especially since he'd gotten permission to leave his job at Home Depot a half hour early. He wanted the extra time to get into his clown garb and set up for his magic act. Katie was so excited about her party that she didn't seem concerned, but her next question echoed Megan's fears.

"Where's Grandpa, Mommy?"

"He'll be here soon, dear," Megan said, as she placed a little party gift at each of the eight sets of decorative paper plates, cups, napkins and place mats with plastic forks and spoons surrounding the cherry wood dining table. There were four more places at the smaller table in the open kitchen. Hovering over each setting was a helium "Happy Birthday!" balloon.

"Grandpa's still going to do magic, isn't he?"

"Of course he is." In fact, he'd been practicing all week, fine-tuning his routines and patter after Katie went to bed.

"Do you hear that, Sophie? You get to see magic."

Katie was addressing a large, lifelike doll with curly auburn hair in a blue silk dress with a frilly organza overlay that occupied one end of a Louis XIV-style sofa. Sophie was one of an expanding family of collectible dolls scattered about the spacious living room that, with the kitchen and dining area, filled most of the second floor of the three-story townhouse. Katie had names for all of the dolls and treated them with the proper respect. She had her own dolls in her bedroom on the third floor, which she played with and cuddled according to her mood. But her mother's collectibles had to be handled with care, and not at all by her friends. Katie had lectured them not to touch, and the same went for her mother's collection of *Limoges* ceramic knickknacks in the Victorian-looking curio cabinet.

"Fifi, your dress is all yucky," she scolded a golden haired, blue-eyed beauty. "Shame on you."

Megan felt a lump in her throat as she watched Katie carefully smooth out the doll's red gingham dress. She looked like a doll herself in her own pink pinafore dress and matching hair bow. If only Artie were alive to see her, to share this moment. She had her father's irresistible smile, his Jewish mouth, his hazel eyes and dark complexion. From Megan came the angelic face, pug nose and dimples. Katie didn't get her mother's red hair, though. Katie's hair was light brown, like her dad's. She was so much like her dad. But mostly it was her smile.

She was smiling now as she smoothed out the doll's dress. "That's better. You have to look especially pretty for my party."

Megan distributed the last party gift, then moved to the tall bay window flanked by sheer white curtains and looked up the two-and-a-half blocks toward North Avenue, where her dad took a bus to and from work. Sometimes she picked him up, which she wished she'd done today. There were a lot of people moving south on the sidewalks, but no one resembling her dad. The bus ran about every twenty minutes. Maybe it broke down, Megan thought. Or got snarled in traffic. Even a fender-bender could create a traffic nightmare. Maybe,

maybe, maybe. If he only had a cell phone, Megan could resolve the maybes. But he didn't. He didn't want one. Stubborn Irishman! she thought with a momentary flash of irritation. He'd also resisted moving in with them. Didn't want to be a burden. But Megan had persisted, and he finally gave in.

Her three-story unit was located near the north end of the sprawling Sutton Place complex that extended from Goethe Street to just shy of Schiller on the east side of Clark. Megan was thankful that she hadn't sold the townhouse after Artie died and bought a smaller unit somewhere else. It was costly, for sure, the monthly assessment being $550, but the balance on the mortgage had been taken care of by Artie's insurance. The main reason she'd decided to stay was the security. A guard manned a security station around the clock at the entrance gate on Goethe, so Katie could play with her friends within the gated complex and be perfectly safe. Of course, she didn't really need the 2,400 square feet, but that was before she found an occupant for the third bedroom. Her dad. And he wasn't a burden.

But where was he?

The beeping of the cordless phone on an end table startled her. Katie scurried over to grab the receiver before Megan could get there.

"Hello. This is the Herbst residence."

Megan uttered a silent prayer. Please, God, let it be Dad.

"Oh, Aunt Karen!" Katie said, then to Megan: "It's Aunt Karen, Mommy!"

Back into the receiver: "Are you coming to my party, Aunt Karen? Grandpa is going to do magic." Listening, all smiles, then handing the receiver to Megan. "Aunt Karen is coming to my party."

"Of course she is, dear," Megan said, putting on a cheerful face. If it wasn't her dad, Karen was the next best thing. "Hi. What's keeping you? It's almost party time."

"Sorry, Meg. Last minute emergency. A new client with a bad case of postpartum syndrome."

"Oh? Is she okay?" Megan said, thankful that it hadn't happened to her after Katie's birth.

"For now. But she'll have to stay with the program."

Which meant ongoing treatment. Whoever she was, Megan knew that the woman was in good hands. Karen was a psychologist who cared more about her client than the $120 an hour she charged. Most of her clients were women either in the midst of a divorce or suffering from its aftereffects. Sometimes she counseled both spouses who were serious about trying to save their marriage. Sometimes she succeeded, sometimes she didn't. For Karen, success was especially gratifying, perhaps because she hadn't been able to salvage her own marriage to a charming but skirt-chasing louse. He'd even put a move on Megan, an incident she'd never revealed to her best friend.

"I got the most darling present for Katie. It's a visit to American Girl. She can select a look-alike doll and a Bitty Baby. Clothes, too. The whole *enchilada*!"

"Oh, Karen, that's wonderful. She'll love it, but you really didn't have to do so much."

"Hey, if I can't spoil your kid, whose kid can I spoil?"

Megan heard the slight catch in her voice. Karen was referring to the child the louse never gave her. "Look, it'll take me five minutes to change, ten to get there. Tell your dad not to start the show without me, okay?"

"I'll tell him…when he gets here." Pause.

"Something the matter, hon?" Karen knew her so well.

"I don't know. I hope not. But Dad should be home by now."

"So maybe the bus got stuck in traffic."

"I suppose that's it." She hesitated, wondering if she should ask the question that she was afraid to ask herself: Had he stopped somewhere for a drink? Karen was way ahead of her.

"Don't even think what I know you're thinking."

"I'm trying not to."

"He's not about to mess up now. Trust me. Or better yet, trust your dad."

"I do. I do trust him."

"Good. I gotta run. He'll be there before I am. See ya."

She hung up. Karen was right. There was really nothing to worry about.

But what if he had stopped off for a drink, if only to bolster his courage? Practicing aside, he hadn't done his magic act for years, wouldn't be doing it now if Megan hadn't saved the trunk of magic tricks he'd accumulated during his boyhood. He'd been bitten by the magic bug in sixth grade and by high school had worked out shows for every occasion with appropriate patter. Kiddy shows, church socials, private parties, country clubs, even a stag party with a stripper—a hard act to follow, he'd quipped—her dad had played them all, fond memories of which he'd shared with Megan many times over the years.

The trunk was stored away when her dad joined the Army. Out it came again during Megan's childhood years, when he'd performed for her birthday parties, then back in the garage loft again, where it remained, collecting cobwebs and dust during the rough years that followed—her father sinking deeper and deeper into alcoholism and depression, bouncing from job to job. And then there were no jobs and no marriage. Her mother had finally had enough and divorced him.

Later, after he disappeared, her mother sold the house in Oak Park. The trunk and its contents almost went with their furniture and household items in a heartbreaking garage sale. But Megan had kept the trunk, crammed it into the storage bin of her townhouse along with the memories of the big, lumbering, handsome, full-of-fun teddy bear Dad she had loved as a child.

The trunk was out again, as if resurrected from the dead, like her dad, as good as dead, maybe worse. Three years on the street, living only for the next drink. Living for forgetfulness. For oblivion. That's why Megan had kept the trunk. As long as she had the trunk, she had hope. Hope that someday he'd come back for it. For her. For a life.

Now he had that life again, and a job at Home Depot. Not much of a job as a lot attendant, but it was a job. And with the job came a restoration of pride. He also had a granddaughter whom he loved as much as his own daughter. And with their love to sustain him, there was no way he would destroy his life again. No way. Her dad would be home any minute. Guaranteed. For sure.

But where was he? Where?!

*7:44 p.m.:* Mack tapped the rim of the rocks glass with his index finger. Angie had anticipated Mack's request and was already hustling over with a bottle of Jack Daniel's. "More ice?"

"I'm fine, Angie," Mack said, thanks to two former encounters with Mr. Daniel's and the beer chaser he was still nursing at the bar of his favorite nocturnal haunt, Joe's Downbeat Bar and Grill.

Long-waisted and buxom, her chestnut hair in a ponytail, Angie filled the rocks glass to the brim. No measuring with a shot glass, just a good, honest if not overly generous portion of bourbon on the rocks. The way it should be.

"Thank you, nurse," Mack said. A little private joke. Not only did Angie administer potent painkillers, she took a maternal interest in his well-being, as witnessed by a question he knew she would ask. She asked it now.

"Are you joining us for supper tonight?"

"I'll get around to it."

"That's what you said last night, dear."

"I filled up on pretzels."

"Not tonight, you don't." Angie removed the bowl of pretzels Mack had been raiding and put it behind the bar. Mack was about to protest when Ella set her tray on the bar at the serving area next to him.

"I need two dry Absolut vodka martinis, straight-up, olives, a Manhattan and Johnny Red on rocks," she said through a mouthful of gum. A young, plump and obviously bleached blonde, Ella was one of the three waitresses who worked the tables.

"Right, coming up."

Mack watched Angie prepare the drinks, marveling at how fast and efficiently she did the job. Other bartenders came and went at Joe's, which required at least two during the week and three on Fridays and Saturdays, but Angie was the anchor, always there, always on the ball, perhaps because she needed the tips to put her two kids through college. Her deadbeat ex-husband would show up once in a while, looking for a touch. Mack hadn't seen him for a while, so maybe she'd finally told him to shove it. He hoped so.

"Here ya go," Angie said, setting the last drink on a tray in what Mack figured was record time.

Ella took the tray and scurried away.

"So what's on the agenda tonight?" Angie asked.

Mack shrugged. He knew the menu by heart. "I'm open to suggestions."

"I've got a rib eye with your name on it."

"Sounds good. I'm in a carnivorous mood. I'll take a pass on the salad, though. What are the sides?"

"Fries or mixed veggies. You'll have the veggies."

"Yes, nurse. And make sure the steak is…"

"I know. Burned. You ready now?"

"Angie, please. Serious food during the cocktail hour?"

Angie made a face and gestured toward a Miller Lite clock on the wall, which showed 7:51 p.m. "The cocktail hour is long over, dear. I'm putting in the order now," she said, and hurried away to serve two men mounting stools at the other end of the bar.

Mack glanced up at one of the TV sets over the bar, which would be muted once the band started to play. The Bulls were battling the Jazz in the third quarter. Ordinarily Mack would have watched the game and cheered the Bulls on. Not so tonight. In fact, the game was an unwelcome intrusion on his present state of mind. Duke Ellington's song, "In a Mellow Tone," seemed to describe his present condition, and it wasn't just the Jack Daniel's tranquilizers. It was the Downbeat's somewhat tacky but soothing ambiance. Framed photos of famous jazz musicians, most long dead, but to Mack like family, crowded the walls along with some large posters of jazz fests and an assortment of old musical instruments. Subdued lighting was provided by Tiffany-style bar lamps that dangled from the high ceiling where massive crossbeams and long-obsolete heating pipes betrayed a previous environment.

Mack knew the history from Joe, the owner. The room was part of a soda pop warehouse in the one-hundred-plus-year-old building just east of State Street on Hubbard before it was converted into a bar frequented by printers and reporters from the nearby *Chicago Tribune, Sun Times* and the long deceased *American*. Joe and a couple of investors had bought the bar in the mid-eighties to feature jazz, liquor and good food at reasonable prices. The going wasn't easy, but the music endured, and a revival of swing had attracted a whole new generation of fans who bolstered Joe's clientele.

The newspaper guys still hung out there. Mack spotted a few clustered around the horseshoe-shaped bar. Fortunately, none of them had taken Mack's usual stool that faced the bandstand. Not that there was any problem hearing the music. The big open room was so conducive to sound that only the singer needed a mike and amplifier. It was just that Mack liked to see what was going on. Be more involved.

The band members were setting up now, eight excellent jazz musicians and a lady vocalist who could render anything from trad to straight-on. But whatever it was, one thing was for sure. It swung. The band, which consisted of a trumpet, two reeds, trombone up front backed by a rhythm section of piano, bass, drums and guitar held forth Tuesdays through Saturdays, and had a loyal following in addition to Mack. Only about half the tables, neatly adorned with checkered tablecloths and candle lamps, were filled, but Mack knew the place would be jammed by the band's second set.

"Good evening, Mack," rasped a voice that betrayed a too-long fondness for nicotine.

Mack turned toward the entrance. Joe Lyman, the owner, was limping over, as he always did at nine o'clock after a late nap. There was an ever-present boutonniere in the lapel of his shiny but neatly pressed double-breasted navy suit. A jaunty yellow bow tie adorned the starched collar of his white shirt. Mack knew he would have his supper and keep an eye on the place until closing time at 2:00 a.m. before retiring to his apartment and office on the second floor of the six-story building.

"Good evening to you, Joseph," Mack said. Mack didn't know why he called him Joseph instead of just plain Joe. Perhaps it was because he was trying to show the proper respect for a fellow jazz *aficionado* who was willing to risk his livelihood to showcase the music.

Joe laid a frail, age-pocked hand on Mack's shoulder, the overhead light glistening off his bald head. "Don't you ever go home?"

"This *is* my home, Joseph. At least my home away from home."

Joe's laugh sounded like coal sliding down a chute. But Mack could see pain flicker in his eyes, as he eased his skeletal frame onto the neighboring stool.

"Joseph, when in God's name are you gonna get that hip fixed?"

"What? And lose my handicap sticker? No way. Besides, I don't think I could survive the knife again. I been cut on so many times I feel like a slab of salami in a deli."

Mack chuckled. It was true, though. At seventy-something Joe had survived a number of operations, including a recent triple bypass. Aside from the fragile ticker, he also kept a respirator at hand to deal with his emphysema, and joked that after his demise he planned to have his liver preserved in a glass jar behind the bar with a skull and crossbones label that read: "Danger! Highly Flammable!" He never complained, though, and his haggard face always wore a smile, as if he were laughing at the Grim Reaper.

"Evening, Mr. L," Angie said, as she set a frozen martini glass in front of her boss, then filled it with the contents of a silver cocktail shaker and dropped in an olive.

"Thanks, Angie," Joe wheezed. He raised the glass with a shaking hand, took a sip and sighed as if the liquid was gin instead of 7-Up. "So how was your day, my friend?"

Mack grunted. "I'm glad you asked that, Joseph. And I'm going to tell you how my day was. But first..." He took a long sip from the rocks glass, and chased the bourbon with a swallow of Amstel Light.

"That bad?"

"Not if you get off watching paint dry."

Joe's laugh terminated in a hacking cough, which persisted for a few seconds before he could respond. "Would you care to elaborate?"

That was another thing that Mack liked about Joe. He was willing to let his patrons unload their troubles on him, then console them with a drink on the house. A psychiatrist would charge a hundred and fifty per hour for the same service, and no free drink.

"Well, let's see. There was this old codger who..."

"Mack, Mack, please. We senior citizens take serious offense at being referred to as codgers."

"Of course. Sorry. Okay, this senior citizen, a resident of the Kingston Manor, a very upscale retirement establishment on Lawrence. You get the picture?"

"I can imagine. Continue."

"Right. Where was I?"

"At the Kingston Manor. I take it this senior citizen went AWOL."

"Correct."

"Alzheimer's?"

"Manic depressive."

"Off his medication."

"Correct again. You've heard this story before."

"I have. So did you find him?"

"We did. At the Lincoln Park Zoo, watching the monkeys jack off."

Another hacking cough laugh. "How'd you know where to look for him?"

"A hunch. The guy worked there for over forty years before he went to the tomb."

"Must have missed the old homestead."

"I guess."

"So that's it? Your day, I mean."

"Oh, no, no, no. We wrapped up another case, my gung-ho partner and I. A missing teen."

"Hey, when am I going to meet this partner of yours? What's his name? Otis?"

"Otis, right. Meet him? Forget it. Anyway, we were working this case a week, off and on. Maybe I told you."

"The Astor girl?"

"Yeah," Mack said. It was the tag the press had given Carroll Ann Van Meter, the daughter of affluent Gold Coast parents on Astor Street. "Anyway, we figured she was on drugs, despite the usual no, no, no, not our little girl bullshit from mom and dad. Parents never give you a straight story about their kids, ya know."

"No, but I'll take your word for it. So you found her. That's good."

"Depends on how you look at it."

"How do you mean?"

"Figure it out. How does a young, attractive girl finance a drug habit on the street?"

"Turns tricks."

"You got it. We flashed her picture around the Damen and California area —the streets are littered with discount whores—and got lucky. A cashier at a White Hen ID'd her. She started coming in a week ago for cigarettes and frozen pizzas. He saw her take them to a fleabag transient across the street. When we found her she was servicing a construction worker on his lunch break."

Joe shook his head. "Sad. Kids today don't know when they got it made."

"A profound observation, Joseph."

"At least it had a happy ending."

"Maybe. I doubt it."

"I mean at least it wasn't a homicide."

"Yeah. I'll drink to that."

Mack took the rocks glass and held it up toward Joe, as though offering a toast, then finished off the last of the bourbon and set the glass down firmly on the counter. "Nurse!" he called to Angie at the other end of the bar.

"Not now, Mack," she hollered back. "You eat dinner first. Then we'll see."

Mack looked to Joe for help, but Joe just started to laugh and cough. "I'm not Angie's boss, Mack. I just own the place."

*9:24 p.m.:* Otis emptied his bladder with a sigh of relief. The two Miller Lites he'd consumed had necessitated this trip to the men's restroom of the Fraternal Order of Police, an aging, three-story building on West Washington where the retirement party for Tony G was still going strong. The catered supper of corned beef and cabbage—a favorite for cop functions—was over, as were the speeches by the Chief of Detectives and Commander that accompanied the coffee and apple pie. The banquet hall was still nearly packed with over two hundred guests, mostly cops who had worked with Tony at one time or another and their wives.

The Commander had presented Tony with a gold watch and an engraved plaque with his affixed badge. A dewy-eyed Tony responded with a few heartfelt and emotional words of thanks, and assured everybody that he would not forget them during his years of retirement. He and his wife, Angela, planned to spend many of those years traveling for pleasure, visiting their three kids and numerous grandchildren and relaxing at their cottage on Lake Delavan in Wisconsin. Small compensation for a lifetime of service, Otis thought.

The dancing had now commenced, mostly to 1950's music as rendered by a four-piece band instead of the usual DJ. Having a live band had hiked the ticket price to forty dollars a head, ten dollars over the normal rate, but no one had complained.

"Hey, GQ. How's it goin'?"

Otis glanced toward a neighboring urinal that was being used by Dan

Manowski, one of his Area 3 associates. The scents of beer and whiskey mingled with the sweet stench of urine.

"Goin' good, Dan," Otis said, not resenting the GQ moniker that Manowski and his fellow dicks had bestowed on him, an obvious reference to his customary attire, which tonight consisted of a black Mani suit, purple Hugo Boss shirt, and purple and gray Armani tie. Otis took as much pride in his appearance as he did in his job. He couldn't say the same for Manowski. Fat and out of shape, he was wearing a wrinkled Men's Wearhouse suit, sweat-stained shirt and garish Tweety Bird tie. A nice enough guy, but in Otis's opinion, burned out. Maybe he'd been on the force so long, seen so much crap, that he just no longer gave a shit. It happened.

Manowski released a deep throated aahhhhhh punctuated by a loud belch followed by an equally loud fart. "Some kinda blast, right?"

"Nothing too good for Tony," Otis said, zipping up. He flushed the urinal and moved to one of the sinks.

"You got that right," came Manowski's guttural voice through the whoosh of water.

Otis spritzed his hands with liquid soap, rubbed them together thoroughly before washing them off. Manowski came over to the next sink, took out a pocket comb and ran it through a tangle of graying hair. So much for sanitation, Otis thought.

"So I see you're staggin' it tonight. What happened to the missus?"

Otis looked up into the wall mirror, where Manowski's beefy face leered at him with a boozy smile.

"Had a previous commitment."

Manowski grunted. "Wish mine had."

Otis understood. Shirley, Manowksi's cranky, matronly wife, would be monitoring his liquor consumption. Otis figured that she hadn't counted on the half pint of Jim Beam Manowski took from his coat pocket.

"Be my guest," he said, offering it to Otis.

"I'll take a pass, thanks."

Manowski shrugged, uncapped the bottle. "Heard you and your new partner cracked the Astor case today."

"Yeah. We caught a break."

Manowski took a pull at the bottle and licked his lips. "How's he workin' out?"

"He does his job." With a chip on his shoulder the size of a telephone pole, Otis could have added, as he yanked a paper towel from a dispenser.

"I knew Mack when I was workin' Area 2 Homicide," Manowski said. He capped the bottle and returned it to his pocket. "Good cop, 'ya know, but fuckin' crazy. Took big chances. Too big. Lost a couple of partners in shootouts."

Otis stopped wiping his hands and stood there holding the paper towel. He had never heard that before.

"That was in homicide, right?" he asked Manowski.

"Yeah."

"I don't think there's much chance of something like that happening in Special Victims. You've been in Special Victims for a long time, right?"

"Fifteen years."

"You ever in a situation where there was a shootout?"

"No, but with a hot dog like Mack, you never know what he'll get you into."

"I suppose that's true," Otis said.

"You can count on it. So my advice is to watch your ass, GQ."

"I intend to." Very carefully, Otis thought. Can't afford to take any chances.

"Better get back. The missus is gonna wanna dance," Manowski said with an obvious lack of enthusiasm.

"Right."

Otis and Manowski left the restroom and walked back to the packed banquet hall. "Where's Tony?" Otis said, looking toward the head table. A banner across the front of the table read: "GOOD LUCK, TONY G!" The dignitaries and their wives were still seated, but the guest of honor and his wife, Angela, were missing.

"Over there. Hey, look at him go, will ya!"

Otis followed Manowski's gesture to a couple on the crowded dance area that fronted a makeshift bandstand, where four musicians on two guitars, keyboard and sax were rendering the dreamy "Moon River." Tony and Angela stood out among the other couples. It wasn't just that Tony was bigger than the other men, with a broad, toothy smile that, to Otis, gave him the appearance of an Italian Teddy Roosevelt, and that Angela was prettier than other ladies her age. It was the fact that they were the only couple on the floor who seemed to know that "Moon River" was a waltz, which they performed like pros. This would have been lost on Otis as well, had it not been for the dance lessons Ava had insisted they take—that *he* take—so he would not embarrass her at the social events which called for a rudimentary knowledge of the basic dance steps— waltz, fox trot and swing. Otis had been informed that the tango and *salsa* were next on her agenda.

"You'd never think a big guy like Tony could move around like that," Manowski said.

"Yeah. He really kicks ass."

"I'm gonna miss that guy."

"Me too."

More than you know, Otis thought. Not just as a mentor and partner, but as a friend. Many were the nights that Tony and Angela had him over for supper at their modest two-bedroom flat in the old Italian neighborhood on the Near West Side. A city guy through and through, Tony had grown up amid the brownstones, fruit stands and groceries of Taylor Street. Some of the best Italian restaurants were still there, the aroma of garlic drifting from their kitchens. The exquisite cuisine at Rosebud and Tuscany, however, was no better than what Angela served up, second helpings of which Otis would wash down with glasses of Chianti.

Unfortunately, there hadn't been many dinners with Tony and Angela after his marriage. Not that he and Ava hadn't been invited. It was just that Ava always seemed to have so much going on. At least, that's what Otis told Tony and Angela. The truth was that Ava was uncomfortable with cops and their wives. The men were either talking shop or sports, she'd complain, and the wives dwelled endlessly on their kids or what they planned for supper every night of the week. This worked both ways. Otis was equally ill at ease with Ava's high society elite, even more so with her academic associates at National Louis, some of whom seemed to regard cops as an American version of the *Gestapo*.

"Think I'll grab another beer," Manowski said. "Wanna join me?"

"Better not. I'm my own designated driver."

"Right. See ya."

Otis watched Manowski navigate haphazardly toward the open bar. He'll be okay, he thought. Shirley would drive him home. Ava did the same for him on the rare occasions when he drank too many martinis.

He thought of Ava now, missing her, missing her bad, and wondered if she was missing him, too, as she did her Ravinia thing. Or was she still too pissed off to miss him. Probably the latter, given the events of the last two weeks which, domestically speaking, had been chilly in the extreme. Not that she'd said anything, given him a verbal bashing. That wasn't Ava's style. It was more what she didn't say than what she said. Despite the silent treatment and the withholding of her body—a woman's ultimate weapon in her formidable arsenal —Otis hadn't caved in.

It was a hollow victory, if he could even call it a victory. As he watched the couples, he wished that he could be out there with Ava now, dancing as close to her as a waltz would allow, feeling her superb body against his. The thought sent an urgent message to his groin. God, he was horny. But there would be no sex tonight, for sure. Zero. *Nada.* Unless...

He glanced at his watch. Only 9:45 p.m. If he took off now, he could hit the Kennedy Expressway and be at Ravinia in half an hour. The festivities would be going until at least eleven. He'd just walk in and surprise Ava. She'd be delighted. All would be forgiven, and his reward would follow. Maybe. But it was worth a shot.

Otis weaved his way among tables and then through big double doors that led to a hallway and the front exit. Sprinting to his Chevy Cavalier, parked a half block east on Washington, he slid into the driver's bucket and inserted the key into the ignition.

He didn't turn the key.

What the hell was he doing? Running out on his partner, that's what he was doing. Running out without even saying goodbye. Oh sure, Tony would come back to the station from time to time, or drop in for a beer at The Slammer, a bar near the station where the cops hung out. The retirees always did, just to say hello, chew the fat, exchange old war stories. But it wouldn't be the same.

Otis got out of the car, auto-locked the door and sprinted back to the banquet hall.

*10:39 p.m.:* Megan stared at the TV on the credenza. She was sitting on the sofa, watching Jay Leno deliver his opening monologue without hearing a word he said. From the bursts of laughter and shrieks from the females in the audience she presumed that his jokes were going over. She'd turned on the TV, hoping it would relieve her anxiety. There was, of course, no way that was going to happen.

Thank God for Karen. She'd been there the whole evening, helping to serve the ice cream and cake to Katie's guests, then monitoring the games, and finally helping to clean up. But mostly she'd been there for Megan. And for Katie, too.

"What happened to Grandpa?" she'd asked for the umpteenth time, as they tucked her into bed. "Why didn't he do magic?"

"He couldn't, dear," Megan had told her. She'd discussed a story with Karen, so as not to alarm her. "He had to do magic at another party."

"But he promised."

"I know, dear," Karen explained. "But this party was for children who don't have mommies or daddies."

"I don't have a daddy."

"Yes, but these children don't have a mommy to love them, either. So you see, your grandpa was just trying to bring a little happiness into their lives. You would want him to do that, wouldn't you?"

"Oh, yes. But will he do magic for me later?"

"Of course he will."

If only that were true, Megan thought. But that wasn't going to happen. Not if he'd done what she was afraid he'd done. Stopped off for that drink. Just one, of course. It was always just one. Then it was just one more, and one more and one more until...

"No!" Megan's voice filled the room. She was on her feet, fists balled.

What was she thinking? No way her dad would let her down. Or Katie. Tonight, of all nights. No way! Something had happened to him! She'd hesitated to do this earlier, but she did it now. Megan picked up the phone and dialed 911.

## Wednesday, May 15

*8:43 a.m.:* Mack filled a styrofoam cup with coffee.

"Good morning."

Mack returned the glass pot to the warmer plate of the Mr. Coffee without looking at his young partner, who had just entered the small refreshment area off the squad room.

"Is it? I didn't notice."

Otis set his coffee mug on the counter and removed a cup from a stack. "Guess you got a good reason for missing roll call?"

"The best," Mack said, tearing open a packet of Equal. "His name is Jack. An old friend." Mack dumped the white powder into his cup and stirred it with a swizzle stick.

"Jack?"

"Jack Daniel's."

"So you gonna tell that to Cronin?" Otis said, filling his mug and the cup with coffee.

"He'll understand."

"Like hell."

"So I get a slap on the wrist. I can live with that." Which meant a verbal reprimand at worst, Mack thought, as he took a sip of coffee. "You look a little under the weather yourself," he said, now observing the puffiness under Otis's eyes.

"Took in Tony G's retirement party." And returned home to a frigid wife and a night of tossing and turning, he thought.

"So? How'd it go?"

"Big turn-out. Even the Commander and Chief of Detectives were there."

Mack grunted. "Those guys might come to my funeral. Might. But for my retirement, forget it." He took another sip of coffee. "So what's on the board this morning?"

Otis took a look at a handful of reports that he and his missing partner had been assigned at roll call and thrust some at Mack. "To add to our already heavy case load we got an elderly abuse complaint, a domestic violence and two missings."

"Wonderful. Some old codger gets ripped off by gypsies, and another wife gets beat on by her loving hubby. To paraphrase Dirty Harry, you've made my day."

Otis took a sip of coffee, grimaced. "Your compassion overwhelms me."

"You'll discover that I'm really a big-hearted humanitarian…once you get to know me."

"Remind me not to hold my breath. Anyway, the missing kid case ought to get your attention. Could be a real heater. A DePaul student. His parents are already screaming at the brass. The father is a big shot neurosurgeon in Detroit. They're flying here as we speak."

"Wonderful. They'll want us to find their kid yesterday. Who reported it?"

"The kid's roommate. They went partying with some buddies, bar hopping, last stop Jake's Joint. The kid got drunk and obnoxious and was asked to leave, which he did. And promptly disappeared."

Mack drank some more coffee. He was beginning to feel almost human. Almost. "This one sounds like it's got possibilities."

"Meaning foul play. Your kinda turn-on, right?"

"If you say so. Let's go talk to the roommate."

"Later. There's a missing dad who comes first. His daughter's waiting in my office. Pardon me, *our* office. She requested that I handle the case."

"Oh? You know her from somewhere?"

Otis handed Mack the report, took a sip of coffee. "Yeah. Her dad was one of my first cases with Tony G. Name's Frank O'Meara. He was a boozer. Lost his job, lost his wife, and finally got lost himself. After a while we wrote him off as deceased. But his daughter never gave up, kept buggin' us to keep the file open. So we put in a little off-duty time on it. Two months ago we got lucky and found him at one of the missions."

Mack scanned the report. The daughter's name was Megan Herbst. The missing father lived with her and her daughter, Katie. No mention of a Mr. Herbst. Probably a divorcee, Mack figured. As for the dad, odds were he was on the street again. He said as much to Otis.

"Probably, but I hope not. The daughter is a really nice person."

"I'm sure. So introduce me."

Otis tucked the reports under one arm and picked up his mug and the cup. "Try not to show too much of the compassion that you claim is overflowing from that big heart of yours, okay?" he said, as they moved through the squad room toward their office.

"I'll make a supreme effort," Mack replied with a smile.

Megan watched the two detectives approaching. She was somewhat surprised. She'd expected to see Detective Winstrom with the older investigator who'd helped her before. But the other man this time was not Detective Giordano. He was younger, harder-looking, fit, like a prizefighter. Megan wondered if an opponent had bitten off his right earlobe, like Mike Tyson. The face looked familiar, but she couldn't place it.

"Here you are, Megan," Otis said, and set the cup of coffee on the computer table where Megan was sitting. "Not exactly gourmet."

"It's fine, thank you."

Otis waited for her to take a sip. He hoped the coffee would help. If he'd had a rough night, he could only imagine what she'd gone through. The dark circles under her eyes were not eye shadow.

"I'd like you to meet Detective McPherson. He'll be working the investigation with me."

Megan looked up at the other detective, who was leaning against the door frame, nursing a cup of coffee but, unlike his partner, looking as if he couldn't care less about her dad. The same went for his attire. While Detective Winstrom was tastefully dressed in a double-breasted charcoal suit, light blue shirt and burgundy tie, McPherson's rust-colored suit looked like it had been slept in and had nothing in common with the yellow shirt and drab gray tie hanging at half-mast from the open collar.

"Detective McPherson," she said.

"Mrs. Herbst. Or is it Ms?"

"It's Mrs. My husband is deceased."

"Sorry."

He didn't look sorry, Megan thought. Just bored. However, had she been able to read his mind, she would have been surprised at the strong first impression she'd already made. To Mack, it wasn't just her small but trim figure, accentuated by tight-fitting black Levi's and a breast-hugging white tee shirt with a red sweater tied around her neck, but the lovely, heart-shaped face, the cupid's-bow mouth, sexy yet demure, framed by shoulder-length hair the intense red of a distant forest fire he'd seen illuminating the sky one night in Montana.

"I thought you were working with Detective Giordano," Megan said to Otis, who slid the desk chair over next to her and sat down.

"I was until two weeks ago. He retired."

"Oh. I hope he enjoys his retirement. Such a nice man."

"The best," Otis said sincerely.

A prince, Mack thought, wanting to get this interview over with. O'Meara was probably sleeping off his binge somewhere and would go home when he sobered up. The DePaul kid was another matter. Easy prey for gangbangers who roamed the streets at night looking for scores, some of whom ended up dead.

Otis took out his Waterman pen and leather notebook from his pocket, then looked at the police report. "It says here that the last time you saw your dad was when he left for work at…" Otis paused to look at the report, "…at seven-thirty yesterday morning."

"Yes. He took the bus at Clark and North Avenue. He works at the Home Depot on North Avenue."

Otis wrote down the current time and began making notes, writing everything down. "You're sure he took that bus? That he went to work?"

"Yes. I called the store this morning and spoke with the manager, Mr. Swope. He told me that Dad was there at eight, as usual."

"What time did he leave?" Otis asked.

"Quitting time is at five, but Dad got permission to leave a half hour early, because of the party…my daughter's birthday party."

"Yesterday morning, before he left, how did he seem?" Mack asked.

Megan was confused by the question. "How do you mean?"

"Did he appear worried about anything? Nervous? Irritable?"

Megan didn't like the direction this was going. "He was fine. In good spirits, in fact, and looking forward to the party."

"You're sure?"

Megan felt her temper begin to rise. "Of course I'm sure. What are you getting at?"

Mack saw the crimson creep into her cheeks. She wasn't going to want to hear what he had to say, but he had to make her face the reality of the situation.

"I'm getting at the possibility that he might have stopped off for a drink."

Megan fought to stay cool. She knew what could happen if she lost control. When she was frustrated or provoked, her temper could flare up in an angry outburst, like a flash of lightning. "He wouldn't do that," she snapped.

"He's an alcoholic, Mrs. Herbst."

"Not any more, dammit! He quit. He promised me he'd never take another drink!" She saw the look of disbelief on McPherson's face. She turned to Otis: "Detective Winstrom, you remember when you found my dad and I met him here at your office and told him that I wanted him to come home and live with me and Katie and especially be a grandfather to her…but not if there was any chance that he might go back to the bottle and the street? You remember how I told him

I would rather she never see him at all than have him come home and she come to love him and then be hurt and disappointed? You remember that…and how he promised me and swore that he would never ever do anything to hurt Katie!?"

Otis was a little pissed off at Mack for causing Megan to lose it, but he knew Mack was right. There was a strong possibility that Frank O'Meara could have relapsed and gotten drunk, then been too ashamed to go home, despite his promises and best intentions. But for now Megan needed to be calmed down.

Otis reached over and put his hand on Megan's arm. "I do remember, Megan. And Frank…your dad…did promise that he would never go back to his old life, that he would begin a new life with you and Katie. So you're probably right. He probably didn't stop for a drink, and we will certainly begin looking for him on the assumption that something may have happened to him, that he could be hurt or sick. But you need to understand that, as police officers, we've got to consider every possibility. Alcoholism itself is a disease, and its stranglehold on a person's life can be very hard to break. So we would be failing in our duty if we didn't at least consider that possibility. You can see that, can't you?"

"Yes. I suppose so…" Megan said. She paused to take a couple of deep breaths, trying to calm herself down. "But I just know something must have happened to him. He wouldn't have missed his granddaughter's birthday party for anything. He was so excited about it, so looking forward to it." She was starting to get worked up again. "He must have had an accident," she said. "That's the only thing that makes any sense. He had an accident."

"Well, we're going to start on that assumption, Megan. We'll check all the accident reports and all the area hospitals." He didn't tell Megan another place they'd check—the Cook County Morgue. But there were also less onerous possibilities to consider. "Tell me, since he got home, has he ever been disoriented, had any memory lapses? Anything like that?"

"No…at least not that I know of. Could that have happened?"

"He was on the street a long time. It could have affected his health."

"Well, he was pretty run-down when he first got home, but all he needed was rest and the proper nourishment. Of course, I insisted he get a physical examination."

"Did he?"

"Yes. At least that's what he told me. I wanted Dad to use a GP at Northwestern Memorial, but he went to a charity doctor he'd seen from time to time when he…was ill."

"Do you know his name?"

"No. I mean he might have mentioned it, but I can't recall it, but I'm sure they know at the mission. The Beacon Mission."

Where he and Tony G had found O'Meara before, Otis thought, writing this down in his notebook. He'd want to talk to the doctor, in case there was anything O'Meara wasn't telling his daughter.

"Was he taking any kind of medication?"

"No. Just vitamins…for his liver. The doctor told him it had to be watched…the alcohol, you know. He gave Dad shots of B-12, too, and I made sure that his diet was low-fat. Why do you ask?"

"Side effects from medication can be unpredictable and often serious."

That was true. Megan remembered getting dizzy once after she'd taken an anti-inflammatory drug for a pulled glute. But her dad wasn't taking anything except the vitamins and an aspirin every morning as a precaution against heart attacks. His heart was okay. His cholesterol was normal. So was his blood pressure. At least that's what he'd told her. Or was he concealing something he didn't want her to know about?

"Is there anything else you can tell us that might help?" Otis asked.

"I don't think so. You'll start right away? To look for him?"

"We'll get right on it. Do you have a picture?"

"Oh, yes, I brought one." Megan reached for her purse on the table and took out a recent photo she'd taken of her dad, which she handed to Otis.

"Great. We'll get this on a missing person's bulletin and circulate it right away."

Megan removed a business card from her wallet, which identified her as a floor broker on the Chicago Mercantile Exchange and gave her cell and home phone numbers. "Here's my card. You can always reach me on my cell phone. You'll call me just as soon as you know anything?"

"We'll keep in touch, Mrs. Herbst," Mack said before Otis could respond.

His remark drew a frigid glare from Megan. Now she remembered where she'd seen him before. On TV, and recently. The "vigilante cop," that's what they called him, the one who they said took the law into his own hands. No wonder she'd taken an instant dislike to him. She was tempted to ask Detective Winstrom how he ended up with him as a partner, but decided against it. Instead, she took the card he offered.

"Don't worry, Megan. We'll find him. But if he comes home, or you hear from him, call me, okay?"

"I will. Thank you," Megan said to Otis.

Otis smiled and squeezed her arm. She saw the compassion in his eyes and felt a degree of comfort and reassurance. But at the same time she decided to attend Mass tomorrow at Holy Name Cathedral. It had been a long time since she'd done this. Although she'd been raised a Catholic and gone to Catholic grade and high schools, she'd drifted away from the church over the years. But she would attend Mass tomorrow. She would kneel at the altar and pray to God to protect her dad. Megan feared that he would need God's help.

*10:25 a.m.:* Otis bought Jess Plunket another latte grande. The young man continued to chew on his thumbnail as he sipped the Starbucks latte and answered the questions that Otis and Mack asked him. Nervous, Otis thought, probably because of a guilt trip. Although his dorm roommate, Brian Bowman, had disappeared Monday night, Jess hadn't reported it until Tuesday afternoon, after Brian failed to show up for a business marketing exam. A straight-A student, Brian never missed a class and for sure not an exam, according to Jess.

Mack saw it otherwise. This was probably the kid's first close encounter with cops other than receiving an occasional traffic ticket.

They were both right.

"Brian was totally blitzed," Jess was saying, a good looking kid, clean cut, wearing a baseball cap over a short crop of sandy hair, jeans, loafers and a DePaul sweatshirt. "I've never seen him like that before. I mean, he drank, sure, but not like seriously. It was more like he was trying to be one of the guys, ya know."

"Any particular reason? I mean, for him to get so drunk?" Otis said between sips from a tall cup of coffee and bites from a huge cinnamon twist. The pastry was delicious. For once Mack had come up with a good idea. Since both of them had missed breakfast, instead of meeting Jess at the DePaul Student

Center on Sheffield, Mack had suggested a Starbucks a short distance away.

"Yeah. He broke up with his girlfriend. Cindy. Cindy Kyser. Or rather she broke up with him. They were tight for over a year. I guess Brian just couldn't handle it."

Otis wrote her name down in his notebook. They might have to talk to Cindy.

Mack was thinking that the Bowman kid must have been really smashed to get bounced out of Jake's Joint, which encouraged a raucous atmosphere from its staff of deliberately obnoxious waiters and waitresses and rowdy patrons, most in their twenties, who came there to swill down pitchers of beer, consume greasy fries and ribs, shoot pool, throw rolls of toilet paper provided by Jake's, and raise a little harmless hell. Mack had made the scene a few times to try to hear a decent Dixieland band through the raucous noise, so he was familiar with the layout. Jake's was one of the occupants of a sprawling, rehabbed, five-story warehouse on North Pier that included a variety of bars, restaurants, shops and business offices.

Mack glanced at the report next to the unconsumed half of his raisin bagel. According to Jess, his friend had been ejected from Jake's at approximately twelve-thirty. He asked Jess to confirm the time.

"That's right," Jess said, now working on a fingernail. "He was totally out of control. Tried to pick a fight with some guys at the next table. Like I said, I never saw him like that."

"Which exit did they use?" Mack asked. There were two: one interior, the other to the pier that bordered a narrow water inlet that extended from the lake and dead-ended at McClurg Court Street.

"They took him to the dock entrance, the bouncers I mean. I went with him to the exit and told him to wait outside until we could settle up the bill. The other guys and me. So we finished our beers and paid up, but when we went outside Brian was gone."

Otis wrote this down. "How long after Brian left did the rest of you leave?"

"Ten minutes or so, I'd say. Yeah, about ten minutes."

Otis looked at Mack, who was taking a sip of coffee. Mack's expression conveyed what Otis was thinking. Things didn't look good for Jess's friend. Even though he was still feeling pangs of remorse for lying to Megan about jumping right on her father's case, he knew Mack was right. The missing kid took priority.

Otis removed a card from his wallet and handed it to Jess. "Thanks, Jess. If you hear from Brian, contact us."

"Yeah, for sure. Do you think he's okay? I mean, well, okay?"

"He'll turn up," Mack said, choosing his words carefully, while feigning as much optimism as he could muster.

After Jess left them with the snapshot of his buddy that Otis had asked him to bring, Mack and Otis stuck around to finish their breakfast and discuss their next course of action, which was routine. Return to headquarters, get the missing bulletins on O'Meara and the kid prepared and circulated on the TRAK system. If nothing turned up, Mack wanted to talk to the night staff at Jake's, but that would have to wait until five. Otis pointed out that they would be working on their own time. Their shift ended at four-thirty.

"I know that," Mack said. "But do you want someone else screwing around with this one?"

Otis knew what he meant. The watch commander might assign the case to another team, who'd prepare a general report on their progress for Otis and Mack to follow up on the next morning.

"No."

"Good," Mack said, and took a bite of his bagel.

*12:17 p.m.:* Mack looked up at the large cross over the entrance to The Beacon Mission. "JESUS SAVES" was the message on the cross. Right, Mack thought with a sardonic smile, as he curbed the police-issue Crown Vic in front of a vintage five-story building at 626 South State Street. So where was Jesus when Kenny needed him? Or the little girls Jason Fry had slaughtered? Or all the innocent victims of the other serial killers, gangbangers, rapists and assorted vermin who contaminated mankind?

Otis had a different take to the message on the cross. His mom was a devout Presbyterian, the spiritual leader of the family, who'd insisted that his dad, two sisters and he attend church every Sunday to hear the word of the Lord and passionate hymns of the gospel choir, to which his mom lent a powerful voice. It was his mom who'd kept him on the straight and narrow through a difficult adolescence, forced him to get an education, and encouraged him to keep trying when he didn't make the basketball team as a high school freshman. His dad was dead now, but his mom at sixty-five was not only alive but full of energy. She still attended church every Sunday, still sang in the choir and still chewed him out if she thought he was out of line. Although not deeply religious himself, the lessons of his mom's faith were not lost on him.

Mack slid out from behind the wheel. "This is a waste of time."

"I'm betting it's not," Otis said, exiting from the passenger side. He'd found Frank at the mission before and was hoping history would repeat. At any rate, Frank wasn't occupying a shelf in the morgue or a hospital bed. The DePaul kid as well. It had taken them most of the morning to have the missing bulletins prepared and faxed on the TRAK system, first to the Cook County Morgue, then to the hospital emergency wards, district police stations and nursing homes in Area 3, and finally to all law enforcement agencies in Cook County. They'd also called the Fire Department dispatch to see if any John Does answering the description of the missings had shown up at a hospital. So far none had. That could change, but meanwhile the next step was to hit the street, which meant checking the numerous missions and overnight shelters in their area. And why not begin with Frank's alma mater, Otis had argued.

"If it's a bet you want," Mack said, "I got a ten that says O'Meara is sacked out on a bench in Lincoln Park and will be home in time for supper."

"You're on."

"And we're not staying for lunch."

"Why not? The food's very nourishing. And free."

"Right. One dip, no lip."

Otis was surprised that Mack knew the hip street reference to how the mission worked when it came to feeding the needy. Diners had to attend chapel first and behave themselves, or no meal. Then they ate: oatmeal and toast for breakfast, usually soup and sandwiches at lunch, and fried chicken for supper, with water for a beverage, no coffee. And one helping, no seconds and no complaints. One dip, no lip.

"And no lip outta you either," Mack added. "We lunch elsewhere."

"Hey, just kidding, my man," Otis said with a grin.

They entered the mission through a large door into a reception area where a bronze plaque on the wall read: "THE BEACON MISSION. FOUNDED SEPTEMBER 17, 1877." A middle-aged man surfaced from behind a counter. His sallow face betrayed a previous life on the street. Otis knew that most of the mission's employees were former homeless converts who had gone through a rigorous spiritual boot camp that helped them stay clean and turn their lives around.

"Good morning."

"Good morning." Otis showed him his badge. "Detective Winstrom, Special Victims. We're looking…"

Before he could continue, a voice interrupted. "I'll take care of the gentlemen, Patrick."

Otis and Mack turned toward an archway to a large room where homeless persons lounged in armchairs and on sofas, watching TV, reading newspapers, sacked out, or a few just staring into space. The man exiting the room was trim-looking with a hardy face and a Van Dyke beard. Athos in *The Three Musketeers*, Mack thought, or was it Aramis? In any event, he didn't look much like a pastor in his natty attire of taupe colored slacks, brown, herringbone sports coat and blue mock turtle neck sweater.

"Hey, Pastor John. Good to see you again," Otis said.

"You too, Otis," the man said, embracing Otis like an old friend of the family. "How's Tony? I heard he retired."

"Tony's doin' good. This is my partner, Detective McPherson," Otis said to the pastor. Then to Mack: "Pastor John Garrett. He's the director of the mission."

Mack took the pastor's outstretched hand. "Nice to meet you, Pastor," he said, surprised that a man this young looking was running one of Chicago's largest missions. He couldn't be more than thirty-five, and had spent some time pumping iron, judging by his strong grip and callused palm, along with bulging chest muscles under the sweater.

"McPherson. Your name is familiar, Detective."

Which meant that he knew the score, Mack thought, but his smile seemed sincere, not snide or condescending. "I've made some print."

"Right. So how can I help you?"

Otis removed the snapshot of Frank from his coat pocket and handed it to the pastor. "We're looking for this man and wondered if he might have spent the night here."

The pastor looked at the photo with a furrowed brow. "I thought Frank was off the street."

"You know him?" Mack said, amazed that he'd recognized O'Meara. There had to be hundreds of derelicts who passed through the mission.

The pastor seemed to read the inflection in his voice. "I try to get to know as many of our guests as possible, Detective." He handed the snapshot back to Otis. "Frank is staying with his daughter, isn't he?"

"Yeah, at least until last night. He went to work and didn't come back."

"You think he hit the bottle again?"

"Looks that way."

The pastor nodded sadly. "A proud man, Frank. If he did, he's probably too ashamed to go home."

He turned to the man behind the counter. "Check to see if Frank O'Meara was with us last night, Patrick."

"Yes, sir." Patrick sat down behind a workstation and fingered the keys on an Apple computer.

"Everyone who stays here has to sign the register, but we also put them in the hard drive," the pastor said.

"No O'Meara, Pastor John," Patrick said.

"Try Cravin." Then to Otis: "Cravin was the name he was using when you found him, wasn't it?"

"Right."

"No Cravin either," Patrick said after a quick scan.

"Maybe he used a new name," Otis said.

Pastor John nodded. "That's possible. It's also possible he joined us for lunch. They don't have to register to have a hot meal." He turned to Mack. "We feed over three hundred people every day here."

"Let's check it out."

"This way."

Pastor John escorted them down a corridor past doors marked "ADMINISTRATION OFFICE" and "CLINIC." Otis already knew the way from his many previous visits. He knew the dormitories on the upper three floors and the adjoining bathrooms, with primitive plumbing but shiny, scrubbed tile floors, where the residents were required to shower before they could spend the night on one of the clean, comfortable beds, which they had to leave the way they found them, sheets and blankets taut with corner folds, hospital-style. Those who converted to the Bible program, like Patrick, were given work assignments, such as cleanup, food serving and helping with security.

Unlike Otis, Mack wasn't really interested in The Beacon's good works. Sure, missions and shelters provided room and board for the homeless and even helped a few get straight. A few. The majority preferred to maintain their lifestyle. The problem with the homeless, in Mack's opinion, was the homeless themselves. Ninety-nine times out of a hundred an alcoholic would spend the rent money on booze, an addict on crack, instead of a warm bed. Still, Mack was impressed with what he saw at The Beacon. Although everything looked more than a little used, the mission was clean and well maintained.

The aroma of chicken soup greeted them when they entered a large dining room at the end of the corridor. Mack scanned the vagrants sitting on folding chairs at long communal tables. A couple of them somewhat resembled the picture of Frank, but he couldn't be sure. Otis and the pastor should be able to ID him, since they knew him personally. "See him?"

Otis shook his head. "Looks like we struck out."

"Maybe not." Pastor John gestured toward a table near the serving station. "The lanky black man in the green jacket. Willie Butler. He and Frank were good friends. Used to come in together all the time."

A vet, Mack figured, by the faded green Army fatigue jacket and hat. "Let's talk to Willie."

As they moved down an aisle between the tables, the vagrant next to Willie spotted them and nudged him. Willie took one look, leaped to his feet and bolted through the swinging doors.

Otis took off after him. Mack followed through the doors and collided with a beefy server. They both went down, Mack on top. Mack swore, pushed himself to his feet and looked around the large kitchen. Cooks and servers gaped, but no sign of Willie or Otis. There was only one other exit, which led to a storage room. Mack ran down an aisle between stacked crates and boxes and exited through an open delivery entrance, where workers were unloading supplies from a truck. He saw Otis chasing Willie down an alley behind the mission and gaining fast. Mack dashed after them and was beginning to feel winded by the time he reached Polk Street. Shit! He was in good shape, but he was a jogger, not a runner, and Otis moved like he was on a fast break for a lay-up.

Almost true. Otis still kept his hand in with pick-up games at the YMCA. Although he had lost some of his quickness, he was still fast enough to easily run down Willie. By the time Willie passed the old Dearborn Street Train Station and dodged through traffic at Clark, he was gasping for breath. Otis grabbed him by the arm and shoved his badge in his face.

"Police, Willie!"

Willie Butler glared at the badge. He didn't need a badge pushed in his face to know the black dude was a cop. The white dude, too. They had cop written all over them when he saw them in the dining room. Not undercover cops, like narc dicks. They could dress down, blend in with the street people. But other detectives had to wear suits and ties. It was regulation. And Willie knew the regulations. That was part of survival on the street, knowing the regulations.

"Fuck you!" he croaked. His chest was pounding and he was having a tough time gulping down air.

Otis was deciding how to play this when Mack ran up, obviously winded and pissed. "Cuff him!"

Otis hesitated. He wanted Willie's cooperation, not the hostility he saw seething on the face of the black man. The face under a graying stubble of whiskers reminded Otis of an old leather jacket, creased and showing the wear and tear of a life on the street, yet still tough and durable. There was something else, too, something lurking in the depths of his hazel eyes. Something beyond life on the street that was telling him that Willie Butler might be a man who could be trusted, even though it was obvious he'd committed some recent crime. Otherwise, why would he have run from the law?

Mack figured the same thing and was in no mood to stroke Willie Butler. "I said cuff him!"

Willie thrust his arms toward Otis, fists balled. "Right. So go ahead. You take me in and be chargin' me with what?"

Willie knew for what. For ripping off a White Hen at State and Illinois early in the a.m. for a lousy ham and cheese on rye from the sandwich rack. He was out of there before the Arab behind the cash register could yell something he couldn't understand and probably reach for the phone to dial 911. Ten minutes later he was wolfing down the sandwich on the Red Line subway train, which he'd boarded a block away at State and Grand, and cursing himself for his stupidity. But what the hell. He was hung over and hungry, and the White Hen was an easy mark. He'd ripped it off before. Now he was thinking that the cops must have ID'd him from the film on the security cameras, even though he knew their location and had been careful to keep his face turned away.

Otis took out his handcuffs and started to snap them on Willie's wrists, then turned to Mack. "Willie would like to know what he's being charged with."

"Tell Willie he's being charged with vagrancy and resisting arrest for openers. We'll get more when we check CHRIS for recent unsolved burglaries."

Willie knew what CHRIS was. Cop talk for Criminal History Records Information System. He also knew that they would find his rap sheet listing a variety of petty crimes with his mug shot. However, if the security camera had caught his face, chances were the data hadn't made it into the system yet. Willie hoped.

"I don't know, Mack," Otis said, giving Mack a wink that Willie couldn't see. "Maybe we should give Willie a break if he cooperates."

"Screw that. Cuff him!"

"Come on. Let's give him a break."

The white cop called Mack glared at Willie as if he'd like to take him into an alley and beat on him. But Willie wasn't sweating that now. Now he got it. The good cop, bad cop routine. Okay, so play along.

"You tellin' me this ain't a bust or what?"

"We'll see," the good cop said. "It depends on the answers we get to some questions."

"And don't give us any bullshit, Willie!"

Willie lowered his hands, but the good cop didn't put the cuffs away, and the bad cop kept glaring at him. "Okay. So what do you wanna know?"

"Frank O'Meara, alias Cravin. A friend of yours, according to Pastor John." Otis saw Willie's face stiffen, and quickly added, "He's not wanted for anything, Willie. We're from Special Victims. Frank's missing, and his daughter wants us to find him."

Willie studied the good cop's face, then the bad cop's, trying to decide if they were on the level. Was Frank really missing, or was he wanted?

"Don't be shittin' me. Frank served in Nam, like me. Us vets gotta stick together."

"I understand," the good cop said. "I'm giving it to you straight, Willie. Will you help us?"

Again Willie hesitated. The good cop seemed sincere, even compassionate. Maybe he really was a good cop. The bad cop was just a bad cop. Decision time.

"You dudes fucked up my lunch, so I guess you're buyin', right?"

Otis looked at Mack and grinned. "Your turn."

*1:22 p.m.:* "So Frank's back on the street, huh?" Willie said, chewing on a bite of T-bone.

"Could be," Otis said as he worked on a slab of deep dish pizza loaded with anchovies, mushrooms and sausage.

Willie washed down the steak with a swig of Millers draft and belched. "I'll kick his ass if he fucked himself up. He's got a daughter, ya know, and a grandkid, a little girl. Family. That's more than I got."

More than I ever had, he thought, or ever will have. His mother, if you could call her a mother, was a crack whore who died from an OD when he was only thirteen. His dad could have been anybody, and he'd hardly known his two sisters. To this day he had no idea what had become of them. When he wasn't running with street gangs, he was spending time in youth centers. He finally found a home in the U.S. Army, but it was Viet Nam that brought his platoon buddies and him together in the closest thing to a family he had ever known. But that hadn't lasted long. Half of them had been shipped home in body bags by the time he volunteered to be a scout sniper. No more family then. After three months of intense training, he was back in Nam, a predator, out there alone in the jungle, even shunned by his own.

After Nam he'd planned to make the Army his career, but blew it by getting drunk and beating the shit out of an asshole second lieutenant. That meant doing time in Leavenworth, a dishonorable discharge and no veterans' benefits. From then on it was all downhill, in and out of shit jobs, in and out of the Cook County lock-up, in and out of missions and shelters. Fun in the Windy City. They said he had an attitude problem, the counselors at the shelters. No shit. At least he'd stayed away from hard drugs. He'd seen what they did to his mother, most of the gangbangers he'd run with and even some of his army buddies. Booze was another matter. A substance abuser, that's what the shit heads at rehab called a drunk. Abuser. A drunk's a *drunk*, which is what he was, and what in the fuck did they know about being abused anyway? Fuck 'em! Fuck 'em all!

All but Frank. Frank was the only guy he could call a friend since Nam. Frank understood, because he'd been there, too. He'd served his time in hell only to find out that there was another kind of hell. Hell on the street. But he was out of that now. He'd gotten clean. He had a life again, and Willie was glad for him.

"When was the last time you saw Frank?"

Otis realized that Willie was off somewhere with his thoughts, and repeated the question.

"I dunno. Two, maybe three weeks ago. He brought me some good time money and some smokes."

"Where was that, Willie?" Mack asked through a mouthful of chicken from a Caesar salad. Back to healthy lunches again after two weeks of pigging out.

Willie hesitated. They'd probably laugh at him if he told them. So fuck 'em. If they did, he'd order another beer. Hell, maybe he'd order it anyway. "The library."

The cops didn't laugh, but they did exchange looks.

"Library?" the good cop said. What was his name? Otis something.

"You heard me. The library. The public library on South State."

"You a bookworm, Willie?" the asshole cop said.

Willie expected to see a smirk on his face, but there wasn't one. "Frank, he likes to read. They got books at the missions, but Frank, he's read all that shit, he told me. So we hit the library. 'Course we couldn't take books out, but they couldn't kick our ass out as long as we didn't fuck up."

Which meant not getting caught having a drink in the men's room, which they had done on many occasions, or causing any disturbances. Willie was often tempted to let loose a loud belch or a fart, just to shake things up, but had restrained the urge. He did this for Frank. An educated man, Frank, but he never made a big deal about it. Or about helping Willie with the words he couldn't understand.

Frank had gotten him into reading, too. It was like a whole new world opened up to him. He couldn't remember the names of most of the dudes who wrote the books, most of them long dead, according to Frank, but he did remember some of the titles. *The Grapes of Wrath, Oliver Twist, The Adventures of Huckleberry Finn* and a bunch of others he'd plowed through with Frank's help. It was tougher now without Frank. He had to check a dictionary to look up the fancy words, or just pass over them if he got pissed, which was often, because the more he read the more he realized that he didn't know shit. But what the hell. He was hooked, and fuck anyone who put him down about it. Not like it was something he talked about, not even to Pastor John.

"When you saw him, how did he seem?" Otis asked. He saw the confusion on Willie's face, and added, "I mean, do you think he was drinking again?"

"Drinking? No. He'd have told me if he was."

Maybe, Mack thought. "He looked okay, did he?"

"Yeah, okay. Put on some weight."

Otis washed down the last bite of pizza with a swig of Pepsi. "Got any idea where he might be?"

"Shit, man, he could be anywhere. But I can tell you where he might have sacked out last night. The Red Line. We used to ride it at night. One of us sacked while the other one stood guard, takin' turns, ya know, 'cause a lot of shit goes down there at night."

Mack and Otis both knew what Willie meant by shit going down at night on the CTA Red Line train that ran between 95th and Howard Street. Thieves would prey on the sleepers, use razor blades to cut their coats or pants to steal their money, or just reach over them to take a purse or bag that might contain anything of value. Worse could happen. A sleeper could wake up in a hospital with a concussion or bleeding from knife wounds. Or not wake up at all.

Otis took a folded-up wanted bulletin from his coat pocket with his card stapled to the corner and laid it next to Willie's beer mug. "Do us a favor, Willie. Flash this around the street. Maybe someone saw Frank. Will you do that?"

Willie unfolded the bulletin. Frank's Irish face beamed at him with its big, lopsided grin, the way he'd seen him last time at the library. "I'll do it. But not for you. For Frank."

"Give me a call if you find out anything."

"That works both ways. You find him, I wanna know. I wanna know he's okay, so you let me know."

"Fair enough. I guess we could leave word with Pastor John."

"Right. Or get in touch with *Street Wise*."

"You got a job, Willie?" Mack said. He was familiar with the publisher of the weekly street magazine that employed homeless people to sell.

"A sometimes job, when I'm in the mood," Willie said, meaning when he needed spending money for smokes and booze. "Les Phipps, he's the honcho over there in charge of the vendors, he'll know what location I'm workin'."

Otis wrote his name down in his notebook. "Thanks, Willie. Any other ideas where we might look for Frank?"

"You might check out the Hilton." He waited for the don't bullshit us looks from the two cops before he added with a sarcastic smile, "That's the Lower Wacker Hilton."

Mack and Otis knew that Willie was referring to the accommodations underneath Wacker Drive, a main drag that borders the Chicago River east/west of the Outer Drive to Congress Street. Aside from providing motorists a fast track across town, Lower Wacker was a sometimes refuge for the homeless.

"You're a million laughs, Willie," Mack said without laughing.

"Fuck you," Willie said, and ordered another beer.

*2:54 p.m.:* Mack drove north on Upper Wacker Drive. When he reached Monroe Street, he descended the ramp to Lower Wacker. Pausing for an opening in the stream of vehicles, he gassed the Crown Vic until he could access an entry into the inner loading lane for the docks of the office buildings and a couple of hotels that lined Upper Wacker. Mack slowed the Vic for the ninety-degree turn east with the river as they cruised along the inner lane.

"Looks like we struck out," Otis said.

"Guess again," Mack said, pointing ahead with a drumstick.

Mack braked the Vic next to a loading dock. Large letters on the dock read: "AUTHORIZED PARKING ONLY!" Ignoring this were three vagrants, who were camped out on the dock, their entire net worth stuffed into Santa Claus bags and shopping carts. Another vagrant was rummaging through the nauseating contents of a huge dumpster. The blatant hostility on their bleary-eyed faces was momentarily erased by the sight of George Washington on the dollars Otis passed out, two to each happy camper along with the missing bulletin for Frank and Otis's card. Unfortunately, no one recognized Frank's face, despite a promise of twenty bucks to anyone who could and did give information as to Frank's possible whereabouts. The offer was open-ended, in case any of them spotted Frank.

"What now?" Otis said. He glanced at the dash clock. 2:55 p.m. "We got a couple of hours before we can talk to the people at Jake's Joint."

"I'm open to suggestions," Mack said, while they drove east on Lower Wacker.

"Guess we could check out some of the other missions and shelters."

"I'm not in a shelter mood," Mack said, stopping for the red at Columbus Drive. "What about that domestic complaint?"

Otis shifted through the missing reports and pulled out one. "How about that? The complainant is a man for a change. Miller, Albert F."

"What's his problem? Not getting any?"

"It says physical abuse."

"Physical abuse? Let's check it out. It might be worth some laughs."

*3:20 p.m.:* Mack and Otis forced themselves to keep straight faces, as Miller, Albert F., a 65-year-old retiree who lived in a low rent apartment in Rogers Park, disclosed the nature of his abuse. Not that there was anything funny about the multiple bites on his neck, face and arm inflicted by his wife. They had required medical attention in the emergency room of the St. Francis Hospital in Evanston. It was the fact that the attack by Mrs. M. had been motivated by Mr. M's inability to get it up, the unfortunate side effect of a drug, Hyzaar, that he was taking for high blood pressure. Ginseng, Viagra and other remedies had been tried to no avail.

When Mr. M. finished his narrative, Otis asked if he wanted to file a charge for aggravated assault. He did not. He loved his wife. If only they, Officers Winstrom and McPherson, would talk to her. Would they do that?

They would, Otis assured him. He also suggested that Mr. Miller have his doctor prescribe another drug to get his blood pressure down. And his dick up, Mack thought with a smile. He wished Mr. M. good luck, but was in no mood to play the marriage counselor and told Otis as much, as they drove north on Broadway to a Jewel store where Mrs. M. worked as a checker.

Otis chuckled. "Comes with the job."

"Then you handle it, Dr. Phil."

*3:55 p.m.:* While Mack listened to dispatch chatter on his radio and did some drum calisthenics on the steering wheel in the parking lot with both sticks, Otis interviewed a distraught Mrs. M. in the privacy of the manager's office. Mrs. M. was Mr. M.'s second wife. She was fifteen years younger than her spouse. She had needs. She regretted the attack. It had not been premeditated, unless consuming a bottle of Zinfandel could be considered premeditation. She had simply lost it. She was sorry. It wouldn't happen again.

*4:26 p.m.:* "Until the next time," Mack said, after Otis briefed him on his conversation with Mrs. M. as they headed south on the Outer Drive to Jake's.

"Probably. Turn the radio down. Got to check in with the boss."

Otis speed-dialed a number on his cell phone. After a couple of beeps, Ava's voice answered.

"Hello."

"Hi, darling. Where are you?"

"On my way home. At last."

"You sound beat."

"Exhausted. Shopping with Mom is always an ordeal. We must have done every mall on the Shore. But I found what I was looking for. I found the fabric."

"Oh? What fabric?"

"For the bedroom curtains. Don't you remember?"

"Oh, yeah." To Otis the curtains looked just fine, but Ava insisted that they didn't blend with the decor and had to go. When it came to the interior decorating of their home, Ava's decisions were law. "So it works, huh?"

"Absolutely. You'll love it. Oh, and I got something for you, too."

"Oh, what's that?"

"It's a surprise, but it's something you really need."

Oh, oh, Otis thought. Things he really needed usually turned out to be things Ava thought he needed but didn't. "Surprise me now. What is it?"

"It's a back support for that awful chair in the den."

"Back support?"

"Yes. I found it at Brookstone. It even has batteries that make it vibrate and give you a massage."

"Fabulous, but I prefer the real thing. Hint. hint."

"Shut up and say thank you, dear."

"Thank you, dear."

Otis meant it. He spent a lot of time in the den, messing with his state-of-the-art Dell 3100 Dimension or working on his model planes, and the back support would be a welcome therapeutic aid. Otis was wondering now if the back support was a peace offering. He hoped so. No matter. He would buy half a dozen roses from a florist on the way home. His own peace offering.

"Oh, I may be a little late. Mack and I got to talk to some people about a missing kid, and they won't be available until five."

"Not too late, I hope. We have plans with the Schlemmers, remember?"

"Sure, no problem," Otis said, now remembering that they were doing supper and theater with Ava's close friend, Marilyn, and her husband. They had a reservation at six-thirty at The Cove, a posh seafood restaurant in Glencoe, and tickets for a play, a revival of *Waiting for Godot*, whoever *Godot* was, at the Apple Tree Theatre in Highland Park. The curtain goes up at eight, so he should be able to make both events. Whatever they learned at Jake's could probably wait until tomorrow.

"Please be on time, dear. And stay in touch."

"Will do. Love you."

"Love you, too."

Otis beeped off with a smile. The cold war was over.

Mack wasn't as optimistic. Otis spent a lot of time on the cell with his wife. Too much time. And he was usually on the defensive, which meant that he was getting heat for something. For a cop there was always something. It was called the job. The job came first, a fact that most wives failed to understand. Mack knew the script from beginning to end. It began with falling in love and ended with divorce.

*4:45 p.m.:* They arrived at Jake's and killed fifteen minutes shooting pool while waiting for the night staff to come on. There were two bouncers, both in their twenties, sporting spiked hair and built like Chicago Bears linebackers. They could have been bookends, except one was blond and the other brunet. The blond, Mike, remembered the incident. He'd escorted the Bowman kid outside when he got out of line.

"How drunk was he?" Mack asked.

"Stinking. But he didn't give me a hard time, even apologized. He wasn't a bad guy, just needed some air, ya know?"

Otis took this down on his notepad. "Did he hang around outside?"

"Don't know. His buddies told him to wait until they settled up, that's all I know. Did you check with security? They might know something."

"We were just going to do that," Otis said. "Thanks for your help, Mike."

The security station was located just off the lobby on the street-level floor. There were three officers on the night shift, two roaming the area and one manning the bank of monitors. Only one of the roamers had been on duty Monday night and couldn't remember seeing the Bowman kid. The monitor officer, Jerry, a short black man, was more helpful.

"Let's check the tape," he suggested.

There were surveillance cameras covering the internal and external areas of the converted warehouse, and Jerry was referring to the tape recorded by a camera located just outside Jake's. It took twenty minutes to get the tape and run it through a player/recorder to the approximate time that Bowman left Jake's. Mack and Otis watched the monitor over the officer's shoulder. The camera panned back and forth along the pier. There weren't many people on the pier at that time of night. A couple were making out on a bench, then left. A group of partying young men and women boarded a power boat and pulled away.

"That him?" Jerry asked, as the camera caught a man exiting Jake's.

"No," Mack said.

The camera panned away, then back.

"There he is!" Otis said. "Hit the slow-mo."

Jerry did. Mike, the bouncer, and Bowman were leaving Jake's, Mike holding the kid's arm to support him. The camera panned away, then back. Bowman was staggering east on the pier. Again the camera panned away. When it returned the kid was taking a leak over the side of the pier into the inlet.

"Lucky we didn't catch him doing that," the security officer said with a smile.

The camera panned away, then back. The kid was gone.

Mack looked at Otis. His face was grim. "Better call your wife and tell her you're gonna be late."

*6:16 p.m.:* Mack and Otis watched the diver submerge again. A police marine boat and unit had arrived at the scene half an hour after they put in the call. The diver was in the water ten minutes later. Another police boat blocked the entrance to the inlet. Uniforms kept a growing crowd of gawkers at a respectful distance. Two fire department paramedics were rolling a gurney down the stairs from McClurg Court, when Mack spotted the CBS TV truck pulling up behind their ambulance. Being only three blocks away, CBS was the first to get its unit on the scene. Mack knew that others would follow.

"Keep those media assholes out of here!" he barked at the uniforms.

Otis agreed. They couldn't stop them from shooting the scene from

McClurg, where they could zoom in on the grim events, or interviewing the grief-stricken parents later, all of which would appear on the ten o'clock news. He'd given an interview himself to the media after finding the Pletcher kid; but this was different. That story had a happy ending. This one wouldn't, and Otis wanted no part in the typical media exploitation of the tragedy.

It didn't take long to find the kid. He was wedged under the pier. Mack and Otis figured that when he fell in, he probably surfaced under the pier and hit his head. An autopsy would tell for sure. That could wait. Informing the kid's parents could not. Otis didn't want them to learn about it from a phone call by someone on the night shift at the station, or worse, see it on the ten o'clock news. They'd left word at the station that they could be reached at the Sheraton.

*7:10 p.m.:* The Sheraton was at Illinois and Columbus Drive, only two blocks away, so they hoofed it. Otis was surprised that Mack agreed to participate in this unpleasant task. However, Mack left the talking to Otis, and seemed more than relieved when they walked from the Bowmans's room on the twenty-second floor to the elevators. The truth was, so was Otis.

They were exiting the hotel when Otis's cell beeped. Otis knew who it was even before he checked the screen. After the kid was found he'd called Ava at the restaurant to assure her he'd meet them at the theater in time for the play. A glance at his wrist watch told him there was no way that was going to happen now. He fingered the talk button and put the phone to his mouth.

"Hello, darling. I was just about to call you."

Mack listened to him apologize. For what? For just doing his job? No, more than just doing his job. Informing the kid's parents in person didn't necessarily come with the job. Mack had to admit that it wasn't something he would have done if he could have avoided it. But Otis was his partner, like it or not, and you had to back up your partner no matter what the situation. Mack would expect the same from Otis. From any partner. That's the way it was.

"Enjoy the play, darling," Otis said after a short, painful conversation. "Love you."

Click. No love you in response this time.

They walked back in silence, this time along the river. The sun was just descending. The sky was clear. A crescent moon had already made its appearance. It was going to be a beautiful night.

Mack wanted to say something, but nothing seemed appropriate. "Hungry?" was the best he could come up with.

"No."

More silence.

"Might as well go back to the station and write up the report," Otis said.

"Can't that wait until tomorrow?"

"It might." More silence. "You got any better ideas?"

"Goddamn right."

"Like?"

"Like I buy us a drink."

"If you're buyin', I'm drinkin'."

## Thursday, May 16

*9:45 a.m.:* Megan knelt down on the knee support in front of the pew where she and Katie were sitting in the nave of the Holy Name Cathedral.

"What are you doing, Mommy?"

Katie's voice could barely be heard above the booming music of the amplified organ that reverberated through the cathedral. Even so, her voice drew a look of reproach from an old lady in a pew across the aisle.

"Shhh, dear," Megan whispered, looking around. There were only a few people in the church, but others were beginning to filter in for the ten o'clock Mass. Megan had decided to bring Katie with her, explaining that this is where her grandpa went every Sunday morning to thank God for helping him come back to them. Katie had gazed in awe at the magnificent nave with its mosaic lancet windows and towering marble pillars that supported the arching oak ceiling.

"What are you doing?" Katie persisted, her voice hushed.

"I'm kneeling so I can say a prayer for Grandpa."

"Can I pray for Grandpa, too?"

"Of course."

Katie knelt down on the support. "Now what do I do?"

Megan clasped her hands. "Clasp your hands together."

"Like this?"

"Yes, dear. And now bow your head."

Katie watched her mother bow her head and did the same. "Do we say the prayer now?"

"Yes. Would you like to say it?"

Katie nodded.

"All right. Close your eyes and ask God to keep Grandpa safe."

"Please, God, keep my grandpa safe," Katie said in a solemn voice. She opened her eyes, looked at Megan, her forehead creased in a frown. "Is Grandpa sick, Mommy?"

"No. No, he's not sick, dear."

"Then why are we asking God to keep him safe?"

"We all need God's help sometimes."

"We do?

"Yes, dear."

Katie stopped asking questions to absorb this. Katie was a bright child and had an inquisitive mind that soaked up information like a sponge. Megan could see that she was still troubled, and wondered if she sensed that her granddad really did need God's help, despite what she had told her, which was that he had gone to visit her Aunt Mary, her dad's widowed sister. Mary Arnett was a warm, wonderful lady who gave kids piano lessons to make ends meet and spoiled Katie with gifts every time she came to Chicago or when they visited her in Kenosha.

"Does God always do what you ask him to?" Katie asked.

"He tries, dear," was all Megan could offer as an answer.

Megan realized that Katie's spiritual upbringing had been sadly neglected, and the fault was all hers. She and Artie had planned to raise Katie in the Jewish faith—Artie's wish—which she respected. Although Artie wasn't orthodox and rarely attended synagogue, he still observed the holy days, with Megan preparing the traditional Passover meal and Artie reading from an abridged version of the Torah. When Artie died, Katie was only three, and Megan couldn't bring herself to follow through on her promise. Maybe deep down she blamed God for Artie's death. This was something she'd avoided discussing with Karen but now realized she had to face, if not for herself, for Katie. As she offered a silent prayer for her dad, she also made a resolution to call Rabbi Secher to arrange for Katie to attend Sunday school.

Katie's hand tugging at her sleeve interrupted her thoughts. "Do you think Grandpa will come home soon, Mommy?"

"I think so."

"I miss Grandpa, Mommy. I miss him so much."

"So do I, dear," Megan said, and bowed her head again, not just in prayer, but so that Katie wouldn't see the tears welling up in her eyes.

*1:20 p.m.:* Mack and Otis listened to the dispatch chatter on Otis's radio as the Crown Vic crept along the old bridle path that ran adjacent to the asphalt bike trail just north of Montrose Harbor. The bike trail was busy with bikers, roller bladers and joggers, although some joggers preferred the softer gravel that crunched under the wheels of the Vic. The lake was also active with a variety of small craft and the big Odyssey cruise ship doing a Thursday afternoon luncheon cruise.

It had been a beautiful morning, warm and sunny, so during breakfast at a Denny's they'd decided to check out Lincoln Park on the chance that Frank was sacked out on a bench. If they struck out, they'd hit some of the shelters and then circulate the missing bulletin both in the area where Megan lived and at the bars near the Home Depot on North Avenue.

The death of the Bowman kid was still very much on Otis's mind. He could be out there this morning, Otis thought, riding a bike, maybe with his friend, Jess, instead of occupying a shelf in the cooler of the Cook County Morgue.

"So how was your night?" Otis asked after a long period of silence.

"Okay," Mack said.

Actually, it wasn't okay. The job was really getting to him, and the Bowman kid's death hadn't helped. So after a couple of beers with Otis at Jake's, he'd gone home, put on some jazz records, turned up the volume and proceeded to drink Jack Daniels…straight from the bottle. But if he thought this would put him in a more mellow mood, he was wrong. He'd continued to brood over the Bowman kid's death…a kid he hadn't found, couldn't have found, until it was too late. But even though he couldn't have prevented his death, the incident reminded him of Kenny. Kenny's death was different. He could have prevented that. But he hadn't. He'd screwed up, and now Kenny was gone. With all this on his mind, it was well after 1:00 a.m. before fatigue and the booze submerged him in a restless sleep.

"How about you?" Mack said. "I hope you made everything okay with your wife?"

"Everything's cool," Otis said, but Mack's grunt betrayed a strong hint of skepticism.

They drove in silence for a while. The dispatcher was relaying a request for assistance by two officers at the scene of a robbery taking place at a liquor store at Stony Island Avenue and 59th. Mack took a drumstick from the dash and began to tap on the steering wheel.

"What's with the drumming, anyway?" Otis asked, hoping that his partner would pick up on the inflection in his voice and stop.

Mack ignored the inflection. "Just keeping the beat to the music."

"What music?"

"The music in my head."

"In your head!"

"Yeah. Used to drive Linda crazy."

No shit, Otis thought.

Mack braked the Vic and pointed the drumstick at a vagrant sacked out on a nearby bench. His back was turned to them, but there was a resemblance to the picture of Frank.

"Our missing Irishman?"

"Could be. About the same build. Give him a wakeup call."

Mack blasted the horn. The vagrant stirred. Another long blast. The vagrant turned over on his side. The angry, withered face behind the shaggy gray beard was not Frank's.

"Sorry, pop," Mack said. He toed the accelerator and resumed his tapping on the steering wheel.

"So I guess you play the drums?" Otis ventured by way of keeping the conversation flowing.

"I keep my hand in."

"So do you play with a group or what?"

"A group? Get serious. I'm a cop, remember?"

"So where?"

"Here and there. I'll sit in on occasion when I know the guys."

"Rock bands?"

"Rock? Not if I can help it. Jazz and swing."

"No shit. I would have thought you'd be into Rolling Stones, Grateful Dead stuff."

"I was, but only to the extent that I had to play it to make a buck back in high school."

"So you were in a band then?"

"Yeah. But once in a while we'd slip in something that swung."

"Swing really moves, I gotta say that. You can get a real workout dancing to it."

"You know how to swing dance?"

"I'm learning. Fox trots and waltzes, too. Ava's idea. She's into ballroom dancing, so we're taking lessons."

"So how's it going? The lessons?"

Otis shrugged. "Okay, I guess. It takes a while to get the hang of it, especially the waltz. Those big bands on the records we dance to, they were pretty good."

Only pretty good? Only great! Mack thought. "My old man probably played in some of those bands."

"No kidding? Was he a drummer, too?"

"No. Dad played the trumpet. He was what they call a side man. Not the lead, but damned good. You had to be to play in those bands."

"Did he play with Glenn Miller? They play a lot of his stuff at the studio."

"No. Miller was late thirties, early forties. Dad made the scene in the fifties. Benny Goodman was still around then. He played with Goodman, Les Brown, Harry James."

"Harry James? I've heard of him. Married some sexy movie star chick, right? Same name as my wife's. Ava somebody."

"Ava Gardner. Ava was one of Artie Shaw's wives. He had four or five. Harry married Betty Grable."

"So what happened to the big bands, anyway?"

"Rock happened to them. It's a lot cheaper to pay four or five guys with guitars and amplifiers than sixteen real musicians."

Otis was beginning to suspect that Mack didn't have much respect for rock. "Too bad. A lot of guys must have had to make some serious career changes."

For sure, Mack thought, including his dad. "There are still a few big bands around, a couple in the area, but most of the guys have regular jobs and play more for the fun of it than the money, which is lousy."

"Maybe we could take one in sometime."

"Are you serious?"

"Sure. Why not?"

"I'll give it some thought, if you promise not to ask me to dance." Otis laughed, and Mack joined in. "Why in the hell am I telling you all this shit, anyway?"

"Good question. Maybe we're bonding."

"Bonding. Right," Mack scoffed.

To Mack, bonding between two partners only took place when they came under fire. That's when it happened and only then. Given his current job, the chance of that occurring with Otis seemed remote. Mack wondered if Otis had ever used his revolver except on the firing range. And would he be able to hit what he was firing at when it counted? Mack wasn't particularly anxious to find out.

"So now that we're bonding, answer me something. Why did you pass up big bucks in the NBA for a badge?"

"I could have made the pros, if I'd bulked up, but I would have been ridin' the pine. A long time ago I decided that if I don't start, I don't play."

Mack knew that Otis had a high opinion of himself, but figured that there had to be more to it than a bruised ego. "Riding the pine still beats a cop's pay."

Otis hesitated. Should he confide in Mack? And if he did, would Mack understand or even give a shit? He decided to take a chance.

"It was like this. I had a cousin. Effie Mae. My mom's sister's kid. She was an only child, because her deadbeat dad took off, so she spent a lot of time with us. I got two brothers and a sister, but they're a lot older than me. I came along late, so Effie Mae was like a little sister to me, and I guess I was like a big brother to her. I was always there for her, you know, to keep her straight and out of shit. But when I went away to college, something happened, I don't know what. Mom, she thinks it had something to do with her asshole father, but Effie wouldn't tell her. Anyway, after that she started to hang out with a gang. She'd miss school, come home stoned at all hours. Then one day she didn't come home at all."

Otis could feel the anger and lingering grief knotting his stomach and paused to keep it under control. Mack knew the ending to this story, but decided to let Otis tell it anyway.

"They found her two months later. Not the police, but some construction workers who were tearing down a condemned apartment building, a gang fortress until they demolished it. The autopsy said she died of an OD. Heroin. End of story."

"Sorry," Mack said.

"Right." Maybe he was sorry, Otis thought. With Mack you couldn't tell. You looked at his face for a clue to what he was thinking and got nothing.

The fact was that Mack was genuinely sorry. But he also realized that he had a crusader as a partner to deal with. His mission was to save all the missing Effie Maes of the world. Good luck. You weren't going to save them by just finding them. In most cases it was too late by that time. They were already screwed up. No, to save them you had to take out the pushers, the gangbangers, even the sicko parents who fucked up their lives. And, of course, you had to exterminate the predators like Jason Fry.

"Okay, so now it's my turn," Otis said after a long moment of silence.

"Your turn to what? You wanna drive?"

"Don't give me any shit. My turn to ask a question that's been bugging me since we hooked up."

"So ask."

"What's with this Rambo shit you're into?"

"Correction. Was into."

"Right. So what about it?"

"Let's just say that I speak from personal experience when I tell you that the legal system doesn't always work."

Otis was tempted to ask Mack if he'd care to elaborate, but decided that was all he was going to get out of him on the subject for now, if ever. "This is getting boring. What say we hit some shelters?"

Mack was about to agree, when the dispatcher's voice on Otis's radio interrupted.

"Twenty-two Charlie to Diversey Harbor. We got a floater."

Mack looked at Otis. They shared the same premonition.

"Wanna check it out?" Otis said.

Mack's response was to gas the Vic.

*1:58 p.m.:* Mack swung the Vic off Diversey Parkway. He pulled up beside a fire department ambulance and a squad car in a parking area and exited the Vic with Otis. They moved across a stretch of lawn toward the sea wall, where two paramedics were lifting a plastic body bag with its grim contents onto a gurney. One policeman, a stocky black man in his thirties, was talking to an old man, obviously a fisherman judging by the two rods, tackle box and net piled by the sea wall. The other cop, white, early twenties and slim, was telling two curious joggers to keep jogging. Behind them Mack and Otis could hear the pop of tennis balls on eight park district courts and the crack of golf balls on a driving range. Pleasure in the park as usual on a sunny afternoon, except for the person on the gurney.

Mack showed his badge to the group. "Detectives McPherson and Winstrom, Special Victims." He moved to the paramedics, both young men in their twenties, one with a crew cut, the other with shoulder-length hair. "What have we got?"

"Hard to say," crew cut said. "The guy's been in the water for a while. Maybe a couple of days." He gestured toward the fisherman. "Would have been there a lot longer if he hadn't hooked him."

"I thought I'd got me a big cat," the old man stammered, obviously shaken. "Like the one I caught last year. Forty pounds, it weighed, maybe more. 'Course I couldn't bring him in...too big...had to cut the line. But this time I knew there was something wrong, 'cause there was only dead weight on the line. No fight. I figured maybe an old tire...I've hooked tires before...but, Jesus, when I saw him there, rising to the surface, face down..." He didn't finish. Mack knew that he'd live with that ugly picture in his brain for the rest of his life.

"Any signs of assault?" Mack said.

Long hair shrugged. "Not that we can tell. Won't know for sure until we get him to the morgue for an autopsy."

While Mack was questioning the paramedics, Otis moved to the gurney. He inhaled a deep breath, took hold of the zipper of the body bag and made a silent prayer. Please, Lord, don't let it be Frank. He felt the bitter taste of his breakfast rising into his throat as he unzipped the bag to reveal what was left of a bloated, puss-leaking face.

"Shit!"

Mack turned. He didn't have to ask Otis if he recognized the corpse. The answer was engraved on his face.

*5:14 p.m.:* Megan stared at the face on the monitor in the viewing room of the Cook County Morgue. At first she didn't recognize him. Where was the color she'd restored to his cheeks with her home cooking? Where were the laughing eyes, the mischievous Irish smile? No, this face couldn't be her dad's. This face was bloated, pale, waxy, gray.

"Megan, are you okay?"

Detective Winstrom's voice seemed far away. Megan didn't answer. Try as she might, she couldn't pry her eyes off the face on the screen. She wanted the face's eyes to open, the lips to move and tell her that he wasn't Frank O'Meara. That he wasn't her dad.

"Are you alright, Megan?"

Detective Winstrom's voice again. Now she felt the gentle pressure of his hand on her arm. "Yes...I'm alright."

Of course, she wasn't. Inside she felt as lifeless as the man whose face filled the screen. When the detectives came to her townhouse an hour ago with the news of her father's death, she was thrust into a state of shock. She tried during the ride to the morgue to prepare herself for the task of identifying his body. But when she saw her father's deteriorating face on the monitor, she felt as though a heavy stone had been rolled across her life, cutting her off forever from his warmth and love and laughter, leaving her abandoned in an alien world from which there was no way home. Megan knew in her head that this feeling would not last, that the grief, the anguish, the tears...and the healing...would come eventually. But not now.

"Is that your father, Mrs. Herbst?"

The other detective's voice. What was his name? McPherson? Of course it's my dad. You saw his picture. Detective Winstrom knew him personally. Neither of you doubted that it was my dad when you came to tell me you'd found his body. So why are you asking me now what you know already? Oh, yes. You have to make it official. Somebody in the family has to identify the body.

"Mrs. Herbst...?

"Yes, that's my father! Of course it's him!" Megan snapped, surprised by the sudden flare of anger burning her cheeks. Why was she angry with them? After all, they'd been thoughtful enough to come to her home to bring her here. Detective Winstrom had always been kind and compassionate. Even the other detective was showing some semblance of sympathy.

She turned away from the monitor to face them. "Can we go now?" she said, feeling as if the walls of the small viewing room were closing in on her, the ceiling descending like the lid on a coffin.

Detective McPherson opened the door. Detective Winstrom took her arm, helped her up, and escorted her out of the room into the reception area.

"If you don't mind, I'd like to sit down for a moment."

Detective Winstrom steered her to a cushioned sofa in the large reception area that reminded Megan of the lobby of an upscale hotel with its comfortable furniture, potted plants and pastoral paintings on the walls. Except here the guests were all dead. A hotel for the dead, Megan thought, as she settled onto the sofa. Never mind the name on the front of the building—COOK COUNTY INSTITUTE OF FORENSIC MEDICINE. Just a fancy name for a morgue— although the sprawling nondescript two-story building of white concrete could just as easily have housed a travel bureau, a real estate office and an insurance agency, rather than its grim operating room, its laboratory, and the refrigerated storage drawers for its transient guests.

Megan's throat felt tight and dry. She looked around and saw a water cooler next to an elderly black lady whose face spoke sadly but eloquently of years of hardship and emotional pain. The only other person in the room was an angry looking young man in a leather jacket and jeans who probably belonged to the Harley in the parking lot.

"Could you get me some water, please?"

"Sure," Detective Winstrom said, and moved to the cooler while Detective McPherson sat down on a chair opposite Megan.

Megan closed her eyes for a moment. She felt completely drained, like a dead battery that could no longer hold a charge. But there were things she couldn't put off, that she'd have to find the strength to tackle right away, so her dad could be laid to rest. She had to call Aunt Mary to tell her that her dad's body had been found and to see if she could drive down from Kenosha tonight to help, especially with Katie. She needed to talk to Karen about the best way to tell Katie that her grandpa was gone and would never come back. She'd already decided to use Fenn & Son Funeral Home on Armitage for the funeral service. She knew the son, John, whose own son, David, was a classmate of Katie's in kindergarten. Of course, Father Kiley at Holy Name Cathedral would be the logical choice to perform the funeral service.

"Here you are, Megan."

Megan opened her eyes and looked at the plastic cup of water being offered by Detective Winstrom.

"Thank you," she said, taking the cup and sipping from it. The water soothed her parched throat, but didn't help to clear her mind. She took another sip, set the cup on the end table next to an array of magazines and looked at the two detectives.

"What happens next?"

"You'll have to arrange for a funeral home to pick up your dad," Detective Winstrom said as he sat down next to her.

"That's not what I meant. What I want to know is how you're going to find out what happened to my father?"

"We're working on that, Mrs. Herbst," Detective McPherson said. "Unfortunately, there were no witnesses. Even if there were, a preliminary examination still has to be performed to determine the cause of death."

"I see. And when will that be done?"

"Depends on the case load. Hopefully first thing tomorrow morning. Tomorrow afternoon at the latest."

Megan nodded, trying to think. She wanted to ask them about the examination. Preliminary, Detective McPherson said. What did that mean, preliminary?

Detective Winstrom leaned toward her. "Megan..."

"Yes?"

"You must be exhausted. Why don't you let us take you home now? You need to get some rest."

"Alright. Are we through here?"

"Yes."

Megan stood and moved on wobbly legs to the entrance. Otis opened the door for her and the three of them walked across the visitors' parking lot to where Mack's car was parked.

The sky had turned overcast, somber, portending rain. No one spoke on the drive back to Megan's townhouse. Megan was wrapped in her thoughts, trying to plan and think through everything she would have to do, yet still in shock. Otis was right. She was exhausted. She needed rest.

They pulled up in front of Megan's building. Otis got out of the car, opened the door for her, and walked her to the entrance to her townhouse.

"You'll let me know when they're finished?" she said, pausing in the doorway. "With the examination?"

"We'll let you know as soon as we know," Detective Winstrom said. "Now go try and get some rest."

"Thanks," Megan said, and turned and entered her home. Yes, she needed rest, but there were so many things that had to be done first. And then there was the question of how her father had died. She would not sleep peacefully until she knew exactly what had happened to him. And maybe not even then.

## Friday, May 17

Mack and Otis had a full case load on Friday morning. First was an elderly abuse complaint at a nursing home by the daughter of her Parkinsons-afflicted mother. The victim was able to identify a surly lady attendant as the abuser, and the attendant was promptly fired. The rest of the morning was spent dealing with a domestic dispute between the affluent resident of a Gold Coast apartment and his girlfriend. An all-night drinking binge had gotten ugly, resulting in a 911 call by the girlfriend. Mack and Otis escorted Mr. Gold Coast to the precinct station, where he was booked and fingerprinted after he'd called his lawyer to post bond.

*12:40 p.m.:* Mack and Otis finally had a chance to sit down for lunch. Otis recommended Stacy's, a restaurant near the precinct station.

"Pass the salt," Mack said. Still on his slim down diet, he was attacking a Caesar salad with chicken.

"Take it easy on the salt, man," Otis said, as he chewed on a thick tenderloin sandwich smothered with melted cheddar cheese and fried onions. "Salt retains water. Bad for the heart."

"Just pass it."

Otis did, and Mack showered the salad with salt. "I can't eat anything without salt. Call me a saltaholic. Besides, who appointed you as my nutritionist?"

"Just trying to be helpful."

"I appreciate your concern, but I haven't seen you laying off the greasy burgers and French fries."

"I never put on weight," Otis said, pulling out his cell phone. "Work out a lot. And I'm type A. Burn off the calories before they have a chance to do their thing." He dialed a number he knew from memory.

"Who are you calling?"

"The morgue. Just want to see if they did Frank yet."

"What's the hurry? You know the verdict."

"Yeah, but I want to get this over with. For Megan's sake." Then into the cell: "This is Detective Winstrom. Have you done the autopsy on O'Meara? Yeah, I'll hang on." Then to Mack: "He's checking."

Mack watched Otis take out his notebook and pen and start writing. "You sure got a thing about that notebook. I never saw anybody write as much stuff down as you do—date, time, place, what you were having for lunch—in addition to what the informant or witness is telling you. Do you really need all that?"

"It helps me remember. Besides, I want to make sure I get all the facts for the reports in case my partner forgets something important."

"I appreciate your confidence in me."

"Don't mention it." Then into the phone: "Thanks. I'll check back later."

Otis pocketed the cell, put his notebook and pen down within easy reach of his plate, and picked up his sandwich. "They won't be able to do Frank until mid-afternoon."

"Good salad," Mack said. He had to admit that Otis was right when he'd recommended Stacy's. "What kind of desserts do they have here?"

"Big time selection." Otis picked up the menu and handed it to Mack. "But

I know what I want. Strawberry cheesecake. It's a specialty of the house. But since you're watching your waistline, I'd recommend the fruit sorbet."

"Thanks, but I think I'll check out the rest of the options myself."

Mack was studying the dessert selections when he heard the clump of heavy boots on the hardwood floor. He looked up and saw a burly young man in jeans and a tee shirt, swaggering from the bar next to the family room and obviously heading for the restrooms near the rear fire exit. It wasn't just the obnoxious smirk on the young man's piggish face or the collage of tattoos on his muscular arms that was drawing stares of disgust from Stacy's patrons, some with small children. In part it was the logo on the front of his grimy tee shirt: "HAVE A GOOD LAY." But there was more. When the young man passed their table, Mack and Otis observed the other message, on the back of the shirt: "WHAT THE FUCK ARE YOU LOOKING AT?"

Mack put down the menu and rose. "Got to take a leak."

"Hey, man. Cool it," Otis said, alarmed by the look in his partner's steel gray eyes.

"If the waitress comes, tell her I'll have the cheesecake—plain, no strawberries."

Shit! Otis thought. Here comes trouble!

Wilber Hossman flushed the urinal and zipped up his soiled jeans. "Sledge" to his buddies, he debated if he should have another beer and whiskey chaser with his pizza before going back to his shit job. Cleaning up the debris at a construction site and loading it into dump trucks was hard fucking work, and the asshole foreman was already giving him a hard time about his goofing off and drinking. Fuck him! Fuck the job! He'd take the afternoon off, claim he got sick, something he ate. So what if they fired his ass? Who gave a shit? Big brother and his wife would put him up until he got another job, one that required less work and paid more bucks.

Sledge turned to leave the restroom, the thought of washing his grimy hands never entering his brain. What did enter his brain was the presence of the dude who was blocking his way.

"I'm sorry, sir," the dude said. "But you'll have to remove your tee shirt before you leave the restroom."

It took Sledge a moment to absorb what the dude was saying. "I have to do what?"

"Remove your tee shirt. It's offensive."

"So it's offensive. Too fuckin' bad."

"I'm sorry, sir, but I'll have to insist."

"Fuck you, and get out of my way before I use your head as a punching bag!" To emphasize the threat, Sledge brandished a huge fist balled up like a sledgehammer, the origin of his nickname, after he'd broken the jaw of a kid with one punch when he was in seventh grade.

The dude didn't budge, and nothing showed on his face but the hint of a smile. Sledge sized him up. No pushover for sure, judging from his upper torso, but he'd busted the heads of tougher looking dudes than this one, even sent the last guy to the ER.

"Take your best shot," the dude said as calmly as if he was ordering a beer.

Not good. Sledge thought. The dude was just too cool. How to play it? A little deception seemed in order. Catch the dude off guard.

"Hey, man, I'm sorry," Sledge said, lowering his fist. "The shirt always got a laugh from my buddies, ya' know. Just a gag. Guess I could turn it inside out..."

Sledge reached up as though to pull the shirt over his head, then swung his right fist at the dude's cleft chin with all of his two hundred and sixty-five pounds of body weight behind it. However, his fist hit nothing but air instead of the dude's chin, throwing him off balance. Before he could recover, a hand grabbed the back of his belt and another fastened on his neck from behind and rammed his head against the mirror. When the cobwebs cleared from his vision, he blinked at his face in the cracked, blood-splattered mirror, his right arm now pinned behind his back, his neck held in a vise-like grip.

"Sorry about that," the dude said. "Now about the shirt..."

Sledge felt his arm being yanked up, and his shoulder exploded with pain.

"Okay, okay! I'll take it off, goddammit!

The dude let go of his arm and neck. In the mirror Sledge saw him back off far enough to deal with a counterattack, which Sledge was momentarily considering as he turned to face him. However, the sudden stab of pain in his forehead convinced him that would be a dumb play, along with the object that the dude took out of his pocket and held up. Shit! The object was a police badge. Sledge cursed himself. Fucking stupid! Now he saw what he should have seen before. The bulge of a hip holster and revolver underneath the dude's rumpled suit coat.

"Hey, man, I ain't done nothin' to get busted for."

"No? I think assaulting a police officer will rate you some serious cell time."

"Shit, man, give me a break! I didn't know you was a cop."

"We'll discuss that after you take off the shirt."

"Yeah, yeah. Okay."

Sledge quickly pulled off the offending shirt.

"Thank you," the cop said. "Now wash your face."

Sledge turned on the tap at one of the sinks and wetted the shirt. Wincing with pain, he used it to dab the blood off the cut in his forehead, thankful that aside from turning purple it didn't look all that serious. Fucking police brutality, he thought. He should raise hell with some public defender and nail the cop's ass. Yeah, sure, and then what? They'd pull his rap sheet and see he'd done time twice for aggravated battery. Then it would be his word against the cop's in front of a fucking judge, and guess which way that would go.

Sledge turned and said: "So are you gonna give me a break or what?"

"Did you read the sign on the front door when you came in?"

"Did I read what sign?"

"The sign that said no admittance to persons not properly attired. Shirt and shoes are required."

"Yeah, yeah, I saw it," Sledge lied. "So?"

"So you're not properly attired, which means I'll have to arrest you for indecent exposure. Of course, if you leave by the rear exit..."

"Hey, no sweat," Sledge said, relieved. "But what about my bar tab?"

"It's on me," the cop said, pocketing his badge. "And I'd advise you to dump the shirt into the nearest trash bin."

"Yeah, okay."

"Good boy," the cop said, patting him on the cheek.

Sledge watched him exit the wash room. When the door closed, Sledge threw the shirt at the door. "Fucking cop!" he spat. But softly.

*6:40 p.m.:* Megan heard the door chime. Who could that be, she thought, as she removed a steamer with Katie's supper from the microwave, a half chicken breast and medley of vegetables. She'd invited Karen to join Aunt Mary and her for supper, but that wasn't until seven. Maybe Karen was coming early.

"Can you get that, Mary?" she asked the robust, grey-haired lady who was keeping Katie company at the kitchen table.

"Of course, dear," her aunt said with a slight, lilting Irish brogue. She had her brother's laughing eyes and a sweet smile to match her personality. However, her aunt was also a lady who would take no malarkey from anybody, including Katie. "Now you eat all your veggies, Miss Katie, and your Aunt Mary will serve you a special dessert she made just for you."

Katie pouted at the mishmash of cauliflower, sliced carrots and broccoli on the plate that her mother placed in front of her. "Do I have to eat them, Auntie Mary? *All* of them?"

"All of them. That's the deal. Okay?"

"Okay," Katie said with a sigh of acceptance. "What is it? What is the dessert?"

"It's a surprise." The chime sounded again. "All right, all right," Mary said. She rose and scurried out of the kitchen.

Katie held up an empty Humpty Dumpty mug. "Can I have some more milk, Mommy?"

"Of course, dear." She removed a carton of skim milk from the refrigerator and filled the mug.

"Thank you, Mommy. I wish Grandpa was here to sit with me while I ate. He always sat with me."

"I know, dear. I wish that too."

Megan realized that Katie still hadn't fully grasped the significance of her grandpa's death. She'd told her about it last night, the words coming easier than she'd anticipated, thanks to the coaching she'd received from Karen. Reinforce feelings of security and love, she'd advised; so Megan thought the best environment to do this was Katie's bedroom, where she was surrounded and comforted by her menagerie of dolls and stuffed animals. Sitting on her bed, Katie cradled in her arms, Megan explained that Grandpa had died from an accident without going into detail.

"Grandpa died? Does that mean he went away?"

"Yes, dear."

"Will he come back for Christmas?"

"No, dear."

"But he'll come back for my next birthday? He'll come back for that, won't he Mommy?"

"No, dear. Your grandpa will never be able to come back. Not even for your birthday."

"Why, Mommy, why?" Katie had sobbed. "Why did Grandpa leave? Is he mad at me?"

"Oh no, dear. He loves you. He would never do anything to hurt you. He didn't want to leave you."

"Then why, Mommy?"

Megan had to fight back her own tears and keep her voice calm when she replied. "I don't know, dear. Everyone has to die sometime. Most people don't die until they're very old. Some people have an accident and die young, like your daddy. God called your grandpa, but he wants you to know that he loves you and he would be with you if he could."

"Is he in Heaven with Daddy?"

"Yes, dear. And watching over you."

Katie snuggled deeper into Megan's arms. "You won't die will you, Mommy? You won't leave me, too?"

"No, dear," Megan said, stroking Katie's head. "I'm not going to leave you. I'll always be here for you. And remember, there are lots of people who love you. Your Aunt Mary and your Aunt Karen."

"Can we say a prayer for Grandpa? Like we did in church?"

"Of course we can."

They did, and Megan held Katie in her arms until she cried herself to sleep, then spent the rest of the night dozing in a rocking chair beside the bed. She'd called Miss Markle, Katie's teacher, this morning to tell her about her dad's death and that she'd be keeping Katie at home for a few days. She wanted to have her home for most of the following week, but Karen had advised her to get Katie back into her regular routine as soon as possible.

Thank God for Karen, and for Aunt Mary, who'd responded immediately to Megan's request to come help her. She'd driven down from Kenosha last night. This morning she'd kept Katie occupied while Megan met with John Fenn at the funeral home making the wake and funeral arrangements and selecting a casket. That had taken most of the morning. That afternoon she lit candles for her dad at Holy Name Cathedral and prayed with Father Kiley, who was more than willing to perform the ceremony. She spent the rest of the day making phone calls to some of her dad's old friends to inform them of his passing. The last call she made was the one she dreaded most. It was to her mother in Florida. Although she could tell that her mother was genuinely shocked and saddened by the news, Megan also knew that she would not come to the funeral. There had been too much anguish, too much pain, and finally too much anger, to be revisited.

"Two detectives to see you, Meg," her aunt said, ushering Detectives Winstrom and McPherson into the living room.

"Who are they, Mommy?" Katie asked.

"They're policemen, dear."

"Why are they here?"

"They're friends of your grandpa, dear. I have to go talk to them, so you finish your supper, okay."

"Alright."

Megan hurried into the living room. "Thank you for coming, Officers. Have you heard anything? I called the morgue twice, but they couldn't tell me anything."

"They didn't get to the examination until this afternoon," Detective Winstrom said.

"You know the results?"

"Yes. We were just there."

Impatient, Megan wanted to ask them what they found out, then realized she was forgetting her manners. "I'm sorry. Won't you sit down? Perhaps you'd like some coffee."

"I could use some, thanks," Detective Winstrom said. "How about you, Mack?"

"Sounds good."

"I'll make it, Meg," Mary said.

"Would you? Thanks."

Megan waited until Detective Winstrom took a seat on her settee. McPherson was about to sit next to him when he saw a Raggedy Ann collectible doll occupying the space. "Oh, sorry," Megan said, and quickly relocated the doll to a rocking chair before she settled into a small armchair across the coffee table from the two detectives. They looked at each other, as if debating who should begin. Detective McPherson nodded to his partner.

"We spoke to the pathologist who performed the examination, Megan. We have a copy of the report, if you'd like to have it."

"Never mind that. What does it say?"

"Nothing we didn't expect. Your father died of asphyxia. There was water in his stomach and duodenum, also the presence of algae in his stomach. Since there were no witnesses, we have to assume he fell into the water and drowned."

"An accident?"

"That's the way it looks."

Megan studied their faces but could only guess what they were thinking. "If you believe that Dad took his own life…"

"No, Megan, that's not…"

"He would never do that. Not to himself. Not to us."

"We're not assuming he did, Megan."

"He had a new life. He had everything to live for."

"I know."

"You said there were no witnesses."

"That's right. At least none who have come forward."

"Then how do you know it *was* an accident? Couldn't he have been… assaulted?" Somehow Megan couldn't bring herself to say "murdered," but she'd had a lot of time to think about her dad's death, and that was the conclusion she was reaching.

"You mean in the course of a robbery?" McPherson said.

"Yes."

"We considered that possibility, Mrs. Herbst, but it doesn't add up. First there's the fact that your father still had his wallet with twenty-three dollars in it, so that would tend to rule out robbery."

"Alright. So it wasn't a robbery, but it could have been a random killing. Every day I read about street gangs killing people just for the fun of it. Isn't that a fact?"

"Yes, it is. But that's not what happened to your father, or there would be some evidence of an assault. According to the pathologist, there were no marks of violence on your dad's body, no internal bleeding either. But he did find something else."

The detective hesitated, as if he was reluctant to continue. Megan had already guessed what that was but didn't want to hear it, especially from stone-faced McPherson.

"Alcohol, I suppose."

"Yes. Quite a bit, I'm afraid. The toxicology report showed that the alcohol content in his bloodstream was over .08."

Megan jumped to her feet, fists balled like a fighter coming out of his corner at the bell, but trying to keep her voice down so Katie wouldn't hear. "I don't give a damn what the report said! My father was not drinking! He promised me he'd never take another drink!"

"Mrs. Herbst, your father was an alcoholic..."

"Not any more! He quit!"

"Alcoholics rarely quit cold."

"Dad did! There was no way he was going to screw up his life again, no way he was going to hurt Katie! Not like this, not right before the party...Katie's birthday party. He was going to perform for the kids, do a magic show. He'd been practicing for days. He knew how important this was for her. Do you think he would have done anything to disappoint her, hurt her like this...after I told him I would rather he didn't come home at all if there was any chance he might start drinking again? Do you really believe that?"

"I guess we'll never know exactly what happened, Megan," Detective Winstrom said gently. "But it wasn't a homicide."

Megan needed to calm down. She took some deep breaths, allowing her gaze to linger on a picture of her dad on the end table. It was an old picture of a young grinning Frank O'Meara in his army dress uniform. "So that's it? Case closed?"

"There is no case, Mrs. Herbst," Detective McPherson said. "Just a tough break. I'm sorry."

Megan glared at Mack. Like hell you're sorry! You just want to get out of here, go back to your station and file this away as just another drunk who fell into the lake and drowned. Screw that!

"I would like to know who did the autopsy."

"Dr. Henderson," Mack said.

"Well maybe Dr. Henderson made a mistake."

"I don't think so. He's been on staff for over ten years. He knows what he's doing."

"I'm sure he does. But did it ever occur to you that Dr. Henderson found only what he was looking for?"

The two detectives exchanged looks again. "What are you getting at, Megan?" Detective Winstrom said.

Megan hesitated, not sure herself, but looking for some answers. "Tell me this. When they bring in a...a body who's been taken out of the lake, what do they look for? Water in the lungs. Okay, there was water in Dad's lungs. Signs of assault. Okay, none. Alcohol in the bloodstream, especially from an alcoholic. Alright, I'll accept the fact that they found alcohol in Dad's bloodstream. But that's it. That's all that Dr. Henderson looked for. Do you agree?"

"It *was* a preliminary examination," Otis admitted.

"Preliminary...and presumptive. But if something doesn't seem right, what do they do?"

"A full toxicological exam, which takes time and..."

"So what if I requested it?"

Silence from the detectives.

"I see. My dad wasn't someone important enough to do a full examination on."

"It's not that, Megan," Otis said.

"And if they don't do it, how do you know for certain that his death was an accident?"

"What do you think they should be looking for, Mrs. Herbst?" Detective

McPherson said.

Megan paced, hands waving. "I don't know. Something in the blood other than alcohol. Maybe in Dad's heart or liver. Whatever they do when they do a complete exam. It's possible they could find something, isn't it?"

"It's possible," Detective Winstrom said. "But it might not have anything to do with your dad's death."

"But if it did?"

Detective McPherson leaned forward. "Look, Mrs. Herbst. If what you're implying is true, then someone went to a lot of trouble to make your dad's death look like an accident. Now why would anyone do that?"

Megan stopped pacing and faced the two detectives. "I don't know. I just want to know for sure, that's all. Is that asking too much? Is it?!"

"No, but only if we were able to show probable cause."

Megan's feeling of frustration was turning to anger, but she quickly put a reign on her emotions when Katie and Aunt Mary entered the room.

"Coffee will be ready in a minute," Mary said. "Miss Katie would like to know if she can have her dessert."

"Can I, Mommy? It's pudding. Chocolate pudding. Auntie made it especially for me."

"Did you eat all of your vegetables?"

"Oh, yes. All of them. Didn't I, Auntie?"

"Right down to the last broccoli stalk."

"Good girl. You can have your pudding just as soon as you wash your dishes. Okay?"

"Okay," Katie said. She turned to Otis. "I've seen you before."

"Yes, Katie. My name's Otis."

"Mr. Otis?"

Otis smiled. "That's right."

"Would you like some pudding, Mr. Otis? It's chocolate."

"Why yes, thanks, but with my coffee."

"I don't know you," Katie said to Mack.

"It's Mack. Mr. Mack."

"You can have some pudding, too, Mr. Mack."

"Thanks, but I'll take a pass."

"Take a what?"

"It means I don't want any."

"Don't you like chocolate pudding?"

"Well, no. Not really."

Katie made a face. "That's weird. My grandpa likes chocolate pudding. It's his favorite next to vanilla."

"Oh? That's nice."

"I wish he was here, but he went away. Mommy says he's in Heaven and is never coming back. Not even for my birthday."

"That's too bad."

Mary took Katie's hand. "Come on, Miss Katie. Let's go wash those dishes and have dessert."

"Alright," Katie said, but her eyes were sad as Mary led her into the kitchen.

Tears welled up in Megan's eyes. As soon as Katie was out of sight, the dam holding back her pent-up feelings broke. Karen had told her this would happen. Covering her face with her hands, her body shaking as if with a tropical fever, Megan began to sob. Otis went to her, put his arm around her shoulder and pulled her against him. His embrace felt comforting. God knows she needed someone to hold her.

"Mrs. Herbst."

Detective McPherson's voice. Megan looked at him through her tears.

"There's a pathologist I know who owes me a favor. I'll ask him to take another look."

Megan could only nod.

## *Saturday, May 18*

*7:35 a.m.:* Mack got to the office early, with a Starbucks coffee and scone, so he would have time before roll call to make arrangements for a full toxicological examination of Frank O'Meara. While he sipped and nibbled at his meager breakfast, he called Megan to see if she had instructed the Cook County Morgue to have her dad's body moved to the funeral home. Yes, she'd attended to that yesterday evening. She gave Mack the name and address of the funeral home—Fenn & Son on West Armitage. Mack told her to call the owner and tell him about the examination, as he would need her approval for it to be performed. Megan said she would and extracted a promise from Mack that he would call her as soon as he knew the results of the exam.

Next Mack called Dr. Alan Greg, the on-staff pathologist he knew at the Cook County Morgue. Mack explained to Dr. Greg what he needed and asked if he could make himself available during the day. He could, but he would have to cancel a golf game to do so. He wasn't happy about that, but since he owed Mack a favor… They agreed to meet at the funeral home at 10:30 a.m.

Otis waltzed into their office with a mug of office coffee as Mack beeped off.

"Hey, wonder of wonders. This is a first."

"A first what?"

"The first time you showed up for roll call before I did," Otis said, settling into the chair in front of the computer. "Something must be up, or am I wrong?"

"You're not. I need a favor."

Oh, oh, Otis thought. Not the best way to start the day. "Which is?"

"I want you to cover me for part of the morning, that's all."

"That's all? Isn't that enough? Enough to get us into the land of deep shit if the brass finds out you're playing hooky while you're on the clock."

"They won't," Mack said with another bite of the scone. "Besides, it's for a good cause." Mack proceeded to tell Otis about the exam of Frank's body at the funeral home.

Otis listened with a scowl on his face but agreed to go along. "How long will the exam take anyway? We still got to follow up on that domestic violence complaint today, and God knows what we'll get assigned at roll call."

"I know, but I don't have to be there during the exam, which could take hours. So after Dr. Greg gets started, I'll take off and meet you at Stacy's for lunch and get back on the job. That should be around noon."

"Okay, sounds like a plan" Otis said, sipping his coffee, "but I want you to know that I'm doing this for Megan, not you. I only hope it will give her some peace of mind about her dad's death."

"It will. The exam will confirm the preliminary autopsy. I know it's a waste of time, but like I said, it's for a good cause."

But as Mack washed down the remnants of the scone with the last sip of coffee, he asked himself a question that had helped him crack seemingly routine cases that turned out to be anything but. The question was: What if? What if Megan was right? What if there was more to Frank's death than an alcohol related drowning? What if the confirmation exam revealed something else?

Something sinister?

What if?

*10:35 a.m.:* Mack pulled into the parking lot of Fenn & Son Funeral Home. The original building was just an old brownstone, but over the years Fenns Senior and Junior had expanded their business and acquired their neighbors' properties, replacing their neighbors' existing structures with a modern addition to the funeral parlor and an expanded parking lot. Two shiny new Lincoln hearses were parked near a delivery ramp at the rear of the lot. Business must be good, Mack thought, as he exited the Bonneville.

Mack walked around to the front door and fingered a button. Chimes from within. A pudgy young man in a business suit answered. Yes, Dr. Greg was there and waiting in the reception room, he informed Mack in a hushed voice that was barely audible over the piped-in organ playing hymns. The young man gestured toward an archway, then moved down a hallway to inform Mr. Fenn that the doctor and the detective had both arrived.

As Mack entered the parlor, Dr. Greg lifted his two hundred plus pounds from an armchair and grunted: "This better be good, Mack. I had two suckers lined up this morning for some easy dough."

Mack smiled and extended his hand. "Sorry about the golf game, Greg. Long crime no see."

"I do the jokes, Mack, okay?" Dr. Greg said, taking Mack's hand in a hearty squeeze. "So what's up with this O'Meara guy?"

"Did you pull the autopsy report?"

"Yeah. I just came from the tomb. The guy got drunk, tried to swim across Lake Michigan and glug, glug, glug. End of story."

"Probably."

"Right. So that being the case, why do you want me to give O'Meara the full treatment?"

"Call it a hunch."

Dr. Greg sighed. "Call it lunacy, but since I owe you..."

They both knew that he was referring to a high-profile case that had made Dr. Greg something of a local media personality. A megabucks plastic surgeon was found in the garage of his Astor Street mansion behind the wheel of a Rolls Royce, the motor running. The preliminary autopsy revealed death from carbon monoxide poisoning. Although there was no suicide note, Mr. Megabuck's second wife, a former sometime model, informed the police that her husband was suffering from clinical depression. This was confirmed by the deceased's psychiatrist, who also revealed that his former patient had displayed suicidal tendencies. Suicide seemed to be the logical conclusion, but Mack wasn't so sure, so he asked Dr. Greg if he would review the autopsy data again.

He did, with Mack looking over his shoulder. The deceased's urine specimen had shown traces of Prozac. No surprise there. The psychiatrist had told them that he'd prescribed the antidepressant for his patient. What he hadn't prescribed was NyQuil, which also showed up in the urine. Probably had a cold, Dr. Greg surmised. Right, Mack agreed, but what would happen if Mr. Megabucks got a really heavy dose of NyQuil? Dr. Greg now shared Mack's hunch. Combined with the Prozac, he'd go beddy-bye big time. This was enough for Mack to put a tail on the bereaved widow, who it turned out was having an affair with her personal trainer. The trainer caved first and drew a twenty year stretch for copping a plea. The widow got life.

Mack had given Dr. Greg the credit for cracking the case, which put him in demand as the forensic expert for WFFD-TV. He loved show biz, which is what he called the news, but was clearly apprehensive about repaying the favor.

"You're sure Fenn & Son are okay with this?" he asked Mack.

"Fenn Junior is. Senior is retired. O'Meara's daughter, Mrs. Herbst, cleared it with Junior early this morning. At least that's what she told me."

"Let's hope."

Dr. Greg nodded toward a slim, middle-aged man entering from the foyer. To Mack, his black suit, white shirt, black tie and styled hair gave him the appearance of a lawyer or stockbroker, but confirming his profession was the somber expression on his pale, rather effeminate face. "Good morning," he said, also in a hushed voice. "I'm John Fenn. Detective McPherson?"

"Right." Very observant, Mack thought. He obviously looked more like a cop than Dr. Greg with his casual slacks, sports suit and loafers. As he introduced Dr. Greg and they all exchanged handshakes, Mack wondered if morticians ever raised their voices or smiled.

"I have to prep a new arrival today," Fenn said, glancing at an expensive looking Rolex, "and we have a funeral scheduled at four this afternoon. How long do you think this will take, doctor?"

Dr. Greg shrugged. "Two, maybe three hours max." He hefted a medical bag from an end table. "I brought along some of my own instruments just in case you don't have everything I need. Could you lend me a surgical garment?"

"No problem. Please come this way."

Fenn led the way through an archway into a larger room set up theater style with folding chairs, a podium, and a casket surrounded by floral arrangements.

"Quite frankly, I'm not entirely comfortable with this," he said. "If Mrs. Herbst hadn't assured me that she would take full responsibility in case there's a legal problem…"

"There shouldn't be any," Mack said. "Next of kin can take charge of the body and do anything they want with it. Right, Greg?"

"Absolutely. I knew a guy who had his wife preserved in pickle juice because she had a sour disposition when she was alive," Dr. Greg quipped, not to the amusement of Fenn Jr, Mack noted, who now escorted them into a hallway that led past the office area to the funeral home's newer addition.

Dr. Greg chortled, always enjoying his own brand of gallows humor. "Don't worry, Fenn. I'm the guy who's on the hot seat. If the esteemed M.E. finds out I'm moonlighting, he'd shit in his baggy greens, and I'd have to find myself honest work at some dreary hospital or, horror of horrors, start a practice."

A blast of cold air hit them as they entered the preparation room, which Mack observed was not unlike the operating room at the morgue, only smaller. There were two stainless steel dissecting tables with blood gutters and tubing, a cabinet of medical instruments, overhead vents spewing cold air, and no windows. Permeating the room was the sweet scent of Formalin laced with alcohol.

"I'd go for the practice," Mack said. "Better hours, bigger bucks. Then you wouldn't have to set up patsies on the golf course."

"You don't understand, Mack. There are so many interesting cadavers that pass through the tomb, I'd be bored shitless having to administer to the living." Dr. Greg set his medical bag on one of the dissecting tables and looked over the array of instruments in the cabinet. "Take the lady who checked in last week. Frozen stiff, literally. Her loving son stored her in a freezer after he put an ax into her cranium. So now she's affectionately known as the 'momsicle'."

Mack laughed. An original Dr. Greg, he thought, that even drew a smile from Fenn Jr.

"Where's the guest of honor?"

Dr. Greg's question was answered by an even stronger blast of cold air from the adjoining storage room as the door opened and Fenn's pudgy employee pushed a gurney into the room with a body covered by a white, plastic sheet.

"Thank you, Arnold," Fenn said.

"Shall we use this table, Mr. Fenn?"

"That will be fine, Arnold."

Arnold maneuvered the gurney up against the side of the other dissecting table.

Dr. Greg came over. "Let me give you a hand."

"It's all right. He's quite light," Arnold said, and quickly slid the corpse onto the dissecting table.

Quite light, Mack thought. O'Meara was a big man, but the form under the sheet couldn't have been more than five and a half feet tall.

"Hold it a minute." Mack was getting bad vibes about this. "Let's take a look at the guest of honor."

Mack pulled the sheet off of the face of the corpse.

"Put him back, Arnold."

"Put him back?"

"Yeah. I don't know who this guy is, but he sure as hell isn't Frank O'Meara!"

*11:43 a.m.:* Megan couldn't believe what she was hearing. She was at the dining room table helping Katie with her homework when Detective McPherson's call came in. For a moment she was unable to respond to what he told her. Not only was the man at the Fenn & Son Funeral Home not her dad, but her father had been cremated!

"How...how could such a thing have happened?!" she said into her cordless phone.

Driving east on the Eisenhower Expressway, Mack could almost feel the heat of Megan's anger coming through the ear vents of his cell phone. "I don't know, Mrs. Herbst. Dr. Greg and I just came from the morgue. All they know now is that the bodies got mixed up."

Mack didn't want to go into detail. The fact was there weren't many details to go into. The body at Fenn & Son was a Thomas Hughes, a suicide, whose closest relative, a brother in LaGrange, had arranged for the body to be delivered to Archer Cremation Services on West Chicago Avenue. Somehow the ID tag on Hughes's foot had ended up on O'Meara's foot, and vice-versa. Officials at the morgue couldn't explain the foul-up. It had never happened before, not at the Cook County Morgue. But it had happened elsewhere. Mack remembered reading recently about a similar goof by a hospital, which had also resulted in the cremation of the wrong body and a lawsuit filed by the family. Mistakes happen. But try explaining that to a justifiably angry Megan Herbst.

"Mixed up? Oh, fine, great! Well, if they think I'm going to just...just accept that, no way! I'll have my lawyer go over there and demand an investigation!"

"They're already doing that, Mrs. Herbst," Mack said, although he wasn't optimistic about the results. Whoever screwed up wasn't likely to do a *mea culpa*. If it *was* a screw-up. Mack was asking himself that "what if?" question again.

Megan was wondering the same thing. "Something's wrong! Something's very wrong here, and I'm not just going to let this go away. I'll hire a private investigator if I have to!"

"I wouldn't do that, Mrs. Herbst."

"Why shouldn't I?"

"You'd probably be throwing your money away. Look, why don't you let me look into this?"

Megan's jaw dropped. This she hadn't expected, especially from McPherson. "Do you mean that?"

"Sure. That is, if that's okay with you?"

"Why, yes. If you really want to."

"Good. I'll begin with your dad's employer. Home Depot, wasn't it?"

"Yes, the one on North Avenue."

"Fine. I'm on my way."

McPherson hung up before she could thank him.

Megan cradled the phone, her anger subsiding. She felt better. Just knowing that somebody would try to do something about her dad's death was comforting, even if that somebody was Detective McPherson. Maybe she was wrong about him. Maybe he was human, after all. She still didn't like him, but what the hell. He was all she had going for her. Not exactly a knight in shining armor. More like a black knight, possibly with his own reasons for helping her other than serving a damsel in distress.

An ironic smile formed on her taut lips. Alright, my black knight. Do it! Go kick ass!

*12:18 p.m.:* Otis took another bite of cheese cake. What in the hell was keeping Mack, he thought, glancing at his wrist watch? Mack had promised to meet him here at Stacy's at noon. If Mack didn't show up soon, he'd just have to forget about lunch. Although they'd wound up the domestic case before Mack took off for the funeral parlor, they'd been assigned two new cases at roll call—a deranged codger who was AWOL from an assisted living community on North Sheridan and a child abuse complaint that could land a teenage girl in a juvenile detention facility if what the baby's parents claimed was true.

Otis glanced as his watch again. To hell with this, he thought, and removed his cell phone from a belt holder. He was speed-dialing Mack's cell number when his phone beeped.

"Hello, partner."

"Where are you? You were supposed to be here twenty minutes ago."

"Sorry, but there's been a new development. You're going to have to cover for me again this afternoon."

"What? No way, or have you forgotten that we have two new cases on our plate? I can't handle them by myself."

"You were doing just fine before you got stuck with me. But that's beside the point. The fact is that Megan's suspicions about her dad's death might have some legs after all."

"Are you saying that the examination turned up something unusual?"

"There was no exam. Frank was a no show. A different stiff was in the cooler. Frank was delivered to another funeral home and cremated."

"Cremated?!" Otis almost choked on a mouthful of cheese cake. "Shit, that must be really tough on Megan."

"To say the least. So now you understand why I need the rest of the day off."

"No, actually I don't. What are you going to do? Play fantasy whodunit? Foul-ups like what happened to Frank aren't all that rare. The other day I read about two bodies at a hospital that got mixed up with the wrong one ending up in the furnace."

"Yeah, I've read that, too, and you may be right...but you know Megan. There's no way she's going to accept this without making a big stink about it. She already threatened to call her lawyer and hire a private investigator, and I was only able to talk her out of it by promising to look into it myself. It shouldn't take all that long. In fact, I should be able to wind it up today. If not, we've got our two day break tomorrow and Monday and I can continue working on it on my own time. And anyway, you've got to admit, for the morgue to get two bodies mixed up is unusual enough to warrant at least some suspicion."

"Mack, you see suspicious things everywhere you look. It's almost like you want to find a conspiracy lurking in every alley and behind every trash can. Well, I can't keep indulging your suspicions. I've got a career to worry about, and I can't, I won't, follow you down that path." Otis waited for a response, but Mack didn't say anything, so Otis continued. "Look, here's what I'll do. You go ahead and spin your wheels, and I'll cover your ass again this afternoon. But please understand, I'm doing this for Megan's sake, and to dissuade her from doing something that will only cause trouble for her, and for you and me, as well. Remember, you've already spent the morning conducting an unauthorized autopsy, and I spent the morning covering for you, so if Megan does raise hell with the city, all that's gonna come out. But don't even think about asking me again."

"Thanks, partner, and don't worry, I won't."

In a pig's eye, Otis thought, then added, "While you're at it, you might try to attend Frank's wake this evening."

"This evening? Megan didn't mention that to me."

"Yeah, well she probably figures that big hearted ol' Mack doesn't give a shit. But if you can make it, it will probably be a pleasant surprise for her as it will show respect for her dad."

"I'll make a point of being there," Mack said, and beeped off.

*12:38 p.m.:* Mack approached the shopping mall on North Avenue that was anchored by the Home Depot. His adrenaline was pumping. It had started pumping the moment he lifted the sheet off the lifeless face of Thomas Hughes. It kept pumping when he discovered that Frank O'Meara had been cremated. Sure, the body switch could have been nothing more than a screw-up. That was the logical explanation and probably the correct one.

But if it wasn't, if the ID tags on the two bodies had been deliberately switched, then it was a whole new ball game. In that case somebody had gone to one hell of a lot of trouble to make sure a more thorough confirmation autopsy on Frank would never happen. To pull that off that somebody had to pay off another somebody at the morgue. It would take a no holds barred investigation to find who the somebodies were and what they were trying to cover up. Only the superintendent could authorize that. Mack fingered his ear with the missing lobe.

Fat chance of that happening without some pretty solid evidence that a crime had been committed. Coming up with that evidence was a very long shot at best, but one that Mack was now determined to take.

Mack pulled into the huge lot of the busy mall, parked near the Home Depot, and made his way to the entrance. A lady at the service desk paged the store's manager, who was on the floor. He was there in a matter of seconds, a tall, slim go-getter type in his early thirties who reminded Mack of Jimmy Stewart. The name badge on his orange Home Depot jacket read "David Swope, Manager." Informed of Frank's death, he seemed genuinely sorry and suggested they talk over coffee in the employee lunch room.

"Frank was a good worker," Swope said, sipping from a Styrofoam cup. "Always on time, always up, you know, enthusiastic, and courteous to the customers. I was going to move him into the stock department. More responsibility, better pay. I'll miss him."

"This past Tuesday, how did he seem? I mean, did he appear as if he had a problem, you know, distressed, uptight?"

"No, not that I can recall. A little tired, maybe. You know, Frank was no kid, and the job's a bit demanding for a man of his age, but he never complained."

Mack took a sip of coffee, his third cup today, and wished it were stronger. "You let him leave early that day, right?"

"Yes. His granddaughter had a birthday party, and I guess he was going to do some kind of show for the kids."

"His daughter said it was about four-thirty."

"That's what he'd asked for, but he actually left at about four, as I recall. I can check his time card."

"There's no need to do that right now. Keep the time card, though. Did he say why he needed the extra time off?"

"Now that you mention it, yes, he did. Nothing specific, just that he had something to take care of before going home. I figured it had something to do with the party and..." Swope was interrupted by a voice on the loudspeaker paging him. He was needed at the service desk. "Another return, no doubt," he said, rising. "I hope it hasn't been used. Some people think they can use the merchandise then bring it back for a refund."

"Or bring in stolen stuff from another store."

"Yeah. Happens all the time. But no sales receipt, no refund. Not at this store." He took a final swig from the cup and dropped it into a trash container. "Anything else you want to know?"

Mack rose. "No. You've been very helpful, Mr. Swope. Thanks."

"Glad to help. Oh, maybe you could tell me where Frank's funeral will be held. I'd like to send a floral display from the store."

"No need. Frank was cremated."

"Cremated? I thought Frank was Catholic?"

"He was."

"There will be a service, though?"

"There's a wake this evening at his daughter's house."

"Good. I'll try to attend. Nice to have met you, Detective."

They shook hands, and Swope hurried away. Good guy, Swope, Mack thought, finishing the coffee. Never asked why he was inquiring about what appeared to be an accident, although he must have wondered about it, or about why Frank was cremated. More importantly, Swope had revealed something Mack hadn't known before. Frank had left the store earlier than originally planned. Why? Something to take care of, Swope had said. That something just could be significant, Mack thought, as he crumpled the cup and pitched it into the container on his way out of the lunch room.

*1:10 p.m.:* Mack nudged the SSE against the curb in front of The Beacon Mission. He found Pastor John in his office behind a tidy desk, talking on the phone.

"Have you had medical attention, Sandy?" The exasperated look on the pastor's face told Mack that the answer was no. "We'll have our on-staff doctor take a look at you anyway, just to make sure, okay? Where's your husband now?" he said, waving Mack into one of the two straight backed chairs in front of the desk. "Alright, now I want you to listen to me. I want you and your baby out of there before he gets back. I want you to pack some things, and not just for overnight. Call a cab...we'll pay for it...and get over here right away. Will you do that?" Listens, grimacing. "Look, Sandy, I'm not giving you any option on this. If I don't see you here in an hour, I'm calling the police and sending them over there with someone from Child Welfare, understand? Now are you going to do what I'm asking?" Pause. "Good. One hour, Sandy, or I make that call."

Pastor John cradled the receiver with a heavy sigh. "You have to get tough with them sometimes. I assume you're here about Frank. Is he still missing?"

"Not any more. He's dead."

Pastor John slumped back into the swivel chair. "Shit! Pardon me, but shit!"

"Yeah."

"How did it happen?"

Mack gave him the official alcohol-related, accidental drowning scenario.

"But you're not so sure?"

Smart guy, the pastor, Mack thought. "I'm exploring other possibilities."

"How can I help?"

"Can you find out if Frank might have paid a visit to your clinic late this past Tuesday afternoon?"

"No problem." Pastor John picked up the phone, fingered an in-house number and put the call on his speaker. "This is Dr. Weese," a voice answered.

"Pastor John, doctor. Were you in the clinic on Tuesday afternoon?"

"No. I believe Dr. Rhodes was working Tuesday."

"Would you check the patients' files to see if a Frank O'Meara came in late Tuesday for some medical treatment? He might have gone by the name of Cravin."

"Sure. Has he been here before?"

"Probably."

"Hold on."

"What makes you think Frank needed to see a doctor, Detective?" Pastor John said, as they waited.

"Just a hunch. His boss at the Home Depot thought he wasn't feeling well and let him off early. He never showed up at home, so whatever happened to Frank happened after he left."

Pastor John frowned, steepling his fingertips. "I see. But if Frank did see a doctor, what could that have to do with his death?"

"I don't know. Maybe nothing. It's a shot in the dark at best."

They waited in silence until Dr. Weese's voice came over the speaker. "I found a file on Frank Cravin, Pastor. His last visit to the clinic was over a year ago. March 22nd, to be exact. He was treated for a viral infection. In short, a common cold."

"Thank you, doctor," Pastor John said. He raised the receiver and cradled it.

"That's funny," Mack said. "Frank's daughter said he was seeing a charity doctor."

"Could be one of our volunteers. They're not on staff, but fill in when we have an overload, which is always. Some will even see our people in their offices. Does his daughter remember a name?"

"No. But if you can give me a list, I'll run them by her to see if one of them jogs her memory."

"Sure. Glad to."

Pastor John swiveled around to a computer station, where an Apple desktop was already fired up. He fingered keys, and a list of names, addresses and phone numbers appeared on the monitor. He clicked on PRINT with the mouse, and an Epson spat out a piece of paper with the data. Pastor John took the paper and handed it to Mack.

"Thanks, Pastor. This may be a blind alley, but it's worth a try."

They both rose and shook hands.

"Good luck, Detective."

Mack exited the shelter and slid behind the wheel of the Bonneville, where he dialed Megan on his cell phone and read off the names of the volunteer doctors.

"None of them sound familiar. Read them to me again, would you?"

Mack did.

"I'm sorry," Megan said, her voice heavy with frustration. "I just can't remember. Is it important?"

"It might be. No matter. I think I know a person who can give me some answers."

Mack beeped off, dialed information for the number of the *Street Wise* newspaper, held on while the operator put him through, and asked for the vending manager.

*1:44 p.m.:* Willie Butler was hoarse from shouting. He'd been hawking *Street Wise* for nearly two hours now and sold only five copies. He was tempted to take a pull from what was left of the half pint of Seagrams 7 in his fatigue pocket, but thought better of it. He'd finish it off later plus a fifth he'd buy with part of the proceeds from selling the street magazine. If he even sold enough to finance the fifth. Of the one dollar per copy, he put sixty-five cents into his pocket, although once in a while someone would hit pretty good with two dollars or even a five spot.

No big hitters this morning, though. Willie tried to keep the anger out of his voice, as he waved a copy at a young exec type hurrying across Franklin Street, a briefcase in his right hand and a copy of *The Wall Street Journal* tucked under his left arm.

"*Street Wise, Street Wise.* Only a dollar. How about you, sir? Help a person out."

Mr. Exec kept moving without breaking stride. "Motha fucker!" Willie muttered. The asshole had seen him, all right. Looked right at him. No, not at him. More like through him, as if he was invisible, which pissed him off even more.

Willie couldn't understand it. Sales on this corner were usually no sweat, even on a Saturday afternoon. It was a prime location. The southwest corner of Franklin and Madison was right in the midst of the ever expanding business district west of the loop and ideally located to catch the flow of pedestrian traffic to and from the Northwestern Railroad Station across the Chicago River. There was also a Starbucks on the corner, which gave him access to its patrons. Maybe it was the threatening storm, Willie figured. It was beginning to drizzle, and people were already taking cover under their umbrellas.

In any event, Willie would have to share the proceeds of his sixty copies of the newspaper with the vendor who had the location locked. His thirty copies and the other vendor's thirty. That was the deal. Otherwise he'd have to find another location and clear it with the vendor service manager before he could use it. Problem was most of the good corners were taken, and the guys who worked them had loyal customers. Willie wasn't about to do this shit on a regular weekly basis, which meant he had to cut a deal with the vendor of a good location like this one.

Willie spotted an attractive young lady emerging from Starbucks with a cup of coffee and some kind of pastry in a sack. Good prospect, he thought, and eyeballed her, so as not to be ignored. "*Street Wise, Street Wise*. Good morning, miss. Buy a copy, only one dollar to help the needy."

"I'll take one," she said. "Hold these, will you?"

Willie held the coffee and sack, while she rummaged in her shoulder bag for a change purse. "Where's Harold? I usually buy from him."

"Harold's sick. I'm subbing for him."

She finally unearthed the change purse and removed two dollars, which she exchanged for her coffee and pastry. "I hope he's alright."

"He'll be fine. Just a cold."

"Tell him to take care."

"I will. Thank you, miss, and God bless you."

His standard response, as if God gave a shit. Nice lady, though. Everyone should be like her, even though she'd probably pitch the newspaper into the nearest trash bin. The view of the world from the street wasn't something most people wanted to look at.

"Hello, Willie. How's biz?"

Willie gritted at the sound of the voice behind him. He didn't have to turn around to know it belonged to the bad cop. "*Street Wise, Street Wise*," he shouted. Maybe if he ignored the asshole he'd go away. Yeah, and maybe pigs could fly. He'd probably tied him into the White Hen job and was here to make the collar.

"I said how's biz, Willie?"

Shit! Might as well get it over with, Willie thought.

"Biz sucks," he said, turning and expecting to see the asshole cop with a pair of handcuffs at the ready. Instead, he was holding a small package wrapped in brown paper. The cop didn't look pissed either, but who the hell knew? You looked at this cop's face and you got no clue what was going on inside his head.

"Too bad," the cop said. "If you want to take a break, I'll buy you a cup of coffee."

"No thanks. I'm busy."

"I thought you might want to know about Frank."

Willie cursed himself. He'd been so busy thinking about his own sorry ass that he'd forgotten about Frank. "So you found him, huh? So how is he?"

"Let's have that coffee, Willie."

*1:55 p.m.:* Willie spiked his coffee with the rest of the Seagrams 7. Since he made no effort to do this under the small table he shared with the cop, this action turned the heads of nearby patrons. Willie could care less. His buddy was dead. So fuck 'em! Fuck everyone!

"So that's it, huh? You cops just write him off, right? Just another bum who nobody gives a shit about."

"What do you think, Willie?"

Willie took a pull at the whiskey-spiked coffee, felt it burn its way down his throat where it only added fuel to the fire of pain and anger raging inside his chest. He was remembering the last time he saw Frank. He would have bet his life that Frank had kicked the booze, that there was no way he'd go back on the street. He had too much goin', a daughter and grandkid who loved him.

"I think it sucks!"

"So do I," the cop said.

Willie stared at him. What in the hell was the cop getting at? He was soon to find out. Willie sipped the coffee, as he listened to the cop tell him about the foul-up at the morgue, if it was a foul-up, and his suspicions that Frank might have been feeling sick. He didn't have to look at the list of The Beacon's volunteer doctors the cop showed him to tell him the one Frank would have seen.

"Needles."

"Needles?"

Willie smiled grimly. "That's what we called him, Frank and me, 'cause he was always givin' us shots, vitamin B and whatever, when we was feelin' shitty, which was often. His real name is Alward, but to us he was Doctor Needles."

"Alward, Lawrence S.," the cop said, looking at the first name on the list.

"That's him."

"620 South Wabash?"

"Yeah. So?"

"Not exactly a high rent district for doctors."

Willie shrugged, took another sip. "So what's that supposed to mean?"

"Maybe nothing. Just a little unusual, that's all."

"Yeah, well Needles ain't no high society doc, ya know. Ain't none of those dudes gonna let street people into their fancy offices. Bad for biz. Might give their patients a heart attack." The cop smiled. Actually, smiled, Willie thought. "So you gonna check him out, right?"

"Yeah. Thanks, Willie. You saved me some leg work. Do me another favor. You still got that missing bulletin of Frank?"

"Yeah, I got it," Willie said, feeling guilty that he hadn't used it yet in an effort to find Frank.

"Keep showing it around on the street. Someone might remember seeing him, okay?"

"I'll do that. You gotta card?"

The cop removed a card from his wallet and handed it to him. "You can always reach me on the cell." He finished his coffee, started to rise. "Oh, almost forgot. I brought you something."

"Oh? Like what?"

The cop handed him the wrapped package. "It's a book. *Les Miserables*."

"Lay what?"

"It's French for the miserable ones."

"Like street people, huh."

"Yeah, you might say so."

"So I guess some French guy wrote it?"

"Right. Victor Hugo."

"Sounds like I heard of him. Yeah, Frank, I think he talked about him. So what's it about, the book?"

"It's about an escaped convict who turns his life around, even becomes a mayor of a town."

"Ex con makes good, huh? That's all?"

"Not exactly. You see there's this cop who's always on his case. Catches up with him years later."

"Bad cop, huh?" Like you, Willie thought.

"Not bad. Just a little inflexible where the law is concerned."

"Yeah, so what happens?"

"Why don't you read the book and find out?"

Willie shrugged. "I might."

The cop rose now. "By the way, I'm just loaning this to you. It's a third edition, so I want it back when you're finished."

"Third edition? Does that mean it's worth some bucks?"

"Big bucks."

"So how do you know I won't cash it in?"

"I don't."

Willie and Mack locked eyes. How do you figure this cop, Willie thought? Was he saying that he trusted him?

"Don't sweat it. You'll get it back."

"Right. Be seeing you, Willie."

Willie reached over and grabbed his arm. "You find out who did Frank, you know where to find me."

The cop nodded. Willie let go of his arm. The cop dumped his coffee cup into the trash bin and exited.

Willie sipped his coffee. It had started to rain outside, but he no longer gave a shit. He had fifty-five more newspapers to sell before he could do what he had to do, which was to hit the street and flash the missing bulletin with Frank's picture. The pint of Seagrams could wait. Finding who did Frank couldn't. For Willie that had now become a priority.

*2:23 p.m.:* Mack headed for 620 South Wabash and kicked up the wiper speed. The drizzle had become a steady downpour that spattered against the windshield of the Bonneville. As he waited for the light to change at Wabash and Harrison, where the 600 block began, he watched a CTA train on the overhead elevated track curl west like a gigantic, metallic snake for half a block over Harrison, then back south behind a parking lot and a row of buildings, the largest of which he figured was 620.

Mack confirmed this by pausing momentarily in front of the aging six-story structure—a candidate for demolition, Mack thought, if the construction of new office buildings and condos continued to upgrade the once seedy environment south of the Congress Expressway. He backed into the only available parking space up the block near the intersection with Balbo. Not bothering to feed the parking meter—the FOP sticker on the windshield exempted the Bonneville from tickets—Mack sprinted past a garage, a Chicken Shack, a wholesale liquor store and a Thai restaurant to the shelter of a steel canopy. A sign on the picture window of an outlet jewelry store advertised that the Gibson Secretarial College was still a tenant. Another sign let it be known that there was office space available for rent and gave the name and phone number of the leasing agent.

Mack entered a lobby that was heavy with the aroma of age. He paused to scan a wall directory next to a small desk and chair. A security station, he figured, not manned during working hours. The first name on the directory was "Alward, Lawrence MD, 310." Down the corridor a bank of two elevators was directly across from the management office. The elevator that lethargically lifted Mack to the third floor made ominous noises and kept him in momentary suspense before the door finally creaked open.

Suite 310 was one of the two suites that flanked the single corridor at the rear of the building. Alward's name was stenciled on the thick, opaque glass portion of the door along with the suite number. A bell pinged as he entered a windowless, almost claustrophobic reception room. There was no receptionist behind the metal desk and there were no patients on the small divan and two chairs, all of which looked like acquisitions from a garage sale. Muffled voices came from behind the office door. The doctor had at least one patient, Mack thought, as he glanced at a yellow legal pad and pen on the desk with a sign instructing patients to sign in with their name and time of arrival.

Mack took a seat on the divan and pulled a *People* from a litter of magazines on the end table. He flipped through the pages of celebs, who apparently had nothing on their minds other than themselves. By the time he reached page seven he was ready to puke, so he exchanged *People* for the latest issue of *Time*. The headline on the cover said "MISSION TO PARIS" and showed President Trippet waving to the cameras as he boarded Air Force One. He was a handsome man in his 50s, trim due to the rigorous exercise routine he was known to work into his busy schedule. Mack thought Trippet's usually robust face looked drawn. No surprise there, he thought, given that the President's "mission" was nothing less than attempting to assemble a coalition of countries to deal with the latest Mideast crisis. Before Mack could find the lead story, the office door opened and two men came out.

"Be sure to take those pills three times a day, Eddie," a thin man said—obviously Dr. Alward, judging from his white jacket and the stethoscope hanging around his neck. Mack pegged him as in his early to mid forties, although a receding hairline and gaunt face made him look ten years older.

His patient, an old man with a week's growth of whiskers, responded with a hacking cough. His shabby, ill-fitting attire gave him the appearance of a human scarecrow, Mack thought. He almost expected to see straw protruding from his ears instead of hair.

Alward took his arm and walked him to the door. "Be sure to take them with meals, Eddie. And Eddie, no alcohol."

"No booze?" the human scarecrow whined.

"No booze, Eddie. Booze and the medication I'm giving you don't mix."

"No booze. Okay, doc."

Fat chance, Mack thought.

Alward opened the door and patted the vagrant on the shoulder. "I want to see you again next Saturday, just to see how you're doing. Can you make it at, say, ten thirty Saturday morning?"

"Ten thirty."

"Ten thirty. Next Saturday, okay?"

"Okay. Thanks, Doc."

Mack watched the human scarecrow shuffle out muttering, "no booze, no booze."

Alward closed the door, then turned to Mack, who rose from the divan. "Good morning? Do you have an appointment, Mr....?"

"No. I'm not a patient, doctor." Mack showed him his badge. "Detective McPherson, Special Victims."

Mack studied the doctor's face for a reaction. Was there just a flicker of alarm in his eyes? Fatigued looking eyes, but intense. The eyes of a man dedicated to his work, Mack thought, confirmed by the fact that he was working on Saturday afternoon.

Alward removed small reading glasses and massaged the wrinkles under his eyes with his fingers. "How can I help you, Detective?"

Mack took out the missing bulletin of Frank and handed it to the doctor. "Do you recognize this man, doctor? Frank O'Meara, alias Frank Cravin."

Alward put on the glasses and studied the picture. "No...I don't think so."

"Really? One of your charity patients, a friend of Frank's, told me that Frank was a patient of yours, too."

"Well, that could be, but I still don't recall the face or the name. I never could remember names, and I see so many, you understand."

"I can imagine. But if he was a patient, you'd have a record of his visits?"

"Absolutely." Alward handed the bulletin to Mack.

"Mind if I have a look?"

"Not at all. Glad to be of help."

Mack followed him into a spacious office that offered a west view through two large windows. Mack could see the Beacon Mission on the other side of a large parking lot that extended from the alley behind the building to State Street.

"I'll just check my files, Detective." Alward moved to a filing cabinet and opened the top drawer. As he fingered through a row of manila folders, Mack took in the area, which obviously served as both an office and exam room. There were the usual medical necessities—examining table, blood pressure gauge, electrocardiogram, some kind of respirator and a cabinet with instruments and medicines. The office space contained a filing cabinet, a bookcase filled with medical books and a desk with a computer and printer. Everything looked very second hand, except a binocular microscope and a high ram HP computer, a kind of mini lab, Mack thought. Mack also observed that there were no pictures of family or friends which most people have in their offices. A lonely man dedicated to his work, he surmised.

"Cook, Cooper...here it is: Cravin, Frank," the doctor said, removing a folder from the drawer. He laid the folder on the desk and opened it to reveal a computer printout of Frank's visits and Alward's hand-written log notes.

Mack scanned the printout, which revealed that Frank's first visit was in April of last year, just three weeks after his last treatment at the Beacon's clinic. "I see Frank has been seeing you for a little over a year."

"Yes, I remember Frank now. The Beacon Mission sent him over. I get a lot of my charity people from the Beacon, the overflow, so to speak. Most of them continue to see me. No long waits," he added with a wry smile.

"So I see," Mack said, returning the smile. "Did Frank have any particular ailments?"

Alward glanced at his log notes before replying. "No, at least nothing unusual. Frank was in pretty good shape for a man of his, well, lifestyle. Let's see, I gave him a complete examination on November 5th. His blood pressure was a little high, not enough for medication, but I told him it had to be watched. I was more concerned with his liver. I gave him a supply of vitamins and recommended a diet which included no drinking." Alward shook his head sadly. "I'm afraid that's advice most of my charity patients don't follow."

"And according to this, Frank's last visit was on the 15th of February."

Again Alward consulted his log notes. "That's right. He was a little run down, so I gave him a shot of vitamin B."

"And you're sure that's the last time you saw him?"

"Yes, of course. Otherwise, it would be in here." Alward's brow creased. "Do you mind if I ask you what you're looking for, Detective?"

"Just making sure we have all the facts, doc. Strictly routine."

"I'm relieved to hear that. I was afraid Frank, well, might have gotten in some kind of trouble with the law."

"No. Frank's troubles are over. He's dead."

"Dead?!" Alward said, as if he'd been slapped in the face.

Mack was expecting a reaction, but shock wasn't the one. To a doctor the death of a patient was not exactly unusual, especially a vagrant.

"I thought...well, I assumed...he was just missing..." the doctor stammered.

"Did you know that Frank had gotten off the street, was living with his daughter, holding down a job?"

"No. No, I didn't."

Could be, Mack thought, since Frank's last visit was before he'd cleaned up his act. If that *was* his last visit. Although there was no reason to doubt the doctor, Mack decided to dig a little deeper.

"Yeah, too bad. It looked like Frank was going to make it, but he apparently hit the bottle again and fell into Diversey Harbor."

"Oh? An accident, I assume?"

"Probably, but we have to follow up to make sure. Like I said, just routine."

"Of course."

Mack gestured toward one of the framed diplomas on the wall that had caught his eye. "I see you got a Ph.D. in biochemistry at Duke."

"Why, yes. I still keep my hand in, so to speak. Actually, I do most of my own lab work, instead of sending it out for analysis. I get quicker information that way and it's cheaper for the patient."

Mack moved to the lab station, where a microscope with what looked like a photo attachment was linked by a line to the computer. "Looks like you're set up pretty good here." He touched a flat device attached to the computer. "What's this thing, doc?"

"That's an automatic analyzer. I feed the data in there and it does the rest for me."

"I guess you store it in these," Mack said, pointing to a rack of CDs.

"Yes."

Mack removed one, looked at the label. "DIAGNOSIS. COLON CANCER. 54783." Alward answered his next question before he could ask it.

"Each CD contains information on my patients for various diseases, which I continuously update."

Mack noticed that the doctor now looked more uptight than before, if that was possible. "And the numbers?"

"Code. There's a medical code for every diagnosis and procedure." Alward glanced at his wristwatch. "I'm sorry to have to rush you, Detective, but I'm expecting a patient. If that's all...?"

"Right. Sorry to have taken so much of your time."

"No problem. I hope I've been of some help."

"You have." Mack replaced the CD in the rack. "I gotta tell you, doc, I really admire what you're doing here. I mean, giving your services to the needy. With your credentials you could be in a suite on Michigan Avenue pulling down six figures and hitting golf balls at some posh country club on The Shore."

Alward's mouth tightened. "Yes, well I always believed that golf was something you took up when you retired."

The ping of the doorbell prevented Mack from probing any deeper on the subject of the doctor's compassion for serving humanity. Maybe it was genuine. Probably was.

"My patient."

"Right." Mack moved to the door, the doctor following, and exited into the waiting room, where a vagrant with his left arm in a sling was occupying a chair.

"Be with you in a minute, Leo," the doctor said.

"Keep up the good work, doc," Mack said to the office door closing in his face. He turned to the vagrant. "Good man, the doc." The vagrant nodded.

As Mack exited the office, he remembered the look of shock on Alward's face when he told him about Frank's death. And how nervous the doctor seemed during the entire interview. Perhaps he was just stressed out from overwork. Perhaps. Or perhaps—perhaps what? Mack had no answer, not even a clue as to what that might be. All he had was a cop's hunch that there *was* something. However, he'd need more than a hunch to follow up on what looked like a dead end.

As soon as the door to his office had closed, Dr. Alward hurried to the telephone on his desk. Picking up the receiver, he poked several numbers and swore. As many times as he'd called this number, he couldn't remember it, probably because at this moment his brain felt like it was going to implode.

He flipped through a Rolodex until he found the name he was looking for with the phone number. His hand was shaking as he fingered the numbers, and it seemed like an eternity before the familiar voice answered.

"This is Alward," the doctor said into the mouthpiece, his voice quavering like a warped phonograph record. "We have a problem!"

*6:22 p.m.:* Willie felt his stomach churn. The cause wasn't indigestion but the thought of spending even five minutes in The New Sphinx Hotel. New! There was nothing new about the narrow, four-story relic between a parking lot and a laundry in the 1000 block of South State Street. Of all the shit holes he'd flopped in during his years on the street, the Sphinx was the worst. However, if he was to play out his hunch about Frank, he'd have to gut out the Sphinx to find the man he was looking for.

Willie paused a moment outside a heavy wooden door flanked by two windows covered with slabs of plywood. Overhead was a fire escape that clung precariously to the front of the building. Good luck to anyone who had to use it, Willie thought. The Sphinx was a four alarm waiting to happen. Willie figured that the hotel had to violate every health and safety code in the book, which was probably overlooked by the City in exchange for payoffs from the slum landlord who lived in some ritzy suburb.

Willie sucked in a lungful of fresh air before he entered into a small, unfurnished lobby. An old man who looked like a zombie surfaced from behind a beat-up reception desk.

"Wanna room?" the zombie croaked.

"No. I'm lookin' for a friend."

"He gotta name?"

"Got lots of names. Try Marcus Washington."

A cockroach emerged from an open sack of Frito Lays and began making its way across the coffee-stained register. The zombie brushed away the cockroach and squinted through bifocals at the names of the guests.

"No Washington. I got two Marcuses. Johnson and Lawson."

"My friend's a big, black dude."

"That'd be Johnson. He's in 415. Tell him he's gotta be outta here by nine a.m. tomorrow."

"You tell him."

"Shit, I ain't seen him since he fell in here five days ago."

"Five days? On Tuesday?"

"Yeah. Paid up for five nights. Haven't seen him since. He's been sending out for food and booze."

Room service, Willie thought, provided by the "skeezers," crack whores who worked the Sphinx for whatever small change and drugs they could scrounge from the all-male residents. Marcus must have hit a big time lick to afford a five-day binge, even at the bargain rate of fifteen dollars a night.

"What time did he check in?

Again the zombie squinted at the register. "Nine-thirty that night."

Nine-thirty, Willie thought. His hunch still might pay off. "Thanks," he said and headed for the stairway next to the desk.

Willie was winded by the time he reached the fourth floor. He had to pause to catch his breath before venturing down a narrow corridor littered with trash and flakes of plaster. He was wishing he had a gas mask to filter out the stench of urine and excrement that came from the backed-up toilets in the community bathroom, one for each floor. Willie was momentarily startled by a large rat that darted out of nowhere and scurried down the hall behind him.

Willie located number 415 and was about to knock when the door opened. A middle-aged black lady, dressed in a mini-skirt, low-cut blouse, torn fishnet hose and pumps, almost collided with him on her way out. Better looking than most skeezers, Willie thought. Must have cost Marcus plenty, this one. Most of them were real dogs, and not all of them were women. They used the rear fire escape to sneak in. Although this did not go unobserved by the security cameras in the hallways, whoever manned the reception desk either didn't give a shit or was paid not to give a shit.

Willie saw the queen skeezer size him up with drug glazed but still calculating eyes that drooled mascara. "Hey, honey. What's up?"

Meaning how about some action, Willie thought. "Forget it," he said, trying not to inhale a nauseous medley of cheap perfume and semen. "Is Marcus in?"

"That his name? Yeah, he's in and he's out, if you follow."

Passed out, Willie thought. "Right. Guess I'll give him a wake-up call."

The whore's bright red lips put on a sultry smile. "You do that, honey. You be here when I get back, I do you both ya'll. We have some fun, the three of us."

"I'll be gone by then. Just wanted to tell my friend that he won the lottery."

"Fuck you, cocksucker!" The whore brushed past him and sashayed down the hall.

"Up yours, bitch!" Willie said, and entered a dark room about as big as a prison cell, except this cell didn't even have a barred window to let in some fresh air to dilute the pungent scent of disinfectant sprayed at the request of the tenant —if he bothered—to discourage the bed bugs. As for air conditioning, forget it, which made it even more sweltering and stuffy in the summer. An old, noisy water heater gave off just enough warmth in the winter to prevent frostbite. Willie never could understand what the chicken wire on the ceiling was for. At least this room had the luxury of a bed instead of just a mattress on the floor.

Willie switched on the light dangling by a cord from the ceiling and shook the broad shoulder of the huge black man sprawled on the bed, face down on the grimy mattress, his naked body partially covered by a semen-stained sheet.

"Hey, man, wake up. You got company."

No response, unless you could call a snore a response. Willie shook him harder.

"Come on, man, wake up."

This time he got a grunt. Marcus Washington rolled his massive head over, eyes blinking into hostile slits. "What the fuck you want?" his voice rasped.

"It's Willie, man."

"Willie?"

"Willie. Willie Butler."

Recognition slowly crept into Marcus's bleary eyes. "Hey, Willie," he said, thick lips between the shaggy beard stretching into a broad smile that exposed a few missing teeth. He rolled over and raised a hand as big as a baseball mitt for a high five, which Willie gave him. "What you doin' here, man?"

"Lookin' for you. You weren't at the Hilton, so I figured you might be here."

"You figured right. Hey, there's a bottle of Ricky's somewhere on the floor. Get it and we'll have a drink."

Willie searched through a litter of empty bottles and fast food boxes, some with leftovers, which had gotten the attention of a convention of cockroaches that seemed immune to the disinfectant. Willie finally found a nearly full bottle of Richard's cabernet, which he offered to his host.

"Take yourself a drink, man."

Why not, Willie thought, taking a seat on a crate, the only other piece of furniture in the room other than the bed. He took a pull and handed the bottle to Marcus. The big man elbowed himself into a sitting position and gulped down half its contents with three swallows.

"I sent the bitch out for food, booze and some blow," he said between burps. "We have ourselves a party."

"Forget it, man. You never see that bitch again, and if you do, she'll give you some shit about being ripped off."

The big man grinned. "Hey, man, you think Marcus is fuckin' stupid? She'll be back as long as she thinks I still got some of my bank."

"Or until she finds it while you're passed out," Willie said, looking around and wondering where Marcus could hide the money without being seen by a next door neighbor through the peep holes in the walls.

Marcus's laugh sounded like he was gargling acid. "It ain't here, man. The bitch done took this place apart. I got it stashed in the bathroom. I go take a piss, I bring back just enough to buy what I need, the bitch included."

"In the bathroom? Man, anyone could find it there," Willie said, referring to the heavy traffic in the bathroom. Some of the skeezers camped out there between tricks, and the wall was a Swiss cheese of peep holes.

"Not 'less they be lookin' under one of the tanks. I got it in a baggie, taped to the bottom, what's left."

"Good a place as any, I guess," Willie said. Then with a sly grin: "Maybe I'll go take myself a piss."

Another gargling laugh. "Yeah, you do that. Marcus be tellin' you this, 'cause I trust you, man. But you fuck Marcus over, I *will* be breaking your leg next time we meet up. Maybe both legs."

Willie smiled, but he knew Marcus wasn't kidding. Marcus was a man you didn't want as an enemy. Although most of his bulked up muscles had long ago turned to flab, sober or drunk, Marcus could be one mean dude. Chicago Bear opponents had found this out when their running backs tried to punch through left tackle, a position Marcus had played for three years before drugs fucked up his football career and the rest of his life.

"Someone die and leave you that wad?" Willie said, wondering where Marcus got his bank. For sure not from the Hilton guests he worked outside the side entrance on Balbo. Wearing his old football jersey, he'd hold a placard with a picture of himself when he played for the Bears and ask people to help a former Chicago Bear down on his luck. It was a good routine, but not good enough to finance the binge he was on.

"Man, this you won't believe. I was doin' my thing when a limo pulls up and this old dude gets out with a young chick. The old dude was really fucked up, and he trips on the curb, so the driver and the chick, they have to pick him up and help him inside. Well, I'm about to split, 'cause I see security headed my way, when I spot the old dude's wallet in the gutter. Man, I ain't moved so fast since my first training camp with the Bears. There was more than five Cs in that wallet, man, which naturally I kept as a reward for trashin' the dude's credit cards."

"Shit, man, with that kind money you coulda shacked up at the Hilton."

"Yeah. I used to stay there, ya know. The Hilton, the Ritz Carlton, shit, all the big time hotels all over. And the food. Shit, man, steaks thick as a phone book and the best booze there is. And the chicks, man, the chicks. Gor-gee-ous! They was always followin' us around, just beggin' to get fucked, ya' know." Marcus sighed. "The good days, Willie, the good days."

Willie saw his smile deflate like a punctured inner tube. For Marcus it had to be more than tough. Willie, he never really had the good life, but Marcus… Marcus had it all. Now he had nothing and knew it. Willie put a hand on his broad shoulder. "Yeah, man, I know. It sucks."

Marcus took another long pull of Ricky's. "Yeah, well, you didn't come here to listen to my shit, man. Right?"

Now Willie played his hunch and showed him the missing bulletin with Frank's picture, even though Marcus knew Frank from his street days. The Hilton was just around the corner from Dr. Needles' office, so if Frank had gone to see the doc Tuesday afternoon, there was a chance that Marcus might have seen him. The hunch paid off.

"Yeah, I seen Frank. First I didn't make him out. He looked good, got himself a shave and haircut, some new rags."

"Yeah. He got clean."

"No shit. You be looking for him, so I guess he's back on the street, right?"

Willie debated whether he should tell Marcus about Frank and decided not to. Marcus would clam up if he thought there was anything about Frank's death that the cops would want to know about. "Yeah. Do you remember when you saw him?"

"I dunno. The other day. Shit, who knows?"

"Which day, man?"

"Which day. Let's see, I was in the Chicken Shack..."

"The one on Wabash?"

"Yeah. Getting myself some grub. I seen Frank goin' by. I yelled at him but he never saw me. By the time I got outside, he was gone."

Figures, Willie thought. The building where Needles had his office was practically next door. But what day was it? Willie asked again.

"Shit, man, one day's like another."

"Could it have been Tuesday?"

"Yeah, I guess so. Yeah, sure, it was Tuesday, I remember now, 'cause that's when I hit the lick. I got hit with a sawbuck from some dude for the grub, so I figured it could be a good night and went back to the Hilton. Lucky I did, right?"

"Right. Hey, thanks, man."

"Shit, for what? You find Frank, you say hello from Marcus."

"I'll do that. Stay up, man."

They slapped palms again, and Willie left. Out on the street he took a few deep breaths to get the stench of The Sphinx out of his lungs, then started walking north on State at a brisk pace. He wanted to get to a phone and call the cop to tell him that his suspicions were right. Frank had seen Dr. Needles before he disappeared. Did that visit have something to do with his friend's death? Willie was betting it did, but maybe he could help get that answer, too. One thing was for sure. He was goddam' well gonna try.

Willie smiled. For the first time in years he felt that he didn't need a drink.

*6:45 p.m.:* Megan could hardly believe her eyes. She was pouring fresh coffee into the silver urn on the dining room table, when the doorbell chimed. Karen had gone to answer it. The last person Megan expected to see walk into her living room was Detective McPherson.

The people she'd counted on being at her dad's wake were there—her Aunt Mary, Father Kiley, Karen, of course, and three of her other lady friends. Only two of her dad's old friends were there, as he'd lost touch with most of them during his years on the street, but she was pleased and grateful to see Detective Winstrom and Katie's teacher, Miss Markle. There were also two people she didn't know: David Swope, her dad's boss at Home Depot, and Pastor John Garrett from The Beacon Mission.

McPherson was a definite surprise, and Megan wasn't sure if he was a welcome one. At least he was showing some respect for the occasion with a starched white shirt and a tie that actually matched the color of the pressed dark blue suit.

"Can I help you, dear?" her Aunt Mary asked.

Megan gestured toward a silver platter on the table, which she'd laid out with her bone china, crystal and silverware. "Looks like your cookies are a big hit."

"I'll fetch some more," her aunt said, beaming with pride.

Justifiable pride, Megan thought. As good a cook as she considered herself to be, she was an amateur compared to her aunt, who now moved to the open kitchen to replenish the empty platter with more oatmeal raisin and chocolate chip cookies. They were not only delicious but light on the calories, due to the absence of sugar in the ingredients. Like Megan, her aunt cooked healthy.

"Aunt Karen wants some more tea, Mommy," a small voice said.

Megan looked down at Katie, who was holding up an empty china cup on a saucer with a silver teaspoon. She reached for the cup, but Katie drew it away. "Let me, Mommy."

"Be careful, dear. It's very hot."

"I will." Katie filled the cup with steaming water from the spigot of the other silver urn. "What kind of tea, Mommy?"

"I think Aunt Karen likes Orange Pekoe."

Katie searched through a crystal bowl of herbal teas until she found the right one. She tore open the packet and submerged the bag into the cup. "There."

Megan watched her move carefully across the room to where Karen was talking to Detective McPherson. She looked so adorable in her yellow gingham dress and matching barrette. The perfect little hostess, Megan thought with pride, and handling the somber occasion with a composure that amazed her.

Not that she wasn't grieving for her granddad. She was. She was simply dealing with it in her own way. All day she'd talked to his picture, the one Megan had chosen to display as a remembrance on a small table flanked with vases of beautiful roses. Megan had heard Katie tell the handsome man in his Army dress uniform that she loved him, that she wished he were here, and that she would say a prayer for him every night. The proud, beaming Irish face in the picture seemed to be saying that he understood. Remembering him as he was then, Megan felt her eyes moisten.

"The cookie lady cometh." Aunt Mary set the platter of cookies on the table.

"What? Oh, right."

Her aunt took her arm. "You okay?"

"Yes. I'm doing fine, considering, thanks to you."

"It's the Irish in me. We take the death of loved ones in stride. Wakes become a celebration of their lives, and, I might add, not without a drop of spirits. Of course, in this case…"

Megan smiled and patted her hand. "There's a bottle of merlot in the cabinet over the stove that I keep for guests."

"Maybe later, dear. Say, you have a late arrival."

Megan followed her gaze to Detective McPherson, who was with Karen and Katie. Katie was giving Karen her tea.

"Yes, I saw. Detective McPherson. He was working with Detective Winstrom to find Dad."

"Yes. I remember. He was here yesterday evening. Handsome man."

"What? Oh, I suppose so."

Hint, hint, Megan thought. Aunt Mary had been on her case for a long time to find another man in her life. At the moment there wasn't one, except Neal, but Neal was more of a friend, not a serious love interest. Aunt Mary was right, though. It wasn't that Megan felt she needed a man to make her life complete. It was more for companionship, a rare commodity that was becoming ever rarer. Except for Karen, all of her girlfriends were married, and couples tend to socialize with other couples. Now there were children in their lives, which left even less time to spend with old friends, especially single old friends.

Thank God she still had Karen to talk to, but unlike herself, Karen was aggressively seeking male companionship, not for a husband—she'd been there, done that, and gotten burned—but to satisfy her basic feminine needs. In fact, Karen seemed to be coming on to McPherson, of all people. Megan had to admit that he was handsome, but in a macho way, and she didn't go for macho types. Too insensitive. Still, when she saw him look at her, she wondered what he was thinking.

Mack was thinking that Megan Herbst looked stunning. Even dressed in simple black pants and blazer with a white blouse, and wearing sparse make-up, her angelic face and flaming red hair still gave her the look of a movie star. Megan was a lady Mack knew he could go for under different circumstances. First, it was obvious that there was no interest at the other end. Second, Mack made it a point not to get involved with anyone related to an investigation, much as he was sometimes tempted.

Mack felt a hand tugging at his coat sleeve and looked down to see Katie's cherubic face gazing up at him.

"I know you. You're Mr. Mack, aren't you?"

Karen answered for him. "This is Detective McPherson, Katie. He's a policeman."

"A policeman?"

"That's right," Mack said.

"But you said you were Mr. Mack."

"It's my nickname."

"What's that?"

"Another name that people call you. It's short for McPherson."

Katie gave him a quizzical look, then said to Karen, "He's strange."

Karen laughed. "Oh no, dear. He's not strange." Then to Mack with a little flirtatious smile. "You're not strange, are you, Mr. Mack?"

"I try not to be."

Mack saw Karen's hazel eyes sizing him up and liking what she saw. That went both ways. Tall and slender, Megan's friend was wearing a navy suit with a short skirt that revealed show-off legs. A little heavy on the cosmetics, Mack thought, especially the blue eye shadow, and her bob-cut chestnut hair gave her face a masculine look she could do without. Nonetheless, one very good looking lady.

"If he's not strange, then why doesn't he like chocolate pudding?" Katie asked Karen.

"I don't know, dear. Why don't you ask him?"

"Why don't you like chocolate pudding, Mr. Mack?"

"I love pudding, but I'm allergic to chocolate."

"Allergic? What's allergic?"

"I break out into a rash if I eat it."

"For real?"

"For real."

"I had a rash one time. Mommy said it was from too much sun. Was it like that?"

"Yeah, only worse."

Katie made a face. "Oooh, that's awful."

"Why don't you ask Mr. Mack if he'd like some coffee, dear?"

"Would you like some coffee, Mr. Mack?"

"That would be fine."

"It won't give you a rash, will it?"

"No."

"Good."

Mack smiled, as he watched Katie scurry over to the dining room table. "Cute kid."

"She's precious. And handling this really well."

"Yeah, must be rough on her."

"I'm sure. She loved her granddad as if he'd been with her all her life rather than only a few months. He was a wonderful man. Did you know him well?"

"No. Not at all, actually. My partner knew him. Detective Winstrom."

"I know. I met him when he was looking for Frank the last time. Such a nice young man. Caring, not like most..." Karen bit her lip.

"Most cops?"

"I'm sorry. That was stupid."

"No apology necessary. We care, most of us. It's just that we keep a pretty tight lid on our feelings."

Karen laughed. "Like a lot of my patients."

"Patients? Are you a doctor?"

"Psychologist. Fixing broken marriages is my specialty. You got a marriage needs fixing, I'm your gal."

Probing, Mack thought. "Too late for that, I'm afraid."

"Oh? Too bad."

"Not really. Some marriages can't be fixed. How's the tea?"

"Ummm, good," she said, taking a sip. "But quite frankly, I could use something a little stronger."

"I was having similar thoughts."

"Maybe when this is over?"

Nothing shy about Karen Wilks, Mack thought, debating if she fell into the category of case-related desirable females. What the hell. "I know a place where you can get a drink and decent food, if you can put up with music that swings. You like jazz?"

"Love it."

"Hey, man, glad you could make it," Otis said, sliding up with a cup of coffee.

"Yeah. Thanks for letting me know. I'm grateful for the opportunity to show respect for Megan's dad." The fact was that he'd decided to attend the wake for more than one reason. Maybe this wasn't the time or the place, but he figured that Megan would want to know what he'd learned—or rather what he suspected —about Dr. Alward as soon as possible.

He'd made a phone call to the AMA after his visit to check out what the doctor had been doing since he got that diploma that was hanging on his wall. Alward had put in eleven years as a lab tech with Abbott Laboratories in North Chicago, then joined the research staff of a small biotech company, Bio-Sci Research & Development, Inc., in Schaumburg. After seven years with Bio-Sci, he'd left the company last July and opened his office at 620 South Wabash. The question was why? According to the AMA data, Alward had a history of giving his services to the needy going back to med school, so maybe it was just that simple. The doc's fervor to serve humanity was genuine, of that Mack was sure. He'd seen the compassion in his eyes when he'd talked to the vagrant, Eddie. In any event, he'd need more to go on than a cop's hunch if he was going to do what he had in mind.

"Did you find out anything more about the screw-up at the morgue?" Otis asked, interrupting Mack's thoughts.

Karen jumped in before Mack could respond. "Wasn't that terrible? How could such a thing happen?"

"Good question," Mack said.

"Well, if I were Megan, I'd sue the shit out of the City, pardon me."

"I think she's got other things on her mind. Personally, I thought this case was closed, but I guess Megan isn't quite so sure," Otis said with a meaningful look at Mack.

"Is there something wrong?" Karen asked. "I mean, about Frank's death, what happened at the morgue?"

"Ask my partner."

Mack debated whether he should tell Otis about Alward. The answer was no, especially with Karen listening. "Probably not."

"You mean there could be something?" Karen said.

The beep of his cell phone was a welcome interruption. "Excuse me," Mack said, pulling it from his coat pocket. He pressed the talk button and put the phone to his ear. "McPherson."

As Mack listened, Otis saw a slight smile form on his lips and wondered if the call had anything to do with what his partner had been up to during the day. Whatever that was, Otis was sure that Mack was not about to share it with him.

"Good work," Mack said when the caller had finished. "I'll keep in touch. And thanks."

"Good news?" Otis said.

"You might say so. Look, if you'll pardon me a minute, I'd like to pay my respects to Mrs. Herbst."

"Of course," Karen said. "We still on for later?"

"We're on."

"Interesting man, your partner," Karen said, as Mack moved away.

"He has his moments."

And full of surprises, Otis thought. Coming on to Karen Wilks, for example. Or was that vice versa? Who knows? Mack never talked about his social life, but he didn't strike Otis as being a skirt chaser. Skirt chasers liked to brag about their conquests. However, Otis was beginning to suspect that there might be something resembling a human being under that cast iron exterior. Maybe he'd find out in time, but right now he was certain of only one thing: During that phone call he'd seen a gleam in Mack's eyes he hadn't seen before. Something had really turned him on, and it wasn't Karen Wilks.

*7:24 p.m.:* Willie decided to play cop. After he finished talking to McPherson, he paid a visit to Dr. Needles on the chance that he'd be working late. Willie knew that he often saw patients in the evening and on weekends, and today was no exception. The uniformed security guard in the lobby, an old dude with wisps of gray hair escaping from beneath a Chicago White Sox baseball cap, told him that Needles was in, but called up to see if the doctor would see Willie. He would, so Willie signed the visitors' register and went on up. He didn't know what he expected to find out, probably nothing, but it wasn't like he had anything better to do. Besides, he was feeling kinda shitty. Fatigued. Maybe it was the four flights he'd climbed at The New Sphinx. In any event, seeing Needles could kill two birds with one injection, Willie thought with a chuckle.

The doorbell pinged as he entered the reception room. There were no other patients waiting. Willie was scrawling his name on the legal pad when the office door opened.

"Come on in, Willie."

Willie entered the spacious office, thinking that the doc looked like he'd just come off a binge. Really washed out. Nothing new there. The dude was a workaholic. "Thanks for seein' me, doc."

The doctor closed the door. "No problem. Got to catch up on my lab work anyway. Besides, you were due here last week, remember?"

"What? Oh yeah," he said, remembering now. Needles had taken his blood pressure, blood and urine specimens, did his thing with the needle and given him some pills to take a month ago with instructions to come back in three weeks. "Sorry. Guess I forgot."

"Not good, Willie. You've got to look after yourself. How have you been feeling?"

"Still kinda shitty, off and on, ya know, but okay otherwise."

"Let's check your blood pressure again."

Willie sat down in a chair next to the apparatus. The doctor wrapped the cuff around his upper right arm.

"I ran tests on your blood, Willie," he said, inflating the cuff bag. "Your cholesterol is still too high. Especially the LDL. Are you taking the medication I gave you?"

Willie felt the cuff tighten on his arm. "Oh, yeah," he lied. He took it when he remembered. "But I'm runnin' low."

"I'll give you some more pills before you leave," the doctor said, squinting at the gauge through reading glasses as the bag deflated.

"Right. So what's the verdict?"

The doctor took off the cuff. "Blood pressure a little low. No problem there. However, I am going to draw some blood again, Willie. Lipitor—that's the medication you're taking—can damage the liver."

"That's bad, I guess?"

The doctor moved to the medicine cabinet and removed a specimen needle. "Yes, but the medication is not my main concern." He attached the specimen tube to the needle. "It's the drinking. Alcohol is the liver's worst enemy. Have you ever noticed blood in your stool?"

"You mean when I take a crap?"

The doctor returned with the needle. "Right."

"No." Not that he ever looked.

"That's good, but if you do, I want you in here fast. Make a fist."

Willie knew the routine, even watched the doctor dab alcohol in the crook of his left arm, probe for a vein, insert the needle and fill the tube. He'd seen lots worse in Nam to be bothered by the sight of blood, even his own. But why was the doctor's hand shaking? He must have done this a million times.

"That'll do it," he said, withdrawing the needle. He capped the tube, then bandaged the puncture with cotton and adhesive tape. "I want to see you again in two weeks, Willie. And this time don't forget."

"Right, doc."

Before he left, the doctor gave him a shot of vitamin B and a refill of the medication.

*8:50 p.m.:* Willie was positioned across the street from Dr. Alward's office building, pretending to panhandle an occasional pedestrian and the students who came and went from a more modern addition to Columbia College. Needles was inside the Chicken Shack getting some food to go. A few minutes later Willie watched him take a sack of food and coffee back into the office building. More lab work? Maybe? Or maybe…what? Who the hell knew?

The more Willie thought about it, the more confused he became. Needles seemed like an alright dude. Otherwise, why would he be doing what he was doing? Not for the bucks, for sure. The only thing for sure in his mind at the moment was that something had spooked the doc. His hand was shaking again when he gave Willie the vitamin shot. And his eyes. Willie had seen that look in men's eyes before. In the eyes of his buddies in Nam when they came under fire.

The cop, Willie thought. McPherson. That had to be it. Willie smiled. Needles was suffering from a bad case of cop-itis. But why? It had to have something to do with Frank, or he wouldn't have lied about Frank seeing him on Tuesday. And why would he want to lie about seeing Frank?

Willie shook his head. Questions, questions and more questions. So he'd hang around awhile longer. Maybe something would break that would give him some answers. Patience, Willie thought.

Patience was something Willie knew about. In Nam, as a scout sniper, he'd spent hours in the jungle, deep behind enemy lines, stalking his quarry, often an important VC, waiting for the opportunity for a clean shot. And getting only one shot. One shot, one kill. The sniper's credo.

Patience. Yeah, and instinct. Gut instinct. The kind that alerts you to danger even before you see or hear it coming. It had saved his life more than once, Willie thought, remembering a night patrol in Nam Dong during his first tour. It was quiet, maybe too quiet. "Get buttoned up," he'd told his platoon buddies. "Charlie's out there. I can fucking feel it." The warning came none too soon, for suddenly the night erupted in a cacophony of automatic-weapons fire and mortar explosions, the screams of men as bullets and shrapnel tore through human flesh. Three of his buddies didn't live through the ensuing firefight, two others were wounded. But, when it was all over thirty-five VC would never see the sunrise, thanks to Willie's gut.

Willie's gut was delivering a message now. Something was gonna happen. Something bad, and if he knew what was good for him, he'd take off now. Too late, though. Get buttoned up, he told himself. He had a feeling a firefight was about to start…and he was right in the middle of it.

*8:58 p.m.:* Dr. Alward also had a premonition of impending danger. The detective's sudden appearance and the shock of Frank O'Meara's death was more than enough to set his heartbeat into overdrive. It was better now after the shot of

Xanax he'd given himself. The coffee and the food he'd bought would help, too
—junk food, deep fried chicken, but better than nothing. Proper nourishment was
something he too often neglected, along with adequate rest to erase the dark
circles under his eyes. When this was over, he would get away, take a long
vacation.

"Got a minute, doc?" Hank said, as Alward passed the security desk.

Alward hadn't bothered to sign out or in again. Hank knew his late night
habits. He also knew how to get free medical advice. Not that Alward minded,
but tonight he was in no mood to listen to Hank's numerous ailments, real or
imagined. "What is it this time, Hank?"

Hank patted his paunch. "It's my stomach. The pain, it come back again."

"How severe is it?"

"Well, it's kinda like a fart that won't come out, ya know?"

Gas, Alward thought. "What did you have for supper?"

"For supper? Let's see, I ate Italian. I love Italian food."

"Pasta and bread."

"Yeah. And lasagna."

Alward sighed. "Hank, I told you before. You've got irritable bowel
syndrome...IBS.  It's very common. I get it myself, when I'm under too much
stress."

"I'm not feelin' uptight, doc. Not that I know of, leastwise."

"No, but in your case it's probably a food allergy. Wheat, is my guess."

"You mean I'm allergic to wheat?"

How many times do I have to go over this before it takes permanent root in
his brain? Alward thought. "Given the fact that your pain often recurs after you
eat Italian food, I'd say that's a pretty accurate diagnosis."

"I know, I know, but couldn't it be cancer, doc?"

"We've already eliminated that, Hank. The colonoscopy, remember?"

"Oh, yeah, but they found some dots."

"Polyps."

"Yeah, polyps."

"They were benign, Hank, and not unusual for a man of your age. Nothing
to worry about."

"You're sure?"

"I'm sure. Now take an Alka-Seltzer and cut back on the Italian food,
okay?"

"Okay, doc. If you say so."

Alward moved to the elevators. For a couple of minutes Hank had
managed to take his mind off his problems. As the elevator moved sluggishly to
the third floor, Alward thought again about Detective McPherson and his
insinuating questions about Frank Cravin. The detective showing up was an
unwelcome surprise, but even if he did suspect something, there was nothing he
could prove, since there was no record of Frank's visit on Tuesday. The shocker
had been learning of Frank's death. They said they'd take care of him, keep him
under observation. He must have gotten away somehow, found a bottle, gotten
drunk and drowned. It was an accident, like the detective said. An accident.

Alward heard the voice when the elevator doors parted. It was coming
from one of the suites down the hall. Not loud—a high-pitched voice, male or
female, he couldn't tell, singing something he didn't recognize. Curious, he
paused to listen. Now he realized the words were in Latin, a language he'd

studied in med school, and the melody was a hymn—a Catholic hymn, he guessed—and the voice was like the voice of a choir boy. Odd. Someone must be working late, he thought, and had a radio on a classical music station. But a Catholic hymn?

The singing stopped as he started down the corridor toward his office. There was no sound from any of the suites he passed, no light showing from underneath the doors. Odd, alright. Very odd. Could the singing have come from his office? A late visitor? Of course not. Hank would have told him if anyone had come to see him while he was getting the food. Especially a choirboy, Alward thought with a smile. Nonetheless, he was apprehensive when he opened the outer door, which he'd left unlocked. To his relief there was no one in the reception room.

His relief was only momentary. He felt his blood surge when he inserted his key into his office door lock. He always locked his office door, even if he was only going to the restroom down the hall. The door was not locked! Had he forgotten this time? There was so much on his mind, he wouldn't be surprised. Yes, that must be it.

But if it wasn't? Alward was tempted to get Hank. Hank had a weapon, enough to discourage a thief. It had happened once before. One of his own patients, an addict, had hidden in the restroom after he left Alward's office and broken in later that night. An alert Hank, making his rounds, had caught him ransacking the medicine cabinet, looking for drugs.

Another thief? Alward almost wished that was the case. A deeper fear was that Detective McPherson was paying him another visit, this time going through his records. There was nothing incriminating in Frank's file, and the detective couldn't get into the computer without a password, but the CD was another matter. If he found that...

Alward shook off his fears. He was letting his imagination run amok. Another Xanax would steady his nerves, get him through the rest of the night to do what he had to do.

He eased the door ajar. The lights were still on, as he'd left them. Good. He opened the door wider. Nothing in the room seemed disturbed. A thief would have ransacked the place. He entered the office, now looking forward to the food and coffee. Maybe he wouldn't give himself that shot, after all.

It happened so fast that Alward didn't have a chance to react—the hand clamped over his mouth, the blade severing his jugular—no pain, just shock—and bewilderment—and the voice of a choirboy, like an angel, singing a Catholic hymn—a hymn that faded away into the silence of death.

*11:01 p.m.:* As soon as Mack turned the corner, he knew he was too late. The street outside the office building at 620 South Wabash was a crime scene—a scramble of cruisers, bar lights flashing, the meat wagon and van from the ME's office, yellow tape and uniformed cops holding back a gathering crowd of gawkers. Someone in the building had kept an appointment with the cooler, and there was no doubt in Mack's mind that it was Dr. Alward.

At Harrison Street Mack pulled the Bonneville up beside a young, uniformed policeman, who was directing traffic over to State Street, and showed his badge. The policeman waved him on. Mack parked in front of Columbia College and crossed the street, while cursing himself for not coming earlier. Karen had proven to be very agreeable company during cocktails and supper at The Downbeat, a fun lady with a great sense of humor. After exchanging cards, they'd gone their separate ways following the band's second set, although Karen seemed to have other activities on her mind. Tempting as that was, Mack had a rule never to go to bed with a lady he didn't get to know first. This eliminated casual sex from his lifestyle, but who needed that anyway when he had Inge.

It was 10:50 p.m. by the time he picked up his car in a nearby lot and headed for South Wabash. The plan was to flash his badge at the security guard with a story about Dr. Alward being a suspect in a drug case and have the guard let him into Alward's office without asking for the usual search warrant. Once inside, Mack intended to take the place apart. If Frank's file had been edited by Alward to reveal nothing, there might be something else that the doctor had overlooked. Too bad he couldn't get into the lab computer. That would take a password. However, he could take the CDs to Dr. Greg to examine. Maybe one of them would tell him something.

That *was* the plan. The plan now was to find out what had happened.

The sight of his badge cleared the way through the swarm of uniforms into Alward's office, which was crowded with techs taking measurements, dusting for fingerprints and shooting photographs. "Hello, Sam. Getting your annual physical?" Mack said to the detective in charge of the investigation.

Sergeant Sam Greiner turned away from an old guy in a uniform, obviously the security guard, with a surprised look on his angular face that reminded Mack of his high school football coach. Mack knew Greiner from when he worked in Area 3 Homicide before being transferred to Area 1. They weren't friends but had gone at each other on the handball court from time to time, contests that Greiner usually won due to his younger age and superb physical condition. A good cop, too, but a strictly by-the-book cop. Trim and neatly attired in a charcoal suit, white shirt and burgundy tie, Greiner took Mack's outstretched hand in a strong grasp.

"Hey, Mack. What are you doing here? I heard you were transferred to Special Victims."

"Buried would be more accurate. The doctor was involved in a missing persons case I'm working, but I see the doctor is out," Mack said, referring to the body sprawled face down near the desk in a pool of blood. "Any suspects?"

Greiner dabbed perspiration from his forehead with a handkerchief. "Not yet. But he was probably an addict looking for drugs."

Addict, like hell, Mack thought, looking around. The room was trashed, alright, but that could be window dressing. He wasn't surprised when he saw that the lab computer was missing. And the CDs. "How did he get it, Charlie?"

The portly Chinese examiner from the ME's office, who was kneeling over the corpse, looked up with a sly grin on his jowl-heavy face. His first name was Richard, but since his last name was Chan, the cops all called him Charlie, for obvious reasons, a moniker he accepted and even parodied. "Unfortunate deceased doctor not appear to have cut self shaving. Obviously victim of foul play," he said in a mock sing-song voice right out of an old Charlie Chan movie. He even looked the part, Mack thought. "Jugular vein severed as neatly as if it was done by a surgeon," he now said in perfect English.

"Any idea how long he's been dead?"

"Not long. One or two hours at the most."

"That jibes with what the security guard said," Greiner added. "The doctor went out to pick up some food and returned around nine o'clock. He must have walked in on the assailant."

"Who found him?" Mack asked.

"I did," Hank said. "The doc, he was workin' later than usual, so I went up to see if I could get him some coffee. What a shame. Real nice guy, the doc."

"How'd the perp gain entry, Sam?" Mack asked.

"Came up the fire escape at the rear of the building and let himself in."

Through the emergency exit, Mack surmised, which was right outside Alward's office. "Any sign of a forced entry?"

"No. The guy knew how to pick a lock."

"And to get in without triggering the security alarm."

"Yeah. He disarmed it."

"Not exactly an amateur."

"Not exactly."

"Does that sound like the work of a hopped-up druggie?"

Greiner unwrapped a stick of gum and popped it into his mouth. "Hell, Mack, I've known street bums who have Ph.D.s. The way I make it, the perp was one of Alward's charity patients. According to Hank here, it's happened before."

"That's right, Detective," the security guard said. "Caught him going through the doc's medicine cabinet, I did, lookin' for drugs."

"This perp was after something else, Sam," Mack said. "The computer. Alward had a lab computer, state of the art."

"Hey, it's gone, all right," Hank said.

"Makes sense," Greiner said. "The perp could raise some easy spending money from a fence."

"What about the CDs?"

"CDs? What CDs?"

Mack went over to the lab station and tapped the empty rack with his forefinger. "Alward did his own lab work, Sam. He kept data on CDs here. They're gone. Ripping off the computer for bucks I can buy into, but why would he take the CDs?"

"How the hell do I know? Probably thought he could sell them, too. We'll find out when we book the guy for first degree murder. And we will book him."

Mack could see that Greiner was getting irritated. He was in charge of the investigation and probably resented Mack butting in. Rather than push what he suspected, Mack decided to back off. "You're probably right, Sam. An addict does make sense. Maybe even one of the doc's own patients."

"That's the way I see it." Greiner gestured toward a uniformed officer filling packing cartons with the manila folders from the file cabinet. "Alward's records of his patients. We'll run all the names through FERC. Odds are the perp has a record. That'll narrow the field."

"Hey, I got a log goin' back 'least six months of the doc's after hours patients," Hank said. "They got to sign in and out, ya' know. You wanna see it?"

"Sure. It might help."

"I got it right downstairs. I'll bet the perp is on that log."

"Could be, Hank."

"You bet he is. Way I see it, he woulda seen the doc at night. That's when I caught the other guy. At night. Hid in the john, then broke in."

"This perp didn't hide in the john, Hank."

"I know, I know, but he'd have cased the place, right? Hey, I'll bet it was the guy who seen the doc tonight."

"He had a patient tonight?"

"You bet he did. A black guy, yeah, a charity case, too. Way I see it, he pretends to be sick so he can make sure the doc's alone. Then he hangs around outside, and when he sees the doc leave, he breaks in not knowing that the doc is just goin' to get some food."

"You may be onto something, Hank. Did you recognize him?"

"No, but I sure as hell would if I saw him again."

"You may get that chance if he's got a rap sheet. He signed the register?"

"You bet he signed it. 'Course, he might not have used his real name, but it's on the register. It's right downstairs. You want me to get it?"

"I'd appreciate it, Hank. And thanks."

"I'll get it now. I'll be right back. It's him, alright. You'll see."

Mack nudged Greiner's arm as Hank made a hasty exit. "Better watch out, Sam. Hank will be taking charge of the investigation before you know it."

"Hey, maybe he's right. It's a lead, in any event." Greiner turned to Charlie, who was rising from beside Alward's body. "You finished here, Charlie?"

"*Finito* for now. When can we deliver him to the morgue for the forensics?"

"He's all yours in half an hour."

"Good. Gives me time to grab a sandwich. Nice seeing you again, Mack."

"You too, Charlie. Give my regards to your number one son."

Charlie grinned and did a little mock Charlie Chan bow. "Unworthy offspring now attending med school at Vanderbilt. Will convey your greeting to same."

"Your missing person," Greiner said after Charlie had left. "One of the doctor's patients?"

"Yeah. A charity case."

"He wouldn't be involved in this in any way?"

"Not likely. He's dead."

"Dead?"

"Yeah. Drowned. Looks like an alcohol-related accident."

"Looks like?"

"Yeah."

A long searching look from Greiner. "Be careful, Mack. Seems to me you're in deep enough shit with the brass already."

"For sure. I don't suppose you'd let me look around a little anyway?"

"Hey, I'd like to, Mack, but…"

"I know, I know. Just asking."

"It'll all be in the report, anyway."

"Right. I'll be looking forward to reading it. Take care, Sam."

"*You* take care, Mack."

Mack realized that Sam was giving him some well-intentioned advice. Still, he couldn't help but take a look at the sign-in pad on the desk in the reception room. This would not be overlooked by Sam, nor would the name of the last person who had seen Alward alive, aside from the security guard…and his killer.

The signature on the legal pad was "Willie Butler."

*11:40 p.m.:* Willie knew he was in deep shit. When the patrol cars and ambulance converged on 620 South Wabash, it didn't take a genius to figure out that a serious crime had been committed and that the likely victim was Dr. Needles. And if Needles was no longer among the living, then Willie would be a prime suspect for his murder. The cops would find his signature on both the security register and the doc's sign-in sheet. To make matters worse, Willie had used his real name. Fucking stupid! Now the cops could access his rap sheet with his mug shot, which the old security dude would probably ID.

Willie had to make sure. If the victim wasn't Needles, or if he was only injured, he was off the hook. So Willie hung around in the swelling crowd of spectators until the paramedics rolled a gurney out to the ambulance with a stiff in a body bag. So much for it not being a homicide. But was the stiff Needles?

*11:52 p.m.:* Otis put the finishing touches on a P-51 model airplane. The sleek, silver Mustang fighter would soon join a variety of World War II airplanes perched on pedestals and dangling by fish lines from the ceiling of his cozy den. It was his private retreat, which contained a variety of memorabilia, including pictures of family and friends dating back to grade school, wedding pictures, and his ribbon for the Indiana High School basketball championship attached to a picture of his teammates and coaches flush with the excitement of victory.

Ava had her private place, as well. It was a sunroom at the rear of the bungalow, where she could grade papers or relax, reading magazines and novels. The rest of the house was functional but far from roomy. It occupied a small lot on North Kildare amidst more spacious and expensive homes in the upscale residential Sauganash neighborhood in northwest Chicago. Although Ava's parents had offered to supplement the purchase of a more prestigious house, Otis had insisted that they buy what they could afford with their combined salaries.

Otis was carefully affixing the insignia to the fuselage of the P-51 when the late news on a small TV over his worktable got his attention—a breaking news story regarding the brutal murder of a doctor at 620 South Wabash. Live coverage at the crime scene followed with a grim-faced mobile unit reporter outside the building interviewing the detective in charge of the investigation, Sergeant Sam Greiner. Greiner was courteous but stuck to the facts as he answered the reporter's questions. The victim was Dr. Lawrence Alward. His throat had been slit by an unknown assailant sometime around 10:00 p.m. Death was instantaneous. The motive appeared to be robbery. No, they had no suspects at this time. Yes, they were pursuing some leads. No, he could not reveal the nature of those leads, as that might compromise the investigation. Could the perp be one of the doctor's patients? It was a possibility they were considering, the detective acknowledged, then excused himself before the reporter could fire more questions at him. The anchorman took over again to assure the viewers that they would stay on top of the story, then moved on to the next juicy item, a sex scandal involving an alderman and a high school cheerleader.

Otis was no longer watching. He was remembering his conversation with Megan after Mack had left the wake with Karen Wilks. Dr. Alward had treated Frank when he was on the street, and Mack was convinced he had seen him the afternoon he disappeared. Megan had willingly shared this information with Otis. After all, they were friends, and Mack was his partner. Otis also had a hunch she'd be grateful if he'd lend a hand. Much as he liked Megan and her daughter, this was something he was not about to do.

Otis put down the model plane and reached for a half empty mug of coffee. Mack was letting his imagination run amok on this whole business. The foul-up at the morgue was just that. A foul-up. As for Alward seeing Frank, Mack only had the word of a vagrant on that one. According to Megan, the vagrant claimed to have spotted Frank near the office building the afternoon he disappeared.

That's assuming the vagrant's booze-or-drug-polluted memory was accurate. Forget it. But Mack wouldn't, for sure. Especially now. Alward's murder would give Mack a chance to do his thing. He'd fasten on it like a dog chewing on an old shoe.

To hell with it, Otis thought, with a sip of now lukewarm coffee. He reached for the remote and silenced the anchorman in mid-sentence as he reported the tragic death of a five-year-old boy on the South Side, the victim of a stray bullet during a shootout between rival gangbangers. Otis didn't need to hear the inevitable interview with the boy's mother. The media's shameless exploitation of what should be the private grief of victims' loved ones really pissed him off. Besides, he had enough on his mind already, which was Ava.

She was still simmering about his passing up the Ravinia charity event for Tony G's retirement party and his no-show for dinner and the theatre with her North Shore friends, despite his efforts to make amends. After Frank's wake earlier this evening he'd wined and dined her at Angelo's, a four-star Italian restaurant in Evanston, but to no avail. Ava had gone into her face-creaming routine as soon as they got home. Otis was too uptight to sleep, so he decided to get his mind off things by working on the P-51.

Gluing another insignia to the top of the left wing, Otis's mind drifted back to the first and only time he'd seen the real thing, a restored P-51 Mustang at the annual air show in Oshkosh, Wisconsin. He was on summer break between his junior and senior years at college, working as a basketball instructor at a boys' camp near Lake Delavan, and had taken a Saturday off to hop over to Oshkosh, where he rendezvoused with the man responsible for getting him hooked on old war planes, Walter Cartwright, his history professor at IU.

Walter was a vet of the Air Force's 99th Fighter Squadron. This distinguished group of all African-Americans and their sturdy P-46 Thunderbolts had put the fear of God into the Germans with dogfights and strafing missions. Two of Walter's buddies made the scene at Oshkosh, along with hundreds of airmen of previous wars. Thanks to Walter, Otis was treated to a free ride in a B25, flown by an old vet who had actually participated in the 1942 Tokyo raid.

Otis was remembering now what a blast that had been. Someday he'd go back to Oshkosh again, get with Walter, retired and walking with a cane now, but still going strong. No retirement community in Florida or Arizona for Walter. He was living in Bloomington with his one and only wife, swimming in the university's Olympic-size pool every day and writing a novel based on his war experiences. They kept in touch, but with less frequency. Otis's fault, not Walter's. He'd invited him to visit many times. As was the case with Tony G, Ava was not interested in making a trip to Bloomington, let alone Oshkosh. At least the Wisconsin Dells trip was still on. It would be an opportunity to connect again. God knows they needed to do that, and soon.

The chime of a Swiss clock in the living room sounded midnight. Thank God he didn't have to get up early tomorrow, Otis thought. It was the first day of his two day break. He wanted to spend Sunday with Ava, but he decided that on Monday he'd get up early to do some fishing. He'd take the RV to Wolf Lake just inside the Indiana border and spend the day. He'd fished Wolf Lake with his dad when he was a kid, so it was kind of a nostalgia trip, as well. Maybe he'd slide over and see his mom in East Chicago, take her whatever he caught, and let her pan fry it for lunch. Of course, he would get the honor of cleaning the fish. A good plan, and it would also give him a chance to talk to her about Ava.

Otis was worried about their marriage, no doubt about that, and he would welcome his mom's feed-back. He'd always relied on her for support and guidance. So had his dad. A great guy, his dad. For years, right up until an aneurysm killed him on the job, he earned a meager living by delivering drugs on a bike from a pharmacy in East Chicago. He knew all the customers, always greeted them with a big smile and a cheerful word. Everyone liked him. For a nobody, he drew more mourners at his funeral than the little Baptist church on East Mulberry could hold.

Otis hadn't known until two years after his death that his dad had never learned to read or write. He kept all the people's names and addresses filed away in his head. Otis missed him, his warmth, his companionship. But it was his mom who provided the counsel, spiritual and practical, that glued the family together. She was also the principal breadwinner. Her housecleaning service to well-to-do families in Merrillville and Crown Point bought twice as many groceries as what his dad made at the pharmacy. She never put him down, though. Never asked him to bring in more bucks, which he could have done busting his ass in the steel mills in Gary. It was enough for her that he was happy doing what he was doing.

Otis knew that the same went for him. She'd give him the same advice now that she'd given him after he graduated from IU. He was on the verge of entering the NBA draft. The fact that he was a candidate for a late round pick and might only survive three or four years as a reserve may have been a hit to the ego but would still put enough money in the bank to buy his mom a nice three-bedroom condo in Merrillville. "Never you mind about me," she'd told him. "You do what your heart tells you to do. What the Lord tells you to do, 'cause the Lord is in your heart. So you listens to your heart, no matter what."

And he had. He'd joined the CPD and entered the Police Academy. Now he was agonizing on whether he should continue to "listen to his heart" and stay with the force. According to the Bible, that's what the Lord would want him to do. To help the afflicted and victims of society. Aside from putting the bad guys behind bars, that's what his job was all about. But Ava didn't see it that way. And she was putting more pressure on him to go the lawyer route. No matter what he did, it seemed like a no-win as far as his marriage was concerned. Caving in would only be a quick fix at best. He'd come to hate not only his job but himself. And, of course, he'd blame Ava. It would be like a cancer, slowly spreading and eventually destroying their marriage. Staying with the CPD could end the same way. So flip a coin, he thought. Heads, you lose; tails, you lose. Great.

If that wasn't enough to keep him awake nights, now he had Mack to worry about. A loose cannon with a short fuse that Otis feared was already lit by Alward's murder. If the cannon went off, the reverberations would be felt all the way to the Superintendent's office. Not *if*, Otis thought. *When*. And even though there was no way Otis was going to get involved, the fallout could still screw up his game plan for promotion, at least for the foreseeable future, let alone his goal of occupying the commissioner's office.

Another no-win? Not if Otis could help it. He'd go see Lieutenant Cronin first thing Monday morning and ask to be teamed with another partner. Even Manowski. Anyone but Mack. If Mack was going to self-destruct—and Otis had a hunch that was going to happen soon—so be it. The fuse was lit. The explosion was inevitable. But when it happened, Otis wanted to be well outside the blast radius.

## Sunday, May 19

*12:10 a.m.:* Willie nursed a beer at the NoName Bar on South State, a couple of blocks from the crime scene, while he watched the late news on the TV over the liquor racks. He'd seen the mobile TV unit at the crime scene and figured the murder would make the news by midnight. It did. A cop in charge of the investigation announced that the stiff in the body bag was the doc and that his killer could be one of his charity patients. Willie gulped down the rest of his beer and hit the street.

*12:28 a.m.:* Mack waited behind the wheel of the Bonneville. He was parked just north of Harrison Street with a clear view of 620 South Wabash. When the last of the investigators, uniforms and forensics finally departed, Mack cranked up the powerful engine, drove the short distance to the office building and pulled up behind the single blue-and-white that remained at the curb. A uniformed officer, a young, muscular black woman, guarded the front entrance. Mack knew her partner would be in Alward's office to secure the crime scene. Investigators would be back for another look-see just in case they missed something the first go-through. He was hoping they had. It was a long shot, but he'd cracked cases before by taking a second hard look and coming up with some clue that had eluded him before.

The officer was in his face as he started to exit the car. "Sorry, sir," she said. "But you'll have to…"

Mack already had his badge and ID in his hand. "Sergeant McPherson, Officer."

"Oh, sorry, Detective. I thought you were finished for the night."

"No such luck. Forgot my notebook, so thought I might as well take another look around as well. Call your partner and tell him I'm on my way up, okay?"

"Will do," the lady cop said, unclipping her hand radio from her belt.

Hank looked up from the *Sun Times* as Mack entered the lobby. A small radio on the desk was tuned to a sports station.

"Hello, Hank. You still on duty?"

"Yeah. Calhoun, he's got the midnight shift, he calls in sick. Sick like hell. Drunk more likely. The guy's an alky. The agency's got no one else available tonight, so I'm stuck with a double shift. It ain't the first time."

Mack gave Hank the same story he'd given the lady cop. He also had some questions for the security guard he hadn't been able to ask earlier.

"Were you on duty last Tuesday, Hank?"

"You bet I was."

"You start at five, right?"

"Right. Never been late, not once."

"That's admirable, Hank. Last Tuesday, do you remember…"

"That's why the boss lets me stay on. I could retire anytime I want, but what would I do? Take walks in Lincoln Park, fish off the sea wall, watch TV. Shit, I'd go nuts."

"Yeah, I hear you, Hank. Now about last Tuesday, do you remember anything unusual happening?"

"Unusual? You mean like a break-in?"

"Yeah. Or maybe someone might have gotten sick, had to be taken to a hospital?"

"No. Nothing like that. I mean it's happened, but not last Tuesday, for sure."

Mack nodded. "You still got that register, Hank?"

"You bet I got it. The detective fella, Greiner, he wanted it, but I got to keep a record, ya' know, so he had one of the cops run it over to Kinko's on State to make a copy."

"Good for you, Hank. Wonder if you'd mind if I took a look at the people who came and went last Tuesday."

"Sure, no problem," Hank said. He removed the register from the top desk drawer and flipped through the pages. "Let's see, that's the fourteenth, right? Here it is."

Mack scrutinized the names of persons who had signed out after five p.m. According to when Frank had left work and what Willie's friend recalled, Frank would have arrived well before five o'clock. He could have also left before five, but if he hadn't, and he'd left under his own will, he would have signed out. However, there was no Frank O'Meara or Frank Cravin signature on the register.

"Find what you were lookin' for?" Hank said.

"Yeah, thanks, Hank. Take good care of this."

"You bet I will. Got to keep a record, ya' know. You get any leads on that vagrant who saw the doc tonight?"

"Not yet."

"Well, you find him, you got your man, for sure."

"Right. Keep up the good work, Hank."

Mack moved to the bank of two elevators wondering what Willie was up to with his visit to Alward. Probably doing a little detective work on his own. Why not? He'd already come through big time. The fact was that Willie was probably the last man to see Alward alive other than Hank and his killer. Maybe he'd learned something. Whatever it was, Mack would have to wait for Willie to contact him.

While he rode the groaning elevator to the third floor, Mack theorized about what had happened in Alward's office on Tuesday. The doctor must have given Frank an injection of something to knock him out. Alward might have gotten him out by himself, but Mack doubted it. More likely he called for help from a person or persons unknown. They'd probably waited until dark and taken him down the fire escape to a car or van in the alley.

Mack was also betting that the same person or persons had murdered Alward. The doctor seemed genuinely shocked when Mack told him about Frank's death. Realizing that he was now an accomplice to murder, he'd probably hit the panic button hard enough to get himself killed. He had to be silenced. Permanently. The big question was why. The answer to that, Mack concluded, probably resided in the hard drive of the missing lab computer and in one or more of the CDs.

A boyishly handsome uniformed officer jumped to his feet from the sofa, a *People* magazine in one hand, as Mack entered Alward's reception room. "Evening, Detective. I mean, good morning."

"Morning it is. Everything quiet here?"

"Like a tomb. And hot."

"Yeah. The air conditioner is off at night."

"Great. I'll be burned toast by the time I'm off duty."

"Comes with the job," Mack said, thinking that the rookie was probably right out of the Academy. "Are you hungry?"

"I'm always hungry. My girlfriend says I got a tapeworm."

Mack grinned, dug out his wallet and extracted a twenty-dollar bill. "There's a Burger King at State and Van Buren. Why don't you get some burgers and coffee for yourself, your partner and me. The feast is on me."

"Hey, great," the rookie said, taking the twenty. "Are you sure it's okay? To leave my post, I mean."

"I'll take that responsibility. And make mine a cheeseburger. With everything."

"Right. Hey, and thanks, Detective…?"

"McPherson."

"Right. Be back soon."

"Take your time. I've got work to do."

And he did. The problem was there wasn't much to work on. Everything in Alward's office that might have provided Mack with a clue had been removed. Not that he'd expected otherwise, but he was hoping they might have overlooked the Rolodex. More than likely there was a name and phone number in there that would give him a lead. Mack even got down on his hands and knees like Sherlock Holmes minus his magnifying glass. Holmes would have found a cigar ash, soil sample or footprint in the well-worn carpet to point him to the criminal, but the forensics had vacuumed up everything, even those things that only Holmes would have found significant, and taken it all to the police lab. The only thing they'd left behind were splotches of black fingerprint powder on the floor and woodwork.

After fifteen minutes on his knees and elbows Mack decided to forget the office and check out the fire escape and alley in case the investigators had missed anything there. He was on his way out of the front door when he almost collided with the rookie.

"Oops, sorry."

"No problem. Put my food on the desk. I'm going to have a look outside."

"Right. Oh, you got change. Three fifty-five."

"Leave it with the food."

"Want some help?"

"No thanks. You go ahead and eat. That tapeworm must be starved."

The rookie grinned as he unloaded sandwiches, fries and cups of coffee from a sack onto the reception desk. "Big time."

"I could use some light, though. Could I borrow your flash?"

"Sure." The rookie unclipped a flashlight from his belt and handed it to Mack. "And thanks again for the food."

"My pleasure."

Mack moved to the emergency door just outside Alward's office. He switched on the flashlight, exited to the third floor landing of the fire escape and panned the light around the landing. The beam revealed nothing but white pigeon excrement on the black iron grating. Mack scanned the stairs and the landings with the flashlight's beam, then descended the fire escape to the alley. An Orange Line train rumbled overhead on its way to Midway Airport while he searched the alley with the flashlight. The area was littered with broken bottles, empty beer cans and scattered trash, but nothing relating to the crime. There were tire tracks in one muddy area, but too many to be of help.

Mack was about to call it quits when the beam startled a big, gray tom cat scrounging for food. The cat let out a menacing hiss, took off down the alley and crouched under a dumpster in back of the Chicken Shack.

"Looking for supper, Ulysses?" Mack said. The cat, with its battle-scarred face and chewed up ears reminded Mack of his Greek warrior statue. The cat's response was a jungle howl. "Okay, my friend, I'll see what I can do."

Mack walked toward the dumpster. The cat seemed to understand and stayed put. Probably hung out there for scraps from cooks at the Chicken Shack, Mack figured. Opening the dumpster lid, Mack waved away a swarm of flies and bees and tried not to inhale its contents, as he shined the light inside. The dumpster was nearly full. Mack found the remains of some deep fried chicken, which he put on a soggy paper plate and laid next to the dumpster. "Not exactly gourmet, Ulysses, but it'll have to do." The cat licked his lips but remained under the dumpster.

Mack was about to close the lid when something caught his eye. He put the beam on it. "Alright!" A CD, half submerged in garbage. Mack reached in and pulled it out. He wiped the label off with a soiled paper napkin and shined the light on it. The label read: "PROCEDURE: HEART DISEASE: 593024." One of Alward's lab CDs, for sure. Mack found a stick and poked around in the garbage until he unearthed sixteen more CDs, all labeled with diagnoses or procedures relating to various diseases. He stuck them in his jacket pockets and probed one more time with the stick. This time he uncovered the fragment of a CD underneath a banana peel. The flash revealed part of a name on the label: "LAZ." Intrigued, Mack probed the refuse and finally came up with another greasy fragment. He fit the two together and shined the light on the now complete label. A single word: "LAZARUS."

Mack stared at the label: "Lazarus." What did it mean? Of course, there was the Biblical reference—the man Jesus raised from the dead. Did that have something to do with what was on the disc? Mack had a hunch that it did. But what? The answer wasn't in the other disks, of that Mack was certain, although he'd run them by Dr. Greg anyway, just to make sure.

Lazarus. Not much to go on, but more than he'd started the night with. "Thanks, Ulysses," he said, looking down at the shaggy warrior, who was now attacking the chicken scraps. While he watched the cat scarf down the food, he made two decisions. First, nothing was going to stop him from finding out what "Lazarus" meant. Second, he was about to adopt a street cat.

*1:14 a.m.:* Willie had been riding the Red Line subway for nearly an hour trying to think through a plan of action. In the army, when you were outnumbered and outflanked, you usually retreated, and that seemed like the best thing to do now. He had enough of a roll to finance a Greyhound Bus ticket to Gary. An army buddy of his—Malcolm what's his name—might stake him to a trip to St. Louis or points West, that is, if he could find Malcolm. Last time they'd connected he was flipping burgers at a Burger King on Broadway. And if he found Malcolm and got the stake, then what? Live off the street, no sweat there, until some smart-ass cop made him from the mug shot on a wanted bulletin.

The alternative to retreat was to advance against the enemy, hoping to do exactly what he least expected and kick ass. Or die in the attempt, of course. In any event, plan two meant staying in Chicago and helping the cop find out who'd done Frank and Needles. If he wound up in the Cook County lock-up facing a murder rap, at least he'd have McPherson covering his ass…he hoped.

When the train stopped at Belmont, Willie was tempted to get off, call McPherson and tell him…tell him what? What did he know other than the doc was running scared? Hell, the cop was smart enough to figure that out for himself.

Okay, so what did he know? There could have been something he'd seen while he was staking out the building that was stored away in his brain. As a scout sniper he was trained not only to work and survive behind enemy lines, but to collect tactical intelligence on his missions. This meant remembering tiny details of what he saw. A discarded tin can might mean something about food supplies or morale. A bunch of cans might suggest the size of the enemy force. Every little thing counted. So was there some little thing this time?

Willie closed his eyes and focused his mind on the scene outside the office building at around 9:00 p.m. He could see the doc exiting the building, walking to the Chicken Shack to order food. No one had entered the building after the doc had left, of that he was certain. Whoever did Needles could have come in earlier and hidden in the building, but Willie was betting that the killer or killers had come up the fire escape at the rear.

What else had he seen? Think, Willie, think! Shit! If there *was* something, he couldn't remember. Well, what could he expect after all the years on the street? He'd lost it, for fucking sure.

Wait a minute. The van! There was a van parked down the street about halfway between the office building and Harrison Street. A dark blue Dodge Caravan, beat up. Willie remembered the name on the side now. Drake's Heating & Cooling. No, not Drake's. Draper's. Yeah, that was it, Draper's. It was just sitting there at the curb. That's why Willie noticed it. That's why he watched it when it pulled away from the curb and paused for a moment outside the Chicken Shack before continuing to Balbo, where it turned west. And to where? Gone on its way to a job? Maybe. On the side under the name it said "24 HOUR SERVICE," so maybe the guys in the van were just taking a break between jobs. Maybe. Or maybe it pulled into the alley behind the office building to do another kind of job.

There had been two dudes in the van, or at least two Willie could see, since there were no rear windows. Willie had gotten a good look at the driver when the van passed by. A Latino for sure, and one mean-looking dude, with a Pancho Villa mustache and a long, jagged scar on his left cheek. Willie couldn't make out the guy in the passenger seat, because he was shielded by the driver.

Had those dudes killed the doc? Willie's gut was sending off some strong signals again, and they were saying yes. There was one way to make sure.

Willie exited the train at Hollywood, descended the stairway from the elevated platform to the street and hurried to a phone stand outside a White Hen convenience store down the block. He picked up a phone book dangling by a chain from the shelf and flipped through the soiled yellow pages until he found the listings for "Heating and Air Conditioning – Service and Repair.". His eyes scanned the alphabetically listed names beginning with "D"—Dave's HVAC Service, Deegan's Electric, Downtown Electric-Heating & Cooling, Dunbar Heating & Electrical. No Draper's.

Willie smiled. He dug McPherson's card from his wallet, inserted fifty cents into the phone slot and dialed. *Now* he had something to tell the cop!

*1:26 a.m.:* Mack slid behind the wheel of the Bonneville.

"Cool it, Ulysses," he said, and jerked his hand away just in time to avoid a swipe of the tom cat's left paw. Must be a southpaw, Mack thought with a chuckle, as he buckled up. He'd returned the rookie cop's flashlight and made a hasty meal of his burger and coffee, saving a scrap of meat for the tom. "Chow down, fella," he said, laying the scrap on the passenger seat. The cat wolfed it down with one bite. Mack was about to cook the engine when his cell beeped. He pulled it from his jacket pocket.

"McPherson."

It was Willie. Willie would make a damned good cop, Mack thought, while he listened to Willie tell him about the van and its Latino occupants.

"It's not much," Willie concluded, "but maybe it'll help."

"Hey, Willie. It's more than I had five minutes ago. Thanks. The Latinos are probably a professional hit team."

"Yeah, and also long gone by now."

"Maybe. And since I'm no longer working Homicide, there's not much I can do about it."

"Why not? Shit, man, you're a cop, right? So put out a wanted bulletin or somethin' on the van."

"Willie, for your information I got dumped to Special Victims by the brass. I won't go into the reasons, but the bottom line is that if they find out I'm sticking my nose into this or any other homicide case, I could be looking at a suspension or maybe even a career change."

"Man, that sucks."

"For sure. But I got a hunch that the guy you call Pancho and his buddy are still around to take care of business, in case anyone else like Frank and Alward get in the way of whatever's going down."

"You got any ideas just what that might be?"

"No, some leads, but I'll have to see where they take me."

"So what's the next move? I'm hot."

"Yeah, I know. How good are you at making yourself invisible?"

"Man, at that I'm an expert. The best place to do that is on the street. They'll be checkin' the shelters and transients, right?"

"Yeah. Look, Willie, I really appreciate your help, but you better keep out of this until it's over."

"Like shit! My ass is on the line. Besides, I got lots of contacts on the street. They can be your eyes and ears, if you need 'em, starting with lookin' for Pancho and that van."

"Okay. Put out the word. How are you fixed for cash?"

"I got a few bucks but not enough to pass around if I want to buy information."

"I can get you two, maybe three C's. Will that do?"

"Make it five, and in small bills. So how do we do this?"

"Let's see. I've got to go to my bank to draw out the money, so it's got to be Monday morning. Give me a place and a time."

"How about Lower Wacker, the south branch. Come down the Monroe Street ramp and get into the delivery lane. I'll flag you down. What are you drivin'?"

"A dark green Bonneville SSE. I'll blink my headlights. Is ten o'clock okay? That'll give me time to get to the bank."

"Ten's fine. See you then, Monday morning."

"Right. And Willie...stay invisible."

"For fucking sure."

Mack fingered the off button and fired up the engine. He was thinking that Willie could be conning him for some easy traveling money to places far away. Could be, but Willie had come through so far, and Mack was betting he'd do it again. In any event, it was worth five C-notes to find out.

"Fasten your seat belt, Ulysses," he said to the cat, then revved the engine and pulled away from the curb.

Halfway down the block, two men in a dark blue Ford Taurus watched the Bonneville take off down the street.

"Let's move," the man in the passenger seat said. Late thirties, just over six feet and trim, he sat upright, displaying a military posture, with a stern, square-jawed face sporting a dark, Clark Gable mustache and crew cut.

"Why bother?" the man behind the wheel said with a Tennessee twang, as he churned the engine to life. He was shorter than the other man and bulkier, although the bulk was all muscle. The freckles splotching his ruddy face matched the red-rust tangle of his short, curly hair. "We know he's goin' home."

"Just do it."

"Yes, sir, General, sir," the driver said through a mouthful of chewing tobacco. He gunned the Taurus after the SSE, which was turning west at Balbo.

"Cut the comedy, Rusty," the other man said, using the driver's nickname. "We stay glued to his ass until we're told otherwise."

"Yeah, well why not check in with the boss and see if we can call it a night. I'm fuckin' beat."

"Hey, watch it!" the other man said, referring to a tire-screeching turn the driver made at Balbo.

"I told you I was beat."

"So am I, but we don't need a cop pulling us over for a DUI test."

"Speaking of booze, I could sure use a drink. When this is over, I'm gonna go back to Nashville, hit a bar where they got some live Country Western, and get totally shit-faced."

The other man couldn't care less what Rusty did, and said so. Ahead they saw the Bonneville pass State Street and turn north on Dearborn.

"Looks like he could be heading for home, alright," he said.

"So make the call, okay?"

The man in the passenger seat removed a cell phone from the coat pocket of his charcoal suit and speed-dialed a number. A voice answered after two rings. "This is Gallagher. The cop just left the crime scene. What are your instructions?" Listens. "Yes, sir," he said, and beeped off.

The driver turned onto Dearborn, this time without abusing the tires. "So?"

"So we stay with him, just to make sure."

"Shit. Now tell me we got to spend the night staking out his place."

"No need. But we have to be back on the job at seven."

"Well at least that's something."

"Maybe you'd rather be pulling phone tap duty?"

"And miss all the action? No way."

"Then shut up and drive."

"Yes, sir, General, sir," Rusty said, and spat out the window.

## *Monday, May 20*

*8:23 a.m.:* Mack found Dr. Greg in the cafeteria at the Cook County Morgue having breakfast.

"What now, my friend?" the pathologist said, while spooning mouthfuls of granola topped with strawberries into his mouth.

Mack laid a small cardboard box on the table next to a steaming mug of coffee. "Got some CDs for some patients' diseases I want you to check out."

Dr. Greg gave him a sly smile. "They wouldn't happen to be the property of the recently deceased Dr. Alward, would they?"

"Either you're psychic or someone at the CPD has been whispering in your ear."

"I have my sources," Dr. Greg said. "What are you looking for?"

"Damned if I know. Anything you find unusual about the various patients' ailments and treatments. When can you get back to me?"

"Let's see," Dr. Greg said, glancing at his wrist watch. "I've got some time between cadavers this morning. Give me a call around noon."

"Will do. And thanks again, Greg."

"Don't mention it. And don't forget that you still owe me for the stiff who wasn't there."

"Got a memory like an elephant," Mack said with a grin.

*9:05 a.m.:* Otis found Commander Cronin chomping on the stub of an extinct cigar when he entered his office.

"What are you doing here, Otis? This is your day off, isn't it?"

"Yeah," Otis said a little nervously. "I plan to do a little fishing, but…well, I'd like to make a request."

"Go ahead."

"I'd like for you to assign another detective to me as a partner."

Cronin's reaction to this was to clench the cigar stub even tighter.

"No way, Otis, unless you have a specific complaint."

What could Otis say? If he blew the whistle on Mack, his partner could be looking at a suspension or worse.

"No. It's just that we aren't exactly what you could call compatible."

Cronin shook his head. "Sorry, Otis. No one else is complaining about their partners, and I'm not about to make waves by reshuffling the deck to accommodate you. You can understand that, can't you?"

"Yes, Lieutenant, but…"

"No buts. That's the way it is."

Cronin rose and came around from behind his cluttered desk. "Look, Otis. I know where you're coming from on this, and I sympathize. Mack's not the easiest guy to be teamed with. But it won't be forever. If he plays by the rules, he'll be back on Homicide in a couple of months." Pause, and a searching look. "He *has* been playing by the rules, hasn't he?"

"Yes," said Otis, trying hard to look sincere and honest and keep a straight face.

"Good. Give it a couple more months, and I'll call the super myself to recommend his transfer."

"Thanks, Lieutenant. I appreciate it."

"Good," Cronin said, clapping Otis on the shoulder. "Now get outta here and enjoy your day off before I put you to work."

*10:05 a.m.:* Mack drove down the ramp to Lower Wacker at Randolph Street and got into the delivery lane, headlights blinking. On the passenger seat was a large manila envelope containing five hundred dollars in fives and tens he'd withdrawn from his bank after seeing Dr. Greg. Willie stepped out from behind a pillar near the Monroe Street ramp and flagged him down. Mack gave him the envelope and told him to stay in touch.

*10:33 a.m.:* Mack entered a large room at the Illinois State Crime Lab, where all the evidence in criminal investigations was examined and stored. Detectives and forensics were busy examining everything from fingerprints on weapons to DNA specimens taken from the bodies of murder victims. Mack was interested in only one item—Dr. Alward's Rolodex, which he requested from Sergeant Cary Rhodes, the detective in charge of the lab, whom Mack knew from his many previous visits.

Sergeant Rhodes returned with the Rolodex after a few minutes and set it on a table. "I shouldn't be doing this. If the brass finds out, I'm screwed."

"They won't unless you tell them," Mack said, taking a seat at the table. He had already given him his b.s. story about a missing person he was looking for who was one of Alward's patients and that the Rolodex might give him a lead. Whether the sergeant believed him or not was another matter.

A rangy man in his fifties, Rhodes ran his hand over a thinning crop of grey hair. "I'm giving you fifteen minutes, Mack, then you're outta here, okay?"

"Fair enough, Cary. And thanks."

The sergeant grunted and moved off. Probably sweating his deferred comp, Mack figured, which would be kicking in soon. Who could blame him?

It didn't take long for Mack to flip through the cards on the Rolodex. There weren't that many. There was the Beacon Mission and a variety of other innocuous names that included a CPA, bank, auto agency, computer help number for Hewlett Packard, Earthlink's help number, a medical equipment company, dentist, cleaners, real estate agent and a furniture rental company. However, the names on two cards did get his attention. One was Patricia Bolles with a New York City phone number, easily identified by the familiar 212 area code. A sister, perhaps a lady friend, Mack figured, jotting the name and number down in his notebook. He'd check it out but didn't expect that it would be significant.

The other card was much more intriguing. The name on the card was "BIO-SCI." There was nothing particularly unusual about Alward having a card for his former employer. He was probably still close to somebody at the company, which would account for the three phone numbers. 847-438-7100 looked like the main Bio-Sci number; the second, 847-438-7221, probably belonged to someone in the company. The third, 438-436-5544, was more likely a cell phone number, since it didn't have the same 847 area code as the other numbers. The number for the friend at the company he was still in contact with? Probably, but still not unusual. For Mack it was the rest of the information on the card that started his adrenalin pumping again. There were three names: "MICROBE438," "JESUS551" and "LORD552." "JESUS551" was X'd out.

Code? Or more likely passwords for a computer. "Microbe" had nothing to do with the other two names, but "Jesus" and "Lord" could relate to "Lazarus," since it was Jesus who raised Lazarus from the dead. Mack slipped the card into his pocket, remembering now what Alward had told him when he'd asked about

Frank: he had a memory problem when it came to names. Thank God for that, Mack thought, because now he had what could be the key to finding out what Lazarus was all about. He also had a strong suspicion that whatever door that key opened would be at Bio-Sci.

*12:17 p.m.:* Mack was sitting at the bar at Stacy's Restaurant washing down a tuna salad with swigs from a bottle of Amstel Light. A good time to catch up on some phone calls. The first was to Dr. Greg. Had he had a chance to examine Alward's lab CDs? He had. Nothing unusual. All were related to Alward's patients and their various diseases.

Mack thanked Dr. Greg and made his second call, this one to Patricia Bolles in New York. A man answered. Mack identified himself and asked to speak to Patricia. The man informed him that he was John Bolles, Patricia's husband, and if the call was related to her brother's murder. It was. Bolles said that a detective had already informed them about the murder, and that he and his wife were flying to Chicago in the morning. Could any questions wait until then? His wife was very distraught and was resting. Yes, the questions could wait.

The fact was that Mack's questions had already been answered. Patricia Bolles was Alward's sister. Mack was also aware that Sergeant Greiner had found her card in Alward's Rolodex and followed up. Good cop, Greiner. The Bio-Sci card would not have escaped Greiner's attention either, but Mack was betting that he would not attach any importance to it. Greiner's focus would be on Alward's charity patients, and especially Willie.

Mack's third call was to what he believed to be the cell number. After two beeps a man's voice answered.

"Kischman."

Mack pressed the end button, then dialed 847-438-7221, figuring that 7221 would be the extension to someone else with Bio-Sci. What he got was a voice saying that the line had been disconnected. Mack beeped off and dialed what looked like the main Bio-Sci number.

"Bio-Sci Research and Development, Arlene speaking. How may I direct your call?"

Mack asked who Dr. Kischman was, and was informed that he was the Director of Research. Did Mack wish to speak with him?

"Perhaps later," Mack said. "Actually, I'd like to speak with your CEO."

"That would be Mr. O'Neal. I'll connect you with his secretary. One moment, please."

Another female voice answered in a few seconds. "Mr. O'Neal's office, Glenda speaking."

"This is Detective McPherson. I'd like to speak with Mr. O'Neal."

"I'm sorry, Detective, but he's on a conference call. Is this regarding Dr. Alward?" Mack told her it was. "Is this important? Mr. O'Neal has already talked with a detective. A Sergeant Greiner. He was here this morning."

"I know, but there's been some new developments in the case, and I was hoping that Mr. O'Neal could be of some help. Can you see if he has some time to see me this afternoon?"

"Could you hold on a moment?"

"Sure."

Mack had time to order the strawberry cheesecake and a cup of coffee while he waited for Glenda to get an answer from her boss. It took over a minute before she was back on the line.

"Mr. O'Neal could see you at three if that's convenient."

It was, Mack told her, and got the directions to Bio-Sci's location in the northwest suburb of Schaumburg before thanking her for her help. As he beeped off, Mack was hoping that O'Neal was indeed a busy man, too busy to put in a phone call to Greiner to check out Mack's phony story. If he did, Mack could look forward to another and even more unpleasant visit to the Hawk's fifth-floor lair at 1121 South State.

*12:52 p.m.:* Otis watched the bobber dancing in the ripples. The trend of the day's events continues, he thought. It had gotten off to a lousy start at 7:00 a.m., when he heard the front door close over the buzz of his electric shaver. Ava was off for her usual three-mile jog before he had a chance to give her a kiss and wish her a good day. Then the visit to Cronin's office, which had got him nowhere. Now he'd been fishing for three hours and all he'd caught as a keeper was an eight-inch bluegill. Fishing usually helped him to relax and forget his troubles, but the fact that he still had Mack as a partner was preying on his mind. He couldn't stop wondering what Mack was up to, what he'd been doing since Saturday night when Alward was killed. And he couldn't stop worrying about when the next bomb would go off, as it surely would if Mack kept imagining that there were sinister goings-on and vast conspiracies behind every event for which a simpler, more logical explanation existed. Well, at least the weather had cooperated. The sky was a brilliant azure blue adorned with lazy cotton candy cumuli.

Parked at the tip of one of the long, narrow peninsulas that extended like fingers into Wolf Lake, he tried to ignore the constant drone of heavy traffic on Interstate 90 that dissected the lake into two interconnected segments. Not exactly a scene of unspoiled pastoral beauty, like The Dells, Otis acknowledged. Part of the east segment was bordered by a small town, Robertsdale, Indiana, but too much of it by industry with smokestacks belching white clouds of pollution. High tension wires supported by huge electric towers hovering over the lake did nothing to enhance the ambiance.

Otis was fishing the shallow water on the west side of the lake along with a few other anglers on the peninsulas and shoreline. Here the shores belonged mostly to Mother Nature, all trees and undergrowth, except for a few campers. An old man and young boy were fishing a few yards away, the man showing the boy how to bait a hook with a worm and then cast. They reminded Otis of his dad and himself years ago, and seemed to be having better luck than he was.

His bad luck continued when he pulled up his line to discover that his worm had been stripped from the hook without even a jiggle of the bobber. Probably a little perch, Otis thought. He reached into the can of worms and extracted one from the damp moss. His plan to have lunch with his mom hadn't worked out either. She had a full day with two housecleaning jobs in Merrillville and another in Crown Point, so Otis would have to cook whatever he caught on the RV's electric range. However, the way things were going, he'd more likely be lunching at one of the fast food joints on Indianapolis Boulevard.

Otis impaled the worm on the hook and cast again. Although he tried to concentrate on the bobber, his mind kept returning to Mack. Two months, Cronin said, and he'd try to get Mack transferred. It might as well be two years, even if the superintendent signed off on it. Otis sighed. No guarantees there, either.

Being preoccupied, Otis didn't react right away when the bobber suddenly submerged. As he yanked up the pole, he felt the hook snag its victim, and judging by the tug on the line, it was no minnow. About time, he thought, working the fish. He let out enough slack so the fish wouldn't break the line, then reeled him closer to the shoreline.

"Looks like you got a whopper there," the old man said.

"Can I see?" the little boy said excitedly.

"Sure. In fact, I can use some help."

"Can I, Grandpa?"

"If he says so."

The little boy ran over. "What do I do?"

"This guy's too big to bring in without a landing net. There's one by my tackle box. Will you get it?"

"Sure."

The little boy grabbed the long handle of the net and came back. "Now what?"

"When I get him near the shore, you get to scoop him up, if you don't mind getting your feet wet."

"Heck, no."

The little boy, who was wearing short pants and no socks, quickly pulled off his grimy Keds.

"Get ready, now," Otis said, reeling the fish closer.

The little boy gripped the handle with both hands like a Samurai hefting his sword to do battle. "Now?"

"Now."

The little boy waded a few feet into the water. It took him three tries to get the fish into the net. Struggling under the weight but beaming with pride, he waded ashore with his captive flopping in the net.

"Ooohh! Look how big it is, Grandpa!"

"It's big all right, Jimmy. Must weigh as much as you do."

"Can I keep it, mister? Can I?"

"Sure. There are lots more where he came from."

"Grandpa, Grandpa! I get to keep it. We can have it for supper. There's plenty for everybody!"

Otis exchanged smiles with the old man. They both knew that carp was not an item you'd find on any fish menu. The old man explained to Jimmy that carp was not a good fish to eat. They were sucker fish, bottom feeders.

The boy's face sagged with disappointment. "Does that make them taste bad?"

"I'm afraid so, Jimmy."

"Then what do we do with it, Grandpa?"

"Let's let the man who caught it decide."

Jimmy extended the net and catch to Otis. "Here, mister."

"Sorry, Jimmy," Otis said, lifting the fish out of the net. Fortunately, the fish hadn't swallowed the hook. He removed the hook from the carp's gaping mouth and threw him into the water.

"There he goes," the little boy said. "I still wish we coulda' kept it, Grandpa."

"Don't worry, Jimmy. You'll catch something that big, something we can eat, like a bass. You just gotta keep trying."

Good advice, Otis thought with a smile. Watching the boy and his granddad move to their fishing poles and cast their lines, he remembered how thrilled he was when he caught his first big fish. It was a twelve pound bass, not huge, but to him it seemed like a monster. Before his dad cleaned it for supper, his mom took a picture of him, fishing pole in one hand, the other hand proudly displaying the bass on a stringer, a triumphant grin on his face. It was a fish that he almost didn't catch. They'd fished all day with little to show for their efforts. Otis was discouraged and wanted to go home to watch TV. His dad persuaded him to make one more cast. Maybe something would happen. It did.

Otis had put the snapshot in a little frame. He had kept it on the dresser in his bedroom as a reminder to hang in there and not give up when things looked bad. He still had the picture. It now resided on the wall of his den with the collage of other pictures and memorabilia, now enlarged and professionally framed, but conveying the same message. Given his current problems, it was a message Otis knew he had to focus on. Perhaps now more than ever.

*2:50 p.m.:* Mack exited the Tollway at Roselle Road. Heading south, he waited for the green at Commerce Drive, the second intersection off the expressway, and hung a left. Commerce Drive meandered past a variety of companies—E Commerce, Mitsubishi, Jewels by Park Lane, Omron and others Mack had never heard of but which all had one thing in common: immaculately landscaped exteriors.

Bio-Sci Research & Development, Inc., its name imbedded in bronze letters on a slab of marble, was no exception. A pole supporting a large American flag was surrounded by a colorful collage of flowers. Sculptured juniper bushes and rows of transplanted spruce trees enhanced the manicured lawn. A geyser of water gushed from a pond occupied by two white swans. Mack spotted some floodlights strategically placed to illuminate the area at night, both to impress and to provide security. Mack had no doubt that the building and grounds were covered by surveillance cameras and motion alarms.

Mack swung the Bonneville into a parking lot lined with light poles at the east side of the building. A sign identified "EMPLOYEE PARKING. VISITOR PARKING IN REAR LOT." Mack slowed the SSE to take in the two buildings connected by a passageway. Judging from the many wide, tinted windows in the two stories of white concrete, the front building obviously housed Bio-Sci's offices. The larger building to the rear had to be the research area. There was a fire escape with emergency exits but no windows.

Driving around to the back lot, Mack saw two workers unloading crates from a truck at one of the two loading docks under the vigilant eyes of a uniformed security guard. Mack nudged the Bonneville into a parking space, exited, walked around to the front of the building and entered into a plush reception area—potted plants, wall to wall carpets overlaid by Oriental rugs, soothing pastoral paintings, expensive looking contemporary furniture. An attractive, well groomed young lady behind a desk greeted him with a smile as bright as the incandescent ceiling lights. The name on her desk plaque read: "Arlene French." Mack was expected.

"Detective McPherson?"

"Yes."

"I'll inform Mr. O'Neal's secretary that you're here. Would you please sign the visitors' register?"

"Sure."

While Miss French phoned, Mack signed his name and the time of arrival, noting that Sergeant Greiner had made his visit at 10:15 a.m.

"Mr. O'Neal will be with you shortly. Would you like to take a seat?"

Mack settled into a comfortable chair and spent five minutes scanning the financial section of today's *Wall Street Journal* that was on an end table with a few magazines. The Dow Industrial Average had moved up 56 points on Friday, he noted. Good news for his deferred compensation plan with Pebsco, which was allocated among a variety of mutual funds. This meant market risk, which Mack was willing to take, since his pension fund with the State of Illinois involved no risk. Well not exactly, Mack conceded. If he lost his badge, he'd blow the pension, and he was risking that possibility now with his unauthorized investigation. Too late to worry about that, he thought, and was just starting to read the market commentary when a tall, slim young lady in a classy-looking coral pantsuit approached, moving like a runway model. She also had a model's striking face with soft curled, brunette shoulder-length hair. Mack wondered if she was as efficient as she was beautiful, or if her boss was more interested in her obvious physical attributes.

"Good afternoon, Detective McPherson. I'm Glenda Ellison, Mr. O'Neal's secretary. Mr. O'Neal apologizes for the delay but can see you now. If you'll follow me…"

Mack did. He managed to pry his eyes off Miss Ellison's beguiling buns long enough to take in the large room they passed through, where numerous employees were busy in cubicles. Arriving at two elevators, Miss Ellison fingered the button of the elevator marked "PRIVATE." The door parted immediately, and the elevator lifted them to the second floor and Miss Ellison's office, a mini version of the reception area.

"Go right in, Detective," she said, gesturing to the open door with O'Neal's name and title stenciled on a bronze plaque.

Mack thanked her and entered the CEO's inner sanctum, a spacious office with a view of the pond and fountain through tinted letterbox windows. Everything from the mahogany conference table and eight chairs at one end of the room to O'Neal's sprawling desk with a computer workstation at the other looked like the best that corporate money could buy. In between was a wet bar, liquor cabinet and glass-topped coffee table surrounded by leather chairs designed for comfort. A large portrait of a gray-haired man dominated the rear interior wall amidst a variety of framed photographs. Other photos and a number of golf trophies resided on shelves and a credenza. The CEO himself was not present.

As Mack waited for O'Neal, he scanned some of the photos. His gaze was drawn to one of a striking teenaged girl. She was sitting on an improvised throne, wearing a pink, strapless formal, a corsage on one wrist and a crown on her head. Long, dark brown hair spilled over her bare shoulders. Beautiful as she was, it was her dark, almost luminous eyes that really stood out. Handing the queen a scepter was a handsome, blond-haired boy in a tux with a white coat. Nearby was a picture of the same boy, but now a young man, again garbed in a tux, this time with a morning coat. He was posing for a wedding picture with his bride, not the prom queen but a radiant looking brunette in a strapless, white dress that accentuated her slim figure. Mack was wondering if O'Neal's wife resented sharing the wall with a picture of his high school sweetheart when he heard a man's voice.

"In here, Detective."

Mack followed the sound of the voice through an open doorway into a smaller room that was filled with a variety of exercise equipment.

"Be with you in a minute, Detective," the man said without looking up from a golf ball on a tee that protruded from a green mat. He lifted a driver over his right shoulder, swung and sent the ball thumping against a large screen that showed a computer graphic fairway. Virtual reality now took over. On the screen a surreal golf ball soared high into the air and landed in the middle of the fairway. A panel in the upper left corner of the screen informed that the ball had traveled 125 yards and was now 47 yards from the green.

Mack was impressed, not only with the golf simulator—he'd heard of these, but never seen one—but with Roy O'Neal's expertise with a driver. The trophies were obviously for real. Mack dabbled at the sport from time to time, but was too impatient to get within range of a respectable handicap.

"Good shot."

"Thanks," O'Neal said. He placed the driver in a rack of clubs and removed a pitching wedge. "This gives me a chance to stay in touch with the game. Don't have much time to get out on a real course or work out at an athletic club, so I decided to bring them to me."

"So I see," Mack said. Judging from the sweat-soaked back of O'Neal's Fila sports attire, Mack figured he'd spent some time on the treadmill or rowing machine before teeing off for a few holes of golf. There were also a Universal station and a rack of weights to address his upper torso. A sports coat, casual shirt and slacks dangled from a clothes rack, loafers and socks underneath. Through a glass door Mack could see part of a shower stall and steam room.

"Quite a layout you've got here."

"It'll do," O'Neal said. He gestured to a computer keyboard on a stand next to the mat. "I can choose the course I want to play with the press of a button. This is one of my favorites, Pebble Beach." He retrieved the golf ball and placed it on the mat. "Of course, it's not like the real thing. You tend to hit the ball too hard on a simulator."

Mack watched O'Neal make an excellent approach shot that sent the computer ball to within a few feet of the pin. The CEO looked in great shape for a man on the near side of middle age, which Mack guessed by the white streaks infiltrating his styled, blond hair. Otherwise, O'Neal's narrow, earnest-looking face showed the same youthful exuberance as the ones in the pictures with only a hint of crow's feet fanning out from the corners of intense, sky blue eyes. Short, about 5'5" Mack estimated, and trim, O'Neal reminded Mack of Alan Ladd in *Shane*, except that O'Neal was gripping the wedge instead of a Colt 45.

"Mind if I finish up here?" O'Neal said, exchanging the wedge for a putter.

"Not at all. Play out the hole."

"Putting is the toughest part with a simulator. It's more like a chip shot, because you have to lift the ball off the ground to hit the screen. More often than not you overshoot the cup, but here goes."

After a couple of practice strokes, O'Neal lobbed the ball against the bottom of the screen. Mack watched the surreal ball roll to the cup and drop.

"A birdie! I'll take it!" O'Neal said, grinning. He racked the putter, removed a hand towel from a shelf and draped it over his shoulder. "Let's go into the office. I'll shower later."

O'Neal waved Mack into one of the leather chairs at the coffee table, as he moved to the wet bar. "Make yourself comfortable. Would you like a drink? I'm having ginger ale."

"Sounds good," Mack said, sinking into soft leather.

O'Neal removed a bottle of Schweppes from a small refrigerator. "Good for the stomach, ginger ale." He filled two tumblers. "Ice?"

"No thanks."

O'Neal handed Mack a gold rimmed tumbler adorned with "Bio-Sci" in gold letters. "Good health," he said, and raised the tumbler.

They drank to it.

O'Neal settled into a chair opposite Mack. "My secretary told me you have other information regarding Dr. Alward's murder."

"That's right."

O'Neal took a drink from the tumbler, then mopped perspiration from his forehead with the towel. "I don't know what I can add to what I told Sergeant Greiner this morning."

"Which was?"

Furrowed brows from O'Neal. "You haven't talked to him? I assumed you were working together."

Mack took a pull at the ginger ale before answering. The dramatic pause which actors used before they delivered the punch line. It worked for cops, too. "No. I'm on another case, but the two could be related. A former patient of Dr. Alward's who drowned in Diversey Harbor."

Mack studied O'Neal's face. Nothing but a perplexed frown.

"What does that have to do with Dr. Alward's murder? According to what I've heard on the news, the police believe that one of Award's charity patients committed the murder for drugs."

"Could be, but I'm betting there's more to it than that. What can you tell me about Dr. Alward?"

"Not a lot other than he was a valued employee. Brilliant, in fact. I hated to lose him."

"You didn't know him personally, then?"

"No, although I make it a point to try to get to know my employees, no matter what their jobs are." O'Neal paused to take another sip of ginger ale. "Loyalty is something I cultivate with my people, not only by providing more than generous wages, medical and retirement benefits, but by simply showing I care about them. In a way, I look at them more as family than just employees. Alward...well, he kept pretty much to himself."

"A loner?"

"I suppose you could say so."

"Do you know if he had any friends here?"

"No. Well, that is, other than Dr. Kischman. He's my director of research."

"Would you say they were close friends?"

"You'll have to ask Dr. Kischman about that. All I know is that it was Kischman who convinced Alward to leave Abbott Labs and work for us. I believe they knew each other when Kischman was teaching at Harvard Medical School."

"Could you arrange for me to talk to him?"

"Of course."

O'Neal rose from his chair and moved to his desk, where he fingered a number on his phone.

Glenda's voice issued from a small speaker. "Yes, Mr. O'Neal?"

"Glenda, ask Diane to meet Detective McPherson at the reception desk.

He'd like to ask Dr. Kischman a few questions."

"Yes, sir."

"Diane, Diane Bates, is Dr. Kischman's assistant. She'll get you through security into the lab."

Mack finished his ginger ale with one swallow and rose. "Thanks. I appreciate your cooperation."

"Glad to be of help."

As Mack set down the tumbler on the wet bar, he looked up at the portrait of the gray-haired man, now observing that the face creased with wrinkles bore a strong resemblance to O'Neal's. "Your father?"

"Yes, and the founder of Bio-Sci. Quite a guy. Served in World War II as a specialist in chemical warfare, then used a GI loan after his discharge to go into business. Would you believe that he started Bio-Sci in his garage with only three employees? Three employees and a dream."

"Looks like his dream came true."

O'Neal gazed reverently at the portrait. "No, not yet, because the dream is ongoing, perhaps never fully realized until cures for all the deadly diseases that plague mankind are developed."

Watching O'Neal look up at his father, Mack now saw more than love and admiration in his eyes. He saw purpose, dedication, an unyielding commitment that Mack guessed went beyond boosting the net worth of himself and his stockholders. Mack decided to do some fishing.

"I guess you got some pretty big projects going here."

"Yes, we do."

"For instance...or can you discuss them?"

O'Neal smiled. "Absolutely. We're a publicly held company, Detective, which means full disclosure to stockholders. For example, we're working on drugs to arrest cancer and viruses that cause such diseases as AIDS and hepatitis B and C. And we're developing an anthrax vaccine that, based on preliminary testing in mice, may be more effective than the one that's currently available."

"That could be big, given what's going on in the world."

"Very big. Homeland Security is looking over our shoulder on this one."

"So, I assume, are your competitors."

O'Neal caught his drift. "You can say that again. At Bio-Sci security is as important as research. You'd be surprised how much thievery goes on in this business. Which is another reason I want to know my employees. Every one of them has had a thorough background check by Global Security Services."

Mack knew Global Security. It was one of the top security companies in the country, with corporate theft only one of its services. Mack figured that the security guards were also GSS people. He also figured he was not going to get anything more about Alward from O'Neal."

"Well, thanks again, Mr. O'Neal," he said, rising. "I appreciate you seeing me."

"Sorry I couldn't have been of more help. Good luck on your investigation."

They shook hands, and Mack exited. A likeable guy, Mack thought, as he rode the elevator to the ground floor. If something was going on here that wasn't on the up-and-up, maybe O'Neal doesn't know about it. Not likely, though. O'Neal impressed Mack as a hands-on CEO, which might include Miss Ellison, he thought with a smile. On second thought, no way. Not in character. Hadn't

Alan Ladd played it straight with Van Heflin's wife in *Shane*?

Mack exited the elevator and moved toward the reception desk, where a lady in a white lab jacket was waiting. Diane Bates, Mack assumed. He'd struck out with Roy O'Neal, Mack thought, but maybe he'd have better luck with his director of research. If not, he'd have to start looking elsewhere for an answer to Frank's and Alward's deaths. However, at the moment, he had no idea where that might be.

"Good morning, Detective McPherson," Diane Bates greeted him. "Dr. Kischman can only spare you a few minutes. He's extremely busy today—not that he's not busy every day—but there's an important project we hope to complete soon." She spoke in a quiet voice as they proceeded along the passageway that connected the office and research buildings.

"I understand," Mack said, noting the security cameras near the ceiling that covered the corridor. "I only have a few questions. It won't take long."

"This is Detective McPherson, Jim," Diane said to a uniformed guard, who stepped out of a small security station at the end of the corridor. "He has Mr. O'Neal's permission to enter the research area."

"Could I please see some ID, Detective?" the guard said politely.

"Sure." Mack handed his wallet with his badge and photo ID to the guard, who scrutinized it, then looked up at Mack to make sure that his face matched the one on the ID. Good man, the guard, Mack thought. On the ball. GSS for sure, and probably a former Marine or Special Forces vet, judging by his sturdy frame and a patch over one eye that had probably seen more than Mack wanted to know about.

The guard returned the wallet. "Thank you, sir. Just push the buzzer and identify yourself on the speaker when you want to exit. The door doesn't open unless I activate it," he said, referring to the heavy iron door confronting them.

"Right."

The guard entered the station, which contained a bank of monitors—an appendage to the main security center, Mack figured—and pushed a button on a control panel. The door slid open like an elevator door.

Mack followed Diane Bates into a room that reminded Mack of his high school chemistry classroom, except that it was at least twenty times as large. Absorbed in their work, white jacketed techies didn't even look up from their microscopes, test tubes and computers as Mack and Diane moved along an aisle between work tables. Mack observed that, unlike cops in the squad room, there was little conversation among the worker bees other than what seemed to relate to their projects.

"There's Dr. Kischman," Diane said.

Ahead, a heavy-set man of medium height was looking over the shoulder of a young lady techie who was feeding data into a computer.

"Good work, Nancy. Very good work. Keep at it. I'll be back later to review it."

"Yes, doctor," the techie said, obviously pleased with the doctor's compliment and the fatherly pat on her shoulder.

The doctor started to move to another workstation when he saw Diane and Mack approaching. "Ah, Detective McPherson," he said before Diane could introduce him. "Mr. O'Neal said you had some questions about Dr. Alward."

Mack detected a slight German accent and a hint of condescension in the voice of a man whom Mack judged to be in his early fifties.

"That's right," Mack replied, holding out his hand, which was taken briefly by Kischman, then released as if he were throwing away a used paper towel. "I appreciate you giving me a few minutes, Doctor. I know you have a lot going on here."

"That's a very accurate observation, Detective." Removing reading glasses from a prominent Roman nose, he massaged the furrows in a long forehead that sloped up to a receding hairline of wavy dark brown hair streaked with gray. "So much going on that I'm afraid I'm guilty of neglecting my home life."

"I keep telling him to give himself more leisure time," Diane scolded. "He works too hard. Much too hard."

Kischman's terse lips formed a weary smile. "Good advice that I don't seem to appreciate. But I do. Diane is more than my very efficient assistant." Kischman gave her arm a little affectionate squeeze. "Among other tasks that are not part of her job, she takes my blood pressure regularly and makes sure I eat a healthy lunch."

"When I stand over him and make him do it," Diane said.

Mack wondered if there was more going on between Kischman and Diane than gratitude on Kischman's part and what he saw as adulation from his Girl Friday. Not so unusual. Kischman was more distinguished looking than handsome, like a senior statesman; and Diane, although a little plump, was not unattractive. A few hours a week on a treadmill and more frequent visits to a beauty parlor might morph her into a pretty decent looker, Mack thought, taking in her freckled, thin-lipped face with minimal cosmetics and light brown hair imprisoned in a bun.

"Mind if I have a cup of coffee while we talk?" Kischman said.

"Fine by me."

Mack followed Kischman and Diane across the room, observing en route a door marked "AUTHORIZED PERSONNEL ONLY." A techie was accessing entry by placing the palm of his right hand on a small screen next to the door.

Mack gestured toward the door. "What's in there, Doctor, if you don't mind my asking?"

"In there? That's where Socrates lives," he said with a sly smile.

"Socrates?"

"That's what we call it. It's our brain, so to speak, the mainframe where all the research data is stored and analyzed."

"Socrates. Good name."

They entered an employee's lounge that, like everything else at Bio-Sci, was first-class. No plastic furniture here, but sturdy oak tables and cushioned chairs. Stretching between a refrigerator and a soft drink dispenser was an oak storage cabinet and counter with a stainless steel sink, hot/cold water filter, coffee station and microwave. Since there were no windows, the walls were covered by a variety of large pastoral murals which conveyed a relaxing atmosphere.

"Why don't you go ahead and talk, Doctor," Diane said. "I'll get the coffee. Would you like some, Detective?"

"Yes, thanks. Black with some sweetener."

Mack and Kischman settled into chairs. "We were all saddened about Dr. Alward's death, Detective. Saddened and shocked, given the tragic circumstances. A terrible thing. Terrible."

"Mr. O'Neal said that you knew Alward before he came to Bio-Sci. That you were his professor at Harvard Medical School."

"That's correct. I was his professor and perhaps something of a mentor as well. Alward was a brilliant student with a great future in biochemistry. I was, of course, delighted when he accepted my offer to work for Bio-Sci."

"Given that Alward and you go back a few years, I guess you got to know him pretty well."

Kischman shrugged and ran an index finger over the bridge of his Roman nose. "Professionally, yes. Personally, not really. You see…Oh, thank you, Diane."

Diane Bates set cups of coffee in front of Mack and Kischman, then took a seat beside her boss with a cup of tea. "Only one cup, doctor."

"Diane also monitors my caffeine intake, Detective," Kischman said as he patted her hand and gave her a kindly smile, which she gratefully returned. "As I was saying, I didn't know much about Alward's private life. He was, well, a solitary man. Kept his feelings to himself. At least he didn't confide them to me."

Mack took a sip of coffee and turned to Diane. "How about you, Miss Bates?"

Diane looked up from the tea bag she was removing from her cup, as if surprised by the question. "About me?"

"Yes. Some men are more comfortable talking to women about their problems than men."

Diane carefully lowered the dripping tea bag onto her saucer. "That's true, but I'm afraid Dr. Alward wasn't one of them."

"Too bad. I was hoping to turn up something in Alward's private life that would tie in with his murder."

Kischman and Diane exchanged looks. "Wasn't he killed by one of his charity patients?" Diane said. "I was listening to the news as I drove to work this morning. They said the suspect was probably a drug addict who the doctor caught robbing his office."

"That's the logical conclusion, but we won't know for sure until we have a suspect in custody. Maybe you can clear up something I'm curious about, and that's why a genius like Alward would leave a job where he had to be making good money to set himself up in a low rent office as a doctor for vagrants."

"I believe I can answer that, Detective," Kischman said. He paused to take a long sip of coffee before continuing. "Alward was a true humanitarian. He had an M.D. degree before he went to Harvard to get his Ph.D. in biochemistry, and he used it to care for the homeless at shelters during the little time he had to spare. I know for a fact that he spent his weekends doing the same thing while he was at Bio-Sci."

"I see but I don't see," Mack said. "I mean, if he was so concerned about serving humanity, wouldn't he accomplish a lot more here than on the street?"

"You just made a very valid point, Detective, and one I emphasized to Dr. Alward when I tried to persuade him to stay on here. But he was determined to do what he felt he had to do. The laboratory was too impersonal for him, he said. He needed to help people on a one-on-one basis. The tragic irony is that he was probably murdered by one of the people he'd dedicated his life to helping."

True, Mack thought, if that's the way it went down. It was beginning to look like that might be the answer. What Kischman and Diane had told him so far certainly didn't give him any other leads. But he wasn't forgetting about the computer disk. Not by a longshot.

"Tell me something else, Doctor. Do you know if Alward could have been working on some research project of his own?"

Kischman's bushy eyebrows arched. "On his own?"

"Yes. He was set up pretty good in his office. All kinds of sophisticated lab stuff. I got the idea he might have been doing his own thing."

"Well, I suppose it's possible."

"But he never mentioned it to you?"

"No. Oh, we talked from time to time. I wanted to stay in touch, hoping I could lure him back to Bio-Sci, if only temporarily, to help us out on a big project we're trying to complete."

"The anthrax vaccine?"

"You know about that?"

"No secret, according to Mr. O'Neal."

"No. No secret that we're working on it. But we're not making it public about how far along we are with the project. If things go right, in two maybe three months we could have a vaccine ready for the Food and Drug Administration. They'll have to test and approve it before it can be put on the market, of course."

"How long will that take?"

Kischman shrugged. "Hard to say. A year, maybe two. Unfortunately, the FDA is notoriously slow in approving any new drug or vaccine, even one as important as this one."

"Important, for sure. O'Neal inferred that some of your competitors would love to get their hands on it."

"That's absolutely correct, Detective. We have to be constantly on the alert for any kind of industrial espionage."

"And it's not just our competitors we have to worry about," Diane said. "There are the drug pirates."

"Drug pirates?"

"That's the term we use to describe overseas counterfeit artists," Kischman said. "So-called pharmaceutical companies that duplicate patented drugs and sell them all over the world at below the market prices. In a very real sense, they're freeloading off our drug research."

"And the countries just let it happen?"

Kischman's smile was heavy with irony. "The public officials in many third world countries look the other way for a percentage of the profits. And even if they don't, the laws are difficult if not impossible to enforce."

"In some countries, like Nigeria, fake drugs are sold openly in pharmacies and outdoor markets," Diane added. "Even on public buses."

Kischman nodded. "And the more sophisticated shoppers have figured out how to point and click to the drugs they want."

"Sounds like a big business."

"Very big. In the billions and getting bigger every day."

"How about new drugs? The ones in development?"

"A priority, Detective. If the pirates can get the technology, they can put the drugs on the black market long before they're approved by the FDA."

"Have you ever had a leak here?"

"No. Not that our people aren't trustworthy, but we aren't taking any chances. All the data on the drugs we're developing goes into Socrates, and only a handful of people have access to that information. It's strictly on a need to know…"

Diane interrupted. "Doctor, you have a staff meeting at three-thirty, remember?"

Kischman glanced at the Piaget on his left wrist. "Oh, yes. I forgot all about it."

Rising and turning to Mack: "I'm sorry, Detective. Do you have any other questions?"

Mack stood up. "No. Thanks for your time, Doctor. If nothing else, you've given me a cram course on what goes on in the pharmaceutical world. But if either of you think of anything that might help, I'd appreciate it if you'd give me a call." He removed two cards from his wallet and handed one each to Kischman and Diane. "You can always reach me on my cell."

"I'll do that," Kischman said.

Before Mack could reach for his cup, the ever-efficient Diane had taken it along with Kischman's and her own and dropped them into a trash container.

"You can find your way out?" Kischman asked, as they exited into the lab room.

"Right. And thanks again."

Mack started to move away, then turned. "Oh, Doctor."

Kischman and Diane paused and turned. Kischman made no effort now to hide his growing annoyance. "Yes? What is it?"

"Just one more thing," Mack said. The question he hadn't asked O'Neal—too cool under fire, Alan Ladd—Mack had deliberately reserved for Kischman and Diane. Now he asked it in the hope that it would catch them off guard.

"'Did you ever hear the word 'Lazarus'?"

"Lazarus?" Kischman said. "Yes, of course. The man Jesus raised from the dead. Why do you ask?"

"It's a name I ran across in my investigation. Probably not important."

Mack turned and moved briskly toward the iron door. The adrenalin was pumping again. Surging, in fact. Mack had observed the look that passed between Kischman and Diane at the mention of Lazarus. Fleeting, but telling. He'd seen that look before, many times, in the eyes of gangbangers staring into the muzzle of a police special. Now Mack knew he was on the right track. The answer to Lazarus was at Bio-Sci, buried deep inside the brain of Socrates.

*3:47 p.m.*: David Blackburn, a tall, lanky man dressed in a fitted, charcoal gray suit, studied the chess board on the monitor of his office computer. The game was merely a diversion from what was becoming a major source of concern for him. When confronted with a problem, he inevitably turned to the chess game and a soothing pipe of his favorite tobacco. Why this worked he didn't know, but more often than not he'd have a solution before placing his computer opponent's king in checkmate. At the moment he was debating whether to move Queen's Bishop 1 to King 3 when a phone beeped.

Blackburn placed the pipe in an ashtray. Ignoring the phone on his mahogany desk next to a framed picture of his daughter, he used a key from a chain to unlock a bottom drawer. It was a call he was expecting. He removed the beeping phone and pressed the receiver against his left ear.

"How did it go?"

"Not good."

Which meant more bad news, Blackburn thought. If his face could have looked more morose than usual, it did so now. "The Moose" is what his frat brothers at Yale had called him, not derisively but accurately. His long, deep-cut face was not unlike that of the moose head that resided over the fireplace of his rustic retreat.

"What happened?"

"Plenty. McPherson knows about Lazarus."

Blackburn absorbed this information before replying. "*What* does he know about Lazarus?"

"I don't know. But he asked Dr. Kischman about it. Kischman is with me now."

"And his response?"

"Negative, of course, other than the Biblical reference to Jesus."

"That's all?"

"Isn't it enough?"

Blackburn paused, retrieved the pipe and took a puff. Not so bad after all, he thought.

"What do you think?" O'Neal continued.

"I think Detective McPherson was on a fishing expedition."

"How do you figure that?"

"If he wasn't, if he really knew or even suspected what Lazarus was all about, he would have been there with a small army of police and waved a search warrant in your face."

Momentary silence. "Yes, that's true enough. But he must have gotten wind of Lazarus somehow."

"Undoubtedly. Probably when he was searching Alward's office, or perhaps when he went through the doctor's items that the police removed. McPherson was at the state police crime lab this morning, snooping around."

"What could he have found there? We know that Alward's files contained no information about Lazarus."

"That's right. But the name must have surfaced somewhere. And that's all McPherson has. Just a name."

"Oh? What about the computer? Whoever killed Alward probably sold the computer. The disks as well. And one of them is dynamite. The fact that they're out there is big trouble."

"I don't think so. Whoever bought them would need a password to get into the Lazarus file. Besides, I don't believe they were sold. I believe they're at the bottom of the Chicago River."

"A nice theory, but what makes you so sure? Isn't it possible that the perp wasn't a druggie? That it was someone working for another biotech company?"

Blackburn massaged his slack jaw with long, tentacle-like fingers, debating whether to tell O'Neal how close he was to the truth. He decided not to.

"That's possible, but they'd still need a password."

"Alright, but we still have McPherson to deal with, and he impressed me as a very savvy cop who won't let go of this until he gets to the bottom of Lazarus."

"That's true," Blackburn said. He'd spent a lot of time going through a file on the detective. It was his habit to try to get to know his adversaries so well that he could anticipate their moves, like anticipating the moves of a chess opponent. "I'm dealing with it."

"You're dealing with it," O'Neal repeated with more than a trace of skepticism.

"Yes."

"Well, I hope so. We're getting close here, very close, and I don't need any more heat from McPherson, that's for damned sure."

"There won't be any."

"I have your word on that?"

"Yes."

"And you'll keep me informed?"

"Of course. You can count on it."

"Yeah, I'll do that," O'Neal replied tersely before hanging up.

Blackburn slowly cradled the receiver. Feeling older than his forty-eight years, he leaned back in the swivel chair and took a long drag on the pipe. He blew a smoke ring and watched it get sucked up by a small ionizer on the desk while he assessed the situation. He was not happy with his conversation with O'Neal. Not that he was worried about the Bio-Sci CEO. O'Neal was a tough guy, who was not likely to crack under pressure. His director of research was another matter. Had Kischman given the detective cause to suspect a connection between Bio-Sci and Lazarus? Blackburn was betting that he had, which was all the more reason to consider a plan that he'd already devised during the chess game.

Blackburn sighed, his eyes straying to a large framed photo on the wall. It showed him at the steering rudder of his 16-foot Hobiecat as it passed the finish buoy to win first place at a catamaran class regatta two years ago. Carol, his daughter, deeply tanned and athletic, was crewing, having replaced Judy, his wife, or rather former wife, who had just emerged from a divorce court with half his assets. Staring at the photo, Blackburn wished he were out there now on his Hobie, a brisk breeze whipping what was left of his sandy hair and propelling the cat at fifty miles an hour across the bay.

Unfortunately, that was not going to happen until this job was finished. Soon, O'Neal had said. Blackburn hoped so. Meanwhile, he had a maverick cop to checkmate. Much as Blackburn disliked his next move, it was one he had to make. McPherson couldn't be allowed to continue his investigation, even though it was unauthorized. There was too much at stake. However, the implementation of this plan was not his decision to make.

Blackburn leaned forward and reached for the phone. Instead of returning it to the bottom drawer, he picked up the receiver and speed-dialed a number.

## Tuesday, May 21

*11:55 a.m.:* Mack eased the Crown Vic to the curb in front of the main entrance to the Chicago Mercantile Exchange on South Wacker Drive. This was where Megan worked, and Mack was looking forward to having lunch with her. He turned off the ignition and started to get out of the car when he was approached by a uniformed security guard.

"I'm sorry, sir, but this is a no parking zone. You'll have to move your car."

"Officer McPherson," Mack said, flipping open his wallet to reveal his badge and ID. "Police business."

"How long will you be, Detective?"

"An hour give or take."

"No problem then."

Exiting the car, Mack moved through the street entrance to the Visitors' Center of the Exchange, a small building bookended by two forty-story office buildings. Another security guard, a young black lady, was waiting with a polite request.

"Please put any metal objects in a container, sir."

Mack emptied his pockets of change and put the coins into the container along with his wrist watch and cell phone. When he removed his .38, the lady's eyes flared with alarm, her right hand reaching for her own revolver in her hip holster.

"I'm a detective, miss. CPD," Mack said, and showed his badge and ID to the obvious relief of the guard before handing her the revolver.

"We'll have to keep the revolver, Detective. And the cell phone. Cells aren't allowed in the gallery."

"Right."

Mack waited his turn to pass through the metal scanner. Ahead, a young man was placing a backpack behind a lady's purse on the conveyer belt that went through an x-ray scanner. Just like at the airports, Mack thought, but the tight security was not surprising. Symbols of American capitalism, such as the New York Stock Exchange, the Chicago Mercantile Exchange and the Board of Trade were prime targets for terrorists, as was the Sears Tower, which was only a block away.

The security guard returned the container to Mack minus the cell phone and revolver after he walked through the scanner.

"You'll need a pass, Detective," she said, handing Mack a numbered sticker.

Mack strapped on the wristwatch, pocketed the change, then peeled off the back of the sticker and stuck it over the breast pocket of his rumpled beige suit jacket.

"This way, please," the guard said.

She escorted the three of them to an elevator, leaned in and punched the button to the fourth floor, where one of the two trading areas was located.

Exiting the elevator on the fourth floor, Mack picked up a brochure at an information desk manned by a pretty young girl identified on a plaque as "Lori Billard," then walked over to the long observation windows where he peered down at a trading floor the size of two basketball courts and wondered how anything resembling business could be taking place in what looked like total chaos—traders jammed in and around octagonal areas, shouting, frantically waving their arms, their eyes darting to the flashing numbers and monitors of the quotation boards that covered the upper walls and hovered overhead. The brochure explained that every trader was his own auctioneer. They were shouting out the number of contracts and prices at which they wished to buy and sell, and also using hand signals to convey the information.

Mack searched the crowd for Megan. There weren't many females among the traders, who, as explained in the brochure, wore red, blue or custom-designed jackets in patterns or other colors affixed with large badges with numbers and initials or names to identify them. Most of the females on the floor were young and garbed in yellow jackets. Consulting the brochure again, Mack learned that these were phone clerks, runners, arbitrage clerks and desk holders, whatever that was, employed by the clearing firms to maintain communication between the phone areas and the octagonal areas referred to as the "pits."

Mack was curious to see how Megan made a living, which is why he'd decided to visit the CME before keeping their lunch appointment. He'd received her phone call on his cell shortly after the morning roll call. Had he found out anything about her dad's death during his two-day break was her anxious question. "Fill you in at lunch" was his reply. They agreed to meet at a café on the ground floor of the complex at noon. "Looking forward to the pleasure of your company," he said, then hung up before Megan could ask more questions, which he preferred to answer in person rather than on the phone.

Mack had to admit that he *was* looking forward to Megan's company, had been all morning, which was spent dealing with a sad child abuse case. Responding to a neighbor's complaint of loud noises and the sound of children crying, Mack and Otis had found five undernourished kids, ages two to nine, occupying an apartment that reeked of refuse and the lingering stench of pot. The children had three different last names, the nine-year-old, a scrawny little girl with a bruised face, subbing in as the missing mother told them. Before turning the kids over to the Department of Children and Family Services, Mack and Otis learned the name of her mother's current boyfriend from the little girl. Not surprisingly, the boyfriend had a rap sheet for drug abuse. His probation officer provided a current address. With a search warrant in hand, Mack and Otis found mother and boyfriend in drug-induced stupors. They booked the boyfriend for violating probation and the mother for five counts of child abuse.

Mack was beginning to suspect that Megan was doing business on the upper trading floor when he spotted a flash of red hair amidst the traders swarming the largest trading pit just under the observation window. She was wearing slacks, loafers and an Irish green jacket with a badge that read "MEG." To Mack, Megan looked like a minnow swimming with sharks, but he was willing to bet that the feisty redhead had held her own with the big boys on the block ever since she was in pigtails.

Mack glanced at his wrist watch. 12:02 p.m. He'd knocked off early for lunch but had promised to pick up Otis at Stacy's by 1:00 p.m. If he was going to have time for lunch, it had to happen now, but Megan seemed in no hurry to leave the pit. Had she forgotten about the lunch date? Not likely. Probably just too involved with whatever she was trading and lost track of the time.

Mack moved to the information desk. "Could I send a message to someone on the floor?"

"No problem," Lori said with a sweet smile. "The name, please?"

"Megan Herbst. She's a trader. She's in the pit just under the window."

"The S&P 500 pit," Lori said, scrawling Megan's name on a memo pad. "And the message?"

Mack gave it to her.

"It'll just take a minute," she said, and picked up the receiver.

Megan was having a good day. She'd made over five hundred dollars trading Eurodollars and another seven-fifty plus in pork belly futures before moving to the S&P 500 pit. She'd hoped that she could close out her short position in the October 1000 future before noon. Unfortunately, the stock market had advanced, forcing her to wait for a possible intraday dip to buy in her position.

Megan was glad to be back on the floor. She'd decided to return to work as soon as possible, not only to get her mind off things but for the more practical reason of paying the bills. She'd kept Katie out of school one more day, which she was spending with her Aunt Mary at one of her favorite places, the Lincoln Park Zoo. Her dad's funeral had gone well. Father Kiley had conducted it in the chapel of the Holy Name Cathedral. Her dad's framed army photo on an empty casket surrounded by floral wreaths had been a fitting substitute for a body. Perhaps it was even better that way. No matter how skillfully morticians prepared the deceased, to Megan the bodies always resembled bloodless mannequins at best. At least the photo showed her dad in the prime of life, his face radiating pride and vitality, smiling as if he was about to deliver the punch line of a slightly off-color joke.

"Hey, Meg. You got a message," a voice yelled into her ear.

Megan turned to one of the runners, Jim somebody, a young man with a ponytail. She took the message slip Jim somebody handed her. "Are we still on for lunch?" was the handwritten question. Before she could respond the runner pointed up to the visitors' gallery. Looking up, Megan spotted the familiar face of Detective McPherson amidst those of a few spectators behind the glass.

Megan gave Mack an exaggerated nod, then glanced at the quotation board suspended over the S&P pit. The stock market was pulling back, the S&P now up only 4.33 points. The clock on the board showed 12:12 p.m. "Tell him five minutes," she shouted at the runner. "At Traders' Deli, as planned."

Jim nodded and scurried to his phone station to deliver the message. The stock market continued to fall. Megan was in the black now, and shouted out for a seller of five contracts at her desired price, also signaling with her hands, since her voice was drowned out by the din of yelling voices. If she waited she might be able to close out with a bigger profit. She'd passed up many a lunch to stay with a position rather than run the risk of being away from the market for even a short time, restroom breaks included. Too much could happen and usually did.

But there was no way she was going to pass up *this* lunch just to make a few extra bucks. She had no delusions that McPherson was here for the pleasure of her company. He had news about her dad, and Megan had a strong feeling it was important.

*12:20 p.m.:* Mack paid a young, dour-faced girl behind a computer cash register at the Traders' Deli.

"Thank you," the girl said as if she could care less, even about the two dollar bills Mack dropped into the tip jar.

"Service with a scowl," Mack said to Megan, as they helped themselves to plasticware, paper napkins and packets of artificial sweetener from a self-serve station.

"You can't have everything. At least the food is decent and the prices reasonable."

Mack had offered to buy lunch at Riverview, a fine dining restaurant next to the cafe, which overlooked the Chicago River. Megan had declined the request. Not only was the service slow, the prices were, in her opinion, on the high side of a rip-off. A frugal lady, Mack thought, while they carried their trays of food through the crowded restaurant to one of the small tables that was just vacated by two red-jacketed traders. When Megan sat down, Mack held her chair.

"Thank you," she said, surprised but pleased by this unexpected display of good manners.

Mack sat down and wasted no time bringing Megan up to date on how he'd spent his two-day break. Megan listened attentively and without interruption, while she nibbled at the Caesar salad between sips of iced tea. What she was hearing was enough to give her indigestion.

When Mack finished, Megan asked, "Do you think he was telling the truth?" referring to Kischman's response to the word "Lazarus."

"No."

"What could it mean? Lazarus?"

Mack shrugged, chewing on a bite of turkey sandwich. "I don't know. Not specifically, that is. A code name referring to some project at Bio-Sci is my guess. Something they don't want anyone to know about."

Megan digested this along with a crouton from the salad. "If that's true, I can't imagine what it would have to do with Dad's death?"

Mack debated whether to answer Megan's indirect question. He was beginning to get the glimmer of an idea but was reluctant to discuss it until he had more to go on. "I can't either."

Megan studied his face and decided that Detective McPherson was probably a good poker player. As a kid she'd eavesdropped many a night at the beer-and-corned-beef-sandwich poker sessions her dad hosted for his friends at the dining room table. She was about to press Mack on the issue when she caught sight of Neil dumping a paper plate and plastic cup into a trash dispenser. On his way to the exit he spotted Megan and came over.

"Hey, Meg," he said, smiling. "How's it goin'?"

"Hi, Neil. Having a good day?"

"Awesome. Made a killing with NASDAQ options. How about you?"

"Rent money, but it will do."

Neil laid a hand on her shoulder. "I'm sorry about your dad, Meg. Are you okay?"

"I'm okay, thanks. Oh, I want you to meet Detective McPherson." Then to Mack, "this is my friend, Neil Rosenbloom."

Neil offered his hand, which Mack took. "Nice to meet you, Detective."

"Likewise," Mack said, sizing up the slender-hipped man in the blue jacket. "ACE" was the name on his ID badge along with a number. In his thirties, fit looking, with a handsome, swarthy face, curly black hair and a smile that displayed movie star teeth which had to have cost major bucks.

"Would you like to join us?" Megan said.

"Thanks, but I've got to get back on the floor. Maybe we could do lunch tomorrow?"

"I'd love to, if the market cooperates."

"Yeah. Look, why don't we knock off early, say two o'clock, give ourselves enough time to talk."

"Sounds good, but let's make it at one-thirty. I have to pick up Katie from school at three."

"Great. One-thirty it is, and at Riverview." Neil leaned over and kissed Megan's cheek. "Nice to have met you, Detective," he said to Mack.

"Likewise…Ace," Mack said as Neil turned and hurried toward the exit.

"Ace?" Mack asked Megan, thinking that Neil and Megan might be more than just good friends.

Megan smiled. "A name some of the traders gave him. Neil is one of the sharpest traders on the floor."

"Let me guess. Owns a Mercedes and lives in a mansion in Highland Park?"

"Close, but the car's a Porsche and the mansion is in Kenilworth."

"Right." Mack took a bite of the sandwich. "I didn't see him at the wake."

"He…he had a conflict," Megan said, wondering where this was going. "He sent a card and a beautiful floral wreath."

"Nice of him," Mack said, chewing. "Married, I take it." It was not a question. The diamond studded wedding band was impossible to miss.

Megan swallowed hard on a leaf of romaine. Now she knew where Mack was going and resented his intrusion into her personal life.

Mack saw Megan's eyes narrow, the flare of crimson in her cheeks. "Sorry," he said, anticipating an angry outburst. "I ask too many questions. It's the cop in me."

Megan took a sip of the iced tea to cool her anger. "It's alright."

Mack gave her a few moments to eat and calm down before he tactfully changed the subject. "I watched you down there on the floor. Looks like a pretty rough environment for a lady."

"It's not the most user-friendly place to work for sure, no matter who you are. But you're right. There is a locker room mentality that some women might find hard to deal with."

"I guess that's true for lady cops as well."

"I can imagine. I enjoy my job, though, stressful and demanding as it is. I guess I get a high from the excitement, the challenge it presents every day I walk onto the floor. You never know what's going to happen, but if you have what it takes, you can do very well."

"I'm sure," Mack said. There was no doubt in his mind that Megan had what it took. "How'd you get into this business, anyway?"

"I was a phone clerk when I met Artie. My husband. He was a floor broker for Bear Stearns until he saved up enough money to buy his own seat. When he did, he asked me to be his assistant. And his wife." Megan smiled wistfully at the remembrance of his proposal of marriage at the top of his lungs in the S&P pit, which drew a volley of cheers and applause from the traders. "I learned all the ground rules from Artie. When he died, I inherited the seat, so here I am."

"Do you mind if I ask what happened? To your husband, I mean. Sorry, another question."

"It's okay," Megan said, her smile wilting. Although she thought she'd learned to cope with Artie's death a long time ago, as she told McPherson about it, she had to make an effort to keep her voice from quavering.

"I was home with Katie…she was just learning to walk…when Artie called me on the cell. He was right outside on the corner, waiting for the light to change so he could cash a check at the bank across the street. He'd had a big day and wanted to know if I could find a sitter so we could go out for supper and celebrate. I never had a chance to answer. An elderly man driving south on Wacker had a heart attack. His car struck several people waiting for the light. Three were severely injured. Artie wasn't so lucky."

Mack now regretted asking the question. He could see this was tough for her to talk about, even after the four years that had passed since the tragedy. Without thinking, he reached over and laid his hand on hers.

"Tough break. Why is it all the nice people get the tough breaks?"

Megan looked into his eyes and was surprised to see something she never expected to see, which was a hint of compassion. "I don't know. Maybe it's to make us stronger, more able to cope, to survive."

"Good point."

Mack squeezed her hand, then withdrew it. Funny, Megan thought. His hand had felt comforting, protective. But now she felt her eyes beginning to mist and stood up. "Excuse me, but I have to use the ladies' room."

"Of course," Mack said, rising.

While Megan was gone Mack dialed Otis on his cell to tell him that he was running a little late.

"Hey, man, our case plate runneth over, and I'm in no mood to put in overtime."

"I hear you. Have another slice of strawberry cheesecake on me. I'll be there at one-fifteen, max."

Mack beeped off before Otis could offer more complaints. When Megan returned, he held her chair again. She thanked him and got back to the business at hand as if nothing had happened since Neil's interruption.

"What's your next move, Detective McPherson?"

"When are you going to start calling me Mack?"

"Alright," Megan smiled. "What's your next move, Mack?"

Mack swallowed the last bite of his sandwich. "Quite frankly, I'm not sure."

"You must have some kind of plan."

"Yeah, but I'm afraid it's next to impossible to implement."

"Which is?"

Mack took a sip of Diet Pepsi, dabbed his mouth with a paper napkin. "Get into Socrates's brain."

"Socrates?"

Mack smiled. "Yeah. That's what the people at Bio-Sci call their research mainframe. If I'm going to find out what Lazarus is all about, that's where I have to go. But the security is so tight there that I haven't the vaguest idea how to bring it off."

Megan gave the poker face a searching look. "No idea?"

"Well, maybe one."

"I have a feeling it's not something in your rules book."

"Not exactly," Mack said without elaborating—but he was gaining new respect for that thing called woman's intuition.

*1:43 p.m.:* Gripping the wheel of the Crown Vic with both hands, Mack swung the car south off North Avenue onto Kedzie.

"What's that address again?"

Otis looked at the case sheet on top of the heap in his lap. "3320 West Evergreen Avenue. You know where that is?"

"Yeah. I spent some time in the Humboldt Park area as a beat cop. I thought you'd been here before."

"If I had, I don't remember it. Or the Soduskys either, for that matter."

"Well, they remember you. Didn't Mrs. S request that you handle the investigation?"

Otis consulted the case sheet again. "Yeah. According to her, I found her missing kid about three years ago when I was with Tony G."

"Well, junior is out and about again. History repeats."

"All too often."

Mack continued south on Kedzie, which bordered the west side of Humboldt Park, until he reached West Evergreen and hung a right onto a narrow street with more than its share of potholes. Things had changed since Mack's last visit to the neighborhood. Once a high crime zone, the area had improved. Most of its residents were Hispanics with whites and African Americans taking up the slack. However, there were still pockets of poverty where it was business as usual for drug pushers and gangbangers.

"I've got a bad feeling about this," Mack said.

"Are you referring to the neighborhood?"

"Partly." Mack debated if he should tell Otis about the nightmare he'd had the night before. He might think he was off his nut. To hell with it, he thought, and told him anyway.

"So you had a bad dream" was Otis's response. "What's the big deal? Everyone has nightmares. What was it about?"

"I don't know. All I know is that I have them once in a while, and although I can't remember them, bad shit has happened to me on more than one occasion afterward."

"Oh? Like what kind of bad shit?"

"Like the time I took a bullet in the hip from a gangbanger."

"Pure coincidence, my friend. Or are you psychic?"

"Maybe. Who knows? My grandmother claimed that she had premonitions of things that happened in her life."

"Everyone has premonitions. Forget it."

For the moment, Mack put his premonition aside and turned his attention back to the neighborhood. The 3300 block of West Evergreen consisted mostly of well-maintained two-flats and single-family homes. Interspersed among these, however, were ramshackle dwellings with weed-choked front yards littered with trash and broken toys. The Sodusky residence fell into this second category.

"There it is," Otis said, pointing to a decrepit A-frame, in front of which a dog was rummaging through an open garbage bag near the curb.

Mack pulled the Vic up in back of a battered Neon with cardboard in place of a rear window and rims without tires propped up on cement blocks. Mack and Otis exited the Vic and climbed cautiously up the creaking wooden steps to a small front porch. Mack stabbed a button under a mailbox stuffed with envelopes that looked like bills and was not surprised when there was no sound of a bell or chimes from within.

"Try knocking," Otis suggested.

"Do we have a choice?"

Mack rapped on the door hard enough to rattle the loose handle. No response.

"I thought we were expected."

"What can I say? Try again."

Mack rapped again until his knuckles hurt. This time a voice rasped on the other side of the door. Neither detective could tell if it was male or female.

"Who the fuck are ya and whadaya want?"

Mack gave Otis a "what gives?" look, then showed his badge and ID to the eyeball filling the peep hole. "Detectives McPherson and Winstrom, Special Victims. You called about a missing son."

"I called about what?"

"Your son," Otis said, looking at the case sheet. "Harold."

"Speak up. I can't fucking hear you."

"Try opening the door," Mack said. He was getting a bad feeling about this.

"Shit."

Sound of a deadbolt being thrown, and the door opened just wide enough, before being stopped by the door chain, to reveal a chalky face that looked like it had been clumsily kneaded out of Play-Doh by a five-year old, topped by a mop of stringy bleached-red hair. The doughy face peered at them with blurry, hostile eyes through the opening.

"Mrs. Sodusky?" Otis said, recoiling from the stench of cheap wine and the pungent odor of someone who hadn't bathed in a very long time.

"No, I'm Madonna, don't ya know." She did a little sexy pose in a soiled kimono that reached down to her filthy, bare feet. "Now what's this shit about a missing son?"

"Your son, Harold. You reported him missing?"

Mack and Otis turned away from the spray of spittle that erupted from the doughface mouth along with what passed for laughter. "Hey, Cal," she screeched at someone in the apartment. "Some cops are here about our son. The fucker's missing again."

A harsh laugh over the babble of a TV program. "You gotta be shittin' me."

"Your son's not missing?" Otis said.

"Oh, he's missing, all right. Last time we heard from the fucker he was doin' ten to fifteen in Joliet for armed robbery and assault. And his name's not Harold. It's Stanley, unless he changed it again."

Otis swore under his breath. False alarms were bad enough, but practical jokes like this really pissed him off.

Mack was having other thoughts about what was going on, and turned to take a hard look at the three-story apartment building across the street, its broken or boarded windows, and the "CONDEMNED" sign on the front lawn.

"Sorry we bothered you, Mrs. Sodusky," Otis said, forcing his voice to remain polite. "I guess there's been some kind of mistake."

"No fuckin' shit. But you can do me a favor by keepin' the fucker locked up and throwin' away the fuckin' key."

The door slammed shut in Otis's face before he could respond. Turning to Mack, he said, "I'd like to get my hands on the asshole who called this one in."

But Mack didn't answer.

"Mack?"

Mack wasn't listening. He had just seen the glint of sunlight on metal in a third-story window of the apartment building and was shouting, "Down! Get down!"

Otis felt himself being shoved to one side, then Mack was leaping over the railing at the rattle of an automatic weapon, hitting the ground, rolling across the lawn, bullets chewing up the turf around him, until he was behind the Vic.

"Take cover, God dammit!"

For Otis there was no cover, but also no gunfire, so he broad-jumped the front steps. A second later he was crouching beside Mack behind the patrol car, his .38 police special in his right hand.

"Where's the shooter?" Otis said, aware only that the gunfire was coming from somewhere in the building across the street.

Mack pulled out his revolver. "Third-story window, the only one not boarded up."

"You're sure?"

"I'm sure. I want you to cover me. I'm going in."

"Going in? Are you crazy?! We gotta call for back-up!"

"Screw back-up! The shooter will be long gone by then. Cover me, or don't you know how to use that?"

"I know how," Otis said, but silently wished he'd spent as much time on the target range as he had practicing free throws in high school and at I.U.

"I hope so. Get ready! And when I tell you to start shooting, do it!"

"Right," Otis said, his palm sweaty against the well-worn handle of his weapon. It was a going away present from his mentor, Tony G, who had told Otis that he rarely had to use it. But Tony G never had a partner like Mack. Manowski had warned him about Mack. Crazy son-of-a bitch could get you killed. Right. Maybe now!

"Okay," Mack said. "Start shooting!"

Otis expected to get a bullet in the forehead as he peered over the roof of the Vic. Gripping his right wrist with his left hand, he started squeezing off rounds. He saw bullets chip into the bricks next to the window and puncture the already broken pane, but the shooter wasn't visible.

Mack didn't hesitate. While Otis fired, he dashed across the street to the front door of the building. He tried the door, not expecting it to be unlocked. It wasn't. A piece of flimsy looking ply board had replaced the glass area. It took Mack only a few seconds to kick it out. He waited a moment beside the door, gun at the ready. No sound from within. He took a deep breath and plunged through the opening into the gloom.

Otis reloaded his .38. He knew what he should do. Call for back-up, wait until they got there, then go in with more firepower. That's what the manual called for in this situation. But Mack had taken that option off the table. Otis knew he was the only back-up Mack was going to get, and he wouldn't have that if Otis didn't get off his butt. There was no sign of anyone in the window, but Otis fired off two more rounds anyway before he ran across the street.

Mack proceeded cautiously up two flights of trash-littered stairs, the .38 extended, then down a hallway to where the two front apartments were located. The shooter had been in the one to the right. Mack pressed his back against the wall next to the open door, listening for a sound. Nothing. He entered quickly, panning the living room with the gun. It was empty except for a few pieces of broken furniture somebody hadn't bothered to remove. He moved to the window used by the shooter and picked up one of the shell casings lying on the floor, a 7.62 mm round.

Mack whirled toward the sound behind him, then lowered his weapon as Otis entered the room. Mack had wondered if Otis had what it took to come through for a partner in jeopardy, but was not putting aside his reservations yet. This wasn't over if the shooter was still somewhere in the building.

Mack pressed his left index finger against his lips, then pointed to the hallway that led to the rest of the apartment. Otis nodded. They started for the hallway, then paused at the sound of a motorcycle revving from somewhere outside.

"Shit!" Mack said, and rushed out the door into the hallway. Otis followed him through a kitchen to the rear exit. The door was wide open. Mack exited to a wooden porch with stairs descending to the other two porches. A man on a Honda, an AK-47 slung over his back, was speeding down the alley behind the building. Mack got off three hasty shots, saw two bullets spark off the asphalt and one take off the handlebar mirror, before the cycle made a tire-screeching turn at the end of the alley and disappeared from view.

"Shit," Mack said again. "I should have nailed his ass."

"Are you kidding?" Otis said, amazed that Mack's shots had come as close as they had—shooting at a moving target with a hand gun from sixty yards away was some kind of shooting.

Mack shoved his .38 into its holster. "Let's collect those shell casings and any other evidence we can find and get out of here."

Otis had no objection to that; he was more than ready to leave.

*2:16 p.m.:* Mack turned onto Western Avenue and headed north to the precinct. They'd have to make a full report of the shooting and turn in the AK-47 shell casings and a bullet they'd pried out of the Sodusky's door frame. Other than those, the shooter had left no evidence.

"So what are you thinking?" Otis said. "All I've gotten out of you for the last five minutes is heavy breathing."

"I'm thinking that there's a contract out there somewhere, and it's got my name on it."

"Hey, wait a minute," Otis said, still shaky from his first shootout. "I admit we were set up, but it must have been gang related. Some gangbanger looking to add two cops to his hit resume."

"That's what somebody wants us to believe. And that's the way it would have gone down if I'd caught one of those 7.62s. But think about it: there was only one target, and I was it."

"Hey, man, I was there, too, in case it slipped your mind."

"I didn't see any bullets going your way."

"So I got lucky. End of story."

"Come on, Otis. This whole thing is way too sophisticated for a simple gang hit. Sure, they could have called about a phony missing kid and taken pot shots at any cops who showed up. But they didn't do that. Whoever made that call asked for you to handle the investigation. And why was that? Because they knew you're my partner. Can you connect the dots?"

Otis had to admit that there was something to what Mack was saying. "Okay, so if what you say is true—and I'm not saying it is—just who are *they* supposed to be?"

"Whoever did Frank and Alward."

"Come on, Mack. You're not going there again."

"Look, if you wanted something to convince you that I'm onto something about Lazarus, now you got it."

"What I got is an extension of your way-out theory. How about one that's more in the realm of reality?"

"Such as?"

"Such as someone you busted once upon a crime decided it was payback time."

"Forget it."

"Mind if I run with the ball on that anyway?"

"Do whatever you want."

Otis intended to do just that. He also decided that the next time Mack had a bad dream, he'd give it serious attention.

*8:53 p.m.:* Megan got out of the taxi in front of Joe's Downbeat Bar and Grill. "LIVE JAZZ" announced the red neon sign in the Downbeat's window. Megan didn't know much about jazz, but the sounds issuing from the bistro reminded her of some of the musical comedies she'd seen on the stages of the Schubert, Oriental and other Chicago theaters. *Thoroughly Modern Millie* and *Chicago* came to mind. Bold, brassy, energetic and, yes, fun, the sounds from the pit bands seemed to move the dancers like puppets on rhythmic strings.

Now Megan wondered if she should go in or not. She made it a rule not to go into a bar without a companion, no matter whether male or female. Single ladies were open season for the lounge lizards, who assumed that they were either prostitutes or females using the bar as a dating service to find that special someone—a fantasy that the lizards were more than willing to exploit. However, Megan would have to break her rule if she was going to find McPherson. She needed to talk to him and, according to Otis, this was his usual nocturnal haunt, which was something of a surprise. Somehow she couldn't associate the stern, tough detective with the good time sounds issuing from the Downbeat.

A frail-looking old man in a neatly pressed navy blue suit and jaunty bow tie greeted her when she entered.

"Good evening, miss. Welcome to the Downbeat. Would you like a table?"

Megan had to raise her voice to make herself heard over the blare of the music. "Yes…well maybe. I'm looking for a friend. His name is McPherson. He's a detective. Do you know him?"

"Oh, yes. He's one of our valued patrons."

"Is he here?"

"He is." The old man gestured toward the bandstand. "But he's a little busy at the moment."

Megan blinked. Was the man behind the set of drums McPherson? He was, and looking and sounding as if he really belonged there, in control, at ease, and smiling. Actually smiling.

"Does he play with the band?"

"No, he's just sitting in."

"Sitting in?"

"A guest drummer, so to speak."

"He's pretty good."

"That he is. Would you like to join him?"

"Yes, thanks. Would you take me to his table?"

"He's at the bar."

"Oh."

Megan scanned the faces around the horseshoe-shaped bar, mostly males, and realized that she had gotten their attention. Her attire, casual but chic, consisted of a scoop white sweater, khaki cropped pants, wedged, slip-on shoes and gold-hoop earrings. Her face was softly made up to complement her total look. Megan wondered if McPherson would be as taken with her appearance as the men at the bar were. She found herself hoping he would, but with the detective, who knew? In any event, she was uncomfortable being at the bar by herself.

The old man seemed to read her thoughts.

"The set will be over shortly, Miss…?"

"It's Mrs. Herbst. Megan Herbst."

"It's a pleasure to meet you, Mrs. Herbst. My name is Joe Lyman, Joe to my friends, and everyone here is my friend. Permit me."

Taking her arm, he escorted Megan to the bar, where a vacant stool fronted by a half-empty bottle of Amstel Light and a bowl of pretzels awaited the return of the missing customer. The old man tapped the shoulder of a heavyset man on the adjacent chair.

"Roy, I wonder if you'd mind moving to another chair to accommodate this lady. She's a friend of Mack's."

A broad smile spread across Roy's jovial looking face at the sight of the "friend." "Hey, no problem, Joe. All too glad to oblige, miss."

Roy pulled his bulk off the bar chair. Joe held it for Megan, who had to step onto the bar rail to lift herself onto the chair.

"Thank you."

"My pleasure." Then to Roy, "I'll have your drink moved, Roy. And the next one's on the house."

"Thanks, Joe, I appreciate it," Roy said, and shambled over to another empty chair, while a pretty lady bartender moved his drink.

"Would you like to order a drink, Mrs. Herbst?" the old man asked.

"Yes, I would, thank you."

The bartender was already back before Joe could call her over.

"Angie, this is Mrs. Herbst. She's a friend of Mack's and she's thirsty."

"You came to the right place," Angie said. "What would you like, honey?"

"A Perrier with a little ice and a slice of lemon," Megan said, aware that Angie was looking her over with what Megan interpreted as approval. Probably knew all of McPherson's lady friends, she thought, if he had any.

"Coming up."

"Excuse me," Joe said. "Got to say hello to some people. Enjoy yourself, Mrs. Herbst."

The old man moved to greet a couple entering the bistro. Moments later Angie was setting her drink on the bar.

"Here you are, honey. Are you going to join us for supper?"

"I might…if I'm invited."

"You'll be invited, trust me."

Angie scurried off to provide another round of highballs for two men on the other side of the bar who were giving Megan boozy "let's-get-acquainted" grins. Avoiding their eyes, she impulsively reached for the pretzel bowl, then drew her hand away. Probably not fat free, she thought. She was hungry but willing to bet that there wasn't anything among the choices of appetizers that wasn't deep fried, unless it was a shrimp cocktail, which was usually overpriced. Perhaps there was a catch of the day on the menu, hopefully salmon.

Megan smiled. She was already planning her choice of food before she was even asked for dinner. Well, if she wasn't, she'd treat the detective. After what he'd been through today, he'd earned a free meal if not a medal. Otis had told her about the shooting. Watching Mack behind the drums, Megan thought he looked like a man who didn't have a care in the world, rather than a man who'd just come very close to being killed. A riddle wrapped in an enigma, this detective, she thought, or vice versa. Whatever. In any event, there was no use trying to figure him out, so Megan took a sip of Perrier and settled back into the chair to enjoy the music.

Mack laid down a heavy beat on the snare and bass drum. He made sure he was in sync with the bass player, as the other six musicians romped through the final sixteen bars of "Lady Be Good." At the conclusion Mack took it upon himself to do a four-bar fill on the snare and floor tom, anticipating that the musicians would catch on. They did, and climaxed the tune with a two-bar coda with Mack providing the exclamation mark on the crash cymbal. The final tune of the set, always a barnburner, drew enthusiastic applause from the patrons.

Mack came around from behind the drums and approached Franz Robinson, the portly black leader and maestro of the reeds, who was setting his clarinet down in an instrument stand next to soprano and alto saxes. A jazz icon, Franz had played with some of the great black swing bands of the forties and fifties with names like Erskine Hawkins and Count Basie on his impressive resume. "Thanks for letting me sit in, Franz," Mack said, always grateful for the opportunity to play with a band, especially one as good as this one, if only for the last three numbers of the first set.

Franz smiled, dabbing perspiration from his forehead with a handkerchief. "Anytime, Mack. You did good."

"Thanks, Franz," Mack said, knowing that if he hadn't done well, if he'd lost the groove, Franz wouldn't have said anything. Getting a compliment from Franz only added to the jazz high he was on.

Stepping off the bandstand, Mack saw Joe limping his way.

"Nice job, Mack." Then with a big grin: "You've got company. And some company!"

Mack followed Joe's gesture toward the bar, expecting to see Inge, who sometimes showed up unexpectedly when her sexual needs required attention.

"I'll be damned! Joe, can you move us to a table?"

"Of course," Joe replied, and went off to tell one of the hostesses to move their drinks to a small table across the room.

Megan watched Mack approach. She tried to read his expression. Was he pleased to see her? At the same moment she wondered why she was even asking herself that question.

"Hello, Megan," Mack said with a smile. "I certainly didn't expect to see you here."

Mack's smile put Megan at ease. She felt reassured that he seemed pleased to see her, and not resentful at her intrusion into his personal life.

"Come," he said, taking her by the arm. "Joe's got a table where we can sit."

Mack led her across the room, moving behind her and holding her chair for her until she was comfortably seated. This was the third time in one day that Mack had treated her the way a gentleman is supposed to treat a lady, and Megan had to admit to herself that she was beginning to enjoy receiving such attention.

"Hey, you were pretty good up there," she said after they were both seated. "I didn't know you were a musician."

Mack gave a little shrug. "I'm not. I just do a good job of faking it."

"Don't be so modest. You sounded really good. Do you come from a musical family?"

"That I do. My dad played the trumpet. He was a side man with some of the big bands in the '50s and '60s. His dad was a top reed man dating back to the late '20s. I gave it a serious shot on the piano and trumpet when I was a kid, but I didn't have it, so I bought a set of drums and took some lessons."

"Why didn't you stay with it? You know, carry on the family tradition?"

"Long story." Mack took a swig of Amstel Light, which was now room temperature. "How'd you track me down? Otis?"

"Yes. He told me where you hang out on your nights off. I tried your home phone and your cell first. No answer."

"Forgot to bring the cell."

"You forgot like on purpose?"

Mack was beginning to wonder if Megan was psychic. "Let's just say that sometimes I like to go fishing."

"Fishing?"

"Same thing. Get off by myself. Relax. Clear my head. Recharge the batteries."

"Sorry I intruded."

"Don't be, and it's no intrusion. But I'm assuming this isn't exactly a social call since you went to the trouble of calling Otis to find me."

"Actually, it was Otis who called me."

"Otis called you?"

"Yes. He's worried about you."

About himself, Mack thought, but kept quiet. "I didn't know he cared."

"No, really. He asked me...well, to reconsider having you investigate Dad's death. He said if your superiors found out about it, you could be suspended, or worse, maybe even discharged. Is that true?"

"It's a distinct possibility."

"He also told me what happened today. The shooting."

"In the line of duty."

"Please don't be flippant. You could have been killed."

"Another distinct possibility."

Megan paused and took a sip of her Perrier.

"According to Otis, you believe the shooting could have something to do with your investigation."

Mack hesitated before answering. He didn't want Megan laying a guilt trip on herself about this. "Possible but not probable. More likely it was a random shooting."

"You really believe that's what happened? A random shooting?"

"That's probably the way it'll shake out. Cops are always open season for gangbangers."

Megan studied his face. Was he being honest with her? She doubted it, but it didn't matter. She'd already made up her mind to ask him to drop the investigation. Much as she wanted to get to the bottom of her dad's death, she had no right to put Mack's career, let alone his life, in jeopardy.

Megan's request drew a long look from Mack. For a moment he didn't know how to respond to Megan's sudden about-face on his behalf.

"Look, Megan. I appreciate your concern. I mean that."

"But you're not going to drop the investigation."

It wasn't a question. Again Mack was impressed with Megan's ability to read him, something that had frustrated friends and associates who'd known him for years.

"No. I can't walk away from this now."

"No, I suppose not." Megan took a sip of Perrier, debating whether she should ask him a question that had been on her mind since she'd spoken with Otis. She didn't know how Mack would react. He'd probably take off on her, but she decided to ask it anyway.

"Tell me something. If you find out who's behind all this, will you…take the law into your own hands?"

Mack smiled. "I see you've been reading my press clippings."

"Why, Mack? Why do you do it? Isn't it enough just to do your job? Make arrests and let justice take its course?"

Mack's smile faded. "It would be, if the justice system always worked, but it doesn't. All too often it comes down hard on the victims while the bad guys walk away."

"That may be true, but don't you see? That doesn't give you the right to be judge, jury and…" Megan bit her lip.

"Executioner?"

"Yes," Megan said softly.

Mack took a sip of beer, then leaned forward and looked thoughtfully at Megan for a moment. "I'm going to tell you a story," he said, then leaned back in his chair and signaled Angie at the bar.  She came over as soon as she finished serving one of her customers seated at the counter.

"Another beer?"

"Yeah. This one's warm. And a double shot of Mr. Daniel's on the side." He'd stayed off hard liquor since he'd taken on his private investigation into Frank's death, but now he felt the need for something stronger.

A stern look from Angie. "If it's a double, it's gonna be the only one you get from me tonight. Is that clear?"

"Yes, nurse."

"So you better make it last."

Mack waited without speaking until Angie returned with the beer and the whiskey. He took a sip of the Daniels and chased it with a swallow of Amstel Light, then leaned forward and looked again at Megan for an uncomfortably long moment, then looked around the room as though trying to decide whether to proceed.

"I had a younger brother, Kenny," he said abruptly, looking directly at her once again. "He was the one who inherited the McPherson family musical genes, not me. When he was only three he was already picking out tunes on the piano. He had the gift, the ear. By the time we were in high school he was good enough on reeds that he could have played professionally."

Mack took another sip of beer, then looked at Megan as though waiting for her to speak.

Megan didn't know what Mack expected her to say. "That's…quite an accomplishment," she ventured, wondering where Mack was going with this, and what his younger brother had to do with his compulsive need to dispense justice.

"We had a band in high school," Mack continued. "Lane Tech, on the North side of town. Kenny played reeds, I played drums, and we had two buddies who were pretty good on guitar. We played lots of gigs, mostly rock, 'cause that's what the kids wanted to hear. But sometimes we got a chance to play ballads and swing at jobs we did for the older people…weddings, college graduations, things like that. Anyway, it was a lot of fun and we made decent money. Decent enough for me to buy a second hand clunker when I turned sixteen."

Mack paused to pick up a pretzel from a bowl on the table and finger it. It was clear to Megan that he was having a hard time telling his story. In fact, Mack was asking himself why he felt such a strong urge to tell Megan? He'd never told anyone about Kenny before, not his partners on the force, not even Inge. Maybe it was because she'd opened up to him about her husband at lunch this afternoon. He wasn't sure. All he knew was that at the moment he felt it was important for her to understand why he did what he did. So he dropped the pretzel into the bowl and continued.

"Kenny and I spent our summers at our grandparents' home on a lake in Indiana. Webster Lake, it's in North Webster, a little town in the northeast part of the state. There's a bunch of lakes in the area. My grandparents had an antique store there. When we weren't working at odd jobs, we were having ourselves a ball, you know, fishing and swimming, and by the time we were in high school, we were making out with the local girls. I guess I was more aggressive at that than Kenny was. Anyway, the girls didn't seem to have a problem with two outsiders from Chicago. The boys, though, that was another matter. They resented our intruding on their turf…and their girls. I had to deal with two or three of them physically before they got the message and didn't mess with us."

Mack took another sip of whiskey and chased it with another swig of beer. "During the summer before my senior year, Kenny did some gigs with a local rock band. The word had gotten around about how good he was. The band had a drummer, but I would go to all the gigs anyway to make sure Kenny stayed out of trouble. Some of the bar jobs got pretty rowdy. Rednecks out to get drunk and pick a fight…and Kenny was no fighter."

Megan noticed the hint of a wistful smile brighten Mack's face as he continued. "Sometimes, on a clear night, Kenny would go out on the pier and play his clarinet. Not rock, but ballads like 'Star Dust' and 'Moon Glow.' You could hear it clear across the lake. When we were in town, shopping or doing some kind of job, like bagging at the supermarket, old folks would come up to Kenny and tell him how much they enjoyed listening to him play those great ballads, how it brought back memories of when they were young and danced with their sweethearts to the music of the big bands that played summer gigs at the dance halls around the area's lakes. That meant a lot to Kenny."

The smile faded as Mack let go of the memory. He reached into the pretzel bowl and removed another pretzel, didn't eat it, just held it while he continued. "Anyway, back to the story. It was late August, our last weekend at the lake before we had to return to Chicago. The band had a gig at a dance hall at one of the lakes. A teen dance. There was one there every Saturday night during the summer. I didn't want Kenny to do it. I had a lousy dream the night before. We were fishing, and Kenny fell out of the boat. He tried to swim, but there was an anchor tied to his feet, dragging him down. I jumped out and tried to save him, but he sank out of sight, like a stone. I couldn't find him. I couldn't save him. I couldn't..."

Mack stopped for a moment as though reliving the agony of the dream, and took another sip of the Daniels. "Then I woke up in a cold sweat. When I told Kenny about the dream, he just laughed. What could happen? It was a teen dance. We'd attended a few of them ourselves. No problems. The county sheriff's deputies were on hand to handle the traffic and prevent any drinking in the dance hall. Although they had to break up an occasional fight, by and large there were no serious incidents. At least not until that night."

Megan waited for Mack to continue. Now he was staring into the shot glass, as though its amber contents harbored a terrible memory that had just escaped from a dark recess in his mind and was rising to the surface to torment him.

"Mack? Are you okay? What happened?" she said gently.

Mack cleared his throat and continued. "Nothing at first. During the first set I hooked up with a girl—Marie. I'd been seeing a lot of her that summer. When the band went on break, I suggested we go outside to my car. A beer would taste good, and I had some on ice in a cooler. Marie was all for it. Before we left, I looked for Kenny, and saw a girl coming on to him. My guess is she was trying to get Kenny to go to her car. I was right. Just for a beer, Kenny said. I told him to forget it. The beer and the girl. I knew this girl. She was bad news. Did drugs. I could see that she was stoned. I told her to get lost. She gave me the finger and walked away. I warned Kenny again to stay away from her, figured that was that, and left with Marie. We went to my car and had those beers."

Another pause. "We also had sex. I guess that's what we both really wanted. It wasn't the first time with her. Afterward, as we were finishing our beers, we heard a girl screaming, shrieking—on and on, hysterically, like something really terrible was happening. I realized right away it was the girl who had come on to Kenny. I also knew in my gut that Kenny was with her and that something really bad was happening."

Megan couldn't see Mack's face. He was still staring into the shot glass, but he spoke more slowly now, in a softer voice, as though he were telling her about a dream he was having at that very moment.

"I got out of the car and ran around the parking lot trying to find them. The screaming had stopped for a moment, but when it started again, I realized the car wasn't in the lot. There was an overflow of cars strung along the side of the lake road, and the screaming was coming from there. I ran down the road as fast as I could. My heart was pounding. At least I didn't have to go far. She was in an open Chevy convertible. She was the only one in the car, but she wasn't alone. There were two boys standing in front of the car. There was a pile of lumber near the road for a house that was being repaired, and the boys were holding two-by-fours. I didn't see Kenny, but I already knew what had happened. I reached into the car and turned on the headlights. Kenny was lying in front of the car near the side of the road. I bent over him. His head was a bloody mess. He was unconscious, but still breathing. For a fraction of a second I just wanted to get up and beat the living shit out of the two boys, but I had to stay focused on Kenny. I was thinking I had to go get help when two deputies rushed up. One of them called for an ambulance on his radio. Then they took the boys and the girl into custody. I waited for the ambulance. When it got there, I rode with Kenny to the county hospital. On the way a medic did his best to keep Kenny alive while I held Kenny's hand and kept telling him to hang in there, that he was going to make it. But he never heard me. He never heard anything. He died on the way to the hospital."

Mack's hand involuntarily clenched and crushed the pretzel, dropping the fragments on the table. Megan reached over and laid her hand on his. "Mack, I am so sorry!"

Mack looked at her, and for a moment Megan thought his usually inscrutable face had softened and she could see his pain reflected in his eyes. Then his face hardened again, his voice regained its edge, and he resumed his normal pace. "Well, that's not the end of the story. I got this later from one of the deputies who happened to be an honest guy. The sheriff called the parents of the two boys and the girl so they could get their lawyers over to the station before they made statements. That gave them a chance to concoct a story. They said that Kenny had tried to rape the girl. The boys heard her screams and came to help her. When Kenny pulled a knife, they had to defend themselves with the two-by-fours. They didn't mean to kill Kenny, just defend themselves. Well, they all lied. Kenny never had a knife. That's what I told the sheriff and the DA, and it's the gospel truth."

"And they didn't believe you?"

"Believe me? The police never even put what I said in my statement. Hell, all they were interested in was covering for the boys. The boys were the home team. And from highly respectable families that carried some big time weight in the community. One of the boy's dads owned a local Ford agency, and the other was the president of a bank. And someone made sure that the boys' and the girl's phony stories had legs. The next morning the sheriff and a deputy went back to where the girl's car was parked. And guess what? They found a switchblade in the grass just off the road. At least that's what they claimed. But it was a plant, pure and simple. Kenny didn't even own a switchblade."

"What happened then?" Megan asked.

"What happened? Nothing happened! Not a damned thing!"

"You mean the boys were never charged with anything?"

"That's right. The DA didn't prefer charges. The knife was entered as evidence to support their stories, and they walked."

"That's…that's incredible!"

"Yeah, well what could you expect. They were all buddy-buddies, the sheriff, the DA, the boys' fathers, even the local judge. I worked part time at a posh country club that summer busing tables, and I would see them boozing it up at the bar after a round of golf. Get the picture?"

Megan did. And it was not a pretty one.

"And that's not the worst of it," Mack said, his jaw clenched tight as a boxer's fist. "The local newspaper made sure that the community bought into the boys' story as well. It wasn't enough that the boys got away with murder and the girl with perjury. They turned it around and made Kenny the bad guy! The murderers were portrayed like heroes! 'High school football stars save girl from rape!' That was the headline—one I'll never forget as long as I live. The rest was all bullshit."

Mack tossed off the rest of the whiskey and slammed the shot glass down on the table. "How's that for justice?!"

"My God, that's infuriating. You must have felt so...so helpless."

"Yeah. Well, I should have stayed with Kenny, made sure he didn't go off with that girl. But I didn't. I was too busy getting laid!"

"Mack, you can't blame yourself...you couldn't...it wasn't your fault."

"Maybe, but telling myself that didn't help. My parents were devastated. Kenny had been the apple of their eye, my dad's hope for carrying on the family musical tradition, and I couldn't get past the feeling that I was responsible for their grief, that what I had done...or hadn't done... had caused this to happen, and them to suffer. They never blamed me, of course, but I know they must have wondered why I hadn't been able to protect Kenny that night like I had in the past. I couldn't tell them I was having sex in my car while Kenny was being beaten to death!"

Mack finished off the last of the beer. "I got really depressed after that. Before Kenny died I wasn't much of a drinker, one or two beers once in a while, but I started hitting the bottle heavy, let my grades go to hell. All I could think about was getting revenge. I even thought about killing the bastards who murdered Kenny, but I could never have dishonored my parents that way. And thank God for my football coach. He came down on me hard, but he got me straightened out. And he gave me some advice that changed my life. He told me, if you want to do something about seeing that justice gets carried out, then join the police force when you get out of high school. I thought about that a lot, and when I graduated, that's exactly what I did. And from the moment I put on a badge, I knew what I had to do."

"You mean taking the law into your own hands?"

"There's more to it than that. Let me show you something." Mack removed the chain with the medal from around his neck and handed it to Megan. "It's a swimming medal Kenny won for his age group when we were at a YMCA camp. He wasn't much of an athlete—I was the jock in the family—but he was a pretty good swimmer. It was only for third place, but it meant a lot to him."

"And to you," Megan said, examining the medal.

"Yeah. After Kenny was murdered, I had it put on this chain so I could wear it around my neck as a constant reminder of a promise I made to Kenny. I swore that I'd never let the bad guys get off scot-free because of money or power or social position, or who their friends were, or how good their lawyer was. And I made another promise, this one to myself. I was careless the night Kenny was murdered. I let my guard down when I left him alone. So I swore I would never let something like that happen again if there was any way I could prevent it. If I ever saw that a crime was going to be committed, and if I could stop it from happening, then I would do everything possible to stop it...to prevent an innocent person from being hurt, or worse."

Megan nibbled at her lemon peel as she sought the right words for a response. "Mack," she said finally. "I understand your anger, your frustration, when criminals escape punishment for their crimes. It's a terrible miscarriage of justice when that happens. But don't you see...what you're doing...it's not the answer."

"To your way of thinking, maybe. But not mine."

Megan looked at the medal again. "It says here 'serving God.' Do you believe that what you're doing is serving God?"

"That depends on what god you're talking about. It seems to me that the god of the Old Testament came down pretty hard on the human race, like a sledgehammer when he thought they screwed up."

"Yes, that's true. The god of the Old Testament could be a god of wrath. But God in the New Testament is different. He's a god of mercy and forgiveness."

Mercy and forgiveness, Mack thought. For vermin like Jason Fry? No way. Vermin like Fry had to be exterminated, not forgiven. But Mack realized that Megan could never understand that. She couldn't understand because for her it wasn't personal.

"Let me ask you a question," he said. "How would you feel if your daughter was raped and murdered, and her killer walked?"

This Megan hadn't expected. It was a question she had never asked herself. She had to think about it for more than a moment before she answered. "I would be devastated, of course. But I wouldn't let it take over my life. I wouldn't let it destroy me or make me do crazy things."

Mack started to speak, then clammed up. Bullshit! Megan could say that now, but if something really did happen to Katie—the kind of things that had happened to the victims of Jason Fry, things that Megan didn't want to confront or couldn't even imagine—then how would she react?!

Megan sensed his anger and raised her glass. "Buy the lady another drink?"

Mack felt his anger defused by the warm smile on the angelic face of this lovely redhead.

"Are you hustling me, lady?"

Now her smile took on a sexy edge. "What do you think?"

Mack waved his hand to signal Angie. "Nurse."

A few tables away, at a booth along the back wall of the Downbeat, Angel Chavez was nursing a vodka and tonic as he watched Mack and Megan engaging intently in conversation. Angel was not his real name. It was Juan. Angel was a name given him by a drunken American tourist when Juan was only six years old. To help support his impoverished family, little Juan would sing the melodies played by his two older brothers on their guitars outside the big hotels in Monterey, Mexico, for whatever small change the *turistas* would drop into their sombreros.

"You sing like an angel, my boy," one *turista* had said before extracting a five-dollar bill from a wallet stuffed with money and tucking the bill into the pocket of Juan's soiled shirt.

The brothers were ecstatic. Five dollars! American money! Enough to feed the whole family a feast of beans, rice, fried pork and tortillas for supper. Perhaps for two suppers. There hadn't been much to eat for a while. Their father, an unskilled laborer, was out of work, and their mother had all she could do just caring for her five children—three boys and two girls.

Yes, the five dollars was a big thing. But to little Juan, it was not the most important thing. It was the sight of all the other dollars in the *turista's* bulging wallet. At that moment little Juan promised himself that someday he would have such money. It was a promise he had kept.

Angel smiled at the memory as he fingered the five-dollar bill in the pocket of his purple, open-necked Zegna sports shirt. He always kept one in his shirt pocket in appreciation for what the *turista* had done for him. If he had not put that bill into Juan's pocket, Juan would not have seen the wallet with the many bills and would not be where he was today.

"Another drink, sir?"

Angel looked up into the smiling face of a plump blonde waitress with a name badge identifying her as "Ella." "I'm still working on this one, thank you," he said with a slight Hispanic accent.

"Just let me know when you're ready," Ella said.

"I will," Angel said, aware that Ella's interest in him was about more than just getting a generous tip. He'd also noticed some flirty glances from other females as he'd followed the elderly host to his table, moving like a flamenco dancer or *toreador*, perhaps resembling one with his medium height and slender waist. Angel smiled. It had happened again. He'd been carded by the old host. His cherubic face topped by a mane of coal black hair often made it necessary for him to show proof of his age, which was twenty-nine, when he entered a bar. This he provided with a Costa Rican driver's license identifying him as Pedro Ruiz.

Angel took another sip of the vodka tonic through a straw. He would nurse the drink until he left. Unless it was necessary to blend in, he stayed clear of alcohol. Drugs, as well. In his line of work his mind must always be clear and focused.

He glanced at his diamond-bezel Rolex. Ten-thirty. It would be eleven-thirty p.m. in Venezuela. He took out a cell phone and fingered "1" on the speed dial. A voice answered in Spanish.

*"La residencia de Senor Ortiz."*

*"Es el su casa?"*

*"No, senor. Senor Ortiz no esta en el pais. Puedo tomar su mensaje?"*

*"No es necessario, gracias. Adios."*

Out of the country again, Angel thought. Ortiz could be anywhere, anywhere in the world, provided it offered the luxuries to which he was accustomed, even if it was a place where he had to take care of business.

Angel poked "2" on the speed dial, Ortiz's cell number. After two tones, another voice answered, this one in English.

"Yes?"

Angel responded in English. For reasons unknown to him, Ortiz rarely used his native tongue of Spanish. His English was flawless but heavily laced with what Angel thought was very highbrow British. Certainly not American. Although not as polished as his employer's, Angel's English was more than adequate, thanks to the instruction he received as a boy at the Templo Iglesia del Sagrado Corazon in Monterrey.

"Good evening. Is this a good time to talk?" Angel said, also not using a name, just in case their conversation should by some electronic quirk, accidental or contrived, reach the wrong ears.

"Ah, it's you, my friend. You have news, I trust?"

"Yes. The detective. He is alive and..."—Angel looked across the crowded bistro to where Mack and Megan were sitting—"doing quite well as I speak."

"Really? A pity."

"Do you want me to take action?"

"No. Not yet, in any event. Let's let the other people handle things for now."

"And if they don't?"

"Then, my friend, you may feel free to take matters into your own capable hands."

"As you wish."

"Good. Keep me informed."

Angel turned off the cell and slipped it into the pocket of his beige Armani sports coat. Suddenly, Angel felt the urge to relieve himself. He got up and entered the men's restroom, which was near his booth at the back of the room. A man was using one of the three urinals. Angel waited until the man washed his hands and dried them with a paper towel before moving to a urinal. Since that time in the church when his whole life had changed, Angel had been unable to expose his penis in the presence of another male.

When the door closed and no one else entered, Angel unzipped the fly of his black Zegna slacks. He had to stand there for a few moments before he could urinate. The graffiti on the wall over the urinals didn't help, especially a crude drawing of a mouth performing oral sex on a penis. Angel closed his eyes to shut out the image and began to sing softly in a high pitched voice that had not lost its melodic pureness since adolescence.

The words were in Latin. The song was a Catholic hymn.

## *Wednesday, May 22*

*7:43 a.m.:* Mack parked in the rear lot of the Area 3 precinct station and moved to the rear entrance with a sack containing a tall Starbucks coffee and a raisin bagel. He was still experiencing the afterglow of the previous night. After telling Megan about Kenny, he'd been able to relax and enjoy her very agreeable company. During and between the band's next two sets, they'd covered a lot of ground about each other. Megan revealed her passion for physical fitness and her culinary skills in preparing food that was both delicious and healthy. But mostly she talked about Katie's progress in kindergarten, where her daughter was already reading at a second grade level and would probably be advanced a grade when she returned to school in the fall.

Mack told Megan about his hobby of collecting and restoring antiques, his still very active mother who ran the antique store in North Webster, and his too infrequent but enjoyable fishing excursions to the mountain streams of Colorado. He was tempted to ask Megan about her married friend, "Ace," but given her reaction at lunch, he decided not to go there. Instead, he attempted to answer Megan's questions about jazz, despite Louis Armstrong's oft quoted response to someone who asked him the same question, "If you have to ask, you'll never know."

Their conversation was sporadic while he took Megan home in a taxi to her condo on North Clark Street. It reminded Mack of one of his first dates when he was a freshman in high school, not knowing quite what to say but just enjoying the presence of a pretty girl. Like that first date in high school, Mack had said goodnight by shaking Megan's hand. No kiss. Had she expected him to kiss her? He could only wonder.

He was also wondering where this thing with Megan was going, and if Megan was asking herself the same question. Maybe nowhere. Just a night out with a special lady. In any event, it was certainly something he hadn't planned. Hoped for, yes, but not anticipated. He'd already decided that he wasn't going to push it. At least not for now. Not until the investigation was over. Then he'd see.

Mack entered the precinct station reception lobby. As he moved through the squad room, he was surprised to see Otis hunched over the computer in their cramped office.

"You're early," Otis said without looking up from the monitor screen.

"Got a wake-up call from Ulysses."

"Ulysses?"

"My cat. He wanted breakfast."

"Since when did you become a cat lover?"

Mack set the sack on the desk and settled into the chair. "I'm not. I owed him a favor."

"I'm not even going to ask you what that's about. Did Megan catch up with you?"

Mack removed the cup of coffee from the sack, pried off the lid to release the aromatic vapor of caffeine, and took a sip. "She did. At least I owe you for an enjoyable evening. Oh, and thanks for bringing her up to date on my resume."

"You're welcome. Need I say that I did it for your own good, as if you give a shit. So what did you decide?"

Mack removed half of the sliced bagel from the sack and took a bite. "What do you think?" he said, munching.

Otis swung around in the chair to face Mack. "So you still believe the shooter had something to do with your so-called investigation?"

"I do," Mack said. Now he saw the smug expression on Otis's face. Something was up.

"To be frank, I was tempted to go along with you on that after I put in a couple of hours on the computer on my own time yesterday. I checked out the guys you'd busted who'd gotten out of stir during the last six months. There were only two. One dude, Kyle Walker, is awaiting trial in the Cook County lock-up for raping a sixty-six-year-old lady after only six weeks on the street."

Mack took another bite of the bagel, chewed and washed it down with coffee. "I remember Kyle. Had a rap sheet of at least a dozen rapes. The judge gave him a light sentence. Guess Kyle promised he'd learned his lesson and would be a good boy."

"I guess. The second ex, Darian Watts, did four out of five for burglary, was paroled four months ago for good behavior. I contacted his parole officer at home. Darian has a job in the service department of a Ford dealer on North Central. The officer gave me the name and phone numbers of Darian's boss. I got him on his cell. Darian did not call in sick yesterday."

"Good for Darian. So much for your revenge theory, I take it."

"Like I said, that's what I thought. So I slept on it and woke up in the middle of the night with another angle."

"Which was?"

"Which was the possibility that a relative of someone in your fan club, like a father, brother, maybe even a son, had pulled the trigger. A long shot, but I did another search this morning and guess whose name came up?"

"I'll bite. Who?"

Otis fingered a key on the computer to enlarge a rap sheet that now filled the monitor screen. Mack blinked. Was that name on the rap sheet what he thought it was? He got up, leaned over Otis's shoulder. It was. Morgan Fry!

"Jason Fry's big bro," Otis said with a hint of smugness. "A man with a motive, wouldn't you say?"

Mack didn't respond. He was looking at Morgan's mug shot, which bore only a slight resemblance to Jason—swarthy, Fu-Manchu mustache, with a tattooed skull and crossbones on his forehead—and reading his rap sheet. The guy had a long history of drug addiction with a laundry list of convictions, ranging from shoplifting to armed robbery, some of which had resulted in convictions and jail time. His latest sentence of three years in Joliet State Prison for strong-arm burglary had elapsed on April 25th.

"Two to one Morgan's our boy," Otis said.

"Could be," Mack had to admit. "But was he acting on his own or being used?"

"Man, you just don't know when to quit, do you?"

"One way to find out. He wouldn't have a current address by any chance?"

"No way. But I got a lead. I called the prison to see if Morgan had any visitors. There was only one. She was there several times to bring him stuff. Name's Sheila Bloeski and, yes, she has a rap sheet. I already printed it out."

Otis handed Mack a rap sheet that showed the dour, scowling face of a bleary-eyed woman with dark, stringy hair and sunken cheeks. She could have been pretty at one time, Mack thought, but her lifestyle and drugs had taken their obvious toll.

"Sheila's a crack whore. Last arrest occurred in a bar on West Wilson when she solicited an off-duty cop. Bad choice. No, she's not in the phone book, but I know a dude who might help us locate her."

Mack was beginning to be impressed by Otis, but he wasn't about to give him an A on his report card just yet. "Let's pay him a call."

*1:04 p.m.:* Otis directed Mack to park the Crown Vic in front of a Dunkin' Donuts near Wilson and Broadway. "So when did you become a donut addict?" Mack asked.

"I'm not. But the dude I want to talk to is. His name's Lionel. Got a stable of hookers and deals some narc on the side. He hangs out here about this time."

"I hope so, since we had to blow off a decent lunch."

True, Otis thought. To work Lionel into their busy schedule they'd have to grab some junk food at a McDonald's or Burger King.

"Speaking of lunch," Mack said. "I'll bet you the tab tomorrow that Lionel's a dead end."

"You're on. Hey, there he is." Otis gestured toward a tall, black man with a goatee coming out of a TCF bank across the street.

"Natty dresser," Mack said, observing the gray fedora, pinstriped charcoal suit, sky blue shirt and burgundy tie. "You guys must shop at the same stores."

"Yeah, like maybe we appreciate presenting a good appearance, unlike some people I know."

They waited until Lionel crossed the street and entered the restaurant before Mack started to get out of the car. "Okay, let's find out who buys tomorrow."

"Not we. I'll talk to Lionel alone. I want information, and you might spook him."

"I'll do more than spook him if he knows something and won't cooperate."

"Relax. I won't be long."

Otis exited the Vic and moved to the Dunkin' Donuts. Entering the restaurant, which was bathed in fluorescence, he inhaled the sweet aroma of donuts. Lionel was ordering at the counter from a young Hispanic girl. The only other person in the place was a bag lady at one of the small, plastic tables, who was muttering obscenities into a cup of coffee.

Otis approached Lionel and tapped him on the shoulder. "Hey, Lionel. How's it goin'?"

Lionel turned. He obviously figured him as a cop, Otis thought, judging by the expression on his face, which looked like he'd just received a request for back taxes from the IRS, assuming he bothered to file a return.

"Do I know you?"

"We met once. I was with Tony G. Detective Winstrom, Special Victims."

Lionel's face relaxed. "Oh, yeah. I remember you. So how's my man Mr. G?"

"Doin' good. He's retired."

"Retired, huh. And you be takin' his place?"

"Nobody can take Tony's place, but I'm trying."

"Here is your order, sir," the counter girl said with a heavy Hispanic accent. She set the cup of coffee and sack of donuts on the counter. "That will be five dollars and fifty-five cents."

Otis took out his wallet. "My treat, Lionel." He handed the counter girl a five and two ones. "*Quedese con el cambio, senorita*," he said. Otis always took advantage of an opportunity to practice his Spanish. He was taking a self-teaching course on cassettes in order to converse with the many Hispanics he dealt with on his job, some of whom couldn't speak English.

"*Muchas gracias, senor*," the counter girl said with a smile that revealed an urgent need to see a dentist.

"*De nada.*" Then to Lionel, gesturing to one of the tables, "Let's step into your office."

"Hey, man. You talk spic pretty good," Lionel said. He set down the sack and coffee and scrunched onto a plastic seat that creaked under his weight.

Otis sat down opposite Lionel. "I'm working at it."

Lionel pried the lid off the cup and extracted a powdered sugar donut from the sack. "I guess you be lookin' to buy more than donuts for Lionel."

Correct, Otis thought. Lionel was one of Tony G's street informants. For a price, of course, and when he was in the mood. "I'm looking for a woman. She's a hooker and a user, and I have reason to believe she's working this neighborhood."

"That be all?"

"That's it. And given your profession, I thought you might know her." Otis took out Sheila's rap sheet from his coat pocket, unfolded it and handed it to Lionel. "Sheila Bloeski. Recognize her?"

"Sheila. Yeah, I knows Sheila. Use the bitch on occasion. Not one of my regular bitches, 'cause she gets too fucked up on drugs and don't bring top dollar."

"Any idea where she lives?"

Lionel took a bite of the donut, aging his goatee with flakes of powdered sugar. "No. Round here somewhere, I 'spect. But I got a phone number."

"That'll do."

Lionel took a pull at the coffee, then removed a memo book from a coat pocket and flipped through the pages. "Here it be. 773-509-9211."

Probably unlisted, Otis thought. He jotted the number down in his notebook, put it back into his pocket and stood up, more than pleased that his hunch had paid off. "Much obliged, Lionel."

"Hey, man, you be forgettin' something?"

"Oh, yeah." Otis removed his wallet, took out a twenty-dollar bill and laid it on the table.

Lionel glared at it with contempt. "Only twenty? My man Mr. G, he took good care of Lionel."

"Sorry, Lionel, but twenty is the going price for one phone number."

Lionel picked up the bill and stuffed it into his breast pocket. "Chicken feed. You be needin' Lionel again, you come up with some serious green."

"Be seeing you, Lionel. Enjoy the donuts."

Otis exited the diner, moved to the Crown Vic and slid into the passenger seat.

"Any luck?" Mack said.

"You owe me lunch tomorrow at Stacy's, and I'm ordering a New York strip."

Mack grunted and fired up the engine.

*4:45 p.m.:* Mack squeezed the Vic between a Cherokee SUV and a Corolla that looked like used car rejects in front of a low rent apartment building on North Malden. Another AWOL from a nursing home and a missing wife, still unresolved, had taken most of the afternoon. Thanks to Mack, they'd bypassed the required procedure to get Sheila's address, which would have involved putting a request through a chain of command beginning with their immediate supervisor and ending with the chief of detectives. That could take forever. Fortunately, Mack had a contact at the Records Division, who provided the address with the usual proviso that the phone call never happened.

Mack and Otis exited the Vic into a light drizzle descending from a gun metal sky. Independently they began scanning the street for signs of a Honda motorcycle.

Mack read Otis's thoughts first. "Guess he wouldn't be dumb enough to park it on the street."

"Guess not."

They walked up to the front door, where a sign advertised studios and one-and two-bedroom apartments for rent, along with the name and phone number of the rental agent. They entered a musty foyer and scanned the rows of alphabetically listed names next to the voice activation buttons on the wall. "S. Bloeski" was there with no apartment number. Mack pushed the button for the superintendent. It took another poke before a voice growled over the speaker. "If you wanna rent, you gotta call the realtor."

"We're the police," Mack said. "Open up."

"All right, all right. I'm comin'."

The door buzzed, and Mack and Otis entered into a hallway. A gaunt, balding man in his fifties approached from the rear.

"You got some I.D.?"

Mack showed his badge and I.D. "We're looking for one of your tenants, Sheila Bloeski."

"Don't recall the name, but that's nothing new. They come and go here pretty fast. Follow me."

The superintendent led them down the hallway and into his combination office/apartment at the rear.

"Bloeski, let's see," he said, consulting a record of tenants. "Here she is. She's on the twelfth floor. 1226."

"Thanks," Otis said. "What's your name?"

A quizzical look from the super. "Lynch. Claude Lynch. I ain't done nothing."

Otis took out his notebook and wrote down the time and the super's name. "No one said you had."

Mack and Otis took one of the two elevators to the twelfth floor. Apartment 1226 was at the end of a corridor at the rear of the building next to a door marked "FIRE ESCAPE EXIT." They drew their weapons, listened. The only sound from inside the apartment was the chatter of a talk show on the TV. Mack started to knock, but Otis touched him on the shoulder.

"Did it ever occur to you that we might be needing a warrant?"

"It did, if we were here to conduct a search. All I want to do is talk to the lady."

"So what if Morgan is in there and armed?"

"Then we talk to Morgan."

Otis felt his stomach coil like a snake. Here we go again, he thought, but damned if he was just going to walk into a barrage of bullets. A little deception seemed in order.

"Mind?" he said, raising his fist to knock.

"Be my guest."

Otis knocked. No response. He tried again, harder this time. Sound of someone shuffling toward the door, then a woman's voice, groggy, as if she'd just been awakened.

"Who is it?"

"This is Lynch, the super," Otis said, doing his best to imitate Claude's growl. "People below you got a leak in the bathroom ceiling. Must be comin' from your place, so I got to take a look."

Nice touch, Mack thought, now willing to give Otis that A.

"Oh, all right."

Sound of a deadbolt, then the chain being unlocked. When the door started to open, Mack burst into the room, Otis behind him, knocking a woozy Sheila aside, guns extended, panning the living room and open kitchenette of the studio. Mack absorbed the scene quickly. Kitchen sink piled with dirty plates. Waste container overflowing with garbage. Room heavy with the odor of nicotine. Ashtrays clogged with cigarette butts. Empty beer bottles strewn about the living room. Air conditioner groaning. Babbling voices on the TV.

Mack turned to Sheila, who was wearing a soiled, floral design caftan that looked like it had been fashioned out of a cheap window curtain. Hazel, drug-glazed eyes in her sallow face now flared with alarm.

"Whadahwant?" she slurred.

"Officers McPherson and Winstrom, Sheila," Mack said. "Special Victims. We're looking for a friend of yours. Morgan Fry."

"Morgan ain't here."

"You wouldn't happen to know where he is, would you?"

"No. Why do you wanna see him? Morgan ain't done nothing."

"We just want to talk to him, Sheila," Otis said.

"Well, I don't know where he is. So you just get the fuck out of here and leave me alone."

Mack grabbed her arm. "You know where he is, all right. Now you can tell us, or look forward to a trip to the Cook County lock-up for drug abuse. I'm sure the shit you're on won't be hard to find."

Sheila pulled her arm away. "You can't do that unless you gotta search warrant. I know my rights. You gotta have a search warrant!"

Otis gave Mack an "I-told-you-so" look, which Mack ignored. He'd seen Sheila's eyes flick for a split second to the closed bedroom door. Morgan Fry was behind that door, for damned sure.

Mack realized that what he did in the next ten seconds could change the course of his life. If Morgan wasn't the shooter, he might be willing to talk to the cops, despite a possible drug rap. No problem there. However, if he was the shooter, and Mack and Otis went by the book to obtain a search warrant—assuming that they could even get one without showing probable cause—Morgan would be long gone by the time they got back. And the evidence linking him to the shooting—the AK-47 and Honda cycle—would probably be residing at the bottom of the Chicago River. Furthermore, Mack would never know if Morgan acted alone or was a pawn of someone who was hell bent on seeing that

Mack's private investigation was terminated.

Otis grimaced. His *own* future was also riding on what happened next, and he was hoping against hope that his partner would do the sensible thing. Of course, there was no way that was going to happen. Mack was pointing to the closed bedroom door. Submitting to the inevitable, Otis followed his gesture and moved to one side of the door, while Mack positioned himself on the other side. Mack reached over and tried the handle. Locked.

"Police, Morgan," Mack said. "I know you're in there. We're not here to do a drug bust. We just want to ask you a few questions about another matter. If you've been behaving yourself, you got nothing to worry about. How about it? Do you talk to us?"

No response.

"One more chance, Morgan. What's it going to be? Do you come out, or do we come in?"

This time there was a response. Automatic gunfire, bullets puncturing the door, raking the opposite wall and blowing out the TV picture tube.

"Get down!" Mack yelled at a screaming, hysterical Sheila.

Mack and Otis waited. Now silence, then the sound of a window being opened.

Mack kicked the door. It didn't budge. Otis wondered what he was doing. Morgan wasn't going anyplace. Mack knew different. He remembered the fire escape exit next to Sheila's apartment. Mack kicked again hard enough to feel the impact into his hip, jumped back to one side, as the door flew open and banged against the wall. No gunfire. Before Otis could react, Mack entered in a crouch, gun extended with both hands. One of the two rear windows was open, curtain fluttering in the breeze. Mack darted to the open window, looked out. Like he figured, Morgan had been able to jump from the window sill onto the landing of the fire escape, which was only four feet away, and was now scrambling down the metal staircase to the 11th floor landing, the AK-47 in his right hand.

"Freeze, Morgan!" Mack yelled.

Morgan reached the landing and whirled with his AK-47. Mack ducked back just in time to avoid bullets from a burst of automatic gunfire.

Mack paused, looked out again. Morgan was halfway down the stairs to the 10th floor landing. Mack steadied his elbow on the windowsill and took quick aim with the .38 at Fry's right shoulder. He wanted to separate him from his weapon, take him alive and talking. Mack squeezed off one round. Mack saw a splotch of red flare in Morgan's shoulder, accompanied with a scream of pain. The bullet's impact jarred the AK-47 from Fry's grasp. It dropped between the stairs and fell to the alley below. But the impact also pushed Morgan forward and down the last three stairs to the landing with enough force to propel his upper body over the railing. For a moment he teetered there, then went over, but was able to grab one of the spokes with his left hand.

Mack holstered his weapon and climbed out of the window. With his feet on the sill, he leapt to the fire escape and grabbed the railing. He felt it give a little, old, unstable, but it held. He pulled himself up and over the railing to the landing.

"Hang on, Morgan!" he yelled, descending the stairs three at a time.

"Hurry, hurry!" was Morgan's anguished cry. "For God's sake, hurry!"

Mack reached the 11th floor landing, started down the stairs and jumped the last six to the landing. He looked over the railing. Morgan was holding onto the spoke just over the floor of the landing, dangling between life and death.

"Okay, Morgan. I'm going to grab your wrist, so hold on!"

"Yeah, yeah, just do it!"

Mack kneeled down, reached between the spokes with both hands and grabbed Morgan's wrist. "I've got you, Morgan. I'm going to pull you up. When I get you to the top of the railing, grab it with your left hand."

"Okay, okay!"

As he did so many times in the gym when lifting a weight from the floor, Mack kept his back straight and pushed himself up with his legs to a standing position.

"Grab the railing."

"Yeah, yeah, I got it!"

"Good. Almost there, Morgan. Now I'm going to get hold of your belt and pull you up. Here goes."

Still holding onto Fry's wrist with his left hand, Mack reached down over the railing for Morgan's belt. This was the dangerous part, because he had to lean far enough over the railing to put himself in jeopardy. Morgan's weight could very well pull him over. Thank God for his upper body work-outs, Mack thought. No way he could do this otherwise.

It took more than a few seconds before he could get low enough to reach Morgan's belt. His fingers curled around studded leather and gripped it tightly.

"Here we go, Morgan."

Mack sucked in air, released it as he started to hoist Morgan. It was a slow, arduous process, taking all of Mack's strength to lift Fry and keep his balance. He almost had Morgan's torso to the top of the railing.

That's when it happened.

Otis saw it first. He was coming down the stairs to the 10th floor landing to help out when he heard the sound of metal tearing away from cement. The upper strut of the railing that supported Mack and Morgan was pulling away from the wall.

Now Mack saw it, felt the railing begin to give. He made one last effort to pull Morgan over. No use. His own feet began to slip on the wet iron landing, his body weight following the now tilting railing. Hands grasped his shoulders from behind and pulled him back. Mack lost his grip on Fry's belt but tried to hold onto his wrist.

"Help me. Help me! For God's sake, help me!"

Mack remembered Jason's cries for help in the inferno of the burning car. Were they the same? That's what he was asking himself, when Morgan's wrist slipped from his grasp.

Mack watched Morgan plunge ten stories, arms flailing as though he were trying to fly, his scream ringing in Mack's ears. The screaming stopped abruptly with the loud thump of Morgan's body bouncing off a dumpster and sprawling onto the alley, where he lay in a heap like a discarded rag doll.

"Shit!" Mack said.

Otis could not have agreed more, but for a different reason than what had just happened. The shit Otis was thinking about was the shit that was about to hit the fan.

*6:22 p.m.:* Mark Jacobs, WFFD-TV's star investigative reporter, was working on his *Deadline Chicago* spot in the 10:00 p.m. news hour—a follow-up about people with suspended licenses who were still driving—when Bernie

Nussbaum entered his small, private office in one corner of the newsroom.

"This just came in from the CPD, Mark. Thought you might want to see it."

"What is it, Bernie?" Jacobs said, not looking up from his computer monitor at the perpetually nervous-looking, middle-aged face of his producer.

Bernie regarded the handwritten information he'd taken from Jacobs's contact on the information trafficking desk.

"A shootout between the police and an ex-con on the northwest side."

"Another shoot out. So what? Happens every day."

"Yeah, but one of the officers involved was Detective McPherson."

That got Jacobs's attention. He'd been following the homicide detective's sordid record for the last three years, even featured some of his alleged vigilante exploits on his broadcasts.

"I thought McPherson was off Homicide," Jacobs said. He'd covered the death of McPherson's last victim, a paroled child molester, which had gotten the detective transferred to Special Victims.

Bernie shrugged. "You got me. Interested?"

"Maybe, if there's an angle that heats it up. Who's the victim?"

"An addict with a record of robberies, three convictions."

"Does he have a name, Bernie?"

Bernie looked at his notes. "Yeah. Morgan Fry."

"Did you say Fry?!" Jacobs was on his feet, grabbing the paper from Bernie's hand.

A bewildered look from Bernie. "Yeah. So?"

"The man's name was Morgan Fry. And I'm betting that Morgan is related to the late Jason Fry, the most recent notch on the handle of McPherson's revolver. Get back on the phone and check it out. Never mind, I'll do it."

After a quick phone call to another contact on the CPD, Jacobs hung up. "I was right. Morgan was Jason's older brother, just released from Joliet State Prison. Let's rock and roll!"

Bernie followed Jacobs into a large newsroom, where the staff was busy with phones and computers at a long table and at desks, putting the finishing touches on the 10:00 p.m. news. The 6:00 p.m. news, now in progress, was visible on a number of monitors scattered about the room.

"What about the driver's license story?" Bernie asked.

"Screw that. I'll do it tomorrow."

Jacobs headed straight for a tall, stocky woman who was looking up at a large storyboard, a clipboard in one hand.

"Janice, I need an ENG and a crew."

Janice Heidinger turned and glowered down at Jacobs. Her masculine face under a short crop of spiked, red-dyed hair regarded him as if he was something she'd like to step on. "No can do, Mark. All the vans are out on stories but one." She pointed toward the story board with a ball point pen. "Last one is practically on its way to cover the V.P. when he arrives at O'Hare."

Fucking lez bitch, Jacobs thought, resisting an urge to pull the earring out of her bulbous nose. Although she'd never made a pass in the newsroom, everyone knew about the assignment editor's sexual preference. Jacobs was also aware that she hated his guts. The feeling was more than mutual.

"Screw the V.P. I got a breaking story on the front burner."

"Mark, in case it's escaped your attention, the V.P. *is* big news again with his remarks trashing the President of France."

So what? Jacobs thought. V.P Woodrow Kearney, "Woody" to the media, was always in hot water for shooting off his big mouth, a continuous source of embarrassment for President Trippet.

"Dammit, Janice, I'm not about to stand here and argue with you! I need the truck and I need it now!"

"And I'm telling you no fucking way!"

Heads were turning now at the sound of the shouting voices, eyes following Jacobs as he stared daggers at Heidinger, then strode across the news room to the office of the news director.

Expecting the worst, Fred Lyles looked up from the news items on his desk at the little man in the plaid sports coat and bow tie who entered his office like a cop about to make a bust.

"Fred..."

"I know, I know, Mark. You need an ENG."

"I fucking well do need an ENG, but I do not, I repeat, do not need the shit that bitch is giving me!"

Lyles brushed crust flakes from a recently consumed pizza off his tufted, graying beard and took a sip of coffee from a mug before replying. Keeping his voice calm but firm, like a parent addressing a child in the throes of a tantrum, he said, "Mark, I understand, believe me I understand. But you're asking me to kill a big story for something that may or may not be worth airing."

"Fred, trust me on this! It's a winner! Have I ever steered you wrong?"

The answer was yes, but Lyles didn't say that to Jacobs. True, his arrogant investigative reporter usually came through, but there had also been some duds. The problem was that no one knew ahead of time if every breaking story would work out. It was always a risk. You just had to send out a reporter and a crew and roll the dice.

"Mind telling me what you've got?"

Jacobs briefly told his editor what he knew. Lyles considered it. It all depended on what Jacobs would be able to dig up at the crime scene, who he'd be able to interview. Without interviews all he had was lard.

"Mark, I just don't know. I mean the V.P. is a sure thing. But..."

Jacobs leaned across the desk, fixing his editor with intense, olive green eyes magnified by bifocals perched on a small parakeet nose. The face of Lyles's star reporter—narrow, with a pointed chin and taut lips and crowned with short, curly, dark brown hair—had nothing in common with the handsome, clean-cut faces of his male news and sports anchors, but was definitely more interesting.

"Fred, I don't have to remind you that the only reason the WFFD's late news is on top of the latest ratings is because of *Deadline Chicago*. Or do I?"

Lyles sighed. The unspoken threat had registered. Jacob's contract was soon to expire, and his agent was already engaged in negotiations with the network. "All right, Mark. I'll take a chance."

"Good. You won't regret this, Fred. Do you inform the bitch or do I?"

"I'll tell her," Lyles said.

Again all eyes were on Jacobs strutting across the newsroom to the storyboard, where he took a marker and scrawled a line through the V.P. story. "Lyles would like to see you," he said to Janice with no attempt to hide his glee at her humiliation.

Not waiting for her to return, Jacobs quickly assembled a crew and marched them out of the newsroom. He didn't have to turn around to know that someone in the room would raise his hand in the *heil* salute. The salute was not a reference to Hitler, but to Napoleon, which was the name the news staff had bestowed on him shortly after he came on board four years ago from the WFFD affiliate in Milwaukee. He wasn't supposed to know about the nickname, but of course he did.

There was, in fact, nothing that happened in the newsroom that escaped his eagle eyes and keen ears. Nor was he offended. He was not here to be loved. And, in a way, he did identify with Napoleon, a little man with big ambitions, like himself. Napoleon had started as "The Little Corporal" and became a great general. Jacobs also had an agenda: New York City, with a spot on national TV, or better yet, his own show, like Geraldo. All he needed as a ticket was a big story. Of course, McPherson wasn't that story, but it would come.

*7:03 p.m.:* The ENG—short for electronic news gathering van— turned north off Montrose onto Malden where a patrol car and two uniformed officers blocked the street. Jacobs showed the officers a letter from Superintendent Hollender that gave him access to crime scenes. This had been obtained out of gratitude for backing Mayor O'Connor's anti-crime campaign and for the support Jacobs knew the mayor would want should he, as rumored, decide to eventually run for governor. Jacobs told the officers to check with Hollender's office for confirmation, which they did.

The driver parked the van just shy of several cruisers that surrounded the meat wagon. Jacobs got out, showed the letter again to one of the many uniformed officers, then directed his crew like a sergeant positioning his troops for combat. The Little Corporal in action. Jacobs placed one cameraman on the top of the van, so he could tape the crime scene and the paramedics, who were already rolling the body-bagged corpse of Morgan Fry on a gurney to the ambulance. That done, Jacobs directed the other cameraman to stand by to tape anyone he could interview.

Jacobs pulled up the collar of his trench coat against the incessant drizzle. He had to wipe off his glasses with a handkerchief before he spotted McPherson and a black detective talking with two other plainclothes detectives under the entrance's metal canopy. Jacobs knew one of the detectives, Sergeant Greiner. Jacobs also knew that Greiner was aware of his clout at City Hall and would not object to his presence. In fact, Greiner had always cooperated with the media, so if need be, Jacobs could count on him for an interview. However, it was McPherson whom Jacobs wanted on camera, a tall order, given the detective's aversion to reporters, whom he treated like carriers of the plague.

Jacobs motioned to a crew member, a pretty girl in her twenties, Gail somebody, whom Jacobs had dated a few times until she let it be known that marriage and children were priorities in her life. Not so for Mark Jacobs. He needed all of his time and energy to make it to the big league. "Hey, Gail, in case you haven't noticed, it's raining, and I'm getting wet."

Gail hustled over with a large umbrella, which she opened and held over Jacobs's head. Jacobs took off his glasses again, wiped them, put them back over the bridge of his parakeet nose, and waited. Maybe this time he'd get lucky.

Mack and Otis were filling in Greiner and his partner on what happened. Old home week, Mack thought. Greiner had just been moved from Division 1 Homicide to Division 3 as Mack's replacement. And Vince Preston, Greiner's partner, was Mack's last partner before Mack was dumped to Special Victims.

Mack knew that the slim, sandy haired young cop, who had a wife and two kids, had not been terribly upset about Mack's transfer.

Greiner's frown said it all but he said it anyway. "The boys downtown are gonna be crapping in their pants about this, Mack."

"I'm aware of that possibility, Sam."

"Dammit, Mack, I told you to steer clear of trouble."

"So what am I supposed to do. Give the asshole a medal for trying to kill me?"

Greiner sighed. "Yeah, I know. It sucks. Well, I guess all I can do is wish you luck."

"That I can use. If you don't mind, Otis and I are going to the precinct to file our report."

"Go ahead. We'll clean up things here."

"Oh, and you might look around for a Honda cycle. Fry used it yesterday when he took those shots at us. It'll have a shot-off rearview mirror. Chances are Fry has it stashed somewhere nearby."

"We'll do that."

"Let's go," Mack said to Otis.

Making their way toward the Crown Vic, Mack spotted a cameraman taping them from the top of a TV van.

"Smile, you're about to be on the evening news," Otis said.

Neither Otis or Mack were looking forward to that prospect, even less to talking to the little man in the trench coat who suddenly intercepted them.

"Mark Jacobs, WFFD, Detective McPherson," he said, thrusting a hand mike into Mack's face, while a cameraman rolled film.

"I know who you are," Mack said. He was all too familiar with the man who'd been on his case for longer than he cared to remember.

"Would you comment on what happened here, Detective?"

Mack was about to tell Jacobs to shove it. He knew how the media could edit what he said to spin the story any way they wanted. This time, however, he decided to take a chance to set the record straight. If he didn't, they'd spin it anyway.

"Officer Winstrom and I had reason to believe that Morgan Fry was the shooter who attempted to kill us yesterday with sniper fire from an abandoned building on West Evergreen. We found out that his girlfriend, Sheila Bloeski, lived here and investigated. Fry was holed up in the bedroom. We gave him the opportunity to come out and answer our questions. He chose to open fire with an AK-47 instead. The sniper also used an AK-47, and I'm certain ballistics will show it was the same weapon used by Fry in Bloeski's apartment."

"You said that Fry opened fire first?"

"That's right."

"You're sure about that?"

"I am. Officer Winstrom here can collaborate that."

"I'm certain he will," Jacobs said.

Mack did not miss the insinuation that cops always stuck together on their accounts of a shooting.

"And what happened next, Detective?"

Mack gave Jacobs a quick account of how he'd wounded Fry and then tried in vain to save him.

"I assume that Officer Winstrom can collaborate this, as well. I mean, that you didn't shoot to kill, that you attempted to save him?"

"He will."

"How about Sheila Bloeski? Did she witness what you've just told me?"

"I don't know. Probably not."

"Let me ask you this, Detective. Do you have any idea why Morgan Fry would try to kill you?"

Mack figured that Jacobs had done his homework and already knew that Morgan was Jason's brother. "In all likelihood it was an act of revenge. A few weeks ago his brother, Jason, made an attempt on my life. He died trying to escape when his car crashed into a diesel tank."

"Oh, yes, I remember. The paroled child molester who, for some reason, also had a grudge against you."

"I was the officer who arrested him for rape and attempted murder of a little girl."

"I believe the attempted murder was never proven. That he wasn't even charged with the crime."

"No. He wasn't," Mack gritted.

"And Fry was paroled on the basis of the opinions of psychiatrists who concluded that he was cured and ready to resume a responsible role in society."

"That was their opinion."

"But not yours?"

"No."

"You still considered him a menace?"

"I did."

"So much so that you felt it necessary to do something about it?"

Mack realized now that he should have blown Jacobs off instead of giving him the interview. Trying to set the record straight with the media was a no-win. "It's all in the police report. If you'd care to read it, you'll know that I was acting in the line of duty."

"What I *know* is that you have a reputation for taking the law into your own hands, Detective. Were Jason Fry, and now his brother, Morgan, two more victims of McPherson justice?"

Jacobs didn't expect a reply to this loaded question, but he got one anyway. As McPherson brushed past him, Jacobs felt an elbow to his chest that punched the wind out of his lungs. Momentarily unable to talk, he gestured to his cameramen to continue to tape McPherson and his partner. Watching them get into the car, and the car move away, he smiled through his pain. Mark Jacobs had his story.

*10:43 p.m.:* Otis was fuming. Sprawled on his king-sized bed, his head propped up on the goose down pillow, he forced himself to watch the entire fifteen-minute segment of *Deadline Chicago* on the 10:00 p.m. news.

Jacobs was doing an even nastier hatchet job on Mack than Otis had expected. By the detective's own admission, McPherson had it in for Jason Fry, Jacobs alleged, and the only account of what happened the night Fry met his death in the fiery inferno—this with a film clip showing the flaming fuel tank—was McPherson's. As for Morgan, Jacobs spun him as an "emotionally disturbed" next of kin, who was merely trying to even the score for his brother, as if being emotionally disturbed justified attempted murder.

The last two minutes featured a live interview with Sheila Bloeski. Looking to Otis like she'd undergone a quick makeover in a beauty parlor, Sheila came across as traumatized by the "unlawful" invasion of her apartment by Officers McPherson and Winstrom. Questioned by Jacobs, Sheila claimed that it was Officer McPherson, not Morgan, who had fired the first shot, and that McPherson had deliberately let Morgan fall to his death. His face a visage of moral outrage, Jacobs demanded that the CPD conduct a thorough investigation into the deaths of both Jason and Morgan Fry.

"We can only hope," Jacobs concluded, "that this mad dog cop will be muzzled before some other innocent victim of Detective McPherson's warped vigilante justice lies dead on the streets of Chicago. This is Mark Jacobs for *Deadline Chicago.*"

Otis aimed the remote at the TV as if it was a revolver and blackened the screen. He suddenly felt the need for something stronger than the glass of iced tea on the night table.

"Why did you turn it off?" Ava said.

"I've had enough bad news for today."

No response from Ava. She'd listened to the entire *Deadline Chicago* broadcast without comment, while removing her makeup and creaming her face at the vanity. Another night without sex, Otis thought. Ava's face-creaming ritual always followed the event. Not that Otis was in the mood tonight, although he was beginning to wonder if they'd ever have sex again, given their ongoing chilly relationship.

"Why don't you turn on Letterman?"

"I'm not in the mood for Letterman. Leno either."

"I just thought it might help you let go, relax, that's all."

"I know."

Otis took a sip of iced tea. Ava hadn't said much about what had happened the last two days, which was plenty. She would, but first she had to internalize it. Rather than react emotionally, she tried to deal with events calmly and objectively after a "cooling off period," as she put it. Otis figured that the cooling off period had about run its course. He was right. The face creaming complete, she turned and asked a question that he hadn't expected.

"Is it true? What that woman said?"

"Is what true?"

"That your partner deliberately let that man Fry fall to his death?"

"No way."

"She seemed very convincing."

"She saw what she wanted to see, if she even saw it at all. Besides, she was stoned out of her mind."

"I hope you're telling me the truth."

"Ava, I was there. Mack did his best to save him, but the railing gave way. If I hadn't pulled Mack back, he might have gone over with him."

Otis was not liking this. Was Ava questioning his word against that of a crack whore who had no love for cops? She must have read his face, because she quickly backed off.

"I'm sorry. I was just afraid that you might be sticking up for McPherson instead of thinking of yourself. Are you going to be okay with this?"

"I think so. Mack and I have to see the superintendent tomorrow at nine. Commander Cronin told me he'd call the super first thing in the morning and go to bat for me."

"What about McPherson?"

Otis shrugged. "I don't know. Probably a suspension pending an investigation."

"Only a suspension? He should be discharged from the force at the very least."

"That could happen, I guess."

Ava rose, slipped out of the matching robe of her slinky, silk, lace-trimmed night gown, draped it over the back of the chair. "I'm just thankful that you'll be rid of him as a partner."

Otis thought that he should be thankful, too. After all, isn't that what he'd wanted, what he'd asked Cronin for? Sure it was. Funny thing though, now that it seemed likely to happen, it wasn't thankfulness he felt. He was feeling sorry for Mack. Sorry and angry at what could happen to him. Okay, so maybe Mack did have it coming, but that didn't change the way Otis felt. Something had happened to him yesterday when he'd had to use Tony's .38, and now he realized what it was. At that moment he'd bonded with his partner. Like it or not, that's the way it was. However, this was not something he would share with Ava, who came over and sat down on the bed.

"You are glad to be rid of him, aren't you?"

"What? Oh, yeah."

Ava slid over next to Otis, bringing with her the fragrance of lavender. Otis put his arm around her shoulders.

"I hope you mean that," Ava said, snuggling into his embrace. "When I think of what happened..."

Otis felt the warmth of Ava's body against his. He felt something else, as well. Her body was trembling. Otis looked into Ava's emerald green eyes and saw something he hadn't expected. He saw fear.

"It's okay, darling," he said, pulling her closer. "It's okay."

Otis held her for several minutes, neither speaking, until her trembling subsided. Then another thing happened he hadn't expected. Her hand slipped under the top of his pajamas and caressed his penis. Otis smiled at the realization that a ritual was about to be ignored.

## *Thursday, May 23*

*9:05 a.m.:* Mack laid his service revolver and badge on Superintendent Hollender's desk. The superintendent wasted no time informing Mack that from that moment he could consider himself suspended from active duty pending a full investigation of his conduct by Internal Affairs. Mack had expected nothing less. Still, the news felt like a karate kick to his groin.

"You can leave now, McPherson," Hollender said. "Ask Detective Winstrom to step in here."

Mack stood there, glaring at the hawk face, at the hint of a smirk on his taut lips. Damned if he was going to leave without speaking his mind.

"Investigator Winstrom and I were only acting on reliable information linking Fry with an attempt on our lives the previous day."

"Let me remind you that you entered the apartment without a warrant, Detective. Mistake number one. And according to the Bloeski woman, you fired without giving Fry a chance to surrender, and that you deliberately let him fall to his death."

"That's bullshit! I fired one shot and one shot only at Fry as he was attempting to escape down the fire escape. And I could have saved him if the railing hadn't pulled away from the wall. It's all in the report."

Hollender picked up papers off the desk and brandished them in Mack's face. "I have your report right here, McPherson. Officer Winstrom's as well. Naturally, he supports your account of what happened."

"Why shouldn't he? It's the truth!"

Hollender slapped the reports on the desk as if he were swatting a fly. "I hope so, Detective. In any event, you'll both have the opportunity to tell your stories to IAD."

"What about my partner? He's not to blame for this. I take full responsibility for entering without a warrant."

Hollender picked up Mack's badge, fingered it. "I'm letting Detective Winstrom off without even a reprimand. He's a fine detective with an exemplary record. But he'll still have to talk to IAD."

Mack felt relieved by this news. A reprimand would have gone onto Otis's record for five years.

Hollender fixed Mack with a frigid stare. "As for you, Detective. If you so much as spit on the sidewalk, you can start looking for a job in the want ads. Do I make myself clear?"

Screw you, Mack thought. Hollender would see that he was fucked no matter how he conducted himself. "Perfectly clear."

"Good. That's all, Detective." Hollender opened a desk drawer, dropped in Mack's badge and looked up at Mack, who was still standing there. "I said that's all."

Hollender reached for Mack's revolver. Before he could think about what he was doing, Mack grabbed the .38 and pointed it at the superintendent. Hollender froze. Their eyes locked. To his credit, the Hawk didn't flinch, Mack thought, but he was willing to bet that if the super didn't have high blood pressure before, he had it now. Smiling, Mack lowered the revolver, flipped open the chamber and emptied six bullets onto the desk.

"Have a nice day, Superintendent."

Mack laid down the revolver, turned and exited the office without closing the door.

*4:20 p.m.:* Willie Butler felt lousy. It was like something inside of him seemed to be slowly sucking the energy out of his body. If Needles were still alive, Willie would have let him give him a shot of vitamin B. Maybe he'd check into a shelter that provided medical service—not The Beacon, of course—give a phony name and get the shot along with a good meal and some sack time on a cot instead of a slab of cement in the Lower Wacker Hilton.

But that would have to wait. Willie had a job to finish first—for the cop and Frank. During the past three days he'd blown about half of McPherson's five hundred dollars—some on food but no booze—but mostly on assholes who'd given him phony leads for the ten spots. Then it occurred to him that the best place to find Hispanic hit men and their van would be on their own turf. Figuring that they were probably Mexican, he'd struck out in two heavily populated Mexican neighborhoods before deciding to try the area called "Little Village" in southwest Chicago.

If anyone knew what was going down on the streets of Little Village, it would be a flamboyant street character who called himself "El Pistolero." Willie knew him as Jose Ortega from his Lower Wacker days before he came up with his *bandito* angle. Garbed like a Mexican bandit of old, El Pistolero pretended to hold up patrons of La Cocina, a well-known Mexican restaurant, who usually parted with a dollar or two for the amusement of being robbed. La Cocina's owner was willing to let El Pistolero do his thing, as were the cops, as long as no one complained. No one did, so infectious was El Pistolero's winning personality.

Willie figured that El Pistolero would not arrive at his place of business until the cocktail hour, so he waited until late afternoon, then took a bus to 26th and California. Willie walked the two blocks west on 26th to La Cocina. As he approached, he saw that he had figured the time right: El Pistolero was brandishing two pearl handled cap pistols at a young *gringo* couple, while an attendant parked their BMW. After receiving a five spot from the man, El Pistolero tipped his sombrero to the pretty young lady and smiled, his gold front tooth glistening in the sunlight.

"*Mil gracias, senor y senorita.* Please enjoy your supper."

Willie approached, hands raised. "Don't shoot, Jose. It's Willie."

"Willie, *mi bueno amigo!*"

Willie inhaled a blend of garlic and tequila, as El Pistolero embraced him in a robust hug. "How's biz, Jose?"

"Please, do not call me Jose, *mi amigo*. Here I am El Pistolero. Business, she is very good, especially with the *gringos*. Let me show you something." El Pistolero twirled the pistols on his index fingers and slipped them into his holsters. "Is good, *si?*"

"Clint Eastwood couldn't have done it better."

"That is true, *amigo*. I should be in the movies, don't you think? But you did not come to Little Village just to see El Pistolero do his act."

"That's right. I got a little business proposition for you if you're interested."

"*Por suspuesto.* Step into my office."

The spurs on his boots jingling, El Pistolero led the way to an alley next to the bistro.

"Pablo, what are you doing?" he said to a scrawny mutt who was rummaging through the contents of an overturned trash bin. "Already I feed you plenty."

The mutt looked up, barked and resumed sniffing through the debris.

"You will pardon my friend, Pablo. He is not so sociable today." El Pistolero paused to stroke his drooping mustache, which he had grown to enhance his *bandito* persona. "Now before you tell me what it is that you want, let me say that if it is something that is not so legal, I do not wish to hear it. *Comprende?*"

"Nothing like that, man. I'm buying information, and I got a ten spot with your name on it if you can help me."

"For information there is *no problema.*"

"I figured as much. I'm looking for a man. A real bad ass. He has a long scar on his cheek and a mustache like yours."

El Pistolero's eyes narrowed. "A scar, you say. Like from a knife or razor?"

"Could be."

"I know of such a man. He goes by the name Carlos Lopez, if that is his real name, which I very much doubt. I pray you do not find this man, *amigo*. He is, as you say, a bad ass. *Muy malo.*"

"I'm not lookin' to get myself killed, but I got a reason to know what Carlos is up to. You wouldn't know where I could find him, would you?"

"Where he lives, no. But there is a bar just a few blocks from here where such men go, and not just to drink tequila. It is called 'El Lobo', the Wolf. A fitting name for such a place."

"'El Lobo', huh? Guess I'll pay it a visit." Willie peeled off a ten from what was left of McPherson's roll, which he really could use now for living expenses, and handed it to El Pistolero. "Thanks, Jose. I mean El Pistolero."

El Pistolero tucked the bill into a pocket of his faux leather vest. "*De nada, mi amigo.* But I must warn you again to be very careful of that man."

"Don't worry, my friend, I will be very careful, *muy* careful, as you say. And thanks for the information...and the warning."

Willie took off and walked the two long blocks south on Sacramento to 28th Street. The bar was just around the corner. It looked as forbidding as Willie had expected, with a grimy, cracked window and a faded sign with the name El Lobo and the image of a wolf, its fangs bared as if about to sink into the neck of a helpless prey. Willie had the feeling that *el lobo* was looking directly at him.

*4:55 p.m.:* Otis paused outside The Slammer, a hangout for cops conveniently located a half block from Area 3 Detective Division Headquarters on Western Avenue. Mack had called earlier that afternoon with a request that Otis meet him at the bar after he got off duty, but he hung up before Otis could ask him why. Whatever it was, Otis figured it would probably mean more trouble, which he definitely didn't need. He'd gotten a mild slap on the wrist from Hollender—a verbal reprimand that would not go into his record as long as he cooperated with IAD. He'd also promised Ava that he'd have nothing more to do with Mack's shenanigans, so now he debated if he should even go inside.

To hell with it, Otis thought. Mack was still his partner, even if he was on suspension pending the results of the investigation. If Mack was cleared, then they'd be working together again. Not only that, but something *had* changed in his relationship with Mack when they were under fire. Call it "bonding" or not, the least he could do was hear Mack out. That wouldn't be breaking a promise as long as he didn't get involved in Mack's investigation, which was going nowhere anyway now that Fry wasn't around to answer questions. If he had been, Otis was confident that his attempt on Mack's life was a clear-cut act of revenge and that he'd acted alone.

Otis shrugged off his apprehensions and entered the cozy neighborhood tavern dominated by an oval bar flanked with small tables. The walls were appropriately adorned with a variety of crime memorabilia—vintage weapons and handcuffs, headlines from old newspapers about famous crimes, and wanted posters of underworld celebrities like John Dillinger and Pretty Boy Floyd. A haze of nicotine hovered over the heads of the usual five o'clock patrons, most of them cops.

Otis spotted Mack at the far end of the bar and started over when a hand grabbed his arm.

"Hey, GQ, how's it goin'?"

Otis looked at the florid face of Dan Manowsky. "Hey, Dan. It's goin' good."

"And congratulations. Word is you made out okay downtown."

"Coulda been worse."

"Fuckin' A. You could be fuckin' dead." Keeping his voice low, Manowsky nodded toward Mack. "Like I told you, McPherson is poison. You're lucky to be alive."

"Yeah, I guess so. Well, hey, I gotta go, Dan."

"Stick around. I'll buy you a beer."

"Thanks, Dan. Maybe later. I need to say goodbye to Mack."

"Goodbye is right. Looks like this time he's down for the count."

"Yeah, well, could be. Hope not, though, Dan. Mack's got good intentions, even if his methods are…unorthodox. See ya later, Dan. Gotta go."

"Just watch your back, GQ, just watch your back."

Good advice, Otis thought, and moved toward where Mack was sitting at the other end of the bar.

Mack was wearing Levi's, loafers and a sweatshirt. He was watching the five o'clock news, which had just started on the TV over the bar.

"Hey, Mack," Otis greeted him.

Mack turned from the TV and looked at Otis approaching. "You're late," he said with a hint of a smile.

"Paperwork. You know how that is."

"I thought you might chicken out. Anyway, thanks for coming."

Otis mounted an empty stool next to Mack. He glanced around the bar and noticed that the stool on the other side of Mack was also empty, despite the fact that several cops were standing nearby.

Mack picked up on what Otis was thinking. "Yeah, I know. They don't have to hang a sign around my neck to know that I'm quarantined."

"I'll take a chance, as long as you're buying."

"You got a deal." Mack took a pull from his bottle of Amstel light. "So what do you think about that?"

"Think about what?"

Mack gestured to the TV with his bottle, where the evening news was in progress. An anchorman was giving an update on President Trippet's meeting with world leaders in Paris to deal with the Mideast crisis.

"About the shit that's hit the fan in the sheik of Araby land."

"The sheik of what?"

"Araby. It's a song. Before your time."

"Figures."

Otis looked at a video clip on the screen of the president emerging from a building with several other world leaders behind him. It was apparent from the serious, almost strained look on his face that the conference was not going well. He waved aside the crowd of reporters who were waiting outside, announcing only that he would not take any questions at this time, and then was hustled by his Secret Service agents into a waiting limousine.

"Not good, for sure. But if anyone can do something about it, it's the prez. He carries a lot of weight overseas."

"Maybe," Mack said. While the anchorman continued to expound, another clip showed an Arab garbed in a general's uniform bespangled with medals reviewing a parade of goose-stepping soldiers and trucks hauling trailers with missiles. "But it's gonna take more than his charm and some half-ass sanctions if that maniac gets enough enriched uranium to go nuke."

"Well, I guess he can get tough if he has to. The guy won a silver star before they carried him out of Vietnam on a stretcher."

"Yeah, he has guts, I'll give him that. But it looks like the pressure's starting to wear him down. Let's hope he can hang in there long enough to pull those other countries into line. Not many of those so-called 'world leaders' are willing to take a stand."

"True enough," Otis agreed, "...but you didn't invite me here to discuss world affairs, did you?"

"No, I didn't." Mack paused and took another sip of the Amstel, then continued. "You're aware of the crap I've been getting..."

"Whadaya havin', Otis? The usual?"

Otis looked up into the jovial face of Lucy Couch, The Slammer's owner, short and plump, with a beehive of light brown hair streaked with gray.

"The usual, Warden," Otis said, using the nickname her cop patrons had given her five years ago, when she'd bought the bar and renamed it "The Slammer."

"How about you, Mack?"

"You can bring me another Amstel. I'll have this one finished by the time you get back. And I get the tab."

Mack turned back to Otis. "Like I was saying, you're aware of the crap I've been getting from the media?"

"I'm aware, all right. I caught *Deadline Chicago* last night."

"Jacobs isn't the only member of my fan club. The other networks climbed on board today, and I guess you've seen the front pages of *The Trib* and *Sun Times*."

"I saw the headlines down at the station, but I haven't read the articles or editorial pages yet. Looks like they've all picked up on Jacob's 'Mad Dog' label."

"It's like a lynch mob. Judged me and demanded I be kicked off the force without even asking if there was another side to the story."

"C'mon, Mack. What did you expect them to do? Endorse you for mayor? The media always spin everything. Sensationalism, outrage...sure they're unfair, but that's what sells papers ...and God knows the press needs all the help they can get these days selling papers...and advertising."

"There was a time when the press reported the facts."

"Mack, I sympathize, believe me. I'm as pissed off about this as you are. But you know from experience how the media are going to treat you. Hell, it's less than a month since Jason Fry went up in flames and the media took off after you like a pack of hounds. Did you expect anything different this time?"

"No, but I'm trying to make a point."

"Which is?"

Before Mack could answer, Lucy was back with their beers. Mack finished off his first bottle and handed it empty to Lucy. "Thanks, Warden."

"You're welcome, Mack. You guys holler when you're done with these and ready for another round."

Mack waited until Lucy moved away before he answered Otis's question. "My point is this. Somebody is using City Hall to turn the heat up on me."

"Mack, you're scarin' me. That's conspiracy thinking."

"Maybe you'll change your mind after IAD gets through with their Q and A. The Hawk as much as said that it will be more like an inquisition than an investigation."

Otis had to think about this. If the IAD investigation wasn't conducted fairly and even-handedly, if it was run more like a witch hunt than a normal investigation, then maybe Mack would have a point. Otis had already completely corroborated Mack's report as to what happened at Sheila Bloesky's apartment. If they took the word of a hopped-up whore over the word of a cop, then it would sure look like something was going on behind the scenes.

Mack took a long pull from his bottle of Amstel. "It comes down to this. The only way I can get my badge back is to find out what's behind Lazarus."

"Mack, for God's sake, get some smarts. At least now you've got a chance of being reinstated, but if you get caught doing your own thing again, you can kiss your badge *and* your pension *adios*."

Mack hesitated, then sighed, "I suppose you're right." He picked up his bottle again, studied it for a moment, then put it down. "Let's watch something else. I think the Sox are playing the Yankees."

"Suits me."

Mack picked up a remote off the bar and channel-surfed to the game.

"Hey, Mack, how about that? The Sox are leading five to three."

"Yeah, how about that."

They nursed their beers and watched the game for a few minutes in silence, giving Otis hope that Mack was ready to take his advice and drop his investigation.

After a couple of minutes watching the game, Mack started the conversation going again. "You're a computer whiz, Otis. Ever do any hacking?"

Uh-oh, Otis thought. Is this just more small talk, or is he gonna try and take this somewhere? "You mean like…serious hacking?"

"Yeah."

"Is this off the record?"

"Of course."

"Well, I messed around a little in high school, you know, like a lot of kids into computers. And there was this one time…" Otis smiled at the memory, "when a buddy of mine and I hacked into the Bureau of Motor Vehicles' database and sent out big bills for overdue parking tickets to the principal, mayor and other dudes on our shit list."

Mack chuckled. "I'll buy you a steak dinner if you'll send one to the Hawk."

"Make it lobster, and you're on."

Mack took a sip of beer. "Joking aside, Otis, there is something you can do for me."

Shit!, thought Otis. Here comes the punch line. "Like what?"

"Like help me crack into the Bio-Sci research mainframe. If I'm going to find out what Lazarus is all about, that's where I have to go."

It took Otis only a moment to see that Mack was serious.

"Let me get this straight. You're asking me to possibly blow off my job, maybe even do some serious jail time, just to help you prove some way-out theory?!"

"I'd do it myself, but I don't know shit about computers."

"Sorry, Mack, but no way. I can't take that kind of risk, and you know it."

"Look, I only want you to lend a hand. And if anyone gets wise, I'll take the fall."

"Mack, you know there's no way you can assure me that I won't go down with you."

Mack was silent. He went to take another pull at the Amstel, but his bottle was empty. He motioned to Lucy and pointed at the table to let her know he was ready for another beer.

"Okay, I understand. Just do me one favor and give me your opinion about this."

Mack took out his wallet, removed a Rolodex card, and laid it on the bar next to Otis's beer. Otis picked it up, looked at it. "It says Bio-Sci. Where'd you get it?"

"From Alward's Rolodex. I've got some questions about it."

"Okay. Shoot."

"For openers, you should know that Alward used to work at Bio-Sci, and I think he was still on the payroll. I think he was feeding information into the research computer. Exactly what, I don't know, but he had all kinds of sophisticated lab equipment in his office that was all computerized."

"So what are your questions?" Otis asked.

"One of the phone numbers is the main Bio-Sci number, one a cell phone for Dr. Kischman. Kischman's in charge of the lab. The third number…" Mack leaned over and pointed to the number 847-438-7221, "is a Bio-Sci number, but it's been disconnected. Any ideas about that?"

"Well, if what you say is right, that Alward was feeding stuff into the Bio-Sci mainframe, he'd need a dedicated line to do it, and 7221 is probably the number."

"Makes sense. And they'd be sure to have it disconnected after Alward was murdered. How about the names—Microbe438, Jesus551 and Lord552? Passwords is my guess. Right?"

"Right, but they could be to Alward's computer, not necessarily Bio-Sci."

"All three of them, with one of them X'd out?"

Otis had to admit that that was unlikely. "Okay, again assuming you're right, Microbe438 is probably the password to get into the Bio-Sci network, since the other two, Jesus551 and Lord552, seem to be related."

"Which means that those two are passwords for Alward's hard drive?"

"Probably. At least Lord is. The fact that Alward X'd out Jesus probably means that the company told him to change the password, which companies do frequently for security."

"And you can bet that they changed the password to the Bio-Sci network again after someone took out Alward. But tell me this. Wouldn't anyone in the lab have access to the research computer?"

"Sure, as long as they have the password."

Lucy returned with Mack's beer and removed the empty.

"So what about a top secret project? Would they be able to get into that, too?"

"Not everyone. The program would be set up to allow only certain persons to access that file. You're talking Lazarus, I take it, if there is a Lazarus?"

"There is, and I'm going to find it. I've got to find it if I want to get my badge back. In fact, I already took a step in that direction this morning after Hollender suspended my ass."

"Oh, really? What was that?"

Mack took a swig of beer before explaining. "Well, I figured that if Alward had a dedicated line to the Bio-Sci research mainframe, a workaholic like Kischman would probably have one too. Right?

"In all likelihood. And what devious thing did you do, as if I didn't know?"

"I drove out to Long Grove and parked across the street from Kischman's house. Of course, Kischman was at work, but I didn't know if his wife was home or not. So I waited around hoping that I'd get an opportunity to do what I needed to do, and got lucky. About a half hour later, a BMW pulled out of the garage and drove away. By the way, the lady behind the wheel was some dish and a hell of a lot younger than Kischman."

"Maybe she goes for the older type."

"More likely she goes for his bank account. Anyway, it gave me the opportunity to find the external phone box. There were two lines coming from a telephone pole between Kischman's house and a next door neighbor. Both lines were identified. One was the number listed in the phone book. The other wasn't."

"So I assume you tapped into the unlisted line?"

"Yeah, with a little help from a 1"x1" Series Telephone Transmitter I borrowed from a cop in Homicide who owed me a favor."

"Congratulations, Mack. You've now got an illegal phone tap to add to your list of offenses."

"Yeah, well that's as much as I know about wiretapping. I've got no idea how to capture the Lazarus file if Kischman does access it. I'm gonna need your help to do that."

"Sorry, Mack, but like I said, I just can't take the risk." Otis drained the rest of his beer and plunked his empty bottle down firmly on the counter.

"Well, I guess I'll just have to forget it then," Mack said.

They turned their attention back to the game. The Sox now led five to four after the Yankee's last batter hit a sacrifice fly to deep center. But Otis's mind was no longer on the game. He was thinking that the information on Alward's Bio-Sci card seemed to make Mack's Lazarus theory at least somewhat plausible. Of course, the only way to find out for sure would be to do what Mack had asked him to do, crack into the Bio-Sci mainframe. No lay-up, for sure, if it was even possible. And while part of his brain kept insisting that he have nothing further to do with the crazy misadventures of Mack McPherson, another part was rehearsing the timing of the commands and mouse clicks he would have to execute to capture the Lazarus file if Kischman logged on to view it.

Otis picked up his empty beer bottle and set it down again. Time to go, he thought. But he didn't get up.

"Hey, partner."

Otis turned and saw the hint of a smile on Mack's face.

"Buy you another beer?"

*9:15 p.m.:* Mack was getting frustrated. "Shit, we've been here over an hour now, and nothing's happened."

"Patience, my man, patience," Otis said, adjusting his headset. "You've been on stake-outs before, I assume."

"More than I care to remember, but this time it's *my* ass that's on the line."

"Don't worry, it'll happen. Just give it time. How about some more coffee?"

"Okay. Good idea." Mack removed his headset and slid out of the dining nook, where Otis had his laptop on the table along with a "black box," a device that allowed data to be encrypted or decrypted. Otis had been able to borrow it before leaving the city from a friend who worked the late shift in the Information Department.

Mack took his and Otis's empty mugs over to the Mr. Coffee on the kitchenette counter. "Great idea using the RV to do a stakeout."

"Why not? If you gotta sit and wait, why not have all the comforts of home?"

Otis's El Monte RV was compact and comfy, with a bathroom and shower stall at the rear and sleeping quarters over the cab. It sure as hell beat spending what could be a long wait in the Bonneville across the street from Kischman's imposing Tudor house.

"I forgot to ask you," Mack said, filling their mugs with coffee. "How did you manage to get away tonight with the RV?"

"I lucked out. Ava's taking in a ballet with her parents. But I've got to have the RV back by eleven."

"Well, that shouldn't be a problem. If Kischman hasn't dialed in to the mainframe by 10:30, then he's probably not going to do it at all tonight."

Mack spotted casting and fly rods and a tackle box in a corner at the rear of the RV. "I see you do some fishing."

"Yeah. Ava and I travel all over. The Dells, Michigan's Upper Peninsula, even motored all the way to Yellowstone."

Mack set Otis's mug on the breakfast nook table. "I fished Yellowstone once, but just once. Too much tourist traffic for me."

"You a fisherman? I never would have guessed it."

"Yeah," Mack said, pacing back and forth with his mug in his hand. He was tired of sitting, and becoming increasingly anxious about nothing happening with the wiretap. "Don't do much fishing anymore, but I spent a lot of my boyhood fishing Webster Lake in Indiana."

"I know where Webster Lake is. Near Wawasee. The parents of a buddy of mine at I.U. had a big summer house there, and I got some invites."

Mack took a sip of coffee. "Wawasee. That's a rich man's lake. Frontage goes for major bucks."

"Out of my league, for sure. I grew up fishing on Wolf Lake. My dad got me hooked, if you'll pardon the pun. Say, what was a big city guy like you doing on a small town Indiana lake anyway, if you don't mind my asking?"

"Not at all. My grandparents had a home on the lake, and my brother and I spent the summers there."

"Yeah? Nice work if you can get it, which you obviously did."

"Hey, it wasn't all fun in the sun. We worked, too. I had all kinds of jobs, like pumping gas at a marina and waiting tables at a country club. Even put in some time with a pyrotechnics company doing private parties and the big Fourth of July shindigs."

"I was a paperboy when I was a kid," Otis said. "Soda jerk, as well."

"Jerk, for sure," Mack said with a smile. Otis didn't react, so Mack continued: "Mind if I watch some TV?"

"Be my guest. But keep the volume down."

Mack set his mug down on an end table attached to the divan and went over to a small TV hooked up to a VHS player on a bookshelf across from the breakfast nook. Scanning the titles of the videos lining several other shelves, he was surprised to see that many were vintage movies of the 30s and 40s.

"I didn't know you were into old movies."

"Yeah. Got a lot more at home. You a fan, too?"

"I guess you could say so, although I'm not a collector, like you. I see you got some World War II aviation flicks."

"Yeah. My history teacher at I.U. got me interested in World War II fighter planes. He was a pilot with the African American 99th Fighter Squadron."

"One of the best in the war. They kicked the Luftwaffe's butt in the air battles over Europe. Let's see what you got here. *Air Force, Thirty Seconds Over Tokyo* and…oh, this one's disappointing."

"Which one?"

"*The Flying Tigers* with John Wayne."

"Don't tell me you're not a fan of the Duke? I would've thought he was your kind of guy."

Mack picked up the remote and moved to the divan. "He is. It's not Wayne. It's how the movie depicts the Flying Tigers."

"Oh, how's that? All I know is that they were flying for China before we got into the war, right?"

"Yeah. They were mercenaries who joined the Chinese Air Force for the adventure and the money. And they were paid big bucks—up to three times what they would have earned as servicemen. In the movie they're painted as gung-ho, patriotic heroes, and they were gutsy, I'll give them that, but when they weren't shooting down Japs in their P-40s, they were carousing in the local bars and brothels. Can you see John Wayne shacked up with a bottle of gin and a sleazy hooker?"

Otis laughed and took a sip of coffee. "Well, I suppose that's the way it has to be during a war. The public has to be pumped up with a heavy dose of patriotism. You can't expect historical accuracy in a movie during wartime."

"That's true," Mack said. "Patriotism does help win wars. When people stop believing in what they're fighting for, they withdraw their support, and you get a Vietnam. But just as important, you can't win a war without accurate intelligence. You know that. You need to know your enemy's troop strength, what kinds of weapons he's carrying, how much ammo he has, where his supply lines are…and most important, what he's thinking, what he's likely to do…and what he thinks you're likely to do. Look, we're in the business of fighting the bad guys, right? You already know all this."

"Well, partner, until you came into my life, I thought I was just in the business of finding missing persons, settling minor domestic disputes...that kind of thing. Now I'm not so sure." Otis picked up his coffee mug, paused, and set it down again. "So you're a student of history, especially military history. What else?"

"I read a lot of psychology," Mack took a sip of his coffee, "and Shakespeare."

"Shakespeare? How come?"

"Shakespeare created some of the greatest villains of all time—Iago, Richard the Third, Macbeth, among others. If you want to understand how an evil person thinks, or how a weak person can be persuaded to do bad things, there's no better place to look than in Shakespeare's plays."

"So the play's the thing, is it?" Otis smiled.

"Yep," Mack laughed. "That's what the Man said. Hey, you've got a satellite antenna, right? Let's see if we can find something more historically accurate to 'hold the mirror up to nature,' as the Man also said." Mack picked up the remote, powered on the TV, and began surfing the channels. "Looks like we're in luck. I've seen this one before. It's an account of the battle of Antietam. Helped change the course of the war for the Union in the east, which up to then…"

"Kill the sound!"

Mack saw that Otis was focusing intently on the laptop monitor.

"What's up?"

"I think we're in business!" Otis said, quickly moving the mouse.

Mack fumbled for the mute button, then hurried over to the dining nook and put on his headset. He could hear the sound of a phone being dialed as he looked at the computer screen over Otis's shoulder. The number for Kischman's second phone line appeared on the screen followed by a request for an ID name.

"Here we go!" Otis said.

They watched "Microbe438" appear in the log-in space, then "Savior553" in response to a request for a password.

"There it is," Otis whispered. "The new password for the mainframe. Now for Lazarus."

Another box opened requesting a file name and access code. "LAZARUS" appeared in the box, followed by "4321KISH" in the code space.

The master file for "LAZARUS" filled the screen.

Otis moved the cursor to "copy" and tapped the mouse.

"Gotcha!"

*9:57 p.m.:* Someone was knocking at Blackburn's door.

"Come in," he said without looking up from his computer. He already knew who it was without having to ask.

The Woman entered. She was slim and appeared taller than her 5'6" due to her 3" high-heeled fashionable shoes. Her face was framed with dark, short-cropped hair with bangs, but was obscured in shadows. The window drapes had been drawn shut, and the only illumination was provided by a small desk lamp and the computer screen, which displayed a chess board and the remaining pieces of an unfinished game. Despite the dim light, Blackburn could see that the Woman was elegantly dressed in a black velvet skirt with a matching blazer accentuating a white tuxedo blouse. Catching the light were pearl earrings and a matching pearl necklace that dangled from her swan-like neck.

"Don't you ever go home, David?"

Blackburn smiled wearily. "I'll get around to it. Sorry to have to drag you away from the party."

"You needn't be," the Woman said, settling into a comfortable leather chair facing the desk. "You know how I hate these affairs."

"I do. Would you like a cigarette?"

"Is it that bad, David?"

"It's not good."

"Then, yes. I think I would."

Blackburn took out a pack of Camels he kept in the desk drawer, reserved exclusively for the Woman. She never smoked in public, and rarely in private. When she did, it meant she was under stress. Blackburn stood and leaned over the monitor to offer the open pack. The Woman extracted a cigarette and allowed Blackburn to flame it with a Zippo before he ignited a fresh pipe of tobacco for himself.

"Thank you, David."

The Woman took a deep drag on the Camel, then exhaled slowly. "What's the problem, David?"

Blackburn lowered his lanky frame into the high-back swivel chair. "Half an hour ago I got a call from our security people at Bio-Sci. There's been an invasion of the research mainframe."

The Woman took this news with her usual calmness, but didn't respond until she took another drag on the cigarette.

"I assume the project file was protected."

Blackburn paused to take a puff on his pipe. "In a matter of seconds after the alert all incoming ports were automatically shut down."

"Seconds."

"Yes."

"Could this have been some kind of computer glitch?"

"It could have been. It happens."

"But you don't think so."

"No."

"The detective? McPherson?"

"In all likelihood. I believe he tapped Dr. Kischman's dedicated line at his home. I called Kischman. He was using the line tonight."

"Do you think McPherson had time to learn anything before the security kicked in?"

"No. But he could have copied the file if he acted quickly."

Another long inhale of nicotine-laden smoke.

"I think we have to assume the worst, David. Do you agree?"

"I do." Blackburn leaned back in his swivel chair, massaged his brow with his fingers. "Until now McPherson has been…just a nuisance. Quite frankly, I thought we had him checkmated. But now…"

"He's ceased to be 'just a nuisance'."

"Yes."

For more than a full minute neither person spoke. The only sound was the muffled drone of traffic outside while the Woman contemplated the gravity of the situation.

Blackburn waited, picked up his pipe, which had gone out, relit it. Finally: "So what are your instructions?"

The Woman ground out the last of her cigarette in an ashtray. "Do what you have to do."

Blackburn nodded. The Woman rose, moved to the door, opened it, then turned. "David. Go home and get some rest." The Woman left, closing the door softly behind her.

Blackburn leaned forward to study the chess board. Holding down the left button on his mouse, he moved his white queen across the board to take out a black knight.

*10:23 p.m.:* Mack stared at the silver Camry. It was parked across the street from his apartment building. Mack had noticed it when Otis dropped him off. There was nothing ominous about the car. It was the shadowy form behind the wheel that moved Mack's right hand to the handle of his backup .38 in the hip holster under his windbreaker. Another Fry? he thought. More than possible. The contract on his life was still open.

Cautiously, Mack crossed the street. When he got closer, he relaxed. The street light provided enough illumination for him to recognize the driver, who was startled out of a doze by the sound of Mack tapping against the side window. Relieved by the sight of Mack's face on the other side of the glass, Megan lowered the window.

"That's a nice way to greet a lady."

"Sorry, Megan. Didn't mean to alarm you, but I wasn't expecting company."

"Well, you've got it, like it or not. Otis told me what you were up to tonight."

"Really? He didn't confide that to me."

"I told him not to. Otherwise, I have a hunch you wouldn't let me in on whatever you found out."

Correct, Mack thought. "I thought you wanted me to drop the investigation."

"I did and still do. But since I know there's no way that's going to happen, the least you can do is keep me in the loop. Did you find out anything?"

"I think so." Mack removed a computer disk from his jacket pocket. "I'll know for sure when I take a look at this."

"The Lazarus file?"

"Yeah."

"Well, are you going to invite me inside or not?"

Mack thought about this for a moment. He was certain that the disk was dynamite. If anyone found out he had it, the price of that contract on his life would go through the roof. And that went for anyone else who knew its contents. Otis had made it clear that he wanted no part of it. Getting the information for Mack was as far as he was willing to go. That was fine with Mack, but Megan was another matter. She had a right to know—or at least a right to choose.

"Megan, if you see what's on this disk, there's a good chance your life will be at risk. You'll become a target, just like I am. You know that, don't you?"

"Mack, what I know is that I have to find out what happened to my father. I can either find out now, or I can find out later, but I'm going to find out, one way or the other. I'm not stopping until I know what happened…and who's responsible…and see that they're…brought to justice. God, I'm starting to sound like you." She gave Mack a weak smile, but he didn't smile back.

"You know you're putting Katie at risk, too."

Megan was silent for a moment. She hadn't thought about that. "Mack, you know I'll do everything in my power to protect Katie. If it comes to that, I can have her go live in Kenosha with Aunt Mary until this is over. But I'm probably already at risk just for wanting to find out what happened to my dad, and I don't think my knowing what's on the disk will make my situation any more dangerous. Whoever's behind this will assume that you would tell me anyway."

Mack couldn't argue with that. Whoever was pulling the strings on Lazarus seemed to have very good intelligence. After all, they'd had Frank's body switched and cremated within hours after Megan made the request for a full autopsy. They must have eyes and ears everywhere. Mack stood up and scanned the street for any unfamiliar vehicles from which someone might be watching them even now, but didn't see any. He leaned over and looked intently at Megan through the car window.

"Okay," he finally said. "Let's go up to my apartment and see what's on the disk."

Megan raised the window, stabbed the unlock button and grabbed her shoulder bag from the passenger seat. Mack opened the door for her to exit and caught the fresh scent of her perfume. Closing the door, he noticed that Megan looked even slimmer and shapelier in her evergreen turtleneck sweater tucked into tight-fitting Levi's.

Megan locked the car door with her remote. As they started to cross the street there was a jagged dagger of lightning over the lake followed by a rumble of thunder and the first raindrops of an approaching storm.

"When is this rain going to stop?" Megan asked as they ran the last few steps toward the entrance to Mack's building to escape the sudden downpour.

"Supposed to clear up tomorrow," Mack shouted over the din of the rain.

"I hope. Katie's been bugging me to take her biking along the lake," Megan shouted back.

Mack opened the outer door of the building and they entered the shelter of a small foyer. "Where is she? With a sitter?" he asked as he shook the rain from his clothes.

"At my house with Aunt Mary. She's decided to spend a few more days with us."

"Nice lady, your aunt," Mack said. He unlocked the inner door with a remote on his key chain. "Makes great cookies. I had more than a few at your dad's wake."

Mack held the door open for Megan and followed her into the lobby. "She'll be delighted to hear that she has another fan," Megan said, accompanying Mack to the single elevator next to the bank of mailboxes. "Would you like to place an order? Aunt Mary is always looking for an opportunity to bake."

"I'll take her up on that," Mack said.

Mack was about to press the elevator button when the door slid open. Charging out and nearly colliding with them was the huge Great Dane, Caesar, with Larry in tow on the leash.

"Sorry, Mack," Larry said over his shoulder.

"Was that a dog or a wolf?"

Mack chuckled and punched the third floor button. "He's really very gentle…if you don't make any sudden moves."

Exiting the elevator, they walked down a short corridor to number 301. Mack unlocked the door and waited for Megan to enter before he followed her, closed the door and switched on track lights. Megan was flabbergasted at what she saw.

"Wow! You said you collected antiques, but this! You've got enough here to go into business."

Mack removed the disk from his jacket pocket, then hung the jacket on a brass hook of the hall tree. "Still got room for a few more." He slipped the holster with his backup revolver off his belt and hung it on another hook.

"Well, I'm more than impressed. Now I know where to go if I'm looking for an antique."

"I'll be happy to oblige." He handed the disk to Megan. "Why don't you get going with this while I make some coffee. The Dell is on the desk."

"Going to put me to work, are you?"

"When it comes to computers, I'm almost illiterate. But I make a pretty good cup of coffee."

"Could you make it tea?"

"I think there's some around."

Mack had to rummage through a cupboard above the sink before he found a nearly full box of chamomile. "I think I'll join you. I've got a feeling I'm going to need something soothing before this night is over."

For sure, Megan thought. All the banter about cookies, antiques and tea couldn't subdue the anxiety she was feeling about what they would discover on the disk. For a moment she wondered if she really wanted to know now that its secret was about to be revealed. With a sense of dread, Megan sat down on a high-back, dark oak chair on rollers and fired up the Dell. She inserted the disk. "EYES ONLY: THE LAZARUS PROJECT" appeared on the monitor with several icons.

"Okay. We're in."

Mack filled two mugs with water and put them into his microwave. "Good. Where do we start?"

"There's an icon that says 'PROJECT'."

"Okay. Go ahead and click it." Mack set the timer for two minutes and hit start.

Megan clicked on the project icon, marveling at how Mack could remain so calm, almost indifferent, when his whole future might depend on what they would find on the disk. She never would understand this cop, she thought. He didn't say a word. He just waited for her to finish reading the data while the microwave droned. When the beeps sounded, Mack removed the mugs and dropped in tea bags.

"The purpose of the project is to find a cure for HCV."

Mack stirred the hot water with a teaspoon. "HCV?"

"Hepatitis C. It's a very dangerous virus that attacks the liver. It can cause cirrhosis, even cancer of the liver. I know a lot about it because I had a friend in college who died from it."

"How do you get it?"

"Injections, accidental needle sticks, tattooing and blood transfusions are high on the list. A carrier's blood has to enter another person's veins. With Julie it was probably from a blood transfusion she had after a childhood accident."

Mack removed the tea bags, dropped them into a trash container. "She had it that long and it wasn't detected?"

"That's the problem with HCV. It's a silent killer. It can hang around in your body for twenty years or more with no symptoms. By the time Julie was diagnosed HCV positive, it was too late. She died eleven months later."

"And there's no cure?"

"It can be treated with antiviral drugs, if it's detected early. But if it reaches end stage, like with Julie, it becomes life threatening, and the mortality rate is high. It looks like that's what the Lazarus Project is addressing. It's trying to develop an antiviral drug for end stage carriers that will arrest the disease for a long time, perhaps permanently."

Mack carried the steaming mugs over to the desk with two coasters and set them down. "I guess that could mean megabucks to Bio-Sci if they succeed."

"For sure. HCV is very widespread. It doesn't get headlines like cancer or AIDS, but it's just as deadly."

"Well, there's no secret that Bio-Sci is working on it," Mack said, pulling up a Victorian era chair next to Megan. "I remember now. Roy O'Neal, the CEO, told me they were working on Hepatitis B and C. So why the secrecy about the Lazarus Project?"

"I don't know. According to this, they've been doing the research for over three years. But the Lazarus Project kicked in July 1st of last year."

Mack sat down and looked at the monitor. "A kind of project within a project, but with the same purpose. What's the answer?"

"Good question. But it must have something to do with the target date for completion."

"Target date?"

"I guess you could call it that." Megan pointed to the screen.

Mack read the following in caps and red letters: "URGENT! A SUCCESSFUL ANTI-VIRAL DRUG MUST BE DEVELOPED BY NOVEMBER 1ST."

Mack scanned the data on the screen. "Not much time left. And there's no explanation for the target date?"

"No. None."

"Interesting. It must be so hot that they don't even want the people who are working on the project to know about it."

"It's…it's bewildering, to say the least. And what does it have to do with Dad?"

Mack took a sip of tea and wished he'd hyped it with honey, lime juice and a shot of Jack Daniel's. "I think I know. Go back to the directory."

"Alright." Megan returned to LAZARUS with the various icons.

"Click on personnel."

Megan did. Two icons appeared. LAB and FIELD.

"Go to FIELD."

Megan clicked on FIELD.

Appearing on the monitor screen:

A - CHICAGO
F - SAN FRANCISCO
M - NEW YORK
R - LOS ANGELES
V - MIAMI

Megan shook her head. "What does it mean?"

"'A' must be Dr. Alward. Chicago was his turf. The other initials are for doctors located in the other cities. No names, just initials, obviously to protect the identity of the doctors."

"Why just these cities?"

"My guess is that the other docs were doing charity work with vagrants, like Alward, and large urban areas obviously provide the most patients. Let's take a look at Alward's file."

Megan clicked on A and brought up a list of twelve patients in alphabetical order: Abrams, Butler, Cravin, Frazier, Horton, Jones, Leman, Norris, Peterson, Stiles, Turner and Underwood.

"There's your dad," Mack said. "Cravin. That was his street name."

Megan looked at Mack with apprehension.

"Go ahead."

Megan moved the cursor to Cravin and clicked. Two icons appeared: LOG NOTES and LAB DATA.

"Let's open the log."

Megan accessed Alward's log notes and gasped at what appeared.

The first entry was dated December 15. The log read: "Subject was sent to me by the Beacon Mission for a routine flu shot, which I gave him. I also injected him with the Hepatitis C virus and instructed him to see me in one month."

"Oh my God! He injected Dad with HCV!"

Mack was not surprised by this revelation. "I figured it was something like that."

"But why?! Why would Dr. Alward do such a thing?!"

"Read the next entry."

Megan did. It was dated January 12. "Inoculated subject with experimental serum X-24." And the next dated February 14. "Subject showing some resiliency to the virus. Results promising but hardly conclusive. Have scheduled subject for a return visit in three weeks and will inject him with X-25."

Megan could hardly believe what she was reading. "This is monstrous! He was using Dad as a guinea pig!"

"Yeah. Your dad and all the other vagrants. The perfect so-called subjects for testing with their experimental drugs. No one to check up on them if they died. But your dad was different. Alward must have panicked when your dad told him that he was off the street and living with you. If your dad went to another doctor for a check-up, all hell could have broken loose."

"So they killed him."

"Yeah. Alward probably injected him with something to knock him out, then called O'Neal and Kischman, who in turn informed whoever is pulling their strings. Some Latino hit men took over from there. They took your dad down the fire escape at the rear of the building and...well, you know the rest."

Megan nodded, slumping back into the chair. Suddenly all the anger seemed to drain out of her. She felt limp, exhausted and sad. "That's why they had Dad taken to another funeral home and cremated."

"Yeah. A full toxicological exam would have set off bells and whistles."

Megan pushed herself out of the chair and walked to the window to stare at the rain pelting the glass. Mack went over and took her arm.

"Are you okay?"

"Yes. I'm just tired...very tired. What are you going to do?"

"Frankly, I'm not sure. There's obviously more to Lazarus than just Bio-Sci, and if I blow the whistle now, we may never know who's calling the shots."

"Do you have any idea who that might be?"

"No, other than they must have *mucho* clout."

"Whoever it is, they tried to kill you before, and they may try again."

"Don't worry. I'm a hard man to kill."

Megan turned. "I mean it. You'll be careful?"

Mack looked into her eyes and asked himself if he was seeing more than just concern for his safety. "I'll watch my back. And remember, you need to watch yours, too."

"Mack…I wonder if I could spend the night here?"

Mack was as surprised by this request as Megan was in making it. All she knew was that she was scared and felt very alone.

"Sure. If you want to."

"Don't get me wrong. It's strictly bed and breakfast."

"Wouldn't have it any other way. Are you sure Ace wouldn't mind…oh, sorry. I said that without thinking. Didn't mean to go there."

To Mack's relief, this time his intrusion into Megan's private life drew a slight smile instead of fireworks.

"No, that's alright. Actually, I'm sure you did mean to go there, but it's okay. I want you to know about Neil and me anyway." Avoiding Mack's eyes, she turned to the window. "I'm sure you guessed that Neil is more than just…a good friend of mine. He's also my…I guess you could say…lover?"

"And he's married?"

"Yes." Megan was uncomfortable with this conversation, but she felt she had to tell Mack about her relationship with Neil so he wouldn't misunderstand. "That's why I chose him."

Mack was bewildered. "You chose him?"

"Yes." She paused for a moment as though searching for the right words. "I just couldn't take the risk of falling in love again. I couldn't go through the kind of pain I went through…when Artie died." Megan turned back toward Mack. "Can you understand that?"

"I know about that kind of pain, remember?" Mack said softly.

Megan let out a sigh of relief. "Then you do understand."

"Yes, I do understand."

"I'm glad. I was afraid you'd judge…"

A loud howling sound pierced the quiet of the loft, startling Megan. "What on earth was that?!"

Mack grinned. "My roommate, Ulysses."

"Roommate?"

"Yeah. He's a street cat I took in."

Mack moved to a window facing Carroll Street and opened it to admit a very wet Ulysses from the fire escape. The big tom padded quickly to the kitchen, where his water bowl resided near a litter box he was just learning to use.

"Poor thing," Megan said. "He looks like he could use a trip to a groomer."

Mack followed Ulysses to the kitchen. "Good luck on that. He's not even housebroken yet, probably never will be." Mack removed a can of Friskies from a shelf, opened it and dumped its contents onto a paper plate, which he set down next to the water bowl. The tom attacked the chicken and gravy with gusto. "He's not much of a hassle, though. Too independent. I figure that someday he'll go out, get licked by another tom or hit by a car and never come back."

"Don't be so heartless. I'll bet you really like him, more than you're willing to admit."

Score another one for Megan's feminine intuition, Mack thought. "I'm getting used to him," Mack said. The fact was he was beginning to warm up to his roommate, even though the cat was still so suspicious and stand-offish that he wouldn't let Mack pet him. "But tonight he has to find another place to sleep, because I'm taking the couch."

"Oh, no you're not. I said bed and breakfast. I should have said couch and breakfast."

Mack went back to join Megan at the window. "Sorry. House rules. I get the couch."

"My, my, just like in those old black-and-white movies. The hero always took the couch. How gallant."

Mack smiled. "Yeah, well, I'm an old fashioned kind of guy. Like my antiques, I guess."

Megan smiled. "Well, I'm glad you are."

Again the image of Mack as her black knight rose up in her mind: brave, honest, courteous, but also with his disturbing dark side: his single-minded commitment to an ideal of justice that would admit no compromise, his unwillingness to accept a world where the wealthy and the powerful could and sometimes did get away with murder, his refusal to retreat no matter how many enemies were arrayed against him. Sure, tonight he was her champion, committed to bringing to justice those who had murdered her father, but could he be there for her once this quest was completed and another victim of injustice rose up to take her place?

She remembered the steady pulsing beat of "Searchin'" by the Coasters that she used to listen to as a child on one of the "Oldies" stations:

*Well, Sherlock Holmes,*
*Sam Spade got nothin', child, on me*
*Sergeant Friday, Charlie Chan,*
*And Boston Blackie.*
*No matter where she's hidin' she's gonna hear me comin'*
*I'm gonna walk right down that street like Bulldog Drummond,*
*Cause I been searchin', searchin', yeah,*
*Searchin' every whi-i-ich a-way,*
*And like the Northwest Mountie,*
*I'm gonna bring her in some day.*

No! No way she could let herself fall in love with Mack. But tonight, at least, she could let him comfort her.

"Mack?"

"Yes?"

"Would you hold me for a little while?"

"Sure."

Mack put his arm around Megan. She pressed up close against him and felt his warmth, and her fear left her as though a blanket of safety had been drawn around her. They didn't speak—there was no need for words—and he didn't attempt to kiss her. He just held her while the rain outside kept up its steady drumming beat against the window.

*11:42 p.m.:* Bryant surfed the TV. "Hey, it's John Wayne," he said when he found a John Wayne movie in progress on the American Movie Channel. Chewing on a bite of a Milky Way bar, his feet propped on a coffee table, he was lounging on the couch of the two-bedroom suite at the Downtown Courtyard Marriott they were using as the base of operations for their surveillance of Detective McPherson.

Gallagher took a swallow of a Diet Pepsi as he worked a *Sun Times* crossword puzzle at the small table next to the kitchenette. "What happened to Jay Leno?"

"I only go for the monologues unless he's got a really cool guest. Too many of them are airhead Hollywood broads. The guitar player is cool, though." Bryant could relate to a good guitar player since he played a pretty mean guitar himself, although he preferred Country Western, having been brought up in Portland, Tennessee, which was only a forty-mile jaunt from Nashville. "I think I've seen this flick before, but I can't remember the name."

"What's an 8-letter word for inert?"

"Inert? Damned if I know," Bryant said, flinching at the impact of the butt of Wayne's Winchester against the jaw of a bad guy who made the mistake of reaching for a Colt .45. "The Duke was special, ya know. They don't make 'em like that today. Eastwood, maybe, and Stallone, but the rest of 'em suck."

"Well, I got news for you, Rusty. Your hero never served in World War II. Jimmy Stewart did. Flew missions in a B-17 over Germany. So did Clark Gable."

"So what? Lots of actors didn't join up." Bryant was getting pissed. Just because Gallagher saw action as a tank commander in Desert Storm, he thought everyone who never wore a uniform could use an injection of courage, Bryant included. Well, fuck him!

"Just thought I'd mention it. Got it."

"Got what? The clap?"

"Funny man. The word for inert. Sluggish."

"Congratulations. How come you keep playing those puzzles?"

"Keeps my mind sharp."

"Yeah, well I gotta give my brain some R and R once in a while. Right now I would appreciate a little Southern Comfort on the rocks."

"Forget it. Just be thankful we got the day off."

"Yeah, well Blackburn is gonna be pissed as hell when he finds out we screwed up today."

"What could we do? Hell, we were lucky we didn't end up in a hospital… or worse."

Bryant agreed. While they were tailing McPherson, they'd narrowly avoided a head-on with a semi that had jackknifed in front of them on the Kennedy Expressway. To make matters worse, they weren't even able to track him on the GPS. The microchip they planted on McPherson's Bonneville made it possible to track him via satellite. But the cop had used a car they didn't know he had, some kind of vintage sedan. That being the case, they decided to take the rest of the day off. Besides, it looked like McPherson had his hands full just keeping his job. Or so Bryant hoped.

"You think the cop is gonna back off?"

"What choice does he have? He's on suspension, and Blackburn made sure he'd get the works if he as much as jaywalks."

"Hope you're right. I'm not liking this fucking assignment, and that's a fact. He didn't have to kill the cop, but that druggie could have done us all a favor if he'd at least put him out of commission."

"The guy was an amateur. They should have let us do the job."

"I guess, but I still don't like it. The cop seems like an alright guy."

"Don't go sentimental on me, Rusty. We got a job to do, no matter who gets in the way."

Bryant snorted, gave his partner a little mock salute. Bryant knew where his empathy for the cop came from. His dad had been a cop, the sheriff of Sumner County, until some drunken redneck had put three bullets into him instead of taking a DUI rap that would have revoked his license. It was a stupid, senseless act that had taken away his dad when he was only eleven. Of course, Gallagher wouldn't understand his feelings, so why tell him. And Gallagher was right. This was no time to go sentimental.

Bryant took another bite of the Milky Way, then mumbled excitedly through a mouthful of chocolate and caramel, "Hey, Dean Martin's in this flick. Now I remember. It's *Rio Bravo*."

"Dammit, Rusty, turn down the volume. I'm trying to concentrate."

"Yes, sir, General sir." Bryant used the remote to lower the sound. "Martin plays a drunk who Wayne takes on as a deputy."

"What's a 5-letter word that describes to look angry?"

"Beats me. Frown?"

"Frown doesn't work. Already tried it. A drunk as a deputy, eh. Some choice."

"Yeah, well Martin kicks the booze and comes through for the Duke in the clutch."

"Good for him. Got it. Scowl."

Which is what Bryant was doing at the sound of his cell phone playing *Your Cheatin' Heart*.

"Shit!" Knowing who the caller was, Bryant picked up the cell from the end table. "Bryant."

Gallagher looked up from the puzzle, also aware that their day off was about to end.

Bryant listened for a few seconds, then explained how they'd lost McPherson. He listened again, this time for nearly a full minute before asking, "What are your orders?"

Bryant nodded glumly. "Right. We'll get right on it." He beeped off. "Shit and double shit!"

"Well?" Gallagher said, expecting the worst.

"Believe it or not, Blackburn didn't have a heart attack, said he understood, that it couldn't be helped. But we got another problem."

"I take it our cop has been a bad boy."

"Very bad." Bryant filled in his partner about the invasion of the Bio-Sci research mainframe. "Blackburn thinks the cop did the break-in and could have copied the file."

"I assume he wants us to find out."

"Correct. And in his words, 'take appropriate action'."

Gallagher rose, took a shoulder holster with a .45 automatic off the table and strapped it on. "I told you we should have done that job."

Bryant pulled his bulk off the couch and moved to his own holster and .45 hanging from a clothes hook on the back of an open closet door. "Well, it looks like you've got your wish."

## Friday, May 24

*6:17 a.m.:* Bryant was slumped over the wheel of the rented Ford Taurus, snoring.

Gallagher winced. Rusty's snoring was getting on his nerves. He was about to nudge his partner awake, but decided against that. If he did wake him up, Bryant would find a Country Western station on the FM, and when it came to Country Western, Gallagher preferred snoring. Gallagher regarded his slumbering partner with disdain. Civilian, he thought. Hell, he'd stayed awake forty-eight hours at a stretch during Desert Storm with only cat naps and short rations to sustain him.

He was wide awake now, but getting impatient. They'd been angle parked with other cars on the east side of May Street between Carroll Street and the railroad tracks for about five hours, waiting for an opportunity to make a move. It made no sense to break into the cop's apartment with a building full of people, some of whom could be light sleepers. Besides, the cop was a dangerous adversary, who just might be expecting unwelcome guests.

Gallagher popped a peppermint into his mouth. Although he hadn't smoked for years, peppermint drops helped subdue the old nicotine urge that resurfaced when he was waiting for something to happen. When it did, he'd have to play it by ear, something Gallagher was used to doing. He'd had to improvise on numerous occasions in combat when things didn't go according to plan.

So far there had been zero chances to do anything. Not surprising. It was early, 6:24 a.m. by the dash clock. The only person he'd seen exiting the building was a guy with a dog as big as a horse. Five more minutes dragged by. The guy with the dog returned. A pretty girl exited the building and drove away in a silver Camry. A Streets and Sanitation truck forklifted a huge dumpster in front of a warehouse and emptied its contents into the truck. Gallagher sucked on another peppermint.

Suddenly, he was shaking Bryant's shoulder. "Wake up, Rusty!"

Bryant jerked up off the wheel, groggy. "What?"

Gallagher pointed. "The cop."

Bryant looked down the street. Garbed in a windbreaker, sweats and sneakers, McPherson had exited the building and was jogging south on May.

Gallagher crunched the peppermint in his teeth. "Let's rock and roll!"

Mack jogged across Fulton Market Street. He was thankful that the rain had finally stopped. However, the pavement was still wet and the air heavy with moisture as the early morning sun fought its way through the overcast sky. When he reached the next street, Lake, he headed east on his usual route.

Faced with a problem, Mack always found it helpful to take a morning jog. It helped to clear away the mental cobwebs. His problem now was to find out who was behind the Lazarus Project without tipping his hand that he knew its secret. He was convinced that the only people at Bio-Sci who had that information were O'Neal and Kischman. O'Neal was a tough cookie, but Kischman might cave if Mack exposed the project now. However, it was more likely that they'd hide behind a cadre of high powered lawyers. So what to do?

By the time he crossed Green Street, Mack was beginning to come up with an idea, which was to bring heat on Kischman and see what developed. Of course, this would put him in even deeper shit than he was already in, but he was fresh out of brainstorms. So Kischman it was. Now he had to work out a plan of action.

Bryant followed the cop in the Taurus. He lagged about a block and a half behind the detective on Lake Street, looking for a chance to take the cop out. None had presented itself, even though at this early hour there was practically no traffic. No people either, until some guy rounded the corner at Carpenter Street and jogged practically in tandem with McPherson on the other side of the street.

Bryant didn't like what he had to do. He wished that he had the job of searching the cop's apartment instead of Gallagher, but when it came to driving, Bryant was far more skilled than the General. As a teenager on a dirt track in Portland, he'd held his own against the pros behind the wheel of a stock car he'd put together himself.

The two joggers paused at Halsted for a red light and a thin flow of traffic. Bryant pulled over to the curb and waited. A CTA train rumbled on the overhead El. At the green the two joggers crossed Halsted. The cop kept going on Lake, but the other guy turned south on Halsted. All right! At least that guy was gone.

Bryant looked ahead to where Lake humpbacked over the Kennedy Expressway on the east side of Halsted. He waited for the cop to get halfway over before easing away from the curb. He was about to floor the pedal when he saw a van approaching. Damn! Bryant was beginning to wonder if he was going to get a crack at the cop when McPherson crossed a narrow street, Union, that bordered the expressway, and stopped in front of a bar on the corner to tie a shoelace.

Bryant quickly checked the rearview, then the street ahead. No cars, no people. Here we go, Bryant thought, and goosed the Taurus.

Mack knew what he had to do. He'd already bugged Kischman's phone, so why not take advantage of it. Mack was still certain that Alward had alerted Kischman about Frank, and Kischman had immediately passed this information along to O'Neal. Or perhaps to someone else. Mack was certain that there was more to the Lazarus Project than just serving humanity, and that O'Neal and Kischman were taking their orders from...who knows? In any event, if Mack paid Kischman a visit at his home and shook him up enough, Kischman just might make another call to Mr. Whoever, in which event Mack would be listening in.

Mack was so absorbed in his thoughts as he tied his shoelace that he didn't hear the sound of the powerful engine behind him. When he did, it was nearly too late. Looking back, he saw a dark blue sedan veering from the other side of the street and bearing down on him. Covering his face with his arms, Mack dove through the bar window a second before the Taurus jumped the curb and sideswiped the building.

Bryant braked, leapt out of the car. Drawing the .45 from his shoulder holster, he climbed through the broken window. Inside he paused for a second to let his eyes adjust to the gloom, then scanned the interior—a sports bar with numerous TV sets, chairs piled upside down on tables. Gun extended, Bryant looked behind the bar. No McPherson. Bryant proceeded cautiously through the bar past the restrooms. There was a fire exit at the rear. The door was open.

Bryant quickly exited into a small parking lot that bordered Walnut Street, more of an alley than a street, that ran east off Union. Only one way the cop could go, but there was no sign of him. Bryant ran down the street to where it ended at Des Plaines and looked in both directions. Still no sign of the cop. Decision time. McPherson could have gone north to Fulton or south to Lake, then in either direction from there. Bryant decided to go back to Lake and get the car. If he couldn't find McPherson, he'd just have to abort the kill and pick up Gallagher. Maybe his partner had better luck.

When Bryant got to the corner, he spotted McPherson running east on Lake. For a moment Bryant debated whether he should pursue on foot. Although the cop had to be fatigued from the jog, Bryant was no great shakes as a long distance runner, and the cop was already two blocks away. Bryant raced back to the Taurus, threw himself behind the wheel. Stomping on the accelerator, he swung the sedan off the curb between two El track pillars and took off after the cop.

Mack was winded. He had just crossed Canal Street, and directly ahead was one of the vintage draw bridges that span the Chicago River. He'd figured that his best bet was to get to Wacker Drive on the other side of the river. Wacker would be fairly busy, even at this hour, which would probably discourage his would-be killer from another attempt on his life. Mack was thinking that if he'd taken his .38—something he never did when he jogged— he would have a fighting chance. No time to dwell on that now. Just keep going, keep gulping air.

Suddenly, an alarm bell was clanging, red lights flashing, barrier arms descending in front of him. Five sailboats were headed under power for the bridge from the south branch of the river. Mack knew they were on their way from their winter dry docks to the harbors on Lake Michigan. Since their masts were too tall to pass under the bridges along the river, the bridges had to be raised. For Mack the timing couldn't have been worse.

Mack looked behind him. The Taurus was coming on fast. Mack looked back and saw the east section of the bridge begin to slowly pivot upward, while the west section where he stood remained level. No choice. Mack ducked under the barrier arm and ran for his life. He was hoping he could leap to the other section before it got too high, or that the operator in the bridge tower on the far side would see him and lower the section. Neither happened. Mack had to stop abruptly at the end of the section. It was too late. The other section was already above his head and rising.

Looking back, Mack saw that the Taurus had pulled over to the curb just beyond the barrier arms. A stocky, red-headed guy in a business suit was getting out. He seemed in no hurry to draw a .45 automatic from a shoulder holster and duck under the barrier arm. Why shouldn't he take his time? Mack wasn't going anywhere, unless he wanted to plunge forty feet into the still frigid waters of the Chicago River, then take his chances fighting the current and dodging bullets at the same time. This seemed like his only option, and it was not a good one.

Suddenly, another entirely unexpected possibility presented itself. It was damned risky, but it was a chance Mack had to take. Backing up a few steps, he rushed forward and leapt off the edge of the section.

Bryant gaped at what he was seeing. McPherson had broad jumped off the end of the bridge and grabbed the mast of a sailboat that was passing close by. For a moment Bryant just stood there, dumbfounded. By the time he ran to the end of the section, McPherson was shinnying down the mast. Bryant got off two hasty shots, saw one bullet spark off the mast just over the cop's head. McPherson dropped the remaining six feet to the deck and ducked behind the front of the cabin, while yelling at an old guy at the helm to take cover. The old guy stayed put. Gutsy, Bryant thought, like the cop.

Bryant lowered the automatic. Watching the sailboat move away, he couldn't suppress a feeling of relief that the cop had gotten away. He was also asking himself if he'd deliberately eased up on the accelerator before the cop dove through that bar window. And could he have nailed McPherson on the mast if he'd taken more careful aim? Or was the memory of his dad taking three bullets in his chest messing with his head? He didn't know. But he did know one thing: if the cop had to die, he was relieved that he hadn't been the one to kill him.

Mack came up off the deck. The old man was still standing behind the wheel, as if nothing had happened. Garbed in jeans, a windbreaker and an old captain's hat, with a craggy, weather-beaten face, he looked as sturdy as the mast of his spotless sailboat.

"I told you to take cover," Mack said.

The old man chuckled, as he guided the boat around the bend of the river where the north and south branches joined and flowed east. "Son, that weren't nothin' to what I went through in the big war. Hell, I had two PT boats shot out from under me and lived to skipper another one."

Mack could well believe it. The vinegary old man appeared very much at home at the helm, and the tattered captain's cap perched at a jaunty angle on his tangle of white hair probably dated back to his Navy days. "Well, thanks for the rescue mission. Or was that an accident?"

"No accident. I seen you was in trouble, so I brought Bessie here—Bessie, that's the name of this here boat, named after my wife—I brought her close enough for you to try for the mast, if you had a mind to."

"Good thing you did, or I would have gotten my feet wet."

"I'd have pulled you out, but in what condition I wouldn't bet on. Someone wanted you dead for sure. If you don't mind my askin', you aren't by any chance a fugitive from justice, are you?"

Mack grinned. "Nope. I'm a cop. Detective McPherson, Special Victims."

"That's a relief, Detective," the old man said, extending his hand. "Dan Hewitt."

Mack took his extended hand, callused, but with a firm grip. "Glad to know you, Dan. *Very* glad, given the circumstances."

"In case you haven't noticed, son, you could use a little medical attention."

Mack looked at his right arm and saw blood seeping through cuts in the windbreaker. Now feeling the pain, he also tasted blood trickling down his cheek from cuts on his forehead. "You're right. Guess I was too busy to notice."

"We can fix that. Bessie!"

A woman's voice answered his yell from the living quarters below deck. "Coffee's comin', Dan, so keep your sails dry."

"Bring up the first aid kit. You got a patient."

"I got a what?!"

The woman's head appeared through the swinging doors of the cabin and regarded Mack with astonishment. "Be right back."

She came up from the cabin a few seconds later with a thermos and first aid kit. A slim, good looking woman with short gray hair and a ruddy face that, like her husband's, showed a love affair with the outdoors, Bessie handed her husband the thermos, then turned to regard Mack with a suspicious look. "Where did *he* come from?"

"He just kinda dropped in," Dan said with a wry smile. "Don't worry, hon. Our guest is a detective. Officer McPherson."

"Nice to meet you, Mrs. Hewitt."

"Shut up and sit down before you bleed to death," she said. Her voice was scolding, but her eyes were kind looking and rimmed with wrinkles that Mack guessed came as much from laughter as from age.

"Yes, ma'am."

Mack sat down on a deck seat. Bessie opened the first aid box and went to work on Mack's forehead. Mack winced from the sting of alcohol-soaked gauze on his cuts.

"Nice boat you got here, Skipper. Catalina 330 Cruiser?"

"Close. She's a 310. You a sailor, son?"

"No, but I got a high school buddy who is. He's got a Catalina 270 Bay at Belmont Harbor. I get out on the lake with him now and then, but he does the sailing and I do the crewing. Ouch!"

"Hold still," Bessie scolded. "You're lucky, young man. Cuts aren't serious, so you won't need stitches."

"Bessie was a nurse in the big war, Detective," her husband said with a loving look. "I met her at a hospital in Honolulu after I took a bullet in the leg from a Jap Zero. We kept in touch, and I looked her up after the war."

Bessie started to cover Mack's cuts with bandages. "Lucky for him he did, or I'd have hooked up with a neurosurgeon from Park Forest and be living high."

"She ain't done so bad, Detective. I went into the boat business, bought a marina on the river. Still own it, but my son-in-law is running the show now."

"That does it," Bessie said, applying the last bandage. "Now let's have a look at that arm. Take off the jacket."

Mack did as he was told.

"That goof must be asleep," the old man said, sounding the boat horn.

Mack assumed he was referring to the operator of the LaSalle Street bridge ahead, which was still down. Dan cut the engine to idle and sounded the horn again.

"For Pete's sake, Dan, stop making that noise!" his wife said. "Why don't you give our patient here some of that coffee. And you might add a little something to put some color into his cheeks."

"Yes, Captain," the skipper said with a wink at Mack. "You see who's really in charge here. I'm just the first mate."

Dan took a mug from a drink holder, filled it with coffee from the thermos, then removed a half pint of Hennessy from his windbreaker pocket and spiked the coffee with a generous slug. "Here ya go, Detective."

"Thanks, Skipper." Mack took the mug, winced again as Bessie dabbed the cuts on his right arm with alcohol.

"Arm looks okay, too," Bessie said. "Just minor cuts. What did you do, anyway? Fall through a window?"

"Something like that," Mack said. He took a pull from the mug, sighed from the warmth of coffee and cognac suffusing his stomach, then told Bessie what had happened.

Bessie shook her head. "You're crazy, the both of you."

"Hey, I ain't had so much fun since I put two torpedoes into the hull of a Jap cruiser off Savo Island. Here we go. The goof finally woke up."

Dan pushed the throttle. Mack watched in amazement as the boat moved forward with the mast passing through the narrow space between the two sections of the bridge as they were just pivoting upward.

"Show off," his wife scolded but with a proud smile.

The old man looked back at the other four sailboats, which were waiting for the bridge sections to be completely upright. "Just wanted to show those weekend sailors how it's done."

"Where are you headed, Skipper?" Mack asked.

"Monroe Harbor. You're welcome to join us for breakfast after I get Bessie docked."

"Thanks, Skipper, but I got a few things to attend to."

Mack took another swig of coffee/brandy. It would take a good half hour or more to pass through the locks in order to reach Monroe Harbor, and Mack wanted to get back to the loft asap. Redhead just might have gone back to search the place if his boss suspected Mack had cracked the Bio-Sci computer. Mack didn't think that was the case, but he wanted to make sure that the disk was still safe. He also intended to make some copies, which he hadn't done, and conceal them at various places outside the loft, which included locking one in his office desk and informing Otis of its location in case anything happened to him. Looking ahead, Mack saw the Marina City dock. He could get off there, catch a cab and be back at his loft in ten minutes.

"Do you mind dropping me off at Marina City?"

"Glad to," Dan said, and turned toward the dock.

"You're not going any place, young man, until I finish this arm," Bessie said.

"You come visit us sometime, Detective," Dan said. "We practically live on this here boat all season. Harbor master will show you where we're docked. You come see us, and we'll do some serious sailing."

Bessie bandaged Mack's last cut. "You're all fixed up. Don't be jumpin' through any more windows, young man. And like Dan said, you come visit. You're welcome anytime."

"I'll do that," Mack said, and meant it.

Mack finished the coffee/brandy and set the mug in the holder. Rising, he gave Bessie a hug and kiss on the cheek she apparently wasn't expecting, but which her smile said she appreciated. When the boat nudged against the pier, he stepped off.

"Thanks again. Both of you," Mack said, and hurried away.

*7:19 a.m.:* Mack entered his loft and swore. The place had been given a thorough going over. Now Mack realized there had been two of them. No way Redhead could have had enough time to do this kind of search. Which meant that Redhead had a partner who'd taken the place apart while Redhead was chasing him. Mack also realized that he had committed a dumb, rookie mistake. He'd underestimated his adversary, who obviously figured that he'd cracked the Bio-Sci mainframe and put the Lazarus file on a disk.

Mack looked toward the rolltop. Ulysses was sitting on the desk, licking himself, but the Dell was missing. No surprise there. Mack hadn't put the file into the hard drive, but they'd taken no chances. It was the disk that they were after. Although Mack hadn't expected a search, he'd hidden the disk in what he considered a very safe place.

Wrong! Mack rushed across the room to where he had at least two hundred

CDs, cassettes and old '78 rpm records stored in cabinets and racks next to the stereo unit. Kneeling, he searched through the many CDs and containers scattered on the floor. He was looking for just one, a Django Reinhardt CD. He'd hidden the disk in the container under the CD. He found the CD first, then the container. It was open. And empty.

*8:33 a.m.:* Roy O'Neal cradled the receiver.

"Well, did they find the leak?"

This anxious question from Dr. Kischman, who had just entered the office and was pacing back and forth in front of O'Neal's desk like a caged animal. Not a lion or tiger, O'Neal thought. Kischman wasn't exactly a tower of courage and ferocity. More like a rabbit, and a very scared rabbit at that, which was something else O'Neal didn't need right now.

"They did. It didn't come from this end, which I guess is good news. Otherwise we'd have someone in the lab to deal with."

"Then how did McPherson break in?"

O'Neal placed the phone with the direct line into a bottom desk drawer and locked it before answering. The fact was he was trying not to show his anger to an already uptight Kischman for the chewing out he'd gotten from Blackburn, as if he could have somehow prevented the mainframe invasion.

"McPherson bugged the dedicated line to your home."

Kischman stopped pacing. "What?! My home line?"

"That's right. Don't blame yourself, Otto. We're dealing with one very smart cop. Besides, if anyone's to blame, it's me." O'Neal had to admit that Blackburn was right. Whatever happened at Bio-Sci, good or bad, was ultimately his responsibility. Kischman resumed pacing, his brow now moist with perspiration. "What are they doing about McPherson?"

O'Neal told Kischman what he'd just learned from Blackburn. Although the detective had survived an attempt on his life, at least Blackburn's men had found the Lazarus disk.

Kischman was not consoled by this news. "How can we be sure that's the only disk?"

O'Neal got up and moved to a coffee maker on the bar. "We can't, but Blackburn assured me that his men did a thorough search of his apartment and are certain that there was only one disk there."

"Well, I hope they're right...but what about McPherson? He's going to be an even bigger problem now that he knows about the Project. What if he talks?"

O'Neal filled a china cup with coffee. "Let him talk. He's already in hot water with the CPD, so who's going to believe him, especially with no proof to substantiate what will be interpreted as wild accusations to save his job. Now calm down and have some coffee, Otto."

"No...no. I've got to get back to the lab. We're running tests on the latest serum today, you know."

O'Neal took the cup and saucer to his desk. "That's right. How does it look?"

"Promising. Very promising. We should know for certain in two, maybe three days."

O'Neal sat down behind the desk. "Good. The quicker we finish this, the better." O'Neal started to take a sip when his phone beeped. He fingered the button for his secretary. "Yes, Glenda?"

Glenda's voice over the speaker: "I have Detective McPherson on the line,

Mr. O'Neal. Do you wish to speak with him?"

Kischman froze in his tracks, but O'Neal only smiled. "Of course. Put him through."

A moment later McPherson's voice issued through the speaker. "Good morning, Roy. Do you mind my calling you 'Roy'?"

"Not at all, Detective. What can I do for you?"

"Tell you in a minute. I'd like to share what I have to say with Dr. Kischman, if you could conference him in."

"No need. He's right here in my office, and you're on speaker."

"Good. I know you're a busy man, Roy, so I'll be brief. I'm sure you're aware that your goons screwed up."

"What I'm sure of is that I have no idea what you're talking about, Detective."

"Of course not, but in case you're curious, allow me to inform you that they not only failed to take me out, they got only one of the Lazarus disks."

An alarmed look from Kischman, which O'Neal waved off with his hand. "How careless of them, whoever they are and whatever Lazarus means. In any event, I don't think you have any such disk, if one even exists."

"I'll let you worry about that, Roy. And here's something else to chew on. Both of you. You want to play hard ball, that's fine with me. Look over your shoulder, you won't see me. But when you least expect it, I'll be there."

Sound of dial tone. O'Neal pressed the disconnect.

"I told you!" Kischman stammered, leaning across the desk, his face ashen. "I told you he'd be more trouble!"

"If you think he has another disk, forget it. It was just a bluff. He wouldn't have made the call if he did."

"Well he wasn't bluffing about the rest. What are we going to do?"

"Not what you're doing right now, which is hitting the panic button. We're going to stay focused, finish the project, and let Blackburn take care of Detective McPherson."

"And if he doesn't?"

O'Neal took a sip of coffee from the cup and smiled. "Well, perhaps I can lend a hand with that."

He index fingered the button for his secretary.

"Yes, Mr. O'Neal."

"Glenda. Put me through to the mayor. And tell him it's urgent."

*1:15 p.m.:* Manuel de Ortiz Hijo was having a good day. One of his horses had finished second in the fifth race at the Calder Race Course in Miami Gardens, something neither he nor his trainer had expected. It was the two-year-old's first race, a début strictly to break in the filly. Now Ortiz was regretting that he hadn't put a bet on his own horse, which would have paid thirty-to-one. This was not the case with Wildfire, the champion of his Kentucky stable, a two-to-one favorite in the sixth. Ortiz had put fifty thousand dollars on his horse to finish first, which would enhance the prize money Wildfire would bring in if he came through again as he had in his previous three starts. It was a bet Ortiz was confident of winning.

Not that he needed the money. His business not only financed his passion for horse racing—he had stables in both Venezuela and England—but supported a lavish lifestyle that included a Learjet 40 that could whisk him at a moment's notice to any place in the world. An experienced pilot with over 3,000 hours log time, Ortiz was also qualified to fly the jet himself. However, he preferred to leave the piloting to an on-call crew while he shared the luxury of the Learjet with a young lovely, such as the one sitting across the table from him how at the exclusive Turf Club.

"Is your horse in the next race, *mi amor*?" she said in Spanish.

"Yes, little one," he replied, also in Spanish. Rosita was still struggling with her English despite the lessons he had provided her. "My champion, Wildfire."

"I do hope he wins."

"I am sure that your lovely presence will bring me good fortune."

The compliment drew a smile and girlish giggle from his latest fling. He'd encountered her quite by accident behind the counter of the pro shop of a private tennis club in San Jose, Costa Rica. During a match with the pro, he'd purchased a new tennis racket when a string of his racket snapped on a powerful first serve. He'd gone on to defeat the pro, then wine and dine the girl who'd sold him the racket, claiming that it was she who had inspired him to victory. Such inspiration should not end tonight, he said. This was an arrangement more than acceptable to the starry eyed sixteen-year-old beauty, as well as her parents when presented with a check for ten thousand American dollars for the employment of their youngest of six children as his private secretary.

The fact that at fifty-three Ortiz was nearly old enough to be her grandfather did not seem to bother Rosita, or for that matter any of the other young girls who'd preceded her. Tall and fit, with the angular face of a Hollywood Latin lover enhanced by a tantalizing satanic beard, Ortiz knew that beautiful women of any age were easy conquests. This was confirmed by the admiring looks from women at other tables, who no doubt were also impressed by his impeccable Bond Street attire—navy blazer, tattersal navy/white shirt, taupe slacks, alligator shoes and red silk ascot.

Ortiz was also aware that Rosita was the center of the men's attention when they weren't watching a race or conversing with their wives or girlfriends. And no wonder, given her long, dark hair that framed an oval face with full, sensuous red lips and a lush, curvaceous body. Since Chanel, Dior and Prada were names Rosita could only dream about, Ortiz had selected her lavish wardrobe himself. Today in her white, low cut tank top and hip-hugging white jeans and gold step-in shoes with three-inch heels, and adorned with gold bracelets, chain belt and dangling earrings, she could easily have passed for a movie starlet or rock diva. If Rosita was aware of the attention she was getting, she didn't show it. Her dark brown eyes that effervesced like the champagne she was cautiously sipping were for him only.

When a voice over the loudspeaker announced that the horses were approaching the starting gate, Ortiz raised binoculars to peer through the picture window at the sleek thoroughbreds on the immaculately groomed track. His prize filly was trotting calmly to her gate, as if she, like her owner, had complete confidence in her ability to win the race.

"Let me see, *amor*, let me see," Rosita said.

"Of course, little one." Ortiz removed the binoculars from around his neck and handed it to Rosita."

"Which one is yours, *amor*?"

"Number seven."

"Ohhhh, he is such a beautiful horse!"

Ortiz smiled. Everything in this new, exciting world of hers was greeted by the same youthful exuberance, as though she were a little girl opening another wonderful present.

Ortiz wondered how long this would last, how long it would take for gratitude and adulation to deteriorate into greed and, worse yet, possessiveness, the first signs of which would put an abrupt end to their relationship. Or would he tire of her first, as he had with some of her predecessors? Once they were gone with a generous check to console their broken hearts, Ortiz neither wondered nor cared what happened to them. Ortiz's credo was to live for the moment, and their moment in his life was over.

Gazing at his lovely companion across the table, Ortiz found himself hoping that Rosita's moment would endure longer than the others'. He also knew that this was not to be. Rosita was very family oriented. She often spoke lovingly of her parents and brothers and sisters. It was only a matter of time before she would bring up the dreaded subject of marriage and children.

Ortiz grimaced at the thought. There was no room in his life of self-indulgence for a wife and children. He had left it to his younger brother, Ramon, to perpetuate the once proud name of Ortiz, which Ramon felt Manuel had besmirched, not only with his scandalous, romantic affairs, but by what he'd done with the family business. At the death of their father, as the older brother, Manuel had assumed command of the modest pharmaceutical business in Caracas and in just a few years transformed it into a worldwide, multimillion-dollar enterprise. His brother would condemn him for the nature of that transformation but at the same time accept a two-million dollar buyout for his interest.

The thought of his brother provoked a sardonic smile and another sip of Dom Perignon. What a pious, hypocritical fool! If he only knew that Angelina, his young, innocent bride, had willingly, passionately, given up her virginity in Manuel's bed on the very eve of her marriage. That she had implored Manuel to continue their affair beyond the exchange of vows with his brother. Of course, this was impossible. The moment of his conquest was over.

Ortiz downed the rest of his champagne and extracted the bottle from the ice bucket. He was about to replenish Rosita's half empty glass when his cell phone sounded. He pulled it from his jacket pocket, annoyed by the interruption.

"Yes."

A familiar voice. "Can you talk?"

"Yes. Go ahead."

Ortiz listened to Angel start to inform him of the latest developments at Bio-Sci. "There they go! There they go!" Rosita shrilled.

"Not so loud, *nina*."

Rosita looked at Ortiz, now seeing that he was on the phone. "Oh, *pardon*. I am so sorry."

"It is alright." Then back to Angel: "What did you say?"

By the time the horses rounded the last turn, Ortiz had gotten a full account of the cop's hack-in to the Bio-Sci computer and his escape from the attempt on his life. At least McPherson had no proof that the Lazarus Project existed, but the fact that he now knew about it presented a new threat.

Ortiz accepted this stoically. He had faced many such problems over the years and always dealt with them successfully. This was in part due to the fact that he anticipated adversities and put people in place to take care of them if they happened. Angel Chavez was one of his recent additions to his cadre of trouble-shooters, and one who had carried out his assignments with total satisfaction. Last year he'd used Angel to eliminate a would-be competitor in Manila, a few months later to silence a foolish Nigerian food and drug administrator who refused the usual bribe to look the other way.

"What are your instructions?" Angel asked.

"Hold on for just a minute," Ortiz said.

The horses were on the home stretch, and Wildfire was pulling away from the pack.

Rosita clapped her hands, as Wildfire crossed the finish line three-and-a-half lengths in front of the nearest horse. "You win, *amor*, you win!"

"Of course, little one. I told you your lovely presence would bring me luck." Then into the cell: "We've given the other people ample time to take care of Detective McPherson, Angel. I will now leave the matter in your capable hands."

"Consider it done."

Ortiz beeped off, surprised to see Rosita's lovely face now wearing a frown.

"Angel? Who is this 'angel'?"

Ortiz understood the pout and laughed. "Angel is a man I sometimes employ in my business."

"Angel. What a strange name for a businessman."

True, Ortiz thought. He knew all about Juan Chavez. He made a point of being fully informed about anyone he employed, especially in Angel's line of work. Aside from the generous money he paid them, their dossiers could be used to ensure their loyalty in case any of them decided to become an informant.

"Angel was a nickname he got when he was a little boy, because he sang like an angel. Now he is like a lost soul seeking retribution. More champagne? We should drink to our victory."

"Oh, *amor*, I am afraid if I drink more, I will become very tipsy. Retribution? What is 'retribution'?"

"Retribution. in Angel's case, was to avenge the sexual abuse he suffered as a boy from his priest."

"Oh, *que terrible!*"

"Yes. The priest must have had similar feelings when Angel slit his throat from ear to ear."

Rosita's eyes bulged. She gulped the rest of her champagne.

"More champagne?"

Rosita hiccupped, then extended her glass.

Ortiz filled it and raised his own glass in a toast.

"To us."

And to the moment, he added silently.

*2:23 p.m.:* Willie was jarred awake by the blare of a truck horn. He'd dozed off again, despite the good night's sleep he'd bought with the cop's money in a neighborhood transient hotel. He'd been staking out El Lobo from a bench in a small playground across the street from the bar since his meeting with El Pistolero, even eating carry-outs there from nearby fast food joints. So far there had been no sign of Scarface and friends. Patience, he thought, reflecting back to his long sniper stalks in the jungles of Viet Nam. It would happen.

The truck horn sounded again, the driver shouting in Spanish at a long-haired kid to move his beat-up Toyota that was blocking the loading dock of a warehouse next to the playground. The kid cursed the driver and gave him the finger. This pissed off the driver even more. He got out of the cab, a big guy with tattoos on his arms, and started to move toward the Toyota to drag the kid out of the car, but before he could reach the car, another kid emerged with a six-pack from a liquor store that adjoined El Lobo. Seeing his buddy was about to get beat up, he ran across the street and jumped into the passenger seat. The Toyota peeled rubber, leaving the cursing driver in a cloud of exhaust.

Too bad, Willie thought. He was hoping the driver would kick the shit out of both of those wise-ass kids before he remembered that he'd been a wise-ass kid himself before he joined the Army. Then it had been his top sergeant in basic training who'd done the butt kicking.

Suddenly, Willie was wide awake and on his feet. The truck, which had moved to back into the loading dock, had blocked his view of two vehicles parked in front of the bar. One was a Ford pick-up. The other was a van. Although it was now painted purple with a *PIZZA ULTIMA* logo on the side, Willie was sure that it was the same Dodge Caravan he'd seen the night Alward was killed.

Now Willie hesitated. Should he call McPherson or investigate further? What happened next gave him the answer. A sporty Alfa Romeo had rounded the corner at 28th and was pulling up behind the van. Willie wondered what a car like that was doing in a neighborhood like this—or the sharply dressed young Latino who exited the Romeo and entered the bar. Not to slum with the scum, for sure.

Willie picked up the wrapper of a Big Mac he'd consumed for lunch and wrote down the license plate numbers of the van and the Romeo. He tucked the wrapper into the pocket of his fatigue jacket and glanced at his Salvation Army outlet wristwatch. It read 2:42 p.m. Willie debated his next move. He could find a phone, call McPherson and report what he had found out. Or he could enter the bar with the hope of getting more information. The second option was risky, but Willie knew it was a risk he had to take.

Angel moved through the grungy room. A pigsty, he thought—plaster-spattered walls with tattered bullfight posters and faded brown photos of famous Mexican bandits, paint-chipped tables and chairs, a scarred hardwood floor littered with cigarette butts and assorted trash. He paused at the bar, where two men were drinking beers and watching a soccer game on a Spanish language channel on the TV. A fat man with a pocked face and greedy eyes, Mario Perez, El Lobo's owner and Angel's contact in Chicago, took Angel's order for a glass of Sprite. When Mario brought the Sprite, Angel pushed an envelope containing five one hundred dollar bills across the bar. Angel carried the Sprite to a booth at the rear and sat down next to the man who called himself Carlos Lopez. Carlos and his two associates, whom Angel knew only by their first names of Julio and Andres, were sharing a bottle of tequila between swigs from Coronas.

"*Que pasa, jefe?*" said Carlos, a heavy-set man with a greasy, drooping mustache and a face as ugly as the scar that disfigured his left cheek. Then he spoke in English with a heavy accent. "Mario says you have more work for us."

"That's right. The detective, McPherson..."

Angel paused, observing a black man in a grimy fatigue jacket and hat entering the bar. An undercover NARC cop was his first thought. Not many people other than Mexicans frequented El Lobo, and it was no secret that Mario dealt in drugs. If he was a NARC, he did a good job of looking like a vagrant. Angel was even more apprehensive when the black man sat down on a bar stool within earshot and ordered a Corona. Mario obviously shared his suspicions, given the look he shot him. Angel waited until Mario turned up the volume on the TV before he spoke again, his voice low.

"I have my orders. We kill the cop."

The three men exchanged looks, not of fear, Angel thought, but certainly of apprehension. Up to now he'd had no reason to doubt their competence. They'd done their share in taking care of the former vagrant and the doctor. The cop was another matter, and Angel hoped they were up to the job.

Their leader, Carlos, submerged the mouth-end of his *cigarillo* into the shot glass of tequila and took a puff before responding. "That will not be easy, *jefe*. Such a job will require more money."

Julio, a thin man with a shaved head and mean, squinty eyes, was quick to agree. "*Verdad*. This cop, he is one *muy peligroso hombre*."

Angel looked across the table at the third man, Andres, paunchy, with a ponytail, bloated face and eyes that betrayed an addiction to hard drugs, which in Angel's opinion made him less reliable than his associates. He was not surprised when Andres made the request for more money unanimous. "Julio is right. Many have died trying to kill him."

Angel regarded the trio with undisguised contempt. Low-life pigs, not professionals, like him, and overpaid at that. He had performed hits when he first got into the business for much less money than they were getting.

"I will kill the cop myself. I will require your services strictly for back-up, in case anything goes wrong, which I do not expect. Nonetheless, I will pay you twice what you received for the other jobs. Agreed?"

Julio and Andres looked at Carlos to make the decision for them. Carlos chased a sip of tequila with a swig of Corona and nodded. "Agreed. When do we do this?"

Angel filled them in on the details of the plan he had already set into motion. Like a general preparing his strategy for a battle, Angel had always given careful planning to any job. This was true with his very first contract, a minor domestic affair involving a woman who wanted the money she would not get from her husband in a divorce court. However, it was the silencing of a key witness in the prosecution of a Mexican drug lord that made his reputation in the underworld. Now he was making big money, so much so that Angel could plan for an early retirement when he accumulated enough wealth in his Swiss and Grand Cayman bank accounts. He was already looking forward to a life of luxury such as that enjoyed by his current employer.

It was a fact heavy with irony that it had been a priest who had launched Angel on his profession. Father Francisco, the *Senor Obispo* of *Templo Iglesia del Sagrado Corazon* in Monterey, had heard young Juan singing in front of the Marriott. In exchange for his voice in the church choir, Juan was permitted to attend the Catholic school, tuition free, an event that his parents considered a gift from Heaven. Such an education would enable Juan to rise from the slums and make something of himself. This he had done but in a way that neither they nor Juan himself could ever have imagined. Although he had sent his parents money from time to time, he'd never attempted to see them again since that day that had changed his life forever.

It had started so innocently. The invitations by the Padre to his private chambers, where he expanded Juan's education in Catholicism, even urging him to enter the priesthood when he was of age. He had listened with the Padre to his recordings of classical music, learning of the lives of the great composers who had created such wonderful symphonies and concertos. Nor had Juan considered it unusual when offered a glass of wine. His father always allowed the children a glass of red wine at festive occasions such as Christmas and Easter. And the hugs from the Padre seemed like genuine displays of affection.

The first time it happened Juan was overwhelmed with shame. Shame for what the Padre had done with him. Shame for the feelings of pleasure the Padre had aroused in him. He had masturbated, yes, but at thirteen he had never had sex. Girls had always made fun of his shyness, which made him even more fearful of their rejection if he approached a girl for a date.

The Padre was consumed with remorse. He said that Satan had filled him with lust. That he would exorcise this foulness from his body. That it would never happen again.

But it did happen again, many times, and Juan felt the Padre's lust gradually contaminate his own body, his very soul. When he could bear the shame and humiliation no longer, he took the Padre's straight razor from his bathroom one afternoon during vespers. He intended to use it on himself, to slit his wrists. Death seemed the only way to rid himself of the Devil and end his suffering. Perhaps it would end the Padre's as well.

But after vespers, when the Padre asked Juan to kneel with him at the altar, to pray with him for God to forgive them and to give them the strength to resist the will of Satan, another thought entered Juan's mind. Killing himself was not the answer. He had not invited the Devil into his body. The Devil had come to him through the Padre. Since the Padre could not perform the exorcism, he must do it for him. Cut out the contamination, like a surgeon would remove a cancerous tumor from a patient. In so doing, Juan would not only free himself from the Devil, but obtain redemption for his sins.

Juan looked around. There was no one in the church other than themselves. If Juan was to do this thing, he must do it now. It was as if God himself had sanctioned this act by first giving him the razor and now the opportunity to use it. He knew this to be true a moment later. After the razor slit through his jugular, the Padre looked at him. His eyes seemed to express forgiveness, his smile relief. He was still kneeling in prayer when his head lolled forward in death, his blood flowing onto the altar.

Of course, Juan could not stay in Monterey. No one would believe the Padre's death was an act of mercy and redemption, and he could not bear to witness his family's everlasting shame. So while his mother was out shopping at the market, Juan hastily packed a few clothes and hitchhiked to Mexico City with the little money he had managed to save. There he learned to survive by singing for pesos, as he had in Monterey, and living in the sewers with other street kids. He also found out that there was better money to be made working for one of the *jefes* whose kids sold candy and gum to the *turistas* while separating them from their wallets or purses.

Juan was fortunate to find a *jefe* who treated his employees generously. Unlike other bosses, Javier Martinez allowed them to keep enough of their hard-earned money to live in a more comfortable environment than the sewers. For four years Juan shared a one-bedroom apartment with three other boys in a hotel that catered to whores and their clients of both sexes, while continuing to sharpen his skills as a pickpocket. But Juan knew that this profession was not one that would provide him with the kind of money he had seen as a boy in the fat *turista's* wallet outside that hotel in Monterey, especially when he had to share his earnings with Javier.

The answer to this dilemma came quite unexpectedly when a pimp insisted that either Juan join his stable of boys who serviced pedophiles, or have his arms and legs broken by men he used to keep his boys in line and recruit new ones. Juan had no choice. He had to use the Padre's razor again. He had kept the razor, finding that it had come in handy to discourage bullies who wanted his money or his body for sex. This act got the attention of Javier's brother, whose first name ironically was Jesus. Jesus was in another line of work. He acted as an agent for people who wanted someone killed. The fee for such contracts was a fifty-fifty split with the men and sometimes women who performed the hits. Angel still used Jesus as his agent in Mexico City, but the split was now ninety-ten with the ten percent going to Jesus. Given Angel's current fees, this was more than agreeable with his former employer.

Unless circumstances required another method, Angel's weapon of choice was still the Padre's razor. He had come to accept the fact that he had not purged himself of the Devil by killing the Padre. However, his own redemption seemed to continue each time he used the razor. It was like killing the Padre again. Some day, when he had his wealth, he would kneel at the altar of the Templo Iglesia del Sagrado Corazon, as he had done so many years ago with the Padre, lay the razor on the altar and implore the image of Christ on the cross for forgiveness.

But this was yet to be. Now there was another neck destined to feel the caress of the Padre's razor. Another neck, another death, another step on his road to redemption.

*2:42 p.m.:* Mack listened to Willie's account of his visit to El Lobo.

"Hold on, Willie. I want to write that down." Mack moved quickly to the roll top, flipped open a notebook and grabbed a ball point. "Shoot." Mack scribbled down the plate numbers of the van and the Romeo and the descriptions of the four men in the bar. The van was almost certainly a dead end, probably stolen as well as the plates, but the Romeo was more likely a rental that could be traced. Unfortunately, Willie wasn't able to overhear their conversation or follow either vehicle after the men left the bar. Whatever they had talked about, Mack had a strong feeling that it concerned him. So did Willie.

"Watch your ass, man. According to my contact, Scarface is one bad dude and his two buddies looked just as mean."

"What about the other guy, the sharp dresser with the Romeo? Did your contact have any info on him?"

"Don't know. I'll have to ask him, but I doubt it. The dude looked like he came from another planet than Scarface and his *amigos*. One thing for sure though. He was the guy giving the orders."

"A go-between or maybe a hit man himself. Thanks, Willie. Good work."

"You still want me to keep an eye on El Lobo?"

"No. Try to find out where Scarface lives or where they keep the van. Could you use some more money?"

"I'm okay for now with what you gave me."

"Okay. Let me know if you find out anything. And call the cell. I'll be on the move."

"Will do."

Mack beeped off. He took time out to feed a howling Ulysses before he resumed straightening up the loft, which he'd been doing when Willie called. At least the searcher hadn't damaged any of the antiques and left his valuable and very breakable collection of original 78 rpm records untouched. Mack searched for a bug as he cleaned up. He'd underestimated his adversary before and wasn't about to repeat that mistake. He was also giving some serious thought to the possibility that he was dealing with more than one opponent. The guy who'd tried to kill him this morning, clean cut and wearing a business suit, seemed to have nothing in common with the three scumbag Mexicans and Mr. Romeo.

Mack was pondering this when his door buzzer sounded. Not expecting company, unless redhead and his crony were returning to finish the job, Mack pulled his .38 from the holster on the hall tree and fingered the speaker button.

"Yes?"

Otis's voice answered. "It's your ex-partner. I've got news and it isn't good. Let me in."

"Stay put. I'm coming down."

Mack holstered the revolver and exited the loft. More bad news was just what he didn't need, he thought on his way down in the elevator. Since Otis was the messenger, whatever it was had to be coming from the CPD brass.

When Mack exited the building, Otis gaped at the bandages on his forehead. "Man, what happened to you?"

"Tell you later. Let's take a walk."

While they walked around the block, Otis filled him in about Roy O'Neal's phone call to his golf buddy, the mayor, and O'Neal's assertion that Mack had accused him of having a strong hand in the death of his former employee, Dr. Alward.

"Well at least that's a fact. What kind of spin did O'Neal put on it?"

"That you claimed that he'd fired Alward when he found out he was selling research info to competitors. And when he discovered that Alward had continued to access the mainframe, he put out a contract to silence Alward and destroy his computer and disks."

"Good, very good. Just way out enough for the brass to dismiss as nonsense except for a wacko cop looking for a big caper to get his badge back. How'd you get this, by the way?"

"I didn't. Cronin did. He passed it on to me, but he was winking when he told me to keep it confidential. Seems he's willing to give you the benefit of the doubt."

"Tell him thanks. I suppose Hizzonor turned up the heat on me?"

"A warrant for your arrest is being typed up as we speak. According to O'Neal, you also threatened him if he didn't come clean."

"Wonderful. You've really made my day."

"Don't mention it. So what really happened at Bio-Sci?"

Mack brought Otis up to date on the attempt on his life and theft of his computer and Lazarus disk.

"Not exactly a coincidence, wouldn't you say?"

"I can buy into that. I hope you found out what was on the disk?"

"I did."

"And?"

"I thought you wanted no part of that."

"That was before I got insomnia wondering what it was."

Mack smiled. He'd had a hunch that Otis's cop curiosity would get the better of him. "Okay, but what I have to tell you could make you a target as well. Still want to know?"

"You may be suspended, but I still consider you to be my partner. So give."

"Okay. So listen up, partner."

Otis did and without interrupting. When Mack finished Otis shook his head.

"Heavy, man. Very heavy."

"And that's only part of it. I still don't know who's pulling O'Neal's strings and the reason for the deadline for finding a cure for the virus."

"Isn't it logical that it's strictly a profit motive? Finding a cure for HCV would mean major bucks for Bio-Sci."

"That's true, but there's got to be more to it than that. I could be wrong, but O'Neal didn't impress me as the kind of guy who'd have two men killed just for the bucks."

They walked in silence for a minute until they reached Otis's Grand Vic.

"So what's your next move?" Otis asked.

"I'm working on some angles, but there's something you can do for me."

Otis hesitated before answering. He'd already gone too far by asking what the Lazarus Project was about. "Alright, just as long as it doesn't cost me my badge."

"It won't even smudge it," Mack said. At least the first request wouldn't, he thought, but the second one was another matter. He handed Otis the paper with the two license numbers and descriptions of the four men in the bar. "Check out the plates. The first is for a van, probably stolen, but the second is for an Alfa Romeo that could be a rental. And run the descriptions of Scarface and Mr. Romeo through CRIS. Maybe we'll get lucky."

"I'll give it a try. How'd you get this, anyway?"

"I didn't. Willie did." Mack explained about Willie's private detective efforts.

"Maybe we should provide Willie with a badge and a .38," Otis teased.

"Not a bad idea. When you get something, call me on the cell. I've got to be out of here before they can serve that warrant. Which brings me to another request. I need wheels."

"What? The last time I checked you had two cars."

"Yeah, with descriptions and plate numbers the cops can alert to every cruiser on the street. Add to that the distinct probability that the bad guys have bugged both cars so they can track me on a GPS. These guys are real pros, which is why we're talking out here instead of in my apartment."

"Okay, so how about a rental?"

"Get serious. They'll check those out as well. That also goes for any place I try to stay. I've got to go underground and still have mobility without being picked up. Which brings me back to that second request."

"Oh, no! No way, man! I can't let you have the RV!"

"Why not? No one will be looking for me there."

"Maybe, maybe not, but I can't take the risk of an aiding and abetting rap."

"Dammit, Otis, believe me, I wouldn't be asking this of you if there was any other option. Otherwise, I'm either in cuffs with no way to expose the Lazarus Project or I'm dead meat! Now what's it gonna be?"

They locked eyes. I can't cave in on this, Otis was thinking, not only because of the possibility of being involved with a fugitive but of how Ava would react if he told her. And he would have to tell her. He'd already broken his promise to her about not having anything more to do with Mack by helping him crack into the Bio-Sci mainframe. And now that their marriage had gotten back on track, Otis was very reluctant to do anything more that might derail it.

Before he could say no again, Mack's cell phone beeped.

Mack pulled it out of his belt holder. "Yes?"

As Mack listened, Otis saw the hint of a smile.

"I think that can be arranged. Where and when can we meet?"

He listened again. "Good choice. I'll be there."

Mack beeped off. He was looking for a break, and this might be it. "That was Diane Bates, Kischman's assistant. She says she's willing to tell me about Lazarus if I can get her immunity to testify. She'll meet me after she gets off work this evening at five-thirty."

"Did it ever enter your cop mind that you might be walking into a bullet?"

It had, especially after what Willie had told him about Mr. Romeo and the Mexicans. They were hatching something, and this might be it. In any event, Mack would be on the alert.

"I'm betting she's on the level. Now how about the RV?"

Otis sighed. Extracting a ring of keys from his coat pocket, he worked the RV key off and handed it to Mack.

"Just bring it back with a full tank."

*5:48 p.m.:* Mack curbed the RV at a parking space across the street from Our Lady of Mount Carmel Church on West Belmont. He'd already checked out the street and the parking lot next to the church for the Alfa Romeo, pizza van and Red's dark blue Taurus. Although none of them were there, that didn't mean that any or all of them weren't somewhere in the vicinity. Still, their absence was a plus, as was Diane's choice of a meeting place. A church seemed an unlikely place for a hit.

While he waited, Mack listened out of habit to the dispatcher on his police radio. Suddenly, Ulysses sprang into the passenger seat with his customary yowl. The tom had been warming up to him and wanted to be petted. Mack had debated whether to give Larry a key to his loft so he could feed Ulysses and change his litter, or take the cat and the litter box with him. He'd opted for the cat and the litter box.

Mack was stroking Ulysses under the chin when Diane approached in a cream colored Honda and parked a short distance from the church. Garbed modestly in a matching navy blazer and pants, white blouse and black sandals, she exited the Honda with a shoulder purse and walked to the church. For a moment she hesitated, as if debating whether to go through with the meeting, then ascended the steps to a traditional Byzantine-style Catholic house of worship with its stained glass windows and rounded arch flanked by twin bell towers.

Mack waited five minutes before he followed. He pulled open the middle of three heavy double doors and entered the tranquil stillness of the vestibule. He paused at the entrance to the nave to scan the vaulted interior. Diane was in the front pew. The only other person in the church was a nun kneeling at the altar in prayer. Nonetheless, as he moved down the aisle, he looked from side to side to make sure no one was crouched down between the rows of pews.

Diane jumped when Mack slid into the pew next to her. "Oh, you startled me!"

"Sorry. Didn't mean to sneak up on you, Diane."

"It's alright. It's just that I'm so distraught."

"I can imagine. What made you decide to talk to me about Lazarus?"

"I found out that the research computer had been invaded. When I asked Otto...Dr. Kischman about it, he said it was a malfunction and not to worry about it. But he seemed upset, not himself, so...well I..."

Mack finished it for her. "You thought I was behind it and got scared."

"Yes. It was you, wasn't it?"

Mack hesitated. He was beginning to suspect that Diane had been sent on a fishing expedition by O'Neal and Kischman, probably to find out if he really did have other disks of the project. He'd already decided that ploy was going to get him exactly nowhere other than to shake them up until they realized that it was just a bluff, which they would certainly do when he failed to expose Lazarus. If that was Diane's mission, then she obviously had no intention of helping him. But they may have made a serious blunder in sending her, Mack thought. Diane *was* scared, and fear made a person vulnerable. Now all he had to do was exploit it.

"Okay, Diane, I confess. It was me. Now let's stop playing games. I know O'Neal and Kischman sent you here to find out if I had other Lazarus disks, right?"

Diane's mouth dropped. "No, I mean...I was just..."

"I'll take that for a yes. Okay, well you can tell them no. I don't have any more disks. The only one I copied was stolen this morning after the goons they sent to kill me screwed up."

This news hit home. "Someone...someone tried to kill you?!"

Mack gripped her arm. "Look, Diane, I think you know or at least suspect that there's more going on with Lazarus than finding a cure for HCV. You've got to realize that whoever is behind the Project—and I don't think O'Neal and Kischman are calling the shots—whoever is behind it will stop at nothing to keep it secret. Frank O'Meara found that out the hard way. So did Dr. Alward."

"I don't understand. O'Meara's death was an accident, wasn't it? And a drug addict killed Dr. Alward. That's what the media said...one of his own patients."

"Don't be naïve, Diane. They couldn't take the chance of O'Meara being examined by another doctor, and Alward was panicking, which meant he was an even bigger risk."

"No, that can't be true! It can't be! I've known Dr. Kischman for years. He could never have anything to do with...with murder. His whole life has been dedicated to *saving* lives!"

Diane said this with such sincere conviction that Mack saw he would never be able to convince her that Kischman wasn't destined for sainthood. He decided to try another strategy. "Okay, Kischman is probably being used, maybe O'Neal as well. But once an antiviral drug is found, they become expendable."

Diane's eyes filled with fear as she thought about this. "Oh, my God! Do you really believe their lives would be in danger?"

"Since they know who's pulling the strings, I'd say it's highly likely. And that goes for anyone they consider a threat. If they knew you were even thinking about talking to me..."

Mack let Diane draw her own conclusions, which her frightened eyes and choked voice told him she had done all too vividly. "Oh, no! What can I do?!"

"You said on the phone that you'd inform about the Project in return for immunity. Well that's exactly what you have to do."

"I don't know! I just don't know!"

Mack knew he had her on the ropes now and kept pressing the attack. "I think you do, Diane. I think you're a decent, caring person. I think that the whole nasty business of experimenting with human guinea pigs has been preying on your mind for some time."

"Yes, yes, that's true. I was opposed to it from the beginning, but Dr. Kischman...he assured me it was the only way if we were to save millions of other people from the disease. Maybe he was right. I don't know. The only thing I know is that I can't live with it anymore! I just can't!" She looked at Mack, her eyes pleading as they filled with tears. "If I do this, if I give evidence, are you sure you can promise me immunity?"

"Absolutely. You understand that you'll be going into a witness protection program?"

"Oh...do I have to do that?"

"If you want to stay alive. But first you have to make a written statement at police headquarters. And it would be a big help if you had some hard evidence to back up your accusations. You have access to the research computer, don't you?"

"Yes."

"And to the Lazarus file?"

"Yes."

"Do you think you can copy the file to a disk?"

"Yes, I suppose so."

"Good. How soon do you think you could do that?"

"I don't know. Maybe tomorrow. It's a Saturday, but sometimes I work Saturdays. I'll have to let you know."

"Right. Call me on the cell when you have it. One more thing. You wouldn't happen to know why the project has a deadline of November 1st?"

"No. Dr. Kischman never confided that to me," she said with a hint of resentment.

That figured, Mack thought. "Okay. I'll be waiting for your call. And Diane..."

"Yes?"

Mack gave her arm a little squeeze. "Be careful," he said as they rose to leave.

At the altar, Angel crossed himself.

"*Pardoname, Dios*, for what I am about to do," he said to the almost lifelike statue of Christ on the cross suspended behind the altar. Even though the expression on the pious face looking down at him showed compassion, Angel did not expect HIS forgiveness. Not now, at least. Perhaps never.

Still kneeling, Angel reached for the razor in the sleeve of the nun's habit he was wearing. His plan had worked to perfection. Not only would he kill the cop, he would perform the act in a Catholic church, just as he had done so many years ago with Father Francisco in Monterey.

Angel looked over his shoulder. The cop was standing, his back to the altar, waiting for the Bates woman to exit the pew. Angel removed the razor from his sleeve, opened it, the blade catching the light from the array of candles on the altar. Gripping the well-worn handle, he rose to his feet and, head bowed, stepped down from the altar. Now!

Diane screamed! Mack spun around. A razor was slashing at his neck. Mack caught the assailant's wrist before the blade could slice his jugular. They grappled in a deadly embrace, crashed against the altar, toppling candles. The man in the nun's habit was strong, but Mack had the advantage in size and weight. He twisted the man's arm behind his back. The man cursed with pain. Mack applied more pressure. The razor fell to the floor.

The next thing Mack knew he was staggering back from a blow on the side of his head from a candleholder that the man had grabbed with his other hand. Momentarily stunned, Mack instinctively reached for the .38 in his hip holster. The man picked up the razor. Mack was faster.

"Freeze, asshole!" Mack said, the revolver leveled at the man's chest.

The man did. Now Mack could make out the face of a young Latino under the hood with delicate, almost effeminate features. Mr. Romeo, Mack figured.

"Drop the razor, *amigo*! I wouldn't want you to cut yourself shaving."

"And if I don't?" the man said in a falsetto voice that could have passed as a girl's.

"You're a dead man."

The man only smiled. "I always wanted to die in church, when my time came. But I do not think this is the time, if you want what I think you want."

Mr. Romeo was right, Mack admitted. He wanted the young Latino alive and talking.

"You've got exactly five seconds to drop it, or take a bullet in the shoulder."

"Are you sure of that, Mr. Detective? Didn't you notice that your hand is shaking?"

Mack didn't, but he did now. His vision was also blurry from the blow on the head. "I'll take that chance, *amigo*. Will you?"

"No. I believe not. Not this time, at least. Would you permit me to lay the razor on the altar. Perhaps that will solicit some measure of forgiveness from the Son of God."

"Go ahead."

Some cool customer, Mr. Romeo, Mack had to admit, which made him even more dangerous. This was confirmed by what happened next. An elderly nun suddenly came out of the door to the sacristy, her face aghast at what she saw.

"What is happening here?!"

"Help me, Sister! Help me!" Mr. Romeo cried out, slumping against the altar.

"Stay back, Sister!" Mack said. "He's…"

Too late! The nun had bought into Mr. Romeo's act and moved to assist him. "My poor sister, let me…"

In one swift, fluid motion Mr. Romeo had the nun in front of him and the razor blade caressing her throat.

"I am sorry, Sister. I do not wish to kill you, but your life is now in the hands of God…and Mr. Detective."

Mack swore under his breath. He'd had a split second to get off a shot, but his shaking hand and foggy vision had made him hesitate.

"For shame, for shame!" the nun said, looking more outraged than afraid. "This is a House of God!"

"I know, Sister, but the detective leaves me no choice. He also has no choice but to allow me to leave. Carlos, bring the van! *Pronto!*"

Mack realized that Mr. Romeo was wired and talking to one of the Mexican thugs. "You're not going anywhere, *amigo.*"

The young Latino ignored the threat. "Now, Sister, we will leave this place of worship. Very slowly, Sister. This razor is very sharp."

With the nun as a shield, the razor at her throat, Mr. Romeo began to back her toward a side door in the nave.

Again Mack hesitated. He could take a shot, but if it wasn't a fatal one, the nun would not survive the razor. Nevertheless, his finger tightened against the trigger.

Angel held his breath. For a moment he was certain the detective was going to shoot. If he did, not only was his own life at stake, but the nun's as well.

Angel had been truthful when he told the nun that he did not want to kill her. The elderly nun reminded him of the *Hermana Superior* at the Templo Iglesia del Sagrado Corazon in Monterey. It was she who had consoled him during the time of his pain and humiliation. Although she never said it, she must have known what the Padre had done to him. You must put your trust in God, she had told him, and pray for God to forgive the Padre for forsaking his vows. It would be unforgivable for him to repay her kindness by murdering a nun.

Fortunately, this was not going to happen. The detective's shaking hand and glazed eyes told Angel that he would not take the risk of pulling the trigger. And for that he genuinely thanked God.

Mack lowered the .38. "All right, *amigo.* I'm giving you exactly one minute. When I come through that door, I expect to see the sister unharmed."

"Agreed. *Hasta la vista.*"

Mr. Romeo reached back, pulled the door open and exited with the nun.

Mack checked his wrist watch.

"I didn't know this was going to happen!" Diane said, her voice shrill. "I swear I didn't!"

Mack watched the second hand. He knew she was telling the truth, otherwise she wouldn't have screamed. And for the scream he was grateful. It had probably saved his life. "Now you know that these people play for keeps."

"I don't understand. Dr. Kischman just wanted me to find out what you knew."

"It's called a setup, Diane. You said Kischman sent you here? What about O'Neal?"

"Dr. Kischman said it was Mr. O'Neal's idea. Oh! I see it now. This was all Mr. O'Neal's doing. Dr. Kischman would never condone…"

"Yeah, yeah, I know. The man walks on water."

The minute was up.

"Stay here!"

Mack moved to the door, stood to one side, then exited quickly, gun extended into a courtyard. The nun was standing at the open gate of an iron fence facing Belmont Avenue. Mack got ready to squeeze off some rounds at a purple van that was gunning away from the curb, then decided against it. Mr. Romeo had kept his part of the bargain, and Mack would keep his.

As Mack moved to the nun, he remembered Mr. Romeo's parting words. "*Hasta la vista.*" Until the next time. Mack had no doubt that there would be a next time. And when it happened, he would not hesitate to pull the trigger.

Mack took the nun's arm.

"Are you okay, Sister?"

"Yes, yes. But that poor young man. May God forgive him."

"That's asking a lot, Sister, even of God."

"Do you think he would have done what he said?"

"Killed you?"

"Yes."

"Absolutely. The man's a cold-blooded killer."

The nun shook her head. "Perhaps, but there is some spark of decency in even the worst of God's children."

No comment from Mack as he walked her to the side entrance. He was thinking that Hitler liked little kids, but still slaughtered six million Jews.

Diane came over when they entered the church. "Are you all right, Sister?"

"Yes, thank you, young lady."

"Why don't you sit down and rest awhile, Sister," Mack said.

"Oh, no. Just look at this mess. I have to straighten up the altar."

"Let me help you."

"No. After what's happened, I'm sure you have more important things to do."

Which was true, Mack thought, turning to Diane, who looked like she needed a blood transfusion.

"That man...if he'd killed you then he might have killed me, too!"

Diane was finally beginning to see the light, Mack thought. "Not *might*, Diane. Aside from being a witness to an attempted murder, just knowing about Lazarus makes you a marked woman."

"Yes, I see that. But you said you could protect me if I made a statement about Lazarus."

Mack thought about this. There was no way now that she could make a copy of the Lazarus file, and without a copy of the file to back up her story, it would be her word against O'Neal's and Kischman's. He could predict how they'd spin it. Diane would be portrayed as a disgruntled, neurotic employee recruited by Mack to support his absurd allegations. Of course, any trace of Lazarus would be purged from the mainframe and stored away in some secret place until the heat was off. And even if there was some breakthrough in revealing the Project, the people behind Lazarus would likely remain a mystery.

"Look, Diane, we can still try to go that route, but the police might not buy it if we don't have any proof, and that would mean no witness protection program."

"Oh my God! Then what *can* we do?!"

Mack wished he had an answer. "Get you someplace safe until I can work out a plan."

"Are you sure?"

"Yes. Don't worry. I've got a place where no one will find you."

"All right. But I'll have to go home first and pack some things."

"We can't risk that, Diane. We'll stop at a mall. I'll pay for whatever you need, okay?"

"Yes, all right. I'll follow you in my car."

"No, you'd better come with me. If they find your car, they find you. Let's go."

They started up the aisle.

"Oh, Detective?"

Mack turned. The nun was holding something in her hand.

"I found this on the floor. Is it yours?"

Mack moved to the nun. "Oh, yes. I must have dropped it during my struggle with the killer."

"I'm glad I found it before you left."

"So am I." The nun handed him the object. "Thanks, Sister."

It wasn't much, he thought, but it might tell him something.

"What was it?" Diane asked.

Mack showed her Mr. Romeo's cell phone.

*6:53 p.m.:* Otis picked up his beeping cell phone. He was in his study, gluing the split tail onto a model B-25 bomber, and the call was an unwelcome intrusion into his private time. He was not surprised when the voice on the cell was Mack's. Nor was he surprised when Mack told him what had happened at the church. Diane Bates's offer to blow the lid off Lazarus had seemed too good to be true.

"I told you it was a setup," he said.

"Yeah, but Diane wasn't in on the hit. She's scared now for real, and for good reason."

"I can imagine. So you've got yourself a witness after all?"

"Yeah. She has no choice if she wants to go on living. Now all I have to do is keep her safe. I'm in a mall now, waiting while she buys some clothes and some other necessities."

"Don't tell me she's gonna play house with you and the cat in the RV?"

"That was the plan, but Diane felt uncomfortable with that arrangement."

"What's her problem? Is she allergic to cats or to you?"

"Very funny. And there is no problem. I'll stash her in a motel that prefers cash to plastic, no questions asked. What did you find out about the van and the Romeo?"

"A Dodge Caravan was on the reported stolen list, like you figured, and the plates belong on a Ford Explorer. You were right about the Romeo, too. It was rented from an agency on Lake Street, dating back to March 14th. The name on the rental application is Pedro Ruiz. Pedro showed a Costa Rican driver's license and paid cash for up to six months."

"Not much help there. The license is probably as phony as his name, and there's no telling when he'll show up to return the car or extend the rental time. Did you check out Mr. Romeo and Scarface with CRIS?"

"Yeah. I went through God knows how many field contact cards. I struck out with Romeo, but had better luck with Scarface. There were about twenty Mexicans with scars on their left cheeks. I plugged in the Little Village area where Scarface hangs out and came up with a guy called Carlos Lopez. He's an illegal, no surprise there, with a rap sheet as long as a roll of toilet paper. Address unknown, of course."

"Of course. Anyway, thanks for trying."

"Hey, no problem. So now that you've got a witness, what are you going to do with her?"

"I'm working on that," Mack said, and explained why he didn't want Diane to make any accusations without any supportive evidence.

"Looks like you're up the proverbial creek."

"Yeah, but you could be a big help if…"

"Whoa! Stop right there. I've already put my marriage in jeopardy, let alone my life."

"Don't worry. I just need some more information that I'm not exactly in a position to get. Mr. Romeo made a mistake. He dropped his cell phone in the process of trying to kill me. I figured he might have programmed some key phone numbers into speed dial and got lucky."

"How lucky is lucky?"

Mack told him. While he was waiting for Diane to finish shopping, he'd found four speed dial numbers. Number one got him an answer from someone speaking Spanish.

*"La residencia de Senor Ortiz."*

Mack had enough high school Spanish to understand what *residencia* meant, but fortunately the guy spoke some English. "Is this Mr. Ortiz?"

"No. I am his...*gerente de casa. Senor Ortiz no esta su casa.* Who is speaking, please?"

"Mr. Ryan. I'm a loan officer with the Chase Manhattan Bank in New York," Mack said, figuring that Ortiz must be pretty well to do if he had a house manager. "Mr. Ortiz requested a loan, but there's been some confusion about his address, and I'm calling to verify it."

*"Por suspuesto.* He is at 246 Avenida de Flores, Caracas, Venezuela."

"Caracas? There must be some mistake. This is the home of Fernando Ortiz, isn't it?"

"Oh, no, Senor Ryan. Manuel de Ortiz Hijo."

"Sorry. I must have the wrong information."

Mack was betting that Senor Manuel de Ortiz Hijo probably had a cell phone when he tried number two.

"Yes?" a voice answered in English.

"Mr. Ortiz?"

A pause. "Who is this?"

"Someone I'm sure you didn't expect to hear from, Ortiz. Detective McPherson..."

Click. Silence.

Mack smiled. Now we're getting somewhere, he thought. He tried number three and was not surprised when a guttural voice answered, "El Lobo."

"I want to speak to the owner."

"This is Mario. I am the owner. What do you want?"

"Could I interest you in a subscription to the *Ladies Home Journal*?"

Mack got an earful of profanity before Mario hung up.

"Score three for the home team," Otis said when Mack finished. "Could it be that Mr. Romeo is working for this Ortiz guy?"

"For sure. Ortiz knew who I was, alright, or he would have asked why I was calling before he hung up."

"Must have shook him up a bit hearing from a man he thought was dead?"

"I hope."

"And Mario must be Mr. Romeo's contact in Chicago, given what Willie told you."

"Right again. But hold onto your jockey shorts on this one. Guess who answered the phone when I dialed number four?"

"I give up. Who?"

"None other than Dr. Otto Kischman. Can you connect the dots?"

"I'm beginning to. The question is, who is this Ortiz guy?"

"That's what I want you to find out. You can start by contacting Interpol. And while you're at it, see if they have anything on Mr. Romeo. He'll come under the category of professional hit man with an MO of using a razor as a weapon of choice."

"I'll get on it in the morning."

"Good, and thanks, Otis." A pause. "Uh, by the way, how is everything going on the home front?"

"You're referring to my marriage, I assume."

"Yeah."

"Well, at the moment it's on hold."

"Oh? Well I hope everything works out okay."

"I'll keep you informed," Otis said, and beeped off.

The fact was that Otis couldn't tell Mack what he didn't know himself. So far things had gone as expected. There'd been no rants and raves from Ava when he explained why the RV was not parked in the driveway. As usual, it would take time for Ava to process the information and come up with a response. In the meantime he was getting the silent treatment accompanied by a deep freeze that put her body off limits.

Otis reached for his mug and took a swig of lukewarm coffee laced with Hennessy. He hoped that the cognac would make him drowsy, but he was already resigning himself to what could be a long toss-and-turn night in the guest bedroom.

*7:52 p.m.:* Ortiz took a long pull of Johnny Walker Black.

"Is something the matter, *amor*? Are you not feeling well?"

Ortiz looked at Rosita. She was reclining on a comfortable lounge chair next to his on the balcony of their luxurious twenty-fifth floor suite at the Mandarin Oriental Hotel in Miami, where they shared a spectacular view of Biscayne Bay. Always a vision of loveliness, Rosita looked like a pagan goddess in her slinky silver hostess gown that emphasized every curve of her voluptuous body. Her look of pain told Ortiz that she had picked up on his reaction to the cop's phone call.

"It is nothing, little one. Just a mild headache."

"Oh. I was so worried. It makes me sad when you are not feeling well."

Ortiz knew that she meant it. He also knew that she really loved him. With the others he never really knew or cared if they loved him or were simply overwhelmed by his good looks, charm and lifestyle. He would genuinely regret the time when his moment with Rosita must end.

Ortiz rattled the ice cubes in his rocks glass, then drank the rest of the scotch. He needed it, and it had nothing to do with Rosita. Something had gone very wrong with his plans for the detective. Not only had McPherson survived Angel's razor, he had somehow gotten his home and cell phone numbers, which had enabled him to find out who he was. This he had confirmed with a phone call to Felix, his house manager. The call from the Chase Manhattan loan officer had to be McPherson. But how had the detective gotten the phone numbers? Had he captured Angel, made him talk? Possible, but Angel was a pro and not likely to divulge the identity of his employer. Of course, he might have been offered a lighter sentence if he cooperated, but Ortiz believed that McPherson was in no position to make such an offer. So what had happened?

Ortiz didn't have long to wait for an answer. He was replenishing his glass from the bottle on the chaise table when his cell phone beeped. The detective again? he wondered, as he pulled his cell from the pocket of his maroon smoking jacket. "Yes?"

This time it was Angel. Ortiz got up and moved to the railing as he listened. At least Angel had escaped the detective, but the rest of what the hit man told him was upsetting, to say the least. Ortiz resisted an angry outburst. McPherson seemed to be living a charmed life. His survival was more a matter of luck than a lack of Angel's skill with the razor.

"Why didn't you call me sooner?"

To Angel, Ortiz's voice revealed only a hint of irritation, as if he'd lost a few dollars in a casino. "I wanted to get another cell phone," he said, and gave Ortiz his new number. "What are your orders?"

"Kill McPherson, of course. But now we have another problem."

"The Bates woman."

"Yes. Do you think she will cooperate with McPherson?"

"Absolutely. She is probably with him now. I checked out her home. She wasn't there."

"Find her and kill her."

"It will be taken care of," Angel said with more confidence than he felt. Locating her would be hard enough, killing her even more difficult if she was with McPherson.

"Another thing," Ortiz said. "I have decided to come to Chicago. I'm leaving early tomorrow morning. This latest development makes the situation more volatile."

"I understand. Where will you be staying?"

"I prefer not to reveal that, even to you. In fact, I do not wish it to be known that I am in Chicago."

Taking no chances, Angel thought. He was aware that Interpol and the Feds knew all about Ortiz's business, and although they had nothing they could take to a judge to detain him, they were keeping an eye on his employer in case he slipped up.

"As you wish. Anything else?"

"No. I'll contact you when I arrive. If something develops in the meantime, call me on the cell."

"The same number?"

"Yes. McPherson already knows who I am, so why change it? And Angel…"

"Yes?"

"Do not disappoint me again."

"I won't."

Angel slowly pocketed his cell phone. Ortiz did not have to explain the probable consequences of another failure. Angel understood that in this event the hit man could very well be the subject of a contract himself.

Ortiz was having similar thoughts as he took a sip of scotch.

"*Amor.*"

"Yes, little one?"

"I got a letter today. From *madre*. Did I not tell you?"

"No. How is she?"

"She is so happy to know about all the wonderful places we have been. She sends you her love and wants you to know that she keeps you in her prayers."

Ortiz smiled. He doubted if anyone had ever kept him in their prayers, except perhaps his own mother, a Catholic, but by no means a devout one. For her, attending church was more an opportunity to show off the latest stylish addition to her wardrobe than to seek religious guidance. A beautiful but spoiled daughter of a prominent Venezuelan family, she devoted most of her life to shopping at expensive boutiques, throwing lavish parties, and pampering Ramon, his wimp of a younger brother. Given this, it was impossible for him to respect his mother, let alone love her.

With his father, it had been different. If Manuel was capable of loving anyone, it was his father, whom he both respected and feared. As he gazed out at the star-studded sky that arched like an enormous vault over the dark waters of the bay, Manuel remembered as he often did the mission his father had given him as a boy, and the strange twists it had taken. He had just turned fourteen, and although his father was an excellent fencer, Manuel had defeated him in a match at an exclusive athletic club in front of a gallery of spectators. He had expected his father to be humiliated, even angry, but he wasn't. Instead he was proud of Manuel and had boasted to the onlookers that his son would soon become the best fencer in the club (a boast Manuel quickly fulfilled).

It was then that his father told him what would become his lifelong quest, his Holy Grail. "My son, always set your sights on the most worthy targets, no matter how distant they may seem. Seek out the most difficult challenges, then use all your skill and knowledge and determination to overcome them, whether in sports, in business…anything you undertake. If you do this," he said, "you will someday achieve *el momento supremo*—the supreme moment."

"*El momento supremo*? Have you achieved such a moment, Father?"

"No, my son, I have not."

This Manuel had not understood. Although Ortiz was a proud name dating back four generations before him, his grandfather had squandered everything away. But his father had scraped up enough money to finance a modest but profitable pharmaceutical business and restore the family name to prominence and respect. Was this not a supreme moment, Manuel had asked?

"No, my son," his father had answered. "Not even that."

"But what then?"

His father had laid a hand on his shoulder and replied: "I do not know, my son, because I have not yet found it for myself, but I do know how you would recognize such a moment: it would be a moment when you finally achieved something very difficult you had been trying to accomplish for a long time, like defeating a worthy opponent after a long struggle, or climbing to the summit of a great mountain. At such a moment, you would feel a sense of pride and accomplishment so profound, so complete, you would be able to say to yourself, 'If I were to die right now, at this very moment, I would die happy, without regret, because I have done what I set out to do.'"

His father had paused, then continued, "That is how it should be for you, my son, but for me, it will be different. I am getting too old to continue my search for *el momento supremo*. But you saw how proud I was of you just now when you were able to defeat me. I will be completely happy when I see you achieve your *momento supremo*. Your supreme moment will also be mine."

With these words, his father had placed on Manuel's shoulders the mantle of power and responsibility. This was liberating—Manuel would never again fear that he might anger his father by surpassing him—but it was also a kind of burden. From then on, every choice he had made, every activity he had pursued, had been for his father as well as for himself. Of course, there was a certain pleasure in this, as it deepened the bond between them. He had discussed with his father every new challenge he undertook, had sought his advice and counsel, and they had celebrated together each victory and accomplishment. At times, however, on those occasions when he and his father had disagreed, or when his father had sought to rein in Manuel's impulsiveness, he had felt a twinge of regret that his father was always looking over his shoulder.

For the most part, however, his father's involvement had spurred him on to ever greater achievements. He had taken up each challenge with fierce determination. He had graduated *summa cum laude*—with highest honors—from Oxford University in England in three years, where he had also captained the soccer team. For the next three years he had played forward on the Venezuela national soccer team, his personal goal being to lead his team to victory in the World Cup. Surely such a world class triumph would be their supreme moment together. At every practice and with every game, he had focused all his energy and attention on achieving this goal, savoring the supreme moment when victory would belong to him…and his father.

But fate dealt him a cruel blow. The night before his team was to play Germany in the finals, he got word from home that his father had just died of a massive stroke. Numb with shock and grief, Manuel had had no choice but to return immediately to Caracas to bury his father. At the funeral he had looked down at his father's rigid face in the open coffin, furious that death had shattered the dream for both of them. The supreme moment, almost in Manuel's grasp, had been stolen from him. If there was a God, which he had always doubted, he cursed him now. Nearly choking with grief and rage, but grim with determination, his hands holding tight to the coffin's edge, he vowed, "Father, I will honor your memory. I will do anything and everything, whatever it takes, to experience *el momento supremo*…for both of us."

Immediately after the funeral, Manuel took charge of the family business. This was his right and duty as the oldest son, and in any case Ramon would have been completely incapable of doing it. Within a few months, he was running the business even more efficiently and profitably than his father had. This was no surprise. He was talented, clever, highly disciplined, and, most important, driven by his quest.

He knew he would need great wealth and power in order to be able to go anywhere and do anything that might bring him closer to his goal. This he had accomplished by expanding the pharmaceutical business into a multi-million dollar manufacturer and distributor of synthetic drugs. Although his father had been an ethical man, with his death Manuel had cast off all moral and ethical restraints. Instead of investing in research to develop new drugs, he simply stole the formulas and processes for making such drugs from the legitimate pharmaceutical companies that developed them, using stealth, bribery and threats to acquire their trade secrets. In short, he became a drug pirate, raiding and exploiting the intellectual property of others to acquire wealth. Achieving victory was all that mattered. He ruthlessly crushed anyone who got in his way, eventually resorting without hesitation to murder whenever he deemed it expedient to do so.

Within a few years he had amassed enough wealth and power to be able to devote most of his time and energy to his quest for *el momento supremo*. Often this was under circumstances that were life-threatening: skydiving from 30,000 feet, driving his own race car in the Grand Prix, even facing a charging rhino in Kenya with time for only one life or death shot from his hunting rifle. These and other adventures provided exhilarating highs, but that was all. *El momento supremo* continued to elude him like a quarry occasionally glimpsed through the scope of a high-powered hunting rifle—but he would find it and bag it. He *had* to for his life to have meaning. He had to keep the vow he made at his father's coffin, and he would explore any emotion and take any risk to do so.

Rosita's voice intruded on his thoughts. "*Amor?*"

"Yes?" he said. Turning, he was surprised to see tears leaving twin trails of mascara down Rosita's pink cheeks.

"What is that you said? About Chicago? Must you go to Chicago?"

Ortiz realized that despite Rosita's limited knowledge of English, her feminine intuition had translated what she hadn't understood in his conversation with Angel. "Yes, little one. There is some urgent business I must attend to."

Very urgent. He'd already made up his mind to go to Chicago when Kischman called him that afternoon. It was good news for a change. Kischman was confident that they had found a successful antiviral drug to combat HCV. Final tests were being conducted that should give them the answer in a matter of hours. Naturally, Ortiz had to be on the scene to make sure everything went according to his plan.

"But you will take Rosita with you, yes?"

"I am sorry, little one, but I will be so busy that I will have little time to spend with you. Besides, you will be much more comfortable here in this wonderful suite." Which was true, given his means of transportation and the place he would stay to keep his movements unobserved by Interpol or the FBI.

"But Rosita will not mind. And she will be so lonely here without you."

Ortiz sat down on the lounge and took both of her hands in his. "I know, little one. It is the same with me. But it will only be for a little while. Two, three days at the most."

"You promise, *amor*?"

"I promise."

Ortiz leaned down and lightly kissed her lips which were now smiling through her tears. He *would* miss her and would have taken her with him if he could. However, he had to be flexible in case he had to move fast, an eventuality that was more than possible.

As for McPherson, Ortiz was actually looking forward to a further dialogue with the cop. The detective might let something slip that would be helpful. Besides, the phone call from the cop had made it personal. It was now *mano a mano*. Not that he would perform the act himself. That was not advisable. Still, an image took shape in his brain: McPherson in the power scope crosshairs of his Safari Grade Browning BAR autoloader that he'd used to hunt wild animals in the jungles of Kenya and Malaysia. Squeezing the trigger. Watching the impact of the perfectly aimed .357 Magnum bullet explode the detective's forehead like a ripe melon. With the thought came an unexpected surge of excitement. And a question.

Could that be *el momento supremo*?

*8:05 p.m.:* Mack waited behind the wheel of the RV. Across the street the red neon sign on the roof of the drab, two-story motel on South Cicero blinked "PARADISE INN." It was a paradise, alright, Mack thought, at least to the hookers who worked the numerous bars strung along Cicero. Most of the other patrons were men looking for a cheap, no-frills overnight flop.

Mack had just dropped off Diane Bates with a small suitcase and necessities she'd purchased at the mall. He watched her through the window of a cramped reception area registering with a geezer behind the counter. Then she exited the office and carried the suitcase to a room facing the parking lot at the south side of the motel. Mack would wait for her cell-to-cell call to make sure she was settled in before leaving to carry out a plan of action he hoped would not only get him off the brass's shit list, but force them to listen up about Lazarus.

Mack had also exercised some gray cells on the subject of Mr. Ortiz while he was waiting for Diane in the mall. He'd remembered what Kischman and Diane had told him about the counterfeit pharmaceutical drug business during his visit to the Bio-Sci lab. When Diane had returned from her shopping to the RV, he'd bounced Ortiz's name off her and gotten an immediate response.

"Everyone in the business knows who Ortiz is. He's one of the biggest drug pirates in the world, and probably the most ruthless."

"I figured as much," Mack had said. "I'm also betting that Dr. Kischman is on Ortiz's payroll as well as Bio-Sci's."

"Are you saying that Dr. Kischman would sell the HCV cure to Ortiz?"

"In a heartbeat."

"No! That's...that's absurd. Dr. Kischman...Otto...would never do a thing like that!"

"Diane, when I recovered that hit man's cell phone, one of the speed dial numbers on his phone was for Ortiz. The other was for Dr. Kischman. Doesn't that tell you that your saintly Dr. Kischman is in cahoots with the devil?"

Diane had looked at Mack with bewilderment. "No. No. That just can't be true. It just can't," she said, shaking her head in disbelief.

Mack had left it at that. He realized that Diane's admiration and obvious affection for Kischman had built a wall of denial around her judgment. Eventually she might recognize the truth—that her mentor was not only a sellout, but an accessory to the murders of Frank and Alward—but not yet.

The roar of a jet passing low overhead for a landing at nearby Midway Airport startled Ulysses, who was curled up on the passenger seat.

"Easy, fella," he said, stroking the cat's head.

The tom made a throaty sound in response. A moment later Mack's cell beeped, and he pulled it from the pocket of his windbreaker.

"Diane?"

"Yes."

"How are you doing? Did the desk clerk give you a hard time?"

"No. He accepted cash on a day-by-day basis. In advance."

No surprise there, Mack thought, but he had instructed Diane to take a walk if the clerk had asked for an ID. "I see your room is facing the parking lot. What's the number?"

"124. I hope I don't have to stay here very long. This place is awful."

"Not the Ritz-Carlton, that's for sure, but you'll be safe. Do you want anything to eat?"

"No, not yet. Perhaps later."

"Okay. Look, I've got something to do that I think will help our cause. It should take a couple of hours, three at the most. If you can hold out 'til then, I'll be back with food. You okay with that?"

"Yes. What is it you're planning to do?"

"I'll fill you in when I get back. Now Diane, remember what I told you. Keep the blinds down and the door locked, double locked if it has a chain lock. Nobody gets in but me. And no phone calls except to me on the cell. If you get a call, don't answer until you check your caller ID and see that it's me calling. I'm the only person I want you talking to. If the room phone rings, don't answer that either. Got all that?"

"Yes."

"Good girl. And Diane, I'm going to get you through this. You're going to be okay if you just trust me. Do you trust me?"

"Yes…yes, I do trust you."

"Good. Keep on doing just that, and hang in there. I'll be back soon, and I think I'll have some good news."

"I hope so."

"I won't disappoint you. Now try and get some rest. And remember, no phone calls except from me. Promise?"

"I promise."

"Good." Mack beeped off.

Diane turned to look at her surroundings. The room was stuffy, and the smell of stale cigarette smoke pervaded everything, almost making her gag. She thought perhaps a blast of frigid fresh air would help, and turned the already groaning window air conditioner to high.

Next she dumped the few things she'd purchased at the mall out onto the bed. She placed some blouses and personal items neatly in the top drawer of a small dresser, then hung her jacket and a pair of cropped pants on hangers in a mini-closet next to a bathroom that reeked of disinfectant.

Entering the bathroom, she arranged her toilet articles on a small shelf over the sink, then looked at her image in the faded mirror on the wall. For a moment she studied herself, turning her head from side to side and brushing back a wisp of hair that had fallen across her forehead. She pouted at her image. Not too bad looking, she thought. I just need to get my hair done, and my nails, maybe a facial. I'll start taking better care of myself as soon as the Project is finished.

The Project! She was suddenly aware how vulnerable she was. Lazarus had become like a shroud hanging over her, a confining, suffocating presence from which she could not escape. With a shiver, she turned away from the mirror.

Diane was suddenly thirsty, her throat parched—but there was no way she was going to drink whatever foul excuse for water might escape from the rusty faucet of the bathroom sink. Fortunately, she'd purchased three bottles of water at the mall along with two apples and an orange. She returned to the bedroom and retrieved them from a shopping bag on the bed, then moved to a small writing table where she placed them on a tray next to an empty plastic ice bucket and two styrofoam cups covered with cellophane. Uncapping one of the bottles, she took a long swallow of lukewarm Ice Mountain.

The water helped a little. She knew she should try to get some rest, but the lumpy mattress on the queen-size bed looked very uncomfortable. Besides, she was too distraught to get any sleep. Memories of the attack in the church kept looming up to haunt her. She had the unpleasant feeling that someone was in the room watching her, although she knew no one was there. She had to distract herself or she would go crazy.

Some television ought to help. She located the remote on the night stand

and settled into a sagging armchair with cotton hemorrhaging from the seams. Activating the TV on top of the dresser, she started surfing the available channels until landing on one of her favorites, Turner Movie Classics. She loved watching old movies as an escape to times when life was less complicated, values were clear, and ethical choices much easier to make. A Doris Day/Rock Hudson movie was in progress. Diane had seen the movie before, but couldn't remember the name. No matter. This light, fluffy romantic comedy was just what she needed to get her mind off her anxieties.

For a few minutes the movie did just that. Then her thoughts returned to the frightening attack in the church...was that just a few hours ago?...and the threat of death that was stalking Mack. She wondered where he was and what he was doing right now. He had seemed pretty upbeat about his plan, although he hadn't disclosed what it was.

But what if his plan didn't work? What if he didn't come back? What if that man with the knife attacked him again, and this time killed him? She would be stuck in this awful place with no one to help her! No, it was worse than that! Like Mack had said, she was marked for death because she knew about the Lazarus Project and had witnessed an attempted murder. It was only a matter of time before they would find her and kill her. For all she knew, they could be outside right now!

Get a grip, Diane, she told herself. Her throat was dry again, so she took another sip of water. It soothed her throat but not her throbbing head. What about Dr. Kischman...Otto, she thought? Mack was so sure that he'd sold out to that ruthless drug pirate, Ortiz, but Diane found that impossible to believe. She knew Otto better than Mack. After all, she'd worked alongside him for years. She remembered the conversations they'd had about the importance of their research, and how the drugs they were developing would save thousands of people from the deadly diseases that afflicted mankind. No, Mack had to be wrong about Otto. He would never have betrayed them by selling the results of their research to a monster like Ortiz!

Diane tried to refocus on the movie, but the thought of Otto's cell number on the hit man's speed dial kept coming back to break her concentration like a mole trapped in her head trying to dig its way out. Was it possible? Could Otto really have sold out? Why would he do such a thing? He wasn't a greedy man. His work was his life, his achievements his reward.

The answer came to Diane in a flash. A flash of rage! It was for Gloria, Otto's wife! If Otto did sell out, he must have done it for her! She was a vain, selfish person who spent Otto's money on expensive clothes, jewelry and other indulgences, including trips that usually excluded Otto due to his commitments to his work. There had even been a rumor circulating in the lab that Gloria was having an affair with the golf pro at the Long Grove Country Club. Diane wouldn't be surprised if that were true.

Now that she thought about it, Otto *had* been acting a little different lately. He seemed distracted and agitated, even giving way to occasional angry outbursts at the lab techs over nothing, which wasn't like him at all. Maybe he'd heard the rumor about Gloria and the golf pro. Or, more likely, it was the anguish and guilt he must be feeling about his pact with the devil Ortiz, which would put the vaccine in Ortiz's hands as soon as it was finished. And that would be very soon, perhaps a few days, perhaps only hours.

Suddenly Mack's words came rushing back to her:

*"Once an antiviral vaccine is found, they become expendable."*

My God! That must include Otto. Especially since he knows who's behind the Project. Of course he's not aware of the danger he's in. I have to warn him. Now!

Diane jumped out of the armchair and went quickly to the writing table, where her cell phone lay next to her shoulder bag. She picked up the phone and turned it on. Otto's number was on her speed dial. She started to finger it, then hesitated as she remembered Mack's warning:

*"No phone calls except to me on the cell."*

Diane turned off the phone and slowly set it down. Sinking heavily into the armchair, she tried to hold back the tears welling up in her eyes, but the strain of the terrifying events of the last few hours were too much for her. She began to sob uncontrollably. Through her tears she watched the blurry images of Doris Day and Rock Hudson. Doris was snuggling into Rock's arms for a final kiss before the closing credits rolled.

If only life was as simple as a Doris Day movie, Diane thought. If only every story had a happy ending!

*8:36 p.m.:* Mark Jacobs took a bite of key lime pie. He was sitting in a booth at the rear of Charlie T's Pub & Grill, which was just down the block from the WFFD studios at Lake and Dearborn. The restaurant, which had been around since the 1940's, had a warm, comfortable ambiance with old movie posters and autographed pictures of celebrities covering practically every available inch of the oak-paneled walls. Jacobs shared his booth with Cary Gant and Lana Turner. And it *was* his booth, at least every weekday night from 8:00 to 10:00 p.m. After one Rob Roy to get the creative juices flowing, he would free-flow tomorrow's *Deadline Chicago* script on a yellow pad and refine it the following morning on his computer. Tonight's broadcast about a recent drug bust and the Mayor's efforts to reduce drug-related crimes, which would begin at ten-thirty, was already prepared with the appropriate film clips.

Charlie T's was also a place where Jacobs's informants could contact him to exchange tips for hard cash. One of his tipsters had shown up earlier with a potentially juicy item. An Illinois State senator just might be on the payroll of a construction company that was bidding for a big slice of a highway improvement bill that the senator was pushing. However, Jacobs would have to dig deeper, check other sources to make sure the story was legit before airing it. He'd learned long ago not to want a story too much. Falling in love with a story could lead to shoddy research. He'd seen more than one reporter go down in flames for committing that cardinal sin.

"More coffee, Mr. Jacobs?"

Jacobs looked up from the yellow pad at an aging, pretzel-thin waiter holding a silver decanter.

"Yes, thanks Roger."

The waiter filled his cup with steaming coffee. "Everything satisfactory, Mr. Jacobs?"

"Excellent, Roger. The vegetables were a bit overcooked, but otherwise excellent."

Which was true. Everything from the shrimp cocktail to the juicy, eight-ounce filet. And, of course, the key lime pie, a specialty of the house, all of which had been deposited in a belly that was beginning to give Jacobs some concern. The intensity of his job had been enough to burn off excess calories in the past, but at thirty-three Jacobs had to acknowledge that he would either have to start counting calories or spend more time in the gym in order to maintain his trim, on-camera appearance. Okay, so tomorrow he'd get with Dave, his trainer at the Lakeview Athletic Club, do some upper body stuff, then run some track. And he could always cut out the key lime pie.

Meanwhile, Jacobs had to prepare a *Saturday Night Special Report*: the ongoing saga of "Mad Dog" McPherson. This had just taken a dramatic new turn. Not only had the detective been suspended, he was now being sought by police with an arrest warrant. It seems that McPherson had made wild and unfounded accusations against the CEO of Bio-Sci Research & Development, claiming that he was responsible for the murder of a former employee, the charity doctor, Dr. Alward. This Jacobs had learned from an even better source than his CPD contacts: Mayor O'Connor himself had called him. He was pissed as hell at McPherson for threatening a well-respected member of the local business community. He wanted Jacobs' help in getting the story out, along with pictures of McPherson, so the public could assist the police in finding him. Although *Deadline Chicago* was usually broadcast only on week nights, Saturday Night Special Reports were occasionally aired when there were news stories of particular importance. The Mayor had asked the WFFD station manager to schedule a Special Report on McPherson on Saturday night so he wouldn't have to wait through the long Memorial Day weekend to get the message to the public. He asked Jacobs to give it to McPherson with both barrels. Not that Jacobs needed any encouragement. His shotgun was already cocked and loaded.

Jacobs finished the script with a blistering demand that the CPD quickly apprehend McPherson and provide him with living quarters at the Cook County lock-up pending formal charges by the DA. He then added a note to his producer to close with a mug shot of McPherson with Jacobs' voiceover asking anyone with information as to McPherson's whereabouts to immediately notify 911. He was dropping his ball point into the breast pocket of his suit coat when Roger arrived with his bill. Perfect timing. Without looking at the bill, Jacobs laid a Visa inside the small, leather container for Roger to take away. He consumed the last bite of the key lime, then removed his glasses, which he laid on the table next to his cell phone. Sliding out of the booth, he moved to the men's restroom in an alcove near the kitchen.

"Good evening, Mr. Jacobs," a white-haired attendant greeted him with a big smile.

"Hello, Henry. How are things?"

"Slow night, Mr. Jacobs, slow night. No conventions in town, ya know."

"Things will pick up," Jacobs said, relieving himself at a urinal.

"I hope so."

Jacobs washed his hands in an old fashioned oval basin with a brass faucet and handles, then accepted the small towel from Henry to dry off. Looking into the mirror, Jacobs ran a pocket comb through his dark crop of curly hair and made a small adjustment to his bow tie, while Henry brushed his coat with a whisk broom before accepting the usual two-dollar tip.

"Thank you, Mr. Jacobs. You have yourself a real nice evening."

Returning to his booth, Jacobs observed that he was no longer alone. A man was in his booth, his back turned. One of his tipsters, Jacobs figured. He figured wrong.

"McPherson!"

The cop removed a pair of dark glasses and looked up from Jacobs's yellow pad. "Hello, Jacobs. I see I'm getting the red carpet treatment on your broadcast tomorrow night."

Jacobs didn't know whether to laugh or yell for help. What in the hell was the cop doing here? One distinct possibility occurred to him and it wasn't one he relished. McPherson would like nothing better than to kick the shit out of the reporter who'd been riding his ass. But in a public place? Not likely. Or would he?

The cop seemed to read his thoughts. "Relax, Jacobs, and sit down before your coffee gets cold."

"What do you want, McPherson? My autograph?"

"Yeah. I'm one of your biggest fans. So listen up, because I'm about to give you a story that could jump start your career to the big leagues, maybe even put a Pulitzer Prize on your mantel. Interested?"

"You're the story, McPherson, and the only thing I'm interested in at the moment is how you knew I was here."

"I called your studio, told your producer I was one of your anonymous informants. Now if you want to listen to me, fine; otherwise I'll talk to one of your competitors on another network. So what's it going to be?"

Jacobs thought about it. Either McPherson was going to feed him a line of bull to get his badge back, or he was a nut case who actually believed what he was going to tell him. In either case, he had nothing to lose by hearing him out, as it would provide him with an actual face-to-face confrontation with the Mad Dog himself.

"Okay. I'm listening."

Before McPherson could begin, Roger returned with Jacob's Visa, the bill and a pen. Jacobs quickly added a generous tip on the bill, scrawled his signature and tucked away his copy and the Visa in his wallet.

"Thank you, Mr. Jacobs. Would your guest like some coffee?"

"Sounds good," McPherson said before Jacobs could answer.

Roger secured a cup and saucer from a nearby coffee station, filled the cup for McPherson and heated up Jacobs's coffee.

"Is the food here as good as the coffee?" McPherson said after a long sip.

"It is. Now what have you got, other than an appreciation for gourmet coffee?"

The cop smiled a funny smile, cryptic, like a code you couldn't decipher.

"Let's play what ifs. What if a blue chip R & D company is using vagrants as unsuspecting guinea pigs to find a cure for a killer virus. And what if this secret project is being protected by political heavyweights."

"I assume you're referring to Bio-Sci?"

McPherson tapped the yellow pad with his forefinger. "You've been getting the City Hall spin on this, Jacobs, and it sucks."

"If it does, so does Mayor O'Connor."

"You got this from the mayor?"

"From his lips to my yellow pad."

The detective nodded, took a sip of coffee. "I know you've got contacts on the fifth floor, Jacobs, but doesn't it strike you as unusual that the mayor would call you personally about this?"

It hadn't, but he thought about it now, and his conclusion was yes, it was unusual. If the mayor wanted Jacobs to push a story, he'd always had one of his stooges call him. This was the first time Hizzonor had picked up the phone himself.

Something else was happening to Mark Jacobs, as well. He was listening to that faint voice deep within his brain, the voice of his reporter's instinct, telling him that he might be on the brink of a big story at that if what McPherson said was true. If Bio-Sci *was* using vagrants to find the cure for a virus, and if City Hall was involved in a cover up, then he had more than a big story. He had his bombshell. His ticket to New York.

But was it fact or fiction? "Okay, you've got my attention. Problem is, even if I buy into what you're telling me, how am I going to sell it to my producer let alone my audience without some kind of evidence to back it up?"

"I'll answer that with another what if. What if I had a witness?"

That voice in Jacobs's brain was getting louder. "A witness? That's different, but I need someone absolutely credible."

"How about the assistant to the director of the Bio-Sci lab?"

The voice was now loud and clear.

"Hold it a minute, McPherson."

Jacobs took his cell phone off the table and speed-dialed his producer. "Bernie, it's Mark. I want you to kill tonight's broadcast on the drug bust story."

"Kill the story?" was Bernie's incredulous response.

"That's right. Kill it. Re-run one of my previous broadcasts. Tell the viewers I'm sick, out of town. Tell them anything."

"Mark, get serious, you can't..."

"I can and I'm doing it. Goodbye, Bernie."

Mark beeped off and signaled Roger, who came scurrying over.

"Some more coffee, Mr. Jacobs?"

"Yeah, and bring me another Rob Roy. Make it a double, and bring one for my guest, as well."

An astonished look from Roger. "Yes, sir. Right away, Mr. Jacobs."

Jacobs put on his glasses, flipped over the hand-written pages of the yellow pad to a blank page and pulled his pen from his breast pocket.

"Okay, McPherson. Shoot!"

*11:36 p.m.:* Mack was keyed up. He'd had time to congratulate himself during the return cab ride from Charlie T's along the Stevenson Expressway to South Cicero. He'd made the right choice with Jacobs to exercise his plan of focusing media attention on the Lazarus Project. Although there was certainly no love lost between Jacobs and himself, Mack had to admit that the little egotist was damned good at his job. He'd also correctly surmised that Jacobs had ambitions that exceeded his current status as a local celebrity, and the Project would be just the kind of big story he'd jump on to elevate his career to the next level.

When they reached the Paradise Inn, Mack had the driver pull over at a side street near the motel. He'd left the RV around the corner in a loading dock area behind an empty warehouse. At least it was out of sight from the street, but Mack knew he was going to have to find a better place to park the camper, so as not to draw the attention of some curious beat cop.

Paying the driver, he exited the cab with two sacks containing plastic containers of food he'd purchased at Charlie T's—a Caesar salad, grilled chicken breast and mixed veggies for Diane, and for himself a hamburger and a slice of key lime pie—Jacobs's suggestion—which Mack would eat in the RV after he delivered the other food to Diane.

As he walked the two blocks to the motel, Mack reflected on the next step of his plan, which was an interview with Diane by Jacobs. Jacobs was all for it, but not a taped interview, as Mack had expected. Jacobs wanted to do it live and in the studio. If he taped it for a later airing, one of his mobile crew would be bound to leak the story to his news director, which would mean forget it. No way his director would take a chance on a story that would bring City Hall down on him like a bunker buster and jeopardize the network, not to mention his job, if it didn't pan out. And it might not pan out if no one involved in the project hit the panic button and confirmed Diane's testimony. The story would go away, and the lawsuits would begin with a vengeance.

Knowing all of this, Jacobs was still anxious to move forward with the interview. Mack was to bring Diane to the studio at 10:15 p.m. tomorrow, fifteen minutes before Jacobs was to begin his *Deadline Chicago Saturday Night Special* segment. Jacobs would tell his boss and his producer that he was going to air the McPherson story, and that he had an anonymous guest to interview whose identity must be kept secret for her own safety. Then he'd drop the bombshell, live, no rehearsal, and let the fallout be what it would be. It was a gutsy call, which could make or break Jacobs's career. But the news hawk was willing to go all the way with the story, a commitment that Jacobs and Mack had sealed with a handshake and a clink of Rob Roy tumblers.

Approaching the motel, Mack turned his head away from a police blue and white cruising amid the still active flow of night traffic on Cicero. No way he was going to get picked up now that things were breaking his way. He was looking forward to telling Diane that her stay in the Paradise would probably be a short one. If Jacobs's boss didn't spring for more desirable living quarters, then the heat the CPD brass would get from *Deadline Chicago* could motivate them to provide room and board for Diane in a police protection facility.

These thoughts were keeping Mack on a high until he reached unit #124. It wasn't the angry exchange of profanities issuing from unit #125 that sent his right hand reaching for the .38 under his windbreaker. It was the fact that the volume of the TV in Diane's room was turned up high enough to cause serious damage to a normal person's eardrums.

Mack set down the sacks of food. He was about to knock on the door when the door to #125 flew open. Exiting quickly and tucking his shirt into his pants was a fat slob who jumped behind the wheel of a pick-up truck and barreled out of the lot onto Cicero. More curses from the woman in #125 before the door slammed shut.

A dispute over the price of the woman's services, Mack thought, which might have been amusing under different circumstances. But Mack wasn't smiling. He was knocking on the door to #124, knocking hard, and getting no response from inside.

"Shit!"

Something was definitely wrong. With a sense of dread Mack slid the .38 out of his hip holster and reached for the door handle. Let the door be locked, he prayed. It wasn't. Before he eased the door open, Mack knew what he would find inside.

Diane was on the bed, a washrag stuffed into her mouth and a pillow case knotted tight around her neck. Mack moved quickly to the bed, took her still warm wrist in his hand and felt for a pulse. None. Just a poor, lifeless Diane Bates, her dead eyes staring in horror at her murderer. Not Mr. Romeo, Mack thought. No slit throat, no blood. One of his Mexican goons, probably all of them. But how had they found her? There was no way, unless…

Mack looked for Diane's cell phone and saw it on a side table next to an armchair. He picked it up and selected "Call History" from the on-screen menu. He wasn't surprised to find Kischman's name and cell number at the top of the list.

So she'd called him after all, he thought. Despite all his warnings, despite everything she knew about his connection to Ortiz and Romeo, she'd called him. She just couldn't believe he was a bad guy. And somehow Kischman had gotten her to tell him where she was. And she'd told him. She'd told him because she trusted him. And now she was dead.

Mack turned off the TV. In the stillness that filled the room he could feel his sadness and anger become palpable. He walked back to Diane's lifeless body on the bed, gently closed her eyelids, and made her a promise: He would get Kischman for this! He would get them all! Whether the Lazarus Project was exposed or not, he was going to even the score, for Diane, for Frank, and for Alward as well.

The silence was broken by a woman's piercing scream behind him!

Mack whirled with the .38, the sight of which only triggered another scream from the disheveled, middle-aged woman in the open doorway.

Mack instinctively reached for his badge before he realized he no longer had one. "I'm a police officer…"

The woman wasn't listening. She was running off. Mack exited the room, saw her screaming her way toward the registration office, an open kimono flapping behind her.

Mack holstered the .38, ran out of the room, and looked around. The obvious escape route was an alley behind the motel. Mack ran down the alley, crossed the side street and kept running until he reached the rear of the warehouse, where he'd parked the RV. Stepping onto the running board, Mack opened the cab door. Ulysses was snoozing on the driver's seat. Mack picked up the tom, slid behind the wheel and deposited Ulysses on the passenger seat.

Ignoring Ulysses's head rubbing against his thigh for attention, Mack inserted the key into the ignition and cooked the engine. "Sorry, fella, but we gotta hit the road."

The tom seemed to understand. As Mack swung the camper onto Cicero and headed south, the tom let out a street howl not unlike the wails of the patrol cars that were converging on the Paradise.

## Saturday, May 25

*2:10 a.m.:* Mack couldn't sleep. It wasn't the cramped sleeping area over the cab, or the cacophony of frogs, crickets and other night critters chattering outside the RV. It wasn't even the fact that Mack was now a suspect for the murder of Diane Bates. It hadn't taken long for the investigating detectives to find out the real identity of the victim, get a description from the prostitute of the man she'd seen in #124 who claimed to be a police officer, put two and two together, and come up with McPherson. This Mack had learned by listening to his police radio for a couple of hours in the camper while dining on a can of tuna and drinking two much needed beers.

Bad as those things were, what kept Mack tossing and turning was the inescapable fact that he had lost his only witness. Without Diane to back up his story, he'd have to find another way to expose the Lazarus Project, and for now he didn't have a clue as to what that might be. Unless he came up with something fast, he might as well start looking for an F. Lee Bailey to take his case.

At least, thanks to Otis, Mack had found a good place to park the RV. While driving south on Cicero, Mack had remembered Otis telling him about fishing Wolf Lake. The lake was just across the Indiana border, only a half hour drive from the Loop via the Outer Drive, through Hyde Park to Stony Island Boulevard, then over the soaring Skyway bridge. After exiting the Skyway at Indianapolis Boulevard, Mack had called Otis for directions to get to the narrow gravel lane that ran along the northwest shore of the lake, a forest preserve, where an RV would strike no one as unusual.

Mack had also filled Otis in on what happened at the Paradise Inn. Otis was naturally very troubled by the news, but maybe whatever he could find out from Interpol about Ortiz and Mr. Romeo would help. Mack gave him a head start with what he'd learned about Ortiz from Diane, but any additional info would be appreciated. Otis reiterated his promise to contact Interpol first thing in the morning.

Mack had also put in a call to Jacobs, but the reporter had already been informed about Diane's murder, this time by Superintendent Hollender.

"The heat's on you, McPherson, and I mean big time."

"Tell me about it. Are you still buying my story?"

"I'm still buying. If I had any doubts before, the murder of your only witness blew them away. Problem is I've got no one to interview now but you, and you're not exactly Mr. Believable."

Mack agreed, and had to waltz around Jacobs's question of where he was going with his investigation now that Diane was dead. "I've been working on some leads, but I'll just have to see where they take me. Meanwhile, I've got to keep a low profile."

"Needless to say, you'll keep me informed. But I've got some bad news. Hollender wanted to know why I was a no-show on *Deadline Chicago* tonight. Said he wanted to make sure that my piece on you was still on track to be aired on the *Deadline Chicago Saturday Night Special Report*. I gave him some bull about having to do more research on the drug bust story before airing that report, which is why I canceled that show. But given this latest development, with you being accused of murdering Diane Bates, there's no way I can't blast you on the Special Report tomorrow night. Sorry, make that tonight, since it's already after midnight. If I don't put on a convincing performance screaming about the threat you pose to the community and demanding the immediate arrest of the 'Mad Dog Cop,' they'll know something's seriously wrong."

"I completely understand. You have my full permission to paint me as a wild cop totally out of control. As for the truth, it might help if you can give me any future feedback you get from your contacts in the CPD."

"You'll be the second to know—after me. And Mack: Good luck."

Good luck for sure, Mack thought, rolling over to his other side in the hope that a change in position would induce some much needed zzz's. Occasional jungle howls from Ulysses didn't help. The tom was used to survival on the streets of the city. The scents and sounds of Mother Nature issuing through the open screened windows of the camper were a new experience. The cat was prowling restlessly about the RV, just itching to get outside to explore his new environment and probably do a little hunting for a juicy field mouse.

"Shut up, Ulysses!"

The tom's response was another howl.

Shit! Mack climbed down from the sleeping bunk and padded on his bare feet to the fridge. He removed a Miller Lite, popped the tab and took a long swallow. He settled onto the small divan to sip his beer and ponder a plan of action. Perhaps Willie would come up with the location of the Mexican's pizza van. Find the van and you find the Mexicans, maybe even Mr. Romeo. However, Mack realized that the chances of this happening were slim to none. By this time the van would be wearing a different color of paint and a new logo. Besides, Willie had already done more than Mack had expected. He couldn't perform miracles.

Mack reached for the remote and turned on the TV. Sometimes he resolved a problem by getting his mind off of it. Sitting down on the divan, he channel-surfed the stations. There wasn't much of interest. The lifestyle of a polar bear on *Animal Kingdom*, a re-run of a Barbara Walters' recent interview of the First Lady, some goofy environmentalist on PBS who was predicting the end of civilization in our lifetime, and an account of the Battle of the Bulge on the History Channel which Mack had already seen. Maybe there was a movie in Otis's collection he could watch, Mack thought, and picked one at random. Judging from the title, *Dancing Lady*, it must be a musical. Although Mack wasn't into musicals, this one starred Joan Crawford and Clark Gable. Since Gable was one of Mack's favorite actors, a man's man like John Wayne, he decided to give it a shot.

It turned out to be better than he thought. Crawford was an aspiring dancer in a burlesque show who wanted to make it to the big time, Gable the demanding director of a Broadway show who gives her a chance. Mack noted the onscreen chemistry between the two stars. He was also captivated by Crawford's eyes— dark, luminous, almost hypnotic.

As Mack watched, something rose to the surface of his brain. He'd seen eyes like Crawford's before. The picture of the prom queen in Roy O'Neal's office came to mind. And something else. Something so fantastic that he had to smile. Forget it, he thought, which he did with the appearance of Fred Astaire in the movie. Astaire was playing himself and doing his best to make Crawford look good as a dance partner. Astaire couldn't do anything about her feeble singing, but with eyes like Crawford's, who cared?

Not Mack. Sipping his beer, he settled back to watch the rest of the movie, now resigned that neither sleep nor the solution to his predicament would come tonight.

*2:34 a.m.:* Willie was having his own problems. He'd checked into the emergency room at Northwestern Memorial Hospital at 1:30 a.m. Since he was a homeless person, the hospital had to accept him for treatment even though they knew that the name he gave, John Smith, was as phony as his social security number. Willie hadn't even bothered to invent an address. The street would have to do, and it did.

Willie knew he was taking a big risk. He'd already been frisked by a security guard, S.O.P. for street people. However, if he was going to feel better, it was a risk he had to take. His energy seemed to have seeped out of his body like air from a tire with a slow leak.

Willie was resting on a hospital bed in one of the cubicles that flanked an aisle in the examination room. A nurse had taken his pulse, temp and blood pressure. Willie had provided a urine specimen for a lab technician, who'd also drawn blood. An athletic-looking young intern with spiked hair and a five o'clock shadow took down data about his symptoms, medication and medical history and told him that a doctor would be along to examine him as soon as possible. Meanwhile, Willie had to endure the screams of a lady in the next cubicle, the victim of an auto accident, until someone gave her a shot of whatever to ease her pain from what Willie overheard was a broken clavicle.

Willie was dozing off when the curtain was pulled aside by the intern. Accompanying him was a not much older looking black lady, short and spry, with a smile that made Willie feel as if he was being welcomed by a friend into her home.

"Hello, Mr. Smith. I'm Doctor Sutton. Sorry I took so long, but we've got a full house tonight. Dr. Young tells me you've been feeling fatigued."

"Yeah."

The doctor took a clipboard from the intern. "How long has this feeling of fatigue been going on?" she asked, reading the data on the clipboard.

"Two, maybe three months, I guess. Wasn't so bad at first, just kinda came and went, but it got worse in the last couple of weeks."

"I see your blood pressure is 102 over 56. Do you have a history of low blood pressure?"

"I dunno. Is that bad?"

The doctor removed a stethoscope from around her neck. "No, not necessarily. It's usually good, but it depends on other symptoms. Take some deep breaths."

Willie did.

"Where have you gone before when you had medical problems, Mr. Smith?" Doctor Sutton asked, as she listened for any heart or lung problems.

Willie hesitated. The doctor's question had triggered a warning signal in his gut. "Is that important?"

"Very important. A record of your medical history could help me make a diagnosis of your problem."

Sounds logical, Willie thought, so why not tell her? Besides, she was bound to become suspicious if he didn't answer her question. And if the Beacon Mission had any medical records for a John Smith, which was more than likely, they wouldn't have anything to do with Willie Butler.

"Here and there. The Beacon Mission mostly."

The doctor lowered the stethoscope and removed a penlight from the pocket of her white jacket. "I'm going to take a look in your eyes, Mr. Smith. Try not to blink."

"Okay."

"I know some of the doctors who work with The Beacon. Which one were you seeing?"

Momentarily blinded in each eye by the penlight beam, Willie felt that warning signal again. "Can't remember for sure. I seen lots of docs there."

Doctor Sutton turned off the penlight and put it onto her pocket. "I'd like to have access to your records over there, Mr. Smith, but I'll need for you to sign a release to get them. Is that okay with you?"

"Sure. Why not?"

"I'm also going to have to keep you here overnight."

"Why? Am I in bad shape or something?"

"I think you're just run down, but I won't know for certain until I see the lab results."

"Okay, but how long will that take?"

"Three, maybe four hours. It depends on how backed up they are. Meanwhile, I'm going to arrange for you to have a room in the hospital so you'll be more comfortable. Do you need something to help you sleep?"

"No. I'm okay."

"Good. I'm going to get a release form now and arrange for that room. Just relax, Mr. Smith. We'll have you feeling better soon."

"Right. Thanks, doc."

Relax, Willie thought, after Dr. Sutton and the intern had left. Screw that! The army had a term for what Willie's gut was telling him now. It was called a red alert!

The intern hustled to keep up with Dr. Sutton.

"What's up?" he said, as she made a beeline for the waiting room.

"I need to talk to Laurie about our patient, Kevin."

Entering the spacious waiting room, Kevin was relieved to see only a few people either watching TV or sacked out on the comfortable chairs as they awaited treatment for a variety of maladies. He'd been on the go since 10:00 p.m. and was feeling the need for a coffee break, which is what Laurie, the receptionist, must be taking, since she wasn't at the window counter adjacent to the Erie Street entrance.

"Where's Laurie, George?" Dr. Sutton asked a burly, black security guard, who was stationed next to the entrance.

"Gone fishin'," the guard said with a big grin.

The intern observed that Dr. Sutton was not amused by this reference to the ladies' restroom, which was not her usual demeanor. He'd sensed that something was bothering her during her examination of Mr. Smith and concluded that it probably had something to do with what she believed was his problem. Unlike many doctors, Dr. Sutton took a genuine and compassionate interest in every patient.

"So what do you think's going on with Smith?"

"What's your diagnosis, Kevin?"

"Testing me, huh?"

"You're here to learn, aren't you? So diagnose."

"Okay. Well, the fatigue he's experiencing could simply be due to his lifestyle. Or maybe he's depressed."

"Could be. How about his low blood pressure?"

"It could mean nothing in itself, like you told him. But coupled with other symptoms…" Kevin paused, feeling his way with this, but beginning to come up with an answer.

"Such as?"

"Such as his face. It had a kind of chalky complexion."

"Go on."

"And his eyes. I didn't get as close a look at them as you did, but they seemed yellowish. Right?"

"Right? And your diagnosis doctor?"

"Hepatitis, and probably C."

"Move to the head of the class, Kevin, but we won't know for certain until we get his labs. Meanwhile, we may have another problem with our Mr. Smith."

"Oh. What's that?"

The appearance in the window of a fat lady with a jovial face forestalled an answer. "Hi, Dr. Sutton. Sorry to keep you waiting. Need some help?"

"Yes, Laurie. I'd like to take a look at the wanted bulletins."

Laurie's face was no longer jovial. "Oh, oh. Don't tell me we have an unwelcome guest?"

"I don't know. I hope not. Go get them, will you?"

"Got them right here," Laurie said.

Dr. Sutton sorted through a number of bulletins that Laurie laid on the window counter.

"What makes you think that Smith is a criminal?" Kevin said.

"When he told me he was treated at The Beacon, I remembered about the murder of a charity doctor who worked with the mission, and that the police were looking for one of his patients as a possible suspect." She paused to scrutinize one of the bulletins. "Take a look at this."

Kevin took the bulletin from Dr. Sutton and studied the mug shot of a black man. "Hey, you may be right. This guy, William Butler, could be Smith."

"George, come over here a minute, will you?" the doctor said.

The security guard ambled over. "What is it, doc?"

"Recognize this man?" she said, handing him the bulletin.

"Shit! I should have made this guy when I frisked him. Nice goin', doc. I owe you. Where is this bird?"

"In the examination room."

"Well, at least we know he's not armed." The guard thrust the bulletin at the receptionist. "Call the number on this bulletin, Laurie. Tell them we've got Butler over here. I'll detain him until they send a wagon."

"Will do," Laurie said, picking up a phone.

"Let's go," the security guard said.

"I'd like to keep him here for a while if possible, George," Dr. Sutton said, as they moved out of the waiting room into a corridor. "Mr. Smith—Butler—could be a very sick man."

"That's the CPD's call, doc, not mine. As far as I'm concerned, he can be sick in the Cook County lock-up."

The guard paused outside the entrance to the examination room to remove a revolver from his hip holster. The sight of the weapon sent a shudder rippling up Kevin's spine. This was his first police experience since he came on staff three months ago. Still, he felt a surge of excitement. It was like watching a police drama on TV with himself as a member of the cast.

"Which cubicle is Butler in, doc?"

"Number five."

"Okay. I want both of you behind me."

The guard led the way into the examination room and down the aisle to cubicle five. Gun at the ready, he pulled the curtain aside.

"Shit!"

Kevin gaped. Their patient was gone.

*3:18 a.m.:* Superintendent Hollender was furious. It had taken dispatch ten minutes after the call about Butler came in from the hospital for someone to call him at home, which had been their explicit instruction. Butler was already long gone by the time two cruisers arrived at the hospital, but that wasn't the point. Hollender had a reason to stay on top of anything regarding Willie Butler.

"Really, Frank, is it absolutely necessary for you to have to go out in the middle of the night?" his wife, Carol, asked from under the silk top sheet of their king-sized bed.

"I'm afraid so, dear," Hollender said, slipping on a pinstriped, double-breasted suit coat. Even at this hour of the morning Hollender adhered to his formal dress code of suit and tie.

"It seems so stupid. I mean can't the police handle whatever it is by themselves without dragging you out of bed at this ungodly hour?"

"Normally, yes, but this is so important that I have to take charge myself."

"What could possibly be that important?"

"I'm sorry, dear, but this is something I'm not at liberty to share even with you without compromising the investigation."

"Well, I hope you won't have to be wherever you have to be for the rest of the night. You need to have your sleep."

"I know, but it's so late now that I might as well go to the office after I finish."

"Oh, alright. But you'll have a proper breakfast, won't you?"

"Yes, dear," Hollender said, trying to conceal a tinge of recurring irritation. When it came to his health, he took his marching orders from his wife. Fully aware of the stress that came with his job, she insisted that he get the proper rest, exercise and three nutritious meals a day, while keeping a low profile on caffeine and alcohol. Although her constant reminders bordered on henpeckery, Hollender endured them with the knowledge that they were offered from a loving wife who had his best interests at heart.

"I'll call you later, dear," he said. "Get some rest."

"I will. And remember to have breakfast."

"I will." Hollender leaned down and kissed his wife, whose lovely, nearly wrinkle-free face showed that she followed her own advice.

"I love you."

"I love you, too," he said, and meant it. Their love was the cement that had held their marriage together for thirty-three years, not only surviving the test of time but the many bumps in the road he'd traveled to achieve his goal of becoming Chicago's top cop.

At the moment, however, as he hurried through the spacious, tastefully decorated living room overlooking Lake Michigan, he was almost wishing that someone else had his job. He closed and locked the door to their two-bedroom apartment and moved down the corridor to a bank of two elevators. While he waited for an elevator, he pulled his cell phone from his coat pocket and speed-dialed a number. A man's voice answered almost immediately.

"What is it, Superintendent?"

Doesn't Blackburn ever sleep? Hollender thought. He sounded wide awake. "It's about the vagrant, Butler."

"Did you get him?"

"No, a near miss. I'll explain in a minute."

Hollender entered an elevator and punched the lobby button. Due to the lack of reception in the elevator, he had to wait until he descended the 25 floors to the lobby before he could resume the conversation.

"Butler checked in at the emergency room at Northwestern Memorial Hospital for treatment," Hollender said, as he exited the elevator, "but by the time the security people realized who he was, he was gone."

"Did they examine Butler while he was there?" Blackburn asked.

"Unfortunately, yes," Hollender said, moving through the marbled lobby of the thirty-story apartment building that dated back to the 1920s, its former elegance recently restored by a savvy condo developer.

"Good morning, Superintendent," an aging doorman greeted him from behind a desk. "Do you want your car brought up?"

"Hold on," Hollender said into the cell, then to the doorman, whose face showed that this early morning appearance by Hollender was unusual: "No thank you, John. I'm having a car sent to pick me up." Back into the cell: "Sorry. What were you saying?"

"I want you to get your people over there right away. I want any urine and blood specimens removed. The same goes for lab results, if they had time to run any tests."

"I'm on my way to take care of it personally."

As he stepped out through the front door of the lobby, Hollender was hit by a stiff wind blowing in off the lake that had dropped the temperature thirty degrees since he came home the night before. Hollender shivered. Damn! Should have brought my trench coat. And where in hell was the car?

"Another thing," Blackburn said. "I have reason to believe that Butler might be working with Detective McPherson."

That was news to Hollender, and not good news. "How do you figure that?"

"Two of my people who were tailing McPherson the day he called on Bio-Sci saw him give an envelope to a black man on Lower Wacker Drive."

"And you believe this man was Butler?" Hollender said, watching a black Crown Vic make the turn off North Lake Shore Drive into a circular driveway and pull up in front of the entrance.

"My men couldn't make a positive ID, but I'm assuming it was Butler, especially since Butler was a street buddy of Frank O'Meara."

"Makes sense," Hollender said, then to the doorman, who had come out of the lobby and was holding the rear car door open for him, "Thank you, John."

The doorman closed the door as soon as Hollender settled into the rear seat. The car pulled away almost immediately. The two detectives in the front seats were on Hollender's staff and had already been given their instructions by their boss when he phoned for the car.

"What do you want us to do with Butler when we get him?" Hollender continued.

"Turn him over to my people. They'll be looking for him, same as your people. Anything new on McPherson?"

"Nothing. But we will get him."

"Call me after you've taken care of things at the hospital," Blackburn said.

"Will do."

Hollender beeped off. He leaned his head back against the seat to try and relax during the short trip to the hospital. Taking care of things at the hospital was no problem, he thought, but his involvement with Blackburn was another matter. When Mayor O'Connor ordered him to cooperate with Blackburn a few days ago, he'd made it clear that if he didn't, he'd no longer occupy the superintendent's office. Asked by Hollender for an explanation, the mayor gave none. Just do it, was his response, or tender his resignation.

Closing his eyes, Hollender thought that perhaps he should have done just that. Resigned. Of course, walking away from a job he'd coveted from the moment he entered the Police Academy thirty-seven years ago was impossible. The job was not only his goal but his passion. And he was good at it. In the short time he'd spearheaded the mayor's anticrime campaign, violent crimes had dropped in Chicago by twenty-two percent.

And this was only the beginning. Hollender was confident that under his command, the CPD would be the shining example of law enforcement for every major city in the country. Still, the superintendent couldn't help but wonder: By cutting a deal with the mayor to keep his job, had he made the biggest mistake of his career?

*8:26 a.m.:* Mack made another cast with Otis's fly rod. He hoped that passing the time fishing would allow the right side of his brain to come up with a possible solution to his problems. Watching TV last night hadn't worked, and so far all he had to show for his fishing efforts were two small bluegills, which he'd thrown back. But after he'd dozed off on the divan, something *had* happened early in the morning that was still bothering him. That something was another bad dream, one that he remembered.

He was lying on a gurney in a morgue, naked, like a corpse about to be stored in a body drawer. Except he wasn't dead. He was paralyzed, unable to move, helpless. Standing next to the gurney was a woman. She was wearing a surgical mask and holding a small, thin object in her right hand. He couldn't make out what it was at first. But then she leaned over him, and the something glistened in the overhead light. It was a hypodermic needle!

The woman pinched a muscle in Mack's stomach and lowered the needle. If Mack hadn't been paralyzed before, he was now…with fear. He realized that the woman was about to inject him with the HCV virus, and he was powerless to stop her. As she leaned closer, he was almost overcome by the sweet odor of her perfume. But it wasn't perfume. It was formalin!

Mack tried to move. It was no use. He could only watch as the needle descended slowly toward the muscle where she would make the injection. Who was she? Why was she doing this? The surgical mask covered most of her face. All he could see were her eyes. Dark, luminous eyes. Joan Crawford eyes!

Mack looked down at his stomach. The needle was touching his skin now. In a moment its deadly contents would flow through his body. With a supreme effort, Mack flailed at the phantom woman with his arms. He gasped for air as the motion jarred him awake. His heart was pounding like a trip hammer, his undershirt soaked with sweat. He sat up, and shook himself to get fully awake. His throat was parched. He got up from the divan and moved to the fridge, took out a can of beer, popped the tab and gulped down half its contents. The first rays of dawn were filtering through the windows. No use trying to get back to sleep now, Mack thought. Not after a nightmare like that.

Two hours later Mack was still trying to make sense of the dream as he made another cast. Dreams are supposed to mean something, which is why patients confide them to their shrinks. But damned if Mack could come up with anything, except that the phantom woman wasn't Joan Crawford. "Elementary, my dear Watson," as Sherlock Holmes would say. Mack smiled. Maybe he could use a shrink himself.

Mack was startled by the crunch of tires on gravel. He looked around to see Megan pulling up in her Camry. She waved as she got out and came over.

"Having any luck?"

"What are you doing here?"

"Watching you fish at the moment. Hey, you're pretty good with that."

Mack made another cast. "I'm full of surprises. So are you. So what are you doing here?"

Good question, Megan thought. She wasn't sure herself. All she knew was that she wanted to help Mack. She'd become aware of Mack's latest dilemma as soon as she picked up the *Sun Times* from her doorstep that morning. If things weren't bad enough for Mack before, now he was being sought as a murder suspect, and she felt somehow responsible. If she hadn't asked him to get involved in her dad's death…. Well, it was too late to worry about that now, but the least she could do was try to help him, which is what she told him.

Mack didn't know whether to be angry or grateful. It was hard to be angry with the flaming redhead, stunning as always, this time in jeans, a white windbreaker and sandals. Still, he felt an obligation to try for her sake.

"You shouldn't have come here, Megan. I don't want you to get involved."

"A little late for that, isn't it?"

"How'd you find me? Otis again, I assume."

"Yes, but I had to pry it out of him. What actually happened last night?"

Mack continued to cast while he filled Megan in on the events of the last twenty-four hours. Megan could hardly believe what she was hearing. Not only had Mack survived two more attempts on his life, but the Lazarus disk had been stolen, and now he was on the run from the police for the murder of his only witness.

"What are you going to do?"

"I wish I knew."

"The TV reporter, Jacobs. Can't he do something?"

"Not without some kind of evidence or another witness."

"How about the street person, Willie what's his name…"

"Butler."

"You said he's trying to locate the Mexicans."

"Yeah, but I haven't heard from him since yesterday afternoon, and I have no way of contacting him. Besides, he'd call me if he had something."

Megan sat down on a tree stump to think. Mack's situation looked next to hopeless.

Mack was thinking the same thing when his cell phone beeped. The number on the small screen was Otis's cell number.

"Hello, Otis. I didn't expect to hear from you yet."

"I got to the station early. Couldn't sleep."

"Same with me. Did you contact Interpol?"

"Yeah. This Ortiz guy is a big-time manufacturer and distributor of synthetic drugs. Does a global biz, and anyone who gets in his way has a nasty habit of ending up dead."

"That confirms what Diane told me. Does Interpol know where he is now?"

"They do. They've been working with the Feds, who would love to get something on him that they could use to either detain him or turn him over to Interpol. At the moment Ortiz is shacked up at the Mandarin Oriental Hotel in Miami with a girl who's not old enough to vote."

"What about Mr. Romeo, his hit man?"

"Cool dude, Romeo. Keeps changing his identity, like a chameleon, but Interpol thinks his real name is Juan Hernando Chavez, known as Angel. This is based in part on his M.O. The guy specializes in close shaves with a razor, *a la* Alward and yourself. It seems that at the tender age of thirteen Chavez cut the throat of a priest who allegedly raped him. Present address unknown."

"Not entirely. He's somewhere in Chicago. Does Interpol have any pictures of Ortiz and Chavez they can fax you?"

"Already have one of Ortiz. Nothing camera shy about that guy. Chavez you can forget. Never arrested, so no mug shot."

"Anything else?"

"Afraid not."

Mack fingered the stub of his right ear lobe. Interpol hadn't been much help, but the least he could do was thank Otis for trying, which he did. It also occurred to him that he had been so busy worrying about his own problems that he hadn't considered Otis's domestic dilemma.

"You been getting any more heat from the wife…about the RV?"

A brief silence. "Well, if you call moving out more heat, the answer is yes."

"Shit! She moved out on you?"

"Yeah. Packed a few duds and went to live with her folks until she can figure out where our marriage is going, which right now looks like down in flames."

"Dammit, Otis, I'm sorry as hell."

"Yeah, well we got deeper issues to deal with than the RV. I'm gonna try to talk Ava into seeing a marriage counselor."

"Mack!"

Megan jumped up off the stump, her face beaming.

"Hold on, Otis." Then to Megan: "What is it?"

"I just remembered…Willie was one of Alward's patients, wasn't he?"

"Yeah."

"Well, when we looked at the names of Alward's so-called subjects on the Lazarus disk, I remember seeing the name 'Butler'."

"You're sure?"

"Yes, I'm sure. I have a good memory for names, dates, stuff like that."

"In a way I'm hoping you're not right. For Willie's sake."

"I know. At least he's only had the virus for a short time, so existing drugs may help. There's one way to find out for sure. And if there's a presence of antiviral drugs in his blood…"

Mack was having the same thoughts as Megan. "Dr. Greg."

"Yes. Do you think your pathologist friend would examine him?"

"I don't know, but it's worth a try. He still owes me that favor."

Otis's voice in his ear. "What's going on?"

"Plenty. Megan believes that Willie was not only a patient of Alward's but also one of his guinea pigs."

"No shit? Hey, that could be dynamite if it's true."

"I'm betting it is. Now all you've got to do is find Willie."

"*I've* got to find him?"

"I'm not exactly Mr. Flexible right now, so it's up to you, partner."

"Shit, why not? I'm on a roll here. I've probably already lost a wife, so I might as well lose my badge, too. But it would make my job easier if he'd call you."

"He may do that. He's on the run, so he'll probably be on the street. You might start with Lower Wacker."

"Will do. One thing's for sure. You're gonna owe me a lot of beers when this is over. On second thought, make that martinis."

"You got it."

As Mack beeped off, he felt a tug on the line. He set the hook and, judging from the fight the fish was putting up, it wasn't a throwback.

"Are you hungry?" he said to Megan.

"Starved. I didn't have time to eat before I dropped Katie off at school."

"Good. Because I think I've just caught breakfast."

And something more important, Mack thought. Thanks to Megan, he just might have caught the break he was looking for.

*10:04 a.m.:* Ortiz was having a moment. At the helm of the sleek 460 Black Thunder S.C., he was zipping across the choppy waters of Lake Michigan at 92 m.p.h. He loved speed, and the sports cruiser was everything he could have wished for to provide it. It was the final phase of his stealth trip to Chicago that had begun at 3:00 a.m. Miami time. That's when he'd exited the Mandarin Oriental Hotel via a service entrance with his briefcase, a laptop and an overnight bag. He was traveling light, fast and, more importantly, unobserved by the Feds.

Ortiz took the same precautions he'd taken three months ago, after Kischman had contacted him about the Lazarus Project. First was an identity change. A passport, driver's license, Visa and business card now identified him as Fernando Salizar, a dealer in rare artifacts from the Grand Cayman Islands. His wallet also contained $2,500 in American dollars.

Second were the contents of the luggage he was taking with him. In addition to another $7,500 American dollars and a variety of passports, driver's licenses and credit cards in different names to deal with any emergency, his briefcase contained an MP-5 with two extra ammo clips. Another precaution was a bullet-proof vest in the overnight bag along with a change of underclothes and a Dopp kit. Given his many enemies, the vest was a necessary traveling companion that had saved his life on two occasions.

Third was his route and method of travel. In addition to his Learjet, Ortiz owned two other airplanes. One was a twin-engine Cessna 340, which was registered in Salizar's name and licensed in the Grand Caymans. He kept it at a private airport near Boca Raton. A limo had been waiting outside the service entrance of the Mandarin Oriental Hotel to take him thirty miles to the airport. Ortiz flew the Cessna from there to the municipal airport in Michigan City, Indiana, a five-hour trip with a refuel stop in Knoxville. He took a cab to the Port Authority Municipal Marina, where the Black Thunder he'd rented was waiting.

Before casting off he'd enjoyed a breakfast of caviar, hard boiled eggs, lox and onions complemented by a bottle of Dom Perignon from the well-stocked fridge in the elegant cabin. With its 6'10" headroom, leather sofas, custom made cabinets, TV/DVD player, microwave and a comfortable double berth, the cabin would be Ortiz's residence while he was in Chicago—another precaution in case the Feds were watching the hotels.

Aside from the thrill of his high-speed race across Lake Michigan, Ortiz was also savoring the good news he'd received late last night from Angel. Not only had the Bates woman been silenced, McPherson was being sought by the police as a suspect for her murder, a welcome development Ortiz hadn't expected. How nice it would be if the cops shot him on sight when they located him, although this might be too much to hope for. In any event, anything he would have to say about Lazarus would be ridiculed now that he no longer had a witness.

It was now 10:16 a.m., and the Chicago skyline was spread out before him under a cloudless azure sky like a gigantic postcard. Breezing past a sailboat, Ortiz exchanged waves with the skipper and his wife, then with two men casting their lines off the back of a fishing boat. The deafening roar of the powerful, twin Mercury 500 EFIs would have drowned out the beeping of his cell phone had Ortiz not taken the precaution of wearing an earpiece connection. Pulling the cell from the breast pocket of his windbreaker, Ortiz was not surprised to see that the name on the small screen was Rosita's. She'd already called him three times on the cell he'd bought her and instructed her to use rather than the hotel phone.

"Hello, *chica*."

"Hello, *amor*. Are you alright? There is so much noise I can hardly hear you."

"It is only the engines of the boat," Ortiz said, raising his voice.

"You are on a boat?"

Ortiz hadn't confided his traveling plans to Rosita and saw no reason to do so now. "Yes. What are you doing, little one?"

"I am watching the television, but I do not understand so much."

"Why don't you go shopping, take a walk along the beach?"

"Yes, I will, but it will not be the same without you. Rosita is so lonely. She misses you *mucho*. Do you miss Rosita, too?"

"Only as much as a flower would miss the sunlight," he said. Which was true. He would like nothing better than to have her sitting next to him in the cockpit's double bolster, her long, lustrous black hair streaming behind her.

"*Esta bien*. Rosita wants you to miss her as much as she misses you."

"I do, little one. But I have to hang up now," he said. He was approaching his destination, Burnham Harbor, and had to pull back the throttle to reduce speed.

"I love you, *mi amor*."

"I love you, too, little one."

I love you, he thought, beeping off. Words he'd said many times before.

They were just words that women wanted to hear. He never meant them. But this time he wasn't so sure.

Ortiz steered the boat through a mass of power and sail boats moored to cans, then around the tip of the peninsula that was once the site of a small airport, Meigs Field. Passing the mammoth convention center, McCormick Place, he speed-dialed a number he'd programmed in that morning. Ahead along a channel were row after row of docks occupied by a variety of big power boats.

"Burnham Harbor Master, Julie speaking," a female voice answered.

Ortiz identified himself, asked for and received directions to where he was to dock the sports cruiser. Since he was familiar with the harbor, it didn't take him long to locate it along big boat row. Ortiz expertly nudged the boat up against the protective tires along the dock and killed the engine. A young, sun-bronzed dockhand was waiting to catch the stern line Ortiz threw him.

"Hey, Mr. Salizar," he said with a big smile. "Welcome back."

Good memory, Ortiz thought, no doubt motivated by the generous tips he'd given him.

"Good to be back...Jimmy isn't it?"

"Jamie, sir. Awesome boat you got there. Want me to tie her down?"

Ortiz picked up his briefcase and stepped agilely from the side of the boat onto the dock. "I'd appreciate that, Jamie."

"You gonna live on the boat while you're here like before?"

"That's right, Jamie. A little cramped, I admit, but I like being on the water."

"I know what you mean. Let me know if you need anything, okay? Food, liquor, anything at all."

Ortiz wondered if Jamie's offer included feminine companionship. "I'll do that, Jamie," he said, and removed a hundred dollar bill from his wallet.

Jamie accepted the bill with an even bigger smile. "Thank you, Mr. Salizar."

"You're welcome, Jamie."

Ortiz made his way along the dock past three launch ramps to the harbor building, a rectangular, white wood structure with a small tower. Inside, Ortiz entered the Ship's Store where two women were browsing through an assortment of refreshments, apparel and boating supplies. Three young ladies in khaki shorts and sky blue tee-shirts with "Chicago Harbors" logos were busy behind a counter.

"Good morning," a plump girl with a ponytail said. "Can I help you?"

Ortiz recognized her voice as the same he'd heard on the phone. "Yes, thank you, Julie. I'm Mr. Salizar."

"Oh, yes. I guess you found the space okay, Mr. Salizar?"

"Yes, thank you."

"I have a rental form for you to sign, and I'll need a credit card. How long do you plan to stay?"

Ortiz handed his Visa to Julie. "Two, perhaps three days."

Julie processed the Visa and laid a rental contract on the counter. "I'll leave it open-ended. Is this your first visit to Chicago?"

Ortiz signed the Visa slip and rental contract. "No. I have been to your wonderful city several times and always found it an enchanting experience."

"Can I call a cab for you, Mr. Salizar?"

Ortiz glanced at his Cartier wrist watch. 10:45 a.m. "No, thank you, Julie. I think I'll take a walk along your beautiful lakefront, perhaps stop someplace for lunch."

"There are lots of really nice restaurants on Navy Pier, but it's quite a walk."

"Yes, I know, but I can use the exercise. An excellent suggestion, Julie." Better than you know, Ortiz thought. Navy Pier, with its many shops, restaurants and amusements, even a theatre, would be crowded with both local people and tourists, a perfect place to conduct business without attracting attention.

"Have a wonderful day, Mr. Salizar."

"I'm sure I will, Julie."

Ortiz exited the building and walked to a bike path on the east side of Soldier Field, which was under renovation to add additional seats and sky boxes. Perhaps he would visit the stadium sometime when the Bears played the Miami Dolphins. Ortiz was not only a big fan of American professional football, he considered himself something of an *aficionado* of the sport. Someday, he thought, he might even buy a franchise, if the price was right.

Ortiz mused over this prospect, while he followed the path at a brisk pace north along the lakefront amidst a crosscurrent of bikers and joggers. When he began to perspire, he paused under a tree to slip off the windbreaker and tie it by the sleeves around his waist. In the distance he could now see the tip of a gigantic Ferris wheel slowly revolving over Navy Pier. Resuming his walk, he speed-dialed a number to arrange what he expected to be a very profitable lunch.

*10:53 a.m.:* Willie was beat. He'd been on the street since he took off from the emergency room of Northwestern Memorial Hospital. For a while he'd considered going back to Little Village to look for Scarface and his buddies. He had enough of McPherson's five hundred dollars left to finance a room in another transient hotel for a couple of days if he kept the food expense down. However, Willie had serious doubts that he had the energy to get the job done. If he could get some sleep, he might give it a try. With this in mind he decided to check in at the Lower Wacker Hilton, the closest and safest place for him to grab a few hours slack time.

Willie also needed some food, and stopped at a McDonald's at Lake and Clark for an Egg McMuffin and coffee to go. He ate his breakfast on the move to nearby Garvey Court, which was more like a ramp than a street that sloped down to the east-west branch of Lower Wacker. The food and coffee helped. Willie was feeling more energized by the time he reached the delivery lane and headed west. He paused by a dumpster to finish the coffee. Pitching the sack and cup into the dumpster, he started to walk again, then froze! About a hundred yards ahead two dudes in business suits were passing out money to three vagrants camped out near a loading dock. Parked nearby was a Ford Taurus. Willie knew the three vagrants, and was about to duck behind the dumpster when one of them spotted him and pointed in his direction.

"Shit!"

Willie turned and bolted. He didn't have to look back to know that the two dudes would be following, but he did. They were, and closing the distance. Furthermore, the taller dude now had a .45 automatic in his hand. Cops for sure, Willie thought. No way he could outrun them, but there was a hotel a short distance away. If he could get in through the loading entrance, make it to the elevators, there was a chance he could lose them in the hotel. But when Willie reached the hotel the loading door was locked.

Gasping for breath, his chest pounding, Willie kept running. What's the use? he thought. Might as well call it quits. Let the cops cuff him. At least he'd get three meals a day and a cot to sleep on in the Cook County lock-up.

But were they cops? The plain clothes dicks drove Ford Crown Vics, and these dudes had a Taurus. So if they weren't cops, who the hell were they and why were they after him? Willie didn't know and didn't want to find out.

Another glance over his shoulder. The dudes were about fifty yards away now and closing. Willie felt his legs about to buckle. He knew he couldn't keep up this pace much longer. Either his legs would give out and he'd stumble and fall to the pavement, or he'd have to slow down. Either way they'd catch him. Then what? If they were cops, they'd cuff him and haul him in. And if they weren't…? All Willie knew was that if he didn't catch a break real soon—like in the next few seconds—it was "Game Over for Willie."

A few minutes earlier Otis was heading east on the Eisenhower Expressway. He took the off-ramp that circled and merged into South Wacker Drive heading north. Staying to the right he took Lower Wacker Drive and eased into the delivery lane, where he cruised along slowly in the Crown Vic looking for Willie. By the time he went several blocks past the point where Wacker curved to the east, he began to think that his search for Willie was a waste of time. He was getting anxious about his regular caseload, which was doubly heavy now that he didn't have Mack for a partner, and he wondered how he would answer Captain Cronin if he were questioned about the cases he had worked on this morning. He figured if he struck out on Lower Wacker, he would just have to get back to his other cases, and Mack would have to wait for Willie to call him.

Otis had been looking to the right as he drove, trying to see into the shadows of the loading docks and around the edges of the dumpsters for any sign of Willie. Just before Garvey Court, becoming increasingly impatient and wondering whether to continue his search, he looked down along the next couple of blocks of the delivery lane to see if he could spot anyone who might be Willie among the few small groups of street people clustered here and there. About a hundred yards away he saw a black guy in a fatigue jacket being chased by two white guys in suits. At that distance he couldn't be sure that the black guy was Willie, but if it was, then Willie was in big trouble. Of course, the dudes could be cops, but Otis had a hunch they were the same guys who had stolen the Lazarus disk and tried to kill Mack.

He didn't waste any time speculating. He stomped on the accelerator of the Crown Vic and blew past Garvey Court, bearing down on the two white dudes. Now he could make out the guy they were chasing. It was Willie alright, looking like a man on his last legs.

Otis blasted the horn, startling the white dudes, who scattered out of the way. A few seconds later he was braking the Vic to a tire-screeching halt in front of Willie.

"Get in, quick!"

Willie opened the passenger door and scrambled inside. Otis gassed the Vic before Willie had the door closed. As the car leapt forward, Otis heard the sound of a gunshot. A bullet punctured the rear window and the windshield between his gasping-for-breath passenger and himself. Shit, how am I gonna explain the bullet hole to Cronin? Otis thought. Oh, well, guess that doesn't matter much now.

"Willie, get down!"

Willie was already sliding down in the seat.

"Thanks, bro," Willie wheezed.

"Don't mention it."

Willie sat up when there were no more shots. Otis slowed to turn at an exit onto the speed lane, then braked for the red at North Michigan Avenue.

"Who the hell are those dudes?" Willie said. "Not cops, for sure."

"No. Not cops."

"Yeah, and why are they after my ass?"

"Long story, Willie," Otis said. He wasn't relishing the thought of having to give Willie the bad news about his having HCV. "I'll fill you in on the way."

"Way to where?"

Otis toed the accelerator when the light turned green and continued east toward Lake Shore Drive. "To Mack and a safe house on wheels."

"A what?"

"You'll see. And fasten your seat belt."

Willie grinned and buckled up.

*11:54 a.m.:* Blackburn parked his hunter green Saturn in the parking lot of The Members Club at Four Streams, an exclusive country club in Beallsville, Maryland, and sat for a moment in thought. There had been both good news and bad news so far this morning. First there was the phone call from Roy O'Neal. The test results on the latest vaccine were extremely promising. In fact, although O'Neal had hedged his enthusiasm with the appropriate cautionary disclaimer —"Well, we need to run more tests to be sure"—Blackburn could tell from his tone of voice that he was really upbeat about the results. Then there was the phone call from Gallagher and Bryant. The vagrant Butler had gotten away from them, rescued by McPherson's partner, Detective Winstrom, just seconds before they would have caught him. Of course, once McPherson got lab work done on Butler, he would go public with his claims and it would be impossible to dismiss him as just a renegade cop trying to save his badge.

Blackburn took a deep breath. Were the challenges of his job starting to get to him? Well, no matter. Time to bring the Woman up to date. Blackburn walked through the parking lot and past the clubhouse, then followed a cart path by a pro shop and a putting green, where golfers were practicing while they waited for their tee time. Up ahead four ladies were preparing to begin their game on the red tee.

The Woman stood out among the middle-aged foursome like a sunflower amid wilted geraniums. Garbed in a yellow Polo top, Bermuda shorts and a brimmed sun hat that covered short-cropped, dark brown hair, she carried her trim figure with the poise of a stage actress, a career she had pursued with success as a young woman.

"Good morning, Mr. Blackburn," said one of the two men standing off to one side at a respectful distance from the foursome.

"Good morning, Alex," Blackburn said to the tall muscular black man. The two men, who served as the Woman's bodyguards, looked very uncomfortable in their dark suits and ties. "Everything okay?"

"Yes, sir. Got the usual flack from the boss, though," he said, mopping perspiration from his brow with a handkerchief. "She wants to walk the course for the exercise, even in this heat, and told us to wait for her in the clubhouse over lunch and some cold beers."

Blackburn smiled. Just like her. Always thinking of other people. "Why don't you get a cart and some bottled water from the pro shop. I don't want you guys passing out from dehydration."

"Thank you, sir," the other man said. White with a ruddy face, he was already pulling off his coat and loosening his tie. "Be right back."

"I guess you want to talk to the boss," Alex said.

"Yes. Go tell her, will you? Oh, wait, never mind."

Blackburn could see that she had already noticed him and was excusing herself from the other ladies.

"Wait here, Alex." Blackburn said. He didn't want his conversation with her to be overheard.

The Woman walked to a golf ball cleaning station, where Blackburn joined her.

"Good morning, Suzanne. Sorry to interrupt your game, but I didn't want to discuss what I have to tell you on the phone."

"Good news, David? I certainly hope so. We sure could use some."

Blackburn looked into her large, dark eyes that brightened for a moment in anticipation of the good news she hoped to hear. Her eyes were the focal points of a lovely, oval face, a Joan Crawford face, he thought, very feminine but with an inner toughness. Although she looked completely composed, Blackburn knew the anxiety, even torment, she was feeling.

"Yes. I got a call from O'Neal this morning."

Her face tensed slightly, in expectation. "And? They found it?"

"That's the consensus from the tests they just conducted."

"They're sure? Absolutely sure?"

"Well, time will tell, and further testing does need to be done to be absolutely certain, but O'Neal was pretty confident that they had an antiviral drug that could arrest the disease for a long time, if not indefinitely."

The Woman clasped her hands, closed her eyes, and turned her face upward. "Thank you, God! Thank you, thank you!" she said with heartfelt gratitude, drinking in the sense of relief that washed over her like a long-awaited welcome rain.

"That's the good news, Suzanne. Unfortunately, we still have a serious problem: Detective McPherson."

"He's still at large?"

"Yes. And what's more, he has one of the Lazarus subjects."

"Oh. I see." As quickly as her face had brightened when she heard the good news, it now turned somber.

"Thanks to the mayor, the superintendent is cooperating. The police will turn over McPherson and the vagrant to us when they locate them."

"If they find them alive, you mean. The other people are looking for them as well, I assume."

"I'm sure they are."

"David, we can't have any more deaths. We just can't."

"I'm afraid that's out of our hands, Suzanne. You know what could happen if we attempt to interfere."

"Yes. I know, but…"

"I don't see that we have any options, do you?"

"Perhaps. Perhaps not."

The woman placed a golf ball in the washer. After she scrubbed it, she dried it off with a towel. Blackburn knew she was processing this latest development before deciding what to do about it. However, he was not prepared for what she said next.

"David, we're going to Chicago."

"What!? You can't be serious?"

"I am. We're going. We'll use Bio-Sci's corporate jet. It will be less conspicuous. Have it flown here...to a private airport."

Blackburn took her arm. "Suzanne, I really wish you'd reconsider this. Let us handle it."

The Woman smiled warmly and patted his hand. "The Project was my idea, David. It's time I got involved personally."

"But what can you do that we can't?"

"Perhaps nothing. I only know that I have to be there in case something happens that we haven't anticipated...haven't planned for. So much is at stake."

Blackburn sighed. He knew that once she made up her mind, there was no way he was going to change it.

"And David, this trip is strictly hush-hush. No one outside the family must know about it."

The "family," he knew, was her affectionate way of referring to the small team he had assembled to support and protect the Project. "Alright. I'll call O'Neal to arrange for the jet."

"Right away, David. I want to be there this evening."

"This evening, Suzanne? That's awfully short notice. The earliest we would be able to leave would be around 5:00, assuming O'Neal can get the jet here that fast."

"Well, do your best, David. You always do." She paused for a moment. "David, you don't think anything will happen tonight, do you, someone getting hurt?"

"You know we'll be doing our very best to prevent that, Suzanne."

"Yes, I know. It's just that the others..." She looked up at Blackburn, and he thought for a brief moment he could see a tinge of fear in her eyes, usually so dark they were unfathomable, revealing only what she allowed them to reveal. Then that look disappeared, and she was once again in control.

"Alright, then, 5:00 o'clock. I'll go directly to the airport from here after I finish my game. I'll arrange to have my bags packed and brought to the airport. I can change clothes on the plane."

"That could be a little cramped."

"You'd be surprised how cramped it got in the closets that passed for dressing rooms during my off-Broadway days," she said with a wistful smile.

"I can imagine," Blackburn smiled back. Then, glancing at the ladies waiting on the tee, "Your friends are looking a little impatient."

"Yes. I'd better get going. You'll take care of everything?"

"Rest assured. And have a good game."

"I will. And David... thanks."

Blackburn watched her stride back to the other ladies. Placing her ball on a tee, she took a practice swing. Then, as if there were nothing more on her mind than a game of golf, she drove the ball a hundred yards straight down the fairway.

*1:16 p.m.:* Ortiz fed another piece of dinner roll to the pigeon that was strutting around and cooing on the ground beside his chair.

"Relax, Otto," he said to his jittery lunch companion at an outside table of Riva Crabhouse, a four-star restaurant on Navy Pier. "Perhaps another glass of champagne?"

"Well, I rarely indulge, but...this latest development..."

"You're sure McPherson has one of the subjects?"

"Yes. Blackburn called O'Neal right after the vagrant escaped his men. And O'Neal confided this to me just before I got your call."

"Regrettable, to be sure, but I'm confident Blackburn's people will take care of the situation."

"I hope so. But I'm still worried."

So was Ortiz, but letting Kischman know this would only make him more distraught than he already was. Removing a bottle of Dom Perignon from an ice bucket, Ortiz filled Kischman's empty glass and replenished his own.

"Let's focus on the good news for the moment, Otto, and the fact that the HCV drug is going to make you a very wealthy man."

Ortiz was referring to the two million dollars that would be deposited into Kischman's Grand Cayman bank account in addition to the one million he had already put there to pay for the doctor's services to date. Ortiz considered this cheap, in view of the millions he would make off the drug in the global black markets.

"Yes, I know, and I appreciate your generosity. It's just...well, when I agreed to our business arrangement, I didn't anticipate that things would become so...so violent. O'Meara, Dr. Alward and now Diane..."

"Yes, I quite sympathize with your feelings, Otto, but we really had no choice."

"No, no, I suppose not," Kischman said, and reached for his champagne glass.

Ortiz frowned. Kischman was having a guilt attack. He also knew it wouldn't be his last if the Lazarus Project was ever exposed. And although Ortiz had considered continuing to use the doctor as an ongoing pipeline to Bio-Sci's new drugs, he now decided it was not worth the risk. Someday Kischman was bound to be found out. When that happened, Ortiz was certain that Kischman would confess, in which event he, Ortiz, would be open season for Interpol.

Ortiz had already considered two courses of action to prevent this from happening. He could have the doctor killed. Or he could continue to use him, but in a different way.

"Otto, how would you like to work for me?"

"Work for you? You mean at your laboratory in Caracas?"

"Exactly. You're already working for me, in a way, so why not go on the official payroll as director of the lab? Frankly, I've been looking for somebody who could upgrade the quality of the drugs we duplicate, a job for which you're more than qualified."

"I don't know, Manuel. That's a big decision. I'd have to think it over."

"Naturally, but I would make it worth your while. Shall we say a million a year?"

"A million dollars?!"

"One million American dollars, and bonuses if you can do the job and still keep the bottom line respectable."

"That's...that's a very generous offer, Manuel. Very appealing, but I'll have to discuss it with Gloria...with my wife. Moving out of the country, living in

Venezuela, that might not appeal to her."

Ortiz thought otherwise. He knew all about Kischman's vain and promiscuous young wife and the big debts the doctor had taken on to support her lifestyle. She was Kischman's addiction, the reason he'd sold out Bio-Sci, and Ortiz was certain that what he was offering the doctor would provide him with an ongoing fix he couldn't refuse.

He didn't refuse, although Ortiz did have to explain to him that in Venezuela a million a year would finance a lavish villa, servants and the ability to travel all over the world—first class.

"Yes, I believe Gloria will be agreeable to that," Kischman said.

"Good. Another thing. I think it would be advisable if you came with me when I leave Chicago."

"Leave with you? I'm afraid that wouldn't be possible. There's so much to attend to for a move like this. Just making arrangements to have everything packed, putting the house up for sale, settling my financial affairs…"

"How long will that take?"

"Four or five days, at least, I guess."

"What about the Lazarus file? Can you download it to your home computer?"

"No, that's no longer possible. After McPherson copied the file by tapping into my home phone line, all outside access to the computer was shut down."

"Ah, yes, of course. That makes sense. So you will have to go to your office to make a copy. And when can you do that?"

"That's not so easy. It's already Saturday afternoon and the office is closed. Tomorrow is Sunday and Monday's Memorial Day. Security is very tight on weekends and holidays. Although I'm in charge of the lab and I often work on weekends, I'm supposed to help maintain security by scheduling any weekend or holiday work ahead of time. It would be much less conspicuous if I copied the file to a disk from my office on Tuesday."

Ortiz thought for a moment. Tuesday was pushing it. One of Ortiz's cardinal rules for achieving success was do what you need to do, then get out quickly. The longer you hung around after your mission was accomplished, the greater the risk that your success would unravel and become a net in which you could get caught.

"Very well. Tuesday. That's three days. We'll leave Tuesday evening. Whatever arrangements you can't complete by then I'm sure your wife can take care of after you leave. The important thing is to get you out of the country now, with the disk, just in case things should get out of hand, so to speak."

Kischman considered this by finishing his second glass of champagne with a shaking hand. "Yes, yes. I see your point, especially now that McPherson has one of Dr. Alward's patients."

"I told you not to worry about that. Blackburn's people will find them."

"But what if they don't?! What if McPherson gets a doctor to examine the vagrant? You know what that could mean!"

Ortiz was well aware of that possibility. "Then I'll deal with them."

"How? You don't even know where they are."

"I'll find a way. Now I think we should order, don't you?"

Ortiz picked up the menu and opened it. He had to admit that at the moment finding a way seemed elusive. However, he'd faced critical situations before and always resolved them satisfactorily. The key was information.

Knowing as much as possible about his adversaries had enabled him to find their weakness, their Achilles' heel.

As he perused the assortment of salads on the menu, Ortiz thought about the information Angel had provided him about McPherson. Angel had done a thorough job, and somewhere in the data was the detective's Achilles' heel that Ortiz was looking for.

"Mommy, Mommy, can I have ice cream now? Can I? Can I?"

Ortiz looked over at a nearby table that was occupied by a young couple and their cute little daughter.

"Yes, dear," the mother said. "But only after you finish every bite of your lunch."

"I will, Mommy, I will!"

Ortiz smiled with the realization that he had just found McPherson's weakness.

*1:56 p.m.:* Mark Jacobs wanted to give up.

"Come on, Mark. One more rep, just one more. You can do it. Go for it!" Dave, his handsome young trainer at the Lakeview Athletic Club, cheered him on.

Easy for you to say, Jacobs thought. Built like a gorilla without hair. You can probably bench press with one arm, without raising a sweat, the eighty pounds for ten reps that I'm struggling to complete. Okay, you fucking sadist, one more push, and that's fucking it!

Sucking in as much air as he could, Jacobs exhaled slowly as, with trembling arms, he summoned up his last ounce of strength to push the bar up and on to the rack.

"Sweet," Dave said with a wide grin of approval.

Jacobs had to acknowledge a deep sense of accomplishment in having survived nearly an hour of Dave's relentless training. Nonetheless, he still needed his trainer's helping hand just to raise his body to a sitting position on the bench.

Dave, looking at his watch: "Say, Mark, you still got time to do some bicep curls."

Screw that, Jacobs thought. "Not today, Dave. I've had it."

"No sweat. Let's sign out of today's session, okay?"

Jacobs stood up on legs wobbly from leg curls and extensions and followed Dave across the weight room to a towel rack. Dave's pen and clipboard with a signature sheet were on top of the rack. Jacobs' Fila sports outfit was dripping perspiration as though he had just come out of a steam room. He grabbed a hand towel and wiped the perspiration from his face and hands, then signed out on the sheet.

"So are we on for next week?" Dave asked.

Jacobs wanted to say no but knew he had to stay with the program if he was going to shed the excess weight he'd put on. "Sure. Same time?"

"I'll have to check." Dave took out a small electronic planner and tapped a few times on the screen. "Got someone at one. How about two o'clock?"

"Two's fine."

"Hi, Dave."

Jacobs looked around at a gorgeous, young blonde wearing a tight-fitting leotard body suit that left nothing to the imagination.

"Hey, Sherry, how's it goin'?"

"Goin' good," Sherry said, turning a pink cheek for Dave to kiss when he hugged her.

Jacobs had observed that Dave gave all of his lady clients a hug and a kiss, regardless of their age and appearance. It was a nice touch that made him the most popular trainer at the club with the female members. Jacobs watched this ritual with a tinge of envy. His trainer would never have to surf the sports bars or join a dating service given the smorgasbord of good looking chicks the club offered.

"Just wanted to make sure you had me down for tomorrow at four," Sherry said.

"Yep, four it is," Dave said, consulting his planner.

"Maybe we could have a Coke or something afterward," Sherry purred. "If you don't have another appointment, I mean."

"Hey, that might work. I got an hour open between clients. I was planning to grab some fruit or a salad at the food bar anyway."

"Wonderful. And it's on me, okay?"

"No way. Dutch or nothing."

"Deal. See ya."

Jacobs ogled Sherry's buttocks as she sashayed over to a lat pull-down. He'd been tempted to ask Dave for an introduction but decided against it. Although being a local celebrity opened the door for some occasional easy scores, the fact that Sherry hadn't recognized him was not good for openers.

"Mark, you did well today," Dave was saying, "but try to get in some workout time before our next session, okay?"

"Will do," Jacobs said, but, he thought to himself, only after I give my muscles a couple of days to recover.

"Good. Take care," Dave said, turning to his next client, a buxom brunette who was drawing the attention of the other men in the weight room. "Hey, Liz. How's it goin'?"

"Goin' good, Dave," Liz said, gliding into Dave's embrace for her kiss.

What a racket, Jacobs thought on his way out of the weight room and down a corridor to the men's locker room. He paused at a water cooler to gulp down three much needed cups of water before heading into a small lounge, where he'd decided to cool down before hitting the shower. Settling into a comfortable recliner, he closed his eyes and tried to ignore the inane babble on the TV of a talk show psychologist advising a bickering husband and wife how they could reconnect. The audience applauded enthusiastically when the couple kissed and made up. This truce would last a day, two at the most, Jacobs thought, before all hell broke loose again with a marriage that was already on the rocks.

His beeping cell phone spared him from listening to the host's next guests, a hysterical mother and her out-of-control drug-addicted teenage daughter. It was McPherson, and what he had to say jerked Jacobs up to a sitting position. Jacobs had figured that the Lazarus story was dead in the water after the murder of Diane Bates, but now that McPherson had one of the project's guinea pigs, it could be a whole new ball game.

"I've got a friend, a pathologist at the Cook County Morgue, who's agreed to examine Willie," McPherson was saying, as he paced the RV. "Do a blood analysis, the works, which will not only reveal the virus but the presence of the experimental drugs."

"He wouldn't be Dr. Greg, would he?"

"Yeah. Why?"

"I know him. I've used Greg as a forensic expert on some of the murders I've covered. Do you think he'll agree to be interviewed?"

"I think so," Mack said when in truth he wasn't sure. Just doing the exam was asking a lot. Going on TV would really put him on the hot seat with the M.E. and probably cost him his job. But if things worked out, and the project was exposed, Dr. Greg would come off as a hero and be on demand with every talk show on network and cable TV. Mack was hoping that this was a pot large enough to tempt a roll of the dice from his friend.

"Okay, his testimony along with yours and Butler's might be enough to trigger an investigation, but I'd feel a whole lot better if there was someone else who could back up your stories."

Mack hesitated. He wanted to keep Megan out of this, but now it might not be possible.

"What is it?" Megan asked, as if reading his thoughts again. She was setting a fresh mug of coffee in front of Willie, who was slouched despondently in the dining nook next to a slumbering Ulysses.

"Hold on." Mack turned to Megan. "Would you be willing to be interviewed by Jacobs?"

"Of course. I said I wanted to help. It's the least I can do."

"I know, and I appreciate it, but it could be dangerous for you and Katie."

Megan's face told him that she was fully aware of this. "Tell him I'll do the interview."

Some gutsy lady, Mack thought. "I've got a person who also saw what was on the Lazarus disk," Mack said into the cell. "Megan Herbst, Frank O'Meara's daughter."

Now it was Jacobs who hesitated. Megan Herbst's testimony would be a big help in selling the story, but it was still a huge risk. The only evidence of the Project would be what the examination of Butler would disclose, which was certainly not enough to convict in a court of law. Jacobs had to hope that the court of public opinion would be enough to trigger an investigation. And this might not happen if the mayor was in on a cover-up, as McPherson suspected, and used his clout to force the CPD to back off. In this event, Jacobs had already decided to demand that the Food and Drug Administration conduct an investigation, which they might or might not do. Added to this was the possibility that his network would drop the story like a hot potato, and Jacobs with it. Well, if that happened there was always a chance that an aggressive cable network like Fox or CNN would take a crack at it. Another big if.

All of this was churning in Jacobs's mind as he asked himself what Edward R. Murrow would have done. Murrow, Jacobs's hero since he was a kid writing for the Austin High School newspaper, had taken a big risk, too, when he'd attacked McCarthy. Woodward and Bernstein as well when they got their first heads-up from Deep Throat about Watergate. Now Jacobs had the opportunity to follow in their footsteps—a realization that blew away any doubts he had about moving ahead.

"Okay, here's the plan," he said. "I want to tape you and Butler asap. I can't get an ENG crew together today, but how about tomorrow at say 10:00 a.m.?"

"The time is fine but forget the crew. You're the only person I want to know where we're camped out...literally."

"Of course. Stupid of me. I'll tape the interviews myself, but I want to do Mrs. Herbst and Greg in the studio live when I break the story. More impact.

Since we probably won't be able to get Dr. Greg to do the blood analysis until Monday at the earliest, possibly Tuesday since Monday is Memorial Day, we should plan on breaking the story on Monday or Tuesday night. Now where in the hell are you camped out, or were you kidding about that?"

Mack smiled, extended his mug for Megan to fill with coffee. "No. We're in an RV at Wolf Lake." Mack gave him directions how to get to their location. "Can you find it okay?"

"No problem. See you tomorrow. And by the way, don't forget that I've still got to blast you on the *Deadline Chicago Special Report* tonight. My heart won't be in it, but I'll still have to make you look dangerous and me look outraged."

"Well, I don't want you coming under even the slightest shadow of suspicion, so go ahead and give it to me with both barrels. In fact, when you think about it, blasting me one night and then breaking the real story a few days later could actually make you look pretty good—able to keep your investigation completely under wraps until it's completed, airing a cover story to maintain the secrecy of your investigation. Very professional."

"Well I'd rather not have to do it that way, but yes, if it's necessary, I'll do my job and be very convincing."

"I'm sure you will. The RV we're in has satellite and a TV, so we'll be watching your performance. Good luck, and see you tomorrow morning."

"Thanks, I'm looking forward to it."

Mack beeped off and took a sip of coffee. "He wants to tape us tomorrow at ten, Willie. You okay with that?"

Willie shrugged. "Why not? I'm not goin' anywhere. I sure wish you had something stronger than this coffee, though."

"There's some beer in the fridge. Will that do?"

"Guess it'll have to," Willie said. He was hoping for a few shots of whiskey, hell, maybe a whole fifth. It wasn't every day you found out that you had a fucking virus that could fucking kill you. He'd come through near-death situations in Nam, but this was different. How in the hell do you fight something you can't see?

Megan moved to the refrigerator and removed a bottle of Miller Lite. "When do I do my interview?"

"Jacobs wants to put you on the air live when he breaks the story. Dr. Greg, too. He figures that will be Monday or Tuesday night. In the meantime, I think it would be a good idea if you and Katie found someplace else to live."

Megan twisted off the cap and handed Willie the bottle. "Well, we could probably move in with my Aunt Mary in Kenosha. It's not far, so I could still get Katie to school and put in some time at the Merc."

Mack frowned, took a sip of coffee. "Forget that. No school, no work, at least for now."

"Katie will have no problem with that, but this gal still has to make a living. Is it really all that urgent?"

"Megan, you're not getting the seriousness of this. They already know who you are. They've obviously been tailing me, since they made two attempts on my life, so they may also know that you've met with me and been in communication with me. They may even know that you've seen the disk. Remember you stayed over at my place the night we saw what was on the disk, and the attempt on my life was early the next morning, shortly after you left. If they were watching my apartment that night, they could have seen you arrive shortly after I copied the

Lazarus file to the disk and then seen you leave early the next morning before they ransacked my apartment. I made the mistake of underestimating these people twice before, and it cost me the disk, and Diane Bates her life. Now please, will you do as I say?"

Megan thought about this for a moment, then reluctantly agreed. "Yeah, okay, you're right, of course. I just hope it won't be for too long."

"Well, depending on how events unfold, you and Katie may have to go into a witness protection program until all the bad guys are rounded up. That goes for you too, Willie."

Willie took a pull at the bottle, swallowed hard. "Why bother? Seems like my number's up anyway."

Megan went over to Willie and put her hand on his shoulder. "It may not be that serious, Willie. You've only had the virus for a short time, and there are existing drugs that can treat it if it's caught early enough."

"Yeah, but for how long?"

"I don't know, but a friend of mine had it in her system for 20 years before they even knew she had it." Megan knew that Willie was at much higher risk of succumbing to the disease quickly because of his life on the street and addiction to alcohol, but of course there was no point in telling him that.

Willie took another swig of beer, then turned to Mack. "Forget the witness protection crap anyway. I got a personal stake in this now. I got a right to be in on the kill!"

Mack had to agree, although he didn't come out and say so. Willie and Megan both had personal scores to settle.

"Well, I better get going," Megan said, glancing at her watch.

"I'll walk you to your car," Mack said.

Megan picked up her shoulder bag from an end table, and she and Mack stepped out of the RV. When they reached Megan's Camry, Mack opened the door but took her arm before she could get in.

"I want to emphasize again, Megan, that you have to be very careful and move quickly. You have to assume that danger is right behind you. Go straight home, pack what you need for a few days, then take Katie and leave for your Aunt Mary's right away."

"Alright, my black knight. I'll do as you say."

"Your what?"

"Black knight. As in Camelot, but without the shining armor."

Mack smiled. "Sorry about that, but I never did look good in shining armor."

"No, I suppose not, but you'll do, Sir Knight."

Megan reached up, pulled Mack's head down and kissed him on the lips. "You'll do just fine."

Astonished, Mack closed the door after Megan slid behind the wheel. With a little wave she started the engine and backed up onto the gravel lane. Basking in the afterglow of the kiss and her subtle lilac scented perfume, Mack watched the Camry move away. A kiss of gratitude, he wondered, or was the unpredictable redhead extending an invitation into her private life? Mack also wondered if he would accept. They had both avoided serious relationships for their own reasons. Megan could be signaling a change of mind. Or was he reading too much into a kiss?

Walking back to the RV, Mack pushed these thoughts from his mind. There was too much going on now to think about a possible relationship with Megan. And he had a cop's hunch that things were about to break big time. The question was: for better, or for worse?

*3:52 p.m.:* Megan turned west off Clark Street onto North Avenue and headed toward the Kennedy Expressway. Her aunt had left for Kenosha a half hour earlier in her own car, and Megan was following her after hastily packing a few things for Katie and herself. "How long will we stay with Aunt Mary?" Katie asked. She was sitting next to Megan with one of her dolls that she'd insisted on taking with her.

"Just a few days, dear. You'll like that, won't you?"

"Oh, yes, yes!" Katie said, clapping her hands. "The park is so fun."

Megan knew that Katie was referring to a park on the lake across the street from her Aunt's house with a well-equipped playground. And fun it was. Megan had always enjoyed pushing Katie in a swing or watching her play while she read a magazine or a book.

Katie's voice interrupted her thoughts. "What about school, Mommy?"

Megan had already thought about that. She'd have to call the school with some reason for Katie's absence. Being sick was the easiest excuse.

"I'll talk to Miss Markle and ask her to prepare some lessons for you," Megan said. Since Monday was Memorial Day, she would do this first thing Tuesday morning. Of course, she'd have to drive back from Kenosha during the day to pick them up. Fortunately, the semester ended on Friday for the summer vacation, but still Megan didn't want Katie to fall behind, even if only for a few days.

"Why are we going to visit Aunt Mary, Mommy?"

Good question, Megan thought. She hadn't had time to consider an explanation. "I've been under a lot of stress, dear. I just want to get away for a few days and relax."

"Is it because of Grandpa?"

"Yes, dear."

"I miss Grandpa so much, Mommy."

"So do I, dear."

Megan reached over and stroked Katie's cheek, surprised to see that it was moist with tears. She was still having a hard time dealing with her granddad's death.

Megan made the green lights at the major intersections of Halsted and Clybourn but slowed as she approached Fremont, where the light was turning yellow. When she reached the intersection, she braked for the red.

Bang!

Megan's head thumped back against the headrest.

"Mommy, Mommy! Someone hit us!"

"Yes, dear. Don't be alarmed. It can't be serious."

Although Megan kept her voice calm, she was seething inside. Glancing into the rearview, she saw a young man getting out of a van. Whoever it was, he would no doubt claim that it was her fault. In rear-end accidents, it was always the driver of the car that was hit who was blamed. Megan wouldn't be surprised if the van driver had rammed her deliberately, just to get a check from her insurance company. It happened all the time. Adding fuel to her anger was the fact that she'd have to come up with the two hundred and fifty dollar deductible for whatever damage was done to her fender.

This was all going through Megan's mind as she unclipped her seat belt. "Wait here, dear. I have to exchange insurance information with the man who hit us."

"All right, Mommy."

Megan reached over into the rear seat for her shoulder bag, opened the door and got out to be confronted with a handsome young Latino who had exited the purple van.

"I am so sorry, lady" he said with an apologetic smile. "It was my fault. I was not paying attention."

Well that's a switch, Megan thought. Then it hit her. Young Latino, good looking, well dressed. Could he be the hit man they called "Angel"? Oh my God! If he was…

What happened next took place so fast that Megan didn't have time to do anything but scream—the Latino suddenly behind her, his right arm around her chest, his left hand holding a straight razor an inch from her neck, the van door sliding open, three thuggish-looking Mexicans jumping out, one opening the passenger door of her car, the other two pulling a screaming Katie out of the car and hustling her into the van, the third sliding into the van behind the wheel, the door slamming shut, muffling Katie's screams and cries for mommy to help her.

And during all of this the young Latino's voice, soft, almost feminine, assuring Megan that her daughter would not be harmed if she did exactly as she was told. Megan stammering her cell number, as requested by the Latino. The Latino telling her that he would call her with instructions, then thanking her, "*Gracias, Senora Herbst*," like a waiter who has just received a generous tip. Then the Latino jumping into the passenger seat of the van, which roared away.

Megan slumped against the Camry. Her head was throbbing with pain, but her mind was in overdrive, trying to think, refusing to panic. What to do?! What to do?! Got to save Katie! Got to call Mack!

Megan jumped back into the Camry, grabbed her cell phone and dialed Mack.

"Mack," she blurted out when he answered, "they've got Katie! They kidnapped her!"

"Damn! I was afraid of this. Tell me exactly what happened."

"We were on our way to Kenosha. I was on North Avenue. I stopped for the light at Fremont and they rear-ended me with their van. I thought it was an accident, so I got my insurance and license and I got out of the car and the man said he was sorry that it was his fault and then I realized he was a young Latino man and I thought it might be Angel but it was too late and he grabbed me and held his razor to my throat while the three Mexicans jumped out and they took Katie…and she was screaming. Oh, my God, Mack, what are we going to do?! We've got to save Katie! I'm so sorry."

"Whoa, Megan. Slow down and take a breath." Mack's voice was comforting. "Now tell me, slowly, exactly what happened, in detail."

Megan took a deep breath, then started over and told Mack exactly what happened, down to the smallest detail, answering his questions as she did so.

"Okay," Mack said when she was finished. "We're going to get through this. We're going to save Katie, but we need to take this one step at a time. We need to anticipate what Angel may do and plan accordingly. I want you to call Otis immediately and tell him what happened. I want him to hear this directly from you. Then tell him to get back to the RV as soon as he can. Then you come straight back here yourself, no stops, as quick as you can, without speeding."

"Okay, I will…but what should I do if Angel calls me before I get back?"

"Then you listen carefully to everything he says and try to remember every detail. Write down everything he says as soon as he hangs up. Then call me immediately. But, Megan, I don't think Angel will call that soon. Look, the only reason they would abduct Katie is to exchange her for me and Willie. After all, I'm the troublemaker, the 'Mad Dog' cop who won't let go of a bone once I've sunk my teeth in it, and Willie is living proof that the Lazarus Project actually exists. Willie wasn't with us until about four hours ago, so I don't think Angel, or his boss Ortiz, had much time to plan this. They'll need to find a place to hide Katie so they can set up the exchange in a way that gives them an edge, and that may take them several hours. It's only been ten minutes since they drove off with Katie. I don't think you'll hear from Angel until this evening. So keep calm and get back here quickly, but safely, okay?"

"Okay, Mack, I'll do exactly as you say."

"Good. I'll expect to see you in about 45 minutes." Mack beeped off.

*4:26 p.m.:* Otis was on the office phone with Ava when his cell phone beeped.

"Hold on, hon," he said, annoyed by the interruption.

He'd been typing his SUP report on the computer regarding a child abuse case he'd investigated that afternoon when Ava's call came in. She wanted to meet him for supper that night at Angelo's to discuss a possible reconciliation, an offer Otis was more than anxious to accept. Of course, he was aware that any damage control for their marriage would be on Ava's terms, namely to exchange his badge for a law degree and a cushy job at her dad's law firm. He'd have to deal with that over cocktails and supper. At least she was willing to talk, though, which was a plus.

However, what Megan told him on the cell put the peace talks on hold, if not deep freeze. He was hoping Ava would understand when he told her about the abduction of Megan's daughter.

"Oh, my God, that's…that's terrible! Of course, you have to help her. We can talk later."

"It could be awhile."

"That can wait. That poor little girl can't. Tell Mrs. Herbst that my prayers are with her."

"I will. Got to go, hon. Love you."

"I love you too," Ava said, her voice choked.

"Sorry, Megan," Otis said into the cell after ending his call with Ava. "Where are you?"

"I'm in my car on North Avenue at Fremont."

"Okay, I want you to get over here right away to make a statement. And bring a photo of Katie. I'll get Homicide on this as soon as I hang up and contact the FBI…."

"No, no, no, we can't do that! They'll kill Katie!"

"Look, Megan, the police can't help you if you don't let us do our job."

"You don't understand. Angel was explicit. He took my cell number and said he would call me with instructions, and he promised that Katie wouldn't be harmed if I did exactly as I was told. And Mack said to just get back to the RV as quickly as possible, you and me both, so we could plan how we're going to rescue Katie."

"Oh," he said, momentarily taken aback, "I didn't realize you had already called Mack. Okay then, we'll do what Mack says. We'll meet at the RV and wait for Angel's call. I've got to clean up some stuff here before I leave. I'll join you, Mack and Willie at the lake in about an hour and a half. And Megan…"

"Yes?"

"We're going to get Katie back, okay? Whatever it takes, we're going to get her back."

"I know you will."

"You need to keep believing that. I'll see you soon."

Otis beeped off and sat for a moment. Frankly, it pissed him off that he couldn't just follow the rules like he had been trained to do for situations like this —get a statement from the witness, get a recent photo of the victim, alert Homicide and the FBI. Not only that, with Mack it seemed like the rules never applied. Everything was an exception. On the other hand, he had to admit that Mack had been right about Lazarus almost straight down the line.

So what good were the rules if you couldn't use them? Well, sometimes you could, but the rules couldn't cover everything that happened on the street. And if you followed the rules strictly, by the book, then too often innocent people got hurt and the bad guys got away. So the rules that were intended to achieve justice, because they were too rigid, too slow, too blind to the real time world, thwarted justice as often as they achieved it.

Maybe it's like basketball, Otis thought. As a point guard he was supposed to set the other guys up to take the shot. That's the general rule. But if he had the opportunity to take the shot himself because of the fluid situation on the court, then he took it, the general rule be damned.

Otis shook his head as though trying to shake off a headache. No way I'm gonna figure this out now, he thought. I've promised Megan we'll get Katie back, "whatever it takes." Certainly breaking the rules. It'll take at least that. Maybe even laying down my life….

Of course, Otis had made a similar commitment with every child abduction case he'd handled. But this time it was different. Very different. This time it was personal!

*5:33 p.m.:* Angel Chavez muttered a curse.

"What is it?" Carlos said from behind the wheel of the van.

"It is nothing."

"I do not think so. I do not think you like this thing we are doing," Carlos said, his voice as heavy with sarcasm as with the pungent odor of his garlicky breath. "It is perhaps you think it is beneath you, *si*?"

Very perceptive, the pig, Angel thought. Child abductions were not in his line of work. Although they were occasionally done for ransom, in most cases the motive was sex by some pervert, like the Padre, who had raped him. To make matters worse, the *nina*, Katie, reminded him of his little sister, Jaunita.

"Unlike you, I do not have to like what I do."

"But we both like the *dinero. Verdad?*"

"Shut your mouth and drive."

"Drive. Drive to where? We have been driving for over an hour now."

Angel was aware of that. They'd been cruising the River West area, searching for a safe place to take the little girl. With its many warehouses, some being gutted for rehabbing into offices or condos, the area seemed like a good place to start. Because Ortiz's call instructing him to abduct the *nina* had been not only unwelcome but unexpected, there had been no time to plan for a place to take her, which is what he told the pig for the third time.

"*Que stupido!* If we do not find a place soon, the police they will find *us*."

"The police will not be looking for us."

"How do you know that? How do you know that the woman will not go to the police?"

"She won't."

"Maybe, maybe not. I say we take no chances. I say we kill the *nina* now and dump her body into the river."

"No! I need her to negotiate with the detective, McPherson."

"So what is the difference if we kill her now or later? She dies anyway, *si*?"

"Not if they do as they are told. I gave my word to the Senora Herbst."

"Your word!" Carlos spat, his saliva spraying the windshield. "*Que noble!* It is like I said. You who have killed so many have no stomach for this."

"I'll do what I have to do," Angel said. Or would he leave that odious task to the pig and his pig *amigos*, as he had with the Bates woman? "And you're still taking orders from me, if you want to get the rest of the money I am paying you."

A harsh laugh from Carlos. "What good will the money do me behind bars? The *nina* could identify us, me and *mi amigos* from our rap sheets. Not you. Oh no. You will be far away with your money, but...*pendejo!*"

Carlos hit the brake in time to avoid ramming into a little VW that had just crossed an intersection in front of them.

"*Idiota! Cuidado!*" Angel yelled.

"Fuck him! And fuck the money, too! I say the *nina* dies no matter what the cop does! The *nina*'s bitch mother, as well!"

"You have nothing to say about this!" Angel barked. "I gave my word to the Senora Herbst. She and the *nina* will be exchanged for the cop and the vagrant. Alive! So shut the fuck up and drive!"

Carlos did shut up, but Angel was apprehensive that when the time came for the exchange, the pigs would carry out Carlos's threat. Even though Angel was carrying a G33 Sub-Compact Magnum, Carlos was armed with an AK-47 automatic assault rifle, Julio and Andres with MP-5 semi-automatics. This would put him at an extreme disadvantage if he attempted to shoot it out with them. But maybe it would not come to that. Carlos had said fuck the money, but Julio and Andres were another matter. They would want to be paid, and Angel would tell them that there would be no money if they killed the *nina* and her mother. However, there was also Ortiz to deal with. Would Ortiz let the *nina* and the Senora Herbst live if the cop agreed to the exchange? Angel didn't know. All he could do now was wait and see what happened. And pray to God, if God was listening, that the *nina* and her mother would be spared.

*6:14 p.m.:* Ortiz was channel surfing on the TV in the cabin of the Black Thunder. Sprawled comfortably on a small sofa, he was savoring the first sip of Grey Goose on the rocks while he searched for a station with the local evening news. Ortiz hoped it would provide him with an update on his nemesis, McPherson.

It didn't take long to find one. An anchorman on Channel 6 was informing his viewers that the detective was still at large and considered armed and dangerous. Thanks to a film clip of a lady reporter being brushed aside by the detective after a shoot-out with a child molester, Ortiz now knew what his adversary looked like. Ortiz had to admit that the detective's appearance lived up to his reputation. He reminded Ortiz of a jungle cat poised to spring. Once again Ortiz had a vision of McPherson in the cross hairs of his .357 Magnum.

The news shifted to another story when his cell phone sounded. He'd been expecting a call from Angel, letting him know if they'd found a place to take the little girl. However, the number on the cell screen wasn't Angel's or Rosita's. The message on the screen said "private number." Since only a very few people had his cell number, Ortiz answered with some apprehension.

"Yes?"

"Hello, Ortiz. Remember me?"

"Ah, Detective McPherson," Ortiz said, amused at the timing of the call. "I was just watching you on television. You photograph very well, did you know that?"

"I'm flattered. And thanks for letting me know that you're in Chicago."

Although Ortiz realized that he'd just made a stupid slip of the tongue, it was of no great concern, since McPherson was hardly in a position to be a threat.

"Yes. I wanted to be here for the kill. You understand?"

"I understand. Now listen up, Ortiz, because I'm only going to say this once, and I want it to sink into that cesspool you call a brain."

"My, you have a way with words, Detective. I'm impressed. Let me assure you that you have my undivided attention."

"Good. I know you gave the order to abduct the little Herbst girl, and I think I know why. You want to exchange her for Butler and me."

"As you Americans so aptly put it, right on. Am I wrong in assuming that this arrangement is acceptable?"

"We'll play along provided the little girl is released unharmed."

"Those are my instructions to Angel. Of course, I can't make the same guarantee for you."

"I figured as much."

"I'm sure you did. And that even knowing this, you would accept the offer. You see, I know more about you than you may have thought. Now is that all you want to tell me?"

"No. Since you did all this research on me, you also know that I'm a hard man to kill. If I live through this, I want you to know that sometime, somewhere, when you least expect it, you'll look over your shoulder and see me coming for you. And that, my friend, will be the last thing you'll ever see. *Comprende*?"

"Perfectly. I'll be looking forward to such a meeting, the likelihood of which I do not anticipate."

"You do that. I'm not saying goodbye, Ortiz. Let's make it *hasta la vista*."

Ortiz beeped off with a smile. The detective had style, he had to give him that. But he was smiling for another reason. The local story that had started when McPherson's call came in was providing him with the perfect place for Angel to take the Herbst girl for the exchange. Not only was it unoccupied, it would give Angel and his *peon* thugs a big advantage in case McPherson tried something devious, which was a distinct possibility.

In any event, Ortiz had made a decision during McPherson's phone call. Angel and his people could take care of the vagrant, the little girl and her mother —of course, they had to die as well—but he would instruct them to detain the detective until he got there. Killing McPherson was a pleasure he wanted to reserve for himself.

*7:12 p.m.:*  Megan was microwaving two of four chicken TV dinners that Otis had picked up at a convenience store on his way to Wolf Lake. She was grateful that this gave her something to do, something to keep her mind off Katie, at least for a few minutes. When the microwave dinged, she removed the dinners and set them down in front of Mack and Willie in the dining nook with some silverware and paper napkins.

"More coffee?"

"Sounds good," Mack said.

"How about you, Willie?"

"Sure." Willie said while attacking his food.

"Otis? How about you?"

"Yes, thanks, Megan."

Megan filled their mugs with fresh brew from the Mr. Coffee, then put the remaining two chicken dinners in the microwave. When the bell rang, she removed them and set them down on the table, one for Otis and one for herself, and sat down to eat.

No one spoke for the next few minutes. Mack and Willie devoured their food, and Otis managed to finish his plate, although with less enthusiasm. Megan had trouble eating. She picked at her food, pushing it around on her plate with her fork, but was too consumed with worry about Katie to eat more than a couple of bites.

When the others had finished their dinners and coffee, Megan got up to clear the table. Suddenly she turned and angrily confronted Mack.

"What's going on, Mack? You said we were going to meet and figure out what Angel might do and analyze everything and come up with a plan to rescue Katie, and all we've done for the last 45 minutes since Otis got here is either make chitchat or sit here eating in silence. Why aren't we figuring out what to do? Angel could call at any moment and...I don't know if Katie is still alive and..." Megan's voice started to break as she struggled to keep from crying."

"Megan, I'm so sorry. You're absolutely right. I've been doing a lot of thinking on my own, of course, but since we're all in this together, we need to discuss what to do as a team. Forget about the dishes. Sit down and let's figure this out, together, right now."

Megan sat back down at the table. "You know," she continued, "I always thought that if anything ever happened to Katie, I'd know it in my heart the instant it happened. Not just the bad stuff. The good stuff, too. It's like we're so close, we're connected inside. Like mothers and daughters should be, I guess. If I think about her, even when she's not around, when she's at school or with Karen or Aunt Mary, it's like I can feel her feelings inside me. All I have to do is just turn my thoughts, my attention, toward her. If she's happy, then I feel her happiness. If she's sad, I feel that. And if she's in danger, then my inner alarm bells go off and I know something's wrong and I've got to do something. But this time, I can't feel her at all. I can't tell if she's okay or not, if they've hurt her, even if she's alive. It's like there's a wall, an emptiness between us, and I can't get through it or around it or over it. I'm just cut off. I'm just helpless."

Mack reached across the table and took her hand. "Megan, trust me, I completely understand. I've been there, remember. Helplessness...and fear and other strong emotions, like anger, or remorse, can do that to you. It's like those strong emotions overload your circuits, and suddenly you can't feel anything except cut off and stuck. But I also know from experience that the best way to get out of that situation is to start taking action. So let's figure out how we're going to rescue Katie, okay?"

Megan nodded, Willie also.

"What are your thoughts so far, Mack?" Otis asked.

Mack took a sip of coffee, then proceeded. "Well, we know that Angel will be offering to exchange Katie for me and Willie. That's the only reason he would have abducted her. He will be using his cell phone to call Megan with instructions as to where we're supposed to go to do the exchange, maybe sending us to a couple of locations near to where he's holding her first to make sure the police aren't following us. He will probably also use his cell phone to give detailed instructions when we get there. The details of how to make the exchange will depend on the physical configuration of the location. If it's a big empty warehouse, for example, Angel may walk forward holding Katie with a gun against her while the Mexicans cover him with their weapons from concealed locations in the corners or along the sides. He might meet us in the middle, or he could have one of us, say Willie, go in first, then bring Katie closer to the entrance, then have me enter, and then release Katie after I'm well inside."

Mack paused and looked at the others for a response.

"You're both dead men if you go through with this, you know. You do know that, don't you?" Otis said.

They looked at each other. Willie responded. "Hell, I'm a dead man anyway. At least this way it's for a good cause."

"Wait a minute," Megan said. "I don't…I can't… Look, neither of you has to do this. Of course I want Katie back, but I don't…I have no right…to ask you to sacrifice your lives to save her. Besides, how do we know this Angel person will keep his word and let her go? He might kill her anyway."

Mack hadn't wanted to emphasize that possibility before, but Megan had obviously figured it out for herself. "Well, from my previous encounter with Angel, I think that he will want to keep his word and release Katie if he can. The problem is both you and Katie can identify him and his Mexican thugs, so even if Angel's willing to take his chances with being caught and identified later, in order to keep his word, which strangely I think he might be willing to do, I don't think the Mexicans will take that chance. They will insist on killing Katie…and you too, Megan. All of us, in fact. And I'm sure Ortiz will agree with them. He won't want any loose ends, like witnesses, left behind."

"So what should we do, then? None of us will survive unless…"

Megan couldn't say it, but Mack knew what she was thinking, because he had already thought of it himself, right from the start. "Unless we shoot it out with them. That's what you're thinking, right? Of course, if we do, you realize that Katie could die even if you survive. Are you willing to risk that?"

Megan hesitated. She was remembering that night in the Downbeat (My God! Was that just four days ago!) when Mack had asked her how she would feel if her own child had been raped and murdered. What had been her answer? She'd have to accept it, live with it. She wouldn't let it take over her life. Something like that.

But Megan's Irish temper was fired up now, and the protective rage of a mother bear for her cub was rising within her to its full height. Accept it like hell! She would not accept a deal with a murderer who would probably kill her child anyway. She would not accept that her child might die while she survived to mourn her. No! If Katie died, Megan would likewise die in the attempt to save her. There was no other way.

"There is only one choice, Mack. I have to take that risk!"

Mack nodded. "Okay. That's the way we'll play it. To the finish."

"Count me in on this, too," Otis said.

Mack gave Otis a long look, a hint of a smile on his face. "I never expected otherwise, partner."

"You hungry, cat?" Willie said to Ulysses, who had just jumped onto the seat beside him. A jungle growl was his answer. "Guess so." Willie laid a scrap of chicken on the seat, which Ulysses quickly scarfed down.

"Okay, then," Otis continued, "let's do a little figuring. We know that there are at least four of them, and we can assume that they're heavily armed, probably with automatic weapons, right?"

"Undoubtedly," Mack said. "So to even the odds we're going to need some heavier firepower than our 38s will provide. Any chance you could get some weapons from the arms wagon?"

A look from Otis. "Sure, and explain to the deputy chief that I need them... for what?"

"Just a thought. But we've got to get our hands on some heavy stuff one way or another."

"Right. The question is where. Even if we could find a gun store that's open at this hour, I'd have to show the owner some ID, which would reveal that I'm a cop. I think you'll agree that that might raise some eyebrows."

"And a possible phone call to police headquarters," Mack added. "Looks like we might just have to indulge in a little grand larceny, Otis."

"What? No way!"

"Wait a minute. How much money you dudes got?" Willie asked. "I mean cash money."

"About sixty-five dollars," Mack said.

Willie looked at Otis. "How about you?"

"Forty-two max. Why?"

Another howl from Ulysses. "Okay, cat, okay." Willie put a scrap of chicken on the seat, which Ulysses quickly devoured. "I know a bro who deals in hardware, and I'm not talkin' Ace Hardware. But it's strictly a cash and carry biz."

"Hey, there's a 24-hour currency exchange near headquarters where I cash my checks. How much are we talking here?"

"Depends on what you're buying."

"What do you think we need, Mack?" Otis said.

Mack took another sip of coffee. "An MP-5, a 20-gage pump shotgun and a hunting rifle with a night scope ought to cover any contingencies. And plenty of ammo."

"That oughta run two, maybe three C's per weapon," Willie said. Then to Otis: "Can you cash a check for that much?"

"Nine hundred? That's not chicken feed, but I think I can handle it, since they know me there and also know I'm a cop. However, I'd appreciate some help on this, assuming we're still among the living when this is over."

"Think positive, partner," Mack said. "I'm not planning on getting us killed. You're going to get your nine C's back, and I'll throw in a double martini as interest." Mack turned to Willie. "Where does your friend conduct his hardware business?"

"Not far from here. Got an auto repair biz on Stony Island. Don't know the phone number."

"I'll call information," Megan said. She removed her cell from a belt clip holder. "What's the name?"

"Andy's Auto Repair."

Megan got the number from information and let the operator put her through. After two rings a deep voice answered.

"Andy's Auto, Andy speaking."

"Just a minute," Megan said, and handed the cell to Willie.

"Hey, Preach, it's me, Willie. Willie Butler."

"Brother Butler. Well, now I haven't had the pleasure of talking with you for a long time. How are you doing? In good health, I hope."

"Doin' okay, Preach, but this isn't a social call. Got some dudes who got a rush order."

"A rush order. It's fortunate I was working late, my friend. What is it they require?"

Willie listed the weapons that Mack wanted.

"I believe I have all of those items in stock."

"How much, Preach?"

"Let's see. The customary price would be eight hundred, but seeing that they're friends of yours, I'll make it seven-fifty."

"Ammo included?"

"Agreed. When can you pick them up?"

"We can be there in about an hour and a half, two max."

"Use the alley entrance, and sound your horn three times. I'll be expecting you."

"Thanks, Preach." Willie beeped off and handed the cell to Megan. "Okay, we're in business. Seven-fifty, ammo included."

"Good work, Willie." Mack smiled. Then to everyone: "Now we've got the first requirement handled. However, in addition to the weapons, we're also going to need an edge. We can't just walk in there, guns blazing, like it was the OK Corral."

"What kind of edge?" Otis asked.

"Well, it would be nice if we had an idea where they're holding Katie, so we could drop in a little early to size up the situation."

"Wouldn't it? Fat chance of that happening though. Angel's obviously a very sharp cookie. He's not going to just give us an address and tell us to drop by when it's convenient. He won't tell us where he's hiding Katie until the last possible moment."

"Maybe, maybe not, but we may still get a break when he calls from something he says. He's got to give some instructions as to when and where we're supposed to go first. Maybe we'll get a clue from that. Anyway, you'd better get going asap. We've got to be as prepared as we can be when Megan gets his call."

"On my way. To save time, why don't I meet you at Andy's."

"Good idea. What's the address?

"Don't know the number," Willie said. "But it's on Stony between 70th and 71st."

Mack turned to Otis. "We'll take Megan's car and wait for you at the corner of Stony and 70th."

"Right."

Otis exited the RV and hurried over to his Cavalier. He was feeling a little better. At least they'd be armed with enough firepower to have a fighting chance —*if* they had an opportunity to use their weapons. That, however, was still a big *IF*.

*8:23 p.m.:* Bryant and Gallagher watched the small Boeing business jet descend. They were sharing an umbrella in a light drizzle beside their Taurus just off a tarmac of the Palwaukee Municipal Airport, where Bio-Sci kept its corporate jet. They'd agreed that the small airport in the northwest suburb of Prospect Heights was an ideal place for the Woman to fly to rather than the more congested, and very public, major airports of O'Hare and Midway.

"Wonder why she decided to come to Chicago?" Bryant said.

Gallagher had been asking himself the same question. "Beats me. Blackburn didn't confide that to me. Just for us to pick them up here."

"Which we're doing. Hold this, will you?" Bryant handed Gallagher the umbrella, took out a stick of chewing tobacco from his coat pocket and bit off a piece.

"Dammit, Rusty, do you have to do that now?" Chewing tobacco was another thing about Bryant that annoyed him. "I'd advise you to get rid of that shit before she gets into the car."

"So what's the big deal? Jesus!" Bryant took a few chews, just to annoy Gallagher. "Blackburn happen to tell you where they're staying by any chance? Like she can't exactly check in at the Ritz Carlton."

"Sharp, Rusty. Very sharp."

"Fuck you, too. One thing's for sure. Something big must be going down for her to take a chance like this."

Gallagher had already reached that obvious conclusion. "At least we have some good news for a change."

"Yeah, but I got to hand it to the cop, ya know. The dude is…"

"Yeah, yeah, don't tell me. Like your hero, John Wayne. Like I told you before, don't let your hero worship get in the way of doing your job."

"Right, sir, general, sir," Bryant said, his mock salute accompanied by a spit of tobacco-laced saliva.

Gallagher struggled to keep his irritation under control. He couldn't allow his dislike of Bryant to interfere with finishing their assignment, which thanks to McPherson seemed to be reaching critical mass. Perhaps that's why the Woman was coming here. To take charge personally, like a general moving from a command post to the front line. Well, they'd know soon enough. In any event, Gallagher had made up his mind that when this was over he was going to put in a strong request to be teamed with another partner, one who wasn't addicted to chewing tobacco or country western music.

These thoughts Gallagher kept to himself, while the jet made a perfect landing, taxied down the runway, and stopped a few yards away.

"I'll get her," Gallagher said.

"Guess I'm driving, as usual."

"Right. And ditch the tobacco."

"Yes, sir, general, sir," Bryant said, spitting out the wad.

Gallagher hurried to the door at the rear of the aircraft. A moment later the hydraulically controlled door pivoted down to reveal stairs on its inside. Blackburn exited the jet first, dressed as usual in an immaculate suit and tie.

"Be careful, Suzanne," he said. Taking the Woman's arm, he assisted her down the steps. "It's slippery."

"Thank you, David."

It had been a while since Gallagher had seen the Woman, but each time he did she made the same strong impression. Garbed in a navy suit, white blouse and walking shoes with small heels, her lovely face partially concealed by large dark glasses and a picture hat with its brim pulled down, she descended the steps like a runway model. However, unlike a model's phony smile, the Woman's smile was warm and genuine when she looked at him.

"Hello, Richard. Nice to see you again."

That was another thing he admired about her. No matter how small their jobs, she knew everybody by their first names and addressed them like friends rather than employees.

"The car's waiting, ma'am," he said, extending the umbrella over her head.

Gallagher escorted the Woman and Blackburn to the car and opened the rear door. The Woman entered first, then Blackburn. Gallagher closed the door, collapsed the umbrella and slid into the passenger seat beside Bryant, who already had the engine running.

"Where to, sir?" Bryant said.

Blackburn gave him an address in Barrington Hills. To get directions, Bryant consulted a GPS system on the dash before he gassed the Taurus. "It's not far. Just a few miles west of here."

Having spent some time in Chicago on previous assignments, Gallagher knew that Barrington Hills was a northwest suburb that rivaled any of the lush burbs along the North Shore. What Gallagher didn't know was that the address was the home of Roy O'Neal, who had suggested to Blackburn that the Woman stay there, since Helen, his wife, was away visiting her parents in San Diego. Blackburn understood O'Neal's desire to keep the Woman's visit a secret even from his wife. If things went wrong, O'Neal wanted Helen immune from what would be a catastrophic fallout and serious jail time for all concerned.

"Any news on McPherson?" Blackburn asked as the car turned onto Milwaukee Avenue.

"Yes, sir, there is," Gallagher said. "We still don't know where he is, but we have a lead on a man who probably does. Superintendent Hollender couldn't reach you on your cell while you were in flight, so he called us."

"Who is he?"

"Mark Jacobs. He's a TV reporter at WFFD."

"I know about Jacobs. He's no fan of McPherson. In fact, he's been on McPherson's case for a long time. So why didn't he inform the police if he knows where he is?"

"We have reason to believe he may be working with McPherson to expose the Project."

"I was afraid of something like this," the Woman said. "If the media gets involved…"

She didn't finish. She didn't have to. This was an unexpected development that they didn't need. "I think I can handle Jacobs, if it comes to that," Blackburn said, trying to downplay the news for the Woman's sake. Then to Gallagher: "How did the police find out about this?"

"A waiter at a restaurant where Jacobs hangs out believes he saw McPherson with Jacobs last night. It didn't register until he saw a film clip of

McPherson on the news this evening."

Blackburn nodded grimly. "It adds up. It looks like McPherson was talking to Jacobs, and Jacobs was listening."

The Woman put her hand on Blackburn's arm. "What do you think we should do, David?"

Blackburn could hear the sense of alarm in the Woman's voice, see it on her face. He took her hand in his. It was ice cold. "Look, Suzanne. Jacobs is smart enough to realize that he doesn't have a story without McPherson and the vagrant, Butler. Which means that we have to get them before he has a chance to break the story."

"Hollender already has his people bugging Jacobs's work and home phones," Gallagher said.

"That's fine, if he's stupid enough to use them instead of his cell, which he's not. What about putting a tail on Jacobs?"

"I was coming to that, sir. It's being taken care of. We also planted a GPS on his car."

"Good. Sooner or later Jacobs will have to get together with McPherson and Butler to tape an interview. When he does, we'll move in with a SWAT team."

The Woman gripped Blackburn's arm. "I told you no more killing, David! I mean it! No more!"

"I understand, Suzanne, but I can't control what will happen if McPherson resists."

"God willing he won't," the Woman said.

Blackburn could only hope she was right. In either event, being a chess player, he felt as if McPherson had put his queen, the Woman, in jeopardy of being checkmated. Blackburn also believed that the next move on this chess board of life and death was his, and he was more than aware that it could be his last.

*9:16 p.m.:* Otis was running late. Only one guy was manning the check-cashing place when Otis got there, and he had closed the store for 10 minutes to go to the bathroom. When Otis reached Stony Island Avenue, he goosed the Cavalier through the yellow off Cornell Drive onto the four-lane boulevard heading south. When he got to 69th Street, he moved into the right lane, then pulled up in back of Megan's Camry at 70th.

Megan saw him in the rearview and fired the engine. "Otis is here. Where to, Willie?"

"Take a right here, then a left at the alley," he said from the back seat.

Megan turned west onto 70th for half a block and swung the Camry into a narrow, trash littered alley that ran behind the buildings on Stony Island Avenue.

"Stop behind that garage door and sound the horn three times," Willie said.

Megan did and cut the engine.

"Stay in the car, Megan," Mack said, as he and Willie exited the Camry. "This won't take long."

"What if Angel calls?"

"Hit the horn."

Otis braked behind the Camry, got out and joined Mack and Willie. "I thought we were expected. So where's your friend Andy, or was it Preach?"

"One and the same. Everyone calls him Preach, 'cause he was studying to be a minister before he got drafted and served two tours in Nam."

Preach must have strayed far from the flock since then, Mack thought. He was about to tell Megan to sound the horn again when the garage door began to rattle up.

A burly black man shambled out of the garage. He was wearing grimy coveralls and a Chicago White Sox baseball cap, a stubble of graying whiskers on a pious looking face that reminded Otis of Pastor Rogers, the minister of the church his mother insisted he attend as a boy. He also had a deep voice which Otis was certain could be heard from the rear of a church without the need of an amplifier.

"Delighted to see you again, Brother Butler," he said as he embraced Willie in a bear hug.

"Hey, Preach. You're lookin' good. How's biz?"

"Fine, Brother Butler, just fine, thanks to the Good Lord." Then to Mack and Otis. "Welcome, brothers, to my humble place of business. But if you don't mind my inquiring, why does Mr. John Law require my services?"

Mack smiled. Preach didn't need an introduction to know that Otis and he were cops. "Let's just say that we're moonlighting, Preach."

"It's okay, Preach," Otis said. "This visit is strictly unofficial."

"Well, seeing as you're friends of Brother Butler, I'm inclined to conclude our business transaction. If you'll follow me…"

Preach led the way into a garage pungent with the odor of oil, grease and gasoline past a dilapidated car on a lift to a tool chest. "I assume you have the agreed-upon remuneration?"

"Seven hundred and fifty dollars," Otis said.

"Excellent, Brother," Preach said. He opened a drawer and removed an MP-5 semi-automatic from a variety of tools.

"I'll take the MP-5," Mack said.

Preach handed Mack the weapon. "And the remuneration?"

Otis took a bulging manila envelope from his pocket and laid it on top of the chest. "Want to count it?"

"That will not be necessary. Brother Butler's word is more than sufficient."

Mack examined the MP-5. "Looks good. How about the rest?"

Preach opened another drawer. "One Remington twenty-gage pump shotgun, as specified."

"You get the shotgun, Otis," Mack said with a little smile. "I figure you can't miss with that."

Otis removed the shotgun from the drawer. "I'm overwhelmed by your confidence in me."

"It would appear that you get the last item, Brother Butler," Preach said. He took a Remington .30 caliber hunting rifle with a scope from another drawer and handed it to Willie.

Willie hefted the rifle. In a way it was like saying hello to an old friend. One problem, however. His old friend's scope was not a night scope, which Willie pointed out to Preach.

"My apologies, Brother Butler. Unfortunately, this is the only one I have in stock at the moment. I hope it will suffice."

"Guess it'll have to." Willie pushed the butt of the rifle into his right armpit and took aim at an imaginary target through the scope.

"Think you can get the job done without a night scope, Willie?" Mack asked.

Willie lowered the rifle. "Hey, man, I was a scout sniper in Nam, remember?"

Yeah, Mack thought, but did he still have the skill of his former trade? It had been a lot of years and a hell of a lot of booze since Willie made his last one shot, one kill.

"What about the ammo, Preach?" Willie asked.

Preach gestured to a metal ammunition container on the floor. "There should be more than enough there to satisfy your requirements."

"One item we forgot to order," Mack said. "Do you happen to have a silencer for the rifle?"

Preach removed the baseball cap, scratched a curly crop of salt and pepper hair. "Well, I don't know, Brother. Not much call for silencers. Let me look around a little."

"Why the silencer?" Otis asked, while Preach rummaged through some drawers.

Willie answered the question for Mack. "Just in case we have to take someone out without announcing our arrival."

"You're in luck, Brothers," Preach said, producing a silencer from a drawer. "Of course, I should charge you for this, but I'm inclined to make you a gift of it out of the goodness of my heart."

Willie took the silencer. "Thanks, Preach."

A horn blared in the alley; Megan's cell phone was beeping. She answered. "Yes?"

Angel's voice. "Are Detective McPherson and the vagrant, Butler, with you?"

"They're with me."

"Good. Now listen closely. There is a 7-Eleven at the corner of Pratt Street and Glenwood. Can you be there in an hour?"

"I don't know. Hold on."

"It's Angel," Megan said to Mack, who had hurried over with the others. "He wants to know if we can be at Pratt Street and Glenwood in an hour. Do you know where that is?"

"Yeah. It's in the Rogers Park area, forty-five minutes to an hour drive, maybe more depending on traffic. Let's cut ourselves some slack. Tell him it'll take us an hour and a half. He doesn't know where we're starting from."

"We can be there in an hour and a half," Megan said into the cell.

"Alright. It's now nine thirty-three. I expect you to be in the parking lot at eleven. I assume you will be driving your Camry?"

"Yes. Is that where you'll bring Katie?"

"No. You are to wait there for further instructions."

"What about my little girl? I want to know if Katie is alright. That you haven't harmed her."

"A reasonable request. Would you like to speak with her?"

"Yes, oh, yes!"

"One moment."

Katie's voice. "Mommy, Mommy!"

"Yes, dear. It's Mommy. Are you all right, dear?"

"Yes, but I'm scared, Mommy. The man said you are coming to get me. Are you coming, Mommy?"

"Yes, dear. Mommy is coming," Megan said, tears welling in her eyes.

"Please, hurry, Mommy! Please! I'm so scared!"

"I'll hurry, dear. I'll be there soon. I love you!"

Angel's voice again. "You see, Senora Herbst, it is as I promised. Your child is safe and will remain so as long as you do as you are told."

"I will, I will."

"That is good. *Adios*."

"What's the story, Megan?" Mack asked. "Do we do the exchange there?"

"No. We're to wait in the parking lot of a 7-Eleven. He said he'd call with further instructions."

"What do you think that means, Mack?" Otis said.

"They're playing it safe. They want to make sure we don't have an escort of blue and whites. One of them will probably check us out, then report back to the others before Angel makes the call to tell us where they have Katie."

"Could be they got her someplace close by," Willie said.

"That's more than likely," Mack said.

"Well, at least that narrows the field," Otis said. "Anyone got any brilliant ideas where that might be?"

"Could be anywhere, but most likely it's an empty house or building. Let's load up and get going. Put the weapons and ammo in Otis's car."

Megan watched them load the weapons into the trunk of the Cavalier with a feeling of dread. She'd seen such weapons so many times in movies and TV programs with the accompanying violence, but that was make-believe. This was different. This was real. For the first time she could appreciate how her dad must have felt before he went into combat. How Mack, Otis and Willie must be feeling right now.

"Let me help you with that," Otis said to Preach, who had picked up the ammo container.

"Thanks, but never mind. In my business I've lifted heavier."

No doubt, Otis judged. He wasn't even breathing hard as he carried what would normally take two men to handle.

"Couldn't help hearing what the young lady was saying," he said, as he lowered the container into the trunk. "Her little girl, she's in bad trouble?"

"Very bad, Preach," Otis said. "She's been abducted by killers."

Preach gestured to the trunk full of weapons. "Looks like you got yourselves a fight on your hands."

Mack closed the trunk. "It could get a little nasty."

The understatement of the year, Otis thought.

"Well, you take care, Brother Butler," Preach said, giving Willie another hug.

"Shit, Preach, I been there before."

"So you have, Brother, but I'll be asking the Lord to watch your back."

"Thanks, Preach."

"Let's get moving," Mack said with a glance at his wrist watch.

"Hold on a minute," Otis said. "If you don't mind my asking…what's the plan?"

"Willie and I will go with Megan to the 7-Eleven and wait for Angel's call. You follow us but park a block away until we find out where they're keeping Katie."

"Then what?"

"I'm working on it."

"Some plan," Otis said, and hurried to his car.

Mack scrunched into the Camry beside Megan, while Willie got into the rear seat. Megan was about to start the engine when she saw the man they called Preach standing outside her open window.

"Don't you worry, Sister. Your little girl, she's going to be just fine."

"I hope so."

"You got to trust in the Lord, Sister. I'm going to go to my church just as soon as I close up here and I'm going to ask the good Lord to protect her and keep her safe."

"Thank you. I appreciate that."

She'll need all of the Lord's help she can get, Otis thought, as he got behind the wheel of the Cavalier. All of us will. Maybe they should all go to church, like Preach, and ask for the Lord's blessing, before they took on Angel and friends. That's what his mother would have said. He could hear her voice now as she rousted him out of bed every Sunday morning when he was a kid. "You get yourself out of that bed, Otis Winstrom, and you get yourself dressed in a suit and tie 'cause you is going to church!"

"Jesus!"

Otis sounded the horn, jumped out of the car and ran over to the Camry.

"What is it, Otis?" Megan said. Otis's face looked as if he'd just won the lottery.

"You said the place we're going is in Rogers Park, right?"

"That's right." Mack said. "Why?"

"I think I know where they've got Katie!"

A dubious look from Mack, astonishment from Megan and Willie.

"Look, this Angel guy has a thing about churches that goes back to his being raped by a priest when he was a kid, right? And he also tried to kill you in a church."

"Yeah. So?"

"Well, it might be a coincidence, but there's a Catholic church in Rogers Park that's a hot local news item. It's empty, falling apart, so the Archdiocese of Chicago wants to raze it rather than spend big bucks to restore it. But there's a Rogers Park Coalition that's bugging the mayor to have it preserved at the city's expense as a landmark."

A pause as the others absorbed this.

"What do you think, Mack?" Megan said.

"I think my partner just got us the edge we needed."

*10:10 p.m.:* Mack's jaw ached with tension. Construction on North Lake Shore Drive had traffic crawling on two of the four lanes, and they had only fifty minutes to get to the church and check it out to see if that's where they had Katie, and then get back to the 7-Eleven.

"Get off at Irving Park," Mack said. "Then we'll take Marine Drive until we pass the construction area."

"Alright," Megan said. "Do you think we'll make it on time?"

"We've got to make it."

It took another three minutes for them to reach the Irving Park exit ramp, which was also clogged with vehicles. Megan had to wait for the green before she could turn west and pass under the Drive to another red at Marine Drive, which bordered Lake Shore Drive. With no oncoming cars close, Megan swung the Camry through the red onto Marine Drive and gave it gas. Fortunately, there wasn't much traffic, and she was able to breeze through two stop signs without making any serious effort to slow down.

"Is Otis still with us, Willie?" Mack said.

Willie looked out of the rear window. "Yeah. Ridin' our ass, so don't go makin' no quick stops."

Let's hope, Megan thought. "Do you know where the church is, Mack?"

"Yeah. It's not far from Pratt and Glenwood, which makes it an even safer bet that that's where they have Katie. Goose it!"

Mack was referring to the light at Montrose, the next major intersection, which was flashing from green to yellow.

Megan did.

Otis white-knuckled the steering wheel. Megan had made it through the yellow, but he had to floor the accelerator to miss an SUV that was turning north off Montrose. Close! Keep taking chances like this, he thought, and they may not make it to the church at all. Not that they had any other options, thanks to the damned construction on the Drive that had them running behind schedule.

At least the traffic on Marine Drive was light, but Otis could only hope that no patrol cops were around to clock them doing sixty plus in a 35 m.p.h. speed zone. They made the green at Wilson and sped around a lumbering CTA bus in time for Otis to avoid a head-on with an oncoming car.

Looking over at Lake Shore Drive, Otis saw that they had passed the construction area. Megan and Mack had obviously observed this as well, because at the next entrance opportunity at Lawrence Avenue, Megan slowed for the red, then turned right as the light flashed green. Otis followed the Camry under Lake Shore Drive, then made a sharp left and continued up the entrance ramp onto the Drive.

Although traffic was moving swiftly again, Otis was forced to keep a heavy foot on the pedal to keep up with Megan, who was weaving the Camry through the flow of vehicles with considerable skill. A glance at the speedometer showed the needle quivering at 72. We might just make it after all, Otis thought…if I live that long.

*10:21 p.m.:* Angel offered Katie another French fry.

"Thank you," the little girl said.

Angel gazed down at her angelic face, eerily illuminated by the moonlight issuing through the narrow, lancet windows, their only source of light other than a flashlight they had taken from the van. How polite, Angel thought. Even though she had to be terrified, she still thanked him for the food. So like his little sister, Jaunita. Pretty and sweet. He was sitting next to her in the rear pew of the nave, just as he had done with Juanita so many years ago in the *Templo Iglesia del Sagrado Corazon.*

"Would you like the rest?"

"Don't you want any?"

"No. I'm not hungry."

Which was true, Angel thought, handing Katie the small container of French fries. He'd hardly touched the coffee, burgers and fries that they'd picked up at a McDonald's on their way to the church. Julio and Carlos were wolfing down their food in a pew across the aisle, while Andres kept watch in the bell tower.

Angel's stomach churned. His plan to save the *nina* and the Senora Herbst by withholding money to the pigs had not worked. They had threatened to kill him if he didn't pay them. He might get one of them in a shoot-out, but surely die in the attempt. To make matters worse, when Ortiz called him to tell him where to take their captives, he made it clear that he wanted them killed along with the vagrant and the cop. Ortiz had not prescribed how it should be done. He did not care about that. The pigs had their own ghastly plans. Angel had heard them arguing about who would have the pleasure of raping the *nina* and her mother before they slit their throats. Carlos had insisted that he get the *nina*. Julio and Andres could have the Senora Herbst. They had drunk to the prospect from a bottle of tequila.

However, if Angel could not prevent their deaths, he could decide how they would die. He would not allow them to be raped and butchered by the slobbering Carlos and his swine *amigos*. He would use his Magnum on the Senora Herbst first. Then he would cradle the *nina* in his arms and release her spirit with one bullet to the back of her head. And as he pulled the trigger, he would pray for Jesus to accept her soul and take her straight to Heaven.

Angel took a sip of coffee, swallowed hard. When Ortiz had ordered him to abduct the *nina*, he should have refused, even at the risk of having Ortiz put a contract on him. Ortiz! *Que animal*! Angel had never had any qualms about the people who had employed him before. In fact, he'd never given them any thought. He did his job, took the money, and that was that. But with Ortiz it was different. To Angel, notwithstanding his wealth, refinement and charm, Ortiz was worse than the three pigs. Ortiz could order the death of someone as casually as if he was ordering dessert at some gourmet restaurant, and not dirty his hands in the deed. Except for the detective. For some reason, Ortiz wanted to kill McPherson himself. For sport, perhaps. The thrill of performing the act personally. In any event, Ortiz had instructed him to keep McPherson alive until he got there.

Easier said than done, Angel thought. He had no delusions that McPherson and the vagrant would just walk in with their hands up. At least Ortiz had steered them to a good place to keep the *nina*. From the bell tower of the condemned church, Andres would be able to see if McPherson, the vagrant and the Senora Herbst were alone and unarmed when they arrived. Of course, they could be carrying concealed weapons, but they would not risk using them. Not with Angel's Magnum pressed against the *nina's* head.

Angel felt Katie's hand tugging at his sleeve.

"Is my mommy coming soon?"

Angel glanced at his wrist watch. The luminous hands showed 10:25 p.m.

"Yes, *nina*. She will be here soon."

"Why do you call me *nina*? My name is Katie."

"I know. *Nina* in my language means little girl."

"I'm not a little girl. I'm six years old."

Six years old, Angel thought. Juanita was six years old the last time he saw her.

"Will you call me 'Katie'?"

"Yes, Katie."

"What is your name?"

"People call me Angel."

"Angel? Like the angels in Heaven?"

"No. I'm...I'm a fallen Angel."

"Fallen Angel? Fallen from where?"

"Just fallen."

"I fell once, off a swing. It hurt awful. Did it hurt you?"

"Just for a little while."

Which was true. Angel hadn't felt that pain for a long time. But he was feeling it now.

*10:28 p.m.:* Megan pumped the brake. Traffic had halted for the red light where Lake Shore Drive ninety-degreed and ended at Sheridan Road.

"Should I take Hollywood or Sheridan?" Megan asked Mack.

Mack looked ahead, saw that traffic was somewhat congested on Hollywood Drive, which ran west. "Take Sheridan."

When the light turned green, Megan followed a line of vehicles making right turns onto Sheridan Road, got into the left lane and promptly exceeded the speed limit.

"How far is Pratt?" she said, her eyes glued on the road and other vehicles.

"Not far. Watch that cycle."

Megan sounded the horn at a burly man with tattooed arms, who had swerved his Harley in front of her, and got a raised third finger in response. "Asshole!" Megan leaned on the horn, which at least encouraged the cyclist to increase speed. They both breezed through a green at Cermak, but had to stop for a red light where Sheridan doglegged past Loyola University.

The cyclist stopped and was about to get off his Harley to confront them.

"We've got no time for this jerk," Mack said.

Mack pointed his service revolver at the biker, who took one startled look and zoomed off right through the red light.

"Stay on Sheridan," Mack said, answering Megan's question before she could ask if they should do that or head west on Devon Avenue.

Megan made the turn before the light changed and accelerated. There were no stops until they reached Pratt and a green light. With no oncoming cars close, Megan nudged the brake and hung a sharp left.

"How far now?"

"Just up the street."

Megan continued west on Pratt. Ahead she could see a CTA train speeding over a viaduct that bridged Pratt.

"Slow down," Mack said. "Glenwood is on the other side of the el."

Megan pressured the brake as they passed under the viaduct. The 7-Eleven was on the northwest corner.

"Pull into the lot."

Megan swung the Camry into the nearly empty lot that fronted the 7-Eleven and parked. Otis and the Cavalier were beside them a moment later. Mack opened the door and got out, as did Willie.

"Wait here, Megan, while we check out the church."

"There's not much time."

"I know. I'll call you when we know something more."

"Please hurry!"

Willie jumped into the rear seat of the Cavalier. Mack got in beside Otis, and Otis gunned the car out of the lot.

*10:35 p.m.:* Ortiz waited outside Gibson's Steakhouse for the valet to bring his car. He'd rented the Buick Century earlier at a Hertz agency on Lake Street with the intention of being at the church when McPherson and the others arrived. Not inside, but parked somewhere close where he could observe what happened without being seen. If things went according to plan, he would be able to get to the church quickly and pay his respects to McPherson before he killed him with the MP-5 in his briefcase.

For the moment Ortiz was basking in the afterglow of the espresso and brandy that climaxed a delicious supper of escargot, lobster and lime sorbet at Gibson's, a four star restaurant on Rush Street, where he'd spent the last two hours. As he watched two gorgeous young ladies exit a cab and enter the bistro, he couldn't help wishing that he had nothing more to do tonight but engage in some stalking of another kind. The bar was active with unescorted ladies, easy conquests all.

Perhaps he would return to the bar later. He'd always experienced an intense sexual stimulation after a kill, which is why he took his lady companion at the time with him on safaris. McPherson being his first human quarry, he could only imagine how aroused he would be after this kill. Ortiz regretted again not bringing Rosita with him to share this sexual high. It would not be as fulfilling with a stranger.

His thoughts were interrupted by the Century pulling up at the curb. The valet, a young black man, jumped out and held the door open. Ortiz tipped him with a ten dollar bill, put the briefcase onto the passenger seat and slid behind the wheel. A glance at the dash clock—10:36 p.m. According to Angel, whom he'd called earlier with routing instructions, he had plenty of time to get to the church.

"Thank you, sir, and have a good night," the valet said before closing the door.

Ortiz smiled as he pulled away. A good night was exactly what he anticipated.

*10:38 p.m.:* Otis saw the pizza van first.

"There it is."

"Slow down," Mack said, as they passed the van, which was parked amidst other vehicles strung along the curb just up the block from the church. "We're only going to get one chance to check out the church, and we can't afford to miss anything."

"I won't miss anything," Willie said. "Us snipers were taught to recon and retain like we was a camera."

"Well, I hope your night vision is just as sharp," Otis said. "This street is as dark as a tomb."

"I'll make out," Willie said. But Otis had a point. The single street light in the middle of the block didn't provide much illumination. Fortunately, it had stopped raining, so there was some light from the full moon when it wasn't obscured by the scudding clouds.

Otis toed the brake as they approached the church, reducing the speed to ten miles per hour, as if he was looking for a parking space. Thanks to an art appreciation course he'd taken at I.U., Otis recognized the church as a traditional Gothic structure, with the arch-roofed nave flanked in front by twin, lantern bell towers. Since he was the driver, Otis didn't have much time to observe more than the gated court on one side of the church, a parsonage on the other and the chains and padlocks securing the three large front doors under an oculus. Yellow caution tape and a large sign fronted the church. The sign read, "WARNING! TRESSPASSERS WILL BE PROSECUTED! THE CITY OF CHICAGO."

"Pull around the corner and park," Mack said after they had passed the church.

Otis made a right at the intersection and curbed the Cavalier in front of a "NO PARKING FROM HERE TO CORNER" sign, where they could still observe the church at a safe distance.

"Okay, so now that we know where they are, do we hit them now?" Otis said.

Mack shook his head. "Not unless we want to be spotted by whoever they probably have as a lookout in one of the bell towers and walk into a firing squad."

"I see what you mean. They made a good choice when they picked the church. And with the front doors sealed, we don't even know how to get in."

"Same way they did," Willie said. "A small section of the wall must have collapsed. It's boarded up now, except for a place where they must have pried open an entrance."

"No shit? You saw that?" Otis said.

"Yeah. It's on the court side near the rear."

"Good job, Willie," Mack said. "You wouldn't happen to know which tower their man is in?"

"Yeah. He's in the one next to the court."

Mack was dubious. The only thing he'd seen in the apertures of the towers was total blackness. "How do you know?"

"The dude lit up a cigarette. I saw the flare of the match. I guess you want me to take him out so you can get in without being spotted."

"Yeah. But you'll need to have a place for a decent shot."

"How about the roof of that apartment building?" Otis said.

"That's what I had in mind," Willie said.

Mack agreed. Not only was it across the street from the church, its four stories made it the tallest building on the street, the others being bungalows and two flats.

"Might be a good idea to wait 'till one of them goes to the 7-Eleven," Willie said. "One less to have to mess with."

"Won't work," Mack said. "They're wired. As soon as he sees we're not there, he'll alert the others and probably kill Megan on the spot."

Willie nodded. "Didn't know they was wired."

"We've got to be with Megan when their guy shows. We'll have a window of opportunity between the time he reports back and whatever time they want us to be at the church."

"That's cuttin' it close," Willie said. "If this mission is gonna come off, I got to have enough time to get up on that roof and set up."

"You'll have enough time if we change places," Otis said. "Chances are if I'm wearing your fatigue jacket and hat, he'll take me for you."

"Good idea," Mack said. "Let's get you up there, Willie. There should be a fire escape in the rear."

Otis already had the Cavalier moving. Turning right into an alley, he pulled up next to the fire escape behind the apartment building. Willie and Otis got out and shed their jackets. Otis put on Willie's fatigue jacket and hat, while Willie removed the hunting rifle from the trunk, then stuffed his pants pockets with .30 caliber bullets.

"How do we stay in touch?" Willie asked.

Otis handed Willie his phone. "Use my cell. Mack's number is speed dial number 'two' on my phone. Just press 'two' and hold it."

"Right."

"Call me when you see their guy leave," Mack said to Willie, who was already starting up the fire escape. "And put the phone on vibrate."

"Okay."

"And Willie."

Willie paused, looked down. "Yeah?"

"When the time comes to make the shot, don't miss!"

*10:43 p.m.:* Angel looked at his wrist watch again.

"Julio. It is time to go," he said, his voice echoing in the empty nave.

Julio spat out a curse. "I have not finished eating."

Or drinking, Angel thought with contempt. He and Carlos were now sharing a bottle of tequila as they finished their food. How stupid. They would need to be sharp tonight if McPherson put up a fight. On the other hand, perhaps it would give them the courage that a fight would also require.

"Take the food with you."

Julio mumbled another curse, slid out of the pew. Shoving the remains of a hamburger into his mouth, he moved to the front of the nave and exited between an opening in the boards covering the hole in the wall.

"Is he going to get my mommy?" Katie asked.

"No. Your mother will come for you after he returns."

"I miss her so much. Do you miss your mommy, too?"

For a moment Angel couldn't respond. The question was unexpected and one he had suppressed from asking himself until now. "Yes, *nina.* I miss her."

"Where does she live? Is she far away?"

"Yes. She lives in Mexico."

"Oh. That *is* far away. I know where Mexico is. I learned it in school."

"You are a very smart little girl."

"Why don't you go see her?"

"Perhaps I will…someday."

Someday, he thought. If only to tell her that he loved her and to ask her to forgive him. The same day that he would return to the church where he had been defiled to seek the forgiveness of the Christ figure. As he steeled himself for what he must do this night, he was thinking that day could not come soon enough.

*10:45 p.m.:* Mack answered his beeping cell phone.

"Yeah, Willie?"

"One of them just left the church. Are you at the 7-Eleven?"

"We just pulled into the lot."

"When do I take out the guy in the tower?"

"Not until we get into position to move in."

"How about using the same place we parked before?"

"As good a place as any. We'll leave here after their man checks us out. Keep the line open and let me know when he gets back."

"Roger."

Mack and Otis exited the Cavalier and got into the Camry, Mack beside Megan, Otis on the rear seat.

"Where's Willie?" Megan said.

"I'm Willie, at least for now," Otis said.

Mack told Megan about the lookout in the bell tower who had to be killed if they were to have any chance at surprising Katie's abductors.

"One of them is on his way here now in the van to make sure we're playing by the rules. Otis and I will go back to the church as soon as he leaves."

"What about me?"

"Sit tight and wait for Angel's call. He'll give you the location of the church and when to be there, which will probably be a matter of minutes. So keep him talking as long as possible. Buy as much time for us as you can."

"Alright, but I'm not staying here. I'm going with you. My little girl needs me!"

Mack realized that it would be useless to try and reason with Megan about this. "Alright, but you stay at a safe distance. And Megan…if we can't bring this off, you get the hell out of there and call 911."

Can't bring this off? Megan thought. That was a nice way of saying that they might not be able to save Katie, or for that matter their own lives.

"That's the deal if you want to come along. Will you promise to do that?"

"Yes." But Megan was wondering if she'd have the will to go on living if Katie died.

"We got company," Otis said.

Mack and Megan saw the pizza van approaching on Glenwood. The van stopped at the intersection. Mack could make out a Mexican with a bald head behind the wheel.

The van didn't move for at least thirty seconds. Looking us over good, Mack thought. After a few more seconds the van turned onto Pratt and headed west.

"Think he bought into my act?" Otis said.

"We'll know soon enough," Mack said, opening the door. "Let's go."

*10:47 p.m.:* Willie felt his old jungle stalking instincts returning. The feeling and the shot of adrenalin it gave him helped compensate for the exhaustion of climbing the fire escape four stories to the roof of the apartment building. Lying prone on the roof, Otis's cell phone at his side, Willie affixed the silencer to the muzzle of the hunting rifle. He rested the barrel on the small ledge along the edge of the roof to support the weapon and help him keep it steady.

Willie peered over the ledge at the left bell tower. He couldn't have asked for a better vantage point: although the tower was at a slight angle to his position, it was about the same height as the apartment building and less than 100 feet away. On a clear night the full moon would have provided ample light for him to make out the figure in the tower, but not now. Tonight the moon's light was almost completely extinguished by a dense blanket of dark clouds. Willie didn't have a night scope, and for as long as the weather didn't cooperate, taking out his target would be difficult at best and impossible at worst. Even when the clouds thinned momentarily, there was not enough light for Willie to make the shot, even with his keen night vision.

Willie started at the sound of an approaching car. Stay calm, he told himself, as he leaned over the ledge to peer down at the street. The pizza van was parking in the same space it had vacated. Willie picked up the cell phone and speed-dialed Mack.

"He's back. Are you guys in position?"

"We're almost there. You all set?"

"All set."

"Keep on the line. I'll tell you when to pull the trigger."

"Roger."

Willie watched the thin, baldheaded Mexican move toward the church. Aware that his heart was pounding, Willie took some deep breaths. Got to keep calm, he told himself. Got to keep deadly calm if he was to take the most important shot of his life.

*10:51 p.m.:* Angel exited the pew to greet Julio.

"Are you sure they were alone?"

"Yes."

"No police cars in the vicinity?"

"I saw none. It is as you expected."

"Perhaps," Angel said, but he was thinking that, with McPherson, it would be wise to expect the unexpected. "Check your watch. You too, Carlos."

"*Si, patron*," Carlos said, his voice heavy with sarcasm and tequila.

"It is now ten fifty-one. I am going to call the Senora Herbst and tell her to be here at exactly eleven ten. So take your positions."

Julio nodded, started to move away.

"Julio. The keys."

Julio turned. "What?"

"The keys to the van."

Julio sneered and tossed the keys to Angel.

Carlos laughed, took a final pull at the tequila and slid out of the pew with his AK-47. "The *patron*, he does not trust you, *mi amigo*. But Carlos, he trusts you."

Angel doubted it. "You have the flashlight?"

"I have it." Carlos pulled a flashlight from the pocket of his windbreaker and followed Julio down the aisle.

"Andres," Angel said into the mini mike clipped to the breast pocket of his suit coat. "You were listening?"

Andres's voice in Angel's wireless earpiece: "*Si*. I heard all."

"They will be here in nineteen minutes. Stay alert."

Angel sat down in the pew beside Katie.

"Is my mommy coming now?"

"Yes, Katie. I am going to call your mother now to come and get you."

"Oh, I'm so glad. I want to go home so much."

Angel reached down to stroke Katie's head. Strange, he thought. It was just as he had done with his little sister, Juanita, when she had come to him for comfort after being scolded by their mother.

"I know you do. Do not worry, Katie. You will be home soon."

Yes, he thought, as he pulled out his cell phone. She would be home soon. But not her earthly home. A new home. A home in Heaven, with the angels.

*10:53 p.m.:* Otis loaded the Remington 12-gage pump shotgun.

"Take some extra rounds," Mack said, removing the MP-5 and two ammo clips from the trunk of the Cavalier.

"Right."

Otis grabbed a handful of 2-3/4 inch Magnum shells from the ammo container and stuffed them into the pockets of his suit coat. He tried to keep his mind focused on the "mission," as Willie called it, not on his rapid heartbeat and parched throat. From their position around the corner he could see the church bathed in thin moonlight one moment, then concealed in almost total darkness when the thick blanket of dark clouds pulled its cover over the moon once again, hiding its light.

"Óne minor problem occurred to me," he said. "With no night scope how are we going to know if Willie made a sure kill?"

"We won't," Mack said. "We just have to hope he comes through."

Hope? Otis thought. How about a few prayers? Megan's hand on his shoulder let him know that she had sensed he was scared shitless.

"I want to thank both of you for doing this."

Mack was also aware of how Otis felt. "It's okay, Otis."

"What's okay?"

"Being scared."

"Don't tell me you're scared, too?"

"Are you kidding? Every time. It might help you to know that once the shooting starts you'll be so busy you won't have time to be scared."

"I'll try to find some comfort in that."

Megan's cell phone was beeping.

Mack hefted the MP-5. "Keep him talking, Megan." Then to Otis: "Showtime, partner. Now it's up to Willie."

Willie sighted through the scope of the hunting rifle.

"Okay, Charlie," he whispered. "Come on and give me a good look at you."

But Charlie wasn't cooperating. Thanks to the moonlight, Willie could see him moving about between the apertures of the bell tower. Restless, Willie thought. Probably keyed up in anticipation of killing Mack and him, Megan and her little girl as well, or worse. Well, Charlie, there was no way that was going to happen. I got a .32 caliber bullet with your name on it. Just give me a chance to deliver it.

It helped for Willie to think of the Mexican thug as Charlie, the GI nickname for the Viet Cong, as if he was still in Nam, doing his thing as a scout sniper. Willie could feel his confidence building, and for a moment he was back in the Mekong Delta, merged with the undergrowth, three hundred yards from a long abandoned house of a rubber plantation that the VC brass had occupied as a temporary CP. All night he had lain there with his Remington 700, at least seven hours, chewed on by insects, his tiger suit drenched with perspiration, even his own urine, as he didn't risk moving even to rig a piss tube, waiting for an opportunity to zap one of the Charlie big shots.

He didn't get that opportunity until the first rays of sunlight filtered through the canopy of pines and broadleaf trees. The VC were stirring, preparing to move out—Charlie was always on the move—when the big shots came out of the house onto the veranda. Willie panned the scope, seeking out the senior officer. Be damned! The dude was a general! Now all he needed was a chance for a clean shot. He got it while the general paused to give an order to his officers. It was the last order he would ever give. Willie put a bullet between the two stars on his hat, then got the hell out of there as all hell broke loose.

It was a major kill that got a Silver Star pinned to the breast pocket of his fatigue jacket. He'd hocked the medal long ago to buy a quart of gin. Now he wished he still had that medal. He wished he had a lot of things he'd pissed away during all those years on the street, especially his self-respect. Well, maybe tonight's mission would restore some of that self-respect.

However, Willie still had to take out Charlie in the bell tower for the mission to have any chance of success. Time was of the essence to bring it off, but the asshole was still moving about, not giving him the opportunity for a clean shot. Willie had waited seven hours for the chance to kill the general. Tonight he'd be lucky to have seven minutes.

Angel was apprehensive. The Herbst woman had asked twice for directions to the church. She had also insisted on speaking with Katie again to make sure she was alright. That's what she said. But was she only stalling for time? And if she was, why?

Angel spoke into the mini mike. "Andres."

"*Si.*"

"Any sign of the Herbst woman's Camry?"

"No. Why do you ask? It is not yet time."

"Just keep a sharp lookout."

Angel hoped Andres would do more than that. He hoped the pig would not run from a fight if it came to that. With an addict like Andres, you never knew.

Andres moved restlessly between the apertures of the bell tower.

"Keep a sharp lookout," he muttered. "*Pendejo!* What do you think I am doing?"

However, Andres had to admit that his *pendejo patron* might have observed that he was a quivering jumble of raw nerves. He needed a fix and he needed it bad. There had been no time to get one before they snatched the Herbst woman's little bitch, and now he was paying for it. When this was over he would use the rest of the money he would get to go on a binge of drugs, women and tequila until the money was gone.

First there was this job to finish. Kill the *gringos*, but not before he and Julio raped the Herbst bitch. Her *nina* they would leave for Carlos. Carlos would get great pleasure from the act. Had he not bragged many times about raping his own little sister? And when it was over, their soft, white throats would feel the caress of their knives. The knife had been his favorite weapon since he was a boy, when he had used it to slit the throats of the chickens his *peon* Padre had raised on his one-acre dirt farm.

He was thinking about that now when the sound of a car motor made him jump. Looking out of a side aperture, he saw a car approaching from the south. There was just enough moonlight for him to see that it was a red car, like the Herbst woman's Camry. But was it the Camry? Andres moved quickly to a front aperture and peered down as the car passed the church.

Willie cursed. Charlie had finally given him a good look. Willie had him in the crosshairs of the scope, his finger about to squeeze off a round, when suddenly the moon went dark again. Charlie was now only a vague form, Willie eased up on the trigger, looked up and cursed again. With the sky covered once more by a dense blanket of clouds, there was no place for the moon's light to penetrate.

Hearing the distant rumble of thunder and feeling the first drops of rain, Willie realized that sure kill or not he should have taken the shot. Barring a miracle, it was probably the last chance he would get.

Otis looked at his wrist watch.

"Dammit, why haven't we heard from Willie?"

"The weather," Mack said. "Or haven't you noticed that we just ran out of moonlight again?"

"I noticed. But we're also running out of time. It's almost eleven, which leaves us with only ten minutes to make our move."

"I know that."

"So how much longer can we wait?"

"We'll give Willie two more minutes."

"Then what?"

"We go in anyway."

Go into what, Otis thought? A hail of bullets, in all likelihood.

"If you don't mind my asking, you didn't happen to have one of those bad dreams of yours last night, did you?" Otis asked.

"If it will make you feel better, the answer is no."

Otis felt better. But not much.

Andres resumed pacing. The fucking car was not the Camry. But why should it be? They weren't due for another ten minutes. But Andres had to admit that the *patron* was right when he told him to stay alert. The detective McPherson was *muy peligroso*. Who knew what he might be up to? Perhaps he would try to catch them by surprise.

Andres checked the MP-5 to make sure it was ready for firing. Shit! He had forgotten to take it off safety. He did so now and cursed himself for taking this fucking job. He was not in the habit of putting himself at this kind of risk. Car heists, muggings and fast food holdups had been enough to keep him in drug money when he wasn't doing time in the Cook County lockup before being deported to Mexico as an illegal alien. If it came to a shootout, he simply surrendered. But tonight he might not have that opportunity.

This was not good. This was not the way it was supposed to be. Fucking Carlos! He had told him the job would be so easy. *No problema*. And the money would be much more than usual.

Fuck the money! Fuck Carlos! Fuck the job! If there was any way out, Andres would take it now. But there was no way out. If he tried to run out, Carlos would probably kill him. Shit, maybe Carlos would kill him anyway when it was over for his share of the money.

Andres cursed at this thought. If he only had a fix. But he didn't. *Un momento*! He did have one more joint. Only one, but it would help calm his nerves. Andres pulled it from the breast pocket of his grimy sports shirt and pressed it between his lips. The sweet scent of the marijuana already made him feel better. He dug a cheap lighter from his pants pocket and flicked it. It didn't light. He tried again. Nothing. Shit! Was it out of fluid? It had lit only a short time ago.

Andres tried again. This time it lit. With a trembling hand he touched the flame to the tip of the joint. It would be alright now, he thought. It would be fine.

Those were his last thoughts. A sharp pain in his forehead. Then blackness.

Mack and Otis sprinted toward the church.

"So what's the plan?" Otis said.

Mack started to respond, but his voice was drowned out by a loud clap of thunder that signaled the beginning of a steady downpour.

"What did you say?"

What could he say, Mack thought, when he didn't know himself? "We'll have to do a quick recon and go from there."

Great, Otis thought. At least Willie had made a sure kill, otherwise they'd be under some serious fire from the dude in the tower by now.

When they reached the church, they ducked under the yellow caution tape and moved past a gate dangling from one hinge of the wrought iron fence into a garden court, a scene of knee-high grass and weed-choked flower beds. Greeting them was an imposing statue of Christ, his right hand raised, as if giving his blessing to a group of disciples. Otis hoped that the blessing included them. They would need the Lord watching their backs this night.

Katie shuddered at the loud thunderclap.

"I'm scared, Mr. Angel!"

Angel could feel her small body trembling against his and put his arm around her shoulder. "It is alright, Katie. It is only a message from God."

"Is God mad at us?"

"No. Not at you."

"I'm scared anyway."

"Don't be, Katie. God loves you and will welcome you into Heaven when your time comes to enter His Kingdom."

"Will my daddy be there?"

"Yes."

"And my grandpa?"

"Yes. He will be there, too, waiting for you."

Katie pressed closer against him when another clap of thunder seemed to shake the church to its foundations. God *was* angry, Angel thought. God was showing his wrath for what Angel must do tonight in the holy place. For what he had done from the moment he slit the throat of Father Francisco. As for redemption for his sins, Angel realized now that he would never receive it. No forgiveness. Only eternal damnation.

Carlos did not fear the wrath of God. For God and the church Carlos had only contempt. In fact, he felt the church was a perfect place to do what they must do this night. He was looking forward to it, especially to raping the little bitch. The mother bitch he would leave for Julio and Andres, but her little girl was his, and he felt his cock harden with anticipation.

Angel's voice in his earpiece. "Carlos, you are in position?"

"*Si, patron.*"

"And the flashlight. Have you checked to make sure it is working?"

"Of course it is working. Did we not use it to get in here?"

"The battery seemed low. Check again."

"*Si.*" Jumpy, the *patron*, Carlos thought, flicking the flashlight on. Always so cool and calm. Something was getting to him other than his obvious distaste of having to abduct the little bitch. "You see. *No problema.*"

"Alright, turn it off. It is now after eleven. They will be here in eight minutes. You know what to do."

Carlos did. He would shine the light on them as soon as they entered through the hole in the wall. The *patron* would order them to move to the altar with their hands clasped behind their heads. He would then tell the Herbst bitch to come up the aisle to get her child. He would keep the beam on the detective and the vagrant. Julio would slip up behind them and slit the vagrant's throat. The *patron* had instructed them not to kill the detective if it was possible. It seems the *patron's* own boss wanted to do this himself.

Screw that, Carlos thought! If McPherson so much as blinks, I will cut him to pieces with my AK-47.

It was now 11: 06 p.m. Mack had come up with a plan. As they knelt by the opening in the wall, he and Otis had heard Angel and Katie talking, then Angel speaking to the man he called Carlos. Judging by their voices, Mack figured Angel and Katie were somewhere near the front of the church. Carlos had revealed his position when he switched on the flashlight. He was in the choir loft in the apse. Good choice, Mack thought. It gave Carlos a field of fire at anyone in the nave.

"I'm going to try to get to Angel and Katie," Mack whispered, his voice barely audible over the sound of what was now a downpour. "If I catch Angel by surprise, I think I can handle him without having to use the MP-5. In any event, he's bound to alert his cronies, and Carlos will use the flash to see what's happening. That's when you take him out."

"What about the other guy, assuming there is only one other guy? We don't know where he is."

"He's our wild card. All we can do is wait for him to use his weapon and watch for the flash. At least we've got the darkness as an ally."

Otis nodded. He didn't like the idea of the dude getting the first shot, but what could they do? "Okay. Good luck."

"You too, partner."

With the M-5 cradled in his arms, Mack crawled through the opening in the wall. He entered the nave just adjacent to the first row of pews and scuttled up the side aisle. So far so good, he thought. The odds of their pulling this off were beginning to look a little better. But just a little.

Angel was still apprehensive. His watch showed 11:08 p.m. Only two more minutes. Soon it would be over, this dirty job, one way or another.

"Andres," he said into the mini mike. "Any sign of the Camry?"

No response.

"Andres. Answer me. Do you see the car?"

Silence.

Angel's apprehension now turned to alarm. Unless there was a malfunction in the wireless transmitter, and Andres wasn't receiving, something was very wrong. Angel suspected the latter.

"Carlos. Andres is not answering."

"I know. What do you think?"

"I don't know. Use the flashlight. See if anyone is in the church."

"*Si.*"

"Julio! Be alert!"

Angel reached for the Magnum in his coat pocket but did not pull it out. He did not want to frighten the *nina*. She would be scared enough when the time came that he had to use it.

Otis hesitated. Crouched just inside the opening in the wall, he debated whether to blast Carlos now or give Mack more time to get to Angel and Katie. Carlos was panning the nave with the flash but hadn't seen Mack. So they still couldn't be certain they had guests. That would change if he opened up on Carlos.

Otis decided to wait. Angel had to be taken out if Katie was to have any chance. Mack and him as well. With Angel's razor at Katie's throat, they'd have no choice but to lay down their weapons. And their lives. But if Mack could get to Angel...

Mack froze. So far Carlos hadn't spotted him with the flash. That all changed when a sudden flash of lightning momentarily illuminated the nave.

Carlos's voice shouting, "There he is!"

Now caught in the flashlight's beam, Mack rolled between pews with the rattle of automatic gunfire and bullets whizzing about him like a swarm of angry bees.

Otis pulled the trigger. He felt the butt of the shotgun's stock jar his shoulder with the recoil. A cursing cry of pain from the choir loft told him he'd hit Carlos. Hit him, but not fatally. The thug was still firing his weapon and calling out for Julio to kill the shooter.

Otis pumped the Remington, aimed at the flashes of Carlos's weapon and fired again. Another scream, this time followed by the shape of a body crashing through the loft railing and plunging with a loud thud to the floor of the apse.

Two down, Otis thought, counting the guy in the bell tower. But what about the other thug, Julio? Where was he? And Mack? Had Carlos hit him?

All this was flashing through Otis's mind when he heard more automatic gunfire behind him and felt the sting of a bullet grazing his left shoulder as he dove over the back of the first pew. The gunfire continued with short bursts that spewed bullets about him. He had no option now but to press himself against the floor and hope that Mack was still alive.

Mack looked for the flash of the weapon. No chance of getting to Angel and Katie now. He had to back up his partner, get the other thug, Julio, then deal with Angel. Mack had seen Otis dive behind the pew when the Mexican opened up on him with an automatic weapon. Otis was pinned down, unable to return fire, wounded for all Mack knew, perhaps even dead. Judging from the flashes of Julio's weapon, he was behind the pulpit. A deranged priest delivering a sermon of death, Mack thought grimly.

Mack realized that from his position in the middle of the nave he couldn't be certain of taking Julio out with his MP-5. But he could get his attention, put himself under fire. If he wasn't able to kill Julio, at least he could give Otis a chance to use the shotgun at close range, assuming Otis was still able to fire it. It was a snap decision Mack executed at once.

"Hey, Julio" he shouted, rising from behind the pew. "It's McPherson. Over here, asshole!"

Mack fired a burst at the pulpit, then hit the floor as Julio returned fire. Mack avoided the spray of bullets by crawling quickly toward the middle aisle. When the gunfire stopped, he rose to a kneeling position behind the back of the pew.

"Nice try, asshole. You're all alone now. Carlos and your *amigo* in the tower are dead, and you're going to join them!"

"*Pendejo*!" Julio's voice shrieking, followed by a long burst from his weapon.

Mack was face down on the floor again, as bullets raked the back of the pew just over his head. Come on, Otis, he thought. Kill the bastard!

Otis pushed himself off the floor. His left shoulder felt like it was on fire, but he wasn't thinking about that. He was thanking God that Mack was still alive. But for how long? Otis realized that Mack was deliberately drawing Julio's fire to give him a chance to take the thug out.

Peering over the back of the pew, Otis readied the shotgun and waited for Julio to fire again so he could fix his position. Julio was somewhere in the apse. But where? He didn't have to wait long for the answer. Another taunt from Mack was quickly followed by a burst from Julio's automatic weapon. Be damned! The thug was behind the pulpit. Otis was quick to respond. He raised the shotgun, aimed and squeezed the trigger.

What the hell?! It didn't budge!

This was no time for the gun to jam, Otis thought. He tried to fire again, but the trigger was stuck. Had he pumped the gun after his last shot? He was sure he had, but tried anyway. It wouldn't work either. Then Otis saw the problem. A bullet had hit the base of the barrel just over the trigger. It must have screwed up the firing mechanism. Who the hell knew? What Otis did know was that now he was going to have to use his service revolver.

Otis drew the revolver from his shoulder holster. He extended the weapon with his wrist resting on the back of the pew for support and waited for Julio to give him another look by firing his weapon again. Otis felt vulnerable without the shotgun, which at least gave him a fighting chance against an automatic weapon. The revolver was another matter. Otis wasn't a crack shot like Mack, and the fact that his hand was shaking did nothing to bolster his confidence.

Julio was panicking. Carlos was dead and the detective, McPherson, was still alive! Carlos was supposed to kill him! Why hadn't he killed him? How could he have missed? Was it the tequila? Too much of the tequila? And Andres. He was supposed to warn them. And now he was dead, too!? Was there someone outside the church who killed him? Or did the cop kill Andres before he entered the church? And what about the man with the shotgun? Was he the vagrant? Julio did not know. Whoever it was, Julio couldn't even be sure that he had killed him with his MP-5. At least the man hadn't returned fire, so if he was not dead, he must be badly wounded. McPherson was another matter. Not only was he alive, the *cabron* was almost daring Julio to try and kill him. Why was this? To make him use up his ammunition? Yes, that must be the reason.

Julio checked his weapon. The clip was empty. Fortunately, he had another, but it was his last. He removed the empty clip from the MP-5, inserted the full one and waited. The detective was not stupid. He was moving around, changing his position. Come on, *pendejo*. Show yourself again so Julio can kill you.

McPherson's voice, as if he had heard his thoughts: "Over here, asshole!"

Julio saw the shape of an upper torso from behind a pew. "Die, *pendejo*, die!" he screamed as he fired the MP-5.

Otis fired, once, twice, three, four times in rapid succession, the .38 kicking in his hands with each shot. Then he ducked down and waited to see if Julio returned fire. Silence except for the incessant pelting of rain on the arched roof of the nave and intermittent rumble of thunder.

"I think you got him."

Otis looked up at Mack, who was standing next to the pew with his MP-5 trained on the pulpit.

"Get the flashlight," Mack said. "I'll cover you."

Otis moved into the apse and picked up the flashlight, which lay on the floor near Carlos's body. Mack was right, he thought, when he'd told him he'd be so busy in a firefight that he wouldn't have time to worry about being scared. But now he felt the bitter taste of bile rising into his throat, especially when he put the beam on Carlos to make sure he was dead. No doubt about that. The thug's upper torso and what was left of his face were pocked with buckshot.

"What about Katie and Angel?"

"They're not going anywhere. Check out Julio."

With Mack covering them with his weapon, Otis followed the flashlight beam to the pulpit, which had taken some bullets from Mack's MP-5. But it was Otis's .38 that had done the job on Julio. He was sprawled on his back behind the pulpit with two bullet holes in his chest.

"Good shooting," Mack said. "Let's get to Angel and Katie."

Mack started up the aisle. Otis followed, while panning the nave with the flashlight. "Where are they?"

"With the front doors chained there's only one place they could be."

"The bell tower."

"Right."

"Question is which one?"

The answer was obvious when they entered the vestibule. The door to the left tower was closed, the one to the right open.

"Looks like Angel's up there with Andres," Otis said.

"Yeah. He'd want to see if he was dead and of no help, maybe even avail himself of his automatic weapon, if he had one."

"Not so good. Well, I guess we'd better go talk to Angel. Maybe we can cut a deal for Katie's life."

"That's what I had in mind, but I'm going up alone, and without a weapon."

"What? Are you crazy?"

Mack handed Otis the MP-5, then his service revolver. "I hope not, but Angel is more likely to listen to me if I'm unarmed."

"And if he doesn't? If he kills you, then uses Katie as a shield to escape?"

Mack had given that some thought. "Let him go. We'll take our chances on Willie picking him off."

Makes sense, Otis thought. Willie had already proven he could make a kill with one shot. "Whatever happens, it better happen fast. Someone might have heard the gunfire and already called 911."

"I'm betting that the thunderstorm gave us some sound cover, but you're right. Here's my cell. Tell Willie what's up."

Otis took Mack's cell phone. "Right."

Mack entered the bell tower and started up a wobbly, wrought iron spiral staircase. "I'm coming up, Angel," he shouted. "I'm unarmed."

And maybe more than a little crazy at that, he thought.

Angel pressed the barrel of the Magnum against the back of Katie's head.

"Ouch! You're hurting me!" Katie cried.

Angel eased the pressure, thankful that the *nina* could not see what he was holding. "I am sorry, Katie. I do not wish to hurt you."

"You said my mommy was coming. Where is she?"

"I am going to take you to her."

Which he would do, Angel thought, if McPherson called off his dogs. He had another man with him in the church, and there had to be a third man outside. The bullet in the forehead of Andres not only explained why he had not given them a warning, it also meant that the third man was a marksman and probably positioned on the roof of the apartment building across the street. Which is why Angel was crouched with Katie between the front apertures, out of sight of the shooter. Getting out of the church and to the van was another matter. Angel could only hope that with the *nina* as his shield they wouldn't risk a shot.

"Angel." McPherson's voice again, and now closer.

"Yes."

"I'm about to enter the tower."

"I want to see your hands above your head."

"Right."

Angel saw the detective's hands and arms, then his head and upper torso rising through the top of the stairwell opening directly opposite his position.

"Stop at the top of the stairs."

"Sure. Mind if I put my hands down?"

"No. Clasp them behind your head."

Mack did so as he took in the scene. Judging from Angel's position, he had obviously figured out that Andres had been taken out by a shooter on the roof of the apartment building.

"Mr. Mack, Mr. Mack!" Katie cried. "Are you going to take me to my mommy?"

"That depends on Angel."

"No, Senor Detective. It depends on you. I want safe passage out of the church and to the van. I do not have to tell you what will happen otherwise."

Mack realized that Angel was not being specific for Katie's sake. "I know. As far as I'm concerned you can walk out of here and out of the country. But on one condition."

"That is?"

"That Katie goes with me."

"That is not possible. I will release her when I reach the van."

"Not acceptable, *amigo*. How do I know you won't take her with you?"

"How do *I* know you will keep *your* word if I do as you ask?"

"I kept my word before. Remember?"

Angel did. After he had released the nun at Our Lady of Mount Carmel church, McPherson had not shot at the van as he escaped. But would he keep his word again? Angel could not take that risk.

"I am sorry. The *nina* stays with me."

"Let me make myself clear, *amigo*. You're going to get time for one shot. Just one. If it's at me, and it's not fatal, I'll be on you before you can pull the trigger again."

Angel studied the detective's face. Was he serious or just bluffing? It didn't take him long to decide that it was no bluff.

"And if I choose another target?"

Meaning Katie, Mack thought. Again Angel was choosing his words so as not to alarm Katie. "You still get one shot. And I promise you that I'll be taking no prisoners."

"I do not think that you will take that chance."

Mack hesitated. That the killer had some feeling for Katie was apparent. But how much? Her life would depend on that. "Not much time, *amigo*? What's it going to be?"

Squinting in the darkness, Mack tried to read a response in Angel's eyes. What he thought he saw was something he never expected to see. Were those tears?

"Let her go, *amigo*. I don't think you have it in you to harm her."

Angel nodded. "Take the *nina*. Take her and leave."

Angel released Katie, who rushed into Mack's outstretched arms.

"I want my mommy! I want my mommy!" she cried.

Mack picked her up. "She's waiting outside, Katie." Then to Angel: "I never expected to ever wish a killer good luck, but I'm doing it now."

"*Gracias...amigo*."

Angel watched Mack descend the stairs with Katie in his arms until they were out of view. He continued to kneel there, as if in prayer, and let a feeling of intense relief wash through him. This dirty job was over. It was the first time he had never finished a job, but he was doing it now, regardless of what Ortiz might try to do to him.

The distant wail of sirens penetrated Angel's thoughts. He had lost track of time, but the sirens sent an urgent signal for him to get out quickly. Rising to his feet, he started toward the staircase when the tower was suddenly filled with a splash of crackling white light accompanied by a deafening clap of thunder. Angel felt his body paralyzed by a jolt so intense that it flung him against the side aperture. For a moment he lost consciousness, then he seemed to be falling...falling through space, like an archangel falling from Heaven, he thought.

Angel didn't feel the impact when he hit the ground. All he knew was that he couldn't move. His vision was blurry, but his mind was beginning to function again. It had happened as he had feared it would. The wrath of God. God had sent a bolt of lightning to strike him down.

Angel blinked at the rain pelting his face. His vision was clearing. He was aware that he was lying on his back, and that the figure of a man was hovering over him. Who was it? The detective? No, he would be gone by now. Who? Then he recognized the figure's pious face. Jesus! Was it Jesus? Could such a miracle be possible?

Then Angel remembered the statue of Jesus in the garden court. He was lying next to the statue. Only a statue. Yet, as he gazed at it, a pale halo of yellow light formed over the statue's head. And the eyes of the pious face looking down at him were effusing a soft glow and showing...what? Pity? Was it pity?

Angel tried to speak, but all that came out of his mouth was a hacking cough of blood. He tried again. This time he was able to murmur the words that were in his heart.

"*Dios...pardoname...*"

When they found Angel, he looked like a man who had died peacefully in his sleep.

*11:22 p.m.:* Ortiz was frustrated. An accident at a construction site on the Outer Drive had halted traffic for nearly forty minutes. He wanted to be at the church to deliver the *coup de gras* to McPherson himself, but when got there, he knew he was too late. The intersection before the church was blocked by a patrol car, and a uniformed policeman was motioning him with a flashlight to turn. Before he did, Ortiz looked up the block. Policemen were swarming about the church, while more cruisers and an ambulance converged from both directions on what was obviously a crime scene.

Ortiz curbed the Century a short distance from the intersection, exited the car into a lingering drizzle and approached the young policeman.

"What happened, officer?"

"I'm sorry, sir. I'm not allowed to discuss that with you."

"Of, course, of course. It's just that I have friends who live next to the church. As a matter of fact I'm on my way to see them. You can understand my concern."

"Yes, sir, but I'm sure they're alright. The shooting appears to have been confined to the church."

"Did you say shooting?"

"That's the way it looks."

"Drug-related, I assume?"

"That's possible, but as I said..."

"I know. You can't discuss it. I suppose I won't be able to see my friends."

"Not tonight, sir. Like I said, I'm sure they're okay, but why don't you give them a call."

"I'll do that. Thank you, officer."

Ortiz walked back to the Century. He was getting a bad feeling about this. The only thing that would have brought the police would be gunfire. But if things had gone according to plan, there would have been none. Had McPherson and the vagrant risked the Herbst child's life by putting up a fight? That didn't seem likely. The stupid Mexicans had probably disobeyed orders and opened up on them as soon as they entered the church. Yes, that had to be what had happened.

Ortiz didn't have to wait long for an answer. Pulling the beeping cell phone from his pocket, he looked at the screen before answering. The message was "Private Number," which could be Angel. Of course, it had to be Angel.

But it wasn't.

"Hello, Ortiz."

Somehow the sound of McPherson's voice came as no surprise. The detective had said that he was a hard man to kill, and he was proving that his boast was no exaggeration.

"Ah, Detective McPherson. So you managed to survive after all. My congratulations. And the others?"

"All safe and unharmed at this end. However, I can't say the same for the three *caballeros*."

"And Angel?"

"I'm afraid you'll have to find yourself a new boy, Ortiz. Angel tendered his resignation."

Which told Ortiz that Angel had released the Herbst child without harming her, probably as his part in a deal with McPherson to save himself. "I'll see that he's well rewarded for his loyalty."

"I'm sure you will, if you live that long. I'll be seeing you, Ortiz, and remember what I told you...keep looking over your shoulder."

Ortiz beeped off. He sat there for a long moment without moving. For the first time in his life he was troubled by something he couldn't identify. It wasn't fear. The only fear he had ever known was the fear of failure. No, this feeling was more subtle, as though something were happening somewhere beyond the perimeter of his knowledge and the reach of his control, but moving in tandem with him, like an animal running along a parallel track toward a point where their paths might suddenly and unexpectedly cross. A premonition? Perhaps. But of what? Ortiz didn't know, and not knowing was what made it so disturbing.

In any event, Ortiz wasn't worried about McPherson. Although the detective knew he was in Chicago, he couldn't possibly find out where he was staying. Besides, McPherson was still a wanted man, wanted by both the police and Blackburn. Even more by Blackburn. However, Ortiz had to consider the possibility that the police would find McPherson first and take him alive. If they did, the detective would tell the whole story about the Project, including Ortiz's involvement. The police might not believe McPherson, but the feds were another matter. They would not only know that he was in Chicago, they would want to know why, and McPherson would supply the answer. Ortiz could not take a chance of that happening. Waiting until Tuesday to leave was no longer acceptable. He would have to leave earlier, Sunday if possible.

Ortiz speed-dialed a number on the cell and waited until a sleepy voice finally answered.

"Kischman."

Ortiz didn't waste any time. Kischman would have to pack a few things and be ready to leave tomorrow.

"I thought I had until Tuesday," Kischman whined.

"Things have changed," Ortiz said, deciding not to tell the doctor what had happened. He didn't need a panicking Kischman to deal with. "When can you be ready?"

"Well, I'll have to go to the bank and draw out some money."

"Don't worry about the money. I can advance you anything you need. What about the HCV cure? Can you go to the office in the morning and copy the file to a disk, despite the fact that it's Sunday?"

"Unfortunately, no. There was a problem this evening with the mainframe cooling system and the whole thing has been shut down for maintenance. It won't be turned back on until tomorrow night."

Ortiz found this news both frustrating and disturbing. It wasn't just the fact that another obstacle had suddenly appeared in his path. He was used to dealing with unanticipated developments and last minute changes in direction. In fact, he always tried to plan for the unexpected as far as that was possible, never relying solely on Plan A, but always having a Plan B and even a Plan C prepared beforehand. No, something more was going on here. Perhaps it was how off the wall this development was, a machine failure that he could never have anticipated or planned for. Perhaps it was the sheer number of things that had gone very wrong recently, including, of course, the loss of Angel and the Mexicans and their failure to kill McPherson and the others. Whatever it was, for a moment Ortiz felt as if he were a piece on a chessboard in a game being played by someone else, and he didn't like that feeling at all.

"Alright, then. We'll leave Monday. I'll expect you at Burnham Harbor Monday night no later than eight. Ask at the Harbor Master's office where Mr. Salizar's boat is located."

"Salizar?"

"Yes. It's the name I'm using."

"Alright. I'll be there."

"See that you are. And with the disk."

Ortiz beeped off, pocketed the cell and started the engine. He was feeling a little better. They would be out of Chicago Monday night and on their way to Venezuela. He had no intention of returning to Miami first. He would send for Rosita later. The important thing was to get out of the country as quickly as possible with the HCV cure. He also smiled at the realization that the entire waterfront would be alive with hundreds of boats out on the lake to watch the fireworks in celebration of Memorial Day. The police would be preoccupied directing traffic and maintaining order, and the boats and fireworks would make the Black Thunder inconspicuous, giving him a degree of cover. So perhaps the day's delay caused by the failure of the mainframe cooling system was actually a blessing in disguise. Perhaps fate was favoring him after all.

Yes, he was feeling much better. But as he pulled away from the curb, Ortiz couldn't suppress the urge to glance over his shoulder.

*11:31 p.m.:* Mark Jacobs was working late. He was organizing the questions he would ask McPherson and Butler when he interviewed them tomorrow morning. He'd have to edit the interview later to allow room for his live interviews with Megan Herbst and Dr. Greg. That couldn't happen for probably a couple of days to give Dr. Greg the chance to examine Butler and run tests on his blood and urine. Jacobs wanted all of his ducks in a row when he dropped the bombshell that would either make or break his career.

Jacobs was wondering again if it was worth the risk when there was a knock at his office door. He looked up at the freckled face of Patty Atwood framed in the glass panel and motioned for the lovely young intern to come in.

"What is it, Patty?"

"I'm sorry to disturb you, Mr. Jacobs, but…"

"But what? I happen to be a little busy right now, or haven't you noticed?"

"Oh, I'm terribly sorry…I just wanted to tell you…a story just came in…a shooting in a church…"

Another shooting, Jacobs thought. Probably a turf war between rival gangs. No big deal there, but he didn't tell Patty that, because he'd remembered that he was hoping to give her a little private instruction over cocktails and supper at Charlie T's. So exercising some damage control, he smiled and said, "Hey, I'm the one who should be apologizing, Patty, for chewing you out for just doing your job. A shooting you said in a church?"

The pained expression on Patty's face now morphed into a smile. "Yes. In Rogers Park. The one that's been in the news that they're trying to save…"

"I know it. Any fatalities?"

"Yes, at least that's what we're hearing, all Hispanics, according to preliminary reports. The assignment editor is sending out an ENG. I thought you might want to cover it."

Gang-related for sure, Mark thought, and probably involving drug traffic. If he wasn't so busy he might tag along with the ENG crew. The fact that the shooting had taken place in a church could give the story some legs, at least for a brief spot on the 8:00 a.m. local news.

"Thanks for telling me, Patty, but…"

Suddenly Jacobs was on his feet.

A startled Patty said, "What is it, Mr. Jacobs?"

"Hispanics. You said they were Hispanics?"

"Yes."

Jacobs was remembering what McPherson had told him about the young Latino hit man and the three Mexicans working for a Venezuelan drug pirate who was after the HCV cure. According to the detective, they had killed Diane Bates and had tried to kill him. Come to think of it, the attempt on McPherson's life had also happened in a Catholic church. Coincidence?

"Wait outside for a minute, Patty."

"Yes, of course."

When she'd closed the office door, Jacobs picked up the phone and dialed McPherson's cell number. No response to the dial tone. Asked by a voice to leave a message, Jacobs did. He tried again. Same thing. Not good. If the detective was involved in the shooting at the church…

Jacobs hung up and headed for the door.

"Come, Patty," he said as he entered the news room. "We're going to church."

## Sunday, May 26

*12:43 a.m.:* Mack pulled the tab off another Miller Lite.

"Why don't you get some sleep?" Otis said from the dining nook where he was drinking beers with Willie.

"Too keyed up," Mack said, plopping onto the sofa next to a slumbering Ulysses.

Aren't we all, Otis thought. Except Megan and Katie. Emotionally exhausted, they were curled up on the over-the-cab bunk, sound asleep. "So who gets the van bed?"

"You guys can have it," Willie said. "It's stopped raining, so I'll flop outside again. I'm used to it."

"It's still wet out there," Otis said. "You can have one of my sleeping bags. Ava and I like to sack out under the stars in nice weather."

"That'll be fine."

"Why don't you go home, Otis," Mack said. "No one knows you're in on this."

"Why bother? It's so late I might as well spend what's left of the night here."

"Is your wife okay with that?"

"No problem. I already cleared that with her on my way here." But without telling her about the shootout, just that they had found Katie. If Ava knew about the shoulder wound and how close he'd come to getting killed, she would have personally escorted him to the nearest hospital emergency room. Fortunately, it was only a flesh wound, which Megan had dressed with the first aid kit he kept in the RV. Besides, Otis had a feeling something else could happen, and told Mack as much.

Mack took a swig of beer, belched. "Sorry. So what could happen with the three *caballeros* headed for the cooler and Angel on the lam?"

"You really gonna take Angel's word on that?"

"Strangely enough, I am."

"Yeah, well, we still got his boss, Ortiz, to deal with. And how about the suit and tie guys who tried to kill Willie and you? They're still out there."

"You're right, but they've got to find us first."

"Who do you think those dudes are anyway?" Willie said.

"Whoever they are, they've got *mucho* clout at City Hall," Otis said. "But why would the mayor be involved in a cover-up of the Lazarus Project?"

"I'm beginning to get an idea about that," Mack said. "And about who's pulling the strings for all concerned."

"You wouldn't like to share that, would you?"

Mack hesitated. His idea was a hunch at best, one that had begun to take seed while he was watching the Joan Crawford movie last night. At the time he'd shrugged it off as too fantastic, and he'd been too busy since to give it any further thought. But tonight he'd done a lot of thinking and asked himself that "what if" question again. If he told the others what he'd come up with, they'd probably think he was delusional. And maybe he was.

"Forget it. It's too far out anyway."

"Well, at this point nothing would surprise me. Maybe you should check in with Jacobs. Bring him up to date on tonight's events."

"Good idea." Reaching for his cell phone, Mack saw a hole in the pocket of his windbreaker. "I'll be damned!" He dropped the cell on the dining nook table. There was a bullet imbedded in the phone.

Willie whistled. "Close call, man, and that's not a joke."

"I'm not laughing, Willie. Otis, let me have your cell."

"Sure."

Mack took the phone from Otis, removed Jacobs's card from his wallet and dialed his cell number. Jacobs answered after two beeps.

"Jacobs."

"It's McPherson."

"McPherson! Where in the hell are you? I've been trying to reach you for the last hour."

"Sorry, but my phone's out of order. It took a bullet."

"No shit. That wouldn't have anything to do with a shootout at a church in Rogers Park by any chance?"

"Yeah. How'd you know?"

"Just a wild guess, given the identity of the bodies they're carting out of the church, which is where I am as we speak. What happened?"

Jacobs listened intently to Mack's account of Katie's abduction and rescue. What a story, he thought! A story within a bigger story, but one that would give the Lazarus exposé a powerful emotional punch when he interviewed Megan live.

"Are we still on for tomorrow at ten?" Mack said after he finished.

"Screw that! Things are moving too fast, and who knows how long you can hide out in that RV. I'll do the interview of you and Butler tonight, if you're up to it."

"That's okay with me. The sooner the better."

"Good. I'll get a camera and be on my way in the next few minutes."

"By the way, how did your piece on Mad Dog McPherson go this evening? I meant to watch it, but I was busy casing a church in Rogers Park at the time."

"Well, I did a real hatchet job on you, as I promised. Half the citizens of Chicago are trembling in their beds tonight because of you. Makes it all the more urgent that we get you and Butler on tape and the lab work done so I can reveal the truth about the Lazarus Project."

"Well, it'll be nice to be on the side of the good guys for a change."

"Don't worry, you'll come out looking like one very shrewd cop. But I've got to get going now if I'm gonna be there in an hour to do the interview. See you soon."

Jacobs beeped off and shouted to the cameraman in charge of taping the usual post crime action. "Hey, Ron. You got another camcorder in the truck?"

"I think so. You need it?"

"Yeah. Just got a tip I want to follow up on. Get it for me, would you, Patty?"

"Right away."

Patty was back in seconds with the camcorder. "Here you are, Mr. Jacobs, and I brought an extra video tape."

"Thanks, Patty. I may need it."

With Patty keeping pace, Jacobs headed for his car, a sporty Lexus, opened the door and put the camcorder and tape in the passenger seat.

"Do you need me to come along, Mr. Jacobs?"

"Not this time, Patty. You go back with the crew, okay?"

"Alright. Is it something important, that tip?"

Probing, Jason thought, like a good reporter. Patty was learning fast. "It could be, Patty, it could be. See you tomorrow, kid. And thanks again. You've been a great help."

Patty beamed. "You're welcome, Mr. Jacobs."

Jacobs settled into the seat and buckled up. Patty closed the door and gave him a little wave as he gassed the Lexus. Good kid, Patty, he thought. He'd need a personal assistant if he hit the big time, and Patty just might qualify for the job in more ways than one. Although it was a little premature to think about that, for Jacobs New York City was beginning to look a lot closer to becoming a reality.

*2:13 a.m.:* The Woman dressed hurriedly. She didn't apply any makeup. Not that she needed any to enhance her natural beauty, but there was no time. Blackburn had awakened her a little after 1:00 a.m. with news that had to be acted on immediately. The TV reporter, Mark Jacobs, had been tailed to an RV on a nearby lake in Indiana, and Blackburn believed that was where McPherson and the vagrant, Butler, were hiding.

Grabbing her shoulder bag and picture hat from the dresser, the Woman exited one of the guest bedrooms of O'Neal's lavish Colonial mansion and descended the stairs to a foyer. In the living room Blackburn and O'Neal rose from an ornate sofa where they were drinking from mugs of coffee. Blackburn was immaculately dressed, as usual, in a pinstriped, charcoal suit. Not so O'Neal, who was wearing a terrycloth robe over his pajamas.

"Would you like some coffee, Suzanne?" O'Neal said.

"No, thank you, Roy."

"I wish you'd reconsider this, Suzanne," Blackburn said.

"He's right," O'Neal said. "Just coming here was risky enough. What if someone recognizes you?"

"I have to take that chance." Then to Blackburn: "How long will it take us to get there?"

"Given the fact there won't be much traffic, about an hour, maybe a little more, according to Gallagher. He's familiar with the Chicago area. He and Bryant are getting the car now."

"What about the police? Have they been informed?"

"Yes. I just called Superintendent Hollender. He's getting a SWAT team together, which he will personally supervise."

"Call him back, David. I don't want them moving in before we get there."

"Be reasonable, Suzanne. They have to secure the area first just in case they decide to put up a fight."

"There can't be any fight, David. I told you, no more killing!"

"I'll call him, but…"

The sound of a car horn outside. "Let's go."

"You go ahead, David. I'll be with you in a minute. And make that call."

Blackburn nodded glumly, removing his cell phone as he left the living room.

The Woman sighed. "A good man, David. He's like the big brother I never had."

O'Neal went over and took her arm. "Don't worry, Suzanne. Things will work out okay."

The Woman smiled wearily. "I pray to God you're right, Roy. I'm just sorry I got you involved in all of this."

O'Neal shrugged. "So what are old friends for?"

A lot in this case, the Woman thought. O'Neal would not only lose everything if the Project was revealed but face the possibility of spending the rest of his life in jail. But aside from her own personal agenda, she knew O'Neal was taking the risk to find the HCV cure for an even bigger cause than serving humanity.

"Roy, I just want you to know how much this means to me."

"I know." O'Neal smiled wistfully. "Do you believe in fate, Suzanne?"

"Fate? I don't know. What do you mean?"

O'Neal took her into his arms and held her. "I mean how different things would have turned out if you had said 'yes'."

The Woman knew the question he was referring to. It was one he had asked after the senior prom at Palatine High School and many times later during their years at Northwestern University, where he had concentrated in the bio sciences, she in drama. Perhaps she should have accepted his proposal of marriage. She probably would have if fate, as Roy put it, had not intervened with the opportunity for her to replace a supporting actress in the road company revival of *The Little Foxes* at the Schubert Theatre. When the show moved on, she went with it across country and eventually to New York City. After a few minor parts in Off Broadway productions, she tried out and landed the starring role in a major play. Her performance established her as a genuine star, and she would remain one for nearly ten years until her marriage, when one career ended and an even more important one began.

Yes, things would certainly have been different had she said yes. That she had loved Roy was never in doubt. But the love she bore her husband was deeper than anything she could have anticipated. They were truly soul mates who were destined to meet. Fate again, she thought.

Again the sound of the horn outside, this time more insistent. "I have to go."

"Yes."

Cradling his face in her hands, the Woman kissed him lightly on the lips. "God bless you, Roy."

The Woman hurried to the door and exited before O'Neal could see the tears welling in her eyes.

*3:33 a.m.:* Willie was having a nightmare. It was a recurring nightmare. He was back in the Mekong Delta, stalking a column of Gooks who were moving along a jungle trail. Suddenly, a Black Hawk gunship was swooping down and spraying Charlie with fifty caliber machine gun bullets. Although Willie knew he was not close enough to be hit, he also knew what would happen next. The Black Hawk would napalm the whole area, and Willie would be cooked along with Charlie if he didn't get the hell out of there. Problem was he couldn't fucking move! It was as if he was paralyzed. All he could do was wait for an agonizing death being roasted alive.

Willie made an effort to move again. This time he was able to sit up. In fact, he was sitting up. And awake. Willie could feel his body damp with perspiration. That fucking dream again, he thought. Or was it a dream? He could still hear the whoosh! whoosh! whoosh! of the chopper's propeller.

Wiggling out of the sleeping bag, Willie stood up and looked toward the source of the sound. The vague shape of a helicopter with blinking lights was approaching low over the lake like a gigantic bat. Willie swore. He didn't have to think twice to know that—like the Black Hawk in his dream—this was a bat from Hell!

Megan was jarred awake by the sound of the chopper. She was so exhausted that she'd dozed in and out of consciousness while the TV reporter, Jacobs, camcorded interviews with Willie and Mack. Katie had slept through it all, but she was awake now and frightened. Cradling Katie with one arm, Megan could feel her little body trembling against hers.

"Mommy! Mommy! What is that?!"

"I don't know, dear." But she did know. It was a helicopter, and getting closer. Looking down from the bunk, Megan saw Willie enter the RV.

"We got company!"

Hyped by the night's events and the coffee they were drinking, Mack, Otis and Jacobs scurried out of the dining nook.

"Is it a police chopper?" Otis said.

"Can't tell. Could be, or maybe those suit and tie dudes."

Mack moved to the door and looked up. The helicopter was hovering directly overhead, but Willie was right. Dark clouds were once again covering the moon, and it was too dark to make out if it was a police helicopter or something else. One thing he knew for sure, however. Whoever it was knew that Jacobs was working with them and had put a tail on him.

"What'll we do?" Jacobs said.

"Stay put. If it's the police, they'll give us a chance to surrender. If it's not…"

Suddenly, a strobe light from the helicopter bathed the RV in a circle of intense light.

"Screw this!" Willie said, grabbing his rifle. "I'm not gonna get my ass kicked again!"

"Hold it, Willie," Otis said. "We got Megan and Katie to think about."

"I am thinkin' about them! Those dudes be takin' no prisoners!"

"Well, there's one way to find out," Mack said. "Stay inside. All of you."

"Mack! Don't go out there!" Megan said.

"Just stay inside!"

Mack raised his hands and was about to exit the RV when a voice blared over a loudspeaker.

"You inside the RV. This is the police. You are completely surrounded by SWAT officers, so do not try to resist. You have exactly one minute to come out with your hands behind your heads! One minute! Beginning now!"

"What do you think, Mack?" Otis said. "Could be the bad guys playing cop."

"It could be, but it's not. I recognize that voice. It's none other than Superintendent Hollender."

"Hollender! So he's in on the cover-up, too?"

"So it seems. How much do you have on tape, Mark?"

"Enough to edit and air."

"It would be a shame if it were to fall into the wrong hands."

"My thoughts exactly." Jacobs removed the tape, injected the spare one and looked around the RV.

"How about my tackle box," Otis said, gesturing to his fishing gear in a rear corner of the camper.

"It'll have to do." Jacobs moved quickly to the tackle box, put the tape inside and snapped the lid shut.

"You have thirty seconds to come out!" Hollender's voice boomed.

"Let's go," Mack said. "Megan, you and Katie stay inside."

"No. We're going with you. Help Katie down, will you, Otis."

"Sure. Come on, Katie." Otis reached up and lifted Katie down from the bunk. "But Mack's right, Megan. Those SWAT guys are the best, but all it would take is for one to have an itchy trigger finger."

"That's just it," Megan said, climbing down the stairs. "They would hardly fire when they see a woman and child."

"Alright," Mack said. "But you exit last after I tell them you're inside."

Hollender's voice again: "You now have ten seconds!"

"Follow me." Then yelling: "We're coming out! And we have a woman and a little girl with us."

With his hands clasped behind his head Mack exited the RV into the glare of the overhead strobe light. Beyond the perimeter of light there was only darkness. But Mack knew that there were at least two dozen SWAT rifles with night scopes trained on him. And perhaps one more. The people who had tried to kill him before could have their own shooter out there. And this would be a perfect opportunity for them to finish the job.

The Woman gasped.

"Did you hear him, David? They have a woman and a little girl with them!"

"I heard. I hadn't counted on this. She must be O'Meara's daughter, Megan Herbst, and her child."

"Which means that she also knows about the Project."

"In all likelihood. McPherson's partner, too. He's the black man who just exited the RV."

The Woman made a decision. It wasn't an easy one given that it could have disastrous consequences for all concerned with Lazarus. But this latest development had eliminated any other options, especially since she was determined to prevent any more deaths.

"David! Tell Hollender to call this off!"

"What? Are you serious?!"

"Tell him to get his people out of here. That you're taking over and will assume full responsibility for McPherson and the others."

"But Suzanne…"

"Tell him, dammit!"

"All right."

Blackburn got out of the Taurus, which was parked off the gravel path that bordered the lake. "Stay here," he said to Gallagher and Bryant, who were standing beside the car.

"Yes, sir," Gallagher said, exchanging a "what's up" look with Bryant.

Blackburn moved past half a dozen squad cars to where Hollender was flanked by two of more than a dozen SWAT officers, the rest of whom surrounded the RV.

"Good work, Superintendent. You can withdraw your men now."

"I can do what?!"

"Withdraw your officers. My people will take McPherson and the others into custody. I don't think they'll give us any trouble."

"You don't?! Let me remind you that McPherson is a suspect for the murder of Diane Bates, and Butler is wanted for Dr. Alward's murder."

"I'm aware of that, Superintendent. I'm also aware that they're both innocent of the crimes."

"You can prove that?"

"I can. Now tell your men to withdraw."

Hollender hesitated, then raised the bullhorn to his mouth and ordered the SWAT officers to return to their squad cars and leave.

"Thank you, Superintendent."

Hollender glared at Blackburn. "You've got the ball, Blackburn, and I hope you fucking choke on it!"

Blackburn smiled. "I'll try not to."

Mack was confused. So were the others. The helicopter had soared away, and the sound of the departing squad cars was growing fainter. Serenaded by chirping crickets and croaking frogs, the group stood in darkness outside the RV.

Otis asked the question that was on everyone's minds. "Why did Hollender call off the show?"

"I'm bettin' it's some kind of trick," Willie said."

"What do you think, Mack?" Jacobs said.

The sound of tires crunching against gravel provided part of the answer to Mack. "I think you're about to get the end of your story."

"I told you it was a trick!" Willie said. "I'm for gettin' our weapons!"

"Hold it, Willie!" Mack said. "If someone wanted us dead it would have happened by now."

The shape of a car approaching down the lane came into view, its headlights out.

"I don't like this," Willie said. "I'd feel a whole lot better with my Remington."

"Maybe Willie's right," Otis said.

As Mack watched the car stop a few yards away, and two men exit from behind the wheel and the passenger seat, he was almost inclined to agree. Although he'd only seen the driver from a distance, he looked like the guy who had tried to run him down and chased him to the bridge. And the car he had driven was a dark blue Taurus. Same car, same guy, for sure. However, instead of drawing a weapon, the man opened a rear door of the car. A tall, balding man got out, while the driver's partner assisted a woman exiting from the other side.

The tall man and the Woman moved toward them, the other two men remaining beside the car. "I'd like to talk with all of you," the Woman said. "Perhaps we could go inside?"

Mack did not take this as a question from the Woman, who was clearly in charge. "Sure. Megan, why don't you play hostess."

"Yes, of course..." Megan said, bewildered by the appearance of the Woman. Who was she? Whoever she was, she exuded an air of authority, and Megan sensed that she was the person who had called off the police.

Megan escorted the Woman to the RV. Katie scampered ahead to open the door.

"Thank you, young lady," the Woman said. "But you go ahead."

"No. You have to go in first. It's good manners."

The Woman smiled, held out her hand. "Let's go in together, okay?"

"All right." Katie took the Woman's hand. "My name is Katie Herbst. This is my mommy. Who are you?"

"My name is Suzanne, Katie," the Woman said, as they entered the RV, Megan and the others following. "But you may call me Suzie. My friends all do. And I hope you'll be my friend, too. Will you, Katie?"

"Oh, yes," Katie said. She led the Woman to the small divan. "Let's sit here. I'll sit on one side and Mommy can sit on the other. But kitty, you have to move."

The tom, who was curled up on the divan, seemed to understand, and after a yawn and a stretch, hopped onto the floor.

The Woman sat down with Katie and Megan. "What an adorable child," she said to Megan, meaning it. Katie was like the little girl she wished she could have had if she'd been able to have children. "You must be very proud of her, Mrs. Herbst."

"Yes...I am." She knows my name, Megan thought, now able to see the portion of the Woman's lovely face that wasn't hidden by the dark glasses and picture hat pulled low over her forehead. She looked familiar. In fact, she looked like...but no. That wasn't possible. It couldn't be her!

Mack thought otherwise. "Now that we're all here, Mrs. Trippet, I suggest that you tell us what this is all about."

Trippet, Megan thought! My God, it was her!

The Woman nodded, wondering how long McPherson had known her identity.

Mack could read the question in her eyes. Dark, luminous eyes, Joan Crawford eyes. During the Crawford movie last night it was the star's eyes that not only reminded him of the picture of the prom queen in Roy O'Neal's office, but of the eyes he'd seen briefly in a close-up of the First Lady's face on the Barbara Walters interview. Could the prom queen and the First Lady be one and the same person he'd asked himself? The prom queen had long hair, he remembered, while the First Lady's hair was short-cropped and banged. He tried to imagine the First Lady with long hair and concluded that there was a resemblance to the prom queen. But only a resemblance. The idea that they were the same person was absurd. A crazy hunch. But those eyes, those Joan Crawford eyes, had stuck in his mind, and the more he'd thought about it the more he began to realize that his hunch might not be so crazy after all.

"Yes, Detective," the Woman said. "I owe you an explanation. All of you, and an apology. If you don't mind, I'd like to make myself more comfortable."

The Woman removed the dark glasses and hat. Stunned silence. It was Katie who spoke first.

"I know you. I've seen you lots of times on TV. You're Mrs. President."

The First Lady smiled. "My husband is the President, dear." Then to Megan: "Ummm, I smell coffee. I wonder..."

"Yes, of course," Megan said, rising.

"Why don't all of you take a seat," the Woman said. "What I have to tell you will take a while."

Otis, Willie and Jacobs slid into the dining nook seats, while Megan filled a mug with coffee from the Mr. Coffee. Mack remained standing, as did Blackburn, who Mack assumed correctly carried an automatic in a shoulder holster under the wrinkle-free charcoal suit coat. Mack also assumed correctly that Blackburn and the two men outside were Secret Service agents, whose job was to guard the President and the First Lady.

"Black will be fine, Mrs. Herbst," the First Lady said before Megan could ask. "May I call you Megan?"

"Of course," Megan said. She didn't know what to make of the First Lady's friendly gesture. Perhaps she was just attempting to put her at ease.

Mack had a different take on it. He was remembering that the First Lady had been an actress. The whole business of cozying up to Katie and Megan was just a way to gain sympathy from her present audience before she opened the curtain all the way to reveal her dark secret.

"Thank you, Megan," the First Lady said when Megan handed her a steaming mug of coffee and a napkin. Seeing that Katie was rubbing her eyes, she said, "You look tired, dear. Why don't you go to bed?"

"Can I Mommy?" Katie said. "I'm so sleepy."

"Of course you can, dear," Megan said. Although Katie probably wouldn't comprehend what the First Lady was going to tell them, Megan shared her obvious wish that Katie not hear it. "Would you help her up, Otis?"

"Sure," Otis said. He lifted Katie off the divan and hoisted her onto the over-the-cab bunk. "Up we go, Katie."

"Can kitty come, too?"

"Why not?" Otis picked up Ulysses and lifted him onto the bunk.

"Good night, Mrs. President," Katie said, snuggling next to the cat.

"Good night, Katie. Sleep tight."

"And don't let the bedbugs bite," Katie added with a yawn.

The First Lady smiled, took a sip of coffee. She waited for Megan to sit down beside her, then got right down to business.

"I assume you all know about the Lazarus Project. What you don't know is that the Project was my idea. I take full responsibility for its conception and implementation."

Blackburn laid a hand on her shoulder. "Suzanne..."

The First Lady patted his hand. "No, David. It's time to put everything on the table." Then continuing to the others: "The purpose of the Project was twofold. Finding a cure for the HCV virus will, of course, be of enormous benefit to mankind. But that was not the primary purpose. The primary purpose was and is to save the life of my husband, the President."

The First Lady took a sip of coffee to let this sink in. No one spoke, but everyone absorbed the news with shock and astonishment. Everyone but Mack. His suspicions had been confirmed, although until now he hadn't known who was responsible for the Project, the First Lady or the President himself.

The First Lady took another sip of coffee. She was finding that this was easier than she had anticipated. Confession was good for the soul, she thought. But would it be good for the country? That remained to be seen.

"Byron was diagnosed with the hepatitis C virus about three years ago by his personal physician, Dr. Kerber, during a routine physical. He was probably infected with the virus years ago from a blood transfusion when he served in Viet Nam. He's been treated with existing drugs, interferon combined with ribavirin, which was keeping the virus under control. According to Dr. Kerber, it could arrest the disease for several years. But that all changed last year. That's when Byron contracted hepatitis B. We don't know exactly how. A simple cut, even a shaving cut, could have caused it. By itself, it's not all that serious. Most people with the virus recover within six months. But not if they also have hepatitis C. The combination of the two viruses is a death sentence. And soon."

"That explains the deadline for finding a cure!" Megan said.

"Yes. Byron would have about a year to live."

"How did Bio-Sci get into the act?" Otis asked.

Mack answered the question for her. "Roy O'Neal is an old friend of Mrs. Trippet's. They went to high school together."

"I see you've done your homework, Detective," the First Lady said. "The fact is that Bio-Sci had been working on a cure for several years and was close to finding one. But Roy said it would take time, and time, of course, was something we didn't have. Then there was the problem of testing the antiviral drugs."

"And not on lab rabbits or mice," Mack said.

If Mack expected the First Lady to avoid his eyes, he was mistaken. She looked right at him when she said, "No, not with lab animals. We had to make sure we had one that would work on human beings."

"Which is where the vagrants came in," Mack said. "Subjects, I think you call them."

Now the First Lady looked away from him. As if to appeal to the others, Mack thought. "Yes. Unfortunately, that was our only option. At first we tested the drugs on vagrants whom our field doctors diagnosed as already being infected with the disease. It's especially prevalent with drug addicts. But there simply weren't enough of them, and we were running out of time so…"

Mack finished what the First Lady couldn't. "So you infected them yourself."

The First lady locked eyes with him again. The detective was making this personal, but she didn't flinch. "Yes, Detective. But none of them have died, and none of them will die. Roy informed me yesterday that they've got the cure. They've developed an antiviral drug that Roy believes will arrest the disease for a long time, perhaps indefinitely. We'll see that all of the…the infected people are not only treated with the drug but given shelter. And for those who want to go through a rehab program, there will be jobs and a new life."

"Hey, does that include me?" Willie said.

"It does, Willie. In fact, you've already been treated. According to the lab data, you were among the first to be injected with the experimental drug that proved to be the right one."

"No shit! Oh, sorry, but I figured I was a dead man."

"You said no one died," Mack said. "Frank O'Meara died."

"We had nothing to do with that," Blackburn said. "Ortiz's people were responsible."

"So you know about Ortiz?" Mack said.

"Yes. About a month ago Interpol informed the FBI about a Grand Cayman bank account that Ortiz's company was funding, and the Feds passed the information on to us. The account is in Dr. Kischman's name, so we put two and two together. As for O'Meara, we weren't aware he was dead until Mrs. Herbst demanded a thorough autopsy. Of course, we couldn't let that happen. So with some help from the mayor's people, we arranged things at the morgue so it wouldn't."

"How'd you get the mayor in your pocket, if you don't mind my asking?" Otis said.

Blackburn looked at the First Lady.

"Go ahead, David. They might as well know it all."

Blackburn nodded. "Every politician has at least one skeleton in the closet. The mayor is no exception. It took a little digging, but we found it. It might not cost him his job if it got out, but it would probably keep him out of the governor's mansion."

Otis understood. It was no secret that Mayor O'Connor was considering running for governor in two years when the next election took place.

"How about Ortiz?" Jacobs said. "If you knew about the Kischman connection, why didn't you do something about it?"

Blackburn shrugged. "What could we do other than keep him under surveillance? Through Kischman Ortiz knew about the purpose of the Project. If we went after him, he'd be certain to blow the story wide open. So he became a kind of unholy partner."

"Yeah, well your unholy partner was also responsible for the murders of Alward and Diane Bates," Mack said. "And the abduction of Megan's little girl."

"Abduction?!" the First Lady said. "What are you talking about?"

The First Lady listened to Mack explain, her emotions a turmoil of shock and remorse at the thought of what could have happened to Katie.

"Oh my God! I'm so sorry, Megan!" she said, her eyes tearing up. "I hope you can forgive me."

Megan didn't answer. The First Lady was not responsible for Katie's abduction or her dad's murder. But what they had done to her dad had ultimately resulted in his death, and forgiving the First Lady for that was another matter.

"I'm not proud of what I did," the First Lady said, addressing the group again. "But I'd do it again to save my husband. However, there's more at stake than just his life. These are perilous times. I think you'll agree that not only the nation but the entire free world needs his leadership. If he is allowed to die, Vice President Kearny will take over, and frankly I don't believe he's up to the job."

The others were inclined to agree. It was common knowledge that shoot-from-the-hip "Woody" Kearny became the VP because he brought with him the extreme element of the party that Trippet had needed not only to get the nomination but to win the election.

"So what's the bottom line here?" Mack said.

"Your cooperation to keep the Project secret," was the First Lady's unhesitating response.

"Are you saying we just forget it?" Jacobs said.

"That's what I'm asking. Let me tell you what will happen if it gets out. The President would not only resign but face criminal charges, even though he knows nothing about the Project."

"He doesn't know about it?!" Mack said.

"That's right. Of course, no one would believe that, but it's true. I told you, the Project was my idea. When Byron's physician informed me about his condition, I told him not to tell the President. He doesn't know, and, God willing, he never will!"

This revelation was startling to everyone, Mack included. He'd figured that the President had to be in on it, but if the First Lady was telling the truth, it put a whole new slant on things. But was she telling the truth?

The First Lady was wrestling with her own emotions. Did they believe her? She could only hope that they did and would agree to cooperate. Since no one was saying anything, she decided to take the initiative. "How about you, Mr.

Butler?" she said to Willie. "Can I count on your help?"

Mr. Butler, Willie thought! He couldn't remember anyone ever addressing him as *Mr.* Butler. So maybe it was just a way of the First Lady to soften him up, get him on her side. Well, if it was, who gave a shit, because he had already made up his mind. The Prez was a Vietnam vet, like himself. Done two tours and been decorated for valor. No fucking way he would see him disgraced. No way!

"I'll go along."

"Count me in, too," Otis said before the First Lady could ask him.

For Otis the choice was a given. The First Lady was right when she'd said that no one would believe that the President wasn't involved in the Project. If it was revealed, the repercussions would make Watergate look like a tea party and leave the country in a state of turmoil for years with disastrous reverberations that would be felt around the world.

The First Lady turned to Jacobs. "This is quite a story for you, Mr. Jacobs."

Quite a story, Jacobs thought! Only the story of the decade, maybe the century, and one that would guarantee him a place in the history books for breaking it! But at what cost? Jacobs remembered other big stories that had been suppressed by reporters, and for good reasons—the breaking of the Japanese Naval code during World War II, Kennedy's deal with Khrushchev to remove missiles from Turkey in exchange for the Russians backing off during the Cuban missile crisis. For that matter the press's deliberate failure to expose Kennedy's many romantic indulgences, including one with an East German spy. So okay, Jacobs, he said to himself. You want to be a real hero, what do you do?

"What the hell. There are other stories."

"Thank you, Mr. Jacobs." The First Lady laid her hand on Megan's. "I know this is asking a lot from you, Megan. Especially considering your loss."

"Yes, it is." Megan had been asking herself what her dad would have decided if he'd known he was being used as a guinea pig. He'd fought a war for his country, risked his life. Given a choice, would he have risked it again to save the life of the President?

"I think my dad would want me to do what was good for the country."

The First Lady squeezed Megan's hand, then looked at Mack.

"And you, Detective McPherson?"

Mack didn't reply. He just stood there looking at the First Lady as though trying to read her heart through her eyes, his face offering no clue as to how he would decide her fate.

Mack felt the gentle touch of a hand upon his arm. Megan was looking up at him, her eyes filled with compassion. She knew what an extraordinarily difficult decision this was for him to make. To do what the First Lady was asking of him, he would have to break his vow to Kenny that he would never let anyone escape justice because they were wealthy or powerful, a vow that he had kept throughout his entire adult life. Please God, she thought, let him let go of the past and choose what is best for the future!

Mack looked down at Megan, then turned back to the First Lady and looked again into her eyes—those deep, haunting, unfathomable eyes. "I've got to think this over," he finally said. "If you don't mind, I'm going outside to get some air."

Mack moved to the door, opened it, then turned to see Blackburn reaching for a weapon in his shoulder holster. "Don't worry. I won't leave the area." Blackburn relaxed and let his hand return to his side.

Mack stepped down from the RV and walked slowly to the water's edge. Aside from the chatter of insects and frogs, it was quiet, tranquil, and peaceful. Rays from the full moon shone through a break in the clouds and shimmered on the dark glassy surface of the lake. Mack sat down on a tree stump. He sat there for several minutes, listening to the lapping sound of the water and inhaling its dank aroma, as he and Kenny had done years ago at Webster Lake before they went to bed. He remembered how sometimes they'd fish by the light of a lantern and talk about what they had done that day and what they planned to do the next day and during the remaining days of summer—and how Kenny would serenade the lake residents on his clarinet. Mack could hear the strains of "Stardust," "Moonglow" and other haunting ballads in his mind, and smiled wistfully at those memories. Here next to the lake at night he could almost feel Kenny's presence, hear his voice.

"Bet I can skip a rock farther than you can."

"Bet you can't," Mack said aloud.

Mack got up and found a flat rock. He flung it side-armed and watched it skip four times across the water before it sank.

"Beat that, Kenny," Mack said.

Kenny never could, but Mack often let him win just to build up his confidence.

Mack took a deep breath and turned his attention to the choice he was being asked to make. The First Lady had conspired with Roy O'Neal to use human beings as guinea pigs without their knowledge or consent. When they could no longer find "subjects" who were already infected with the virus, they had deliberately infected others, exposing them to sickness and death, in order to continue their experiments. While the First Lady had never ordered anyone killed except Mack himself, she had set in motion events that resulted in the deaths of Frank O'Meara, Dr. Alward, Morgan Fry and Diane Bates. She had broken the law, and the law applied to everyone, the First Lady included.

On the other hand, if she was telling the truth, not acting—with those intense glistening eyes of hers, it was hard to tell for sure—then she had done what she did almost exclusively for unselfish reasons: out of love for her husband, who she claimed knew nothing about Lazarus and was even unaware of his own approaching death; out of concern for her country, which sorely needed his leadership in these deeply troubled times; and in the belief, unfortunately but almost certainly true, that the President's death or resignation could send the country into chaos and the world to the brink of war.

Mack picked up another flat stone, but didn't throw it, just held it loosely in his right hand. He reached under his shirt with his left hand, drew out the swim medal, and held it up so it glistened in the moonlight. Should he keep his promise to Kenny again? Is that what Kenny would have wanted him to do?

"What about it, Kenny? Is it?"

Mack thought he knew. He was remembering an incident that occurred on their grade school playground when he caught a bully giving Kenny a rough time. Mack was beating the crap out of the bully when he felt Kenny tugging at his arm.

"Stop it, Mack! Stop it!" he pleaded. "He's had enough!"

Yeah, he knew what Kenny would have wanted him to do. But the decision wasn't Kenny's. It was his. And the time to decide was now: Should he keep his promise to Kenny that he would never let anyone escape justice because of money or power or position—a promise that had been his lamp and compass for more than a quarter century—or participate in a massive, historic, unprecedented cover-up?

Then there was the other promise Mack had made when he became a cop, and that one was made exclusively to himself. He had sworn that if he ever saw that a crime was about to be committed, he would do everything in his power to stop it so that innocent people would not be hurt. Would he be violating that promise if he let Suzanne Trippet go unpunished? Apparently not. If the vaccine that had been given to Willie would in fact cure the disease, as she said it would, then there would be no more experiments and no more killing. In fact, some of those addicted old men, whose lives were like a living death, like Frank's had been, and Willie's, might get a real life back again. And that would certainly be a fitting conclusion for the Lazarus Project.

A few drops of a light rain began to dance on the surface of the lake. Mack smiled, remembering Portia's judgment in *The Merchant of Venice*: "*The quality of mercy is not strained. It droppeth as the gentle rain from heaven upon the place beneath.*" Looking up at the moon sailing free beyond the rack of clouds, he let a few drops of rain fall onto his face, opened his mouth and tasted the sweetness of the water, then tucked the swim medal back under his shirt. He tossed the flat stone he was still holding in his right hand into the lake, not trying to skim it this time, just letting it sink below the surface of the water.

Turning, he walked unhurriedly back to the RV, where the others were waiting anxiously inside. When the door opened and Mack entered, all eyes turned toward him, trying to read his decision in the expression on his face. But Mack's face gave them no clue.

He walked over to Suzanne Trippet and stood in front of her for what seemed like a long time, saying nothing, but looking deep into her dark eyes, as though searching for something…a reaction, an emotion, anything that would reveal her true character, whether she was sincere or just manipulating all of them with her consummate acting skills. But he had already made his decision.

Without a word, he turned and walked to the rear of the RV where some fishing gear was stacked in a corner and removed an object from the tackle box. Returning to the divan, he offered it to the First Lady. It was a camcorder tape.

"I think you'll want this," Mack said, with the hint of a smile finally brightening his face.

The First Lady took the tape, which she correctly assumed was of the interview Jacobs had recorded. "Thank you, Detective," she said, "thank you very much." Then to the others, "Thank you, all of you. I'm very grateful." She turned to Megan, her taut lips relaxing into a warm smile. "I wonder if I could impose on you for another cup of that coffee?"

"I've got a better idea," Otis said. He slid out of the dining nook, opened a cabinet over the microwave and took out a bottle of brandy. "Hennessy XO. I've been saving it for an occasion."

The offer, which was received with a chorus of enthusiastic cheers, relieved the tensions of everyone, Mack included. Why the hell not, he thought? He still wasn't a hundred percent sure he had made the right decision, but, right or wrong, he was going to drink to it.

## Monday, May 27

*10:30 a.m.:* Mack picked up his badge. Superintendent Hollender had just laid it on his desk. Mack correctly assumed that this required a supreme effort by The Hawk, as did what he was about to say.

"You'll be pleased to know that you've been officially cleared of the murder of Diane Bates and any misconducts have been removed from your record."

"That's good. I assume you were able to pin her murder on one of the dead Mexicans via his DNA?"

"We were. His rap sheet ID'd him as Carlos Lopez, an illegal who did time and is wanted for about everything in the book."

"That figures. How about my revolver?"

Hollender removed Mack's service revolver from a drawer and laid it on his desk. "We also cleared Butler of Alward's murder. We found a razor on the body of the hit man, Chavez, and DNA on the razor matched Alward's."

Mack leathered the .38 in his hip holster under the windbreaker, while waiting in vain for The Hawk to thank him for tipping him off about the razor. "So what kind of spin are you putting on all of this?"

Hollender leaned back in the swivel chair and regarded his clasped hands. "For the record, and this is Blackburn's record, not mine, but for the record it goes this way: Roy O'Neal asked you to investigate a possible leak at Bio-Sci. You suspected Dr. Alward, who was still doing some research for the company. When Alward hit the panic button, Chavez had to take him out and..."

"Hold on, hold on. Kischman is the real heavy. He was the sellout, not Alward."

"Not according to Blackburn."

"Are you telling me that Kischman walks?"

"He walks. That's the way Blackburn wants it, for reasons known only to himself. Besides, with all the witnesses dead, all we have on him would be circumstantial at best. Any half-ass lawyer could get him off."

"Too bad," Mack said, but he understood why Blackburn would not want any charges pressed against the doctor. If they brought too much heat on him, he'd be sure to reveal the Lazarus Project and the First Lady's involvement. "I assume that goes for Ortiz as well."

"It does. We can say that Chavez was presumably working for a foreign drug pirate, but that's all, unless we want to get our ass sued big time by Ortiz, which the DA is not about to let happen."

"What about Diane Bates's murder?"

"Alward was only part of the picture. One of the lab techs was also on the drug pirate's payroll, and Bates suspected who it was. Fearing for her life, she offered to cooperate with you if you could get her into a witness protection program."

"Let me finish it for you. Chavez and the Mexicans got to her before she could reveal the tech's name."

"Right. But Chavez didn't know that. Since his boss would stand to lose millions if his pipeline to Bio-Sci was shut down, you had to be taken out. To accomplish this, Chavez abducted the Herbst child."

"Well, at least that part has a ring of truth."

Hollender cracked his knuckles. "What's true and what's not true I don't want to know. I was never in the loop on this, and that's fine by me."

"Okay, wind this up for me. Since it can't be Kischman, who takes the rap as the tech sellout?"

"No one. O'Neal will let it be known in time that an internal investigation has resulted in the resignation of an employee whose name he prefers not to reveal to avoid any possible legal repercussions."

"Cute. One more little detail, and that's Frank O'Meara's death. How's that going down?"

"As it stands. Accidental drowning."

"I hope Megan Herbst can live with that." But Mack already knew that she would. No way she'd go back on her promise to the First Lady. "So when are you going to break the story?"

"I'm not. It's the mayor's request that we let Jacobs do that."

More likely the First Lady's request via Blackburn, Mack figured, in appreciation for Jacobs's cooperation. As for himself, Mack cared only about getting his name cleared, but he wondered how he would come off in what would be a big story for Jacobs. "And how about me? How will I be spun in all of this?"

Hollender's smile looked like it could curdle cream. "Why you come off as the super cop. In fact, I'm putting you in for an award for valor. Detective Winstrom as well, for helping you rescue the Herbst child and take out the bad guys."

"Thanks, but it's too bad you can't pin a medal on Willie, too. We couldn't have done it without him."

"Don't worry. Jacobs will make a hero out of Butler as well."

"He deserves it. And a lot more. Maybe there's some kind of job with the city he could have?"

"I'll see what I can do."

"Thanks," Mack said, reassessing his opinion of The Hawk. Maybe he wasn't such an asshole after all. "And I appreciate you seeing me on a holiday."

"Holiday?" Hollender said with a wry smile. "For the good people of this city, maybe, but not for me or the department. It's Memorial Day, and there's a big fireworks show tonight off Navy Pier, and you know what that means."

Mack did. The lakefront would be a mob scene requiring more cops to handle the heavy traffic and deal with the pickpockets and gangbangers who would turn out in full force.

"But there is something you can appreciate," Hollender said. "Mayor O'Connor has instructed me to reassign you to Homicide, which I'm doing as of right now. You report to Area One tomorrow morning."

"Extend my thanks to the mayor," Mack said. He'd hoped that eventually he'd be transferred back to Homicide, but now that it had happened, he wasn't as up about it as he thought he'd be. Maybe it was the fact that he'd lose a partner whom he'd come to both like and respect.

Hollender cracked his knuckles again. "One last thing, and this time it's my turn to do the appreciating, and that's if from this moment on you'll do everyone a favor and stick to the book."

"I think I can handle that," Mack said.

"See that you do," Hollender added firmly.

Then Mack did something that neither of them expected. He held out his hand. For a moment The Hawk glared at it as if it were the head of a rattlesnake. Then he took it in a firm grip.

Mack nodded, turned and exited the office. By the book, he thought. Yeah, that's the way it would be…unless…. No, he wouldn't think about that, wouldn't go there right now. But he was thinking about a little unfinished business he wished he could take care of.

*10:49 a.m.:* Mack spotted the Taurus. Since it was parked beside his Bonneville in the headquarters lot, it was obviously not there to be overlooked. But Mack had to get closer to see that the man behind the wheel was Blackburn. He was smoking a pipe, and he was alone. As Mack approached, the driver's window slid down to release the aroma of roasted chestnuts.

"How did it go with Hollender?" Blackburn asked.

"Since you gave the orders, I guess you already know. Is this a social visit or what?"

Blackburn tapped the pipe on the edge of the window, dumping smoldering ashes onto the asphalt. "Something like that. Let's take a ride."

Mack wondered what kind of ride. Maybe Blackburn didn't believe that he would keep his promise to his boss. However, if that was the case, he'd have his two agents with him to provide some further persuasion. No, Blackburn had something else on his mind.

"Sure. Why not?"

Mack moved around to the passenger side, opened the door and ducked into the seat. Buckling up, he said, "Mind telling me where we're going?"

"You'll see."

Blackburn fueled the engine and drove to the exit, where he braked the Taurus at the guard shack long enough to show his ID again to a policeman at the security station. After the barrier arm raised, Blackburn gassed the sedan, hung a right onto 35th, and stopped at Michigan Avenue. He waited briefly for an opening in the flow of traffic before turning left and heading north on Michigan.

"I wanted to take this opportunity to apologize for what we put you through."

"You mean for trying your damnedest to kill me?"

"That was not my original intention, Detective. I was certain that you'd survive an attempt on your life by a doped-up petty hood like Morgan Fry."

"Very considerate of you. So why did you sic Fry on me?"

"Call it a warning shot across the bow."

"The idea being that I should back off my investigation."

"Exactly. I knew that the shooting would go down as a revenge motive, but that you were smart enough to get the real message. Unfortunately, it was a message you chose to ignore. And when you were able to break into the Bio-Sci computer…"

Mack finished it for him: "You kicked things up to the next level."

Blackburn shrugged. "It wasn't an action that I would have taken if there had been any other options. Again, my sincere apologies."

"Thanks, but not accepted. So now that you've got that off your conscience, what is this little ride all about?"

Blackburn hard righted through a green light at 31st street and headed east before replying. "It occurred to me that we still have a problem."

"*We*? The last time I checked I wasn't on your payroll."

"No, but knowing your penchant for taking the law into your own hands, I'd say that's definitely the case."

"You're referring to Ortiz and Kischman."

"Correct. It would be a shame to see them escape justice for their crimes."

"As well as eliminate the risk that one or both of them might reveal the Lazarus Project at some future time."

"That possibility had occurred to me."

"I'm sure. But you're right. Aside from dispensing justice, I've got a personal score to settle with Ortiz. One problem. I haven't a clue where he is other than he's in Chicago."

"Fortunately, I do. We've been keeping Mr. Ortiz on our radar screen ever since we found out about the Kischman connection. With some help from the FBI, it wasn't too difficult to track him to Chicago. He always carries a briefcase with him. Aside from a variety of phony ID's, credit cards and cash, it's loaded, literally, with an MP-5. Before Ortiz came to Chicago, he was shacked up with a girl in a suite at the Mandarin Hotel in Miami. One of our people, posing as a maid, managed to plant a GPS chip in the briefcase."

Mack had to hand it to Blackburn. The man was very good at his job. "So where do I find him?"

Blackburn swung the Taurus onto the entrance ramp to the Outer Drive and merged with the northbound traffic before responding. "You'll know in a minute. One more thing. If something is to be done about Ortiz and Kischman, it has to be soon, because they're leaving for Venezuela tonight."

"And with the Lazarus cure, I assume?"

"You assume correctly. Thanks to some wiretaps in Ortiz's place of residence and a car he rented, we've been listening to his conversations with the good doctor, which is how we know about their traveling plans."

Mack nodded glumly. "That doesn't give us much time, for sure."

"No, it doesn't." Blackburn angled the Taurus into the right lane as they passed the McCormick Exhibition Center. "Do you have any experience with power boats?"

"Some when I was a kid, but usually behind them on water skis," Mack said, wondering about the question. "Other than that, most of my boating experience comes from crewing for a buddy on a Catalina."

"That so? I'm a part-time sailor myself, but on a catamaran. I can handle a small power boat but when it comes to the big, powerful racers, a pro I'm not. Which poses another problem."

"How so?"

"Because Ortiz is."

Mack was beginning to get the picture. Blackburn had exited the Drive onto 18th Drive and was heading toward Burnham Harbor. "Don't tell me Ortiz is holed up on a boat?"

"He is. He's been living on a Black Thunder sports cruiser since Saturday morning under the name of Salizar. He rented it at the Michigan City Marina after flying his Cessna there from Boca Raton."

"A pilot, too. A man of many talents, Ortiz."

"And a crack shot, I might add," Blackburn said, pulling into the parking lot. "Big game hunter."

"Is that information intended as a heads-up?"

"You can call it that." Blackburn eased the Taurus into a parking space, braked and killed the motor. "This won't be easy."

"It never is. So how do we deal with our mutual problem?"

"Good question. I'll be right back."

Blackburn got out of the Taurus and walked to the harbormaster's building. While he waited, Mack pondered the situation. By the time Blackburn returned Mack was beginning to come up with an idea.

"Just wanted to make sure that there was no change of plans by Mr. Ortiz," Blackburn said, as he slid behind the wheel. "There isn't. He's already settled his bill and is scheduled to leave at 9:30 p.m."

"This boat, the Black Thunder. How fast will it go?"

"Up to 95 miles per."

"Would a cigarette boat match that speed?"

"I think so."

"So as long as we're here maybe it would be a good idea to rent one."

"I was thinking along those lines myself. But since we're both amateurs, it would be nice if we had someone who could handle it. Any suggestions?"

Mack smiled. "Well, I can't say for sure he'd accept, but I think I know a man who'd love to be asked."

*9:32 p.m.:* Ortiz guided the Black Thunder away from the dock. It was shortly after dusk, and the moon was just appearing on the horizon as though rising majestically out of the lake. With only a slight, cooling breeze out of the east and a cloudless sky, for Ortiz it was a perfect night for the first leg of their journey across the lake. However, he was aware that his traveling companion, sitting next to him in the cockpit's double bolster, was a jumble of raw nerves.

"Relax, Otto. Have another drink."

"Yes, yes, I believe I will," Kischman said. Removing a cold bottle of Grey Goose from an ice bucket, he splashed vodka over ice in his rocks glass. "I can tell you that I'm more than relieved to be leaving earlier than I had expected."

"If you're still worried about McPherson, don't be. Although he survived my plans for him at the church, he's still wanted by the police."

"Yes, but I'd feel better if he was in custody."

"So would I, Otto. Or better yet, dead. And I can assure you of the latter, even if he gets himself exonerated for the murder of your assistant."

"How can you be certain of that?"

"Because one of my first actions when we reach Caracas will be to put out multiple contracts on him. My only regret is that *I* won't be the one to pull the trigger."

A perplexed look from Kischman. "*You* want to kill him yourself?"

"Yes. Not only would it provide me great satisfaction, but it would remove any uncertainty about his demise. However, I have to admit that I've never met an adversary as challenging as McPherson."

And one who was still giving him recurrences of that disquieting feeling, Ortiz thought, that premonition. But of what? Ortiz didn't know. What he did know was that the disk inside his briefcase would soon double his already considerable wealth, which he celebrated with another sip of Grey Goose.

"Aren't you going to answer your phone?" Kischman said.

Absorbed by his thoughts, Ortiz hadn't heard the cell beeping. Pulling it from the pocket of his windbreaker, he inserted the earpiece into his right ear before answering. McPherson again? No, the number on the cell screen was one he both knew and welcomed.

"Yes, little one?"

"*Amor*, I am so sad. You have not called your Rosita for so long."

"I know. I'm sorry but my business has taken so much of my time."

"So much time that you forget your Rosita?"

"That would be like forgetting my own name. You are always in my thoughts, little one. And I have good news. I have concluded my business sooner than I expected and am leaving Chicago now."

"Oh, that is wonderful, *amor*. You have made me so happy. How long will it take you to get here?"

"I'm not going to Miami. It is necessary for me to fly directly to Caracas."

"To Caracas. I do not understand."

"I'll explain later. My private jet will fly you to Caracas tomorrow morning at 11:30. I have already settled the hotel bill and alerted the crew. A limo will pick you up at nine. The money I have given you should take care of any necessities.

"Oh, yes. You give me so much money it makes me nervous. You will be at the airport, *si*?"

"No. You will get there before I do. My servant will meet you and drive you to my *hacienda*. When I arrive, we will have a very grand celebration."

"Oh, that is so wonderful. I will be waiting for you, *amor*. I miss you so much."

"I miss you, too, little one."

Which was more than true, Ortiz thought, pocketing the cell. He was smiling at the thought of their sexual reunion, the warmth of her young, lush body against his, as he swung the Black Thunder east after passing Soldier Field. It was dark by the time they reached the open water beyond the harbor, but Ortiz maintained the speed at 10 m.p.h. due to the numerous boats on the lake, their running lights sparkling in the dark water like a swarm of fireflies.

"Are there always so many boats out at night?" Kischman asked.

"No. There's a fireworks show tonight to celebrate your Memorial Day. We will be able to observe it. It should be quite spectacular."

"If it's all the same to you, I'd prefer we get to where we're going as soon as possible. You said Michigan City?"

"Yes. We'll have supper on the boat when we reach the harbor. Only cold cuts and caviar, but I think you'll find it more than satisfactory. And a limo to take us to the airport."

"You think of everything, Manuel."

"I pride myself in doing just that, including sandwiches and thermoses of coffee that we'll need during our long fight to Caracas."

"What about the weather?"

"I've already used my laptop to access the internet and file a flight plan with the Flight Service Station. There might be a couple of bumpy moments but most of the flight should be comfortable."

"I must confess that I'm a little nervous about the flight. This will be my first experience in a small plane."

"Don't worry, Otto. Unlike a big jet, the Cessna will glide if by any chance both motors were to fail, which would give me a chance to put her down somewhere. And, of course, we could use the parachutes."

Grimacing at that prospect, Kischman took another long pull from his rocks glass. "I certainly hope it won't come to that!"

So did Ortiz, but if it did, given his jumping experience, he was fully prepared to survive. That thought reminded him that he hadn't done a jump for some time. He missed the thrill of plunging through space before releasing the main rectangular chute and gliding blissfully to earth. By pulling down the toggles about twelve feet off the ground, he was able to walk the chute in. Ortiz was making a mental note to arrange another jump when the Black Thunder moved beyond most of the boats that were gathered for the fireworks.

"Better put down the drink, Otto." Ortiz said. "I'm going to open her up." Ortiz set his tumbler into one of the drink holders embedded into the custom console, as did Kischman. "Hang on."

Ortiz pushed the hammer-shaped throttle forward. He felt his back pinned against the bolster as the bow of the sports cruiser rose briefly out of the water with a roar of its dual Mercury 500 EFIs.

"My God! How fast are we going?" Kischman shouted.

"Only 65 miles per hour. This boat has a top speed of over ninety. I find it very exhilarating, don't you?"

"No, I can't say I share that feeling."

As attested by his hands braced against the console, Ortiz thought. Kischman was such a...how did the Americans put it? Such a wimp. Ortiz detested such men. If he didn't need the scientist, he'd push him overboard with the greatest of pleasure. Ortiz was musing about this when he heard the cell phone beeping in his ear. Rosita again, he thought, picking the phone off the dash and raising it to his mouth.

"Yes, little one?"

"Sorry to disappoint you, Ortiz."

"McPherson!"

Kischman gasped. "It's the detective! I knew it!"

"Shut up!" Then into the cell: "Ah, detective. Nice to hear from you again. I assume you are still a fugitive from justice?"

"Not any more, *amigo*. I've been cleared of all charges. Even got my badge back. But that's not why I called you."

"Oh? And why did you call me?"

"To refresh your memory. Do you remember what I told you before?"

Ortiz did. That someday he would look over his shoulder, and McPherson would be there. But such a thing was not possible. It couldn't be. Yet, when Ortiz looked over his shoulder and saw a cigarette boat bearing down on them, he not only realized that it *was* possible, but that his premonition had become an alarming reality.

Mack tapped Dan Hewitt on the shoulder.

"He's kicked up the speed," he shouted in order to make himself heard over the roar of the dual MerCruiser engines.

"I know," Dan shouted back from behind the helm of the powerful cigarette boat. "But we'll catch his ass."

Mack had every confidence that he was right. According to Dan, the boat would do over 100 m.p.h. The vinegary former World War II PT boat skipper had been a good choice to drive the racer. And Mack had been right when he figured that he would be a willing volunteer for the job. More than willing, Mack thought, judging by the big grin on his weathered face.

"Why did you give..." Dan yelled, but the rest of it was drowned out by the roar of the engines.

Mack leaned toward the old man in the twin bolster seat beside him. "Say again."

"Why did you give them a wake-up call?"

"Call it psychological warfare."

Hewitt nodded as if he understood. Maybe, but Mack doubted it. He wanted Ortiz and Kischman to do some sweating. He wanted them to experience at least some of the terror that Alward and Diane must have felt when they were murdered. And a scared man was more vulnerable, more likely to make mistakes, easier to take out. Kischman, for sure, but Ortiz was another matter. The big game hunter would be more likely to remain cool under fire.

At the moment, Mack judged that they were trailing the Black Thunder at about a hundred yards and gaining. Ortiz had turned off the running lights, but the cruiser was visible in the moonlight. So were the other boats they had passed before they reached the open water. Nevertheless, Dan had wisely kept their navigation and stern lights on. A collision with another boat was something they didn't need.

When they closed the distance to about seventy yards, Mack lifted the MP-5 off his lap, figuring that they were close enough now for him to use the weapon. If he could put a bullet into the Black Thunder's fuel tank, the boat would eventually run out of gas or, better yet, get blown out of the water. Of course, the same applied to them. Mack wasn't forgetting that Ortiz also had an MP-5 and knew how to use it, which made getting off the first shots a priority.

"Let's give them something to think about," he shouted.

Mack stood up with his elbows braced against the console and prepared to fire a burst over the windscreen. Too late. He couldn't hear the automatic gunfire over the engines' noise, but the flashes from the stern of the Black Thunder were visible.

Dan pulled back the throttle, as bullets sprinkled the water about ten feet in front of the bow.

"What are you slowing down for?" Mack yelled.

"Getting out of harm's way," Dan yelled back.

Mack was surprised. This had to be a picnic compared to what Dan had been through in World War II. "Mind telling me why?"

Dan gestured behind them. "You're forgetting that we got an ace in the hole."

Mack grinned, clasped the old man's shoulder. "Aye, aye, Skipper." The cagy old cuss was thinking smart, Mack thought, and congratulated himself for having the foresight to bring along the hunting rifle Willie had used. With the Remington they could fire away at the Black Thunder while staying out of the effective range of Ortiz's automatic weapon.

Mack turned and shouted to the man in the rear bench seat who had the rifle. "Okay, Blackburn, the ball's in your court."

The secret service agent nodded and moved forward between Mack and Dan.

"I forgot to ask before," Mack said into his ear. "But how good are you with that?"

"Good enough."

Mack could only hope. "Okay. Go for it."

Kneeling, Blackburn rested the barrel of the Remington on the windscreen for support, took aim and squeezed off three rounds.

Ortiz couldn't hear the shots. It was the bullet that decapitated the head of the stern light and sprayed the cockpit with glass fragments that alerted him. Not that he hadn't expected to be fired on. He had. But when he'd seen the cigarette boat pull back after he fired his MP-5, he thought he might have bought himself some breathing space. Wrong. McPherson obviously had a weapon with a greater range than his MP-5. It was probably a hunting rifle, and Ortiz was wishing he had his own Browning BAR.

But he didn't. What he had was a bad situation. At this range his MP-5 was ineffective. All he could do for the moment was to zigzag the Black Thunder to make it more difficult for the shooter in the cigarette boat. Evasive action at best, but Ortiz knew it would only be a matter of time before a bullet would either hit him or the fuel tank. If it hit the tank and it didn't explode, the boat would eventually go dead in the water.

That wasn't his only problem. He also had a panicking Kischman on his hands. The doctor was cowering down behind the bolster, his face chalk white in the moonlight.

"How could he have found us?! How?! How?!"

Ortiz didn't answer, but he had a good idea how. The FBI must have planted a GPS microchip in his overnight bag, computer case or briefcase while he was in the Mandarin Hotel in Miami. An agent posing as a service maid, in all likelihood, and probably in the briefcase, since he always took it with him. He could deal with that later. For the moment he had to stay calm, keep his mind clear and devise a plan of action to escape McPherson and whoever else was in the cigarette boat.

Continuing across the lake was not an option. Somehow they had to get on shore. To do that, Ortiz had to elude his pursuers. An opportunity might present itself if they could lose themselves in the boats gathered for the fireworks show.

Ortiz cranked the wheel hard to port, bringing the Black Thunder in a sharp 180-degree turn that tilted the boat and flung Kischman against its side.

"My God, are you trying to kill us?!" Kischman shouted.

Ortiz righted the boat before answering. "I'm trying to save our lives, so stay down, if you want to go on living!"

Kischman did. Ortiz looked over his shoulder. The Cigarette boat was about eighty yards behind them and gaining. Ortiz knew he had to take some kind of evasive action.

The appearance of a cruise ship, the Odyssey, which was making its nightly dinner run, provided Ortiz with that opportunity, and he headed directly toward it. Its decks and picture window dining areas were crowded with passengers who were now in the line of fire of the shooter in McPherson's boat. As Ortiz expected, the shooter withheld fire.

Ignoring the repeated warning blasts of the ship's horn, Ortiz maintained his course. Just when a collision seemed imminent, he spun the wheel to the right, nearly sideswiping the ship's hull. Then he swung the Black Thunder in front of the Odyssey's bow in a sharp U-turn that put the ship between himself and the cigarette boat.

Momentarily out of view of his pursuers, Ortiz breathed easier. But only a little.

Mack clung to the bolster. The sharp turn by the cigarette boat had nearly thrown him out of the seat. This was not a concern. What was a concern was the fact that Ortiz's maneuver had put the Black Thunder out of sight for too many precious seconds. If that wasn't bad enough, when Dan brought the racer around the stern of the Odyssey, he had to yank the throttle back to avoid a head-on against the side of a power boat that was idling with its two occupants engaged in more than watching the fireworks.

"Asshole!" a young man at the helm yelled, breaking a clinch with his girlfriend long enough to brandish his fist.

"Sorry," Dan said, and got the boat moving again, but now at about 30 m.p.h., the reduced speed necessitated by the heavy boat traffic.

"Damn! We lost him!" Mack said.

"Not good, for sure," Dan said.

Blackburn lowered the Remington. "A slippery fellow, Mr. Ortiz. He'll be even more so if he gets to shore."

Mack had to agree. "Looks like all we can do is cruise around and hope we spot him."

"You do the spotting," Dan said. "I got my hands full avoiding a collision."

For sure, Mack thought. The lakefront was crowded with boats of every description, and too many were the size of the Black Thunder. Suddenly, a salvo of booming shells signaled that the fireworks show was beginning. At least the fireworks helped the visibility, Mack thought. A canopy of exploding rockets illuminated the area, their contrails filling the night sky with a collage of reds, whites, yellows and greens that were mirrored on the dark water. With a little luck they could still find the sports cruiser. However, once the fireworks show was over, the boats would disperse to various harbors, the Black Thunder with them.

Meanwhile, time was running out, and Mack had a sinking feeling that so was their luck.

Ortiz felt more confident. He'd eluded the cigarette boat and was cruising at 15 miles per hour amidst the boats massed for the fireworks. And now—thanks to his knowledge of the lakefront and its harbors—he'd thought of a way to get ashore before McPherson found him. Once there, he would take no chances flying out of O'Hare or Midway airports. He would use one of his phony IDs to rent a car and drive to another city, perhaps Milwaukee or Indianapolis. From there he'd take a commercial flight to Caracas via Mexico City.

A good idea, Ortiz thought, if he had time to carry it out. If McPherson believed or even suspected that he was dead, it would buy him more time, at least until he was safely out of Chicago. But how to accomplish this? Ortiz was considering a plan of action when Kischman's anguished voice reminded him that he still had another problem.

"Are we safe now?"

"For the moment," Ortiz said, pulling the throttle back to idle. "There's a canvas bag on the floor behind the bolster. Get it. I'll be right back."

"Alright." Kischman leaned over the bolster and picked up the bag by its handle, while Ortiz descended into the cabin. After making sure his wallet with its valuable contents were secure in a zipped pocket of the water-resistant windbreaker, he shed the jacket and removed the bullet-proof vest from his overnight bag. Ortiz had a hunch that he would need the vest before this night was over. In any event, he was taking no chances in case his plan failed. He slipped into the vest, then put on the jacket as he moved back onto the deck.

"What is this?" Kischman asked.

"An inflatable rescue raft. We're abandoning ship."

"What? Why are we doing that?"

Ortiz unzipped the bag and pulled out a four-man raft and two small, collapsed paddles. He was familiar with the Winslow Super-Light Rescue Raft. He had one for each of his three airplanes in case of a crash landing on the water. "There's still a strong possibility they'll find us on the boat, but they won't be looking for us on this. Stand back."

Using an attached CO2 canister, Ortiz inflated the circular raft.

"What are we going to do when we get ashore?"

"I'll tell you when we get there."

Ortiz grasped the raft by one of its handles and hoisted it over the gunwale into the water.

"Hold onto this."

Kischman took the raft's lifeline that Ortiz handed him. "I'm still worried. Maybe we should give ourselves up."

Ortiz climbed over the side and stepped agilely onto the raft with the MP-5. "You do that, Otto, if you're foolish enough to believe that they'll take you alive."

"They wouldn't just kill us in cold blood?!"

"Wouldn't they? With what we know about the Project?"

"Yes, yes, you're right. I wish I'd never gotten into this!"

"Too late for that now. Get the briefcase. It's under my bolster."

Kischman reached under the seat and pulled out the briefcase. "Be careful," he said, handing the briefcase to Ortiz. "I'd hate to lose that disk after all I've been through to get it."

Ortiz placed the briefcase on the raft. "My sentiments exactly, Otto. Now throw me the rope."

"What?"

"The lifeline. Throw it to me."

"But I have to get in first."

"Sorry, Otto, but there's been a slight change of plans."

"Change in plans? I don't understand."

Ortiz did. Kischman was now a liability he didn't need if he was to survive. "Perhaps this will explain."

Smothered by the booming fireworks, a burst from Ortiz's MP-5 tattooed Kischman's chest with bullets that flung him back against the side of the boat. His eyes glazed with shock, he hung onto the lifeline as if he was hanging on to life itself. Ortiz had to yank it hard from his grasp before Kischman toppled backwards over the gunwale into the water. Strange, Ortiz thought. This was his first kill of a human being, but it hadn't given him the feeling of exhilaration he'd anticipated. Too easy, of course. No challenge. Certainly no *momento supremo*. More like just stepping on a cockroach.

Ortiz didn't dwell on this. He had to take the next step of his plan. Laying the MP-5 down in the raft next to the briefcase, he reached over the gunwale with his left hand, grasped the handle of the throttle and waited until the bow of the Black Thunder drifted to where it was pointing directly toward the shore.

Ortiz knew that what he did now would take perfect timing if the raft was not to be swamped and possibly overturn. Shoving the throttle forward with his left hand, he pushed the raft away from the cruiser with his right hand. Ortiz had to kneel quickly and grab the top ring-strap of the raft, which rocked precariously from the turbulent wake churned by the powerful engines as the boat surged forward. When the raft settled in the water, Ortiz pulled out the handle of one of the paddles and began to propel the raft through the water.

A smile creased Ortiz's lips. He'd carried out the risky part of his plan. The rest should be easy.

Mack was on edge. They'd spotted the Black Thunder racing toward shore and taken off after it. However, the cruiser was making no attempt to avoid collisions with other boats, which were sounding their horns and scrambling to get out of the way.

"Is he crazy or what?" Dan shouted.

Mack was asking himself the same question. Ortiz was driving like a maniac, as if he'd hit the panic button. But would a man who'd faced wild animals be likely to panic now?

"I don't know," Mack yelled. "Watch out for the sailboat!"

Dan had already seen the two-master and skillfully steered the racer around its stern.

Blackburn kneeled between their bolsters. "At this rate they'll get ashore before we catch up."

"Not if Ortiz maintains his present course," Dan said. "He's headed toward the breakwall, and for that matter so are we."

"Maybe he doesn't see it."

"Then he must be blind."

Mack agreed. The fireworks provided enough illumination for him to make out the wall. Yet the Black Thunder sped on, as if Ortiz and Kischman had a death wish.

"If he doesn't turn now it will be too late," Dan shouted.

The cruiser didn't turn. It rammed the wall with an impact that cartwheeled it over the wall. When the boat splashed upside down in the water, its engine was smoldering. A moment later the fuel tank exploded, showering debris and burning gasoline.

Dan yanked the throttle back to idle. "Jesus! Nobody could live through that!"

"Looks like Ortiz did our job for us," Blackburn said.

"Think so?" Mack said. "I'm not so sure."

"Want to take a look?" Dan said. "They'll be floating if they're wearing vests, maybe even if they aren't."

Mack gestured to a police boat that was speeding toward the wreck. "Let the police look. They may find Kischman, but I'm betting Ortiz is still very much alive and figuring that we'll waste valuable time looking for his corpse while he gets away."

"Well, he's not swimming if he wants to take the disk with him," Blackburn said.

"No, but he could be paddling," Dan said. "The Black Thunder probably has an inflatable life raft. Most big power boats do."

"It figures," Mack said. "Where do you think he's heading, Dan?"

"Probably a harbor. Monroe Harbor is the closest. The entrance through the breakwall is just off our port. Want to give it a try?"

"We've got to start somewhere," Mack said.

"Roger," Dan said, reaching for the throttle.

"Hold it, Dan," Blackburn said. " Don't you think Ortiz might do something other than the obvious?"

Mack continued to feel a grudging respect for the secret service *honcho*, despite his personal dislike for the man who had nearly caused his death. "Such as?"

"I don't know. I'm not familiar with the lakefront. Where's the next entrance through the breakwall?"

"South," Dan said. "Not until you get to the Shedd Aquarium, which is quite a distance for a man with only a paddle."

"How about north?"

"No entrance. The wall dead-ends at the Marine Safety Station. But there's a drive there that goes to shore."

"Yeah, and what amounts to a path on the other side of the wall," Mack said.

"Which means he could walk to shore if he got onto the wall," Blackburn said. "How hard would that be, Dan?"

"No sweat for an agile man, given the big boulders at the base of the wall he could climb up on. 'Course, he'd have to have more than a little knowledge about the lakefront if he went that route."

"Which Ortiz may or may not have," Blackburn said.

Dan grunted. "Well, what's it gonna be? Monroe Harbor or do we cruise north along the wall? We haven't got time for both options."

"You're right," Blackburn said. "We've got to make a decision now!"

For sure, Mack thought. And if it was the wrong one, Ortiz would be home free.

Ortiz looked over his shoulder and tensed. A big power boat was heading his way. It was cruising slowly along the breakwall but gaining on him every second. Could it be McPherson's cigarette boat? Ortiz couldn't tell. It was too far away—more than a hundred yards, Ortiz judged—to make out clearly. Although it could be any one of the many powerful cruisers on the lake, Ortiz wasn't taking any chances. The crash ruse would have worked against any other adversary. But McPherson wasn't any other adversary. The detective may not have been deceived. And if he hadn't been, he could also have anticipated Ortiz's plan of escape. However, if it was McPherson, at least he hadn't seen the raft yet, or the cruiser would have increased speed. But Ortiz realized that he had about a minute at best before it caught up with him.

The situation forced Ortiz to improvise again. Fortunately, there was an opportunity for concealment—the fireworks barge. The barge was directly ahead. Paddling vigorously, Ortiz propelled the raft past the bow of the barge and then around to its north side. Enveloped by the dense smoke billowing from the mortars, Ortiz was now in a perfect position to observe the cruiser when it passed by without being seen by its occupants.

Now Ortiz was faced with two possible courses of action. If it wasn't the cigarette boat, he would still carry out his plan to reach shore along the breakwall. If it was McPherson's boat, Ortiz would head back south to Monroe Harbor, or better yet, flag down a power boat, give the occupants a story about running out of gas, and get a faster ride to one of the harbors or yacht clubs. In either event, Ortiz believed he would be able to escape.

However, as he waited for the cruiser to appear, Ortiz realized what tempting targets its occupants would be. Even though his eyes were tearing from the smoke and ash, and his eardrums ached from the percussion of the mortars,

Ortiz was sure he could take out McPherson and anyone else in the boat with his MP-5.

Ortiz picked up the automatic weapon and hefted it. No, don't be stupid, he told himself. The sensible thing to do was to get away. Forget about killing McPherson. One of the hit men he would hire would accomplish that. Yet, Ortiz felt his index finger caress the trigger of the MP-5, as it had the trigger of his Browning BAR before he imbedded a bullet into the skull of a wild animal. To him it was like caressing the sex of a woman, to arouse her—and himself—before entering her.

Ortiz felt the sensation now. Should he surrender to it? The temptation was great. But so was the risk if he missed and a firefight ensued. Of course, missing his targets was something he didn't anticipate. He'd never missed before. If he had, he'd be dead by now. Besides, it probably wasn't the cigarette boat. Just another cruiser. Probably. But if it wasn't?

Mack was worried.

"This doesn't look good. We should have spotted him by now."

"Maybe," Dan said. "Unless he made it onto the breakwall."

"Not likely," Blackburn said. "If he had, we would have seen the life raft."

Dan nodded. "We got no choice now anyway. It's too late to go back to Monroe Harbor. The Marine Safety Station is still a ways off. We might see him once we get around that damned fireworks barge."

Mack could only hope. The barge, which they were approaching, blocked their view of the breakwall. Also hindering visibility was the dense smoke issuing from the mortars. Mack pressed a handkerchief against his nose and mouth to keep the pungent fumes out of his lungs. A smoke mask would be preferable, he thought, like the ones he'd worn as a kid in high school when he'd worked for the pyrotechnics company in North Webster.

Mack observed that the lake show was remotely controlled, as were most displays, many by computers and choreographed to music. The pyrotechnics team, barely visible in the smoke, was working on a small barge off the stern of the larger fireworks barge. A windowed, wooden barrier kept them protected from any misfires. Mack hadn't been so fortunate. Most of the small events he'd worked had required that the mortars be fired manually, and Mack still carried a scar on his left arm from a shell that had exploded prematurely.

Mack unconsciously fingered the scar now as Dan maneuvered the cigarette boat around the barge's bow.

"Damn!" Dan said, coughing. "I ain't seen so much smoke since my PT got strafed by a Jap Zero in the Sealark Channel. My crew and I hit the water seconds before the fuel tank blew."

"We'll be clear in a second," Mack said. He tried to look ahead for any sign of the raft, but his eyes were tearing from the smoke swirling from a sudden gust of wind.

"Take cover!"

Blackburn's voice, shouting and pushing Mack down. Although he couldn't hear the shots, Mack felt the sting of a bullet that grazed his left cheek, while Blackburn rapid-fired the Remington.

Dan immediately kicked up the speed in a U-turn that flung Blackburn on top of Mack. "Where is the s.o.b.?"

"Next to the north side of the barge," Blackburn said. "I couldn't see him—too much smoke—but I saw the flashes of his weapon."

"Lucky you did," Mack said. He tried to rise, but Blackburn's body still had him pinned down.

"Give me a second," Blackburn said. With his right hand braced against the console, he grunted with pain as he pushed himself up to a sitting position. "Like Reagan said, 'I guess I forgot to duck'."

Then Mack saw the blood seeping from a hole in Blackburn's windbreaker over his left shoulder."

"You did more than that," Mack said. "You took a bullet that was probably meant for me."

"Let's say I owed you one."

"Debt repaid," Mack said. And meant it.

Ortiz couldn't believe what had happened. Crouching on the life raft, he'd waited for the cigarette boat to pass by. He didn't have to wait long. As he'd anticipated, it was McPherson's boat, and his vision was still clear enough for Ortiz to make out the detective and two other men. Ortiz raised the MP-5 and drew a bead on McPherson.

That's when it happened. A gust of wind obscured the boat in smoke as Ortiz squeezed the trigger. Now Ortiz didn't know if he'd hit McPherson or either of the other two men. What he did know was that he was immediately under return fire. When he saw the flash of a weapon, he felt the punch of a bullet against the bullet-proof vest right over his chest. Once again the vest had saved his life, he thought, as he flung himself prone onto the raft. The raft was another matter. The hiss of escaping air meant it had been hit. Ortiz didn't hesitate. The barge was only three feet above the water, so grabbing the briefcase with his left hand, he leapt easily on board.

Dan pulled the throttle back to idle. He'd brought the cruiser back south of the barge and far enough away to be out of harm's way. At least for now. The question was: What was their next move? Judging from Blackburn's bloody shoulder, there seemed to be only one choice.

"We'd better get you to a hospital, partner."

"That can wait. Mr. Ortiz can't. We've got him checkmated now. If one of my bullets didn't get him, chances are I put a few holes in the raft."

"He ain't goin' nowhere for sure," Dan said. "Especially if he's dead."

"There's only one way to find out," Mack said. "I've got to get onto the barge."

"Don't be crazy, son," Dan said. "If he's alive, he's probably on the barge. We try to get you on, we'll all be easy targets."

"He's right," Blackburn said. "But I see your point. We have to take him out now. When the fireworks are over, he can flag down a boat."

"Why not leave him for the cops?" Dan said.

Blackburn looked at Mack. They both knew that they couldn't bring any charges against Ortiz for fear that he'd reveal the Lazarus Project. "With Ortiz's money, he can hire the best legal brains in the country and probably walk."

"Not if I can get to him first," Mack said. "I've got another idea about getting on the barge." Mack offered the MP-5 to Blackburn. "Think you can handle this?"

Blackburn took the weapon. "I've still got one good arm."

"Good, because I may need some cover."

And a hell of a lot of luck, he thought.

Ortiz waited in suspense. The cigarette boat had moved south of the barge and taken up a position about fifty yards away. The fact that the boat was still there was not a good sign. Ortiz had to assume that nobody in the boat had been killed by his shots, perhaps not even wounded. And even if he was wounded, McPherson would still be dangerous.

For the first time in his life Ortiz could appreciate how a wild animal must feel when trapped by its hunters. In this event the animal usually attacked its adversary. And died—which Ortiz reasoned would be his fate if he fired at the boat again. Not only would that reveal his position but in a firefight he would be outnumbered and outgunned.

Unlike the trapped animal, Ortiz had another possible way out. It was one he detested, but he had no alternative. Somehow he had to surrender to the police. They would be his bodyguards until his lawyers arranged his bail, whatever the price. Of course, he would have to throw the MP-5 into the water. If the police tried to tie him to Kischman's death, there would be nothing they could prove without a weapon. The Lazarus disk would have to go over the side, too. However, this would not stop him from eventually getting the HCV cure. Like Kischman, someone else in the Bio-Sci lab could be bought once Ortiz was back in Venezuela.

This all flashed through Ortiz's mind as he continued to watch the cigarette boat. When the fireworks ended, the boats on the lake would disperse, which should give him the opportunity to hail one. McPherson would not dare gun down an unarmed man in front of witnesses.

Ortiz smiled. Once again he would outwit the detective.

Mack slipped over the gunwale into the water. With the barrel of his .38 clenched in his teeth to keep it reasonably dry—Mack hoped—he began to breaststroke toward the south side of the fireworks barge. The plan was to get onto the barge and surprise Ortiz. That was assuming that Ortiz was still alive and, even if he was wounded, able to use his MP-5. Mack had to assume that he was.

Mack also knew he'd need the smoke screen provided by the mortars to get onto the barge unobserved by Ortiz. So far, so good. But as he got about twenty yards from the barge, a barrage of rockets filled the night sky with multiple bouquets of exploding fireworks and booming shells in a spectacular finale. As debris showered down, a cacophony of boat horns sounded the spectators' appreciation for the show.

For Mack, the end of the fireworks was bad news. The smoke would clear soon, and if it was too soon, he'd be a sitting duck—a very dead one.

Ortiz realized he had to act now. The fireworks were over, but so far he hadn't been able to carry out his plan. Other than the cigarette boat, there were no other boats close enough to signal for help. Fortunately, there was an alternative, which was to swim over to the control barge, even if that meant having to shed the bullet-proof vest, and seek the security of the pyrotechnicians.

First he had to get rid of the MP-5 and the briefcase. But as he raised the weapon to throw it overboard, he froze. There was a sound—very faint—but a sound coming from the south side of the barge. What was it? Now he knew. A splashing sound. Something was in the water. Or someone!

Mack quickly submerged. As he did, he heard the rattle of Ortiz's MP-5 and felt the sharp stab of a bullet in his left shoulder. Not serious, he thought, since the water had cushioned the bullet's impact. What was serious was the fact that when he saw Ortiz materialize out of the smoke, he'd only had a split second to drop the .38, gulp a lungful of air and dive. Thanks to his summers spent on Webster Lake as a boy, Mack was an excellent swimmer and able to hold has breath underwater for a long period of time.

Mack knew he would need to do this again, not just to survive, but to take out Ortiz. Success would depend almost entirely on the element of surprise now that he had no weapon. His first attempt had failed, but he had one more chance...but only one. Mack knew it would be his last.

Ortiz readied the MP-5. Although he couldn't be certain he'd hit McPherson, he knew the detective would have to surface soon and somewhere in the vicinity of the barge. When he did, and before he could submerge again, McPherson would be visible long enough for Ortiz to get off another burst from the MP-5. And this time he wouldn't miss.

Mack surfaced. Even fully clothed, it had taken him less than a minute to swim under the barge to the north side. Filling his lungs with air, he made his way toward the stern in case Ortiz remembered his advice to "look over his shoulder." Mack hoped that Ortiz would expect him to come up on the other side of the barge or assume that one of his bullets had finished him. In either case, Mack wanted to put more distance between himself and Ortiz before he climbed onto the barge. Once he was on board, he could look for an opportunity to catch Ortiz off guard. However, the pain throbbing through his left shoulder was another problem. If it came down to hand-to-hand combat, *mano a mano*, Ortiz would have the upper hand if his bullet had done more damage to Mack's shoulder than Mack could feel. There was no way to tell. Or to know what would happen next. But Mack did know, when this was over, one of them would leave the barge in a body bag.

Ortiz was startled by the blast. Turning, he saw a rocket shooting up from one of the mortar tubes affixed in rows of wooden racks. A belated misfire, Ortiz assumed. He was about to turn away to look for McPherson when the barge was momentarily illuminated, first, by the bright explosion overhead, then by a fading weeping willow of contrails. Although his vision was still clouded by the lingering smoke, Ortiz saw something else he hadn't expected. A man was climbing onto the barge near its stern.

McPherson!

Ortiz quickly panned the MP-5, fired...and swore. After only a short burst of two or three rounds, the trigger went limp. By the time Ortiz replaced the empty clip with a full one from his briefcase, the detective had scrambled behind a huge, construction-size roller-dumpster.

Again Ortiz had to acknowledge the ingenuity of his adversary...and his own good luck. Had the rocket not misfired, he would have been in for a very unpleasant surprise. But now the detective had run out of surprises...and the ability to fire a weapon. If he still had one, which was unlikely, it would be useless now that it had been immersed in the lake.

Ortiz moved cautiously, one step at a time, toward the dumpster, musing how dramatically things had changed in only a few seconds. Now he was no longer the hunted. He was the hunter again—in control—with his quarry, McPherson, trapped and defenseless.

His heart was pounding with excitement. After a lifetime of searching, he was finally going to experience *el momento supremo*!

Mack crouched behind the dumpster. It was the only place of concealment on the barge—used, Mack knew, to secure the big mortars in sand to prevent serious damage in case of a misfire. Being able to get there without being hit told Mack that the clip in Ortiz's MP-5 had run out of ammo after only a short burst. But Mack also figured that Ortiz probably had an extra clip in his briefcase. The sound of Ortiz's voice confirmed that assumption.

"Very good, McPherson. I never expected you to swim under the barge."

Mack looked around. There was still a chance to survive if he found what pyrotechnicians called a "ready box."

"Did you hear me, Detective?"

"Loud and clear, *amigo*."

Mack spotted the box. Fortunately, it was only a few feet behind him.

"Good," Ortiz said. "I can't tell how much I've looked forward to meeting you. And, of course, killing you."

The asshole was really enjoying this, Mack thought, as he scuttled over to the large box and raised the lid. Good. Keep him talking, buy some time. "Sorry to disappoint you, *amigo*, but I've got you covered. So I'd advise you to drop your weapon and surrender."

A derisive laugh from Ortiz. "I think not, Detective. I think if you had a weapon, and it functioned, I would not be given the opportunity to surrender." Right about that, Mack thought.

Mack quickly scanned the contents of the ready box, which contained extra mortar tubes and shells. "Maybe. Maybe not. Do you want to take that risk?"

"But most certainly. What is life without taking risks? But in this case, I believe the only risk I am taking is being apprehended by the police. A temporary inconvenience, I assure you."

No doubt, Mack thought, and quickly selected a three-foot tube from the box. Against the high-powered lawyers Ortiz could hire, the DA would have a tough time proving anything that would stick if Ortiz threw the MP-5 and his briefcase overboard, which he would surely do. "The FBI might not make it so temporary," Mack said, grabbing a 6-inch long cylindrical "Spider" shell with a long fuse.

Another laugh from Ortiz, now closer. "Not if I am deported to my native country, Venezuela, on a previous charge—fictitious, of course—for which my very good friend, *Presidente Herrera*, would pardon me if he wishes to continue receiving ten percent of my company's gross profits."

Mack removed the final item he needed from the box—one of the road flares that were used to ignite the fuses. "Looks like you've got it all figured out."

"But of course. That is why I have always prevailed...and prospered. I plan ahead. Now would you care to step out and die like a man, or must I hunt you down like an animal?"

Mack scurried back to the dumpster. "You'll have to do it the hard way, *amigo*."

"As you wish."

Mack figured that Ortiz would try to outflank him. The question was: on which flank? To find out he had to take a chance of being hit. The dumpster was so high that Mack had to grab the rim and pull himself up to peer over the top. Ortiz was about forty feet away and angling toward Mack's left flank. Mack dropped down as a burst of bullets from Ortiz's MP-5 whizzed overhead.

"Sorry, *amigo*, but no cigar."

"*Esta bien*. There would be no satisfaction ending your life instantly by putting a bullet into your head. I think three or four in the belly would be more appropriate."

"Whatever turns you on," Mack said, moving quickly to the left side of the dumpster.

Mack knew he had to act fast. Ortiz would be on his flank in seconds. He dropped the shell into the mortar tube with the long fuse protruding out of the muzzle. Pulling off the red safety cap from the end of the fuse, he flamed the flare by scratching the tip against the dumpster and ignited the fuse. Now it was a matter of timing—and guesswork. As he watched the sparks of the burning fuse race into the tube, Mack knew from experience that it would take between ten and thirty seconds before the fuse would ignite the gunpowder in the lift charge that propelled the shell. If he exposed himself too early, Ortiz could easily cut him down before he had a chance to use the mortar. The same fate awaited him if he delayed too long, and the mortar fired before he could draw a bead on Ortiz.

Mack lay down on his back next to the left end of the dumpster, cradling the mortar in his arms. He figured that ten seconds had already elapsed. He counted off ten more, then rolled left onto his stomach so he was just beyond the end of the dumpster, propped up on his elbows and holding the mortar so he could sight along its length. Ortiz was about thirty feet away near the side of the barge.

Mack took quick aim. "Here, put this in your belly."

Ortiz was momentarily confused when he saw Mack lying prone on the ground, presenting a smaller target than if he were standing as Ortiz expected. He lowered his weapon to point where his target was lying and managed to get off a short burst of three or four rounds. Bullets clanged off the dumpster just as the mortar fired. Its recoil rolled Mack over and pushed him back behind the dumpster. He lay there stunned, not knowing if the shell had hit Ortiz, not knowing if bullets from Ortiz's MP-5 were about to rip into his body.

Ortiz saw the flash. Instantaneously the two-pound shell, traveling at more than 200 miles per hour, slammed through the bullet-proof vest into his stomach, hurling him backwards off the barge and out over the open water of the lake.

For a moment, Ortiz could not comprehend what was happening. He wanted to scream, but couldn't breathe. What was embedded in him so deeply? Why was he falling through space? He reached instinctively toward the tail of something protruding from his stomach, as though to wrench it out, but his hands jerked away when his skin was seared by the heat. What was it, this hot alien lump boring into him? Then he remembered the flash and understood what it was. Fireworks! He'd been shot with a mortar, and in a few seconds the shell was going to explode!

His body plunged into the lake, and he felt the water close over him, but the burning pain was like a fire in his belly so intense that the water could not cool it, but instead seemed to be boiling around him. He felt as if his lifelong hunger for *el momento supremo* had suddenly turned into a voracious animal that was tearing him apart, cooking him and consuming him from inside.

*El momento supremo!* He remembered his father's words: "At such a moment, you would feel a sense of pride and accomplishment so complete, you would be able to say to yourself, 'If I were to die right now, at this very moment, I would die happy, without regret, because I have done what I set out to do.'"

Something was terribly wrong! He had not set out to do this! Instead of achieving *el momento supremo*, he was dying an agonizing death at the hands of a superior enemy! Instead of pride and accomplishment, he was feeling only shame.

During the last few heartbeats of his life, he thought he saw his father look over his shoulder, then turn away in bitter disappointment. A huge cry—"*No, Father, no!*"—reverberated through him. Then the shell exploded.

A geyser of water, blood and body parts rose for a moment above the surface of the lake, then subsided, while light trails from the Spider burst dimmed and faded in the water's darkening depth.

## Saturday, June 22

*9:15 p.m.:* Mack was late. The band was on break between the first and second sets when he arrived at the Downbeat. Scanning the room—packed with the usual Saturday night patrons—Mack spotted Otis waving him over to a table near the bandstand. As he weaved through the tables, he was intercepted by Joe, who was making the schmooze rounds of his loyal patrons.

"Mack, good to see you. It's been a while."

"That it has, Joseph. Too long."

"How's your shoulder?"

"Doing good. The wound is nearly healed."

"Glad to hear it. Close call, my friend. By the way, did you know that you look pretty good on television?"

Mack chuckled. Joe was referring to his interviews by Jacobs on two of the *Deadline Chicago* broadcasts to discuss his part in solving what the media were calling "the drug-pirate murders."

"If I did, it was unintentional," Mack said.

"Well, you had me glued to the tube," Joe said. "That was one hell of a story."

More than you know, Mack thought. And with a new twist that was closer to the truth. With Kischman and Ortiz dead, they could be revealed as the bad guys. Alward now came off as a victim who was doing some private research for Bio-Sci when he found out that his old friend, Kischman, was selling lab secrets to the drug pirate, Ortiz, and made the mistake of confronting him about it. The same fate befell Diane Bates, after she sought protection from Mack for her cooperation in revealing her boss's betrayal of Bio-Sci and his part in Alward's murder. To keep the lab pipeline open for Ortiz, Mack also had to be silenced, this to be accomplished by the abduction of Katie by Ortiz's hit men in exchange for Mack. The church shootout and boat chase with the deaths of Kischman and Ortiz went down as they happened, except for Blackburn's participation. The presence of a Secret Service agent in the case would arouse unwelcome curiosity by the media. The same went for the contents of Ortiz's briefcase, which Mack had found on the barge and turned over to Blackburn.

"What would you like to drink?"

"What?" Mack said, still thinking how well things had turned out, not only with the media, but with the brass, Mayor O'Connor included. With an eye still on the governor's mansion in Springfield, Hizzonor had let it be known that he had personally sanctioned Mack's "unofficial" investigation of the Bio-Sci murders.

"I said what's on the beverage agenda? Jack Daniel's?"

"No. Have Ella bring me an Amstel Light, will you?"

"My pleasure. The good-looking young black man. Your partner, I assume."

"Ex-partner. I'm back in Homicide."

"And I take it the gorgeous black lady is his wife."

"She is. I've never met her, and I'm afraid she's not exactly a fan of mine."

"How about the redhead? Megan Herbst, as I recall."

"You recall correctly."

"Also a knockout. Anything serious?"

Mack smiled his cryptic smile before answering. "Joseph, did anyone ever tell you that you ask too many questions of a personal nature?"

Joe's laugh became a hacking cough before he could reply. "All the time. My apologies."

"You're forgiven," Mack said, patting Joe on the shoulder. "And the answer is *que sera sera*."

"Like the song."

"Like the song. Oh, and have a bottle of your best champagne sent over."

"How best is best?"

"Well, let's say about eighty dollars' worth of best."

"Will do. Is this an occasion?"

"Of a sort. Tell you about it later."

"I'll be all ears. And I'll serve the champagne personally."

"Thank you, Joseph."

Moving toward the table, Mack observed that Otis, Ava and Megan looked like they had just stepped out of a Neiman-Marcus display window. Although Mack had taken more than usual pains with his own attire—tan slacks, yellow shirt and a beige sports coat that actually matched color-wise—he paled in comparison to Otis in his navy slacks, red polo-style shirt and white windbreaker sporting a Ralph Lauren logo. The ladies presented appearances of casual elegance. Megan was wearing a silky looking, low-cut apricot-colored dress that complemented her flaming red hair, while Ava's white, strapless body-hugging dress accentuated her tall, slim figure.

"Hey, Mack," Otis said, grabbing Mack's outstretched hand. "Good to see you."

"You too, Otis."

"I'd like you to meet my wife, Ava."

Mack extended his hand to Ava, wondering if the warm smile on her lovely face was sincere. "Hello, Ava. I've been looking forward to meeting you."

Ava took his hand. "So have I, Detective."

"Call me Mack. I'm off duty."

Ava laughed. "Sorry…Mack."

The ice broken—Mack hoped—he released Ava's hand and turned to Megan. "Hello, Megan. You look great, as usual."

"Hi, stranger," Megan said, rising. "Does an old friend who hasn't seen you for ages rate a hug?"

"Sure." Mack gave Megan a polite hug and, once again surprised by the feisty redhead, got a kiss on the cheek in return.

"That's from Katie. She said it would make the pain go away."

"Pain?"

"Your shoulder."

"Oh, yeah. Well, it's practically good as new. Tell her thanks."

"I will."

Mack held Megan's chair before sitting down. "Sorry I haven't been in touch with everybody, but I've been kinda busy."

"So has the prez," Otis said, gesturing toward a TV over the bar, which was on during the band's break. It was muted but showed President Trippet hosting a press conference about his Mideast mission. "Looks like he got the job done big time in Paris."

"That he did," Mack said. "Frankly, I didn't think he could pull it off."

"Well, if you didn't already know that, you could tell by just looking at him," Ava said.

This drew stares from Mack and the others.

"My darling wife comes from a long line of psychics," Otis quipped.

"And my darling husband comes from a long line of corny jokesters," Ava countered, which drew laughs from the others. "Seriously, you must admit he hasn't seemed like his old self lately. You know, exhausted, both physically and emotionally. Like he had the weight of the whole world on his shoulders."

"Which he did and has," Megan said.

"Exactly," Ava said. "But just look at him now. A picture of high energy and confidence. It was as if his successful Paris mission gave him a new lease on life."

Mack and the others exchanged conspiratorial looks and smiles.

"Did I say something funny again?" Ava asked.

Otis reached over and took her hand. "No, darling. It's just that you're very observant…and right, as usual."

"Thank you, my darling husband," Ava said with a rewarding kiss on Otis's cheek. Then to Mack: "I understand congratulations are in order."

"Congratulations?"

"Yeah, that's right," Otis said. "For breaking the Feingold case."

"Oh, yeah. I guess it made some news."

Only some? Otis thought. The murder of the wealthy spinster was a headline grabber from the moment her severely beaten body was found in her North Dearborn brownstone. Given the missing jewelry, the murder went down as robbery related until Mack made the connection between the victim's nephew —one of the three heirs—and an ex-con who worked as a bouncer at a riverboat casino in Hammond, Indiana.

"How did you run down the bouncer?" Otis asked.

"He made the mistake of trying to hock the jewelry with a fence who keeps me informed—for a price, of course. The jewelry was part of the payoff for doing the hit. The nephew was a frequent high roller, and big loser, at the casino. The bouncer knew who he was and made a pitch that would set both of them up with big bucks. End of story."

"Well, you certainly do rate congratulations," Ava said.

"Thanks, but it was no big deal," Mack said. Then, to the bleach-blonde waitress, who was setting a bottle of Amstel Light on the table: "We'll be having supper, Ella, and the check goes on my Visa."

"You got it," Ella said, and scurried off to another table.

"Okay, what's the occasion?" Otis asked. "It must be something really special if you're buying."

"Tell you when Willie gets here," Mack said. "I wonder what's keeping him?"

"Willie?" Ava said. "Is he the vagrant who helped you save Katie?"

"Ex-vagrant. He's got a job with the Chicago Park District."

"No kidding?" Otis said. "That's great. I don't suppose you had anything to do with it?"

Mack took a swig of Amstel. "You can thank The Hawk. All I did was make a request."

"I'm surprised you didn't invite Mark Jacobs, as well," Megan said.

"I did, but by this time he's probably on his way to New York."

"Oh, what gives?" Otis asked, spearing an olive in his half-full martini glass.

"A job with Fox News as a field reporter, for openers. Jacobs did some follow-up reports of the Bio-Sci murders about the international market for synthetic pharmaceutical drugs and the pirates who manufacture them. The reports got Fox's attention, especially O'Reilly, who interviewed Jacobs on two of his programs."

"Good for him," Megan said. "I'm sure Jacobs will do well at Fox."

"With his ego, he'll fit right in," Otis said, drawing laughs from everyone. "Hey, here comes Willie now."

"Is that Willie?" Megan said. "I hardly recognize him."

She was referring to Willie's now clean-shaven face and formerly tangled hair that betrayed a recent visit to the barber shop. Added to that was his attire: clean, new-looking Levi's, a sky blue open-neck sports shirt and a beige windbreaker that had replaced the grimy, tattered fatigue jacket.

"Hey, Willie. Lookin' sharp," Otis greeted him before introducing him to Ava.

"It's a pleasure to meet you at last, Willie," Ava said, accepting his callused hand. "Otis has told me so much about you."

Willie looked a little embarrassed when he replied. "I guess that's good."

"Don't be modest, Willie," Megan said. "We're all very proud of you."

"Pull up a chair and sit down, Willie," Mack said.

"Yeah, and I hope you haven't eaten, because supper and drinks are on Mack," Otis said.

"I'd like to, but I promised Pastor John I'd help out tonight at The Beacon. He wants me to talk to some of the street guys, help them get straight."

"That's wonderful of you, Willie," Ava said. "Otis and I are going to do some charity work for The Beacon, too. Aren't we, dear?"

"Sounds like a plan."

"Maybe we'll meet up there sometime," Willie said. "I just dropped by to tell you I couldn't make it," Willie laid a small object wrapped in brown paper in front of Mack, "and return this."

"What is it, Willie?"

"The book you loaned me. *Les Miser*...something."

"*Les Miserables*?" Otis said.

"That's it. You read it, too?"

"Yeah, as part of an English Lit course at I.U. What did you think of it?"

"Well, I liked it okay up to the end. I mean, I was glad to see the ex-con... what's his name?"

"Jean Valjean."

"Right. Like I said, I was glad the cop finally got off his case. But then the cop kills himself. I don't get it."

"You see," Mack said, "the cop had this thing about the law. Justice had to be served, no matter what. So when he let Valjean go, he was breaking the law he'd dedicated his life to uphold. Therefore, he became his own judge, jury..."

"And executioner," Megan said, shooting a glance at Mack.

"Well, I still don't get it," Willie said. Then to Mack: "Anyway, thanks for the book. I'd better be going."

"Wait a minute, will you, Willie," Mack said. "I've got an announcement to make, so sit down and have a glass of champagne, okay?"

"Well, I'm not drinkin' much anymore. A beer on occasion."

"This *is* an occasion, Willie," Megan said, still looking at Mack.

Mack wondered if Megan was getting inside his head again. He wouldn't be surprised if she was.

Willie pulled up a vacant chair from a neighboring table. "Well, I guess I can stick around awhile."

"Okay," Otis said. "We're all here, so spill it."

Mack gestured toward Joe, who was limping toward them with a bottle of champagne in an ice bucket and a stand. "Will do, just as soon as Joseph serves the bubbly."

"Which I'm about to do," Joe said. He set the bucket on the stand and removed the bottle. "Ella will be right over with the glasses."

Otis whistled. "Hey, *Moet Chandon*. That's drinking first class, Mack. I didn't know you were a wine connoisseur."

"I'm not. I leave that to Joseph."

"Good choice, Joe. But are you sure the host can afford it?"

"He doesn't have to," Joe said, popping the cork to release an aromatic vapor. "This is on the house, compliments of Charlie."

"Charlie?" Megan asked. "Who's Charlie?"

Mack chuckled. "Charlie is the resident ghost of a former owner. He spent a lot of time in the cellar where the liquor is stored, imbibing from the inventory. The story goes that Charlie is still hanging out there."

"A spirit among the spirits," Joe quipped. Then to Ella, who was placing champagne glasses on the table: "A glass for me too, Ella."

An astonished look from Ella. "Are you sure, Mr. L? I mean…"

"I know, I know. But a few sips won't kill me, and if they do, I'll go join Charlie in the cellar."

Ella grimaced. "Don't even say that, Mr. L."

Joe smiled and, despite a shaking hand, filled the six glasses with champagne without spilling a drop. "None of the waitresses will go down there. Right, Ella?"

"No way," Ella said over her shoulder, as she headed toward the bar.

Joe raised his glass in a toast. "Okay, Mack. Here's to…here's to what?"

"Got your notebook with you, Otis? Mack said.

"Yeah."

"Well, get it out and write this down."

"Okay." Otis removed his notebook and pen from his pocket. "Shoot."

Mack got up. "At exactly 10:45 a.m. this morning I walked into Superintendent Hollender's office and requested that I be transferred from Homicide." Momentary stunned silence.

"Is that really true, Mack?" Megan said.

"It is. In fact, I've already submitted it to The Hawk. Furthermore, the request contains my desire to return to Area 3 Special Victims."

"Oh, no!" Otis said. "Don't tell me I've gotta put up with you as a partner again?"

"Afraid so…partner."

Otis put down his notebook and pen and raised his glass. "Well, then all I've got to say is…Hip, Hip, Hooray!"

Everyone applauded this revelation, clinked glasses and drank to it.

Taking his seat, Mack had to admit that he was somewhat astonished himself with his decision. Maybe it was the absence of the usual supercharge he got when he put a bad guy behind bars—or for that matter, on a slab in the morgue. Or maybe it was the memory of a grateful young mother asking God to bless them when Otis and he returned her missing little girl.

But if Mack didn't know, Megan did. "That's wonderful, Mack. I couldn't be more pleased." This was followed by another kiss on his cheek.

"That goes for me, too," Ava said, delivering a kiss on his other cheek. "And for my loving husband, as well. Right, dear?"

"If I don't have to kiss him, I can live with it. But I do have one condition."

"Oh?" Mack said. "Such as?"

"Well, if I've gotta listen to you banging on the steering wheel again, the least you can do is let me hear you give a real set of drums a serious workout."

"Hey man, you play drums?" Willie asked.

"He does," Megan answered for Mack. "And he's really good."

"More like okay," Mack said. "But it's not like I can just walk up there and sit in without an invitation."

"I've already arranged that," Joe said, gesturing toward the bandstand, where the musicians were assembling for the second set.

Mack saw Franz motioning him over.

"Come on, Mack," Otis said. "Go for it."

"Okay," Mack said, getting up. "I'll give it a try."

The fact was that he'd been looking forward to an opportunity to play again and had been practicing for the past two weeks despite some residue of pain in his shoulder.

"Hey, Mack. Good to see you," Franz greeted him, as Mack stepped up on the bandstand.

"You too, Franz," Mack said. "Thanks for letting me sit in."

"Always a pleasure," Franz said, picking up his clarinet from the stand.

Mack made his way past the four up-front musicians to the four-man rhythm section in the rear.

Johnny D., the black drummer, handed Mack the drumsticks with his usual broad smile. "Welcome back, Mack. Looks like you got an audience."

"Yeah, so if I screw up, come and rescue me."

"You'll do just fine," Johnnie D. said.

Mack adjusted the stool to accommodate his height before sitting down to do a few practice rolls on the snare. When the other musicians were ready, Franz turned to address them.

"We'll lead off with "I've Found a New Baby" in D-minor. I'll do the first sixteen bars— Mack, give me a tom-tom beat—and everyone comes in on the bridge. Okay, here we go. One—two—one-two-three-four..."

When the band finished the first song—with Mack providing a four-bar fill on the snare and floor tom before the band's two-bar second close—the audience erupted with applause, the most enthusiastic provided by Otis.

"You know something," he said. "The guy's not bad."

Megan watched Mack, relaxed and smiling, like she'd seen him the first time behind the drums. For a moment their eyes met, his as if asking a question, hers giving the answer.

"Not bad at all," she said softly.

## About the Author

**Richard Rose** hails from  Kokomo, Indiana. Teen dances, basketball and too many greasy French fries gave way to a BA at Wabash College. After 3 1/2 years fighting the Cold War on the East/West German border, Richard began a long career as a First V.P. with a major investment firm in Chicago, where he did market reports on TV and radio. Richard's wife and true love, Kay, supports his passion for writing, which includes short stories, novels and screenplays. She also keeps him healthy. No more greasy French fries.

http://www.richardroseonline.com.

Photo by Jorge Medina Photography

If you enjoyed *The Lazarus Conspiracies,* consider these other fine books from Savant Books and Publications:

*Essay, Essay, Essay* by Yasuo Kobachi
*Aloha from Coffee Island* by Walter Miyanari
*Footprints, Smiles and Little White Lies* by Daniel S. Janik
*The Illustrated Middle Earth* by Daniel S. Janik
*Last and Final Harvest* by Daniel S. Janik
*A Whale's Tale* by Daniel S. Janik
*Tropic of California* by R. Page Kaufman
*Tropic of California* (the companion music CD) by R. Page Kaufman
*The Village Curtain* by Tony Tame
*Dare to Love in Oz* by William Maltese
*The Interzone* by Tatsuyuki Kobayashi
*Today I Am a Man* by Larry Rodness
*The Bahrain Conspiracy* by Bentley Gates
*Called Home* by Gloria Schumann
*Kanaka Blues* by Mike Farris
*First Breath* edited by Z. M. Oliver
*Poor Rich* by Jean Blasiar
*The Jumper Chronicles* by W. C. Peever
*William Maltese's Flicker* by William Maltese
*My Unborn Child* by Orest Stocco
*Last Song of the Whales* by Four Arrows
*Perilous Panacea* by Ronald Klueh
*Falling but Fulfilled* by Zachary M. Oliver
*Mythical Voyage* by Robin Ymer
*Hello, Norma Jean* by Sue Dolleris
*Richer* by Jean Blasiar
*Manifest Intent* by Mike Farris
*Charlie No Face* by David B. Seaburn
*Number One Bestseller* by Brian Morley
*My Two Wives and Three Husbands* by S. Stanley Gordon
*In Dire Straits* by Jim Currie
*Wretched Land* by Mila Komarnisky
*Chan Kim* by Ilan Herman
*Who's Killing All the Lawyers?* by A. G. Hayes
*Ammon's Horn* by G. Amati
*Wavelengths* edited by Zachary M. Oliver
*Almost Paradise* by Laurie Hanan
*Communion* by Jean Blasiar and Jonathan Marcantoni

*The Oil Man* by Leon Puissegur
*Random Views of Asia from the Mid-Pacific* by William E. Sharp
*The Isla Vista Crucible* by Reilly Ridgell
*Blood Money* by Scott Mastro
*In the Himalayan Nights* by Anoop Chandola
*On My Behalf* by Helen Doan
*Traveler's Rest* by Jonathan Marcantoni
*Keys in the River* by Tendai Mwanaka
*Chimney Bluffs* by David B. Seaburn
*The Loons* by Sue Dolleris
*Light Surfer* by David Allan Williams
*The Judas List* by A. G. Hayes
*Path of the Templar - Book 2 of The Jumper Chronicles* by W. C. Peever
*The Desperate Cycle* by Tony Tame
*Shutterbug* by Buz Sawyer
*Blessed are the Peacekeepers* by Tom Donnelly and Mike Munger
*Purple Haze* by George B. Hudson
*The Turtle Dances* by Daniel S. Janik


Soon To be Released:
*The Hanging of Dr. Hanson* by Bentley Gates
*Imminent Danger* by A. G. Hayes


http://www.savantbooksandpublications.com

29350464R00203

Made in the USA
Charleston, SC
09 May 2014